# DICKENS

The Pocket Edition

Peter Ackroyd's most recent novels are
*(The House of) Doctor Dee*, *English Music*,
*First Light* and *Chatterton*. He has written
one other major biography, *T. S. Eliot*,
which was awarded the Whitbread Prize
for biography, and was joint winner of
the Royal Society of Literature's William
Heinemann Award. He is currently
working on a biography of William Blake
and lives in London.

# PETER ACKROYD

# DICKENS

Abridged from the
Sinclair-Stevenson *Dickens*

Mandarin

**A Mandarin Paperback**
DICKENS

*Dickens* first published in Great Britain 1990
by Sinclair-Stevenson Ltd
This abridged edition published 1994
by Mandarin Paperbacks
an imprint of Reed Consumer Books Ltd
Michelin House, 81 Fulham Road, London SW3 6RB
and Auckland, Melbourne, Singapore and Toronto

Reprinted 1994, 1995

Copyright © 1990 by Peter Ackroyd
The author has asserted his moral rights

A CIP catalogue record for this title
is available from the British Library
ISBN 0 7493 1685 3

Printed and bound in Great Britain
by Cox & Wyman Ltd, Reading, Berkshire

# Contents

# Acknowledgements

The pages from the first edition and corrected proofs of *Bleak House* and the picture of Dickens, Catherine and Mary Hogarth are reproduced courtesy of the Board of Trustees of the Victoria and Albert Museum; the portrait of Wilkie Collins is from the Mary Evans Picture Library; the drawing of Dickens by Samuel Laurence is reproduced by permission of the National Portrait Gallery, London. All the remaining pictures are reproduced by kind permission of the Dickens House Museum.

# Prologue

"... deeper than all, if one has the eye to see deep enough, dark, fateful, silent elements, tragical to look upon, and hiding amid dazzling radiances as of the sun, the elements of death itself."

Thomas Carlyle on Charles Dickens.

"Remember that what you are told is really threefold: shaped by the teller, reshaped by the listener, concealed from both by the dead man of the tale."

*The Real Life of Sebastian Knight.*
Vladimir Nabokov.

"Ippolit Kirillovitch had chosen the historical form of narration, preferred by all anxious orators, who find in its constraints a check on their own exuberant rhetoric."

*The Brothers Karamazov.* Fyodor Dostoevsky.

CHARLES DICKENS was dead. He lay on a narrow green sofa — but there was room enough for him, so spare had he become — in the dining room of Gad's Hill Place. He had died in the house which he had first seen as a small boy and which his father had pointed out to him as a suitable object of his ambitions; so great was his father's hold upon his life that, forty years later, he had bought it. Now he had gone. It was customary to close the blinds and curtains, thus enshrouding the corpse in darkness before its last journey to the tomb; but in the dining room of Gad's Hill the curtains were pulled apart and on this June day the bright sunshine streamed in, glittering on the large mirrors around the room. The family beside him knew how he enjoyed the light, how he needed the light; and they understood, too, that none of the conventional sombreness of the late Victorian period – the year was 1870 – had ever touched him.

All the lines and wrinkles which marked the passage of his life were now erased in the stillness of death. He was not old – he died in his fifty-eighth year – but there had been signs of premature ageing on a visage so marked and worn; he had acquired, it was said, a "sarcastic look". But now all that was gone and his daughter, Katey, who watched him as he lay dead, noticed how there once more emerged upon his face "beauty and pathos". It was that "long forgotten" look which he describes again and again in his fiction. He sees it in *Oliver Twist*, in the dead face which returns to the ". . . long forgotten expression of sleeping infancy", and in that same novel he connects "the rigid face of the corpse and the calm sleep of the child". In Master Humphrey's death, too, there was something "so strangely and indefinably allied to youth". It was the look he recorded in William Dorrit's face in death; it was the look which he saw in the faces of the corpses on view in the Paris Morgue. This connection between death and infancy is one that had haunted him: sleep, repose, death, infancy, innocence, oblivion are the words that formed a circle for him, bringing him back to the place from which he had begun. Here, in Gad's Hill, close to the town in which he had lived as a small child, here in the house which his father had once shown him; here the circle was complete.

A death mask was made. He had always hated masks. He had been frightened by one as a child and throughout his writing there is this refrain – "What a very alarming thing it would be to find somebody with a mask on . . . hiding bolt upright in a corner and pretending not to be alive!" The mask was an emblem of Charles Dickens's particular fear; that the dead are only pretending to be dead, and that they will suddenly spring up into violent life. He had a fear of the dead, and of all inanimate things, rising up around him to claim him; it is the fear of the pre-eminently solitary child and solitary man. But was there not also here some anticipation of the final quietus? The mask was made, and he was laid in his oak coffin. This wooden resting place was then covered with scarlet geraniums; they were Charles Dickens's favourite flowers and in the final picture of the corpse covered with blossom we can see a true representation of Dickens's own words echoing across the years — "Brighten it, brighten it, brighten it!" He always wanted colour about him, and he was notorious for his own vivid costumes. Especially in youth: and, on the wall above the coffin, his family placed a portrait of him as a young man. It was no doubt that painted by Daniel Maclise, and it shows the Dickens of 1839 looking up from his desk, his eyes ablaze as if in anticipation of the glory that was to come. Georgina Hogarth, his sister-in-law, cut a lock of hair from his head. On his prior instructions, his horse was shot. And so Charles Dickens lay.

The news of his death, in that age of swift communication, soon travelled around the world. In America Longfellow wrote that "I never knew an author's death to cause such general mourning. It is no exaggeration to say that this whole country is stricken with grief." But this perhaps is no surprise in a country which had greeted the arrival of the latest sheets of *The Old Curiosity Shop* with cries of "Is Little Nell dead?" Carlyle wrote, "It is an event world-wide, a *unique* of talents suddenly extinct . . ." And at once a certain aspect of his significance was seen clearly; as the *Daily News* wrote on 10 June, the day after his death,

"He was emphatically the novelist of his age. In his pictures of contemporary life posterity will read, more clearly than in contemporary records, the character of nineteenth century life."

And yet, if he was the chronicler of his age, he also stood apart from it; he was always in some sense the solitary observer, one who looked upon the customs of his time as an anthropologist might look upon the habits of a particularly savage tribe. And there is no more direct evidence for this than in his own will, read now as he lay in his coffin. ". . . I emphatically direct that I be buried in an inexpensive, unostentatious and strictly private manner . . . that those who attend my funeral wear no scarf, cloak, black bow, long hat-band, or other such revolting absurdity . . . I conjure my friends on no account to make me the subject of any monument, memorial or testimonial whatever. I rest my claims to the remembrance of my country upon my published works . . ." It was presumed that this meant that he wished to be buried quietly in the vicinity of Gad's Hill and his childhood haunts, and at once a grave was prepared for him in the crypt of Rochester Cathedral.

But a compromise was reached between Dickens's family and what might be called the interests of the nation; he was to be buried in Westminster Abbey, after all, but with a completely private service. He had once said, ". . . the more truly great the man, the more truly little the ceremony . . .", thus emphasising that simplicity which was an essential part of the man. And so it was on Tuesday morning, 14 June, that his body was taken from Gad's Hill to Higham Station, and from there conveyed in a special train to Charing Cross. A small procession of three coaches made its way down Whitehall, and the great bell of the Abbey began to toll as they drove under the archway into Dean's Yard; then the small group of family and friends entered Westminster Abbey, where Charles Dickens was to be laid in Poets' Corner. Around him were the busts of Shakespeare and Milton, and at the end of the short ceremony the organ sounded the Death March. In Rochester, the city in which he had as it were begun life and in which his last novel was set, the bell of the cathedral tolled as he was interred. His grave at Westminster Abbey was left open for two days. At the end of the first day, there were still one thousand people outside waiting to pay their respects. So for those two days the crowds of people passed by in procession, many of them dropping flowers onto his coffin — "among which," his son said, "were afterwards found several small rough bouquets of flowers tied up with pieces of rag."

There, in the ragged bundles of flowers, no doubt picked from the hedgerows and fields, we see the source and emblem of Charles Dickens's authority. Even to the labouring men and women there was in his death a grievous sense of loss; they felt that he had in large measure understood them and that, in his death, they had also lost something of themselves. It is often said that the great Russian novelists of the nineteenth century capture the soul of the Russian people with their fervour, their piety, and their wonderful tenderness; but can we not say that Dickens captured the soul of the English people, as much in its brooding melancholy as in its broad humour, in its poetry as well as in its fearlessness, in its capacity for outrage and pity as much as in its tendency towards irony and diffidence? And can we not see something of the national outline, too, in Charles Dickens's brisk, anxious stride across the face of the world — a man of so much assurance and of so much doubt, of so much energy and so much turmoil? It might be said, in fact, that it was his peculiar genius to represent, to bring together, more aspects of the national character than any other writer of his century. As a man he was sharp, exuberant, prone to melancholy and a prey to anxiety; as a writer he was filled with the same contrasts, so concerned with the material world and yet at the same time so haunted by visions of transcendence. The evidence for that divide is to be gathered throughout his work. In the nineteenth-century Russian novelists, the material and the spiritual are in a certain sense interfused; and in the French novelists of the nineteenth century it is the very genius of the material world to have no transcendental echoes: it remains splendidly itself. But, in the work of Charles Dickens, the real and the unreal, the material and the spiritual, the specific and the imagined, the mundane and the transcendental, exist in uneasy relation and are to be contained only within the power of the created word. The power of Charles Dickens.

To all Victorians, then, the death of Dickens came as the evidence of a giant transition; in these last decades of the nineteenth century, the English people were witnesses to the fatal disruptions of an old order and the unsteady beginnings of a new. There are times, when looking at Dickens, or when looking at the people who mourned him, the years between his time and our own vanish. And we are looking at ourselves. Just as these who came to mourn in the Abbey were looking at themselves. When they buried him, and surrounded his grave with roses and other flowers, they were registering in symbolic sense the end of an age of which he was the single most visible representative; more so than Palmerston, now dead, more so than Gladstone, who stood in an uneasy relation to the period yet to come, and more so than the Queen herself who had not, like Dickens, seen all the transitions of the century. He had more than seen them; he had felt them, had experienced them, had declared them in his fictions. From a distance, then, he embodied the period from which he sprang; and in the course of the succeeding pages we will see how it was his particular genius to turn his life itself into an emblem of that period – instinctively, almost blindly, to dramatise it. But when we come closer to him still, when we observe his life and his work in continuous

xiv

motion and combination, will these biographical certainties remain or will they dissolve?

For there is a sorrowfulness, a self-contained sorrowfulness, almost a coldness, about aspects of Dickens's life on earth – just as the same sorrowfulness and coldness can be glimpsed within the heart of his narratives. We might use here the imagery of the seascape which fascinated him always: on the surface there is the light and the turbulent water, the currents and the cross-currents, the whole vast edifice of the natural world seen as a wall of glass, or as foam, or as wave, or as rainbow. There are often great scenes of tempest on the face of this water – and how Dickens seemed to live in the storm – but even at quieter times there is still the track of the sailing vessel, the current of the steam-ship; always activity; always busyness. But if we go further beneath the water, beneath the active and busy world of light, what then? If we dive down deeper, dive into the unfathomable depths, what then do we see of him? Lost objects which have drifted down, now flattened beyond recognition. Darkness and silence. Strange phosphorescent images. Is this what Carlyle meant – a man whose radiance contained the presence of death itself?

But this is to move ahead of our history, and surely it is from Dickens, of all writers, that we learn that it is in details that the spirit fully lives. And if it is true, as David Copperfield says, that ". . . trifles make the sum of life", will we see in the "trifles" of Dickens's life all the constituents of his great works – see in them, too, the true shape of the world in which he lived? For this is the challenge, to make biography an agent of real knowledge. To find in a day, a moment, a passing image or gesture, the very spring and source of his creativity; and to see in these details, too, the figure of the moving age.

# One

CHARLES DICKENS was born on the seventh of
February 1812, the year of victory and the year
of hardship. He came crying into the world in a small
first-floor bedroom in an area known as New Town or
Mile End, just on the outskirts of Portsmouth where his
father, John Dickens, worked in the Naval Pay Office. His
mother, Elizabeth, is reported to have claimed that she
went to a ball on the night before his birth; but no ball is
mentioned in the area for that particular evening and it is
likely that this is one of the many apocryphal stories which
sprung up around the birth and development of the great
writer. He was born on a Friday, on the same day as his
young hero David Copperfield, and for ever afterwards
Friday became for him a day of omen. Whether like his
young hero he was born just before midnight, when the
tide was in, is not recorded; but this strange association
between himself and his fictional characters is one that he
carried with him always. He said once, during a speech in
memory of Shakespeare's birthday, that: "We meet on this
day to celebrate the birthday of a vast army of living men
and women who will live for ever with an actuality greater
than that of the men and women whose external forms
we see around us . . ." He was thinking here of Hamlet
and Lear, of Macbeth and Prospero, but is it not also true
that in this small front bedroom in Portsmouth, in the

1

presence of a surgeon and a monthly nurse, there was born on this February day Pecksniff and Scrooge, Oliver Twist and Sairey Gamp, Samuel Pickwick and Nicholas Nickleby, Pip and David Copperfield, Miss Havisham and Little Nell, the Artful Dodger and Wackford Squeers, Thomas Gradgrind and Little Dorrit, Sydney Carton and Paul Dombey, Fagin and Edwin Drood, Uriah Heep and Wilkins Micawber, Quilp and Sam Weller, Barnaby Rudge and Bill Sikes, Tiny Tim and Tommy Traddles, all of them tumbling out into the light? It is impossible to say precisely how many characters Charles Dickens has created — almost two thousand of them, born with Dickens but not dying with him, living on for ever. Whether Dickens himself shall turn out to be the hero of his own life, therefore, or whether that station will be held by others, these pages must show.

There was already one man who had set his mark upon him, and in the local newspaper there was inserted an advertisement: "On Friday, at Mile-end Terrace, the Lady of John Dickens Esq., a son." Three weeks later John Dickens and his Lady, whom their son was later savagely to satirise, walked through the lanes and fields to the church of St Mary's Kingston. Here the infant was christened with the names of Charles John Huffam Dickens — Christopher Huffam, who will later play no inconsiderable part in this story, being a friend of John Dickens and godfather to the child. Then they walked back to their small house — not exactly genteel, despite the flourish of John Dickens's announcement in the newspaper, but certainly respectable, in a semi-rural neighbourhood away from the clamour of Portsmouth, a home for someone of modest means but one who could lay definite claims to being a part of the middle classes. It may seem strange that Charles Dickens, who in his work was excessively nostalgic about the years of his childhood, never showed any signs of sentimental interest in the house of his birth:

"I can't say I usually care much about it," he once wrote and indeed on the one occasion he seems to have revisited the area he could not find the exact dwelling.

Charles Dickens was not the first child – eighteen months before John and Elizabeth Dickens had had a daughter, Frances Elizabeth, called Fanny all her life. A servant lived with them, too, so this was by no means a large house for them all. The infant memories of Dickens, if such they be, would have been of people moving around in small rooms; mainly female voices, female tears, echoing through the small house. And is there not in his constant description of parts of the body – the face, the hand, the leg, seen in distinction to other limbs – some mark of the first stages of infant perception? No other memories can be traced from a period almost as remote to him as it is to us, unless it be the fact that the first object remembered by David Copperfield is of ". . . my mother with her pretty hair and youthful shape". In later life Dickens was heard to deny the belief that a child had any "divine instinct" of love for its mother, but his own helpless and instinctive affections do not always consort easily with his ordinarily articulated opinions. It is also in *David Copperfield*, after all, that David identifies himself with a baby at the breast, just as at the opening of *Master Humphrey's Clock* the narrator was "happy to nestle in her breast – happy to weep when she did – happy in not knowing why".

And what of the rest of the Dickens family at this time? Charles Dickens never seemed to know much about his grandparents, and even less about those who had come before them, and yet there is no doubt that they always stood silently around him. The actual origins of his family remain quite unknown. There was a Dickens family of Babbington, Staffordshire, who were lords of the manor of Churchill from 1437 until 1656, and a contemporary biographer records that ". . . it is said that from this family Mr Dickens, the author, is descended", "it is said", always,

3

in this context, being a synonym for unreliable gossip or conjecture. There was also a long line of John and William Dickens (the names of his father and grandfather respectively) who had first lived in Derbyshire but who were memorialised frequently in London records of the seventeenth and eighteenth centuries: and, if there is to be an origin for Dickens, it is perhaps more appropriate to look for it here in generations of Londoners. Surely the image of the city which Dickens creates comes from sources as deep as himself, as deep as his own inheritance?

More is known of those immediately preceding him. His mother's maiden name was Barrow, and the Barrows came from Bristol. There appear to have been clerics in this family but, more importantly, they were the makers of musical instruments. Both his maternal grandparents were connected with this business, and his grandfather also practised as a music-master – although his later and less worthy activities were to leave a different kind of mark upon his grandson. And yet the figures who influenced him most are to be found on the father's side of his family. Dickens's paternal grandparents were both servants, a fact which was not revealed until after his death. William Dickens was butler or steward for the Crewe family, who possessed houses in both London and the country; all the available evidence suggests that he was a thrifty and conscientious man, one who could not have risen to that level of service without considerable administrative abilities and with a reputation for financial probity. These were all qualities which his grandson possessed, even to abundance.

But there were also characteristics which Dickens inherited from his grandmother, the only grandparent whom he ever really knew. She was a housekeeper for the Crewe family, and in his fiction he shows an especial fondness for such conscientious old ladies. She had married her husband early in life; before her marriage she was a servant to a certain Lady Blandford in Grosvenor Square, and there are unconfirmed reports that she came from a small village named Claverley, near Tong, and that she had been housekeeper at Tong Castle. The only interest to be found in these shadowy reports lies in the fact that it is often claimed that Little Nell meets her quietus in the church at Tong; if so, a strange pilgrimage for one of Dickens's small and sickly heroines – towards death in a place marked by the presence of his grandmother! After her marriage in 1781, however, she joined the Crewe family and was eventually promoted to the post of house-keeper, a post she retained until she was seventy-five. She, too, was trusted and competent. But, more importantly, she was known as a fluent story-teller; one of the Crewe children later recalled that ". . . not since that time had she met anyone who possessed so surprising a gift for extemporising fiction for the amusement of others".

His grandfather dead before his birth; his grandmother dead when he was twelve; and his father's brother died childless: he had really only a small circle of relations, therefore, not at all like the extended Victorian family which he was later both to celebrate and to curse. And yet the image of the family haunts him. Practically all of his novels are concerned with the life within families, after all, specifically in the degradation and unsatisfariness of familial relationships. This is the fount from which all forms of social evil are seen by him to spring, but the conclusions of his novels tend nevertheless to reinstate some idealised family group which can withstand change and the world. In Dickens's fiction that idealised family becomes an image both of social and religious life; so, by that strange alchemy of his genius, he turns private long-ings for a more ordered and stable life into a positive social force. Does it also come as a surprise, then, that he all but destroyed his own family, and that he was perpetually beset by the failures and weaknesses of his own relatives?

We must look for the origins of these compulsive, contradictory feelings in those closest to him – and no one ever came as close to him as his parents, John and Elizabeth Dickens. In them we see half of his strength and half of his weakness, and in his baffled troubling relations with his parents we observe also the root source of that art through which he was later to encompass them.

Elizabeth Dickens, his mother, was twenty-three at the time of his birth – a young woman, then, and it would be most unwise to transpose all of the stories about her in later life to this much earlier period. Still more unwise, therefore, to take the stock portrait of Mrs Nickleby, assumed to be Charles Dickens's portrait of her, and use this as a stick with which to beat her. His relationship to his mother was central to his life, but it was necessarily a complex one established upon guilt and rejection but combined with a kind of hopeless love. All the maternal figures in his novels are in fact ways of reinstating someone else in her place. He did not want to see her too clearly. He did not want to get too close to her. And yet there are occasions when the reports of others, and Charles Dickens's own casual asides, help us to see the mother of the genius more clearly. "It is an undoubted fact that all remarkable men have had remarkable mothers, and have respected them in after life as their best friends" – these words are put into the mouth of the put-upon and somewhat foolish Mr Tetterby. An early biographer records that "her famous son, it is said, resembled her greatly in his later years. She was a cheerful soul, fond of joining in the amusements of young people, and especially in dancing . . ." He was fond of dancing, too, but he did not like to see his mother dance; he is said ". . . to have regarded her performances with disfavour". And here also we trace the strange alchemy of the mother–son relationship, the son despising in his mother what is implicit in himself, just as in his fiction he sees her as a stranger without realising that he is also looking upon his own face.

As for John Dickens, Charles's father, there is also a great deal known, some of it verifiable and some of it apocryphal. He had been brought up by his mother in the various Crewe households, his father having died a few months before his birth; it is often claimed that Dickens draws his fictional orphans from his own blighted experience as a boy, but can we not also see in his father's own partial orphanhood a ready source of fantasies and stories? He had a brother, William, who was three years older and who seems to have inherited his parents' sense of responsibility and fiscal caution which John notably lacked. William died as the keeper of a coffee house in Oxford Street, not a particularly exalted occupation, and one which the Dickens family never seems to have mentioned. But on the available evidence he appears to have been his mother's favourite son; John, on the other hand, was called by her "that lazy fellow . . . who used to come hanging about the house" and one "against whose idleness and general incapacity she was never tired of inveighing". Certainly she left him nothing specific in her will, stating that instead he had obtained diverse sums from her on different occasions; in other words, the pattern of his life was set early and in succeeding years he would dun his son much more heavily than ever he dunned his mother.

John Dickens stayed with his mother in the Crewe household until he was about twenty or twenty-one, and there is no doubt that by then his character was almost completely formed. Perhaps with the influence of Lord Crewe, he went to Somerset House in 1807 as an extra clerk in the office of the Treasurer of His Majesty's Navy; here he met another new recruit, Thomas Barrow, the brother of Elizabeth. Two years later he was given a more permanent position of assistant clerk in the Pay Office, and in succeeding years he steadily moved forward through the ranks of promotion, but even before this welcome security of employment he began his serious pursuit of his colleague's sister. By 1808 he had been transferred to a more responsible position in Portsmouth, which must have entailed a certain amount of commuting in his courtship of Elizabeth Barrow who still lived in London. On 13 June 1809 they married at the Church of St Mary-le-Strand, and then travelled back to Portsmouth and to their new house in Mile End Terrace. Frances was born in the following year, and Charles two years later.

And what of the father in these early years? He was a clerk, but the work was not of that ordinarily bureaucratic kind which the word now suggests. He was with others responsible for paying both the naval workmen in port and the crews upon ship, which meant physically handing over the money; sometimes, with a crowd around them, it might lead to disagreements, and sometimes even to fights. He was always well-dressed, always polite, always affable. He was good-looking – better looking than his children, it was generally thought – and well-built, although inclining to stoutness in later years. According to one contemporary in the Navy Pay Office he was ". . . a fellow of infinite humour, chatty, lively and agreeable". This seems to be the general report. "A chatty pleasant companion"; "most genial and courtly . . . of kindly disposition"; ". . . possessing a varied fund of anecdote and a genuine vein of humour"; "very courteous, imposingly so"; ". . . the jolliest of men". He described himself as an optimist and once compared himself to "a cork which, when submerged, bobs up to the surface again none the worse for the dip". Strangely enough his son, in one of his earliest pieces of journalism, describes just such a man as "one of the careless, good-for-nothing, happy fellows, who float, cork-like, on the surface, for the world to play at hockey with . . . always reappearing and bounding with the stream buoyantly and merrily along". He may have been jolly, but he had a fearful temper; on one occasion, according

8

to a story, he had been asked to allow no one behind the scenes during the course of one of his son's theatrical ventures and, on entering the green room, flew at his own reflection in the glass and bruised his knuckles. He was always short of money, always spending money, always borrowing money. This improvidence and recklessness, when seen in combination with his courteous and amiable personality, also suggest that there was a callowness or even a coldness at his centre. There is a sort of emptiness, an infantilism, a refusal to confront himself. This is no more than in a million other men: it comes to our notice only because it was noticed and recorded by his son. "How long he is," Dickens once complained, "growing up to be a man." And we recall in Dickens's fiction how universal it is that the child looks after the adult, and how the adult remains so dependent upon the child that he becomes something worse than merely child-like.

In fact Charles Dickens's relations to his father were of the most complicated sort; not the "half-admiring and half-ashamed" response of Little Dorrit to her imprisoned father, but something at once more violent and less easy to understand. There were times in later life when John Dickens became for him a creature of nightmare, forever weighing upon his life, but long before that time it is clear that the image of his father haunted him in some generalised and unspecified way. He is even mentioned in his first published story. It seems that John Dickens liked to tell an anecdote about the time he escorted Sheridan's wife in a coach to London, and how once he kissed Sheridan's hand – Sheridan being the Paymaster to the Forces between 1807 and 1812 – and there, in Dickens's first published piece, we find a grandiloquent and "little smirking man" who has been "endeavouring to obtain a listener to some stories about Sheridan".

But his attitude to his father was not one that could be resolved by parody or imitation; there were other feelings

9

at work. If he admired him he despised him, too, but he also recognised the presence of his father within himself so that, at times of great distress, his own self-pity spilled over into pity for the man who had begotten him. He was forever accusing him during his life of rapacity and ingratitude but, after his death, his constant refrain was "my poor father".

The Dickens family did not stay long in the little house in Mile End Terrace, and five months after his birth they removed to Hawk Street, the first of many moves which were to mark Dickens's childhood and which even at this very early age must in some sense have affected him. This particular street was beside the port itself – for John Dickens it was no more than three minutes' walk to the small naval pay office just within the gates. The street has now gone (although its name and the pay office itself remain), but at the time it was considered a perfectly respectable thoroughfare where many officers were placed in lodging houses. In *Dombey and Son* Dickens recounts in vivid detail a certain Mrs Pipchin, boarding-house keeper, and in particular he dwells upon her clothes like "the . . . black bombazeen garments of the worthy old lady [which] darkened the audience chamber". After he had composed this his older sister, Fanny, is reported by him to have exclaimed, "Good heavens! What does this mean? You have painted our lodging-house keeper and you were but two years old at the time." Whether it was indeed a portrait of the lady, or whether it was simply based upon fugitive infant impressions, is one of those conundrums which regularly occur in trying to assess the processes of Dickens's extraordinary imagination. Eighteen months later the family were on the move again, this time to the new extension of Portsmouth which was known as Southsea, at 39 Wish Street. The rent here was twice that of their previous house, which confirms what the records themselves demonstrate, that John Dickens was steadily climbing through the preordained ranks of preferment. (He had also subscribed to Campbell's *Lives of the Admirals* which suggests, if nothing else, a certain attachment and even affection for his profession.) They were joined here by Elizabeth Dickens's sister, Mary Allen, known as Aunt Fanny, who no doubt contributed her own portion of the larger rent.

They spent New Year's Day in that house, a New Year's Day apparently remembered by Dickens forty-six years later in an article for his journal, *Household Words*. "So far back do my recollections of childhood extend," he wrote, "that I have a vivid remembrance of the sensation of being carried down-stairs in a woman's arms, and holding tight to her, in the terror of seeing the steep perspective below." This has the ring of truthful memory, a recollected experience of anxiety, and so does the picture which greeted him when he peeped into the celebrations in the ground floor room – ". . . a very long row of ladies and gentlemen sitting against a wall, all drinking at once out of little glass cups with handles, like custard-cups . . . There was no speech-making, no quick movement and change of action, no demonstration of any kind. They were all sitting in a long row against the wall – very like my first idea of the good people in Heaven, as I derived it from a wretched picture in a Prayer-book – and they had all got their heads a little thrown back, and were all drinking at once." This is an extraordinary picture; it was one that he said always haunted him when anyone talked of a New Year's Day party. But in this vision of a row of strangely silent people, leaning against a wall with their heads thrown back, there also is revived the picture of a lost age, a vanished age – lost to Charles Dickens himself when he looks back, but also how much lost to us.

Three months later there was a birth in Wish Street; a male child, on 28 March, who was christened Alfred Allen Dickens. Those who profess to understand the nature of

11

infant consciousness might suggest that the emergence of another male child when Dickens himself was just a little over two years old would have inspired anxiety and resentment in the sibling's breast – that he would have felt, as Dickens put it in another context, "an alien from my mother's heart". Would he have been denied the pampering which he might have desired, and would he then have felt rejected by his mother? It is difficult to be sure; certainly the idea of maternal rejection is a very strong thread both in his fiction and in his own reminiscences. And then six months later Alfred Allen died, of "water on the brain", and for reasons which remain unclear was buried in the churchyard of the obscure village of Widley. If the infant Charles had harboured resentful or even murderous longings against the supplanter, how effectively they had come home to roost! And how strong the guilt might have been. *Might have been* – that is necessarily the phrase. And yet when the adulthood of Dickens is considered, with all its evidence that Dickens did indeed suffer from an insidious pressure of irrational guilt, and when all the images of dead infants are picked out of his fiction, it is hard to believe that this six-month episode in the infancy of the novelist did not have some permanent effect upon him.

Then in January of the following year the family were on the move again; the Portsmouth administration was being curtailed after the ending of hostilities, and John Dickens had been recalled to Somerset House. And so for the first time Charles Dickens entered London, a journey about which he remembered nothing except the fact that they left Portsea covered with snow. But already the capital must have been associated with privation, if not exactly hardship – John Dickens had a reduced income in the city, largely because he was not paid an Outport Allowance. They went into lodgings at 10 Norfolk Street, now 22 Cleveland Street, on the corner of Tottenham Street.

The house is still there; now the ground floor contains a sandwich shop, but then it was a grocer's. The grocer was also the landlord, a certain John Dodd who was later to become one of John Dickens's many creditors, and it seems possible that it was during this London period that Dickens's father first ran into debt. They stayed here two years — Aunt Fanny and perhaps a servant with them — and although nothing else is specifically recorded of their life in that period there can be no doubt that it affected Dickens. It was not only that another child was born in this period, Laetitia Mary Dickens in April 1816, but, rather, that it was in his third and fourth years that the infant Dickens gradually awakened to further consciousness of the world. A world that was now not one of fields, but of streets. Of course there were areas close to Tottenham Court Road which were still rural — the fields of Camden Town were relatively close — but the sense of urban reality was quite a new one. Dickens was later to shed tears when he paced some London streets and, although it would be too much to say that the small child was aware of the miseries which existed close to him, it would be a foolish person indeed who did not believe that the strange mysteries and sorrows of London did not in some way pierce or move his infant breast. And what is that cry repeated more than once in Dickens's fiction, the words of the dying child who cries out, "Mother! . . . bury me in the open fields — anywhere but in these dreadful streets . . . they have killed me"?

It was in January 1817 that they returned to those "open fields"; to Sheerness, which was John Dickens's next posting, a somewhat isolated port and about which little is known in connection with the migratory Dickens family. It seems that they rented a small house next door to the Sheerness Theatre, and one mid-nineteenth-century chronicler said of John Dickens that "of an evening he used to sit in this room, and could hear what was passing

13

on the stage, and join in the chorus of 'God Save the King' and 'Britannia Rules the Waves' ''. Songs and theatres are to feature large in Dickens's childhood, and here is perhaps the first intimation of that long-forgotten world – in the vision of John Dickens singing patriotic songs in his sitting room, listening eagerly to the sounds coming from a small wooden theatre. A world in which nautical or comic songs and theatrical farces were the most popular form of entertainment. This is the world beside which Charles Dickens grew up.

Four months later, at the beginning of April 1817, they moved from Sheerness along the coast to the much more populous port of Chatham. It is here, in what was sometimes called "the wickedest place in the world", twinned, as it were, with the cathedral town of Rochester, from which it is impossible geographically to separate it, that we first begin to see Charles Dickens *in situ*; that we first begin to see Dickens's childhood clearly, and can trace from it the lines which connect his infancy with his maturity, his childish imagination with his later fiction. It is the area with which he felt himself to be most closely associated, and it is the one to which he returned in later life. Rochester provides a setting for his first novel and for his last; Chatham itself, once described by him as a "mere dream of chalk, and drawbridges, and mastless ships, in a muddy river", was also to become one of the primary landscapes of his imagination.

# Two

THEY moved to Ordnance Terrace, on the brow of a hill – "the most airy and pleasant part" of the parish, Dickens was to say later. It was a comfortable although by no means a spacious house; John Dickens always seemed to prefer *new* buildings, and the houses in this terrace had only recently been constructed. And it was a typical building of its period: the narrow hallway, the dining room on the first floor, and the parlour above it. There was a bedroom on this floor, too, for the parents and then up a further staircase to two attic rooms, one for the servants and one for the children. Charles Dickens seems to have spent half his childhood in such small rooms; and in his fiction also we find attic rooms, musty rooms, parlours, tiny kitchens, sets of chambers, all of them suggesting that Dickens's fictional imagination could best work within the ambience of the small spaces he had known as a child. In Ordnance Terrace there were now three children, two nurses, Aunt Fanny and the Dickenses themselves – a complement of eight in what was effectively a six-room house.

Chatham was of course a naval town, and from the window of his attic bedroom the young Dickens would also have looked out across the hayfields to the prospect of the harbour and dock beyond; he would have seen the tall masts of the sailing ships and the chimneys of the dockyards outlined against the hillsides and orchards beyond them. And beyond them, too, were the Chatham Lines, that system of hollows, pits, drawbridges, subterranean passages and bomb-proof rooms where the soldiers garrisoned in Chatham would engage in manoeuvres or what today would be defined as "war-games". These Lines, Dickens wrote later, were "grassy and innocent enough on the surface, at present, but tough subjects at the core". There were to be found here mysterious "dark vaults" with gratings and with a "smell so chill and earthy". That grave-like odour is one of the most significant of his childhood – it will occur in other contexts, both in Rochester and in Chatham – and it is as if he smelled it for the rest of his life. Ordnance Terrace itself was on the brow of a hill which led to Fort Pitt, one of the many fortifications around the Medway, and beyond the small front garden of the Dickens residence the ground ran down to the old town and to the river beyond. There was a field just in front of the house where the young Dickens used to play with his sister and with his nurse; when he returned many years later, that field had been removed in order to make way for the railway which linked London to Chatham, and here as in so many aspects we may discern how the childhood of Dickens was spent in an older country which was already receding into the far distance when he reached maturity.

The Dickens family lived here for four years. One of the earliest accounts of this period talks of him as "a lively boy of a good, genial, open disposition, and not quarrelsome as most children are at times"; certainly these were some of the happiest years of his childhood, and in later evocations of the area he was to describe "the sheaved corn . . . in the golden fields . . . Peace and abundance". And yet Chatham itself hardly deserved so golden a description. It was a rough and dirty place, the haunt of the sailors and soldiers who were stationed there at a time when the

Napoleonic Wars had just come to an end, leaving the inheritance of wasted lives, maimed bodies, popular discontent and a repressive domestic government. A place known for being "as lawless as it is squalid" and one in which the numerous frowsy drinking places were matched only by the number of equally frowsy brothels. We can be sure that the young Dickens noticed all of this; how much he understood is another matter. But, at a time before the moral restraint of what we have come to call the "Victorian period", the less salubrious sights and odours were simply taken for granted, and there is nothing of the prude or puritan about the later Charles Dickens which would suggest that he was in any way horrified or repelled by what he saw as a boy. Quite the contrary; there is evidence to suggest that "low life" in a certain way always exhilarated him, and the tone of Mr Pickwick's remarks about the Medway towns (no doubt Chatham in particular) has all the hallmarks of Dickens's own ebullient spirits: "The streets present a lively and animated appearance, occasioned chiefly by the conviviality of the military. It is truly delightful to a philanthropic mind, to see these gallant men, staggering along under the influence of an overflow, both of animal, and ardent spirits; more especially when we remember that the following them about, and jesting with them, affords a cheap and innocent amusement for the boy population."

Chatham itself imperceptibly merges with the cathedral town of Rochester, which was of course considerably more "respectable" than Chatham itself; it was an ancient market-town with its own castle, cathedral, and guildhall. Almost as soon as he arrived in the neighbourhood, John Dickens subscribed to *The History of Rochester* which, like his earlier subscription to the *Lives of the Admirals*, suggests his urgent need to become a part of whatever environment in which he found himself, to fit in and as it were to aggrandise himself by attaching himself to the grander

17

elements of the reality around him. The experience of Rochester for his son was quite a different one; it has a narrow high street and on market days it must have been especially crowded and noisy. And yet in Dickens's later descriptions it becomes "the silent High-street" which, with its gables, its ancient clocks, its fantastically carved wooden faces, and its "grave" red-brick buildings, is an emblem of past time. Of course, in the early chapters of *The Pickwick Papers*, Rochester and its environs become the scenes of farce but even during this sport of excitement and of activity, fuelled more than anything else by Dickens's own youthful high spirits, the atmosphere of the cathedral and of the ruined castle cast their own shadow; "frowning walls," says Alfred Jingle, "– tottering arches – dark nooks – crumbling staircases – Old cathedral too – earthy smell – pilgrims' feet worn away the old steps . . .". Thus in his first book; and thus also in his last when, in *The Mystery of Edwin Drood*, Dickens describes the ancient city in just such terms, "A monotonous, silent city, deriving an earthy flavor throughout"; and when a certain Grewgious peers through the great western doors into the cathedral he mutters, "Dear me . . . it's like looking down the throat of Old Time." In his beginning is his end but, in the years between, Dickens constantly sees Rochester in similar terms as reflecting "universal gravity, mystery, decay, and silence" and as thus reflecting upon his own precarious existence: ". . . what a brief little practical joke I seemed to be, in comparison with its solidity, stature, strength, and length of life." Age; dust; mortality; time. These are the images of Rochester drawn from him again and again, and is it too much of a hyperbole to leap from the adult Dickens to the child once more and to suggest that this low, mournful note was one that sounded for him throughout his childhood?

Yet of course there were other notes. Other sounds swirling around him. And none more evocative for him than "the splash and flop of the tide". Dickens grew up beside water – beside the sea, beside the tidal waters, beside the river – and there is no doubt that it runs through his imagination. From a very early age he was acquainted with the sea and the things of the sea. There were occasions, for example, when with his sister Fanny he used to accompany his father on expeditions on the Navy Pay yacht, a very old boat known as the *Chatham*, and upon this he travelled up the Medway to Sheerness. The river itself was then filled with ships and schooners and barges and yachts: here he would have seen the two prison ships, the *Euryalis* and the *Canada*, and the hospital ship, the *Hercules*. In the dockyard itself he glimpsed those vast wooden walls which loom up and which only by an act of imagination can be seen as the sides of ships; and in the dockyard, too, he would have heard the pile-driving and the sluice-driving, the blacksmiths and the carpenters, the mills and the mast-houses, the oar-making and the rope-making; and, everywhere, "the smell of clean timber shavings and turpentine". It was in the Chatham dockyard that he felt the ". . . gravity upon its red brick offices and houses, a staid pretence of having nothing worth mentioning to do, an avoidance of display, which I never saw out of England". And yet even in this aspect of his childhood there was a sense of change all around him; the end of the sailing ship was approaching, and already steamers plied between Dover and Calais.

As a child, too, he first nourished that love for the naval service which is everywhere apparent in his fiction, no less in the wrinkled countenance of Captain Cuttle than in the heroic adventures of shipwrecked mariners. Hence the many nautical expressions which he uses or on some occasions misuses and hence, too, the connection which Dickens generally makes between sailors and neatness or cleanliness; as if life on board ship was for him the epitome of the safe, private and carefully arranged world to which

19

he was always drawn. In his last novels, also, those things which are most cherished by his imagination are those things which are connected with water; with the running tide, the drifting river, the enormous sea, even the reflection of the moon upon water which as a very young child he believed "was a path to Heaven, trodden by the spirits of good people on their way to God . . ." And then there were the ships themselves "filled with their far visions of the sea". On more than one occasion in his published writings he quotes from Campbell's "Ye Mariners of England":

> As I sweep
> Through the deep
> Where the stormy winds do blow . . .

And all through his life he loved to read accounts of maritime travels. Of course it would be wrong to point to Dickens's childhood and say: This is where it all began. Here are the origins of his genius. But the child hears and sees without needing to understand the meaning of its perceptions; the atmosphere of earliest childhood can seep into later writings without the writer himself being aware of any such source.

That Dickens was an observant child, we know; that he was also a very clever one is no less open to proof. His mother was his first teacher; she taught him every day and, to the best of his own recollection, she taught him well. (The fact that she later instructed him in Latin tells us two things – that she was a much better educated woman than has been suggested and that, despite her son's later animadversions against her, there was no sense in which she neglected him.) "I faintly remember," he once told his friend John Forster, "her teaching me the alphabet; and when I look upon the fat black letters in the primer, the puzzling novelty of their shapes, the easy good nature of O and S always seem to present themselves before me as they used to do." We might say, then, that it was to his mother that Dickens owed the first awakening of his childish imagination, the first entry into that world of words which so enthralled him; and even here, in his first steps forward, it is clear how the words themselves satisfy him, how he finds peace in the letters. Was it some such concatenation of reasons that led him once to claim that "I dreamed my first dreams of authorship when I was six years old or so . . .", a sufficiently startling claim, but one which he subsequently modified to the age of eight.

Then in 1818, with his sister Fanny, he was sent to a dame-school in Rome Lane. These archaic institutions – which lasted well into the nineteenth century but had their roots back in the fifteenth – were based on nothing more than the belief that an old lady who could write or read, and who had a few chapbooks at her command, might profitably be employed as the educator of infant minds. That there were some good dame-schools it is impossible to doubt but Charles Dickens was implacable in his hostility to them, and it is likely that his attitude was acquired from his own experience. In later life he said that his particular dame-school was "over a dyer's shop", but in a speech he once gave he seems to come closer to the actual feelings of that time when he was ". . . under the early dominion of an old lady, who to my mind ruled the world with the birch"; and under her auspices, too, one senses the power which the young Dickens found and felt in words. "I never now see a row of large, black, fat staring Roman capitals, but this reminiscence rises up before me." What rises up before him, especially, are the *clothes* which his fellow pupils wore – a brown beaver bonnet, a black dress, a pinafore. The dyer's shop, too, suggests nothing so much as odours. And, yes, these are the perceptions which a child would have, perceptions which he is quite likely to recall.

In this period he was educated with his slightly older
21

sister, Fanny. What we know of Fanny herself is that she was both quick and gifted. In later life she was described as possessing "decision of character" as well as a "natural buoyancy of spirits and fondness for society"; she was also said to be self-reliant "in no ordinary degree – together with almost restless activity and practical energy". In some respects she resembled her younger brother, therefore; together, they seem actively to have differentiated themselves from their parents in a way that their younger siblings were not to do. There is a difference, however; it was said that "there was nothing of the romantic in her composition".

So it was that in these infant years he went to school with his sister, was taught by his mother, and began to read. His first companions were 'picture books', as he said later, ". . . picture books: all about scimitars and slippers and turbans and dwarfs and giants and genii and fairies, and Blue-beards and bean-stalks and riches and caverns and forests and Valentines and Orsons: and all new and all true." He would later recall certain of the picture books at which he gazed; *Jack the Giant-Killer* was one and *Little Red Riding Hood* was another, "my first love," he said of the latter. No doubt she has been the first love of other small children, too, and in the rhymes and stories of the nursery we can trace a real human continuity in the life of this country over the last two or three centuries. It has been said that the childhood of most men and women is, through the generations, much the same. This may or may not be true – the conditions of the early nineteenth century are in some ways now irrecoverable, so the statement can be neither proved nor disproved – but it is the case that much of its imaginative climate remains the same. No doubt that is why the work of Dickens still retains such a powerful hold; it springs from the roots that we all in some part share.

There are other sudden illuminations of this shared past

from Dickens, and characteristically he remembers a particular scene or image which for some reason has never left him – a coloured engraving of Mrs Skipton "in a florid style of art", the picture of a bull pulling a bell rope in the *Cock Robin* saga, a shaft of light illuminating Cain as he murders his brother, a Russian serf amid the snows; all these images returned to him. But not all these memories were to do with death or deprivation, and in a later essay he was able to recall the verses printed in a picture book entitled *The Dandies' Ball, or High Life in the City*.

But he was not only a reader; like all good children, there were times when he was an avid listener. Children's stories. Nursery stories. Bedtime stories. Whether these were told by a nurse or by his mother is now no longer clear. There were two young female servants with the family at Ordnance Terrace – a Mary Weller and a Jane Bonny – but in later essays he also describes one called Mercy and another called Sally Flanders. One of these figures was apparently "a sallow woman with a fishy eye, an aquiline nose, and a green gown, whose specialty was a dismal narrative" of a landlord who turned his guests into meat pies. And Dickens goes on to say that this narrator "had a Ghoulish pleasure, I have long been persuaded, in terrifying me to the utmost confines of my reason" as well as making disparaging comments about his friends and relatives. Then there was the nurse who told him stories about a certain Captain Murderer, about the curse of a talking rat with its cry "Oh Keep the rats out of the convicts' burying ground!". That last phrase has a convincing resonance with the more Gothic elements in Dickens's fiction; but for that reason alone we would be wise to be cautious about its plain matter-of-fact truth.

And so these early years passed, with little to report except for the slow increase of the Dickens family and the somewhat insecure ability of John Dickens's finances to support them: in August 1819, just three weeks before the

23

birth of another daughter, he borrowed the large sum of two hundred pounds from a certain James Milbourne, at an annual repayment of twenty-six pounds for life. In March of the following year Dickens's salary was raised according to precedent but nevertheless he never managed to keep up with the necessary repayments and eventually his brother-in-law, Thomas Barrow, whom he persuaded to countersign the debt, was forced to repay it for him; this in part accounts for something of the later coolness of Elizabeth's family towards her husband, and the document itself, known as "the Deed", was later to figure largely in Dickens's childhood. Then in August 1820 another child emerged – this time a son, Frederick, who was in succeeding years to be a source of great annoyance to his famous brother. So already there are signs here of all the calamities which Dickens was later to visit upon his fictional families: the burgeoning household, the debts, the threats of legal action all suggesting an atmosphere of strain, if not exactly of anxiety, which the young Dickens himself knew well.

But John Dickens was not without resources, and the pursuit of esteem under difficulties is clearly a mark of his character: thus it was that in March 1820 he reported for *The Times* on a fire at Chatham. Even if this did not earn him immortal fame, it at least ensured him a place on the vestry committee which was organising help for those affected by the disaster. It would be too much to claim that his son's subsequent interests, both in journalism *and* in fires, owe anything to John Dickens's activities; but there is one mark of paternal influence of which there can be no doubt. A young companion of Charles Dickens in these Chatham years – a certain J. H. Stoqueler who in a late reminiscence called his friend "Charley Wag", no doubt on the principle that a childhood companionship earns at least the right to be jocular – describes how he and the young Dickens used to idle their time together on
24

Rochester Bridge or walk up the road which leads to a house known as Gad's Hill Place. It was, it seems, a favourite journey of Dickens and there is no doubt that his goal was of a private character. For it was this house which his father had once pointed out to him; Dickens used to tell the story to his friends whenever he later passed it, and he recorded it at least twice in print. So, for once, we can be sure of its authenticity: ". . . upon first seeing it as he came from Chatham with his father," Forster once wrote, "and looking up at it with much admiration, he had been promised that he might himself live in it or in some such house when he came to be a man, if he would only work hard enough." And so, thirty-six years later, he bought it. Anyone who doubts the influence of Charles Dickens's childhood upon his later predilections and obsessions may take their scepticism no further, for without doubt only a man heavily influenced by his father's praise would spend the next thirty years of his life trying to earn it. Gad's Hill Place might have been a house that his father picked at random, a convenient emblem of prestige and property; and yet it continued to haunt his son. It is intriguing, too, that as a boy he did so often walk to this house outside Rochester: he wanted to see it again and again as an image of his possible future, he wanted a fine house even then. Even at that time he seems to have wanted to escape the narrow and over-populated domesticity of his real home.

There are other less striking memories to be drawn up from the depths of his childhood and, once again, it is better to rely upon Dickens's stray asides than upon his more elaborate attempts either at autobiography or at fictional reconstruction. Thus it is we can believe him when he was passing through Chatham and pointed to a particular wall, exclaiming, "I remember . . . my poor Mother, God forgive her, put me on the edge of that wall so that I might wave my hat and cheer George IV – then Prince Regent – who was driving by." One can believe the

25

brief memory of ". . . the kite that once plucked at my own hand like an airy friend". One can believe that he really did have his ears boxed "for informing a lady visitor . . . that a certain ornamental object on the table, which was covered with marbled-paper, 'wasn't marble'", for it fits in with the evident fact that, as we shall see, the young Dickens had a great belief in literal meaning. Certainly we can believe a strange episode that his sister seems to have confirmed, when, for reasons that he could not remember, and in a period about which he is vague, ". . . we stealthily conducted the man with the wooden leg – whom we knew intimately – into the coal cellar, and that, in getting him over the coals to hide him behind some partition there was beyond, his wooden leg bored itself in among the small coals . . ." There were a lot of gentlemen with wooden legs in this naval port (it was, you might say, an occupational hazard) and this anecdote has all the hallmarks of some small intrigue between the servants "below stairs". In fact Dickens seems to have had something of an obsession with wooden legs – they pop up time and again in his fiction – and the recollection of this man with his stump thrust among the small coals was to be revived in *Our Mutual Friend* as the spectacle of Silas Wegg with ". . . his self-willed leg sticking into the ashes about half-way down". So are childhood scenes revived in fiction, the lost images restored.

But, if we are to talk of his infancy in these terms, then there is one aspect of early nineteenth-century England which, perhaps more than anything else beside his own solitary reading, marks him out for his eventual fate: it is his childhood love for the theatre, for pantomime. There were occasions when he was taken by relatives to London, and there can be little doubt that this was primarily to visit the theatres; he specifically remembers, on one occasion, being taken to see Grimaldi, "in whose honor I am informed I clapped my hands with great precocity". And

John Forster adds this in his biography: "By Lamert, I have often heard him say, he was first taken to the theatre at the very tenderest age." Lamert was a friend of the family – his stepfather eventually married 'Aunt Fanny' – and the theatre was the Theatre Royal in Rochester, on the New Road which leads out of Chatham and connects it with the cathedral town. The building survives still, a small, narrow place, in which it is hard to see the crucible of young Dickens's imagination. And yet so it proved. "The sweet, dingy, shabby little country theatre" Charles Dickens was to call it, with the odour of sawdust, orange-peel and lamp-oil which he savoured all his life. And it was here that he saw *Richard III* and *Macbeth*, Lillo's *The London Merchant or the History of George Barnwell* and Rowe's *Jane Shore*; the world here was transformed into farce and melodrama, and in all his accounts of his childhood expeditions to the theatre there can be sensed the unmistakeable hunger and intensity of Dickens's gaze. He missed nothing; the funny man "in a red scratch wig" who sings a comic song about a leg of mutton while imprisoned in the deepest dungeon, the hole in the green curtain, Richard III pretending to sleep on a sofa that is too small for him, the reappearance of the Witches and King Duncan in various walk-on parts, the words of the irate rustic ("Dom thee, squire, coom on with thy fistes then!"); and he believed everything. He loved the bad acting and the stage costumes, the absurdity of the actors and the banality of the plays, almost as if they were simulacra of life itself, and in all these accounts he conjures up the rapt vision of the child sitting in that "Dear, narrow, uncomfortable, faded-cushioned, flea-haunted, single tier of boxes" in the Theatre Royal. It was a vision which never left him, even though it might fade each time he left the bright theatre in order to return to the dreary, dull and settled world beyond it.

But if there was one theatrical art which truly inspired

him, it was that of pantomime, "that jocund world," he called it, ". . . where there is no affliction or calamity that leaves the least impression . . . where everyone, in short, is so superior to all the accidents of life, though encountering them at every turn". A bright, safe, world in which comedy mingled with tragedy, scenes of farce with scenes of pathos, love and death, Pantaloon and Columbine, dark scenes and transformation scenes, processions and patriotic songs, comic dances and rhymed couplets, everything to be sung and not spoken. "No words can express," one contemporary wrote, "the animation, the gaiety, the boldness, the madness, the incoherence, the coarseness, the splendour, the whimsical poetry, the brutality of these Christmas pantomimes." In *Great Expectations* there comes a point when Pip remembers how he had laid down his head after a Fair because it had been "too much for my young senses". And we must picture the young Dickens in a similar way — over-wrought, over-eager, screaming with delight, watching everything and forgetting nothing. In later life he enjoyed nothing so much as imitating the postures and the manner of the clown; on one occasion, he "began playing the clown in pantomime on the edge of a bath" and then by accident tumbled into the warm water, and, on another, he demonstrated on a train journey how the clown "flops and folds himself up like a jack-knife"; he was also adept at improvising the "patter" between clown and pantaloon. We see that same spirit in the older Dickens who, even in the years close to his death, would still stoop down in order to read the bills advertising the London pantomimes.

It is in this spirit, too, that we must see him constructing and working a toy theatre in his more wretched childhood years after Chatham; he had it in Camden Town, London, complete with the sheets of characters (penny plain and twopence coloured) to be cut out, pasted onto cardboard and glued to wires or sticks. These then would be pushed onto the small stage, with its backdrops, props and scenes;

in full costume, and in suitable postures, the tiny cardboard creatures would then act out the play. Here it was that Dickens performed *The Miller and His Men* and *Elizabeth, or The Exile of Siberia*; his brothers moved the little players, which sometimes had an unfortunate habit of creasing up or becoming unglued, while Charles himself read and acted out the scenes. He was even writing now, and he said later that his first piece was composed when he was nine or ten years old – *Misnar*, a tragedy based on *Tales of the Genii* and concerning a gracious and wise young prince (no doubt Dickens himself) who has a habit of uttering wise thoughts when surrounded by demons or monsters. Dickens once declared that "I was . . . an actor and a speaker from a baby" and in this vision of the young boy, book in hand, taking on the roles in this miniature theatre we see, in miniature too, an emblem of Dickens's own relation to the world. His daughter once observed that, when he was writing his fiction, he would literally act out the words in front of a mirror before placing them down on paper, and of course eventually he came to read out the words of his novels to the audiences of England and America. He never abandoned his inheritance; when many years later he was living at Gad's Hill Place, a toy theatre was given to his son and at once Dickens became fascinated by it – he set to work to produce the first piece, called *The Elephant of Siam*, and, his son recalled, he "pegged away at the landscapes and architecture of Siam with an amount of energy which in any other man would have been something prodigious, but which I soon learned to look upon as quite natural in him". So, in his later life, in his constant attendance at the theatre, and in his own skills as a performer, we understand how much the garish light of the stage represented for him both the memory and the intensification of childhood experience.

One component of that experience was something which Dickens himself called "conviviality". The idea of entertainment, of an audience sharing in a certain pleasure, the idea of friendship, the idea of the family, all things which he tried helplessly to resurrect throughout his life precisely because they derive from the memory of his early childhood. Mary Weller, his young nurse at Ordnance Terrace, has a distinct recollection of him in that light. "Sometimes Charles would come downstairs and say to me, 'Now, Mary, clear the kitchen, we are going to have such a game.' "There is no doubt that this is a true memory, and here for the first time we have a clear echo of Charles Dickens's voice; it is one repeated in his own writing, with "I've got sitch a game for you, Sammy" in *The Pickwick Papers* and "There's *such* a goose, Martha" in his public reading of *A Christmas Carol*. So does the voice of the child re-emerge in the man. George Stroughill, a friend from Ordnance Terrace, would sometimes bring in his Magic Lantern but also "they would sing, recite, and perform parts of plays". Charles himself had a "favourite piece for recitation" which was "The Voice of the Sluggard" by Dr Watts; "the little boy," according to Mary Weller, "used to give it with great effect, and with *such* action and *such* attitudes" (one sees here also the older Dickens, head thrown back, hand in the air, reciting from his novels):

'Tis the voice of the sluggard; I heard him complain,
   You have wak'd me too soon, I must slumber again.

He would have recited passages from the classics, too, and no doubt much of his acquaintance with Shakespeare came from such a source. And then he liked to sing. He had a "clear treble voice" and at this time, Mary Weller remembers, "sea-songs were . . . his especial favourites".

The young Dickens sang at birthday parties and at Twelfth Night parties. He was also writing his own songs; he composed and sang a comic number entitled "Sweet Betsy Ogle", and this delight in comic performance is to be seen also in his rendition of a "mono-polylogue" in the manner of the great comedian Charles Mathews; these performances consisted, as the name suggests, in one person playing all the parts of a short play and in doing so by means of stock phrases, comic mannerisms and the mimicry of dialect. All these features would later reappear in his mature fiction, of course, and it will soon also become clear what a gifted mimic Dickens was; but it is here, in these infantile performances, that we see the beginning of the use of such gifts. It is one of the most important images of Dickens's childhood – the young boy, beaming, eyes shining, singing, striking attitudes, giving a perfect performance, being cheered and applauded.

At some point during the early months of 1821 Dickens left the dame-school in Rome Lane and moved to a larger and more promising school in Clover Lane – a school run by a young man of twenty-three, William Giles, the son of a Baptist minister and himself a Dissenter. Giles had a reputation in the Chatham neighbourhood "as a cultivated reader and elocutionist". He seems to have spent some time at Oxford, teaching at a school there, but although he was debarred from residence at the university because of his nonconformist faith it is possible that he was given permission to attend certain courses. Certainly he was a well-educated young man and some indication of the nature of his Chatham establishment can be glimpsed in an advertisement for another of his schools which he placed some years later – "The English Department is distinguished by an approved analytical method of tuition, by due attention to Letter-writing, Translating and the composition of Theses and Essays. In the Commercial department, great care is observed in securing to the Pupils a good hand-writing . . ." This is close to the syllabus in which the young Dickens himself would have been instructed, with the addition, too, of lessons culled from Lindley Murray's grammar, a book to which the

31

schoolmaster Wackford Squeers alludes in *Nicholas Nickleby*. "It's me, and me's the first person singular . . ." Dickens himself was equally punctilious about such matters of grammar and, although there are occasions when the momentum and expansiveness of his style lead him to neglect the niceties of syntax, he was always able to spot and pounce upon the mistakes of others.

Dickens remembered many details of his time at this Chatham school; he remembered its playing fields where, according to his daughter, Mamie, "he and his friends went through — in play — all sorts of wonderful and heroic achievements"; he remembered the time of his first school examination when he recited some verses from the *Humourist's Miscellany* and received, according to his own memory of the occasion, a double encore from all those present. In a letter to his schoolmaster many years later Dickens observed that ". . . you magnify, in my bewildered sight, into something awful, though not at all severe". We may acquit Giles, then, of being the prototype for any of the grotesque schoolmasters in Dickens's fiction. During the course of his two years at this school Dickens came to be on close terms with the Giles family itself; two of William's younger brothers were also enrolled here, and William's sister remembered him as ". . . a very handsome boy, with long curly hair of a light colour".

The Giles family seem to have played some part in the next move of the Dickens family for, soon after Dickens entered the school, the family migrated to a house at 18 St Mary's Place (known as "the Brook") which was next to the Baptist meeting house where William's father was the minister. It was a "plain-looking whitewashed plasterfront" sort of house, complete with the regulation small garden before and behind, a semi-detached six-room affair. It could not have been much smaller than the house in Ordnance Terrace, but there is a definite possibility that it was in social terms a step down for John Dickens from the airy and pleasant purlieus of the Terrace to an area which was essentially for humble dockyard officials. It was of course conveniently closer to the dockyard itself, and other contemporaries have described it as an area "of singular architectural beauty and charm" — even if that charm might have been of a somewhat poignant kind, since from the upper windows of the house the young Dickens could see the church and churchyard which he later memorialised in "A Child's Dream of a Star". It is not clear, then, whether the Dickens family had begun that slow descent which was eventually to lead to a debtors' prison, but certainly there seems to have been some change of atmosphere here; and Mary Weller has recalled that "there were no such juvenile entertainments at this house as I had seen at the Terrace".

Yet what better place could be found to speculate about Dickens's own religious leanings during his childhood years? He does not seem to have leaned very far in any particular direction, his most striking religious memory being of the fireplace in St Mary's Place, of which the tiles were illustrated with scenes from the Scriptures (he gave it to Scrooge, perhaps in revenge, in *A Christmas Carol*). There is one more lengthy memory of his childhood experience of religion, but again it is not designed to make converts; the little Dickens, according to Dickens himself, was on occasions "dragged by the hair of my head" to listen to a preacher, or, as he puts it, ". . . to be steamed like a potato in the unventilated breath of the powerful Boanerges Boiler and his congregation". This may be a reminiscence of a time when he was taken to the Baptist chapel next door — perhaps under the combined influence of the Giles family weighing down upon the Dickenses — but, since this narrative is part of his writing as the "Uncommercial Traveller", it is also possible that Dickens is only imagining the scene. That he did undergo some form of religious education does seem likely, however;

in one letter he specifically mentions ". . . the immense absurdities that were suggested to my own childhood by the like injudicious catechising" about such matters as "the Lamb of God".

In any case, even if Charles Dickens was not properly introduced to the beauties and mysteries of Christianity, he found beauties and mysteries elsewhere. For it was in this little house, in St Mary's Place, that he himself locates his first awareness of books and his first entry into literature. In the room next to his own, his father kept what seems to have been a standard set of volumes: "From that blessed little room, *Roderick Random*, *Peregrine Pickle*, *Humphrey Clinker*, *Tom Jones*, *The Vicar of Wakefield*, *Gil Blas* and *Robinson Crusoe* came out, a glorious host, to keep me company. They kept alive my fancy, and my hope of something beyond that place and time – they, and *The Arabian Nights*, and the *Tales of the Genii* – and did me no harm . . ." *My hope of something beyond that place and time* – here are the irremediable longings, the aspirations, of the small boy in the somewhat nondescript little house.

Reading is the other significant image of Dickens's childhood, to be placed beside that of the young boy singing and acting upon a tavern table – it is the image of the solitary child, lost in his book, preoccupied with his own fancies, creating his own world. Creating his own world so vividly that it supplanted the one around him. There is a reflection of this when, in *A Christmas Carol*, Ebenezer Scrooge is led helplessly back to his childhood and sees "his younger self, intent upon his reading. Suddenly a man, in foreign garments: wonderfully real and distinct to look at: stood outside the window, with an axe stuck in his belt, leading an ass laden with wood by the bridle. 'Why it's Ali Baba!' Scrooge exclaimed in ecstasy . . . One Christmas time, when yonder solitary child was left here all alone, he *did* come, for the first time, just like that. Poor boy!"

Of course such a picture of the young Dickens is quite

different from the memories of him in the same period. One contemporary at William Giles's school recalled his "marked geniality" and "his proficiency in all boyish sports such as cricket etc.". There will be many similar descriptions of Dickens's maturity, too, but in a very real sense they are deceptive; there was that within him which avoided the notice of other people, a stiller and more attentive person, a darker and deeper temperament which he literally kept to himself. It is not surprising, therefore, that in his later semi-autobiographical accounts of childhood another self steps out of the gaiety and the good humour; there emerges a child who is guilty and anxious, sensitive and quick to anger, filled with apprehensions but never expressing them to anyone.

So what kind of imagination was being formed by this boy who appeared cheerful and gregarious, but who believed himself to be weak and lonely? It is hard to forget those images of death which the mature novelist seems particularly to associate with childhood, in part deriving from self-pity, but perhaps also an echo of his two siblings who died in infancy. More significantly, however, it is clear that for Dickens childhood is often associated with the experience of sudden terror and of inexplicable fear, just as Scrooge's blood was ". . . conscious of a terrible sensation to which it had been a stranger from infancy".

That he was a sensitive child is not now in any doubt, of course, and his last years at Chatham would for him have been marked, if not by the slow decline of his family at least by the gradual increase in its problems. Although his father was progressing through the ranks of the bureaucracy in pre-ordained fashion – he became a third clerk in Chatham in 1821, and in the December of that year was transferred from the Pay Office to the branch which inspected seamen's wills and powers of attorney – his own financial position was less secure. In May, as a result of his inability to pay the interest owed on the money he had borrowed from James Milbourne, his brother-in-law was forced to cancel the Deed by paying John Dickens's creditor a total of two hundred and thirteen pounds; from this date, relations between the Barrows and the Dickens were little short of frosty. Then the family itself began to change, an experience which is uniquely unsettling to a small child. His aunt, Mary Allen, married Thomas Lamert in December 1821 and the newly wedded couple moved to Ireland, together with one of the servants, Jane Bonny. The next year, however, was one which remained more prominently in Dickens's memory – in March 1822 a child was born, and christened Alfred Lamert Dickens in memory of the infant who had died eight years before. But this birth was followed by the calamity of another death; Dickens's infant sister, Harriet, died from the smallpox (the disease which disfigures Esther Summerson in *Bleak House*). Again the death of the sibling may have provoked in him feelings of fear and of guilt: this cannot be known, although it is curious how often in the lives of writers there is to be found the early death of a younger brother or sister. Whether Harriet died in Chatham or in London is not clear, because it was in June of this year that John Dickens was formally recalled to work at Somerset House. The house in St Mary's Place was relinquished, and there was a sale of some of the Dickenses' household effects; a local shipwright, who was about to marry Mary Weller, bought the best set of chairs. Mary Weller herself left, and an orphan from Chatham Workhouse was taken on as the new servant. The remaining furniture was sent ahead by water and the Dickens family made their way to London in a carriage; they travelled to Camden Town and settled in a new house in Bayham Street.

For reason or reasons unknown, Charles Dickens did not travel with them. He remained behind in Chatham, staying in the house of his schoolmaster, William Giles, for about three months. Perhaps he asked to stay in order to complete some phase of his education – even as a ten-year-old boy he was no doubt determined and ambitious – or perhaps his parents, knowing his sensitive disposition, wished him to remain there until they were properly settled in the capital.

# *Three*

L ONDON. The Great Oven. The Fever Patch. Babylon.
The Great Wen. In the early autumn of 1822 the
ten-year-old Charles Dickens entered his kingdom. He was
met at the end of his journey from Chatham, and rejoined
his family in their new house in Camden Town – 16 Bayham Street, a recently erected house (no more than ten
years old) in what was then an area only just being
developed. He was given a tiny garret room at the top of
the house, which looked out over a small garden surrounded by a wall. There were two rooms on the first
and ground floors, as well as a basement, and within this
somewhat confined space there were now the Dickens
parents, their five children, the servant whom they had
brought from Chatham Workhouse and James Lamert, the
stepson of the man whom Aunt Fanny had married. He
was a lodger, whose payments must materially have
helped the family but whose effect upon the life of Charles
Dickens was to be little short of catastrophic.

Camden Town itself was a quiet and respectable semi-
rural area, almost "genteel" despite the problem of rob-
beries which always beset those whose houses abutted
upon lanes and open fields. There was grass growing up
in the newly paved road, and water was to be taken from
a pump almost opposite Dickens's new house. To the south
was Somers Town, but there were fields between; to the

north the wooded heights of Highgate and Hampstead; to the east and west there were fields and market gardens, notable amongst them the tea-gardens of the famous Mother Red Cap, a place of resort, and if not quite a sylvan retreat at least something very different from the gin shops of the metropolis. Where Euston Station now stands there were fields of sheep and cows. The road between Camden Town and the hamlet of Kentish Town led through open fields, unlit, solitary and the haunt of footpads. Bayham Street was in fact one of the few roads already put down upon this area, of which the chief occupations were still haymaking and cricket, and to one contemporary at least it was nothing less than the countryside itself: "To my childish apprehension it was a country village. It seemed a green and pleasant spot."

Dickens's recollections were somewhat different. Some thirty-two years later he was to describe it as touching "the outskirts of the fields" but "at that period it was as shabby, dingy, damp and mean a neighbourhood as one would desire not to see . . . quiet and dismal . . . crazily built houses – the largest eight-roomed – were rarely shaken by any conveyance heavier than the spring van that came to carry off the goods of a 'sold up' tenant . . . we used to run to the doors and windows to look at a cab, it was such a rare sight". And he remembers, too, the band playing in the Mother Red Cap tea-gardens. ". . . They used to open with 'Begone Dull Care' and to end with a tune which the neighbourhood recognised as 'I'd rather have a Guinea than a One-pound-note'." To John Forster, he described his house itself as "a mean small tenement, with a wretched little back-garden abutting on a squalid court". In fact neither the house nor the area was as mean or as dismal as the locale of Dickens's imagination: it is as if the young child, distracted by his own unhappiness from seeing the actual nature of the place, had already fastened his misery upon his surroundings.

For the fact was that the young boy remembered Camden Town as the place where he first fell into neglect. Of his father he wrote in an autobiographical fragment, ". . . in the ease of his temper, and the straitness of his means, he appeared to have utterly lost at this time the idea of educating me at all, and to have utterly put from him the notion that I had any claim upon him, in that regard, whatever. So I degenerated into cleaning his boots of a morning, and my own; and making myself useful in the work of the little house . . . and going on such poor errands as arose out of our poor way of living." He seems to have referred to this episode to John Forster on many occasions, and his first biographer recalls his words: "As I thought, in the little back garret in Bayham Street, of all I had lost in losing Chatham, what would I have given, if I had had anything to give, to have been sent back to any other school, to have been taught something anywhere!" It is to be noted that Dickens here re-emphasises the loss of schooling; in the unlikelihood of any more education all the agony of the little boy seems to be encompassed. The future was snatched away, the dreams and visions of his youth thrown off, all the hope he had of becoming a famous man and all the knowledge of the talent within his own breast (for even children have that knowledge) were of no account. For a talented and ambitious child there is no hell worse than this; all the dirt, all the dreariness, all the poverty which he summons up in his account of Bayham Street spring from it. James Lamert built him a toy theatre, and he seems to have written small sketches (one of a deaf and elderly lady who waited on them at table); but these could only have been stray and brief entertainments, all the more sorrowful because they reminded him of the life he had left behind and the skills which seemed to him now about to waste away for ever; as if, when his consciousness of himself were soiled, then his whole small world became soiled also.

He makes his little hero, David Copperfield, ten years old when he begins work at Murdstone and Grinby's – "a little labouring hind" – which is precisely the age when he came to London, and there are countless passages in his fiction where he places all the poverty and horror of the world in London, all of its peace and seclusion in the neighbouring countryside of Kent. Yet sometimes the reality seemed to him worse than anything he could profitably put in his fiction; in the published version of *David Copperfield*, the sentence which describes the onset of this period in his life reads, "And now I fell into a state of neglect, which I cannot look back upon without compassion". But an examination of the emendations in his manuscript revives the lost sentence which he originally wrote: "And now I fell into a state of dire neglect, which I have never been able to look back upon without a kind of agony." And in his fiction, too, the house of Bayham Street is recalled; it is the house where the poor Cratchits celebrate their Christmas feast in *A Christmas Carol*, and it is the house of Mr Micawber in *David Copperfield* which displays an air of "faded gentility" in a "rank and sloppy street"; his own old garret room appears in the same novel as ". . . a close chamber; stencilled all over with an ornament which my young imagination represented as a blue muffin; and very scantily furnished".

It was here, then, that he sank into what he once described as "a solitary condition apart from all other boys of his own age". Alone, friendless, bereft of any possible future or any alternative life, he would sometimes walk down the little paved road of Bayham Street and look south towards the city itself just as he had once looked out to sea in Chatham; from here the great city, smoky in the grey light, might have seemed to him like "a giant phantom in the air". There was death at home, as well; it is possible that his young sister, Harriet, died here and not

41

in Chatham; certainly his Aunt Fanny died, in Ireland, in the autumn of this year.

That the city was, however, in part for him an enchanted place is not in doubt. In an essay, "Gone Astray", he records how in this period he was taken by an unnamed "Somebody" to see St Giles, and how he somehow managed to become separated from his adult companion. So he wanders through the streets of London quite alone, all the time noticing how "grand and mysterious" everything seemed; he meets a dog, eats a sausage, sees the giants of Guildhall and thinks of every City merchant as a creature of fable. Even in his forlorn lost condition he was "inspired by a mighty faith in the marvellousness of everything". How precise a recollection this is may be a matter of dispute; he himself says, however, that it was "literally and exactly how I went astray. They used to say I was an odd child, and I suppose I was." Indeed the image of the little boy, filled with both wonder and apprehension, seems genuine enough. And there is one other incident in the story which carries a certain conviction; he decides to visit the theatre and: "Whenever I saw that my appearance attracted attention, either outside the doors or afterwards within the theatre, I pretended to look out for somebody who was taking care of me, and from whom I was separated, and to exchange nods and smiles with that creature of my imagination." Here is a timely reminder of the potential horror awaiting some children in the streets of London but here, more especially, is an image of the ten-year-old boy who is already something of an actor.

For the skills of his Chatham youth had not completely been abandoned. John Dickens still retained the friendship of Christopher Huffam, Charles Dickens's godfather, and there were many occasions when the young boy was taken to Huffam's house and shop in Limehouse. Christopher Huffam, together with his brother, was a sail-maker and ship's chandler who lived in Church Row, just behind the great Limehouse church of Nicholas Hawksmoor, and their business was in Garford Street almost opposite Limehouse Hole. It was in the house of this prosperous merchant that John Dickens placed his young son upon the dining room table and prevailed upon him to sing. "The Cat's Meat Man" was one of his favourites:

> Down in the street cries the cat's meat man,
> Fango, dango, with his barrow and can.

And on one occasion, according to Charles Dickens himself, he was declared by one of the audience of neighbours to be nothing less than a "prodigy". But there were other reasons for the young boy to remember this place with affection. In his novels marine-stores like that of Solomon Gills in *Dombey and Son* are treated with great affection, as Dickens always did with the sea and with the things of the sea, and it seems likely that the atmosphere of Limehouse reminded the young boy of the ambience of Chatham which he had known just a few months before. On his journeys to see Christopher Huffam he would have passed forges, ropeyards, mast-makers, oar-makers, boat-builders. All the familiar smells and sights of his recent childhood would then have returned; and beside the Huffams' brick-walled workshop, where they made sails, stored rope and piles of chain, the Thames still flowed. So did he here discover the comfort of childhood associations? Yet was it also in the prosperity of the Huffam household that he began to feel the disparity between this life and the life of Bayham Street?

Certainly John Dickens was, all the time, coming closer to bankruptcy. The poor-rate due to be paid in April of 1823 was only met by him after a summons, and in the following year he seems not to have made any attempt to pay the local rates for paving and lighting. By moving to London he had also lost various 'outport allowances' and it has been calculated that his salary dropped by some ninety pounds a year. This would not have been a welcome development but nonetheless, on a salary of approximately £350 per year, he ought to have been able to meet all the expenses of his household. Instead there seems to have been a steady drain on his resources, the reasons for which remain unclear. It has been suggested that he drank, evidently on a stray remark of Charles Dickens many years later that a man might procure bread and meat on credit but that — gesturing at a bottle — ". . . has no right to do this sort of thing in the same way". It is hard to believe that he was a drunkard, however, and there is no evidence to support that fact. It has also been suggested that he was a secret gambler, and this on the evidence of Little Nell's grandfather in *The Old Curiosity Shop*, whose addiction to gambling Dickens describes with such success. But these speculations are perhaps not necessary; the fact is that John Dickens was simply and recklessly improvident, one of those people to whom no thought of responsibilities can avert the need to assuage the pleasure of the moment.

When Dickens first came to Bayham Street, the "night-life" of London fascinated him; particularly he was struck by the world of Seven Dials — ". . . what wild visions of prodigies of wickedness, want, and beggary, arose in my mind out of that place!" But now there came a time when that life would come all too close to him. It began with James Lamert. He was no longer living with the Dickens family — no doubt the want of space and the noise of small children had something to do with his decision — but he had been approached by his cousin, George Lamert, to become the chief manager of a business he had just purchased. This was Warren's Blacking of 30 Hungerford Stairs, a manufacturer of boot blacking, and it was James Lamert's suggestion that Charles, now entering his twelfth year, should also be employed there at a salary of six or seven shillings a week. Dickens himself put the matter baldly: ". . . the offer was accepted very willingly by my father and mother, and on a Monday morning I went down to the blacking warehouse to begin my business life." The date generally fixed for this inauspicious occasion is Monday, 9 February, 1824, just two days after his twelfth birthday. It might have seemed to him ". . . some dark conspiracy to thrust him forth upon the world", to use the words in *Oliver Twist*, but to his parents it must have been a welcome opportunity for their son to be gainfully employed and to help with their own straitened finances. In a business run by their kind relative, after all, what rungs might their son not climb on the journey towards gentility?

And so on that fateful Monday he walked the three miles from Camden Town to the Strand, down Hampstead Road and Tottenham Court Road, crossing the High Street which leads into Broad St Giles's and then down St Martin's Lane. Then across the Strand into an area of squalid corners and alleys, and descending Hungerford Stairs to the river itself. His destination was the last house on the left, beside the Thames itself, ". . . a crazy, tumbledown old house, abutting of course on the river, and literally overrun with rats. Its wainscotted rooms and its rotten floors and staircase, and the old grey rats swarming down in the cellars, and the sound of their squeaking and scuffling coming up the stairs at all times, and the dirt and decay of the place, rise up visibly before me, as if I were there again."

This was the place to which the twelve-year-old Dickens came, then. James Lamert greeted him, and took him to the counting house on the first floor; there was an alcove there, looking down at the Thames, which was to be his place of work. A boy who worked downstairs, Bob Fagin, was called up to show Dickens of what that work would consist: he was to take the bottles of blacking and prepare them for sale. Not bottles exactly, but receptacles rather like small flower pots made of earthenware and with a rim around them for string. Dickens's job was ". . . to cover the pots of paste-blacking: first with a piece of oil-paper, and then with a piece of blue paper; to tie them round with a string; and then to clip the paper close and neat all round." When he had finished a few gross of these, "I was to paste on each a printed label". He worked for ten hours a day, with a meal break at twelve and a tea-break in the late afternoon. The boy himself, ". . . of singular abilities: quick, eager, delicate, and soon hurt, bodily or mentally", now sitting at a work-table with scissors and string and paste, looking out at the dreary river just beneath him, bearing away his hopes. It is not too much to say that his childhood came suddenly to an end, together with that world of reading and of imagination in which the years of his childhood had been passed. But it was not gone; it had ended so suddenly that it did not gradually fade and disappear as most childhoods do. Instead it was preserved entire in the amber of Dickens's rich memory. "My whole nature was so penetrated with the grief and humiliation of such considerations, that even now, famous and caressed and happy, I often forget in my dreams that I have a dear wife and children; even that I am a man; and wander desolately back to that time of my life."

It was not the only catastrophe of that time since, no more than a few days after the boy's introduction to Warren's, John Dickens was arrested for debt. It was at the instigation of a certain James Karr, a baker who lived round the corner of Bayham Street in Camden Street, and the contested amount was a large one, forty pounds. It was not the only debt of John Dickens – there were still claims outstanding even from Rochester as well as London – and after his arrest he was taken to a "sponging house" or "half-way house" where debtors about to be imprisoned tried to obtain relief before the prison doors closed upon them. Now "with swollen eyes and through shining tears" his young son ran errands and carried messages for John

Dickens, no doubt some to his father's mother and brother. But it seems that John Dickens had either claimed too much in the past or on this occasion had gone too far; no aid was forthcoming. On 20 February, he was incarcerated in the Marshalsea Prison as an insolvent debtor. It was a common offence in this period and for some years after — it has been estimated, for example, that in 1837 there were between thirty thousand and forty thousand arrests for debt — but nevertheless the insolvent debtor was classed as a quasi-criminal and kept in prison until he could pay or could claim release under the Insolvent Debtors' Act. It often happened that such a prisoner remained indefinitely within the prison and John Dickens himself, immediately before being taken away, announced that "the sun was set upon him for ever".

Marshalsea was the place and the area which haunted Dickens throughout his life, the place he had come to as a child. In his autobiographical fragment he could recall scenes and details as clearly as if they had happened just the day before yesterday; how his father had drawn up a petition and, when it was being read out loud by another prisoner, how he had listened "with a little of an author's vanity, and contemplating (not severely) the spikes on the opposite wall"; how as a visitor he watched and noted everything which happened within his view as a prisoner might study with wide eyes the cracks and surfaces of his cell; how he ruminated on all the peculiarities of the prison and the prisoners as he sat over the blacking bottles in Warren's; how "in that slow agony of my youth" he made up histories for the shabby and wretched people whom he saw here.

Dickens's parents never mentioned this episode in their lives to their son in later years, and their silence might suggest that they were as traumatised by it as he; but we can never be certain. But of Charles's reaction there can be little doubt. The image of the Marshalsea never left him.

47

The high wall with the spikes on top of it, the shadows cast by the prison buildings, the lounging shabby people – all of these images return again and again in his narratives. But the gaol is even more central than that; there are times when within his fiction the whole world itself is described as a type of prison and all of its inhabitants prisoners; the houses of his characters are often described as prisons, also, and the shadows of confinement and punishment and guilt stretch over his pages.

The uncertainty of these months continued, and no more distressingly so for the child than in continual changes of address. For a few weeks after the incarceration of John Dickens, Elizabeth and her children remained at Gower Street North; most of their possessions had now been sold and they were encamped in two or three rooms, the meagre remains of their furniture and their other belongings around them. It seems that she was, in someone's immortal words, waiting for something or someone to "turn up" to solve her husband's financial problems – probably a member of his family or of her own – but, at the beginning of April, despairing of any immediate aid, she and the youngest children moved into the Marshalsea alongside John Dickens. Charles was taken to lodge with a friend of the family, a Mrs Roylance who lived only a short walk away from Gower Street North in Little College Street.

John Dickens was still drawing his salary from the Pay Office but, a month after entering the prison, he applied for retirement with pension; no doubt he feared that his bankruptcy might lead to his dismissal, and wanted to preclude that possibility. But he lodged his appeal on the grounds of his ill health; he was, according to the medical report he sent with his application, suffering from "a chronic infection of the urinary organs" which in his covering letter he described more grandiloquently as an "unfortunate calamity". There is no doubt that he was

48

suffering from just such a painful complaint – indeed he died of it – but his application seems to have lapsed as events in his life took a different turn. On 26 April his mother died at her son's house in Oxford Street at the age of seventy-nine and, although John Dickens was not named as an executor in her will, without a doubt this was something that had indeed "turned up".

There were no immediate consequences, however. John Dickens remained in the prison, and his eldest son remained in Little College Street; every Sunday he spent the day in the Marshalsea. On Sunday evenings he took his solitary way back to Camden Town; all that can safely be said about these days is that Charles Dickens's feelings on the matter were as usual kept within his own secret, struggling, anguished self. There was one outburst, however: after three weeks or so he complained to his father about his isolation "so pathetically, and with so many tears . . . It was the first remonstrance I had ever made about my lot, and perhaps it opened up a little more than I intended." Here one notices again the extraordinary reserve and secrecy of the boy, just like the child Pip in *Great Expectations* who feels everything and says nothing, but the effect of this single disclosure was beneficial. He was removed from Little College Street, and a new lodging was found for him in Lant Street, a small narrow street, dull, restful enough to the senses to provoke "a gentle melancholy upon the soul", and within two minutes' walk of the Marshalsea itself. Here Dickens was placed in a house owned by a certain Archibald Russell, an agent for the Insolvent Court and therefore used to transactions of such a kind; the landlord and his wife, according to Dickens's own account, were later immortalised as the Garlands in *The Old Curiosity Shop*. His was a garret room once again, and its "little window had a pleasant prospect of a timber yard" but in comparison to what had gone before it seemed to him to be "a Paradise". Yet paradise

49

had really been lost, and it was in this attic room that one night the young boy once more fell into a spasm which lasted until the morning.

For this was the shape his life had taken; in the morning he would lounge around the old London Bridge until the gates of the prison were opened – this was the bridge which was completely roofed over with houses and buildings and where, as he loitered, he would entertain the Chatham workhouse servant with his own vivid fictions of the life around him – and then he would breakfast with his family before setting off for the blacking factory. When his day's work was completed, he would return to the Marshalsea, generally crossing Blackfriars Bridge, turning into Great Surrey Street until he took a side-turning into Great Suffolk Street. He would have supper with his family, and then at nine go back to his lodgings in Lant Street.

It is possible at this time that he contemplated the idea of escape; escape back to William Giles's house, perhaps, and to the scenes of his happier years. Back to the hope of being "learned and distinguished" once more. Or at least of "going away somewhere, like the hero in a story, to seek my fortune . . ." Certainly this is the dream he gives to David Copperfield, who leaves the warehouse in which he works and makes his own pilgrimage to Chatham, where Dickens had once lived, and to his kind aunt there. Yet if he had such dreams they soon faded; ". . . transient visions," as he records in *David Copperfield* again, "day dreams I sat looking at sometimes, as if they were faintly painted or written on the wall of my room, and which, as they melted away, left the wall blank again." So he suffered, but he suffered in secret; never once did he complain to his working companions, or even to his parents. "I never said, to man or boy, how it was that I came to be there, or gave the least indication of being sorry that I was there . . . I kept my own counsel, and did my work." This repression of his feelings, this silence, will be seen to be characteristic of the mature Dickens – never wanting to show himself as he truly was, to express how he truly felt, is a remarkable characteristic of the man who in his fiction seems so open to all the sentiments of the world.

# *Four*

IT was impossible to say for how long John Dickens might be incarcerated; so, in other words, it was impossible for his son to know the length of his service in the blacking factory. But that John Dickens, unlike William Dorrit, did not intend to settle in the gaol is obvious from the fact that, very soon after his arrival in the Marshalsea, he was preparing for his freedom under the Insolvent Debtors Act. This meant that he could be released after being declared insolvent, if he could demonstrate that his debts were incurred unintentionally, that all property of his own was surrendered, and that all goods over a combined value of twenty pounds would be used to pay off his debtors.

John Dickens's case was brought before the Insolvent Court, described later by Dickens in *The Pickwick Papers* as a badly lit and badly ventilated room which was ". . . always full. The steams of beer and spirits perpetually ascend to the ceiling, and, being condensed by the heat, roll down the walls like rain: there are more old suits of clothes in it at one time, than will be offered for sale in all Houndsditch in a twelve-month; and more unwashed skins and grizzly beards . . ." and so forth, all the stench and noise of the place being recaptured in what reads like an act of memory on his part. Here his father was placed in an enclosure to the left of a panel of judges, his case reviewed, debts both in Rochester and in London detailed, and an appointee assigned to handle the payment of these (in fact John Dickens had to find a considerable sum in the November of the next year, and a further sum in the following November). Case over.

And so, on 28 May, having spent fourteen weeks in the Marshalsea, John Dickens was released into the world. If he was not taken in procession to the prison gates, as happens both to Samuel Pickwick and to William Dorrit, the relief and celebration must nevertheless have been much the same. At first the whole Dickens family, with the exception of Fanny, went to stay with Mrs Roylance in Little College Street; the orphan servant seems to have been discharged at the same time, one further example of the severity of behaviour in a period when people had to struggle for mere survival. They came "not as lodgers", Mrs Roylance's grand-daughter later explained, "but as welcome guests". It is not clear how long they stayed here – and who indeed would have bothered to record the wanderings of a poor family? – but at some point they moved further north, to Hampstead, remaining there until late in December. Then at the end of this year the Dickens family moved to 29 Johnson Street, in Somers Town, only a few minutes' walk from their original house in Bayham Street; in an area which soon declined into squalor but was then what might be called "shabby genteel", the home of shopkeepers and clerks. The street was some thirty years old, and overlooked the fields which still bordered Camden Town; it was narrow and had a sort of intimacy – a "family circle" was the way in which it has been described – but it could not have been entirely unaffected by the closeness of the city. For one thing no gas light had as yet reached it and, since most of the inhabitants would have been too poor to afford an inexhaustible supply of oil-lighting, the street would have been plunged into profound darkness at the end of the day.

John Dickens continued his work as a clerk in Somerset

House, his first application for retirement having lapsed; and, with the knowledge that most if not all of his colleagues had heard about his imprisonment for debt, this could not have been the easiest of periods for him. Certainly he was soon reapplying for retirement, which suggests that he was no longer happy with the work upon which he had been engaged for some nineteen years. Yet he went to the office every day still, walking from Somers Town to the Strand. On these journeys he would have been accompanied by his son, himself working in that same neighbourhood, and it is tempting to speculate upon their relationship to each other in this period – the father continuing with a job he was finding more and more disagreeable (and of course still troubled by that infection of the urinary organs which seems to have flared up at times of crisis), and the son going daily to a place he hated and feared in equal measure.

Yet not all Dickens's experiences in this period of his life, not all his experiences of London, were of a disagreeable sort. The world of theatres and "penny gaffs" was just around the corner, almost literally so, but he makes particular mention of one aspect of his reading during this period – it was a twopenny weekly, *The Portfolio*, which professed in conventional style to combine instruction with amusement but which was essentially a compendium of horror stories, fables, executions, disasters ("All Of Us In Danger of Being Buried Alive"), murders, and sketches of London life. Dickens always loved reading of such things and, at this particular stage of his life, it is not premature to view the formation of his genius within the context of a very popular culture. Indeed within the culture of London itself.

And indeed his stay in the blacking factory was at last coming to an end. At the close of 1824 John Dickens had once again requested permission to retire from the Navy Pay Office on a fixed pension – the circumstances, according to his superior who backed the application, being of a "mixed nature" but including his urinary infection and his release under the Insolvent Debtors' Act. The petition was accepted on this second occasion, and John Dickens retired from his naval work on 9 March, 1825 after service of some twenty years. He had a pension of one hundred and forty-five pounds a year but he was in the process of paying off his debts, and was still poor; still what his son might later have called "shabby genteel". Some months before his final departure his son's place of work had changed, when Warren's left the mouldering warehouse by the Thames and moved to Chandos Street just off Covent Garden. This was a larger establishment, but, more importantly, it seems that Dickens had now attained as much dexterity in his tasks of pasting and tying as Bob Fagin. The two boys sat in front of a window, to gain the light for their tasks, ". . . and we were so brisk at it, that the people used to stop and look in. Sometimes there would be quite a little crowd there. I saw my father coming in at the door one day when we were very busy, and I wondered how he could bear it."

In fact, it seems that John Dickens, for reason or reasons unknown, finally could not bear it. His son was the object of a fierce quarrel between himself and James Lamert, letters were exchanged, and Charles Dickens left the establishment in Chandos Street with a ". . . relief so strange that it was like oppression". The cause of the quarrel is not known; Dickens himself suggested that it was the sight of his son working in the window which prompted his father to act, but this seems unlikely. It may have been to do with money; it may have been to do with pride. Or perhaps that combination of the two which would have been so important to a person in John Dickens's position; he, like his son, was always susceptible to slights and it is not hard to understand why eventually he did choose to quarrel with the employer of his labouring

55

child. So the boy went home — relieved, as he said, and no doubt also oppressed because his sudden departure meant that he had to begin a new kind of life altogether. Then his mother stepped between Lamert and her husband; in a move for which Dickens never forgave her, she resolved the quarrel between them and came back from Chandos Street with "a request for me to return the next morning". But John Dickens, in a moment which perhaps more than anything else saved Dickens for posterity, refused. He wanted his son to be sent to school, to retrieve all those hopes and ambitions which father and son seemed to share.

The time which he spent at Warren's is unclear, and he himself did not seem to be sure. "I have no idea how long it lasted; whether for a year, or much more, or less." Recent commentators have varied their estimates between a matter of six months to a year, but the real point is that the young boy did not know how long he was likely to remain in that employment. He might, as far as he could see, be thrown away for ever. The episode itself was never discussed in his later life and remained his secret. He told Forster, who was to become his biographer, but it was still a matter of dispute whether he ever told his wife. Certainly he never told his children. Just as secrecy and guilt are some of the characteristic themes of Dickens's fiction, so reticence was the key to his own life.

And yet of course it haunted him; the image of boot blacking appears in *The Pickwick Papers* and carries through his novels to the last, *The Mystery of Edwin Drood*. Blacking bottles, blacking brushes, boot black advertisements, even a blacking warehouse itself, make their appearances in Dickens's novels like some secret transaction between his fiction and his private self; as if in the repetition of this episode he was signalling one of the sources of his strength.

So in a sense his adult imagination and character were formed by the experience of Marshalsea and of Warren's.

One cannot help but think that, when Dickens was abandoned in the blacking factory, he fantasised about kind strangers looking desperately for him and seeking to relieve him, just as he saw adults who he thought were beating him down and using him with no regard for his welfare. In moments of crisis or uncertainty, the adult Dickens often returns to that childhood and to that childhood apprehension of reality. These were the figures he carried in his head, and the figures which he transposed to his fiction. Why else is it that adult reality is always, and at every turn, threatening? – how different a sense of life from his Augustan forebears who described death and disaster but never accompanied them with that calamitous low note which sounds so loudly throughout Dickens that there are times when the reader says, "I can't bear it if this happiness is destroyed, or this outing ruined, or this little boy's money stolen, or this child kidnapped!" And yet these are precisely the things which come to pass. For throughout the novels we are left with the image of the child who still dwells somewhere within. Insecure. Maltreated. Starved. Frail. Sickly. Oppressed. Guilty. Small. Orphaned. Of course there are healthy children to be found in his pages but, like the schoolchildren in *The Old Curiosity Shop*, they are merely players. *His* children are somehow separated from the world, forced to keep their distance. " 'Has my dream come true?' exclaimed the child again, in a voice so fervent that it might have thrilled to the heart of any listener. 'But no, that can never be. How could it be – Oh! How could it!' "

# Five

AND so Charles Dickens left the blacking factory and, with it, the formative years of his childhood. Almost at once he was enrolled by his father at Wellington House Academy, a school only a short walk from their house in Johnson Street and one which had a good reputation in the neighbourhood. He was to remain for two years, and what is surprising about the record of his stay there is the extent to which he had changed from the passive, suffering "labouring hind" of only a few months before; all his contemporaries concur that he was lively, agreeable, high-spirited, healthy, and very clearly the "son of a gentleman". Dickens had, as it were, "come through" the experiences which had so secretly scarred him; he was in that sense self-created and already in the thirteen and fourteen-year-old schoolboy we can discern the lineaments of the mature Dickens. The fact that he made the transition so successfully suggests how supple and yet how sturdy a temperament he possessed; he was not one to be bowed down by misfortune, but to use and to conquer each calamity as it arose.

The school itself stood in the Hampstead Road, facing the fields of a large dairy farm (on his way from Johnson Street, Dickens's quickest route would have been a road alongside the fields), and was of a conventional kind. One large schoolroom, made of timber and holding something

58

like two hundred boys with their "rough notched" forms arranged in rows; there was a modestly sized playground outside, with the house of the owner and headmaster just beside it. We must imagine the schoolroom divided by learning abilities rather than age, the boys conning their lessons by rote (an older boy often being deputed to teach the younger ones) amid the noise of voices, slate pencils, and quill pens being sharpened. Charles Dickens's own memories of this school are far from complimentary, and in a speech much later in life he declared that "the respected proprietor of which was by far the most ignorant man I have ever had the pleasure to know, who was one of the worst-tempered men perhaps that ever lived, whose business it was to make as much out of us and to put as little into us as possible . . ."

His training at the school does not seem to have been of any remarkable kind. "Depend on it," one contemporary wrote, "he was quite a self-made man." Which echoes John Dickens's remark that his son "may be said to have educated himself!" (a phrase which Dickens later liked to imitate in his father's own manner). And yet at Wellington House Academy Dickens was taught Latin, and seems to have distinguished himself enough to carry off the Latin prize one year; in return he gave his tutor a copy of Horace's verses. Other people have disputed Dickens's claim that he was taught the language, but on the evidence of his novels themselves there seems little doubt of it — indeed, at a much later date, he is to be found consulting the works of Virgil. He was also apparently taught the violin, according to an early biographer, "which study Dickens could by no means make progress in, and had to relinquish". Even if his knowledge of the English language was acquired, as one colleague remarked, "by long and patient study after leaving" it still seems that he already possessed more than the rudiments of his tongue; he astonished his schoolfellows by being the only one able to spell

59

theatre, a feat which suggests not only his own early attachment to that place of entertainment but also the woeful ignorance of his classmates.

Most of the memories of his time at school, however, concern not his academic or literary prowess but his "animation and animal spirits". He is remembered for having sung "The Cat's Meat Man" and entering "into all the vulgarity of the composition"; how touching, this, that the young boy still sang the songs he learnt at the time of his privation. Similarly he was remembered for improvising upon the "lingo" or the "gibberish" of the schoolboys, and for posing as a poor boy in order to beg from old ladies before whom he "would explode with laughter and take to his heels" – how strange that already he should begin mimicking the fate which only a few months before had in fact been his, although it is true that his ability to translate the events of his life into theatre was a natural and permanent gift. One of his first jokes is also remembered – one friend remarked that his trousers seemed well worn and that they needed a rest.

*Dickens*: "Ah yes! You are right, it *is* a long time since they had a *nap*."

The young Dickens was also remembered for his interest in the theatre and in amateur theatricals. It is recorded how with two schoolfriends he "used to act little plays in the kitchen" of a friend's house. One contemporary observed that ". . . he was very fond of theatricals. I have some recollection of his getting up a play at Dan Tobin's house, in the back kitchen . . . we made a plot, and each had his part; but the speeches every one was to make for himself". He was still adept with the toy theatre constructed for him by James Lamert at Bayham Street, and for that small but fiery stage he condensed such plays as *Cherry and Four Star* and *Elizabeth, or The Exiles of Siberia*, a *roman sentimental* describing the plaintive adventures of a young girl who journeys to Moscow to meet the Czar.

It is not known what role Dickens himself played in this little romance but the nature of his interest is clear; these innocent plots with their heightened dialogue and strident effects, these "cut-outs" moved to and fro upon small rods, these small but perfectly detailed sets, are at the centre of Dickens's imaginative response to the world. It is not a theatre which encourages anything like psychological exploration or social realism, but these were not matters that ever moved Dickens; he was entranced by the bright surfaces and the powerful stories, the vivid unnatural colours and the shuffling movement of the cardboard creations.

He stayed at Wellington House Academy for only two years, once again his father's wastrel habits confounding his son's ambitions. The point was that, despite his pension from the Pay Office and the strong possibility that he was already working as a journalist, John Dickens's means did not encompass his ends. Some debts were still being taken directly from his pension, and sums had to be disgorged to his debtors in both 1825 and 1826; as a result, in October 1825, he was in arrears with the payment of an outstanding debt and he wrote a letter to the administrators explaining that "a circumstance of great moment to me will be decided in the ensuing term which I confidently hope will place me in comparative affluence . . .", these rolling words being precisely the sound which his son so carefully adopted and parodied. Then seven months later, "comparative affluence" having eluded him once again, he asked to pay off his debt in monthly instalments.

But it cannot be said that John Dickens was a lazy man, even though he was an improvident one. At some point in this period – and the likelihood is that it was very soon after his retirement from Somerset House – he began what was for him a new career as a journalist. He was employed by *The British Press*, both as a parliamentary reporter and also as a contributor of articles on the subject of marine insurance. He was now entering his forties, and it is a sign of his undaunted spirit that he should so quickly embark upon a quite new career; if, as seems probable, he also undertook to learn the difficult art of shorthand then his application and industry have to be admired. J. P. Collier, who was working for *The British Press* at this time, suggested that John Dickens was "a gentleman of no great intellectual capacity", but Charles Dickens himself said that he was "a first-rate shorthand writer on Gurney's system, and a capital reporter . . ." In the latter role he had already had a certain amount of practice – he had described the fire at Chatham for *The Times* – but evidence of his journalistic skills is no longer at hand. The only articles of his which can be identified with any certainty are those on the subject of marine insurance when, in a prose as fulsome as it is precise, he extols the claims of Lloyds over competing agencies.

The particular link with *The British Press* could not have lasted long, however, since the newspaper collapsed in October 1826. John Dickens then took the not unusual step of applying for money from the firm, Lloyds, which he had championed in print; they responded by giving him ten guineas. But such small sums were not enough to avoid a further visitation of financial chaos; a few months later the family were evicted from their house in Johnson Street, and took lodgings just around the corner at The Polygon in Clarendon Square, so named because it consisted of five blocks facing inwards with their courts and gardens running into a central point. This was in fact a more "respectable" area than Johnson Street, and it is unlikely that temporary lodgers of the Dickens sort were entirely welcome. Nine or ten months later the family had returned to Johnson Street, however, whether in a midnight sortie, through a composition with the rating authorities, or by a technique which later became known in this same area as "Home Rule" (possession being nine tenths, etc.), is not clear. In fact these have been called Charles Dickens's "silent years" and certainly one of the aspects of Dickens's adolescent life which can never now be recovered consists of those slights or indignities to which he must necessarily have been subject, and which in a young man of his sensitive disposition must have rankled.

In the short term, John Dickens's financial failure meant that his son had to be removed from Wellington House Academy; he was now fifteen and had, as he said in a letter some years later, "to begin the world". His two years of schooling were over but, curiously enough, there is no sign or sense that he resented this abrupt removal from a standard middle-class education. Perhaps he really did wish to "begin the world" and held the belief which David Copperfield possessed at a similar juncture ". . . that life was more like a great fairy story, which I was just about to begin to read, than anything else". Certainly he seems never to have regretted not attending a university and, if further proof were needed, perhaps it lies in the fact that he showed no great inclination for his own children to do so – he seems to have preferred that they left school young and went into "business" or some allied worldly pursuit.

The "business" in which Charles Dickens now made his way was the law. His parents, and once again particularly his mother, made the first move. Elizabeth Dickens was the niece of a certain Mrs Charlton, who kept a boarding house in Berners Street. One of her lodgers here was a young lawyer, Edward Blackmore, to whom Mrs Dickens was introduced. Blackmore explained what happened: "His mother expressed a great wish to get him employment in my office, and the boy's manners were so prepossessing that I agreed to take him as a clerk . . ." He was also, Blackmore says, ". . . extremely good-looking and clever". And so in May 1827 Charles Dickens began the world as a junior clerk in the office of Ellis and Blackmore, "a poor old set of chambers of three rooms" in

Holborn Court, at a starting salary of 10/6 a week eventually rising to fifteen shillings. The firm moved at the end of the year to Raymond Buildings, a short walk away; it was on the second floor, and it seems that the young Dickens used to amuse himself here by dropping cherry stones on the hats of passers-by, confronting any complainant "with so much gravity and with such an air of innocence, that they went away . . ."

He was, it seems, a "universal favourite" at Ellis and Blackmore. For one thing he was that great comic relief in any office, a good "mimic". There was an old laundress in Holborn Court – a particular type of dirty, snuff-taking servant at which Dickens was later to excel in his fiction – and Dickens "took great interest in her and would mimic her manner of speech, her ways, her excuses etc to the very life". He had seen her, understood her, had perhaps even been drawn to her by what he later called the "attraction of repulsion", and reproduced her in his own person – only clever people become good mimics, because the primary act is one of understanding and empathy, a kind of helpless abnegation of one's own character in favour of that which has supplanted it. Even as he worked in the dingy chambers he was still watching, and learning. Observing, for example, how at the beginning of each day, as he was to put it in *The Pickwick Papers*, "Clerk after clerk hastened into the square by one or other of the entrances, and looking up at the Hall clock, accelerated or decreased his rate of walking according to the time at which his office hours nominally commenced; the half past nine o'clock people suddenly becoming very brisk, and the ten o'clock gentlemen falling into a pace of most aristocratic slowness."

Of course the law itself appears in many of his novels, even if its entry is sometimes by humble means. In the petty cash book of Ellis and Blackmore there are such names as Weller, Mrs Bardell, Corney, Rudge and Newman

Knott — all names which he would use, one way or another, in his later work. Newman Knott, according to a colleague, was a man "whose eccentricities and personal history were a source of great amusement to the clerks", and he was popularly supposed to be the real antecedent of Newman Noggs in *Nicholas Nickleby*; apparently there was also in this period a Little Old Lady of the Court of Chancery upon whom Miss Flite was later based. But such derivations have to be taken very cautiously — there is no doubt that on many occasions Dickens used certain salient characteristics of the people whom he met or knew, but there are very few instances when he simply transcribed what he had seen and heard onto the page. The novelist's art is not of that kind: Dickens perceived a striking characteristic, or mood, or piece of behaviour, and then in his imagination proceeded to elaborate upon it until the "character" bears only a passing resemblance to the real person. In his fiction Dickens entered a world of words which has its own procedures and connections, so that the original "being" of any individual is subsumed into something much larger and generally much more conclusive.

Dickens's life ahead at this point promised nothing but unrelieved drudgery, but there were compensations. There was the theatre. He was, as his employer noted, "very fond of theatricals" and some years later Dickens recalled that "I went to some theatre every night, with a very few exceptions, for at least three years: really studying the bills first, and going to see where there was the best acting . . . I practised immensely (even such things as walking in and out, and sitting down in a chair) . . ." He is talking about a period just a little later than his days at Ellis and Blackmore, although even in these early years he was a keen and frequent attender at all forms of dramatic entertainment. It is a moot point whether the young Dickens himself acted around this time, although most of the evidence suggests that at some point in this period as a clerk he may well have put at least a tentative foot upon the boards. Many years later he told John Forster that he had once played the character of Flexible in a now forgotten drama entitled *Love, Law and Physic*, and George Lear records that "he told me he had often taken part in amateur theatricals before he came to us". He may have been referring here to private family gatherings, but a school-friend does state that "at about the age of fourteen Dickens took parts at the small playhouse in Catherine Street". This was the Minor Theatre where Lear and Dickens went to see Potter attempt his own parts but, since the charge for playing such roles as Othello was then approximately fifteen shillings, it is unlikely that the schoolboy Dickens could afford such sums even if he had the ambition to take the largest parts: he may have been one of those who attend a scene or two, and in later years was quite happy to forget the fact. Hence the paucity of references.

Dickens stayed with Ellis and Blackmore for approximately eighteen months, during which time, it seems, "he grew so very much"; this from George Lear, who goes on to say, "I remember his having a new suit of clothes, brown all alike, coat cut like a dress coat, and with a high hat: he seemed to grow into a young man at once." After he left Ellis and Blackmore in November 1838 he spent a brief period in similar employment at the office of Charles Molloy – it seems that he moved here on the recommendation of another clerk, a certain Thomas Mitton, who knew Dickens well. He did not stay long in the office of Charles Molloy, however, even with Mitton for company. His previous employer, Blackmore, assumed that Dickens did not continue with his legal life because of its "drudgery" and Dickens later told Wilkie Collins that he "didn't much like it". This seems fair enough, but it is not simply a case of weariness or boredom. Dickens was and remained a most ambitious person – how could he, who

66

had already suffered so much and proved to himself that he could rise above such suffering, how could he endure the life of a "writing clerk"? In fact, even while he was with Ellis and Blackmore he was planning a new career. He was learning shorthand, and this specifically to become a reporter in the press gallery of the House of Commons. This may not appear to be a particularly exalted position but, in that period, it was a well-established commencement for many great careers and, in addition, it was the best-paid work then available for a stenographer. And so he set to work to master a system which, on average, took a person of moderate capacity some three years to learn. Dickens seems to have managed it in almost as many months. He taught himself the Gurney method (no doubt persuaded to do so by his father or even by his uncle, who had both gone through the same tuition) and while teaching himself what he called "a very difficult art" he was "walking miles every day to practise it all day long in the Courts of Law".

There were advantages which accrued to the study of shorthand, even if they were ones which he might not then have fully valued. His use of phonetic spelling, and the graphic embodiment of speech which is a part of shorthand, led him to listen very carefully to the sounds of words; and, once he had distinguished them, to put them down very quickly and with absolute accuracy upon paper. It is often said that his transcripts of Cockney or American speech are to a certain extent exaggerated, but in almost all instances one finds Dickens noting down very exactly the phonetic variants of local demotic. Shorthand also taught him literal "short" cuts in the transition from speech to writing, so that something of the freedom and spontaneity of speech is retained within his own prose. That is also why his novels are never harmed by being read aloud – Dickens himself was eventually to make another career out of doing so – since the elements of sound and

67

speech are as intrinsic to them as the more literary virtues which critics have uncovered. It was a skill which Dickens never lost: when he dictated letters to a secretary he would often make the same movements as if he were himself taking it down in shorthand, and an old colleague, George Dolby, noticed that when Dickens was interested in a speech being delivered he would "follow the speaker's words by an almost imperceptible action, as if taking down the speech in shorthand".

It was with these skills that Dickens now wanted to start a new career, working for himself as a freelance transcriber. Dickens had wanted to enter the parliamentary press gallery, like his father and uncle before him, but either there were no vacancies or his lack of experience momentarily told against him. So he resolved to gain experience elsewhere, and at some time in the spring of 1829 – in his eighteenth year – he enrolled at Doctors' Commons. It was not a place which in itself encouraged ambition, just two quadrangles with their main entrance in Knightrider Street south of St Paul's Cathedral, with the paved stone and red-brick buildings which in the secluded recesses of the City harboured nothing but somnolence, stunted trees and dusty sparrows (there are some such places left still, although Doctors' Commons itself is long gone). Here were a series of courts which were convened in the same Hall and which, for a variety of reasons, took for their jurisdiction both ecclesiastical and naval matters. A Consistory Court, a Court of Arches, the Prerogative Court, the Delegates Court and the Admiralty Court; in his later fiction Dickens used the tangled legal system to mirror the confusions of the world, and there is no doubt that his experience as a young man, caught up in a system of which the absurdity was palpable, helped to strengthen this sense of life as convoluted, indeterminate, capable of infinite complexity and procrastination. ". . . always a very pleasant profitable little affair of private theatricals", as Steerforth says in *David Copperfield*, "presented to an uncommonly select audience".

For the first few months, it seems, Charles Dickens was hired by one particular firm of proctors — "very self-important-looking personages" Dickens called them in a later sketch — to take notes on evidence and on judgments (there is the legend of the stool he sat upon, one of the material props which always seem to haunt the reputations of the great). But it was not long before he established himself as an independent shorthand reporter; he rented a reporter's box in the Court itself, and also shared the costs of a probate office or transcribing room in Bell Yard nearby. He even had a business card engraved to give definite announcement of his independent status: "Mr Charles Dickens/Short Hand Writer/10 Norfolk Street, Fitzroy Square". This latter address was the first in a series to which the Dickens family would move over the next few years, each one in turn seeming to be a way to escape the attentions of creditors.

It was arduous and monotonous work. "It wasn't a very good living (though not a *very* bad one)," he wrote later, "and was wearily uncertain . . .". It is the precariousness of it which lingers in his memory, then, and indeed the post of a freelance shorthand writer, so dependent upon the patronage of proctors or upon sudden commissions, would not necessarily have appealed to anyone as sensitive and anxious as the young Dickens seems to have been. We must imagine a young man, already aware of the powers latent within him but still living with his family in difficult circumstances, walking each day through the City to his tedious work. ". . . I could settle down into a state of equable low spirits," his hero David Copperfield says, "and resign myself to coffee; which I seem, on looking back, to have taken by the gallon . . ." The general impression of Dickens in these "silent years", the period of incubation (you might say) between his eventful childhood

69

and his no less eventful maturity, is of someone both ambitious and purposeful but as yet uncertain in which direction his ambitions were to be driven.

# Six

F IRST love. This was not infantile love, nor was it the love for his mother and sister. This was infatuation. Her name was Maria Beadnell; she was fifteen months older than Charles Dickens. She was quite short – apparently her nickname at one time was "the pocket Venus" – dark-haired, dark-eyed with that kind of slightly plump beauty which can so easily dissolve in later life; and, from all the available evidence, she was something of a flirt if not quite a coquette. Her "Album" contained verses and drawings from more than one admirer, but it has the honour of being the volume to contain Charles Dickens's first extant writing, an acrostic on the name of Maria Beadnell which opens:

> "My life may chequered be with scenes of
>     misery and pain,
> And it may be my fate to struggle with adversity
>     in vain . . ."

How Dickens met her is not known, although a friend, a young bank clerk by the name of Henry Kolle, is thought to have been one possible intermediary. Her father was a banker and they lived next door to the "shop", as it were, in Lombard Street. They met in the spring of 1830, as

Dickens commemorated in a set of verses he wrote for the Beadnell family in the following year:

"And Charles Dickens, who in our Feast plays a part
Is a young Summer Cabbage, without any heart;
Not that he's *heartless*, but because, as folks say,
He lost his a twelve month ago, from last May."

The name "Charles Dickens" then meaning nothing – just another admirer, a friend of the family, an amateur versifier.

In Dickens's memory of this time many years later, at a time of great distress in his own life when a sudden letter from Maria opened the floodgates of the past, he characteristically recalls small objects and scenes – a pair of blue gloves, a "sort of raspberry coloured dress", "a tendency in your eyebrows to join together"; such disparate memories can in turn be compared with David Copperfield's recollection of Dora, with "a little black dog being held up, in two slender arms, against a bank of blossoms and bright leaves". This is not any Proustian exercise of memory, because it is neither elaborately perceived nor fully *felt*: Dickens sees things vividly and instantaneously, describes them, and then moves on. But if his memories of Maria Beadnell are of her clothes or of parts of her face – *disjecta membra* indeed – his real nostalgia about this aspect of his past is reserved for himself and for his own feelings. ". . . there never was such a faithful and devoted poor fellow as I . . ." he told her later and, in another letter, he wonders if it is not ". . . ungrateful to consider whether any reputation the world can bestow is repayment to a man for the loss of such a vision of his youth as mine". Dickens was a man of infinite nostalgia about himself; what is real, and what remained real for him, is the ambitious boy moving through adolescence to maturity. That is why this period of struggle, which really "made" him long before he achieved success, was the one which he could never forget. The one which he continued to interpret in his fiction. The one around which he was most willing to cast a roseate light.

But struggle he did. He fought to make headway – with Maria Beadnell, with the world, with his own career. Even while he was working as a shorthand reporter in Doctors' Commons, at some point early in 1831 he joined the parliamentary staff of the *Mirror of Parliament*. His uncle, John Henry Barrow, was both editor and proprietor of this periodical; and, since his father was already working in the same capacity in the press gallery, it hardly comes as a surprise that the young man should join the ranks of its reporters. The journal had been founded three years before, specifically to provide a weekly account of the proceedings in the House of Commons and the House of Lords; in this it had already succeeded, and had acquired a reputation higher than that of its rival, *Hansard*. After a while Charles Dickens played some role in the management and editing of the newspaper, but his primary duty consisted in attending Parliament and keeping an accurate shorthand record of what transpired there. It was well-paid but exhausting work. In the days of the old Parliament – the building was destroyed by fire in 1834 – reporters were consigned to the back bench of the Strangers' Gallery, where it was hard to hear what was taking place on the floor of the chamber below them. In addition, as one parliamentary reporter recalled, "It was dark: always so insufficiently lit that on the back benches no one could read a paper and so ill-ventilated that few constitutions could long bear the unwholesome atmosphere . . .", a reminder that, in those days, the washing of bodies and the cleaning of clothes were not considered to be absolute priorities.

It is possible that he engaged in more than parliamentary reporting as a young man and in the Dexter collection of Dickens material, housed in the British Library, there is a report of the trial of a certain Williams, Bishop and May for the murder of "the Italian boy". It took place on 12 February, 1831, and on the frontispiece it is stated that the court proceedings were "taken in shorthand". There is no direct evidence to link it with Dickens, but in the descriptions of the murderers there is something which seems very close to the kind of prose Dickens was writing only a few years later: "Bishop advanced to the bar with a heavy step, and with rather a slight bend of the body; his arms hung closely down, and it seemed a kind of relief to him, when he took his place, to rest his hand on the board before him. His appearance, when he got in front, was that of a man for some time labouring under the most intense mental agony, which had brought on a kind of lethargic stupor . . ." And of a co-defendant the unknown shorthand reporter writes, ". . . his look was that of a man who thought that all chance of life was lost . . . there appeared that in his despondency which gave an air of – we could not call it daring, or even confidence – we should rather say, a physical power of endurance . . ."

Perhaps the work of Dickens; perhaps not. All that we can say with certainty of this period is that his skill as a shorthand reporter was growing, and that as a result of his work on the *Mirror of Parliament* he was becoming more widely known among the London journalists. Certainly he was asked to do occasional work for another journal, the *True Sun*, on its inception in March 1832; the nature of the work is unclear and now impossible to verify, but the salient fact is that Dickens was becoming deeply involved in the reporting of political affairs at precisely the time when the life of the nation was undergoing a profound change. Yet, in his novels and journalism, Dickens rarely mentions this period of his life in such terms; in his own accounts of his distraught and thwarted existence, political conditions go unregarded. But he did not disregard them at the time and in a speech he gave five years before his death he makes it clear how much he knew and understood about the world around him: ". . . the newsman brought to us daily accounts of a regularly accepted and received system of loading the unfortunate insane with chains, littering them down on straw, starving them on bread and water, denying them their clothes, soothing them under their tremendous affliction with the whip, and making periodical exhibitions of them at small charge, rendering our public asylums a kind of demoniacal Zoological Gardens. He brought us constant accounts of the destruction of machinery . . . In the same times he brought us accounts of riots for bread, which were constantly occurring and undermining the State, of the most terrible animosity of class against class, and of the habitual employment of spies for the discovery, if not for the organisation of plots, in which the animosity on both sides found in those days some relief. In the same times the same newsmen were apprising us of the state of society all around us in which the grossest sensuality and intemperance were the rule . . . This state of society has discontinued in England for ever." These are Dickens's clearest memories of the period in which he was brought up and went to school; how far away he must have seemed from them when he made this speech in the spring of 1865 and yet, as we shall see, they remained an inalienable part of his imaginative life.

Indeed, his imaginative life would find an outlet and, even at the time when he was recording the parliamentary debates on Reform, and working as a more general reporter on the radical *True Sun*, he was seriously considering the idea of a career in the theatre. There is even a suggestion that, while he was reporting the proceedings of Parliament, he was also appearing nearby at a minor theatre called The Westminster in Tothill Street. But this is probably false. What is without doubt however is that in March or April of 1832 — still only twenty — he wrote to the stage manager

75

of Covent Garden, a Mr Bartley, ". . . and told him how young I was, and exactly what I thought I could do; and that I believed I had a strong perception of character and oddity, and a natural power of reproducing in my own person what I observed in others".

The significant point here is that he was deliberately modelling his routine upon that of Charles Mathews, a comic actor whose smartness and quickness had already made him the idol of the hour – "the beau ideal of elegance," one contemporary wrote. "We studied his costumes with ardent devotion." Dickens himself was always greatly interested in the possibilities of sartorial display, but there were other reasons which drew him towards Mathews. It is worth recalling, for example, that this actor's real skill lay in the swiftness and dexterity with which he could change both voice and dress so that he could represent "seven or eight different, and very varied, characters in an evening". The ability of one man to assume a variety of characters and voices was of extreme significance to Dickens, suggesting as it does both a mastery of the world and an evasion of the personality. In years to come such versatile acting would indeed become for him a way of lifting the burden of selfhood – an American observer in those later years noted of Dickens that "his rapid change of voice and manner in the impersonation of character was almost like what we read of the elder Mathews". A newspaper subsequently declared that Dickens was very much like Mathews in his walk and manner and voice – although it was quick to point out that the author possessed an "earnestness" which the comic actor lacked. It is worth recalling, too, that the characters whom Mathews most often imitated were those of the garrulous female, the urchin, the foreigner with his broken English – these had always been stock types, but they are also precisely the types which Dickens introduces into his fiction. Dickens would also have known the staccato monologue which

Mathews had perfected in a now forgotten piece by Thomas Holcroft called *The Road to Ruin*, since it is one the novelist later immortalised in Alfred Jingle, the first truly comic character he ever created. It would be wrong to press these resemblances too hard, but no great artist works in a vacuum and there seems little doubt that it was under the direct inspiration of Charles Mathews that Dickens first explored the comic possibilities latent within him.

But a career on the stage was not to be his, after all. Mr Bartley, the stage manager to whom Dickens had addressed his letter, wrote back quickly enough. "There must have been something in my letter that struck the authorities . . ." Dickens told Forster later. "Punctual to the time another letter came, with an appointment to do anything of Mathews's I pleased, before him and Charles Kemble, on a certain day at the theatre." Fanny was to go with him in order to accompany him on the piano, here re-enacting their childhood roles when the young Dickens sang for his father's companions. Yet on the appointed day Dickens was "laid up", as he put it, "with a terrible bad cold and an inflammation of the face". Never can there have been a more fortunate illness. He would not have been a great stage actor; he was too small for romantic leads, and there was a certain spareness and lightness about him which would have made him suitable really only for servants, dandies and assorted comic roles. The stage was not his destiny, and so he became ill on the day which that particular future opened for him. Somehow he knew – or at least his body knew – that this was not the life for which he was intended. There is in great artists a secret momentum that always draws them forward so that they can ride over obstacles and avoid side-tracks without even realising that they are doing so – so it was with Dickens. Whether it be called a power of will or of ambition, whether it is a form of self-awareness or even of self-ignorance, there was something which ineluctably led him forward to his proper destination. He told Bartley that he would renew his application the following season, but he never did so.

This period – spring 1833 – was notable also for something else: it marked the final stage of his separation from Maria Beadnell. "Separation" is perhaps not quite the right word, since they seem not to have been in any tangible sense together. It is a familiar story, but its familiarity does not render it any the less painful for the young men and women who experience it for the first time – passion on one side and reserve on the other, the love of love on the one hand and the love of intrigue on the other. What seems to have happened is this: for some three years Dickens had been paying court to Maria Beadnell. His advances were at first favoured and then neglected and finally rebuffed; there was a slow but steady falling off between them, and in the period towards the end of their acquaintance Dickens would, in the early hours of the morning, walk after work from the House of Commons to Lombard Street just to see the place in which she slept. There were clandestine letters, conducted through mutual friends like Henry Kolle. But by March 1833, almost three years after he had first met her, he began to lament the futility of his pursuit. The attitudes of the parents of both parties are not recorded, although it is clear that there must have been something like coldness or indifference on the part of the Beadnells. Maria's mother called him "Mr Dickin" and it is possible that the Beadnells did not approve of the young Dickens, although surely his ambition and his post in the press gallery would have weighed against the fact that his father was a convicted debtor and had at the end of 1831 once again been taken to the Insolvent Court: nevertheless there are suggestions in Dickens's extant correspondence that his family during this period felt in a sense "unwanted" and were more than usually susceptible to real or imagined slights.

That he was thwarted and stalled and frustrated and wounded there is no doubt; he was always afraid of being rebuffed and now, for the first time, he had been rejected. Three years marks a long period in the life of a young man, and now three years of courtship had come to nothing. Wasted. His heart laid bare, and also wasted. In later life he seemed to regard it as a traumatic event – one which he had "locked up" in his own breast and which, he said, had led directly to a "habit of suppression" which meant that he could never display his true feelings to anyone, not even to his children. This is true enough of his mature character – no author can have been at more pains to conceal his emotions than Dickens, despite the "emotion" of his fiction – but it is by no means the whole story. His rejection by Maria Beadnell was the one which he could most plainly lament and most clearly feel, but the fact that it provoked such deep emotion within him suggests that it was in a sense an echo or reprise of earlier abandonments; those by his mother and by his sister were prominent in his own memories of his childhood, and there is every reason to suppose that the experience of female rejection determined much of his emotional life. He had an appetite – indeed a demand – for total love, which no human being could really satisfy; in addition he seems to have sought a total identification with the object of his love, and in so desperate a situation any sign of resistance or retreat would be treated by him as a severe calamity.

The abortive romance with Maria Beadnell sets the pattern for these years in Dickens's life in another sense, also, marked as they are by apparent uncertainty and confusion even as the real direction of his life was implicitly being set. There were of course still the problems of his family to waylay and beset him. John Dickens had again been declared insolvent in November 1831, and his name had appeared in the *London Gazette* as being sued in the Insolvent Debtors' Court, but he carried on with his new career;

he was working for the *Mirror of Parliament* (one of his duties being to send MPs proofs of their speeches for correction) and had joined the parliamentary reporting staff of the *Morning Herald*. He had, like his son, also become a reader in the library of the British Museum — which suggests, if nothing else, that despite the difficulties of these years he had not entirely abandoned certain literary aspirations. There was another child in this already overstretched family, little Augustus, known as "Moses" or "Boz" after the son of Doctor Primrose in *The Vicar of Wakefield*. Dickens's two other brothers, Alfred and Frederick, were now being sent to a school in Hampstead; they only attended the school for two years, however, since once again John Dickens's improvidence meant that he could no longer afford to keep them there. (It seems to have been one of Dickens's duties to collect his brothers from school at the end of the day and, in a real sense, he would have to look after these siblings for the rest of their lives.)

Uncertainty, then, in his domestic life; uncertainty in his romantic aspirations; and great uncertainty, too, concerning his eventual destiny. He had already approached the purlieus of three occupations — the stage, the legal profession, and journalism — but it seems that at some time during this period he also took very seriously the possibility of emigrating to the West Indies. A relative, a certain Mrs Margaret Hadfield, had just returned from there and "on the occasion of that visit," a cousin later recalled, "and whilst he was still brooding over the choice of a career, Dickens questioned her very closely as to the prospects for pushing his fortune in the West Indies, wanting but a little encouragement to try his luck there."

Any writing of his own was of an appropriately desultory kind, and the most complete examples of his compositions are in fact the occasional verses which he composed for Maria Beadnell's album. They are not without merit, however — "The Devil's Walk", "The Bill of Fare", "The Churchyard", and "Lodgings to Let" show great skill in versification and demonstrate his ability to evoke a mood of sentimental pathos as well as one of comic parody. These are the familiar characteristics of the poetry of young writers, and would not be remarkable, perhaps, except for the name which was being appended to them.

Not much here to divert the attention, or to detain the reader, except as a symptom of Dickens's general restlessness. His main work was simply to earn his living in a family which he must also have helped to support. In December 1832 he found work as a polling clerk (the Member for whom he was working, Charles Tennyson, was the poet's uncle but perhaps more significantly a Reformer), and in the parliamentary recess of 1833 he was trying to obtain extra employment as a shorthand writer: he asked a friend to recommend him as such if "the opportunity arises". A little later in the same year, he went to dinner with a certain John Payne Collier who was on the staff of the *Morning Chronicle*. His uncle, John Barrow, wanted to obtain a position for his "clever nephew", as Collier put it, on that paper and had brought the two men together. Collier retold the story many years later: ". . . [Barrow's] nephew wished of all things to become one of the parliamentary reporters of the *Morning Chronicle*. I asked how old he was, and how he had been employed before he had connected himself with the *True Sun*. The answer was rather ambiguous; the uncle only knew that his father's family distresses had driven Charles Dickens to exert himself in any way that would earn a living . . . at Barrow's instance, I agreed to meet Dickens at dinner, his uncle also informing me that he was cheerful company and a good singer of a comic song." And so it proved, although it seems that Dickens "would not make the attempt until late in the evening and after a good deal of pressing". Eventually he sang "The Dandy Dog's-Meat

Man" and his own composition, "Sweet Betsy Ogle"; both songs of his youth. But the dinner was wasted in all other respects — Collier either could not or would not help Dickens in his journalistic progress, and it was not until late in the following year that he fulfilled his ambition and joined the *Morning Chronicle*.

# Seven

DICKENS began seriously to write at some time in the summer or autumn of 1833, perhaps spurred on by Maria Beadnell's rejection of him, perhaps wishing to make good use of his time during the parliamentary recess, or perhaps just rising into his own gifts at the appropriate moment. It was a short story entitled "A Dinner at Poplar Walk". There were revisions for later editions (and indeed its title was eventually changed to "Mr Minns and His Cousin") and in its final version it opens, "Mr Augustus Minns was a bachelor, of about forty as he said – of about eight-and-forty, as his friends said." Mr Minns was "a clerk in Somerset-house", just as John Dickens had been, and the story is a light sketch concerning the misadventures which happen when families pursue putative legacies with too much earnestness. One senses here the pressure of the young Dickens's own concerns with money and familial pride, and there can be no doubt that in his early writing he grabbed almost blindly at any material close to hand. Yet the general mood of the piece is theatrical and almost farcical; it reads largely like a piece for the stage which has been transmitted onto paper. But funny, nonetheless.

Later he said that, in his first stories written for publication, he had used "plain penmanship and a sheet of paper large enough to hold the lines"; and, for that first publication, he had chosen the Monthly Magazine, a

83

periodical of no great reputation or circulation (it had just been taken over by a certain Captain Holland). It was published in Johnson Court, off Fleet Street, and Dickens had brought his piece which he "dropped stealthily one evening at twilight, with fear and trembling, into a dark letter-box, in a dark office . . ." But the darkness did not last for long. When he went back to the same address to buy the next issue of the magazine, he found printed there "A Dinner at Poplar Walk". "I walked down to Westminster Hall, and turned into it for half an hour, because my eyes were so dimmed with joy and pride that they could not bear the street, and were not fit to be seen there." All the excitement and barely suppressed emotion here say more about the pleasures of authorship than any later and more experienced reports: to see his work in print for the first time was, for Dickens, something like a revelation of himself and yet, more importantly, a revelation of what he might become. His eyes could not bear the streets because his interior sight had beheld a larger and more capacious vision than anything which his present reality could encompass; it was a vision of his own fame. Quickly he wrote a letter to Henry Kolle, who seemed to have surpassed him in affairs of the heart, in order proudly to announce the publication – "I am so dreadfully nervous," he wrote, "that my hand shakes . . ."

Over the next few months he wrote another eight stories for the *Monthly Magazine* (for none of which, incidentally, was he paid). In January 1834 he wrote a story about some amateur theatricals which go awry (the play was *Othello*, which of course he had already parodied elsewhere), and in the following month a story about a draper's assistant whose manner belies his "low" status. There are flashes of acid if high-spirited wit in all these sketches (in some respects like Jane Austen's juvenilia), but both plot and humour are generally farcical and almost vulgar – like that of the kind of London "spark" Dickens was later to satirise. These stories are about loss of face or respectability, of the perils involved in trying too hard to impress, of theatrical mannerisms which go wrong; all themes, of course, likely to be of some consequence to a young man who was himself intent upon rising in the world. And it is clear, in fact, that this particular young man already had larger ambitions than could be easily satisfied by a small magazine; he was planning a series of sketches or stories to be entitled "The Parish" and by the end of 1833 he had already been talking about a "proposed Novel". It has been suggested that this plan concerned *Oliver Twist* and, since it is undoubtedly true that most proposed first novels contain more than their fair share of autobiographical material, it is likely that Dickens would have hit upon some such theme — the poor boy rescued from oblivion and misery — which would so closely touch upon the events and fantasies of his own childhood.

And already the characteristic style of Charles Dickens was beginning faintly to emerge — in a story published in April 1834, "The Bloomsbury Christening", there is a foretaste of Scrooge in a misanthropic old party, Nicodemus Dumps, and in the Kitterbells an anticipation of those happy, helpless, feckless families which later became something of a Dickens speciality. In another story two months later there is a preview of another type of Dickensian humour: in a love letter within that story we find an anticipation of Jingle in "Ere this reaches you, far distant — appeal to feelings — love to distraction — bees'-wax — slavery". And finally, in August of 1834, another very funny story (the important thing to remember about these early stories is just how comic the young Dickens could be) is succeeded by the pseudonym, "Boz". At one stroke he created an identity which could unite these scattered pieces, while at the same time fabricating a minor mystery about the author himself. That he had good reason to be proud of his authorship is not in doubt; there were already

85

appearing favourable if short reviews of his stories, and he had also received the further if unwelcome compliment of being reprinted — or pirated, rather — both in England and in the United States. What he had always wanted, "the fame . . ." It was beginning to happen. One of the recurring words in his correspondence now is "flare", a term which he uses variously to describe an appearance in print, a party, an argument, and any kind of concerted or violent activity. But the real meaning is clear enough: to brighten, to erupt, to come alive at last.

But he was not as yet a *successful* author. Not yet. He still had to earn his living in the employment of others. In the autumn of 1833 he was helping his uncle, John Barrow, with business on the *Mirror of Parliament* but he soon found a larger sphere in which to move. It so happened that in the earlier part of the following year a Liberal politician, Sir John Easthope, became the new proprietor of the *Morning Chronicle*, a serious London daily newspaper that under its previous owner had somehow lost its way. Easthope's purchase of it, primarily as a mouthpiece for the Whig and reformist cause, heralded a re-organisation of its journalists. A certain Thomas Beard had joined its parliamentary staff, and suggested that Charles Dickens should also become its representative in the press gallery. Easthope was not an easy man, in any case — his employees called him "Blast-hope" — but eventually Dickens was enrolled upon the staff.

The *Morning Chronicle*, in its new incarnation, became a paper of some stature; John Stuart Mill described it as "the organ of opinions much in advance of any which had ever before found regular advocacy in the newspaper press", by which he meant that it was the first serious daily newspaper to introduce Benthamite theory "into newspaper discussion". In other words, the *Morning Chronicle* was on the more intellectual and fervent end of the Liberal spectrum. In fact it increased its popularity as a result —

its circulation rose within a few years from one thousand to six thousand. Its editor, John Black, seems to have shared generally in Benthamite principles, and John Stuart Mill said of him that he was "the first journalist who carried criticism and the spirit of reform into the details of English institutions". Of course Dickens was at this stage a radical but not, as we have seen, necessarily of the same Benthamite stamp as Black and Easthope – indeed he was later to engage in arguments with Black about the results of that Benthamite measure, the New Poor Law, which in the cause of political theory had organised a system of poor relief both barbaric and simplistic. The important thing about Black, however, was that, like any good editor, he knew talent when he saw it and it was not long before he became, in Dickens's own words, "my first hearty out-and-out appreciator".

Yet Dickens was certainly not spared the ordinarily rigorous and arduous life of a general reporter. At a salary of five guineas a week he was employed as one of twelve parliamentary reporters of the paper but over the next two years his duties included theatre reviews and, during the parliamentary recesses, he travelled widely to report on election campaigns, dinners, public meetings and the like. For once his internal energy and restlessness had found a suitable outlet, and Dickens has left his own record of how "I have often transcribed for the printer from my shorthand reports, important public speeches in which the strictest accuracy was required . . . writing on the palm of my hand, by the light of a dark lantern, in a post chaise and four, galloping through a wild country, all through the dead of night . . ."

There is also a possibility that at this stage Dickens did not envision a literary career for himself since he wrote to the Steward of New Inn stating that he intended ". . . entering at the bar, as soon as circumstances will enable me to do so". In fact Dickens seems on other occasions to have considered the possibility of a legal career – there would even come a time when he would apply to become a magistrate, like Henry Fielding before him – but in this period it seems most likely that Dickens simply wanted to find chambers for himself. He wanted his independence, in other words, and he wanted to put some distance between himself and his family; a fact about which his father seemed a little bitter, since he referred to "Charles's determination to leave home, on the first occasion of his having an annual engagement . . ." with the *Morning Chronicle*. The wisdom of Dickens's decision was soon evident, however, for only a week after he wrote to New Inn his father was once more arrested for debt – this time on the initiative of wine merchants to whom he owed money. Once again, just as the young man was beginning to find the world and to make his mark upon it, his old childhood humiliations and miseries threatened to descend upon him. And this time matters were worse than usual; Dickens had apparently backed some of his father's bills and would therefore also be liable for arrest. "I have not yet been taken," he wrote to Thomas Mitton when asking for his help, "but no doubt that will be the next act in this 'domestic tragedy.'" His father was escorted to Sloman's detention house for debtors at 4 Cursitor Street; Dickens was too busy with his newspaper work that morning to deal with the problem, and asked Mitton to visit him instead. Dickens then went to Cursitor Street at six, just two hours before starting work on the night's session in the parliamentary gallery, and managed to give his father enough money to escape the immediate consequences of his debts (some of this money came from Dickens's "French employer", about whom nothing is known – an indication, at any rate, of the extent to which he was forced to take many and varied employments in these first years). What is most interesting about this episode, however, is not the helplessness with which the father relied upon the son, nor the precariousness of Dickens's family life, but rather the fact that no more than two months later he used the experience in a story which he wrote for the *Monthly Magazine*. "A Passage in the Life of Mr Watkins Tottle" has a long section in which the aforesaid Mr Tottle is taken to a "lock-up house in the vicinity of Chancery Lane", this establishment and its guests being described in great detail and with an obvious air of authenticity. "The room – which was a small, confined den – was partitioned off into boxes, like the common-room of some inferior eating-house. The dirty floor had evidently been as long a stranger to the scrubbing-brush as to carpet or floor-cloth; and the ceiling was completely blackened by the flare of the oil-lamp by which the room was lighted at night." Dickens was using his private family experiences even though they have no direct relation to the plot of the story which he was composing – either he was being a good reporter and wanted to make use of the material which he had observed so woefully at first hand, or he simply had to put down the episode in fictional form in order to deal with it properly and so come to terms with his own feelings. That is why there are times in Dickens's sketches and stories of the period when a somewhat penny-drama plot is redeemed by intense observation, by exactly that "intensity of . . . nature" which he had diagnosed in himself.

His father was released, but only at the expense of his son's borrowing from his friends on the security of his own salary. But this did not deter John Dickens himself from almost immediately writing to those same friends in turn asking for money; he informed Thomas Beard, for example, that the household was about to break up, with various members of the family going into lodgings but "your humble servant 'to the winds'". His son, Alfred, he told Beard in a subsequent letter, "is walking to and from Hampstead daily in dancing Pumps". Colourful letters –

certainly more colourful than apologetic – and it is hard not to be entertained by that air of self-dramatisation which the father brings to the most dismal situations. Which was a gift, of course, he transmitted to his famous son.

The son, meanwhile, had, as it were, fled; in December 1834 he moved with his younger brother, Frederick, into chambers at Furnival's Inn. He rented what was then known as a "three pair back" at what was then the not inconsiderable rent of £35 a year – three modest rooms, a cellar and a lumber room in a not very prepossessing congeries of buildings which had been expressly built as chambers. It was a "good" address but somewhat gloomy, according to all reports, and in his later writings Dickens always referred to the loneliness and dilapidation of such places – describing them once as "that stronghold of Melancholy" and dilating on the unpleasant habits of the "laundresses" who were supposed to clean them and look after their tenants. One can be sure, then, that the "gloomy thoughts", of which Dickens admitted he was a prey, would still have visited him even at this time when his whole career seemed to stretch before him in bright prospect. Yet, as he noted during this period, "We have much more cause for cheerfulness than despondency after all; and as I for one am determined to see everything in as bright a light as possible . . ." This is always to be remembered about Dickens: cheerfulness keeps on breaking through.

At this time he was writing his sketches which, fortuitously, found a slightly wider audience. For it was at some point in the autumn or winter of 1834 that he made the acquaintance of George Hogarth, who was about to become the editor of the *Evening Chronicle* – a tri-weekly offshoot of the *Morning Chronicle* which was delivered mainly to the rural areas around London. Hogarth "begged" the young man to write sketches for his new venture, to which Dickens graciously assented – although adding, in a not unfriendly manner, that he would expect "*some* additional remuneration" above his *Morning Chronicle* salary. Upon that everybody seems to have agreed, and for an extra two guineas a week Dickens embarked on a series which was to become known as "Sketches of London".

George Hogarth, however, was to play an even more important role in his life. Hogarth was a music critic and journalist. He had known Walter Scott – his sister married Scott's printer, James Ballantyne – and had had a relatively distinguished if peripatetic career as editor of local newspapers in Exeter and Halifax. He had moved to London in the early autumn of 1834 in order to take up a position as musical and dramatic editor of the *Morning Chronicle* but, as we have seen, he was soon appointed as editor of the *Evening Chronicle*. He had taken 18 York Place, one in a terrace of houses the gardens of which bordered the south side of the Fulham Road (the area of Fulham was in those days known for its nurseries and tulip gardens, but perhaps as a result was also a byword for dullness). He soon established a friendship with Charles Dickens, the young man whose occasional journalism he so obviously admired, and it was not long before Dickens was making social calls to Fulham.

Dickens became a welcome guest at the Hogarths, and he in turn welcomed them. Hogarth's eldest daughter, Catherine, told her cousin in a letter of February 1835 that she had attended a birthday party for him at his chambers in Furnival's Inn: ". . . it was a delightful party I enjoyed it very much – Mr Dickens improves very much on acquaintance he is very gentlemanly and pleasant . . ." And so was heralded one of the most famous marriages of the nineteenth century. Three months later, Charles Dickens and Catherine Hogarth were engaged. She was the oldest of the Hogarth children – nineteen when she met Dickens, whereas her sister Mary Hogarth was fourteen and Georgina seven — but all three girls were to exercise a permanent influence upon Dickens's life, in one capacity or another. Mary, for example, was not yet of an age to marry but there is no doubt that the affection between her and the young Dickens was strong; she gave him presents, a fruit knife and silver inkwell, very soon after he had come to know the Hogarths and it is clear from all later reports that her gentle and selfless nature deeply impressed the young man. But little else is known about her — only a "spiritual" quality which she seemed to possess and, since she died at an early age, it can only be said that her proper character remained as it were in the womb of time, leaving behind only the faint intimations of a personality from which Dickens in later life was to create his own beloved "Mary".

Catherine, by contrast, is a much more tangible and definite figure. There are many descriptions of her, but the most comprehensive and accurate comes only a few years after her meeting with Charles Dickens: ". . . a pretty little woman, plump and fresh-coloured, with the large, heavy-lidded blue eyes so much admired by men. The nose was slightly retroussé, the forehead good, mouth small, round and red-lipped with a genial smiling expression of countenance, notwithstanding the sleepy look of the slow-moving eyes." In other words she was the same physical "type" as Maria Beadnell, Dickens's last romantic attachment, and this similarity may give added weight to Dickens's childhood wish "to marry a Columbine". But Catherine seems to have been quite without Maria's flightiness or flirtatiousness — clearly Dickens, now so busy with his journalism, could do without the strain of these.

Dickens was already getting into his stride with his "Sketches of London" for the *Evening Chronicle*, and his development as a writer is to be observed even as he worked upon these occasional pieces of journalism. For one thing he was extending his range. In his first months he had rigidly separated his "stories" from his "sketches" but it would always be part of his genius to reconcile the opposing tendencies of his mind, and now in a new series he began for the *Evening Chronicle* – it was entitled "Our Parish" and was certainly related to the novel he still wanted to write – he began to combine fiction and observation in new ways. The stories had always tended to be more supercilious, more farcical, owing a greater debt to the theatre. The sketches are more benign, more purposeful, more concerned with elucidating the world. It is as if the creative side of Dickens was still being held back by his early allegiance to the stage, while his hitherto untried powers of observation were growing ever stronger. What was interesting now, too, was the intermittent expression of his social indignation; he was no longer the ironic or supercilious farceur and in his first pieces for the *Evening Chronicle* his social concerns began to emerge very clearly. In a short piece entitled "Gin Shops", for example, he made the connection between intemperance and poverty which he maintained for the rest of his life. And all the time Dickens knew the direction in which he was going; he was in the position of someone who is "fighting to get on", as he said of another colleague later, and he was quite aware how in that position the exposure of a name "before the public", as he put it, was very important. In later life he tended to disavow these sketches as the product of a juvenile sensibility, but at the time he was very concerned to get them right; there is no doubt, either, that it was their publication, rather than that of *The Pickwick Papers*, which first gave Dickens a measure of fame.

At the same time, Dickens was working in the press gallery of the House of Commons. He was becoming increasingly weary, in other words, often working until dawn and then sleeping until ten or eleven in the morning. And then getting up to write at once to Catherine: "I wrote till 3 oClock this morning (I had not done for the paper till 8) and passed the whole night, if night it can be called after that hour, in a state of exquisite torture from the spasm in my side far exceeding anything I ever felt." So on occasions of more than usual stress the pain in his side, the legacy of his childhood, still returned. (It was generally allayed, however, by potions from Thomas Beard's brother, Francis, who was then a medical student and who later became Dickens's family doctor.) Already he was doing too much: in June 1835 he stopped writing his "Sketches" for the journal of his putative father-in-law, but began writing them for a magazine called *Bell's Life in London*. This was partly because they offered him more money, and partly because to appear on the front page of that metropolitan journal was better than being tucked away inside a newspaper primarily designed for the rural areas. In addition he had a great admiration for its editor, Vincent Dowling. It was to Dowling that he sent his famous "business card", written on the spur of the moment in an inn opposite Dowling's offices: "CHARLES DICKENS, Resurrectionist, In Search of a Subject". The "resurrectionist", or grave-robber who took corpses and sold them to medical faculties for dissection, had been lately in the news; and Dickens, with his own subdued infant fear of the dead coming alive, was still fascinated enough by the profession in later days to place one of its exponents in *A Tale of Two Cities*. But in this instance he seems to be no more than poking macabre fun at his own life as reporter and observer rather than active participant.

All the while he was trying to balance the needs of his career against his duties to Catherine who, on occasions, seems to have been disturbed by his attention to his work at the expense of herself. It was not unreasonable for her to be so: it must have looked as if this was the shape their marriage was about to take, and indeed in that she was not much mistaken. Nevertheless, in order to be closer to her he had moved to lodgings in Selwood Terrace, a row of houses just north of the Fulham Road and only a short walk from the Hogarths' own house. He took the place in May, at the time of his engagement, and remained here for six months – thus assuming the obligation of rents both here and at Furnival's Inn. Despite minor and temporary disagreements, in fact, the course of their engagement was a relatively smooth one; at no stage was she anything other than what he described as "My dearest life" or "My dearest love", "dearest Pig" or simply "Mouse", and there is evidence, too, that their affection for each grew during the course of their engagement.

Still the work piled up. In January 1836 he began once more writing sketches for the *Morning Chronicle* and during these months, also, he wrote frequent theatre reviews, carried on working in the press gallery of the House of Commons (according to one report he was so overpowered by a speech by Daniel O'Connell on the hardships of the Irish peasantry that he burst into tears and could not continue), he reported on a dinner for Lord John Russell in Bristol, reported on a fire at Hatfield House, and attended a by-election which he summed up as ". . . bells ringing, candidates speaking, drums sounding . . . men fighting, swearing drinking, and squabbling . . .", during the course of which Dickens holed up in a hotel room with other representatives of the press and played bagatelle. He also attended a stone-laying ceremony (which ceremony he later used, to great effect, in *Martin Chuzzlewit*). His life as a journalist, then, was a wearying if various one. But he was indisputably a success, and the favourable wind of his career seems, as often happens, to have given him self-confidence and even stridency in his dress: ". . . a fresh, handsome, genial young man," one of his parliamentary colleagues described him now, "with a profusion of brown hair, a bright eye . . . rather inclined to what was once called 'dandyism' in his attire, and to a rather exuberant

95

display of jewellery on his vest and on his fingers." Another colleague has a similar story: ". . . he had bought a new hat, and a very handsome blue cloak, with black velvet facings, the corner of which he threw over his shoulder *à l'Espagnol*." The same colleague recalls an incident which epitomises the merry side of Dickens: they were walking together through Hungerford Market "where we followed a coal-heaver, who carried his little rosy but grimy child looking over his shoulder; and CD bought a halfpenny worth of cherries and, as we went along, he gave them one by one to the little fellow without the knowledge of the father. CD seemed quite as much pleased as the child." And as he walked through the market Dickens, in that expressive but comic manner of his, alluded to the difficulties which he himself had experienced as a child – "He informed me, as we walked through it, that he knew *Hunger*ford Market well, laying unusual stress on the two first syllables." Yet within a matter of months Dickens's life was to change in ways that he could not, even in the days of his childhood fantasies, possibly have imagined.

# *Eight*

IN the autumn of 1835 a young publisher, John Macrone, approached Dickens with the idea of reprinting his stories and sketches in volume form, offering £100 for the copyright. Dickens seems to have leapt at the chance, not least because it would provide a welcome additional income just before his marriage, and almost at once he began to plan and arrange the proposed collection. The title was one difficulty; "Bubbles from the Bwain of Boz and the Graver of Cruikshank" was the first suggestion, by Macrone himself, but Dickens considered the idea of bubbles emanating from a steel engraver to be a little far-fetched. He in turn suggested the less facetious but more accurate title of "Sketches by Boz and Cuts by Cruikshank" – the important name in both titles, however, really being the second. It was something of a coup for Macrone to enlist the services of this illustrator, George Cruikshank, in the cause of a young author of only modest fame. To have his name on the title page was, if not a guarantee of success, at least a provident hedge against failure. He was called the "Illustrious George", and was already very well known as a caricaturist and illustrator of books – he was in some ways a difficult man, with powerful perceptions but equally powerful opinions. He could be truculent and assertive, even though this self-assertive manner often gave way, in his famous drinking bouts, to one of drunken clowning and gaiety. He was dark-haired, swarthy, with prominent eyes and nose; he looked as if he might have walked out of one of his own caricatures, and indeed he most resembled his own later illustration of Fagin in his condemned cell, of which G. K. Chesterton, perhaps Dickens's best critic, said that ". . . it does not merely look like a picture of Fagin; it looks like a picture by Fagin". Cruikshank called Dickens "Charley", and although at first their working relationship seemed perfectly amicable (with Cruikshank quite aware of his preeminent position) it soon became clear that the young author was in no sense about to defer to the older and more famous man. Quite the opposite, in fact; with a self-assurance and even self-assertiveness which are entirely characteristic of Dickens even when young, he began to badger Cruikshank for the illustrations to his first book – an event which Cruikshank, in a letter to Macrone, described as an "unpleasant turn". But clearly it was important for Dickens to assert control over his own project – in the first edition of *Sketches by Boz* he paid fulsome tribute to Cruikshank, but all subsequent editions removed references to him in anything but a nominal sense. His relationship with the artist was in later years to be a most uneasy one (Cruikshank said in the 1860s, "When I and Mr Dickens meet on the same side of the way, either Dickens crosses over or I do") and this small preliminary skirmish did in fact delay the publication of the first edition for some two months. Eventually it appeared in February 1836.

It was a great success. Dickens had not organised his stories or journalistic pieces to any discernible plan, and in fact seems to have been at pains to suggest the range and heterogeneity of his talent (in a preliminary puff for the book in his own newspaper, he added the word "versatile" in proof to describe himself). But he had gone to some trouble to prepare the material for this more permanent form of publication – he had written an essay on

Newgate, perhaps the most powerful of his short pieces, solely for publication in the volume. In fact he would always have an intuitive and astute notion of public taste and public response, and on this first occasion he deliberately revised the sketches to make them more suitable for the readership of a book rather than that of a newspaper; he cut opening and closing paragraphs which were no longer relevant or suitable, he softened some of his social criticism, erased political or topical allusions and, as far as possible, removed any harshness or clumsiness which had inevitably crept in during the course of their rapid composition.

But a more important proposal, and more significant enterprise, was just about to come. *Sketches by Boz* appeared on 8 February, and just two days later a certain William Hall called upon Dickens at his lodgings in Furnival's Inn. At once Dickens, with his power of visual recognition, remembered him to be the man who had sold him, more than two years ago, over the counter in Johnson Court, the issue of the *Monthly Magazine* which had contained Dickens's first story. William Hall was now one of the partners in the publishing firm of Chapman and Hall, a relatively new venture for which Hall supplied the financial acumen while Thomas Chapman provided the "literary" dimension (not an uncommon divide among publishers, and it may have been one that contributed to Dickens's later portrait of "Spenlow and Jorkins").

The previous year Chapman and Hall had engineered a success with a publication called the *Squib Annual of Poetry, Politics, and Personalities*, which was more or less a vehicle for the cartoons of Robert Seymour; now they wanted to repeat that success and Seymour had come up with the idea of publishing in shilling monthly parts a record of the exploits of something known as the "Nimrod Club"; this would concern the misadventures of a group of Cockney sportsmen (a familiar comic subject at the time, suggesting as it does that growing awareness of the uniqueness of urban experience). Seymour's drawings would be the important thing, however; the provider of the words, or "letterpress", definitely the subsidiary. The job of appending those words had been offered to Charles Whitehead, a writer who had just taken up the post of editing the *Library of Fiction* for Chapman and Hall, but he demurred; and it seemed that it was he who suggested the newly fashionable Boz for the task. No doubt Seymour was consulted before any decision was made but, when it came, it was entirely in Boz's favour. So Hall had arrived at Furnival's Inn in order to offer the job to Charles Dickens, for a payment of nine guineas per sheet and at a rate of one and a half sheets per month (a sheet being a publishing term for sixteen pages of the finished product). He accepted almost at once, and that evening Dickens wrote to Catherine saying that "the work will be no joke, but the emolument is too tempting to resist". Especially since now they were making active preparations for their marriage and, a week after receiving the offer from Hall, Dickens moved to larger quarters in Furnival's Inn at an additional cost of fifteen pounds a year. He was buying furniture, too, for this new home – rosewood for the drawing room, mahogany for the dining room. It would be here that he began the novel which would bring him world-wide fame.

But there were other matters to settle in advance: once again Dickens's self-command and determination prompted him to change the nature of the task he was about to perform. He may not yet have known the nature of his especial genius but, with the instinct of a "professional" writer, he knew what to avoid; the idea of a sporting club had been worked to death in recent years, as had the notion of "Cockney sportsmen", and from the beginning Dickens decided to turn the project on its head in order to give him room for the full use of his particular powers. He told Hall that ". . . it would be infinitely better for the plates to arise naturally out of the text; and that I should like to take my own way with a freer range of English scenes and people, and was afraid I should ultimately do so in any case." In other words, he had no intention of being a mere accompanist for Robert Seymour's illustrations. As in all the projects he ever undertook, he insisted that he should take the pre-eminent role. He was being all the more assertive because, at this time, Seymour was, as one contemporary noted, "the most varied and the most prolific" caricaturist of his day. Chapman and Hall, with the grudging acquiescence of Seymour, concurred.

It was almost time to begin. He needed a title, and a hero. In deference to Seymour's original notion he imported the idea of a club or society of urban "types", although they would have very little to do with the "sportsmen" whom the artist had envisaged. More significantly, he needed a name. Names would always be very important to him. In later years he could not begin a book until he had hit upon the right title, and in a notebook he made lists of fanciful or odd surnames to assist with his inspiration. It is simply that, without the name, the essence could not and did not exist; he was a man who trusted in the power of words and the name seemed to call forth the character whom then he could begin to portray. So it was with this new project: he remembered the name of a coach proprietor from Bath, a man whose coaches he would have seen or used during his peregrinations as a journalist on the *Morning Chronicle*. This man was Moses Pickwick. And so Mr Pickwick was born. And, with him, *The Pickwick Papers*.

Charles Dickens had now moved into his new chambers. The House of Commons was not sitting, so he had his mornings and evenings for his own writing. He needed all the time he could get. He had agreed to provide the first number by early in March, and the second at the end of the same month — each number would be longer than anything he had ever written before, some twelve thousand words, but the length did not daunt him. He sat down, on 18 February, 1836, and began.

The form and manner of *The Pickwick Papers* heralded a revolution in the circulation and appeal of narrative fiction. Of course the idea of shilling monthly parts for this enterprise had originally been that of Robert Seymour, and the form itself was not a particularly new one; there had been similar excursions in the same field of light humour and *facetiae* with heroes such as Mr Jorrocks and Dr Syntax. Serialisation of fiction in magazines was equally common (much of the work of Marryat and Galt was first published in this way) and there were even examples of fiction being published in monthly parts — the difference being that such serialisation was really only employed for old and familiar tales like *The Pilgrim's Progress*. What was unfamiliar about Dickens's venture was the idea of a *new* story being marketed in this way, and within a matter of months it became clear exactly what it was that Dickens had initiated.

By the end of March the first instalment was published of *The Posthumous Papers of the Pickwick Club, containing a faithful record of the Perambulations, Perils, Travels, Adventures and Sporting Transactions of the Corresponding Members*. It was "Edited by 'Boz'"', came in green wrappers, with 32 pages of print and 4 engravings by Seymour, and was priced at one shilling. The exact number printed is in doubt, but it can be assumed that approximately 400 were distributed by Chapman and Hall. It had been hard work, but it was finished. He wrote his own advertisement for the *Library of Fiction* in which facetiously he heralds the appearance of a work to be placed alongside that of Gibbon's *The History of the Decline and Fall of the Roman Empire*.

Buoyed up by his exhilaration at a labour completed he

now went on to the next event of his life, his marriage — "went on" being the appropriate phrase here, since there was a sense in which these extraordinary months in the life of the young writer were like a series of hurdles, over each of which he leapt as he went along. Certainly it was the success of *Sketches by Boz*, and the prospect of extra financial reward from *The Pickwick Papers*, that persuaded him to marry sooner than he had originally intended. He and Catherine Hogarth had been engaged for less than a year and, since she was still a minor, Dickens had to return to the scene of his old employment, Doctors' Commons, in order to obtain a special marriage licence. The ceremony itself took place on 2 April in the Hogarths' parish church, the newly built St Luke's in Chelsea. As a wedding present Dickens gave his wife a sandalwood work-box inlaid with ivory, and after the breakfast at York Place he took his bride down for their honeymoon to a small cottage (a two-storey wooden building, whitewashed) in the Kentish village of Chalk; this was only a few miles from Rochester, and it seems that the letting of the cottage was arranged by the Dickenses' old neighbour, Mrs Newnham, from Ordnance Terrace days. The decision to take his honeymoon in an area he had known as a child is not perhaps as sentimental as it seems: it is quite likely that Dickens, at a time when he was deluged with work, decided to take the easiest option and rely upon the help of old family friends to secure him a place to rest. And, since he was in the process of writing a narrative set in the same area, no doubt the thought of returning to it for an additional examination was a welcome one.

The newly-married pair stayed in Chalk for less than two weeks, and then returned to the new lodgings at Furnival's Inn; the three rooms here were larger than those which Dickens had originally possessed but nevertheless they must have seemed somewhat small to Catherine after her life in the capacious Hogarth household. But at once Dickens went back to work. On the eighteenth of the month he had his first meeting with Robert Seymour; he had invited him to Furnival's Inn together with Chapman and Hall, to "take a glass of grog" (his younger brother, Frederick, to whom Dickens was especially attached, was also a member of the little party), but in the same letter Dickens asserted his proprietorial rights over their venture by suggesting that Seymour alter one of his illustrations – a task which Seymour, no doubt against his wishes, carried out. Nothing is known of the ensuing party, and it is noteworthy now only because, two days later, Seymour went into the summer-house of his garden in Islington, set up his gun with a string on its trigger, and shot himself through the head.

The suicide of Seymour was of course a most unwelcome surprise both to Dickens and his publishers since the whole project, originally established on the popularity of the artist, might quickly founder without him. More immediately, the second number was about to be printed and at once a search was made of the artist's working-room; three engravings were found, and these were duly published as Seymour's last contribution to *The Pickwick Papers*. But the essential problem remained: since his return from his honeymoon Dickens had already written half of the succeeding number, and some decision about the future shape of the series without Seymour had to be made. At once the search began for a suitable artist.

Dickens it was who eventually chose the illustrator who more than anyone else came to be associated with his work – Hablot Knight Browne. He was a little younger than Dickens and, although he had had no academic training, had been apprenticed to an engraver; he had left his apprenticeship a short while before, and was still making up his mind whether he wanted to be a painter or an illustrator when he encountered the novelist. He had already been working with him on a small pamphlet and, although he had had little experience in etching, he was chosen to continue work on *The Pickwick Papers*. This may have been for personal reasons as much as anything else: Dickens had already met him and no doubt saw in him those qualities of steadiness, perseverance and, above all, pliability which he knew that he needed. Browne was a quiet, unassuming, unobtrusive and almost painfully shy man; he hated going out "in company" and to the end of his life remained something of a "loner", a man who was content with his lot in life and performed it satisfactorily. In some ways he resembled Thomas Beard, in fact, and it seems that Dickens was attracted to just this type of character – not necessarily because it complemented his own more vivacious and gregarious temperament, but rather because these qualities of self-effacement and shyness were precisely the ones he admired and precisely the ones which he felt most lacking in himself. Thus, paradoxical though it may sound, his friendship with the artist in a way helped to recompense him for his own strengths. So Browne was chosen and, as we shall see, no better illustrator could have been found – not only did he at once fall into compliance with Dickens's ways and requests (even adopting the name of "Phiz" to complement "Boz") but he learned from the novelist's own art and, in a sense, grew with it.

By early May Dickens had signed an agreement with John Macrone to write a novel entitled *Gabriel Vardon, The Locksmith of London*. This may have been the novel he had been proposing to himself ever since he began writing the sketches and, if so, since it only eventually emerged in completed form as *Barnaby Rudge*, it has the claim to being the novel most delayed by Dickens. He received two hundred pounds for this, and then three months later accepted a further one hundred pounds when he agreed to write for Thomas Tegg a children's book to be called *Solomon Bell the Raree Showman*. Then in the same month he made an agreement with yet another publisher, Richard Bentley, for two novels, each to be of the conventional three-volume length. He had also agreed to write sketches for a new weekly paper, *The Carlton Chronicle* – and all this at the time he was writing *The Pickwick Papers*, continuing with his parliamentary duties for the *Morning Chronicle*, and preparing another volume of *Sketches* to be published by John Macrone. In other words, he had committed himself to the eventual publication of some five books while still heavily engaged upon his first novel.

The reasons for placing such an extraordinary burden of work upon his shoulders are various, however, the first being that he needed the money. No doubt he was already planning to leave the *Morning Chronicle* (a step he eventually took in November) and no doubt he was even now trying to measure his funds for the months and years ahead, estimating the loss of the *Morning Chronicle* income against the payments for the proposed works of fiction. Throughout his life Dickens had an obsessive need for the security which money could bring – it ought to be remembered that he would soon be casting the childhood of the miser, Ebenezer Scrooge, at least partly in the image of his own. It is clear enough that he knew as well as anyone, at least as well as any of his biographers, from what troubled origins this demand for money came. It was not that he himself was a miser or loved money for itself. He was on all occasions a most generous and open-handed man. It was just that his early experiences in the Marshalsea and blacking factory provoked an anxiety which only the assurance of financial well-being could assuage.

No doubt it was partly the pressure of constant hard work, just as much as the early Victorian belief in a "change of air", that persuaded Catherine and her husband to take a cottage in the country during the late summer – in August and September they absconded to Petersham, from which rural retreat Dickens made occasional sallies into London until they returned on 24 September. It was here, during this interval, that he placed Pickwick drunk in a wheelbarrow and that he introduced to his readers the legal partnership of Dodson and Fogg.

By October his publishers, Chapman and Hall, were already discussing a possible sequel to *The Pickwick Papers*, for throughout this period that narrative was moving slowly ahead, growing in power as it proceeded. He was writing quickly but such is the sureness of his invention that the manuscript in his strong and confident hand is remarkably free of corrections. He numbers each page at the top as he goes along with his flowing quill pen – there are two or three small deletions on each page which look as if they were made at the actual time of writing, and there are others which were clearly made when he looked over the manuscript after he had completed it. He was often writing early in the morning or late at night, and often when exhausted from his reportorial duties. The narrative, as a result, contains a few repetitions and obvious occasions when the seed for a later scene has been sown in Dickens's mind as he went along. There is a vignette in the Fleet Prison where a poor man's mind is slowly breaking down as he "was riding, in imagination, some desperate steeplechase . . .", for example, and this image is worked up into a whole story a few numbers later. Dickens's imagination caught fire as he went along, then, the energy and speed making it burn all the brighter. It is this sense of moving life which runs through it almost from the beginning, and within a few weeks he had started to tie the month of the fictional narrative to the very month in which that number would appear. By October he had already planned the probable course of the next three numbers and, in the December issue, he is looking forward to the events of the next spring. By the conclusion of his labour he had so harnessed the time of his narrative to the real time of chronology, and had been so successful at relating the impact of brief stories and events to the larger movement of each episode, that in *The Pickwick Papers* he came close to incorporating the rhythm of life itself.

The writing of *The Pickwick Papers* is in a sense the education of Charles Dickens; education in public response, education in his powers of human observation, education in his talent for comic narrative. Just as he finds new meaning and new life in the figure of Mr Pickwick as he proceeds – Mr Pickwick soon ceases to be merely a humorous figure and becomes instead the embodiment of natural benevolence – so Dickens discovers new power and capacity within himself. And it is a young man's book, too, because it has no sense of an ending. All of his life up to that point is somewhere within these pages, and in that spirit *The Pickwick Papers* becomes an exercise in self-definition as well as in the telling of a story. That accounts for its charm, that instinctive, compulsive, exhilarating sense of discovery. The scenes in Rochester, no less than the scenes in prison, testify to the sense of enlargement and liberation which Dickens was now feeling; the real Rochester, the real Bull Inn, the real debtors' prison, were not as large and as echoic as they become in these pages where they are labyrinthine, incalculable, chaotic. There were times when Dickens was overworked and ill – violent headaches, and something he described as "rheumatism in the face", afflicted him in the winter of 1836. Such apparently minor ills were not insignificant in a period when even a common ailment such as a cold might prove fatal and where the techniques of medicine and surgery were quite rudimentary. But even during such periods of stress Dickens managed to work on, his invention and humour undiminished.

The success of *The Pickwick Papers* was not long in coming. Chapman and Hall had printed approximately four hundred copies of the first monthly number. By the end, they were selling some forty thousand. It began to happen at the time of the fourth number, or instalment, when Sam Weller is introduced and when Hablot Browne's illustrations appear for the first time. In July, also, Boz's identity was first revealed, and in that same month William Jerdan printed extracts from the novel in his influential *Literary Gazette*. And, since *The Pickwick Papers* appeared monthly, it reaped the benefit of being mentioned or reviewed each month in the other public prints – although there seems to have been some difficulty in categorising the material from which they were quoting. Some journals placed it not under fiction but under journalism or "miscellanies". But there is no doubt that its comic appeal – its human appeal – was steadily being seen and its audience steadily growing. That is also why in the fourth number there first appeared the "Pickwick Advertiser", a section of advertisements placed in front of the main text like advertisements in a newspaper. In this first edition of the "Advertiser" the only goods to be sold are books, among them *A Popular Treatise on Diet and Regimen*, *Les dames de Byron* and *The Angler's Souvenir*, but the success of Pickwick was such that by the ninth number there were more pages of advertisement (some thirty-nine) than pages of text (thirty-one). The range of the advertisements had also widened from the merely literary, and now included Rotterdam Corn and Bunion Solvent, Simpson's new Antibilious Pill, a gentleman's water-proof cloak "in all respects superior to the shabby-looking India Rubber" and – a firm favourite, this – Rowlands's Macassar Oil.

The extent of the advertising was an indication of one significant fact: *The Pickwick Papers* had become an extraordinary success. ". . . no sooner was a new number published," one contemporary wrote, "than needy admirers flattened their noses against the booksellers' windows eager to secure a good look at the etchings and to peruse every line of the letterpress that might be exposed to view, frequently reading it aloud to applauding bystanders . . . so great was the craze, Pickwick Papers secured far more attention than was given to the ordinary politics of the day". Lord Denman used to read it on the bench while jurors were deliberating their decisions and the fashionable doctor, Sir Benjamin Brodie, read it in his carriage as he travelled between patients. One gentleman on a "grand tour" in 1840 found "Pickwick" inscribed on one of the pyramids, and there is the famous story of the dying man who seemed to find no comfort in his spiritual minister but who was heard to say, "Well, thank God, Pickwick will be out in ten days, anyway." But perhaps the most important evidence for the success of Dickens's work is to be found in the report of one of his first biographers who, at the time of the novel's appearance, had visited a locksmith in Liverpool: "I found him reading Pickwick . . . to an audience of twenty persons, literally, men, women and children." It was hired by them all for twopence a day from the circulating library, because they could not afford a shilling for the monthly number, and the observer never forgot how these humble people, who themselves could not read, laughed with Sam Weller and cried with "ready tears" at the death of the poor debtor in the Fleet prison. This was the audience which Charles Dickens had found – not only the judges and the doctors, but the labouring poor. By some miracle of genius he had found a voice which penetrated the hearts of the high as well as of the low. Truly he had created a national audience.

# Nine

NOW at last he could make his own way. He could make his own terms. He could shake off his old employers, and work fully for himself. So it was that at the beginning of November 1836 he signed an agreement with Richard Bentley, the publisher, to edit a new magazine which was originally to be called the *Wits' Miscellany* but which was later changed to *Bentley's Miscellany* — "Would not that be going to the other extreme?" one real wit asked at the time. He had already agreed to supply Bentley with two three-volume novels, as we have seen, and this agreement to edit Bentley's new enterprise tied them even closer together. Dickens had agreed to edit the journal for one year, and set to work upon it with no misgivings. It was his first experience of editing, although he had been involved in the more technical administration of the *Mirror of Parliament*, and had spent enough time on the *Morning Chronicle* not to be overawed by the responsibility; almost at once he began to write to various authors whom he hoped would contribute, perhaps the most famous of them being Douglas Jerrold. Jerrold himself, a radical journalist who had literally worked his way upwards like Dickens from humble origins, was indeed the type of writer and man with whom Dickens seemed most at ease and most in sympathy; he always preferred the company of writers of working-class or lower-middle-class origins and suitably robust views. Dickens was part of a radical generation growing to maturity in the 1830s, and it is important to see his fiction, as well as his journalism, in the sometimes fierce and polemical light which his colleagues or contemporaries cast.

It seems that John Macrone, the publisher of *Sketches by Boz* for whom Dickens had agreed some time before to write a novel, *Gabriel Vardon*, only now heard about Dickens's agreements to publish two novels with Richard Bentley – and this only when Dickens sent him a letter asking if he might withdraw from his previous contract. It was a difficult situation, especially since Macrone was just about to publish the second series of the *Sketches*, and Macrone was not sure how to proceed. Certain colleagues advised him to keep Dickens to his earlier contract, although the publisher himself must already have at least guessed the self-willed and stubborn determination of Dickens in matters of this kind. Even as Dickens and Macrone argued over the withdrawal from his agreement, the second series of *Sketches by Boz* was issued. On this occasion it appeared in one volume only, partly because of Dickens's usual niggling disputes with Cruikshank, but largely because Dickens himself, overworked and sometimes ill, was not able to provide enough material for two volumes. He gave Macrone much of the material which he had left out of the first series, but also some more recent prose – this collection, it has to be said, is rather less carefully edited than the previous series but is nonetheless an important clue to Dickens's development during this period. The problem with Macrone remained, however, and it was only after some complicated negotiating – settling largely on the question of whether a quid pro quo could be worked out by assigning Macrone the copyright to the *Sketches* – that the matter was finally resolved. Dickens would now only be writing novels for Richard Bentley.

He had handled these negotiations himself, but there now entered his life a man who was in future years to take many of these business burdens from him. It was in late 1836 that Dickens encountered John Forster. They met at the house of Harrison Ainsworth. How Dickens had fist come across Ainsworth is not clear, although it seems likely that their joint publisher, Macrone, at some point introduced them. And they, too, had become friends. It could be said that they were well matched. Ainsworth was seven years older than Dickens, and only two years before he had won enormous acclaim as a novelist for his *Rookwood*. Certainly he was as well known as Dickens himself, and the later publication of *Jack Sheppard* even seemed at one point to be eclipsing Dickens's own *Oliver Twist*.

If anyone is connected with Dickens's name, it is Forster; and indeed he was the most likely person to walk down through posterity as the friend and companion of genius. He was the same age as Dickens and, when they met, they would have already known or at least soon discovered how much they had in common. Forster, too, had come from lowly origins; he was the son of a Newcastle butcher (in later life he was infuriated by enemies who taunted him behind his back as a "butcher's boy"), and it was said that his mother was the "daughter of a cow-keeper". But he was one of those young men who, at this period in English history, seemed ready and able literally to push their way forward through the world — a feat only a little more easily achieved at this time of social transition and political confusion. Forster was a kind and generous friend, as this narrative will show. But the fact remains that there were some people who never could understand how it was that Dickens became so attached to him. Forster could, after all, be very difficult indeed. He seems to have felt keenly his low origins, and there were often occasions when he became uneasy or defensive. He was inclined to bluster as a result, had an almost comical sense of his own dignity, and frequently assumed an air of overpowering infallibility: there is the notorious occasion when he corrected Macready, one of the greatest nineteenth-century actors, for his delivery of Shakespeare. In fact he often gave the impression, typically to those who did not know him well or had not become accustomed to his foibles, of being rude, pompous or just ordinarily bad-tempered.

He was everybody's friend – no one in the nineteenth century had such a wide acquaintance among social, political and literary figures – but pre-eminently he remained Dickens's friend and companion. Within a few weeks of their first meeting Forster was aiding and advising him in various tangled matters of publishing business, and it is not going too far to say that he became Dickens's literary agent, editor, proof-reader and critic. Dickens himself seems to have realised quite soon just how astute Forster was, and in literary matters tended to use him as a representative audience; that is why there were many times when he also gave him literal *carte blanche* to alter or amend his manuscripts. Forster had a hatred of sensation and melodrama for their own sakes, and it is quite probable that Dickens curbed his natural tendencies in these directions in implicit recognition of his friend's disapproval. Of course there were many differences between them; no men of such unequal temperaments could hope to avoid them. There were periods of coolness, there were sometimes terrible arguments and, towards the end of Dickens's life, when Forster became a fully paid-up member of Society at precisely the time when Dickens had become totally disenchanted with it, there was a definite lessening in the warmth if not in the attachment between the two men. Yet he was always Dickens's best friend and staunchest ally; in a sense it might be said that he devoted much of his life to Dickens, perhaps seeing in him all the genius which he knew that he himself did not possess. And it was Forster who said, after Dickens's death, that ". . . the duties of life remain while life remains, but for me the joy of it is gone for ever more". Thus does our knowledge of later events reflect our understanding of those which precede them, and in the beginning we see something of the end.

Their world then was full of venture and change, of optimism and reform – the "circle" of Dickens and Forster was soon to be filled with other young men who had the same confidence and enthusiasm as they. Perhaps with a hint of that period's coarseness or vulgarity, too, because this was still a time when men and women were hanged in public and when it was common for a deformed or crippled person to be openly mocked in the streets. These new friends were, in another sense, all of a type. They were "outsiders" in one way or another, most of them having found their way to eminence after severe hardships and struggle and self-denial. One of Dickens's closest friends was Daniel Maclise, for example, an Irishman just a year older than he, who had left school at fourteen in order to concentrate upon a career as an artist. In that he was highly successful – he came to London at the age of sixteen, and two years later won a gold medal at the Royal Academy for the best historical painting; in his period he was best known for his idealised "story-book" canvases, sometimes executed on a large scale, although it is one of the ironies and perhaps injustices of history that he is now best remembered for his portrait of Charles Dickens. By the time he met the young novelist, however, he was an artist of great reputation. But he was a paradoxical man, with a complexity of temperament that appealed to Dickens. On the surface he seemed to have an air of ease and almost of indifference, even in the most difficult circumstances. But he was also something of a solitary, and there is some evidence that his moods varied wildly from

115

enthusiasm to depression. Certainly in later life he became a sick and moody recluse, from which isolation not even Dickens's fondest promptings could move him. But we must see him in this early period, when he was one of Dickens's closest friends and, responding to Dickens's own gaiety and energy, a young artist with as great a future before him as the novelist.

Another close friend was an older man, William Charles Macready. By the time he met Dickens he was already the most famous Shakespearean actor of his day, and someone for whom Dickens would have felt immediate respect and sympathy. He was in some ways acutely theatrical, with an expressive face, a powerful voice, and sonorous manner, but in addition he would have appealed to Dickens's own sense of professionalism by being an absolute professional himself. As a colleague wrote, "He was a thorough artist, very conscientious, very much in earnest." His dramatic style would also have attracted Dickens for, although Macready took on the great roles, he seems to have been better at those expressing passion rather than nobility; he was a master of pathos, remorse, the more bravura aspects of melodrama, and nothing moved Dickens more than these.

In this period, then, the inner circle of Dickens's friendships comprised Forster, Ainsworth, Maclise and Macready (this is not of course to forget his earliest friends, Beard and Mitton, who remained close to him). But there was also an outer circle which reflects if nothing else the kind of people, and the kind of world, in which Dickens felt most comfortable and which most clearly embodies his own interests and predilections. This world was, essentially, of a socially radical nature. There was Albany Fonblanque, editor of *The Examiner*, to whom Dickens was introduced by Forster: he was never close to Dickens, being for one thing a much older man, but he was a leading "philosophic radical", had been a close friend of Bentham, and was most associated with the cause of law reform. Dickens's friendship with Bulwer-Lytton was established for similar reasons; although he was by no means the "self-made" man so common in Dickens's acquaintance, he would first have met Dickens when he had a reputation for radicalism. Then there was T. N. Talfourd, an example of early nineteenth-century catholicity of talent; by the time he came to know Dickens, he was a Serjeant at the Bar (a peculiar position, like that of barrister, but one only allowed to practise in certain courts), a Liberal MP for Reading, and a successful playwright. He was seventeen years older than Dickens, and bore the traces of the eighteenth century perhaps more obviously than his young friend: "I remember how he kept the tradition of the then past generation," one contemporary noted, "and came into the drawing room with a thick speech and unsteady legs." He had been a friend of Lamb and Coleridge (we must remember how the Romantic movement, as it has become known, spilled over into the nineteenth century to such an extent that Dickens might even be seen as its true heir), which would have impressed, if not necessarily endeared him to, Dickens. But he was sometimes vain and self-centred, albeit innocently so; he also had an unfortunate inability to pronounce his "r"s, a habit which Dickens used to imitate and mock.

At this time Dickens and Catherine were still living in Furnival's Inn but his brief reminiscences of this period have characteristically much more to do with Catherine's sister, Mary Hogarth, than with Catherine herself. He does seem to have grown very close to her; on the New Year's Day of 1837 he bought her a desk, and in a later diary he notes the day of his first son's birth with a further account of Mary:

"*Saturday, January 6, 1838*: This day last year, Mary and I wandered up and down Holborn and the streets about, for hours, looking after a little table for Kate's bedroom

117

which we bought at last at the very first Broker's we had looked into, and which we had passed half a dozen times because *I didn't like* to ask the price. I took her out to Brompton at night as we had no place for her to sleep in; (the two mothers being with us). She came back again next day to keep house for me, and stopped nearly the rest of the month. I shall never be so happy again as in those Chambers three Storeys high — never if I roll in wealth and fame. I would hire them to keep empty, if I could afford it." Later events were to be partly responsible for this tone of melancholy, but the essential facts of Dickens's domestic life in this period can be glimpsed easily here: Mary a welcome and often long-staying guest with the young couple, and a general air of happiness which was not in later life to be recovered.

Following the birth of her first son it seems that Catherine suffered from some post-natal disorder, the first signs of that nervous condition which was frequently in later years to recur. Mary Hogarth wrote to her cousin about her sister's condition: ". . . my dearest Kate . . . I am sorry indeed to say has not got on so well as her first week made us hope she would. After we thought she was getting quite well and strong it was discovered she was not able to nurse her Baby so she was obliged with great reluctance as you may suppose to give him up to a stranger. Poor Kate! it has been a dreadful trial for her . . . It is really dreadful to see her suffer. I am quite sure I never suffered so much sorrow for any one or any thing before . . . Every time she sees her Baby she has a fit of crying and keeps constantly saying she is sure he will not care for her now she is not able to nurse him." Catherine was suffering from severe depression, therefore, which sounds like the exacerbation of some general nervous anxiety.

Dickens was a conscientious and practical husband, and since Catherine's health did not seem to improve he decided that, at some inconvenience to himself at such a

118

busy time, they should move to the healthier air of Kent. With Mary in attendance, they returned to Chalk; and with them, of course, came the baby soon to be christened Charles Culliford Boz Dickens, the "Boz" apparently an error, resulting from John Dickens's shouting out the name beside the font. (Dickens's father, by the way, was not always so benign a presence: even now, so early in his son's career, he was trying to "borrow" money from the publishers, Chapman and Hall, "recollecting how much your interests are bound up with those of my son".)

Dickens could not himself rest at Chalk, and during the two months they stayed there he was constantly engaged in all the work to which he had committed himself. He was now of course an editor, and he estimated that he was reading some sixty or eighty manuscripts a month for possible publication in *Bentley's Miscellany*. But that was only one aspect of his editorial work, which also included proof-reading as well as the revising and cutting of articles. He arranged the payments for each contributor, and worked upon his own article each month. It ought to be remembered, too, that he was collaborating closely with George Cruikshank who, as the official illustrator of the magazine, had a position of some significance; they worked together amicably enough, however, despite their recent arguments over the *Sketches*, the general plan being that Dickens suggested which articles ought to be illustrated and then left it to Cruikshank to decide upon a particular passage or scene. There is no doubt that he enjoyed his work. On one occasion he compares being an editor to that of being a stage manager, and it is clear that he brought the same skills to this editorial venture which he had brought to bear upon his management of amateur theatricals. In both areas, after all, he liked to be an impresario of all the talents even while reserving the central position for himself.

It ought to be remembered, too, that he was still writing

a whole number of *The Pickwick Papers* each month, and the pressures of work and ambition were now so intense that he was composing right against the deadline, sometimes not finishing a particular instalment of the novel until a few days before its actual publication. The reason for such haste was, largely, because Dickens found himself embarked almost at once upon another series. The first number of the new magazine, in January 1837, had opened with a sketch by him entitled "The Public Life of Mr Tulrumble" and then the next month another sketch, a continuation of the first, appeared under the title "Oliver Twist". The first had been set in "Mudfog", a pseudonym for Chatham, and was a pleasant enough satire on the idiocies of provincial authorities with the moral that "puffed-up conceit is not dignity". The second, with "Oliver Twist" as its title, begins in a workhouse in the same town of Mudfog. In other words, at this point, harassed by family difficulties, exhausted by overwork, and suffering from a variety of ailments, Dickens himself did not at first seem to realise that he was embarking upon the novel which in later years would perhaps more than any other be identified with his name. He had the idea only of a series of articles in mind ("The Chronicles of Mudfog" perhaps), but then almost as soon as he began he found that he had "hit on a capital notion". For he had created the figure of Oliver, the child born and brought up in a workhouse, the child who dared to ask for more, and at once he saw the possibilities which could be extracted from it. The idea of a series of sketches was abandoned.

There is some dispute about the origin of *Oliver Twist*, largely engineered by George Cruikshank who many years later (and after the novelist's death) insisted that he had been the principal begetter of young Oliver and of his sad history. On the face of it this is unlikely – Dickens was not the kind of writer or person who acquiesced in the ideas of others — but it is at least possible that Cruikshank suggested the notion of writing something like an Hogarthian poor boy's "progress" through poverty and misery. In any case Cruikshank and Dickens shared many of the same preoccupations; they were both fascinated by London, particularly in its more squalid and darker aspects, and by images of prison or punishment. There is no doubt, for example, that Cruikshank had sketched the "condemned cell" of Newgate long before he made Fagin its occupant. This proves nothing about *Oliver Twist* itself, only the fact that author and illustrator were eminently well suited to work together upon this saga of London "low life".

What *is* clear is that as soon as Dickens had hit upon his "capital notion" of the deprived and abused child, the whole conception caught fire in his imagination. It is even possible that this was in essence the "proposed Novel" which he had been contemplating ever since he began seriously to write, and it has been said, rightly, that *Oliver Twist* is the first novel in the English language which takes a child as its central character or hero; a revolution, perhaps, although not one which was widely noticed at the time. This is largely because factual "orphan tales" were actually quite common in the period, and Dickens himself had often read autobiographies which emphasise the miseries and privations of childhood: even Johnson's life of Richard Savage has a long passage on the horrors of his infancy. There was also an ancient but still healthy tradition of "rogue literature", which in part chronicled the dramas of lost or abandoned children. So the theme of *Oliver Twist* was not in that respect new. Nevertheless it was one that directly appealed to Dickens's own sense of himself and his past, and was therefore one in which all the resources of his imagination could be poured. In the original sketch Oliver was born in Mudfog or Chatham, the site of Dickens's own infancy, and the figure of the parish boy's

121

"progress" was one that at once attracted a cluster of childhood feelings and associations. Oliver Twist's forced association with Fagin, which seems like a savage reprise of the young Dickens's companionship with Bob Fagin in the blacking factory; Oliver's flight towards respectability; his journey from dirt to cleanliness and gentility. Thus does Dickens seem able to work through his own childhood in disguised form, both in its troubled reality and in its disturbed fantasies of escape. The life of Warren's, the foul streets of London, the sheer helplessness of the lost child resound through a narrative which becomes the echo chamber of Dickens's own childhood. In the March number of *The Pickwick Papers* Tony Weller had mentioned "Warrens's blackin'" and in the following month's episode of *Oliver Twist* a "blackin' bottle" is mentioned by the notorious beadle. The associations come flooding back as Dickens writes.

But his childhood does not pass untrammelled into his fiction; that is one reason why he was an artist and not a memoirist. And that is also why it is important to realise that he was working on *The Pickwick Papers* and *Oliver Twist* at the same time – in fact he was writing the opening chapters of the poor boy's progress, filled as they are with suffering and abandonment, at precisely the time he was also writing some of the most comic passages in *The Pickwick Papers* concerning as they do the misadventures of Bob Sawyer and the skating party at Dingley Dell. In fact Dickens soon adopted the characteristic rhythm of writing *Oliver* first, and *Pickwick* after, and it could plausibly be maintained that as a result *The Pickwick Papers* assumes a more buoyant form, as if much of the pathos which he had once introduced into the comic narrative has now been transferred to the monthly serial in *Bentley's Miscellany*. But the relationship between the novels cannot be taken too far since they have quite different forms. For one thing *Oliver Twist* is much shorter, with some nine thousand words in each episode compared to *Pickwick's* eighteen or nineteen thousand; in addition, the publication of a narrative in monthly parts was quite a different undertaking, with quite different rules, from that of publishing a monthly serial in a magazine. *Oliver Twist* was surrounded by other fiction (although it was always placed *first* in *Bentley's Miscellany*) and those who came to read it would approach it with habitual assumptions about the kind of "adventure" it was likely to provide: monthly magazine serials were commonly of the adventure or mystery sort, and relied to a large extent upon formal devices of suspense and plot to maintain that mood. In that sense, it could not be said that *Oliver Twist* disappointed them. It conformed to type even as it transcended that type, and in the brilliant exploitation of familiar material part of Dickens's genius is to be found.

Dickens worked quite instinctively, making it up literally as he went along. Apparently the name of Oliver had come from an omnibus conductor's conversation which Dickens overheard; he had seen a pauper's funeral at Cooling Church (how often that church upon the marshes is connected in Dickens's mind with death) and transposed it to the novel; he knew of a magistrate, Mr Laing of Hatton Garden, whom he went to see before turning him into Mr Fang of *Oliver Twist*; an enquiry was being conducted into the deaths of workhouse children who had been "farmed out" (that is, adults were paid to take care of them in private houses), and he used *that* too. At first he had difficulties with the length – the first instalment was too short – but within a matter of weeks he was getting into his stride. There had been nothing quite like it before – *The Pickwick Papers* and *Oliver Twist* running together, two serials of quite different types appearing simultaneously. What was admired then, and what one admires still, is the sheer fluency and easy flow of these narratives; the humour itself lies almost as much in Dickens's unflagging

123

invention as in the scenes themselves, since it is the laughter and gaiety of human creativity. For Dickens is enjoying it, too; never can a writer so young have had such easy access to all the resources of the language, effortlessly wielding what was for him an instrument of power, the only instrument of power he had ever possessed.

Of course Dickens had to return frequently to London from Chalk – he was commuting between his family and the city on editorial business – but one of his major preoccupations in this period was also to find a larger house. The birth of their son meant that he and Catherine would have to move out of the chambers in Furnival's Inn, and Dickens's own growing fame would also seem to have demanded it. He offered for one house, but did not get it, and then rented temporary lodgings at 30 Upper Norton Street when the family returned to Furnival's Inn; it is possible that he needed somewhere quiet in which to work. He was so busy, in fact, that he employed house agents on his behalf, although he also found time to travel around London with Mary Hogarth in order to inspect available premises. And at last he came across the right one – on 18 March, 1837 he made an offer for 48 Doughty Street and, after agreeing to a rent of eighty pounds per annum, he moved in two weeks later. It was a pleasant house of the last century, situated in a private road with a gateway and porter at each end. He had borrowed money from Richard Bentley in order to pay for such things as moving expenses and, at the time, it struck him as a ". . . frightfully first-class Family Mansion, involving awful responsibilities". It was indeed larger than anything in which Dickens had ever lived before – a twelve-roomed house on four floors, for which relatively large edifice Dickens also employed a cook, a housemaid, a nurse and, eventually, a manservant called Henry. So far had the young author already come. His study was on the first floor, at the back of the house and overlooking the garden.

On the floor above were two bedrooms, in one of which Mary Hogarth seems often to have slept, and on the ground floor there was the dining room and back parlour. The drawing room, where the family would often sit, was next door to Dickens's study. It is difficult now to evoke the actual living presence of the house, although it is clear that at once it was given several Dickensian touches – the woodwork was painted pink, a veined marble hearth was brought in, a complete set of "standard novels" was purchased to furnish his study, and bright flowered carpets introduced. (Since he seems to have had a nervous terror of fire, one of his first moves was to insure everything with the Sun Fire Office.) The furniture would have been of the Regency and William IV style, and it was one which for the rest of his life Dickens preferred over more gloomy and more sober mid-Victorian interiors. He loved elegance but just as importantly he loved brightness; that is why he installed mirrors in whichever house he occupied. An era in which candles and oil lamps provided interior lighting was surely one in which the use of mirrors to reflect light was of paramount importance, although some unkind critics have suggested that Dickens's love of mirrors was based on vanity as much as anything else.

Of course, in Doughty Street, Dickens would have arranged and rearranged all of the furniture as well; one of the most remarkable of his characteristics was his ability to visualise exactly where every piece of furniture was in any room in which he had stayed. Order was of extreme importance to him, and he had a nervous habit of placing chairs and tables in *precisely* the right position before he could get down to a day's work. He could not bear anything to be out of place and, when he stayed in hotels or rented houses, one of his first tasks was to rearrange the furniture according to his own interior plan. Even in this trivial way he stamped his personality upon everything around him, since he could not breathe in an atmosphere which was not permeated by him. He always had a superstitious habit, by the way, of turning his bed in a north–south direction – a lifelong habit since, according to one friend, "he maintained that he could not sleep with it in any other position; and he backed up his objections by arguments about earth currents and positive and negative electricity. It may have been a mere fantasy but it was real enough to him ... Nervous and arbitrary, he was of the kind to whom whims are laws, and self-control in contrary circumstances was simply an impossibility".

Here in Doughty Street he gave dinners and entertained his friends (as well, no doubt, as his parents); on so grand a scale, in fact, it seems that some people believed that he was spending money too lavishly even for so young and successful an author. There are a few reminiscences from friends about this period, all of them suggesting a perfectly happy domesticity of the kind which Dickens had not enjoyed since the first years of his childhood – he had one son already, and with the constant attendance of his brother, Frederick, and with his sister-in-law, he already had the makings of a suitably large family. That it was a happy family there is no doubt, even though in much later life Dickens would insist that almost from the beginning he had felt estranged from his wife. At the time Catherine herself had no such doubts – "Oh dear Mary," she wrote to her cousin, "what pleasure it would give me to see you in my own house, and how proud I shall be to make you acquainted with Charles. The fame of his talents are now known all over the world, but his kind affectionate heart is dearer to me than all." It might have seemed that this domestic idyll was set indefinitely to continue, as Dickens slowly made his way forward in the world. He was already now "accepted"; he had been elected to the Garrick Club; and on 3 May he had delivered his first public speech. It was at the anniversary festival of the Royal Literary Fund, and when a toast was made to "the health of Mr Dickens and the rising Authors of the Age" it was received with "long-continued cheering". But then, four days later, an entirely unanticipated event changed everything.

# Ten

O N 7 May, 1837, Mary Hogarth died at the age of seventeen. She had been the previous night with Dickens and Catherine to see a performance of his farce *Is She His Wife?* at the St James's Theatre. They had returned home to Doughty Street at about one in the morning; Mary went to her room but, before she could undress, gave a cry and collapsed (the doctors were to diagnose her condition as one of heart failure). Mary's mother, Mrs Hogarth, was called, and in her grief became insensible; Catherine and Dickens stayed with Mary as she lay in her bed in the little back room, but she never recovered. At three o'clock the following afternoon she died in Dickens's arms. Or, rather, it seems that she was dead for some time before he fully appreciated the fact. An undertaker was summoned – in an essay many years later he recalled "the one appalling, never-to-be-forgotten undertaker's knock" on the door – and she was placed in a coffin which remained in the bedroom overlooking the garden of 48 Doughty Street. She was buried six days later. Mrs Hogarth became hysterical after her collapse and had to be kept from the bedroom by force, while Catherine on the other hand showed surprising and what seemed to Dickens almost excessive calmness and strength. But, in this situation, clearly it was she who had to remain strong.

For the effect upon her husband was of the most extraordinary kind. His grief was so intense, in fact, that it represented the most powerful sense of loss and pain he was ever to experience. The deaths of his own parents and children were not to affect him half so much and in his mood of obsessive pain, amounting almost to hysteria, one senses the essential strangeness of the man. He cut off a lock of Mary Hogarth's hair and kept it in a special case; he took a ring off her finger, and put it on his own. These are all very natural reactions but, more eccentrically, he kept all of her clothes and two years later was still on occasions taking them out to look at them – "They will moulder away in their secret places," he said. He also dreamed of her every night for the next nine months – he called these nocturnal phantoms "visions" of Mary – and continually expressed a wish to be buried with her in the same grave. To keep the clothes of a seventeen-year-old girl, and to desire to be buried with her, are, even in the context of early nineteenth-century enthusiasm, unusual sentiments.

Mary became for Dickens the idealised image of the female. "Young, beautiful, and good" were the words he had inscribed upon her gravestone, and he uses the same words in his later descriptions of Rose Maylie, Little Nell and Florence Dombey. He had said in one of his mourning letters that "the love and affection which subsisted between her and her sister, no one can imagine the extent of . . .", and again in his fiction there is a constant tendency to idealise the relationship between sisters as if in their happy companionship there dwells some holy bond. And of course the image of the virtuous and innocent girl – "she had not a single fault," he said – is one that emerges throughout his fiction and acquires a mystical, semi-religious, significance; it would not be going too far to state, in fact, that Dickens's own religious sensibility began to develop as a result of Mary's death. It is known that he started regularly to attend the chapel of the Foundling

Hospital in Great Coram Street nearby, and since he mentions a visit to church in the immediate aftermath of her death it seems likely that it was at this time in particular that he began to feel the need for religious hope or consolation. He was consoled "above all" by "the thought of one day joining her again where sorrow and separation are unknown"; when we come to consider Dickens's Christianity it is as well to remember from what private roots of suffering and relief it sprang. And hence, too, the religious significance which he attached to the concept of memory; as soon as she was dead he was reminiscing about their lives together. "I can recall everything we said and did in those happy days," he said, and for him the memory became a blessed faculty aligned with fancy and the imagination, linking the living with the dead and thus earth with heaven; it became a way of infusing reality with spiritual grace, and there can be no doubt that it was the death of Mary Hogarth which awakened those elements in his nature which had up to this time been overshadowed by his appetite for fame. Dickens had learned another hard lesson early – he was still only twenty-five – but in a sense it was his good fortune that the profound experiences which shape a writer's imagination happened to him sooner rather than later.

But he could not write just yet – for the first and last time in his life he missed his deadlines, and the episodes of *The Pickwick Papers* and *Oliver Twist* which were supposed to be written during that month were postponed. Instead he went with Catherine to a rural retreat, Collins's Farm in Hampstead, which, curiously enough, is in much the same location as the one to which Dickens was soon to consign Bill Sikes after his murder of Nancy. They remained here for a fortnight, although in the last week Dickens was travelling back daily to Doughty Street. Quiet and rest were certainly needed since, although Catherine had seemed so calm at the time of Mary's death, she had

130

in fact suffered a miscarriage – although it is possible that this was as much in reaction to her husband's hysteria as to her own grief. But clearly the thought of death was now very much on her mind; she wanted to have her infant son, Charles, christened as soon as possible and wrote to ask her cousin to take the place of Mary as godmother. "We have learned from sad experience," she wrote, "the uncertainty of life."

By the beginning of June they were back in Doughty Street and Dickens at once began work on the postponed chapters of *Oliver Twist*. Much critical acumen has been expended in trying to locate the time when Dickens first decided that this series should take on the definite shape of a novel and not be simply a parish boy's "progress" in the conventional sense – when in other words he provided a circular rather than simple linear shape to the narrative, and began to tie up all the loose ends which previously he had been happy to leave trailing on the ground. But there is another change which has been less widely noticed since it is in the episode after the death of Mary Hogarth, and in those that follow, that Dickens begins to lose interest in the topical and polemical intent of the first chapters. The suppressed poetry of the narrative begins more clearly to emerge as a result, and what had been in part a series of sharp satirical sketches turns into a narrative at once more romantic and more mysterious. It may be unwise to suggest a firm connection between this transition and the death of Mary, but her presence does also become visible in certain direct ways. So it is that he now creates Rose Maylie, a young girl of seventeen ". . . so mild and gentle; so pure and beautiful; that earth seemed not her element . . ."; and so it is that she passes through a perilous illness, comes close to death, but then miraculously recovers. He raises Mary Hogarth in his words, and the theme of loss and return is one that becomes central to the story as Dickens now begins to develop it.

This is not to suggest that chapters or passages are uniquely determined by Dickens's experience of Mary Hogarth's death — the pull of the narrative comes from sources deeper and darker than even the most appalling of recent events — but rather that certain aspects of Dickens's creative imagination were thereby strengthened or aroused. That is why there now develops in *Oliver Twist* a constant sense of the need for sleep, for forgetfulness, for that blessed slumber "which ease from recent suffering alone imparts"; and there are episodes in the book now where Oliver hovers between sleep and wakefulness, in which suspended state he experiences what Dickens calls "visions" — visions in which "reality and imagination become so strangely blended that it is afterwards almost a matter of impossibility to separate the two". Was it in that state that he had his own "visions" of Mary? Yet it is also appropriate to the nature of the novel itself.

There is a poetry in the novel, also, which is quite unlike anything which is to be seen in previous fiction, a poetry of barely whispered notes that sets up a deep refrain within the text, for it was Dickens's great achievement to bring the language of the "Romantic" period into the area of prose narrative. He was the first novelist really to possess the "sympathetic imagination" of his great poetic predecessors, through which he was able to grasp and integrate an entire world. So, when we come to consider the inconsistencies and difficulties of his view of the world, perhaps we ought to remember Sir Henry Taylor's contemporaneous remarks on the Romantic poets themselves: "A feeling came more easily to them than a reflection, and an image was always at hand when a thought was not forthcoming." These remarks might well be applied to the novelist, too, but it is not enough to say that he inherited the imaginative dispensation of the Romantic poets. Even in *Oliver Twist* itself we see another poetry, the poetry which appears in certain Gothic novels and which in

Dickens's writing becomes the poetry of London, the poetry of darkness and isolation, the poetry which Bulwer-Lytton described only a few years later as "the vast and dark Poetry around us – the Poetry of Modern Civilisation and Daily Existence . . . He who would arrive at the Fairy Land must face the Phantoms".

Of course it is not to be imagined that each mood or feeling of Charles Dickens can be formulated and expounded in an analytical way; what one observes are various appetencies and reactions, instincts and memories, each jostling against or working with one other, a bundle of striving impulses for a few of which at any time we give appropriate names. Clearly the Charles Dickens who emerges through the pages of *Oliver Twist* would not be easily or immediately recognisable to those who knew him; indeed, after his brief sojourn at Collins's Farm, he returned to London and to his working life for, to those who mixed with him, it might have seemed that nothing in particular had happened. He had already inserted advertisements in *Bentley's Miscellany* explaining the omission of the usual *Oliver Twist* episode and, in the next number of *The Pickwick Papers*, he explained why the June number had not been published as the result of "a severe domestic affliction of no ordinary kind". But now he went back to work at once. Back to his old activities. He went to the prison at Coldbath Fields (at Clerkenwell, and so within walking distance of his house in Doughty Street) with Macready, and they had dinner with the comedian, Harley, afterwards – "Our evening was very cheerful," Macready wrote in his diary; on another evening he had dinner at the house of Talfourd with Macready and Forster; he attended the wedding of his sister, Laetitia, to Henry Austin (an architect and engineer who, with Dickens's assistance, became an active proponent of sanitary reform); he attended a dinner at Greenwich for the Literary Fund; he was even planning a comedy, and discussed the project with Macready. And, for a week in July, he travelled to France and Belgium together with his wife and Hablot Browne. At this stage in his life he did not seem particularly interested in other countries at all; he was, in one sense or another, devoting all of his energies to understanding and conquering his own. It was only when his position in England became more assured that he felt the need to get away.

Dickens and family went down to Broadstairs at the end of August, taking with them Mrs Hogarth, Mary's mother, who had still not recovered from her daughter's sudden death four months before. So it was here at the beginning of September that he recommenced work on *The Pickwick Papers* (having refused to write a number of *Oliver Twist* for *Bentley's Miscellany*) but now, in this penultimate instalment of a narrative that had taken him so far, there are certain signs, if not of weariness, at least of his creative interests being diverted elsewhere. He was in a sense tired of Mr Pickwick, and he was already thinking of new novels he wished to write – the much-postponed *Gabriel Vardon*, or *Barnaby Rudge*, was clearly on his mind, and he was to begin work on *Nicholas Nickleby* within three or four months. So he reverts to his earlier borrowings from the contemporary theatre, and tries to round off *The Pickwick Papers* as if it were a play; he reintroduces characters like Bob Sawyer, Mr Pott of the *Eatanswill Gazette*, the red-nosed preacher Mr Stiggins, the notorious Fat Boy, and engineers the final appearance of other characters such as Jingle and Job Trotter, Mr Dodson and Mr Fogg. But the book ends as it began, with the "immortal Pickwick" whom Dickens had created when he was a struggling reporter in his lodgings in Furnival's Inn. It ends with Dickens, the most famous author of his day, writing these words in his study in Doughty Street: ". . . he is invariably attended by the faithful Sam, between whom and his master there exists a steady and reciprocal attachment,

134

which nothing but death will sever." But of course death has not intervened, for Mr Pickwick is indeed "immortal" – his narrative will never die because it is imbued with the irresistible energy and the unfeigned humour of creativity which Dickens enjoyed throughout the period in which he wrote it.

Following the completion of *The Pickwick Papers*, Dickens found that he had time on his hands, and at once he began to employ what might have seemed to him to be the merely wasted days of not working. Of course he still had the same two proposed novels in mind – *Nicholas Nickleby* to be published by Chapman and Hall in monthly numbers from April 1838, and *Barnaby Rudge* to be published by Bentley at some time in the autumn of that same year. But neither of these projects was as yet ready to begin; for one thing, Chapman and Hall had started publishing *Sketches by Boz* in monthly form, and he did not want to clog the market with too much material. So instead, after some prompting, he agreed to fill the empty days by editing the memoirs of the famous clown, Joe Grimaldi, and by writing a short pamphlet entitled *Sketches of Young Gentlemen*. The latter need not detain us long; it is a volume of sharp and well sustained comic sketches in which Dickens characteristically turns human beings into various "types" in the approved early nineteenth-century manner. *Memoirs of Joseph Grimaldi* is another matter. Dickens began it unwillingly, since the task of bringing order and purpose to Grimaldi's papers (already once revised) was a cumbersome business, and he only eventually agreed when the payment for his editorial services was increased by Bentley. It was to be published in time for the pantomime season, and Dickens's method was to cut an already abridged account and then dictate the results to his father who came to Doughty Street for the purpose.

In the first weeks of 1838, just at the time he was revolving in his mind the possibilities for his next novel (the first episode of which was promised to Chapman and Hall in the spring), he decided to travel with Hablot Browne to Yorkshire. But this was no "jaunt" – he had a definite aim in mind, and planned his trip accordingly. As a child he had heard vaguely about the notorious Yorkshire schools, and in particular he remembered the story of a "suppurated abscess that some boy had come home with in consequence of his Yorkshire guide, philosopher and friend" – in other words, the schoolmaster – ". . . having ripped it open with an inky pen-knife". He remained "curious" about these schools, which were in many instances nothing but convenient dustbins for unwanted children, bastards or orphans; the advertisements for them often included the chilling words, "No Vacations", which meant that the children were retained there indefinitely. And the conditions, to judge by contemporary reports, were often as harsh as it is possible to conceive. Clearly Dickens had been encouraged by the success of his topical allusions in *Oliver Twist*, and determined that he could direct his polemic against new targets; the idea of poor children being almost literally imprisoned in squalid conditions, and of being tyrannised by brutal adults, was one that in any case struck to the centre of his imagination. So once again his childhood reading, and the memories or fantasies of his own childhood, helped to fashion his ideas for a new novel; the inter-animating process had begun. He became "bent upon destroying" the Yorkshire schools, and, with that aim in mind, he concocted a scheme in which he would pose as the friend of a widowed mother who wished to place her child in just such an establishment. The trip was intended to be a "mighty secret" but a legal colleague of Thomas Mitton knew a lawyer who practised in that Northern neighbourhood, and he gave Dickens a letter of introduction. For the occasion Dickens took the name of Hablot Browne – it is clear that he did not want his own identity, as the author of *Oliver Twist*, and the attacker of workhouses, to be revealed to his new intended subjects or victims – and at the end of January he and the real Browne travelled up to Yorkshire in order to investigate the conditions under which these poor schoolchildren existed. (He took his illustrator with him so that he might have the benefit of seeing the landscape and its figures for himself.) They stayed in Yorkshire for only two days, but during that time Dickens, with an ability to organise his impressions as successfully as he organised everything else (he variously compared his brain to a number of pigeon-holes and to a photographic plate sensitive to the slightest impression), absorbed everything of significance for his own design.

They travelled up on Tuesday morning by a slow coach, paradoxically called the "Express", which left the Saracen's Head at Snow Hill at eight o'clock in the morning; they stayed at Grantham overnight then took the Royal Glasgow Mail to Greta Bridge, and eventually reached Bowes, a small village on the moors near the River Greta.

It was here that Dickens encountered Mr William Shaw and his academy. He wrote later in his diary, "Shaw the schoolmaster we saw to-day, is the man in whose school several boys went blind sometime since, from gross neglect ... Look this out in the Newspapers." It is clear that Dickens did not go up specifically to find Shaw, and the information about his neglectful conduct probably came from a disgruntled usher (or teacher) whom according to local report Dickens met at the time. Shaw himself was obviously less communicative; it seems that Dickens's real identity was discovered, and that Shaw's attitude towards the novelist's investigations into his establishment was not particularly friendly. But Dickens had seen all he needed of the school and its owner; it is probable that all along he knew approximately how he would deal with the subject, and was looking merely for those details which might give his imaginative design a local habitation and a name. It was while at Bowes, too, that he wandered into the local churchyard and found there many tombs of dead school-children; in twenty-four years, some thirty-four young "scholars", from the cheap schools of the district, had died at ages varying from ten to eighteen. In particular Dickens was struck by one gravestone which read: "Here lie the remains of GEORGE ASHTON TAYLOR Son of John Taylor of Trowbridge, Wiltshire, who died suddenly at Mr William Shaw's Academy of this place, April 13th, 1822 aged 19 years. Young reader, thou must die, but after this the judgement." It was a dismal winter's afternoon, with the snow laying thickly about, as Dickens read the epitaph. "I think his ghost put Smike into my head, upon the spot," he told a friend later in the year.

Almost at once Dickens tried to begin work on the novel itself, combining the new enterprise with his labours over *Oliver Twist* and *Bentley's Miscellany*, but he could not settle down to the task until he had clared his mind of the anxiety he felt over yet another novel; this was *Barnaby Rudge*, which he had promised to Richard Bentley by October. Of course none of it was written, or was likely to be under present circumstances, and so he wrote to Bentley suggesting that it should appear in monthly instalments in the *Miscellany* after *Oliver Twist* had completed its run there – thus buying time, and clearing the ground for *Nicholas Nickleby*. Or, to give the novel its full title, *The Life and Adventures of Nicholas Nickleby, Containing a Faithful Account of the Fortunes, Misfortunes, Uprisings, Downfallings and Complete Career of the Nickleby Family. Edited by "Boz"*. Bentley acceded to this new request and Dickens, able to forget about *Barnaby Rudge* for the time being, set to work, fitfully at first, on his Yorkshire novel. It is worth noting, too, as he begins to write, that there is in this period a change in his handwriting; he has finally lost the old school-formed style and has evolved his own distinctive, clear but nervous hand. In fact to see a chronological selection of his signa-
138

tures is to see a pattern of contraction and expansion — the earliest letters signed in approved schoolbook fashion and then slowly drawing inward, becoming bunched up with a certain kind of intensity which reaches its peak in 1837 before beginning to broaden and expand into the more elaborate signature of his later years. In addition, in 1836 he stops placing the "flourish" of his signature under *Charles* and puts it instead under *Dickens*; and, approximately from the end of January 1837, he begins to write out in full the dates of his letters at the top of his notepaper, as if signifying a new self-consciousness about the chronology of his life. Certainly the change in his handwriting at the time he was writing *Nicholas Nickleby* suggests that, at last, he was beginning to see himself as a major novelist.

All the evidence suggests, too, that Dickens, after he had surmounted his fitful start, was working quickly and easily on the new novel; the surviving manuscript pages of *Nicholas Nickleby* show that it was written very clearly and smoothly, with very few deletions and additions. Since it opens with an account of the Nickleby family quickly followed by scenes at the inauguration of the United Metropolitan Improved Hot Muffin and Crumpet Baking and Punctual Delivery Company, there is almost certainly an intention on Dickens's part to recapture that inventive, free-wheeling and almost picaresque spirit which had been so much the inspiration of *The Pickwick Papers*. And yet, if the narrative were to be improvised in this way, how was it that Dickens had taken such trouble to enquire into the conditions of the Yorkshire schools with clear reference to their use in the same novel? The reason lies with Dickens's own ambitions at this point in his career; he wanted to do something larger than either of his first two novels, and this mainly by combining their best elements. He knew that the pathos of *Oliver Twist* had been just as much a success as the comedy of *The Pickwick Papers*; and he realised, too, that at a time when, he said later, "the stability of my success was not certain" he did not want to lose either his reputation as a topical and polemical novelist or his fame as a comic one. So in *Nicholas Nickleby*, he devised a plot capacious enough to include both aspects of his genius; and so congenial a task was it that, after some initial hesitation over the first pages, he was, as we have seen, working with very little difficulty upon it. He began seriously in the last week of February and had finished the preliminary number on the ninth of the following month; many of the main characters had thus been introduced, among them Ralph Nickleby, Mrs Nickleby and the rest of that unhappy family, Newman Noggs and the ineffable Mr Squeers. Clearly he knows in which direction he is travelling – a metaphor much employed by Dickens himself when discussing the process of his fiction – but he is in no hurry to get there and, in the interim, he is quite happy to employ all the effects he has already used and which he knows to work. He had a broad overall conception of the general story, but he is playing it by ear as he goes along. So it is that in the final chapter of the first instalment he takes young Nickleby to Snow Hill, where he and Browne had set out for the North and where Fagin had been only a few weeks before in *Oliver Twist*: the landscape of Dickens's wonderful imagination was, in a physical sense, small indeed. As soon as the first number had been finished, in his elation and relief he summoned Forster for a ride (these riding jaunts by the two of them were now very common until the time came when, for reasons of health, Dickens gave up riding for walking). But he started working on the next episode of *Oliver Twist* almost immediately afterwards, until eventually he was able to settle down into a more congenial routine whereby he wrote *Oliver Twist* before embarking upon that month's number of *Nicholas Nickleby*, generally finishing the latter task only two or three days ahead of publication.

At the end of his labours on *Nicholas Nickleby* Dickens told his friends that it "had been to him a diary of the last two years: the various papers preserving to him the recollection of events and feelings connected with their production". This may be Dickens's own understanding of the fact that his novel reminded him of the circumambient world in which it was written — his moods and difficulties over certain sections, the locales where he composed them, and so forth. But it raises, too the question which bedevils *Nicholas Nickleby* perhaps more than any other of his novels. To what extent, and for what purposes, did Dickens base his characters upon "real" people? There is the obvious case of Squeers and Dotheboys Hall, since the description of both provoked many threats of libel writs from various real Yorkshire schoolmasters; notably, it seems, from William Shaw himself who eventually came to realise the folly of suing the famous "Boz". Many scholarly articles have been devoted to exploring the precise degree of truth and fiction in Dickens's account of that Yorkshire school, with the perhaps predictable conclusion that in some cases he exaggerated, in some cases he under-emphasised, and in some cases faithfully recorded, the reality. Of his exaggerations there can be little doubt, since the physiognomies of Mr Squeers and his spouse are clearly based upon the grotesques of the Hogarthian tradition; it also seems possible that he exaggerated the moral villainy of the schoolmaster since, after the publication of *Nicholas Nickleby*, various voices were raised in William Shaw's defence — all to the effect that he was, in the context of his period and of his profession, by no means the worst of a motley collection. Yet there are also parts of the narrative which are very firmly modelled on the actual conditions of the period, not least in the absurd advertisements which the Yorkshire schoolmasters (in fact Shaw himself was a Londoner) placed in the public prints. Shaw's own advertisment includes the fact that "YOUTH are carefully

141

instructed in the English, Latin and Greek languages . . . Common and Decimal Arithmetic; Book-keeping, Mensuration, Surveying, Geometry, Geography and Navigation . . . No extra charges whatever, Doctor's bills excepted. No vacations, except by the Parents' desire." It is clear from examination of the surviving exercise-books from Bowes Academy that his pupils were in fact proficient only in handwriting and in the mere copying by rote from various text-books, but no doubt it was the absurdity of including "Navigation" in the list of special subjects that prompted Dickens's own version of the advertisement in which the subjects include "fortification, and every other branch of classical literature". The somewhat ominous last sentence of Shaw's real advertisement must in turn have prompted Dickens's "No extras, no vacations, and diet unparalleled". There is a clear connection here, then, between Dickens's observations and his subsequent composition, just as the episodes on his trip to the North were re-employed in the novel itself.

But there is also a great deal of evidence to suggest that Dickens actually underplayed the horror of life in the Yorkshire schools; that, for reasons of decorum or credibility, he purposely ignored the worst excesses of which men like William Shaw were capable. When he looked up the old prosecution against Shaw in 1832, for example, he would have read a real account of the conditions at Bowes Academy by a pupil who had been afflicted by blindness while there: ". . . their supper consisted of warm milk and water and bread, which was called tea . . . five boys generally slept in a bed . . . On Sunday they had pot skimmings for tea, in which there was vermin . . . there were eighteen boys there beside himself, of whom two were totally blind. In November, he was quite blind and was then sent to a private room where there were nine other boys blind . . . Dr Benning used to come to the school when the boys had nearly lost their sight. He merely looked at the boys' eyes and turned them off; he gave them no physic or eye-water, or anything else. There was no difference in his fare during his illness, or his health."

But the public confusion of fact and fiction is not simply a matter of his characters' reality being impressed upon the readers by Dickens's own unparalleled imagination, a process exemplified by one young woman, who saw an illustration in a bookseller's window and rushed into her house screaming, "What *DO* you think? Nicholas has thrashed Squeers!" It is easy to laugh at the credulity of such readers, perhaps, but it is no different from the reaction of audiences to most television soap operas, where the activities of imagined people become as real as those of anyone actually living in the world. The most significant effect was of a slightly different kind, however, since it was the *difference* between what was real and what was imagined which became wholly confused by a reading of Dickens's novels. This could of course have beneficial results, for it was said at the time that Dickens's accounts of the poor and the neglected actually increased the amount of concern for, and knowledge of, those real people who lived in the vicinity of Saffron Hill and Field Lane. Yet, in hindsight, this seems doubtful; the movements for social reforms and for social analysis were part of that same early Victorian ardour which Dickens's own novels exemplify but did not necessarily create. We must see Dickens's own writings and the social movements of the period as complementary, animated by the same energy and faith, but as distinct. Much more likely, however, is the contemporaneous belief that Dickens's loving accounts of the middle-class and lower-middle-class actually brought those classes more vividly present *to themselves* and as a result rendered them more confident, more aware, more completely alive. It was his ability, as one contemporary account puts it in somewhat elaborate fashion, "to describe impressions respecting peculiarities in persons or objects around them which, without such ready hints, they would never perhaps have been susceptible of''. Dickens opened up the world for those who were already living in it. It comes as no surprise, for example, that a police commissioner reported that young thieves spent their time playing games like pitch-halfpenny and reading books like *Oliver Twist*. Characters like Mr Micawber, Mrs Gamp and Smike became wholly real to those who read of them; their verbal expressions were copied and terms like ''Pecksniff'' or ''Gamp'' were used to describe certain types of people. The identification was, in that sense, complete. There were also Pickwick clubs, in which each member took on the name of a Pickwick character. The verger at Rochester Cathedral seemed to enjoy being known as ''Mr Tope'', the name of the chief verger in *The Mystery of Edwin Drood*, and when Dickens was instrumental in sending one boy to Ragged School, he became known to his companions as ''Smike''.

There were even occasions when Dickens himself would deliberately behave in a Dickensian manner. When showing American friends around Rochester and Chatham, for example, he ordered an old coach in the style of Pickwick. But, more importantly, the reality of his characters was impressed as much upon him as upon any of his readers. In a short letter to his office manager he once wrote, ''Scrooge is delighted to find that Bob Cratchit is enjoying his holiday . . .'' And, when he was manager of his amateur theatricals, he was often addressed by his cast as ''Mr Crummles''. In other words Dickens relished the idiosyncrasies and mannerisms of his characters; once they had been created they continued to live within him as so many imaginary companions whom he delighted to introduce to others on appropriate occasions. What is more significant, perhaps, is the fact that he ''saw'' his characters in the same way that he had seen the characters of his childhood reading. He said that, while writing *A Christmas*

*Carol*, Tiny Tim and Bob Cratchit were "ever tugging at his coat sleeve, as if impatient for him to get back to his desk and continue the story of their lives". More curiously, perhaps, as one friend remembered, "he said, also, that when the children of his brain had once been launched, free and clear of him, into the world, they would sometimes turn up in the most unexpected manner to look their father in the face. Sometimes he would pull my arm while we were walking together and whisper, 'Let us avoid Mr Pumblechook, who is crossing the street to meet us'; or, 'Mr Micawber is coming; let us turn down this alley to get out of his way.' He always seemed to enjoy the fun of his comic people, and had unceasing mirth over Mr Pickwick's misadventures."

The adjective to stress here is "comic"; he saw comedy everywhere and with a novel such as *Nicholas Nickleby*, so often diagnosed and analysed, it is at least appropriate to suggest that it is primarily and overwhelmingly a comic narrative; that Dickens himself, the novelist of a thousand moods, is also primarily and overwhelmingly the greatest comic writer in the English language. That is why, as he was toiling over the more solemn adventures of poor Oliver Twist, all the humour of the recently completed *Pickwick* is reaffirmed in *Nicholas Nickleby* which has some title to being the funniest novel Dickens ever wrote; it is perhaps the funniest novel in the English language.

There is of course the grotesque humour of the Squeers family —". . . here's richness!" Squeers exclaims as he pours out thin milk and water for the abandoned children and, in his later encomium on his lovely wife, he declares, "One of our boys — gorging his-self with vittles, and then turning ill; that's their way — got a abscess on him last week. To see how she operated upon him with a pen-knife! Oh Lor! . . . what a member of society that woman is!" And of course there is the Mantalinis who emerge from Dickens's imagination complete and inimitable, Mr

145

Mantalini forever trying to hold off the wrath of his rich wife by the most agreeable endearments.

But if one character emerged from this novel as the comic favourite, it was Mrs Nickleby, the garrulous old party who always experiences difficulty in remembering what she is talking about. " 'Hackney coaches, my lord, are such nasty things, that it's almost better to walk at any time, for although I believe a hackney coachman can be transported for life, if he has a broken window, still they are so reckless, that they nearly all have broken windows. I once had a swelled face for six weeks, my lord, from riding in a hackney coach – I think it was a hackney coach,' said Mrs Nickleby reflecting, 'though I'm not quite certain, whether it wasn't a chariot; at all events I know it was a dark green, with a very long number, beginning with a nought and ending with a nine – no, beginning with a nine, and ending with a nought, that was it, and of course the stamp office people would know at once whether it was a coach or a chariot if any inquiries were made there – however that was, there it was with a broken window, and there was I for six weeks with a swelled face . . .' " And so she goes on, the first and perhaps the finest example of those women in Charles Dickens who simply cannot stop talking.

Dickens's high spirits and his theatrical comedy existed as much in his own life as they did in his fiction, and if there is one constant memory of him among his friends and contemporaries it was precisely this quality of humour; "he had an inimitably funny way," one remarked, and there are memories of the time he "roared" with a friend during a dinner party, of the occasions when he literally cried with laughter, of his quickness and animation, of his enthusiasm in telling a funny story, of "his strangely grotesque glances" when he was dramatising a comic scene, of the way in which the sides of his mouth quivered when he was trying hard not to laugh.

146

His own son noted that, of all the men he knew, Charles Dickens was the quickest to see the ludicrous aspect of any situation. Misplaced gravity especially amused him, and there was one occasion when he had to leave a church service which was taking place on a steamer during a heavy sea. He simply could *not* help bursting out in laughter. One remembers here the immoderate and sometimes hysterical laughter of the boy attending Mr Jones's school in Hampstead, the boy who laughed during the service in chapel and complained that his potatoes would be spoiled. There is that same hint of suppressed hysterics in an incident when he and Cruikshank attended a funeral. Funerals often provoked hilarity in Dickens, and he himself recounted how he "cried" with laughter at some of Cruikshank's philosophical asides during the ceremony; and, when Cruikshank was decked out in a black coat and a very long black hat band by an undertaker, "I thought I should have been obliged to go away". There were times like this when Dickens could only just manage to control himself, his laughter often relieving stress or panic but also acting as some destructive or purging force and overpowering all the conventions of the world.

But his greatest social talent, apart from the telling of stories, droll or macabre according to the occasion, was his enormous skill as a mimic. Sometimes it was a physical mimicry; once he told some friends how he had seen a man, as a cure for sea-sickness on a boat, begin to cut up slices of brown paper in order to plaster them on his breast and in a wonderful manner Dickens mimicked this man's "sympathetic motions of the jaw" as he used his scissors on the paper. He liked, too, to imitate the movements of animals — of, for example, a lion in a cage (a situation in which he sometimes found himself) — and once he "gave a capital imitation of the way a robin redbreast cocks his head on one side preliminary to a dash forward in the direction of a wriggling victim". But above all he liked to

147

imitate his closest friends; "he delighted to recall," one of those friends remembered after Dickens's death, "the peculiarities, eccentricities and otherwise, of dead and gone as well as living friends." He imitated Forster and Hood and Sydney Smith; he mimicked the slow drawl of Samuel Rogers and the sometimes absurd longueurs of Macready. This gift extended to his writing also and, on one occasion when Wilkie Collins seemed to be too ill to complete a series, Dickens offered to write it for him "so like you as that none should find out the difference". In some ways, perhaps, a rather insulting offer.

Of course he could also imitate himself; he liked to tell stories against himself, and on more than one occasion seemed to parody the excesses of his own style. He said of a peculiarly affecting episode in *David Copperfield*, when David's mother dies: "Get a clean pocket-handkerchief ready for the close of 'Copperfield' No 3; 'simple and quiet, but very natural and touching' – *Evening Bore*." This was part of the comedy he found in quoting advertisements out of context – "No family should be without it," he would say of one object or another. We have here intimations of a man who found it difficult, if not impossible, to take anything absolutely seriously for very long; often in the middle of scenes of distress and poverty in the worst rookeries of London, for example, something would strike him as "irresistibly comic". Nothing was excluded from the range of his humour, whether it took a farcical or satirical turn, and although it is proper that the work of Dickens as a social reformer and even propagandist ought to be made plain (he would have been horrified if these activities were to be ignored, since he invested so much energy in them) one should never lose sight of the fact that his anarchic, liberating and sometimes harsh laughter was his immediate and even instinctive response to the world. And one can see him, also, withdrawing into himself once more after he has amused everyone; going back to his own communings, where the steady low note of his melancholy is not to be separated from that constant spring of humour that was with him always. We will leave him as he left the company of others in just such a mood: "Just as we were in a tempest of laughter over some witticism of his, he jumped up, seized me by the hand, and said goodnight."

# *Eleven*

S O the daily life of Charles Dickens continued as, in the first years of his fame, he worked on *Oliver Twist* and *Nicholas Nickleby*: his writing in the mornings, his riding in the afternoons, alone or with Forster, his supper at five and then more work, or a trip to the theatre, or perhaps an evening at home. He was a man of relatively fixed habits, even when young, since a regimen of work and rest was the only one that could have supported such continuous and energetic production; that and the knowledge of his success, emphasised all the more when the first number of *Nicholas Nickleby* sold fifty thousand copies (it did not significantly fall off from that number for the whole of its run). There were problems, however. Catherine had given birth to her second child on 6 March, 1838 – this was Mary, generally called Mamie – and once again she was plunged into that condition of physical debility and post-natal depression which had afflicted her after the first child. Dickens took her to Richmond for a few days to help her to recuperate, and then in June they moved for the summer to 4 Ailsa Park Villas in Twickenham, a peaceful and rural retreat, perfect for those long rides which he enjoyed but also for the multifarious sports of summer – bagatelle, battledore, quoits, bowling, bar-leaping. There were, as always, frequent open invitations to his friends to come and stay with them (Dickens always liked to create around him a family more extended than his immediate one); there were boating trips up the Thames; there were expeditions to Hampton Court. Of course he was still busy here with both novels and, with the sometimes unwelcome assistance of Bentley, he conducted all his usual work on the *Miscellany*. Quite regularly he commuted to Doughty Street, however, and not just for business reasons: this was the time of the new Queen's coronation (and thus the proper beginning of the Victorian era, to be dated some years after Dickens's rise to eminence), and he attended the festivities in Hyde Park about which he wrote an article for *The Examiner*.

There were other trips in this period of his fame; at one point he fell ill just when he should have been finishing his fictional instalments and later told a friend that he took a steamer for Boulogne, hired a room in an inn and there "secure from interruption" was able to get on with his postponed work and "to return just in season for the monthly issues with his work completed". He was also speculating about a journey to America, and it is possible that even now he was chafing against the strains of domesticity, with two infants around him and a wife who found it difficult by herself to cope. There is often a sense in his life of his wishing to break away from bonds even as he was tying them for himself. His most important task, however, was to finish *Oliver Twist*. In March he was ". . . sitting patiently at home waiting for Oliver Twist who has not yet arrived", and only days later "fallen upon him tooth and nail".

He went to the Isle of Wight in September in order to work undisturbed – staying at Alum Bay and then at Ventnor – and such was his fluency that he managed to write eight chapters in the twelve weeks from July to the end of this month. As soon as he came back, he applied himself to *Nicholas Nickleby*, but then once more turned his attention to the last chapters of *Oliver Twist*. He pretended

151

to many people to be "out of town", managed to see hardly anyone, and composed few letters; in this period he also frequently wrote after dinner into the late hours, a practice which in later life he regarded with abhorrence. But it was of this closing sequence that he told Bentley ". . . I am doing it with greater care, and I think with greater power than I have been able to bring to bear on anything yet . . ." These were indeed the most powerful scenes. He killed Nancy – "I shewed what I have done to Kate last night who was in an unspeakable *'state'* " – and then went on to hammer out the flight of Sikes, the pursuit of him by the mob, his death, the trial and punishment of Fagin. While of course leaving Oliver, the parish boy, at the end rich and happy. He managed to write the final six chapters in three weeks but, as always, he hated to leave his creations once he had brought them so vividly to life; he became as much a part of their world as they were part of his, and at the end of his narrative he wrote, "I would fain linger yet with a few of those among whom I have so long moved . . ." But he could not. The book was complete. It would appear in *Bentley's Miscellany* for a few months yet, but the three-volume printed edition was about to be published. He had finished it at last, "this marvellous tale" as he called it.

It had become a superstition with him that he should be out of London on the day of publication, so almost as soon as he had completed *Oliver Twist* he was off. On this occasion, however, the superstition was combined with the opportunity to "work up" some more scenes for his remaining novel, *Nicholas Nickleby*: he left on a tour of the Midlands and North Wales with Hablot Browne. Their main destination was Manchester, for it seems that Dickens had arranged to visit some of the cotton mills with the express purpose of somehow fitting them into the plot and once more reasserting his claim to be the single most important topical and polemical novelist in

England. He had already been impressed by Lord Ashley's attempts to alleviate the plight of child labourers in England, and at this stage he was clearly in accord with what was known as the Ten Hours Movement, which campaigned to limit the amount of time children could be employed; now he decided that he wanted to see for himself the conditions of the operatives in the factories and "to strike the heaviest blow in my power for these unfortunate creatures". And so, a week after he had completed *Oliver Twist*, and entrusting the reading of the final proofs to Forster, he set out.

He returned in time to see the final proofs of the book edition of *Oliver Twist*, and at once took exception to some of Cruikshank's final illustrations; he seems to have been disappointed with the whole series but had the good sense to curb his temper with the "illustrious George" and ask him to remove only one, a painfully sentimental print of Rose Maylie and Oliver by the fireside. Cruikshank at first prevaricated, limiting himself to making minor changes in the existing plate, but finally he agreed to substitute another for the next printing. Dickens had already made his own changes for the volume edition of the text, by not only altering such minor details as the Artful Dodger's height (originally three foot six inches but altered to a more credible four foot six inches), but also excising those passages from the original instalments which had emphasised the serial elements and origins of the tale. Thus did Dickens attempt to transform it into a much more coherent and consistent piece of work. He also suddenly decided to use his real name; the first printing had its author as "Boz" but all subsequent ones amended this to "Charles Dickens".

One reason why Dickens treated his second novel with much more seriousness than his first was that even as he was writing *Oliver Twist* he had decided that he wanted to dramatise it for himself, perhaps hoping in this way to knock out of the field any inferior imitations. Nothing came of this idea but there was a dramatisation at the St James's Theatre on 27 March; since this was the theatre with which Dickens had been heavily involved, and since Harley and Braham were still in charge there, it has been suggested that Dickens himself did in fact write this first adaptation. Certainly he may have had some involvement with it – no doubt attending rehearsals, if nothing else – but the more likely candidate for authorship is Gilbert à Becket, a man of Dickens's age but one who epitomises the fate of moderately successful nineteenth-century "hacks" who wrote a plethora of cheap plays and edited a variety of unsuccessful cheap journals. The play was not a success, however, and the reaction was such that it closed after two or three nights.

There were six versions of *Oliver Twist* in 1838, representing at least in a literal sense the most dramatic aspect of what was called "Bozmania" or "Boz-i-ana" and although at one such version Dickens, embarrassed by what was being perpetrated upon his book, lay down in his box from the middle of the first act until the end of the play, the sentiments of such adaptations are some indication at least of the taste of the audience; a taste that Dickens himself found that he needed to satisfy. It is not that Dickens objected in principle to the dramatisations of his novels, just that he disliked the poorer ones. He did in fact admire or at least enjoy some aspects of an adaptation of *Nicholas Nickleby*, for example, which was running simultaneously with the dramas made out of *Oliver Twist*: in particular he appreciated the portrayal of Smike by Mrs Keeley, although he took exception to her uttering sentiments about "the pretty harmless robins".

At the beginning of 1839 Dickens turned his attention to the serial novel which he had promised to bring out in *Bentley's Miscellany*, in May, immediately after the final chapters of *Oliver Twist*. By this stage he seems to have had

154

no more than a rough idea of the nature of the story he was going to write; it was to be called *Barnaby Rudge*, and was in part to be concerned with the Gordon Riots of 1780; but the thought of having to complete the first episode by May, even as he continued his work on *Nicholas Nickleby*, seems to have exacerbated his belief that he was being exploited by Richard Bentley. That there was no ground for such a belief is not the point; he saw his work being applauded and dramatised, but he also saw Richard Bentley taking a large share of the proceeds from the serialisation of *Oliver Twist* which he believed ought to be his. So he stopped working on *Barnaby Rudge*. Then he seemed about to break off the agreement to write the novel altogether but, at Forster's urging, he decided merely to postpone its appearance for six months. Bentley, perhaps somewhat rashly, agreed to this proposal on condition that Dickens himself should extend his contract to edit the *Miscellany* for a further six months; and on condition, too, that he should engage in no other writing except *Nicholas Nickleby* until *Barnaby Rudge* was ready. At this Dickens lost whatever self-control he possessed: ". . . if you presume to address me again in the style of offensive impertinence which marks your last communication, I will from that moment abandon at once and for ever all conditions and agreements that may exist between us . . ." Here, when aroused, is the clear sense of his own dignity and worth. And then, two days later, he resigned from the editorship of *Bentley's Miscellany*.

*Nicholas Nickleby* paramount, then, in this period when he had no other book upon which he was engaged; it was the first time since the early days of *The Pickwick Papers* that he had only one novel to write. But there were always domestic preoccupations to mitigate his literary ones. He had to dismiss his manservant, Henry, for some unspecified but obviously glaring "impertinence to his 'Missis'", Catherine; then he hired a small man with very bright red hair, William Topping, to take his place (as always, he preferred to deal with smaller men). More serious were his problems with his parents, and particularly with his father whose importuning and indebtedness were becoming a perpetual trial to his son. John Dickens seems to have made a habit, for example, of begging — the word is scarcely too strong — from Chapman and Hall, Dickens's publishers. Many letters between son and father were destroyed, both by Dickens himself and by his executors after his death. What these letters contained is obviously not known but Georgina Hogarth, who was responsible for destroying many of them, said that ". . . there were letters to CD from his father, from his mother, brothers and other relations, almost all of them in the same tone, money difficulties, applications for money . . . *And most especially from his father* . . . not only debt and difficulties, but most discreditable and dishonest dealing on the part of his father towards his son . . ." More evidence for this "discreditable" behaviour will emerge later, but it was in this period that matters once more reached a crisis. John Dickens's debts had come to such a point that bankruptcy proceedings must again have been threatening; and Dickens took an immediate decision. In the February 1839 number of *Nicholas Nickleby* he had despatched Kate and Mrs Nickleby to a country cottage and now, at the beginning of March, he decided to find a similar place for his parents; just as in his fiction he had a tendency to dispose of characters who were no longer necessary for the narrative, there is a sense now in which he wanted to remove his parents from the scene of action. And by what better means than those he had already found in his novel?

He travelled quickly down to Devon and, with his usual impatience and impetuosity, found a new house for them the same day; it was called Mile End Cottage, Alphington, just a mile outside Exeter, and, to judge from Dickens's descriptions in his ecstatic letters back to his wife and

Forster, you would think that it was indeed a cottage constructed in his fiction. It was a "jewel of a place . . . in the most beautiful, cheerful, delicious rural neighbourhood I was ever in . . . excellent parlour . . . a capital closet . . . a beautiful little drawing-room . . . noble garden". He found it by accident, simply by walking along the road, and at once decided that this was the place. Not only did he arrange for it to be rented by his parents, looked over and signed the necessary documents, but he also furnished it and purchased such things as the crockery, the glass, and the stair-carpet. No detail was too small for his attention – just like the details of his fiction – and of course by the time he had finished ". . . the neatness and cleanliness of the place is beyond description".

The fact that Dickens wanted his mother to come down to Alphington to help with the arrangements, just as he was to ask her to attend during Catherine's next pregnancy, suggests that she was a more willing and practical person than is to be presumed from the descriptions of those who take her to be the living original of Mrs Nickleby. Clearly, too, it was John Dickens who was most at fault on this as on other occasions. They had been living in King Street, Holborn, and Dickens wanted to get them off to Devon without alerting his father's creditors; in addition he gave his father an allowance of seven pounds and ten shillings a quarter, no doubt on condition that he did not return to London. The parents acquiesced in the move, although they really had no choice in the matter and in any case could hardly withstand the force of their famous son's will. Indeed it seems that their relationship to him had altered somewhat since the days of his newspaper reporting. One friend saw Dickens with his family in this period and noted that "they appeared to be less at ease with Charles than with anyone else, and seemed in fear of offending him. There was a subdued manner, a kind of restraint in his presence . . . because his moods were very variable." In other words Charles Dickens had become the master of the family, and was already playing the role of "father", both supporter and disciplinarian; the parents had become children again, just as Mrs Nickleby becomes a child to be guided by her son.

And all the time he was ". . . thinking about Nickleby", working hard on it, or "powdering away", to use one of his favourite expressions. Its story itself is the familiar one of a young man's journey through life, with the cry "The world is before me, after all", and his subsequent encounters with villains and misers and virgins; but Dickens has added to it suffering children, insufferable or crazy women, comic or broken-down wretches, and a family life which is seen characteristically as a place of torment. He is trying to introduce everything within the confines of the prose narrative − romance, melodrama, tragedy, comedy − but if there is one large distinction between this novel and its predecessor it is that in *Oliver Twist* Dickens used a romantic vocabulary whereas in *Nicholas Nickleby* he uses a theatrical one. Perhaps in mute recognition of the fact that he was introducing so many different styles in the novel, they remain precisely that − *styles* − and the characters always seem to be enacting a role which has been given to them. The book itself was eventually dedicated to Macready, and everything about it has the feel of the theatre; it is as if Dickens saw human life conducted among the bright lights of the stage, making it somehow larger and brighter than the reality. If he had any image of the world in his head as he wrote, it was that narrow and highly magnified one which he observed from the stalls or from the pit. One could put it differently by noting that *Nicholas Nickleby* is written by someone whose understanding of appearance, of gesture, of speech and of character has been very strongly influenced by his experience of acting; the effect is heightened by Hablot Browne's illustrations which characteristically portray everything as if it were indeed
158

taking place upon the stage. But if the novel is close to the theatrical conventions of the period (which were also the conventions employed by most popular literature) this is not to suggest that it lacks power or effectiveness as a result. Quite the contrary. The most obviously theatrical scenes in the book – the rescue of Madeline Bray from the clutches of the hideous miser Arthur Gride, the discovery that Smike is really Ralph Nickleby's son – are moments of great power which still have an enormous ability to intrigue and to move the reader. One of the lessons in reading Dickens comes from understanding how little our responses to this form of action have changed, and how close we still are to our ancestors who wept and laughed in the small theatres of London. And yet at the same time Dickens, with that extraordinary double-awareness he possessed, satirises the theatre even as he displays his love and admiration for it; much of the novel is concerned with parodying bad acting, for example, a subject which always fascinated him. On the other hand, some of the serious scenes and events in the novel are themselves parodied with the same élan. Many learned disquisitions have been devoted to the parallels between the comic and serious elements of the action, but surely they can be seen as another aspect of Dickens's high-spirited inventiveness in which he plays with ideas and events as lightly and as gaily as he invents a comic scene or describes a character, the very epitome of what is described here as ". . . those strange contradictions of feeling which are common to us all".

Yet so much of the theatrical momentum within Dickens's novels depends upon his own personality. There is, first of all, that constant delight which he took in mimicry. His ferocious humour. His ability to parody himself. His delight in acting. But he also performed in his novels the roles which he adopted in his amateur theatricals; in his fiction, too, he is both stage manager and central performer. In *Nicholas Nickleby* and elsewhere, there tends to be the same troupe of players surrounding him, to each of whom he gives instructions about pitch or tempo or rhythm, and who come on or go off like actors at the appointed time. The endings of novels are extremely important clues to a writer's real intentions, because it is often at that concluding point (when the novelist has, as it were, come to an end of the self-imposed tasks and the necessary difficulties) that real meanings emerge in the most relaxed and unhindered way. That is why it is so significant that most of Dickens's novels end with the same kind of tableau and curtain that marked the dramas of the period. The actors all return, their past and futures mapped out; they link hands and bow; then suddenly the curtain comes down and they are gone.

By the end of April Dickens wanted to get away from the city, so he and Catherine took a place in Petersham, Elm Cottage, where they remained until the end of August. Of course, Dickens's hospitality and appetite for company were in no way abated; there were constant invitations to friends to spend the weekend there. On one occasion he visited the Hampton races close by, and used the material he gathered in the next number of *Nicholas Nickleby*. Of course the novel was his main task even while he was resting in the countryside of Surrey; there were times when he was "shut up" in the cottage in order to write, and he would frequently send his copy direct to the printers, Bradbury and Evans, in London. In fact he generally stayed at Petersham from Saturday until Monday, and then during the week made various commuting excursions to London.

Soon the idea of a new venture, a *Miscellany*, had taken a hold upon him, and it led him to neglect his work on *Nicholas Nickleby*, and induced "great worrying and fidgeting of myself"; again one sees how even the most tentative plan, once it is conceived by him, is seized as if it were

160

already a burning reality which had to be put into practice immediately. He could not sit still. The idea of a weekly periodical for which he would receive a regular income without having to extend his energies once more on a long novel clearly appealed to him, together with the fact that a periodical under his sole guidance and authority would confirm that link with his audience for which he was always searching and which might have been in danger if he had simply embarked upon another monthly series. He had a good idea of his audience and he knew that, to keep it, surprise and novelty were potent instruments. Of course this new idea had the great merit of binding Chapman and Hall even closer to him, but in a partnership as beneficial to himself as it was to them – he proposed the idea of *Master Humphrey's Clock*, as the new weekly periodical was to be called, at the same time as he suggested that in the matter of *Nicholas Nickleby* they "behave with liberality to me". In fact they paid him an extra £1,500, and it seems partly the fact that he had outlined a new agreement for future co-operation which persuaded them to be so generous; the pattern emerges here which was to become constant in Dickens's later career, of dangling both the carrot of a future work and the stick of his well-known wrath to keep his publishers in line. The agreement with Chapman and Hall which he eventually signed for *Master Humphrey's Clock* was almost ideal from Dickens's point of view; he was paid a weekly salary while Chapman and Hall covered the expenses, and he shared equally in all profits. Henceforward in his career, having suffered from fixed payments in the past, he insisted that he would always participate in the profits and thus increase his own income as his sales increased. He was perhaps the first professional author to *act* as a professional, and to put what would have been notable skills as a Victorian businessman to good use. And, as he became more and more enthusiastic about his ideas for the new periodical and his own future, *Nicholas Nickleby* itself began to suffer from slight inattention; those episodes written at Petersham show no evidence of flagging invention, but they do show some sign of his loss of interest in construction.

Dickens still did not want to return to London, however, and this largely because he was no longer happy with Doughty Street. He had given notice that he did not intend to resume the tenancy agreement which was just about to expire, and no doubt the presence of two children, with his wife pregnant yet again, made the somewhat cramped rooms of the house seem even more constricted. So as soon as they left Petersham they went down to Ramsgate to search for lodgings. There were none to be obtained there, and instead they went back to the nearby town of Broadstairs; they no longer stayed in the small house in the High Street, but instead took a commodious house on the sea-front. It was here, at 40 Albion Street, that he set to work on the final number of *Nicholas Nickleby*. And here, too, he experienced one of those episodes concerning servants which might have been pathetic but which always seemed to Dickens to be irresistibly comic: his cook "got drunk – remarkably drunk – on Tuesday night, was removed by constables, lay down in front of the house and addressed the multitude for some hours . . ." Not that he did not miss London; and, in one of those strangely self-revealing letters which on the surface seem merely animated and cordial, Dickens suggests that because of his absence any number of dreadful events might have taken place in the capital. "I almost blame myself for the death of that poor girl who leaped off the Monument . . . neither would the two men have found the skeleton in the sewers", and he goes on to describe an imaginary portrait by Cruikshank of someone stuffing a dead child down the little hole of the privy. Another aspect of a vision which was sometimes truly grotesque.

Fred was with the family at Broadstairs. Of all Dickens's

brothers he was undoubtedly the favourite, and Dickens took a constant interest in his welfare; together they climbed down to the beach one night during a ferocious storm, and crept within the shelter of a boat beside the little pier in order to observe the breaking sea. But for most of the time here his diary mentions just one word – "Work". Writing at his study looking out at the turbulent sea, composing the final chapters of *Nicholas Nickleby* in which Squeers is undone, Ralph Nickleby's treacheries unmasked, the terrible story of his son, Smike, is told, Dotheboys Hall breaks up at last and everything ends cheerfully for the hero and his bride, for the hero's sister and her betrothed. Nicholas Nickleby becomes "rich and prosperous" just like his creator but the novel ends with a vision of the grave of poor Smike, a character so much like a simulacrum of the author as he might have been if he had remained a ". . . labouring hind". But now dead and buried for evermore. Then, on Friday, 20 September, 1839 Dickens wrote in his diary: "Finished Nickleby this day at 2 o'clock, and went over to Ramsgate with Fred and Kate, to send the last little chapter to Bradbury and Evans in a parcel. Thank God that I have lived to get through it happily." He had already written his preface to the newly completed novel, in which for the first time he adopts that fond and agreeable tone towards his audience which he wished to continue in his projected journal, *Master Humphrey's Clock* – his aim being, he said, that of ". . . one who wished their happiness, and contributed to their amusement". Here is Dickens as the man of feeling, uniting all his readership in a concord of affection and brotherhood.

The completion of *Nicholas Nickleby* was celebrated by a dinner which Macready described as "*too* splendid". It was held at the Albion in Aldersgate Street, and Maclise's painting of Dickens was given pride of place on the occasion – a painting, incidentally, of which the engraved copies

163

became so popular that the plate from which the impressions were taken deteriorated beyond repair. Apparently it was not a particularly inspiring occasion. In a speech in honour of Dickens Macready compared him to Wordsworth, which seems to have prompted Dickens to tell a fellow guest that he enjoyed Wordsworth's pretty but somewhat morbid poem, "We Are Seven", one of the few indications that Dickens admired the first generation of Romantic poets. The party broke up "very late". Very late, and then back to Doughty Street, where Catherine was now in the last stages of her fourth pregnancy; in fact she had been pregnant for most of the time since her marriage, despite what must have now become the evident fact that she suffered post-natal depression and anxiety of a particularly severe kind. Her health was slowly being drained away.

And what of Dickens himself? High-spirited, energetic, apparently unaffected by arduous labour and by equally arduous leisure; and yet a man who was, as his children will later testify, much less affectionate and easy with his immediate family than he was with his friends. He was often taciturn, often something of a martinet in household matters, and notably irritable and impatient with his wife's "slowness". But how did he see himself? It is significant how in these early books, written in the full flood of his success, he so often projects himself into images of privation and imprisonment. "Dick", the name by which he was known to Cruikshank, Maclise and others, is also the name he gives to a blind blackbird in *Nicholas Nickleby*, and to the frail orphan boy destined to die in *Oliver Twist*. He seems to have felt himself to be in some profound manner ill-used, and again in *Nicholas Nickleby* there is an image of a child which might come from Dickens's own childhood — "It is a sad thing . . . to see a little deformed child sitting apart from other children, who are active and merry, watching the games he is denied the power to share in." With the
164

exception of the deformity, this is very much the image of his own infancy which Dickens remembered, and such references manifest an overwhelming and almost helpless self-pity. There is a sense in which Dickens always imagines himself to be neglected, and no doubt this permanent vague dissatisfaction with the world must on occasions have been directed at his immediate family. The birth on 29 October of Kate Macready Dickens, the child who in many respects was to be the one most like her father, could only have served to increase that sense of imprisonment which was one of the disadvantages of his domesticity.

And one of the reasons, too, why he wanted to move — as soon as he had returned to London from Broadstairs, he began to search in earnest for a new house. Dickens suggested that he should leave Doughty Street by the Christmas of 1839 on condition that the landlord bought from him all the fixtures he had installed, yet another example of his practical canniness in financial matters, and at the beginning of December the Dickens family and servants moved into a much larger house. One Devonshire Terrace was on the Marylebone Road, almost opposite the York Gate into Regent's Park; in some ways it was a grander address than Doughty Street and certainly a grander house. It was the last in a terrace of three and stood on the corner of Marylebone Road and Marylebone High Street, its square garden protected by a high wall. It was on two floors, contained some thirteen rooms, and was soon to be well furnished with candelabra, rosewood chairs covered with silk, silk damask curtains, large mirrors, sofas, sofa tables and — the only homely touch — a cottage piano which Dickens had originally bought for his lodgings in Furnival's Inn. He also had the front door and exterior railings painted bright green, one of his favourite colours, although this did not prevent it from being seen by some observers as a rather conventional and even dreary mansion.

The move to Devonshire Terrace had taken up a great deal of time, and he had to make up for the loss by cancelling most other engagements in order to work on *Barnaby Rudge*, which he had begun again in October only to break off. But he contracted a bad cold in his chest and, in addition, had agreed to write another selection of essays, *Sketches of Young Couples*. This is in many respects a particularly bad-tempered selection of portraits of the marital state but it does contain one notable article of faith which Dickens was to maintain for the rest of his life: ". . . all men and women, in couples or otherwise, who fall into exclusive habits of self-indulgence, and forget their natural sympathy and close connection with everybody and everything in the world around them, not only neglect the first duty of life, but, by a happy retributive justice, deprive themselves of its truest and best enjoyment." This is a fine statement – the fine statement of an *idea* – yet it ought to be remembered that, as even these slight sketches demonstrate, Dickens's imagination most closely and naturally twined itself about the actual conduct of human beings. But these *Sketches of Young Couples* were light work. He had more important tasks ahead of him. There was *Barnaby Rudge* . . . and then, even as he was working on his much postponed novel, he saw an advertisement which had been placed by Bentley in the *Morning Herald* and which announced *Barnaby Rudge* as "preparing for publication". At once he wrote to his solicitors, Smithson and Mitton, charging them to tell Bentley that the book would not be ready on time; and that, in fact, he refused altogether to produce it. He gave as his principal reason the fact that Bentley had for some time past been associating Dickens's work with that of his other authors (such as Harrison Ainsworth) and "hawking them about in a manner calculated to do me serious prejudice". Now it is certainly true that Dickens had a dislike, amounting almost to a phobia, of having his own novels associated with those of other writers, but in truth he was desperate to get out of his contract to supply *Barnaby Rudge* to Bentley. It was not even close to being finished, he was about to begin work with Chapman and Hall on the new periodical he had proposed, and he had in any case no high regard for Bentley himself; so he seized upon the advertisement as an excuse to cancel his contract. Of course Bentley himself was astonished by Dickens's sudden and peremptory declaration – "one of the most extraordinary effusions that even Mr D ever sent forth," his solicitor commented, and Bentley's son later added, "It is a brick in the building of Dickens's character. He wished to break his agreement, and so he made up the account herein. Dickens was a very clever, but he was not an honest man."

This was not the only occasion on which Dickens was charged with dishonesty, and his enemies sometimes accused him of being an outright liar. Of course he was very fond of superlative expressions, and he had an innate taste for excessiveness: never has he been so willing to do something, never has he had so large an audience, never has he sold so many copies, and so forth (although it is often odd to see these superlatives, in his correspondence, couched in his characteristically neat and tidy hand). It is also undeniably true that he would make up or at least embellish incidents when it suited his purpose to do so, even though this native tendency towards exaggeration also had its more beneficent side; as one contemporary noted, he was often guilty of "the amiable magnifying of the merits of persons . . ." But the point is more complicated than that, and certain comments which Dickens made at different times of his life all point in the same direction: ". . . any impression of mine is, I need not say, much better than a fact . . . I promised to tell you the truth, and this is the truth, as I feel it . . . I have created a legend in my own mind – and consequently I believe it with the utmost pertinacity . . ." And so forth. This comes

167

close to the truth of the matter: Dickens believed what he saw, or what possessed him, at that moment. If he felt something, it became at once true for him; in the same way that he *saw* his characters, immediately he seized upon an opinion or a belief it possessed absolute truth and reality in his own mind. Everything in the world, therefore, took on the shape of his own principles or obsessions; this has nothing to do with lying unless creation itself is a lie. And, although it may be poor comfort for those who suffered from his misrepresentations (his wife principal among them, in the end), there is no doubt that Dickens would have felt able to put his hand upon his heart and swear that he was always telling the truth.

Which was precisely why his animus against Richard Bentley was inspired by a real sense of outrage, even though it was Dickens himself who was principally in the wrong. From that time forward it was, as he put it, "war to the knife . . . with the Burlington Street Brigand". He was no doubt counting on Bentley's unwillingness to take him to court – it is rare for a publisher to sue an author – and in that belief it turned out he was not very much mistaken. And in the meantime, having abandoned work on *Barnaby Rudge*, he turned his attention eagerly to his proposed periodical, *Master Humphrey's Clock*. He proceeded very much as he had planned; he conceived the idea of a club, and began writing a series of tales which were linked to the members of that club. This idea of the "framed tale" was one that satisfied some aspect of his imagination; stories had appeared within the narratives of *The Pickwick Papers* and *Nicholas Nickleby*, too, and it is probable that this notion of linked but separate tales was closely connected with his memory of his childhood reading; not only his reading of periodicals like the *Bee* and *The Spectator*, but also, and most importantly, of *The Arabian Nights*, the fantasies of which had so deeply stirred him. What is unusual about the first number he was now writing of *Master*

*Humphrey's Clock*, however, is the narrator, for here Dickens casts himself in the role of an old man whose essential memory is of his childhood as a "poor crippled boy". Just as Somerset Maugham gave the hero of his *Of Human Bondage* a club-foot, as some physical symptom of the inadequacies Maugham believed himself to possess, so in the figure of Master Humphrey we see once again that projection of injury and vulnerability which Dickens had already explored in earlier characters and which he would use once again in such creations as Tiny Tim.

And there is London, too, the London which he celebrated in *Nicholas Nickleby* and which once more is defined in his new periodical as a place which contains "within its space everything, with its opposite extreme and contradiction", holds together a "thousand worlds"; a city where the narrator has "some thought for the meanest wretch that passes". Here Dickens is establishing the framework in which he will tell his stories, but once again he is firmly drawing the boundaries of his own imagination. The first stories he wrote were certainly of a London kind. He opens with an episode concerning the twin urban deities of Gog and Magog, no doubt partly inspired by his original plan to write a book about old London with Harrison Ainsworth but also clearly linked with his own imaginative interests at that time. The first chapters of *Barnaby Rudge*, which he had already written, were concerned with eighteenth-century London, and it is significant that all the ensuing short tales in *Master Humphrey's Clock* were set in the sixteenth or seventeenth centuries. His whole thinking was revolving around the past, therefore, and in the month he began writing *Master Humphrey's Clock* he visited an antiquarian bookseller, a Mr Upcott, who called himself "bibliophile and publisher", and wrote in the visitors' book — ". . . this most extraordinary antiquarian mansion, whereto I mean to return at the earliest possible opportunity to refresh myself with a few dusty draughts from its exhaustless wells." Old London. The crippled childhood of the narrator. Old books. So in *Master Humphrey's Clock* the idea of the past, the specific past of London and his own lost childhood are once more intertwined. As if in exploring the history of the city he was in some way exploring and animating his own past. Combining ". . . past emotions and bygone times". Which adds substance, perhaps, to G. K. Chesterton's comment that in these periodical tales lay "the stuff of which his dreams were made".

Around this time too a friendship was made which was to be of great importance to Dickens. At the house of Edward Stanley, a Whig politician who had "taken up" the famous novelist as so many others in the fashionable world had done or were at least attempting to do, he met Thomas Carlyle. In later life Dickens told one of his sons that Carlyle was the man "who had influenced him most" and Dickens's sister-in-law said to Carlyle himself that "there was *no one* for whom he had a higher reverence and admiration". There is the famous photograph of Dickens on the lawn at Gad's Hill Place, reading Carlyle's *History of the French Revolution*. In his admiration for him, of course, Dickens was by no means alone and there is a strong case to be made for Carlyle being the single most important writer in England during the 1840s; Dickens, although he was by no means intimately acquainted with his writings when they met, would have known of him by repute in the radical circles in which they both moved and was certainly aware of some of his work.

Dickens's own first impressions are not recorded, although he would no doubt have considered Carlyle to be in the same "camp" as himself; not just because of his radical sympathies but also because, earlier in this year, he had given a course of lectures which were later published as *Heroes, Hero-Worship and the Heroic in History*. Dickens was always to have reservations about Carlyle's worship of power, and the men of power, but he could not have helped but be stirred by Carlyle's encomia on "The Hero as Man of Letters" in which he declared that ". . . since it is the spiritual always that determines the material, this same Man-of-Letters Hero must be regarded as our most important modern person. He, such as he may be, is the soul of all. What he teaches, the whole world, will do and make . . . Men of Letters are a perpetual Priesthood, from age to age, teaching all men that a God is still present in their life . . . I say, of all Priesthoods, Aristocracies, Governing Classes at present extant in the world, there is no class comparable for importance to the Priesthood of the Writers of Books . . ." This of course, shorn of its Idealistic elements, is precisely the position which Dickens was moving towards; and precisely the role which he seems to have wanted to assume.

And yet it cannot be said that Carlyle had any very high opinion of Dickens's merits as a writer – this primarily because Dickens was a novelist and thus consigned to the world of Appearances rather than that of the Real. Of course he was entertained by Dickens's writing, and sometimes moved by it, but there is no doubt that his most permanent attitude was one of slight disparagement aptly expressed in his idea of Dickens as a "little fellow". He said as much later when in *Past and Present* he obliquely described Dickens's progress through America: ". . . if all Yankee-land follow a small good 'Schnuspel the distinguished Novelist' with blazing torches, dinner invitations, universal hep-hep-hurrah, feeling that he, though small, *is* something . . . Possible to worship a Something, even a small one . . ." And when describing the idea of Genius he again disparages the very kind of work on which Dickens was engaged – "What! The star-fire of the Empyrean shall eclipse itself, and illuminate magic-lanterns to amuse grown children? He, the god-inspired, is to twang harps for thee, and blow through scrannel-pipes; soothe thy sated souls with visions of new, still wider

171

Eldorados, Houri Paradises, richer Lands of Cockaigne?"
Yet at the same time as he hated the sin he liked the sinner.
"I truly love Dickens," he once said, "and discern in the
inner man of him a tone of real Music, which struggles to
express itself as it may . . ."

Of course Dickens's beliefs were on the whole instinctive, passionately held but not necessarily carefully considered, and in Carlyle's writings he would have found a
strenuous idealism, a high purpose and an essential
seriousness which would help to bind his own notions into
a coherent whole. Certainly Carlyle's speculative idealism
and his distrust of philosophic radicalism would have
helped to set Dickens's own more scattered ideas into
some sort of order. Both men agreed, for example, or
would come to agree, on the parlous state of England at
this time, a time which seems to us so strident and so
fruitful but which seemed to them to be barren of meaning
and empty of faith. In *Past and Present*, published three
years after their first meeting, Carlyle spoke of the condition of the country in terms that Dickens would have
understood and admired: "All England stands wringing its
hands, asking itself, nigh desperate, What farther? Reform
Bill proves to be a failure; Benthamee Radicalism, the gospel of 'Enlightened Selfishness' dies out, or dwindles into
Five-point Chartism, amid the tears and hootings of men:
what next are we to hope or try?" These were times when
the men of the early Forties were ". . . mumbling to ourselves some vague janglement of Laissez-faire, Supply-
and-demand, Cash-payment the one nexus of man to
man: Free-trade, Competition, and Devil take the hind-
most, our latest Gospel yet preached!" These were some
of the assaults that Dickens himself was to direct against
his contemporaries, and, like Carlyle, over all social and
political matters Dickens erected a vast shadowy symbolic
structure so that the London of *Bleak House*, for example,
might be said to act as an echo-chamber for Carlyle's words
172

on "Sooty Manchester, — it too is built on the infinite Abysses; overspanned by the skyey Firmaments; and there is birth in it, and death in it; — and it is every whit as wonderful, as fearful, unimaginable, as the oldest Salem or Prophetic City. Go or stand, in what time, in what place we will, are there not Immensities, Eternities, over us, around us, in us . . ." This is the vision of Carlyle, but it is also the vision of Charles Dickens. It is the true vision of the first half of the nineteenth century.

To say that Carlyle was the single most important philosophical writer of his period, then, is to throw a different light upon an age which has often seemed in retrospect to represent no more than the beginning of a staid Victorian dispensation. It was nothing of the kind. It had its own unique energies and patterns; we see how in Carlyle and in Dickens they spread and eddy, reaching from the innermost imagination to the large circle of readers who picked up each episode of *Oliver Twist* or the latest of Carlyle's pamphlets. Indeed from this greater distance we can see distinct resemblances between them. Both writers marrying philosophical or social analysis with the vivid scene or detail, both of them moving away from that strict separation of genres which had marked eighteenth-century writing, both of them uniting the most unlikely opposites — a private self-communing speech with public rage and denunciation, an almost apocalyptic vision with a strict determination to tell the "truth", a Gothic stance with the need also to be "real" and to be "immediate". All of these elements are contained as much within Carlyle's prose as that of Dickens; in both men we may discern the true lineaments of the 1830s and the 1840s, that period of passion and responsibility, of faith and scepticism. But Carlyle was the older man, and it was Dickens who really came to maturity in an age of transition.

# *Twelve*

AT the beginning of April 1840 Charles Dickens travelled to Birmingham with Catherine and Forster; he
had already written a "little child-story", introducing Nell,
for his new periodical, the story which was eventually to
become the first chapter of *The Old Curiosity Shop*. No doubt
he visited this manufacturing city for some more general
purpose connected with his new venture, but in any case it
was his practice to be out of London when anything of his
began publication; and, on the day after they left for the
Midlands, the first number of *Master Humphrey's Clock* duly
appeared. It cost threepence a week (monthly parts sold
at a shilling) and in appearance it was very distinctive. It
was larger than the regular monthly parts of *Nicholas
Nickleby*, on creamy white paper, and with twelve pages
of text; the engravings were not placed at the beginning
of each issue, as they had been with the monthly numbers,
but were "dropped" into the text. All this demonstrates
Dickens's fine eye for detail, and the care he lavished upon
the project was matched only by his hopes for its success.
The prospects were, he said, "beyond calculation". It was
a "very difficult game" but "with very high stakes before
me" and, when he heard that the first number had sold
some seventy thousand copies, he was elated. At this rate,
he told Macready in the first flush of his optimism, he
could make ten thousand pounds a year. And already he

was devising ways of improving the effectiveness of the magazine; he was going to insert the story of the child into the third number but then changed his mind and decided to put it in the fourth, his primary aim at this stage being to lend coherence to what was an assemblage of different materials. He wanted to give his journal "a less discursive appearance". And his instincts were right: the page proofs of numbers five and six were already prepared when it became clear that the public appeal of this heterogeneous collection of essays was not as great as Dickens and his partners had anticipated. Within two weeks sales had dropped almost thirty per cent to around fifty thousand copies, and it was at this juncture that Dickens decided to cut his losses. He realised that the public had been expecting another story from him, and, like the professional journalist he was and always remained, he set out to provide them with just that; it is likely that he had already seen possibilities in the "child-story", this story of the little girl whom Master Humphrey finds wandering in the streets of London, and perhaps intended to return to this charming theme from time to time. But now he decided to elaborate upon it and to transform it into a story of weekly instalments. There is no doubt that it exercised a strong fascination for him in any case; at this juncture, as he later told a friend, Little Nell "followed him about everywhere", as did so many of his creations once he had imagined them. As with *Oliver Twist* what had once been simply a short story about a child had grown almost at once into an entire narrative. It is as if the plight of a solitary child provoked Dickens into full-scale conceiving and scheming and designing, as if it would not let him rest until he had (in Little Nell's case, literally) laid it to rest.

And so the fourth number of *Master Humphrey's Clock* opened with the new story. He had other material which he wanted to use up, of course, and so we find the tale of Little Nell preceded by a short story about the murder of

175

a child and followed by a piece of romantic parody — " 'Can you?' said he with peculiar meaning. I felt the gentle pressure of his foot on mine; our corns throbbed in unison . . ." — displaying, if nothing else, the essential amorphousness of Dickens's talent at this stage. He was ready to try his hand at anything. But so it was, out of occasional pieces and stray inspirations, that the great story of Little Nell and her grandfather emerged. By the time the novel had finished its run sales of *Master Humphrey's Clock*, which had now become its vehicle, had reached one hundred thousand. John Forster, who took on for Dickens the task of reading the final proofs of the novel, said that thus *The Old Curiosity Shop* emerged "with less direct consciousness of design on his own part than I can remember in any other instance throughout his career". Yet it was this particular narrative which more than any of his other works made "the bond between himself and his readers one of personal attachment". By the beginning of May he was writing the third, fourth and fifth chapters and already the characters were emerging in abundance; Little Nell herself, Quilp the rebarbative dwarf, Kit Nubbles the golden-hearted "grateful fellow" and Dick Swiveller.

It was clear by now that he was again embarked upon a long story, and it was with the intention of concentrating all his energies upon it that he decided quite suddenly to go down to Broadstairs; but the evident fact that he wished to work undisturbed did not prevent him from sending letters to such friends as Beard, Mitton, Maclise and Forster asking them to join him and his family by the sea. They were back in Albion Street, along the sea-front, and it was here that he really embarked upon *The Old Curiosity Shop*. The first thing he did, however, was to rearrange and tidy his rooms; "the writing table is set forth with a neatness peculiar to your estimable friend," he wrote to Beard, "and the furniture in all the rooms has been entirely rearranged by the same extraordinary character." Here, in the half-

John Dickens

Elizabeth Dickens

From an unsigned miniature,
said to be the earliest portrait

Dickens at twenty-four
from a painting by Samuel Laurence

Charles Dickens
painted by Daniel Maclise, 1839

Georgina Hogarth,
painted by Frank Stone

Catherine Dickens,
1842

Catherine Dickens
in later life

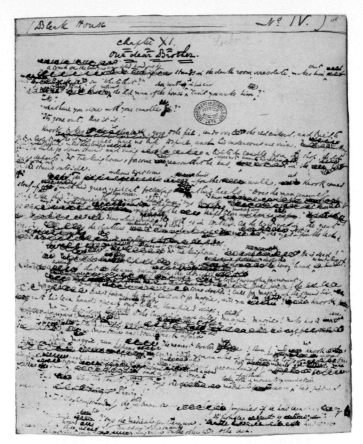

The opening of chapter 11 from the manuscript of *Bleak House*

## CHAPTER XI.

### Our dear brother.

A TOUCH on the lawyer's wrinkled hand, as he stands in the ~~death~~ room, irresolute, makes him start and say "What's that?"  *dark*

"It's me," returns the old man of the house, whose breath is in his ear. "Can't you wake him?"

"No."

"What have you done with your candle?"

"It's gone out. Here it is."

Krook takes it, goes to the fire, ~~bends~~ over the red embers, and ~~tries~~ to get a light. The dying ashes have no light to spare, and his endeavours are vain. Muttering, after an ineffectual call to his lodger, that he will go down stairs and bring a lighted candle from the shop, the old man departs. Mr. Tulkinghorn, for some new reason that he has, does not await his return in the room, but on the stairs outside.  *stoops*

The welcome light soon shines upon the wall, as Krook comes slowly up, with his green-eyed cat following at his heels. "Does the man generally sleep like this?" inquires the lawyer, in a low voice.

"Hi! I don't know," says Krook, "I know next to nothing of his habits, except that he keeps himself very close."  *run on*

Thus whispering, they both go in together. As the light goes in, the great eyes in the shutters, darkening, seem to close. Not so the eyes upon the bed.  *is shaking his head and lifting his gesture*

"God save us!" exclaims Mr. Tulkinghorn. "He is dead!"

Krook drops the heavy hand he has taken up, so suddenly that the arm swings over the bedside.

They look at one another for a moment.

"Send for some doctor! Call for ~~Maggie~~ up the stairs, sir. Here's poison by the bed! Call out for ~~Maggie~~, will you?" says Krook, with his lean hands spread out above the body like a vampire's wings.  *Flite*

Mr. Tulkinghorn hurries to the landing, and calls "~~Maggie, Maggie~~! Make haste, here, whoever you are!" ~~Maggie~~!" Krook follows him with his eyes, and, while he is calling, finds opportunity to steal to the old portmanteau, and steal back again.

"Run, ~~Maggie~~, run! The nearest doctor! Run!" So Mr. Krook addresses a crazy little woman, who ~~is~~ his female lodger, who appears and vanishes in a breath, ~~and~~ who soon returns, accompanied by a testy medical man, brought from his dinner, ~~and~~ with a broad snuffy upper lip, and a broad Scotch tongue.

"Ey! Bless the hearts o' ye," says the medical man, looking up at them after a moment's examination. "He's just as dead as Phairy..."

Mr. Tulkinghorn (standing by the old portmanteau) inquires if he has been dead any time?

H

Caricature of Dickens,
1861

whimsical references to himself, one detects at least a brief note of genuine pride. And at once he began his routine. He rose at seven, started work at about 8.30 and generally finished before two – an arduous enough schedule, but he found the difficulties of working within the limits of weekly numbers (as he had done with *Oliver Twist*) no less exhausting.

At the beginning of the story he was only working two weeks ahead of the printer, which, in a venture so much depending upon regular appearance, was cutting it somewhat fine. The nervous strain upon him, the constant need for unwearying effort in order to meet his commitments to what he now considered to be his "public", were severe: perhaps this is the best explanation for his sudden decision to escape, to travel, to go on a "jaunt". For, after about four weeks in Broadstairs, he visited Chatham and Rochester with Forster and Maclise. He always found a kind of sustenance in his returns to his childhood haunts, and it is almost as if they reminded him of how far he had already come; of how far he might yet travel. Yet even the longest journey had the same necessary end; it was on the occasion of this visit that he is reported to have said of the little burial ground just beneath Rochester Cathedral, "There, my boy, I mean to go into dust and ashes." Then he was back in London, back in his study at Devonshire Terrace, where he complained that "I am more bound down by this Humphrey than I have ever been yet" and where he continued the narrative of Little Nell's wanderings, of the meeting with Mrs Jarley and her waxworks, of the machinations of Quilp.

But he was restless as he worked on *The Old Curiosity Shop*, a story he found difficult to "turn". He went down with Catherine to see his parents at the cottage in Alphington which he had found for them. "They *seem* perfectly contented and happy," he told Forster. "That's the only intelligence I shall convey to you except by word of

mouth." In that last sentence, of course, lies all the difficulty of biography, for how is it possible now to guess at
what was passed by mouth, by the sudden expression or
by the unintentional phrase? The whole meaning of a life
may be evoked in such moments which cannot now be
reclaimed – like the life itself disappeared utterly, leaving
behind just written documents from which we can only
attempt carefully to reconstruct it. But the biographer does
know some things which may not even have been clear
to Dickens himself as eagerly he moved forward through
the world, each day a new confirmation and extension of
his being; we know that the parents were *not* happy, for
example, and that John Dickens would soon be forging
bills with his son's signature.

After the short visit to Alphington Dickens went again
to Broadstairs and rented a larger place, Lawn House, for
the rest of the summer. Once more he was close to the
sea, and once more he invited friends and relatives to join
him. It was an unusual holiday only in one respect, inas-
much as a certain Eleanor Christian, a friend of the family,
left a detailed account of her stay with the Dickens entour-
age and gave in particular a sharp portrait of Dickens himself. He does not emerge particularly well largely because,
in Eleanor Christian's account, he is marked by facetiousness, a propensity for a certain kind of savage fun, and
a wilful unpredictability in his moods. The small details
are right; how his clothes were too *"loud"* ("Young as I
was, I was aware of the vagaries of dress indulged in by
authors and artists; but this was something unusual . . ."); 
how, like his brothers and father, he had a slightly thick
speech and tended to talk in low and hurried tones; how
when he was concentrating he would suck his tongue and
pull upon his hair; all these things are confirmed by other
contemporaries. And in his behaviour, too, Eleanor Christian remembers what others also saw; how his humorous
remarks "were generally delivered in an exaggerated,
178

stilted style", and how misleading was the "rapt, preoccupied, far-off look" which he sometimes adopted when in the company of others. In fact he was "taking in" everything and would eventually indulge in "most amusing but merciless criticisms" of everything that had been said. But above all else she remembered the variability of his moods. There were times when he was boisterous and amicable, even though some of the effects of his high spirits, like dragging Eleanor Christian into the sea while she was wearing her new and only silk dress, were not altogether pleasing. He would sing snatches of popular songs as they travelled in carriages on various excursions, he would attend the local dances (even though he stayed in the shadows so that he would not be recognised), he played charades and party games with all the excitement and gusto of his nature – at one time, during charades, putting on a lady's broad-brimmed hat with bedraggled feather. But there were also times when he was moody, silent and unsociable. There were even occasions when his eyes were like "danger lamps" and it was then that "I confess I was horribly afraid of him".

There is one refrain here. A little while after Broadstairs Eleanor Christian was about to go, uninvited, to a charade party at Dickens's house. But the friend who was to take her demurred: "If it was anybody else but Charles Dickens I should not hesitate an instant," she told Eleanor Christian. "But he is so odd!" His brother, Frederick, also said that he was "*odd* sometimes" and this is a description repeated by others. Odd. Mercurial. Unpredictable. Talking in low and rapid tones. This was the man who was then engaged upon a novel where tearfulness and grotesquerie, farce and tragedy, lie side by side. A novel which reads like a cross between *The Pilgrim's Progress* and *Tales of the Genii*, where the little heroine mixes with dwarves and giants, where the child-like are parodied by the childish, where there are dead children and waxworks, where the

179

impulse towards Gothic historicity is continually displaced by the distorted figures of contemporary nightmare, where sexuality is everywhere apparent but nowhere stated. A novel, too, where there are constant references to wildness and to the wild.

There were other reports of a "wildness" attributed to Dickens, too, which seemed to have been passed around very quickly; that he had "fallen under the power of the demon Drink" and, most persistently, that he was mad and was undergoing treatment in an asylum. It is said that these reports of his madness originated from a joke about the raven which Dickens kept at Devonshire Terrace, a creature called Grip in whose attitudes and behaviour he took a keen interest. And, so the report goes, Landseer had said that Dickens was "raven mad". But this seems unlikely. It is more probable that the feverish pace which he maintained, as well as the usual rumours which surround someone already so celebrated as he, had crystallised into some easy formulation about insanity. That it was a serious report is not in doubt, since Dickens himself went to the unusual step of denying it in the preface which he was soon to write for *The Old Curiosity Shop*.

At Broadstairs he kept up the momentum of *The Old Curiosity Shop*, and one night as he walked along the cliffs he had a sudden vision of the stars reflected in the water and of "dead mankind a million fathoms deep" after the Flood. It was a vision which he placed within his story when Little Nell sees the same stars reflected in the river and then ". . . found new stars burst upon her view, and more beyond, and more beyond again, until the whole great expanse sparkled with shining spheres . . ." And all the time new images were crowding in upon him – images "in my mental Museum", he called them – images of the sea, of dreaming faces, of the road between Birmingham and Wolverhampton which he had travelled with Catherine and Forster at the beginning of the year, images of the mob, images of the pilgrimage of Little Nell and grandfather towards her death, wonderful images of the firewatcher who sits before the furnace of a factory. "It's my memory, that fire, and shows me all my life."

Images of sublimity, then, even as his own diurnal life continued. He was not feeling well; he was suffering from severe pain in his face, which he ascribed either to rheumatism or *tic douloureux*. Then, as soon as he returned from Broadstairs to London at the beginning of October, he discovered that the profits he had expected to accrue from *Master Humphrey's Clock* were not, after all, there; the expenses of producing what was a very handsome periodical were proving heavy. And he managed to contract a bad London cold – "I have been crying all day," he said. But of course tears could not stop him working. He was helping to supervise Frederick Yates's adaptation of *The Old Curiosity Shop* at the Adelphi, although he could not eventually bring himself to attend any of its performances. He was already planning to begin *Barnaby Rudge* in *Master Humphrey's Clock* immediately after the conclusion of the present novel. And he was "revolving" the general idea of *The Old Curiosity Shop*, bringing Little Nell to live by the old church, and foreshadowing her death. All the themes came together in these winter months of 1840: the interest in death, the pre-pubescent girl, the ruins of the old church all speaking of some time of innocence so unlike the industrial landscape of the Midlands through which his heroine had passed. Yet there can be no permanent innocence. The buildings must fall into ruins. The girl must die.

Indeed there was an aspect of his character which exulted in Little Nell's death – "I think it will come famously," he said in a letter in which he described his own grief. In fact there is no doubt that he deliberately worked himself up into a state of pity and holy terror in order to write of this death with the proper sympathy – that is why he had begun thinking once more of the death of Mary Hogarth, almost as if he were relishing the experience of the pain of loss. And then a strange reversal takes place, a reversal which is of considerable importance in understanding Dickens's own sense of his fiction. Clearly he needed to remember the pain of loss in order properly to describe the death of Little Nell – this is a familiar importation of life into art – but then, strangely, the art begins to affect the life. The very state which Dickens provokes in himself in order to write is transferred to the world so that, for a while, his heart actually becomes as open to real people as it does to his own creations. It was while he was killing Little Nell, for example, that he tried to resolve a quarrel between Forster and Ainsworth and gave his experience of writing *The Old Curiosity Shop* as the crucial reason why he was "sorry in my heart that men who really liked each other should waste life at arm's length".

Of course his own grief at the death of Little Nell was matched by the public response. It is always said that the crowds gathered on the harbour front of New York and asked the incoming passengers from across the Atlantic, "Is Little Nell dead?" The response at home was also very encouraging to Dickens; Little Nell was even compared to Cordelia, perhaps the first but certainly not the last occasion when the names of Dickens and Shakespeare were placed together. Lord Jeffrey was found in tears after reading the death scene, and Daniel O'Connell threw the book out of a railway window exclaiming, "He should not have killed her!", a complaint echoed by many others who sent letters to Dickens imploring him to avert that unhappy fate.

But what was it about the death of Little Nell which provoked such a response – such a significant reaction, in fact, that one later critic described it as "a movement in the history of modern sensibility"? Of course this is an exaggeration, and even at the time not everyone found the death-bed of Little Nell as moving as the author intended. There were many readers who disliked the "sentimentality" of the scene just as much as anyone in the latter part of the nineteenth century. But that it did have a marked effect upon others is not in doubt, and it is as if in the death of the virginal child there were many readers who lamented the death of their own innocence. Some of the feeling aroused might be seen, therefore, as a form of vicarious self-pity, which is surely the most potent form of emotionalism, then and now. But there is more to it than that. Dickens was lamenting the death of a child when the deaths of children in ordinary life were quite familiar; in 1839, for example, almost half of the funerals in London were conducted for children under the age of ten, carried off by sickness or malnutrition.

Yet despite its tragic element *The Old Curiosity Shop* is illuminated throughout by Dickens's wild humour, making light of the things that most closely touched him, parodying the very passions he could barely withstand. Above all, too, the sheer joy of invention and of creativity. Many years later – in fact only two years before his death – a friend found him reading the novel once more and "laughing immoderately" because the story of the sad pilgrimage reminded him of the circumstances in which the book was written. He had not forgotten the sorrow he felt when coming close to the death of Little Nell, but that sorrow is subsumed in a larger and more powerful burst of laughter. And at this point, perhaps, it is appropriate to consider the question of Dickens's own sentimentality, since it has often been assumed that the ready emotionalism in his fiction somehow spilled over into his own life. It has been reported that in *The Old Curiosity Shop* someone weeps about every tenth page, and in *Dombey and Son* Florence Dombey is calculated to have broken down in tears on eighty-eight separate occasions. (By the Fifties, however, the fashion for fictional tears somewhat abated and Dickens's characters remain much more firmly dry-eyed in his later books.) But Dickens himself was not inclined to weep, and it may be significant that he tended to shed tears only when reading books or watching action upon the stage.

After he had completed *The Old Curiosity Shop*, at four o'clock on a January morning, there were only a few extra editorial tasks he had to perform on the complete story in order to prepare it for the volume edition; he had to remove certain extraneous material concerning Master Humphrey himself, for example, and in the extra space provided he added a few paragraphs. It is interesting that at this point he adds a remark about the presence of "wild grotesque companions" around Little Nell and obliquely alludes to *The Pilgrim's Progress*; it is clear that both these elements of his art had occurred to him only as he was writing the story. In addition one perceptive reviewer had noticed a few months before the allegorical tendency of the story, and Dickens himself took up the hint by now saying of Little Nell that ". . . she seemed to exist in a kind of allegory". Thus it is that novelists come to understand what they have actually been doing. But once more, at the end of his labours, he found it difficult to break away from the characters he had invented, and can we not see his own reaction to this work completed in his recent description of Sir Christopher Wren regarding St Paul's: "I imagined him far more melancholy than proud, and looking with regret upon his labour done."?

Little time for regret in Dickens's case, however, since at once he turned his attention to that much-delayed story, *Barnaby Rudge*, which he had decided to serialise in *Master Humphrey's Clock* as soon as *The Old Curiosity Shop* had finished its run; it was the best way of maintaining the circulation of the periodical and, of course, the attention of his public. He had already written two chapters at the time of the abortive negotiations with Richard Bentley, and to give himself more room for manoeuvre he now added a few passages which turned the two chapters into three – enough material for two numbers of the magazine. But there were problems and distractions. Catherine was now expecting another child and, once again, she began to suffer from the illness or illnesses which had left her prostrate in the past. Dickens felt compelled to remain at her side, and for forty-eight hours got no sleep at all. There was also the difficulty of turning his mind to *Barnaby Rudge* when he had been so recently exhausted by Little Nell; but a few days later, as he told Forster, "I imaged forth a good deal of *Barnaby* by keeping my mind steadily upon him". He began writing on the twenty-ninth of January, just eight days after finally completing *The Old Curiosity Shop*, and managed to finish a third number of the new story. But he was restless. Even though Catherine was still in acute distress, he had to get out. He had to walk around. He went to see Forster at about ten in the evening, and rapped on his window with his stick; but his friend was out, and instead Dickens went on alone to the Parthenon Club where he met someone else and sat drinking gin and water till three in the morning. A few days later, on 8 February, his second son, Walter, was born; in the census return for this year Dickens described himself in the usual Victorian manner as "Gentleman", and declared that his household at Devonshire Terrace now consisted of one wife, four children, four maid-servants and one man-servant. He had come a long way from the Marshalsea.

At the end of the month the family went down to Brighton, largely in order to enable Dickens to work undisturbed on the new novel, and remained there for a week. On his return to London he suffered a small private loss. His pet raven, Grip, had died. He had always been fascinated by the bird, and followed its antics closely – comparing its clumsy run to that of a "playful cow", for example, in one of his touches of exact observation. The death provoked a series of facetious letters to his friends, wherein

185

Dickens expatiates upon the life and death of the bird: "On the clock striking twelve he appeared slightly agitated, but he soon recovered, walked twice or thrice along the coach-house, stopped to bark, staggered, exclaimed 'Halloa old girl' (his favourite expression) and died. He behaved throughout with a decent fortitude, equanimity, and self-possession, which cannot be too much admired." And so on and so forth; facetiousness was Dickens's one besetting vice. But there were also domestic affairs of a more troublesome kind. His family were still a burden upon him and would remain so for the rest of his life; he had just written a letter of recommendation for his brother, Alfred, who wished to begin a career in New Zealand as an engineer (he was in fact the only Dickens brother who made any kind of name for himself). But the real problem was with his father, since it was only now that Dickens realised that John Dickens had not only been continuing his wastrel ways in Devon but had also been forging his son's name, or using his son's name as a guarantor for certain debts. It is not difficult to imagine Dickens's reaction to this news; he had sent him down to Alphington precisely in order to avert this kind of fecklessness, but the terrible shadow of his parents — first glimpsed when they consigned him to the blacking factory so many years before — now once more threatened him. He took swift action, and placed an advertisement in all the leading London newspapers that "certain persons bearing, or purporting to bear, the surname of our said client" had been obtaining credit, and that Charles Dickens would not be responsible for any debts so incurred. It was the most public manner he could possibly contrive to distance himself from his father. He refused to speak to him personally, and demanded through his solicitors that John Dickens should leave England altogether and reside on a fixed stipend on the continent. In fact John Dickens, for reasons unknown, continued to live in Alphington with his wife but the whole

186

episode only served further to deepen the antagonism between father and son.

So it is not very surprising that the early episodes of *Barnaby Rudge*, upon which he now set to work again, should themselves be animated by conflicts between fathers and sons, and that the theme of filial rebellion is central to the development of the entire novel. Of course the novel had been with him now for five years, ever since he had first contracted to write it, and there is no doubt that its major public theme – the civil riots of 1780 – also continued to fascinate him. Much of the research had already been done; he had read the main historical narratives, and had even ranged further afield in the quest for accuracy and detail. His copy of Waterton's *Essays on Natural History* has pencil marks beside the chapter on ravens. But although *Barnaby Rudge* is an "historical novel" it is one, which, like all good historical novels, is actually concerned with its own time. His interest in the London mob which had rampaged through the streets of London and set fire to Newgate Prison, for example, must have been considerably increased by the fact that now in his own period Chartism and the Chartists seemed about to provoke civil rebellion of a similar kind. It must be remembered that the passage of the Reform Act in 1832 had not appreciably affected the vast body of wage-earners, who remained underpaid and unrepresented. 1837 had been a year of severe depression, not really alleviated until the end of the decade, and it was in such a climate that the disillusionment over the political reforms of 1832 emerged in the demands of "the Charter" – demands which included universal male suffrage, the secret ballot, the payment of Members of Parliament, the abolition of the property qualification for Members of Parliament, equal constituencies and annual elections. But these demands were in turn fuelled by popular hatred of the New Poor Laws, and by increasing public clamour for factory reform. Dickens clearly sympathised with the thrust of working-class grievances in regard to those last two elements, if not to the parliamentary demands, and it is equally clear that in his fiction he was attempting to put the case of those who felt themselves to have been actively neglected by "the system" in these recent difficult years.

And so as the story gradually took possession of him, he began his wanderings through London "searching for some pictures I wanted to build upon". He had always been interested in the historical essence of London, that deeply imbued spirit of dirt and misery with which he could bind his own past to that of the city itself, and in these first weeks of composing *Barnaby Rudge* he visited "the most wretched and distressful streets" to find images which could move him. He also went to see in prison a certain William Jones who had been charged with unlawfully entering Buckingham Palace and who was generally considered to be of "unsound mind"; on Dickens's visit, no doubt, he was unwittingly posing for Barnaby. In fact he entered gaols on at least two occasions in one week – another visit was to see a tailor, whose wits were considered to be "ricketty" and who once again might stand in for Barnaby as Dickens closely watched him. Watching as his own imagined character comes alive in front of him.

After he had completed the first three numbers he stopped for a week – he felt "lazy", he said – but then once more he began work upon it in earnest. There could never be any real repose for him. In any case the life of London never pressed so heavily upon him as when he was trying to write; there were constant dinners or gatherings and constant attempts to enlist him in the service of one cause or another. It was now, for example, that he was offered the candidature of MP for Reading, an offer he declined principally on the grounds that he could not afford the expense of running for parliament. In the meantime he busied himself with a project for establishing a

Sanatorium for the middle-classes, on a subscription basis. Such duties occupied too much of his time, however, and there is no doubt that he was both depressed (he admitted as much) and desperate to get away. So once more his thoughts turned to Broadstairs, and he opened negotiations for the rental of another house there for the summer; in the meantime he took up an invitation which had been proferred to him during the spring, a proposal that he should visit Edinburgh in order to be publicly welcomed and entertained there. He wrote back to a Scottish friend, ". . . I would not for the world reject any compliments they, or any of them, sought to offer me. Therefore I say, stop *nothing* . . ." in the way of dinners or ceremonies. He was also thinking of Catherine, whose native home was Scotland, and plans were quickly made for a visit of some three or four weeks. Once he had made the arrangements he was, as usual, very anxious to put them into effect as quickly as possible. ". . . I am on the highest crag of expectation," he wrote – while all the time composing as much as he could of *Barnaby Rudge* before he went away. And indeed he was working very fast upon it; at the beginning of June he finished four chapters within six days, on average about 2,300 words a day.

On 19 June he and Catherine left for Scotland, a journey both by the new railway and by road which took some three days. The first engagement of this tour was a public dinner to be given in his honour in Edinburgh which, as he said many years later, was "the first public recognition and encouragement I ever received . . ." It was in fact a striking occasion, one spectator noticing this "little, slender pale-faced, boyish-looking individual" arriving in the Waterloo Rooms to an extraordinary reception: "I felt as if the tremendous cheering which accompanied his entrance would overwhelm him." Another guest noticed his "cheeks shaven like those of a comedian, black stock surmounted by no collar, in accordance with the fashion of

189

the day, elaborate shirt front and general showy get-up". He dined at the top table, raised upon a platform, and himself noticed how odd it was that so young a man should be surrounded by so many elderly worthies who had come to honour him; "I felt it was very remarkable to see such a number of grey-headed men gathered about my brown flowing locks." Here was the man who had written *The Pickwick Papers*, *Nicholas Nickleby*, *Oliver Twist*, *The Old Curiosity Shop*; and he was not yet thirty years old. After the dinner was completed, Catherine Dickens and the other ladies arrived in the gallery to hear the speeches. Professor John Wilson, a remarkable writer under the name of Christopher North, rose to propose Dickens's health by saying that they had come "to honour one that has outstripped them all in the race", a sentiment which led to "great cheering", according to the newspaper reports; Wilson went on to talk of Dickens's "genius" and of his being "perhaps the most popular writer now alive".

In fact there was a sense in which he was now becoming public property. He was given the Freedom of the City of Edinburgh and when he made a chance entry into one of the theatres there "the whole audience rose spontaneously in recognition of him, the musicians in the orchestra, with a courtly felicity, striking up the cavalier air of 'Charley Is My Darling'". And yet, even as he wrote of his success, he wanted to return to the familiar ways of home and his friends. "For God's sake be in waiting," he told Forster when he mentioned the longed-for date of his return to Devonshire Terrace, yet another indication of the way in which Dickens craved for the comfort of what was essentially his extended family. One senses here in "For God's sake" his terrible appetite for affection even at this time of triumph. A time when he attended dinners and various receptions or parties in Edinburgh. A time for playing the part of the famous author. But no time for some things: it is odd that he did not bother to accompany Catherine when she visited the Edinburgh house in which she was born.

As soon as he returned to London in the middle of July, he at once began work on those scenes of riot that feature in *Barnaby Rudge*; he was writing very quickly, and managed to finish six chapters in twelve days before setting off for Broadstairs with the family. Once again his friends were invited to come and stay with them and, in a curious letter to Maclise, Dickens intimates that the painter might like to favour the prostitutes of Margate – "I know where they live". He himself confined his attentions to the novel. "I am in great heart and spirits with the story," he said, although this may have been just his own way of cheering himself up: he knew by now that the sales of *Master Humphrey's Clock* with the new novel had fallen markedly since the end of *The Old Curiosity Shop*, and were now running at something like 30,000 a week. In addition the magazine itself was so expensive to produce that there were still no real profits at all. That is no doubt why Chapman and Hall, publishers who had been signally generous to Dickens, were keen to discuss with him the possibility of a new novel, to be published in monthly parts and to begin in the spring of the following year; they knew that large sales, at least, could be expected from the old and tested formula. Dickens came up to London to discuss the matter with Forster; he was early as usual and, walking around Lincoln's Inn Fields, where Forster lived, he was suddenly seized by something which seems part inspiration and part fear. He suddenly had a vision of himself as a feeble and broken man: he seems always, in fact, to have had an irrational fear of incapacity, of going "dry". He had now been continually before the public for five years. He may even have considered the possibility that the low sale of *Barnaby Rudge* owed something to his own fatigue or over-familiarity. Whatever the cause, he decided there and then that it was time "to *stop* – to write no more, not one

191

word, for a whole year – and then to come out with a complete story in three volumes . . . and put the town in a blaze again". Of course the three-volume novel would be for him, at least, quite a new form: and almost at once the prospect invigorated Dickens. He explained his proposals to Forster who, acting as Dickens's intermediary even when Dickens was present, explained the plan to Chapman and Hall over dinner. The publishers were astonished, not least because Dickens wanted his year "off" to be financed in advance by them, even though he already owed them three thousand pounds over the purchase of his copyrights and contracts from Richard Bentley; but Dickens's will was not one that was easily brooked, and eventually, after some discussion, they agreed to the new proposals. They would pay Dickens another eighteen hundred pounds, in order to finance his year of idleness, and he would reward them with a story the following spring (in fact he realised soon after that it would be easier for him to revert to the old monthly numbers, written as the months went by, rather than compose a three-volume novel which would necessarily have to be completed during the preceding year). In other words, he had purchased a temporary freedom from his responsibilities but only at the cost of leaving himself heavily in debt to Chapman and Hall. But he was elated by that prospect of freedom, and went back to Broadstairs in something like a "holiday" mood even though he was still in the middle of writing *Barnaby Rudge*. "I have just burnt into Newgate," he told Forster – of that point in the narrative when the rioters storm the great prison – and then, a week later, "I have let all the prisoners out of Newgate . . . I feel quite smoky when I am at work." And no doubt his smokiness was increased by this sudden burst of vicarious radical anger. At times like these he *becomes* the rioters, and the scenes of burning London in the novel are some of the most extraordinary in all of his fiction. One can sense behind them

192

the eagerness of Dickens's research as if in his pursuit of the past he were also pursuing the secrets of his own mysterious self, just as one can sense in his furious prose the alacrity of his own long walks along the London thoroughfares which in his imagination were bathed in blood red. And yet, and yet . . . the prospect of a year's idleness was beginning to affect him; he was, he said, becoming "hideously lazy" and was only just finishing each instalment of *Barnaby Rudge* in time for the printer.

He was becoming preoccupied, too, with other matters since, for some time past, he had been revolving in his mind the idea of visiting America. Originally he had the idea of writing a series of essays for *Master Humphrey's Clock*, or perhaps a little book, on the subject of travels there; there were in these years no end of studies of American life by various English worthies, but no doubt Dickens thought that he might supply something of a novelty for that particular market. The idea had remained with him, and a fulsome letter of tribute from the American writer, Washington Irving, seems to have been the deciding factor – Irving told him that ". . . if I went, it would be such a triumph from one end of the States to the other, as was never known in any Nation". But there were problems, chief among them being Catherine who did not want to go, and who certainly did not want to leave the children behind. Walter, after all, was a still only a baby of nine months. She "cries dismally" every time Dickens mentioned the subject. But he was not a man to let family considerations stand in his way and by the nineteenth of September, only six days after he had broached the plan with Forster, he had finally decided to go. At once he fell into the "stir and bustle of anticipation" which always preceded the enactment of any plans he made; "he was in his usual fever," Forster wrote, "until its difficulties were disposed of." The major difficulty, at this juncture, still being Catherine. She still remained to be convinced, and he asked Macready, who had travelled to America on just such a tour as he was planning, to write to her and to reassure her. Dickens was still not sure if he should take the children, and all these preliminary problems "to a gentleman of my temperament, destroy rest, sleep, appetite, and work, unless definitely arranged". Somehow or other, Catherine was brought round to agreement; no doubt Dickens's own fevered impatience and impetuosity carried her in the direction she did not really want to travel. For in his own mind the trip had become "a matter of imperative necessity" and not even the tears of his wife could affect it. It was agreed that the children should remain in London, under the care of his brother, Fred, and that Anne Brown, Catherine's maid, should accompany her across the Atlantic. In fact Catherine was eventually able to face the prospect with more equanimity, although even now Dickens did not tell her precisely how long they would be away. Perhaps this was because there were times when she was still uneasy – "I have seen her *looking* (very hard) at the Sea, but she has *said* nothing." It should be noted at this point that it was he who persuaded her to leave behind the children, despite the insinuations he would make against his wife in later and more troubled years. But, even as he was impatiently making his plans for America, he was in his imagination anticipating his return from that country to the delights of home and the arms of his friends. He told Forster at the end of September, three months even before he sailed, "I am already counting the days between this and coming home again." How *odd*, as his friends would no doubt have said.

Just before finally returning to London from Broadstairs, he set off for a short visit to Rochester with Forster and Catherine but, while there, began to feel the agonising pains which heralded the onset of a fistula – a gap in the rectal wall through which tissue had been forced. He had suffered from rectal pains just recently, ascribing them to the fact that he spent much of his day sitting at his desk, and seems to be recollecting them in a short passage of *Barnaby Rudge* which he wrote in Broadstairs, where the sleeper's consciousness of pain is described as "a phantom without shape, or form, or visible presence; pervading everything . . ." The pain had now grown worse; he went back to London with Catherine, and three or four days later endured an operation at the hands of Frederick Salmon, a surgeon famous for his work in that area of the human body: thirteen years before he had published *A Practical Essay on Stricture of the Rectum*. The fact that he was in capable and experienced hands did not of course minimise the pain of the operation.

Dickens, now, was assiduously studying for his trip. He had something like twenty-seven different American guide books and, when he was interviewed by an American journalist some weeks before his departure, the reporter noticed that "his study was piled with Marryat's, Trollope's, Fidler's, Hall's, and other travels and descriptions of America, and blazed with highly-coloured maps of the United States . . ." Of these bright maps the novelist made a typically Dickensian remark: "I could," he said, "light my cigar against the red-hot State of Ohio." Nevertheless the last month of 1841, the month before the departure of Dickens and his wife, was a very quiet one. He had finished the novel, of course, and had wound up Master Humphrey's clock, and now dined out with friends and relatives. The last week in particular he wished to spend with his children, who would not see their parents for another six months, but he also paid farewell calls upon Macready and other friends. These must have been difficult interviews for him because he had a rooted distaste for saying "Goodbye" to anyone, even those closest to him; this may have been part of his own emotional reserve on the most deeply felt occasions but it suggests, also, that

195

fear of estrangement and separation which he had experienced so deeply in his younger days.

Then on the second day of the new year, 1842, in company with Forster, together with Dickens's siblings Alfred and Fanny, Charles and Catherine Dickens left London for Liverpool. They were to sail on the *Britannia*, a steamship of some 1,154 tons and capable of carrying 115 passengers. In *American Notes*, the book about his travels which even now he was contemplating, Dickens conjures up an animated scene at their departure. "Three cheers more: and as the first one rings upon our ears, the vessel throbs like a strong giant that has just received the breath of life; the two great wheels turn fiercely round for the first time; and the noble ship, with wind and tide astern, breaks proudly through the lashed and foaming water." Charles Dickens was on his way to America.

# *Thirteen*

I T was not an easy journey. A fellow traveller made a
sketch of Dickens on the deck of the *Britannia*; he
seems to be wearing some kind of cap and his hands are
plunged deep into the pocket of his overcoat; he looks
somewhat woebegone. And well he might. He always suffered greatly from sea-sickness, until in later life he literally
willed himself to withstand its effects, and for the first two
days he stayed in his cabin. The sea remained rough and
then, five days out, the little steamship was caught up in
a mighty storm – "Picture the sky both dark and wild, and
the clouds, in fearful sympathy with the waves, making
another ocean in the air." This is from Dickens's own
account in *American Notes*, and he went on to say of the
*Britannia*, ". . . she stops, and staggers, and shivers, as
though stunned, and then, with a violent throbbing at her
heart, darts onwards like a monster goaded into madness,
to be beaten down, and battered, and crushed, and leaped
on by the angry sea . . ." Perhaps these passages owe
something to his own childhood reading of travellers'
adventures but, even though other passengers' recollections of the same journey are not so fearsome, there is no
doubt that there was a terrible storm which might, just
might, have killed them. Catherine "was nearly distracted
with terror", as she herself wrote, "and don't know what

I should have done had it not been for the great kindness and composure of my dear Charles".

Their destination was Boston and as soon as the ship had reached its berth a group of editors and journalists rushed on board in order to see and to interview Dickens; he was still dressed in his pea-coat and, when Catherine gently remonstrated with him about changing clothes, he replied that such formalities did not matter now that they had reached "the other side". At once he was grabbed, his hand shaken, his comments taken down, his appearance scrutinised, until he could be rescued by Francis Alexander, an artist for whom Dickens had agreed to sit, and taken to the Tremont House Hotel. One of the many people waiting to see and to greet him noticed how he "flew up the steps of the hotel, and sprang into the hall. He seemed all on fire with curiosity, and alive as I never saw mortal before." Then, when he entered the lobby, he greeted the curious bystanders with the old pantomime phrase: "Here we are!" He dined that evening in the hotel with the Earl of Mulgrave, who had also been a passenger on the *Britannia*, and then at about midnight on a bright cold night he went out with him into the streets of Boston. A boy, who was later to become a great friend of Dickens, James Fields, was one among a number of people who watched and followed Dickens in his first visit to the town; he records how he was "muffled up in a shaggy fur coat" and "ran over the shining frozen snow . . . Dickens kept up one continual shout of uproarious laughter as he went rapidly forward, reading the signs on the shops, and observing the 'architecture' of the new country into which he had dropped as if from the clouds."

The first important public event for Dickens in America was the dinner given to him by the "Young Men of Boston" on the first evening of February. Not the first public dinner in his honour (Edinburgh, as we have seen,

198

had had that privilege) and certainly not the last, but in some ways typical of a nineteenth-century social entertainment which had become something of an institution. For this was a lengthy affair; it began at about five in the evening and continued till one in the morning and, beside the meal itself, there were long speeches punctuated by songs, comic or otherwise, so that the whole occasion had something of the gaiety of a stage performance. The president of the occasion rose at one point to greet their guest and remarked how "a young man has crossed the ocean with no hereditary title, no military laurels, no princely fortune, and yet his approach is hailed with pleasure by every age and condition . . ." This emphasis upon Dickens's unaristocratic if not exactly lowly origin marked precisely the bond which he hoped to form with the United States, and in his speech in turn Dickens emphasised what might be called the democratic or egalitarian aspects of his particular genius. "I believe," he said, "that Virtue shows quite as well in rags and patches as she does in purple and fine linen." In other words, he was setting himself up as an unofficial laureate of the nation and its beliefs; there is no doubt that at this stage, fêted on all sides, he felt some *consonance* with this new country. Yet it was not to last, and there were warning signals already when in this first major speech he touched upon the question of international copyright, by politely alluding to the fact that his work and that of other British authors was being generally pirated by American publishers and American magazines without any recompense being paid. He did not mention the subject before his visit, but the fact that he raised it so soon suggests that it had been very much on his mind; later he was indignantly to deny that it was the primary reason for his visit to America, but the very fact that he did not mention the subject in advance to anyone might only suggest that the prospect of earning more money from his American sales was one that he was wary of

199

mentioning for fear of seeming mercenary. Certainly it was not the message which the Americans wished to hear from the great young novelist.

In his account of Boston in *American Notes*, Dickens does not remark upon his own reception but instead dwells upon the case of Laura Bridgman, a deaf, dumb and blind girl whom he had encountered at a Boston institute for the blind; how strange, perhaps, that at this time of his greatest triumph (for nothing in England had ever equalled the treatment he was receiving in the United States) he should revert to the plight of a young girl struggling towards communication from the depths of her entombed spirit. In his speeches, also, he referred frequently to the sorrows of Little Nell. It is almost as if in this royal progress he felt it necessary to keep a quiet heart by sympathising or identifying with the plight of a suffering child. A child, he liked to think, as he had been.

In fact *American Notes*, and much of his own travels through the United States, are largely concerned with what might be called the mournful institutions of American life; the asylums, the workhouses, the prisons, the orphanages, the blind institutes. Of course this was not uncommon in other travellers' accounts of America; in this new age when the role of the state and social provision was being endlessly debated, public institutions of all kinds were at the centre of contemporary argument. Indeed, in a period of social transition, such places were almost the touchstone of national progress. In England eighteenth-century attitudes towards various forms of governmental control, in prisons and asylums in particular, were only gradually being displaced by the sometimes more "stream-lined" and sometimes more humane methods of the radicals and utilitarians. But in America the experiment had as it were started from the beginning and, in the accounts which Dickens wrote of the Boston institutions in particular, it is clear that he believed himself to be witnessing a much more effective and modern form of public care. He had seen the future here, and it worked.

They had been in Boston for two weeks, and on Saturday, 5 February they took the three o'clock train for Worcester; it is reported by several witnesses how crowds waited along the line to get a glimpse of "Boz"; even as the train was moving in or out of the station heads would be thrust through the window with the enquiry "Is Mr Dickens here?", and at each station the crowds surged towards the train in order to catch a glimpse of the famous novelist. They spent Saturday and Sunday in Worcester, their time now filled by the characteristic dinner parties and levées. It was here that the Governor of the state, when discussing the Bostonians with Dickens, enquired, "Did they sound *hash* to you?" By which he meant, did their accent sound disagreeable? Dickens replied, "I beg your pardon. What did you say?" It took time for a translation to be given to him, but in that question – "What did you say?" – one can hear an echo of Dickens's fascination with American speech which was at once so familiar and so alien to him. He noted how "Possible?" was used as a mere habit of reply; how "Yes?" was also used as a simple interrogative; how "Where do you hail from?" meant "Where were you born?" Dickens had a wonderful ear for the quirkiness of speech – phonetic analysis of Cockney speech in the 1830s suggests how accurate and natural the conversations of Sam Weller would have read to a native Londoner – and he stored up all of these Americanisms for use at a later date. But even at the time he could not resist imitating it, and in one letter to Forster managed to include a number of words and phrases which were quintessentially "Yankee" – ". . . it does use you up complete, and that's a fact . . ."

Eventually they reached New York, which fascinated Dickens; from his hotel-room on Broadway he could see a scene almost like any in London but somehow with more vivacity, more animation, more colour than in his own city. Here were omnibuses, hackney cabs, coaches, phaetons, but among them all the pigs which wandered through the city. Pineapples and water-melons on display. Bowling saloons. Ten-pin alleys. Oyster bars in basements. The ladies with their brightly coloured dresses. The hum. The stench. The sheer momentum of the city. It was an energy and display which he was soon to experience at first-hand, in fact, since the great coming event here was the "Boz Ball" to be held in the Park Theatre. The theatre itself had been turned into a ball-room with chandeliers and drapes and candelabra; the walls had been covered in white muslin and punctuated by large medallions representing each one of Dickens's novels; and in the centre was a portrait of Dickens with a laurel crown hovering over his head in the grip of an eagle. The stage had been extended, turned into a Gothic set and, in front of some three thousand people and between dances, there were tableaux vivants representing scenes from his fiction. In fact Dickens seemed to thoroughly enjoy this extraordinary tribute, dancing until he and his wife were so tired that they slipped out and went quietly back to their hotel. Now, at last, he had really seen the *éclat* of his fame.

But he became sick; he retired to bed with a sore throat, and stayed within his hotel for the next three days. How much this was genuine illness, and how much the need simply to rest, is not clear. Certainly, despite his conviviality and his need for friendship and love, he was in many respects an utterly private and enclosed man. He needed time alone; time for writing, of course, but also time for the kind of self-communing through which, as he said, he was able "to understand my own feelings the better". The isolated child was also the isolated man and he needed that isolation, however temporary it was; he hugged it to him as if in its enclosure he might remain true to himself. But here he had obtained no rest and no privacy; "everything public, and nothing private," he exclaimed. He hated, it was reported, "giving himself up as a spectacle". One of his great fears, as we shall see in later accounts of his dreams and imaginings, was of becoming an *object* in the world, one bead among thousands of beads on the great chain, one strand among many strands, one thing among many things. But this was what was happening to him now. When he arrived at any railway station the crowds peered in the window at him "with as much coolness as if I were a Marble image". There were other indignities. "If I turn into the street, I am followed by a multitude. If I stay at home, the house becomes, with callers, like a fair . . . I go to a party in the evening, and am so inclosed and hemmed about by people, stand where I will, that I am exhausted for want of air. I dine out, and have to talk about everything, to everybody . . . I can't get out at a station, and can't drink a glass of water, without having a hundred people looking down my throat when I open my mouth to swallow."

Of course no one could have had such a reception, even allowing for the uncomfortable aspects, without being in some way moved by it. "They are friendly," he said of the people, "earnest, hospitable, kind, frank, very often accomplished, far less prejudiced than you would suppose, warm-hearted, fervent, and enthusiastic . . . when they conceive a perfect affection for a man (as I may venture to say of myself), entirely devoted to him . . . The State is a parent to its people; has a parental care and watch over all poor children, women labouring of child, sick persons, and captives." And he made friends on this visit who would remain attached to him for the rest of his life and with whom he had the closest relations. There was Charles Sumner, one of the leaders of the anti-slavery faction; David Cadwallader Colden, a philanthropist; Jonathan Chapman, the Whig Mayor of Boston. In particular he struck up a close friendship with Cornelius Felton, who was Professor of Greek at Harvard University. This was not the kind of friend he made in England but Felton was quite different from his English counterparts; he was the son of poor parents who, like Dickens himself, had made his way in the world through effort and industry. These were the kinds of Americans he most liked – Bostonian (except for Colden, who was a New Yorker), "self-made" men, liberal, courteous, magnanimous.

On 5 March they travelled from New York to Philadelphia. Dickens was determined to make no more public engagements, though this was forestalled by the always eager and determined attitudes of his putative hosts. A local politician had visited them after their arrival, and asked if he could introduce the famous author to a few friends; Dickens assented, no doubt somewhat wearily, and in the next day's newspapers there was an announcement that he would "receive the public" at a specified time. In his own account, Putnam describes how "at the time specified the street in front was crowded with people, and the offices and halls of the hotel filled". Dickens was indignant but, informed that a refusal on his part would now provoke a riot, agreed to meet everyone; he stationed himself in the hotel parlour and for the next two hours shook the hands of a steady stream of Philadelphians. One journalist noticed that he simply "shook the proffered hand feebly, and let it fall", although Putnam himself remembers how "the humorous smiles played over his face . . . the thing had its *comic* side".

From Philadelphia he and Catherine travelled on to Washington. From this time forward, his resolution to travel merely as a private citizen was to a certain extent maintained; press reports about him became scarcer after this date, also, although that may simply be due to the evident fact that his "novelty value" had by now all but vanished. But of course there were many who had not yet met the distinguished stranger; he was taken to visit

President Tyler, for example, who on seeing Dickens remarked, "I am astonished to see so young a man, Sir." He also attended the President's levée where, once again, he became the main object of attention; when he moved among the guests, according to one report, it had the same effect as corn thrown before chicken. It was while he attended a private dinner in the capital that news came of the arrival of long-awaited letters from England: he left the dinner as soon as he decently could, and rushed back to the hotel. Catherine was waiting for his arrival before she opened the letters, which demonstrates how submissive or self-sacrificing she could be, and together they read them until two in the morning.

It was now that their real travels in America began. From Washington they travelled to Richmond; in particular Dickens wanted to visit the tobacco plantations there, and to see a "slave state" in action. From Richmond they travelled back to Washington. From Washington to Baltimore. Then, from Baltimore the Dickenses travelled on the mail coach to Harrisburg – what he thought to be a parcel on the roof of the coach turned out to be a small boy who, observing the heavy rain that was falling as they made their way, remarked to Dickens, "Well now, stranger, I guess you find this, a'most like an English a'ter-noon, hey?" Dickens liked small boys, although he often pretended not to, and adds in his letter on the incident, "I thirsted for his blood." And then across a wooden bridge, roofed over, for more than a mile, with all its echoes and its rumblings, so that it seemed to Dickens to be like a journey in a dream. From Harrisburg onto the canal boat which was to take them to Pittsburgh – in frowsy and dirty shared sleeping quarters where all the men spat and where no one washed except, of course, Dickens and his party. "I make no complaints, and shew no disgust. I am looked upon as highly facetious at night, for I crack jokes with everybody near me until we fall asleep."

Then Pittsburgh, where once more he was surrounded and hemmed in and bothered and bewildered by callers both expected and unforeseen. Anne Brown and George Putnam were stationed at the door of his hotel room, to take cards and to announce each visitor in turn. He held one conversation in the course of which an American apologised for his seeing the country under such unfavourable circumstances with "commerce and manufacture destroyed, credit paralysed and spirits of people depressed in a corresponding degree". This was something which interested him for two days later, in a letter to Macready, he made much the same point – "Look at the exhausted Treasury; the paralyzed government; the unworthy representatives of a free people . . ." It was in Pittsburgh, too, that he encountered an Englishman he had known many years ago in London; he had failed in business and was now a portrait painter, and such was the hospitality of Dickens that he dined with them for each of the three days they remained in the city.

Then onwards again. Dickens having arranged this tour so that they were almost continually moving, they went now by steamboat down the Ohio River to Cincinnati. From Cincinnati they continued by boat to Louisville, and then on to the farthest extension of their journey, down the turbid Mississippi to St Louis. Then back by steamboat to Cincinnati; then on from that city to Columbus in a stage-coach, Dickens taking his favourite seat on the box with the driver. By now Dickens he had seen all that he really needed to see (although there were to be two or three small outings later), had more than enough material for the travel-book he intended to write, and was now relaxing into a broadly comic mood brought on by the imminent end of their American journey and the prospect of their return home. Already he had arranged to travel back across the Atlantic by sail rather than by steam, and their passages were booked on the *George Washington*.

But first they visited Niagara where Dickens eagerly awaited the sound or the sight of the Falls; Nature in its more gigantic forms always appealed to his imagination. Then, as they arrived at the station, he saw "two great white clouds rising up from the depths of the earth". All at once he was frantic to see it, and immediately he ran off to the ferry which took travellers to the very Falls themselves. "I dragged Kate down a deep and slippery path leading to the ferry boat; bullied Anne for not coming fast enough; perspired at every pore . . .", as if he himself were like the waterfall, the sweat pouring from him. Once on the boat he saw what it was: blinded by spray, deafened by the roar, he was close enough to see more than that "vague immensity" which at first he had glimpsed. Then he rushed to the inn where they were to stay for the next few days, changed his clothes and hurried out again to see the phenomenon; this time he went down into the basin and looked up at the cascading waters. "There was a bright rainbow at my feet; and from that I looked up to – great Heaven! to *what* a fall of bright green water . . ." Here he felt at peace again, that peace of wonder and self-communing which had been snatched from him in America. No more crowds. No more levées. No more curious spectators watching him, noting him, writing about him. Here was "Beauty, unmixed with any sense of Terror" and "Peaceful Eternity" and as he gazed upon it, as he continued to gaze upon it over the ten days they remained here, he began to recover that sense of his inner life which had been denied him on his travels. And here, once more, he thought of the dead girl, Mary Hogarth. Her image was presented to him in this other image of the eternal, and there can be very little doubt that he did truly believe her to be a "spirit" looking down upon him from some place of eternal repose. All these images and associations sanctified Niagara Falls for him, and so his anger was compounded when he read in the visitors' books various facetious or indelicate expressions from those who had visited the spot before. "If I were a despot," he wrote, "I would force these Hogs to live for the rest of their lives on all Fours, and to wallow in filth expressly provided for them by Scavengers, . . . every morning they should each receive as many stripes [whippings] as there are letters in their detestable obscenities." Which, if nothing else, is an apt indication of the kind of anger to which Dickens could on occasions be roused.

At the end of the month they travelled back south again to New York. They were within a week of their departure and, to pass the time now already filled with so much anticipation, they made an excursion up the Hudson River for one last look at another part of the country. They visited a "Shaker" community, part of a religious sect for which Dickens apparently had nothing but contempt; he was never a devotee of the more extreme forms of religious worship, and the Shakers impressed him as nothing so much as irresponsible or depressing bores. "I so abhor," he wrote later in *American Notes*, "and from my soul detest that bad spirit, no matter by what class or sect it may be entertained, which would strip life of its healthful graces, rob youth of its innocent pleasures, pluck from maturity and age their pleasant ornaments . . ." And what he seems to have noticed among them, too, was their hypocrisy and their cant – in that respect his reaction against them was part of his general reaction against America itself. Certainly it is no coincidence that his next novel would be primarily concerned with that theme, since there was no other aspect of human behaviour which struck him more forcibly in all these months of travelling. Cant everywhere. Cant in the newspapers. Cant from the self-styled leaders of public opinion. Cant from the businessmen. And did he now, having at first identified himself with this new world, sense a certain amount of hypocrisy also within himself?

But at last the day had come. On 7 June, 1842, he had

208

breakfast with some of his more steadfast American friends; then he and Catherine embarked upon the *George Washington* in order to begin their voyage home. They had taken various mementoes with them – amongst them two American rocking chairs, of which Dickens became especially fond, and a small white spaniel whom he christened "Timber Doodle" just as if he had trotted from the pages of one of his own novels. Dickens had chosen to come back by sail rather than steam because he feared drowning by water much less than he feared death by fire; as a result, the journey home had few of the terrors which had afflicted them on board the *Britannia*. By Dickens's account it was a pleasant and uneventful crossing; he organised a facetious little club, called the United Vagabonds, and entertained himself with various games of whist, chess, cribbage, backgammon and shovel-board. But he noticed, too, the poor passengers who kept "below decks" in their own "little world of poverty", and he took pains to find out from some of them their histories as they sailed on to England. Home. Dickens was leaving behind a country which, despite the friends he had made there and the progressive state institutions he had visited, he seems to have viewed with little emotion other than contempt. In fact his dislike intensified even as he returned to England; no doubt reflecting, all the while, upon the way he was treated both by those idle crowds who had watched him and by those newspapers which had attacked him. What had he found in that country? Everywhere business and money, money and business, coarseness of manner and a dismal concern with commerce. More enlightened penal and social policies, certainly, but no humour. No laughter. And newspaper politics; it was the newspapers which had attacked him, and it was with the newspapers that he was primarily indignant. In that sense he suffered a sea-change on the journey back from America and, even though it is unlikely that he reflected

209

upon his own identity in any general sense, it is quite clear that he returned to England a very different person, a very different writer, from the one who had so eagerly embarked at Liverpool six months before. He had taken everything for granted before – England, his own success, his political radicalism – but his experience of the United States opened his eyes to the particular nature of all those things which characterised him and which gave him life. Dickens's American journey had truly been a journey towards himself.

# *Fourteen*

IN the early morning of Wednesday, 29 June, 1842, the *George Washington* docked at Liverpool. Charles and Catherine Dickens had come home. They returned to London by train and then in the evening arrived at Osnaburgh Street, where Fred and the children were staying. Mamie Dickens, who was then four years old, remembers a hackney coach coming up to the door and "before it could stop, a figure jumped out, someone lifted me up in their arms, and I was kissing my father through the bars of the gate". The shock of their sudden arrival – they had not been expected until the next day – sent Charlie into convulsions; Dr Elliotson was called at once, and the boy quickly recovered. He was "too glad", he said and some time before had told the washerwoman (his "confidential friend", as Dickens described her) that he would "shake very much" when his parents returned. But there was also Dickens's extended family to visit. He went straight to Macready's house, hurried in and before Macready could see who it was found "dear Dickens holding me in his arms in a transport of joy". Then Dickens rushed off to see Forster at his house in Lincoln's Inn Fields – but he had gone out to dinner. Dickens found out where he was dining and sent a message by servant to tell him "that a gentleman wanted to speak to him". But Forster realised who it was, came out of the house, jumped into the carriage and began to cry. So much for the sternness and masculine reticence of the "Victorians".

They moved back to Devonshire Terrace the day after their arrival, with all the domestic upheaval which this entailed, and it seems that from this time forward Catherine's younger sister, Georgina, came to live with her sister and brother-in-law in order to help with the children. She became a sort of unofficial governess, known after a time as "Aunt Georgie". She was eager, punctilious, and helpful; indeed, what young woman would not have tried to impress a famous brother-in-law, leading a life so much more glamorous than any she had known before? More importantly, perhaps, she came to the Dickens household at the age of fourteen and thus was only a little younger than Mary Hogarth when Dickens first knew her; it seems, in fact, that at once he noticed a resemblance between the two girls: ". . . so much of her spirit shines out in this sister," he wrote of Mary, "that the old time comes back again at some seasons, and I can hardly separate it from the present." Was this one of the reasons why Dickens invited Georgina to join his family? If so, there is no cause to suppose that Catherine, at this stage, disapproved of such a decision.

Such was the energy of Dickens himself that immediately after his return he launched into several projects at once; he composed a long circular on the absence of copyright in America and sent it to various writers, and at the same time wrote a letter to the *Examiner* in which he publicly declared that he would never sign a publishing contract with an American firm (a promise which he did not in fact keep). He also became marginally involved in a scheme for a Union or Guild of writers, a project which at this time came to nothing but which he would revive with more success at a later date. Then a few weeks later he wrote a long letter to the *Examiner*, supporting the provisions of Lord Ashley's Mines and Collieries Bill, which

212

was about to prohibit the employment of women and children in the mines. It is indicative of his real politics, however, that he attacks the aristocratic owners of the mines (in particular the vacuous Lord Londonderry) rather than the industrial civilisation which depended upon them. He signed it merely "B", for "Boz", but all those who knew him recognised who the writer was. Clearly he was troubled by the idea of children being involved in such a dangerous and dirty trade (did he remember his own time in the blacking factory as he wrote this eloquent condemnation of the aristocratic mill-owners who were trying to defeat the Bill?) but clearly, also, he had come back from America with a greater awareness of his own fame and a greater sense of his power as a public figure.

Within two weeks, he had also begun work on an account of his travels which he finally entitled *American Notes for General Circulation*. He had gone there with the idea of writing such a book, and there was no reason to believe that it would not achieve a high sale; and, if there was one thing he needed now, it was money. Money to help pay back the debt to Chapman and Hall. Money to support his ever-enlarging family. Money to support his spendthrift father and younger brothers who seemed incapable of making their own way. And so, with the images of the New World fresh in his mind, he began. His opening chapter was a salvo directed against what he anticipated to be a hostile American reception; he read this to Macready almost as soon as he had written it, but the actor was not impressed by Dickens's excessively defiant and almost hostile tone. "*I do not like it,*" Macready wrote in his diary and in fact, at Forster's instigation, Dickens later and reluctantly dropped the offending chapter from the published book. Of course accounts of American travels by English notables were not at all rare phenomena: in *The Pickwick Papers*, the elder Weller is heard to say of Mr Pickwick: ". . . let him come back and write a book about the 'Merrikins as'll pay all his expenses and more, if he blows 'em up enough." If Dickens did not exactly blow them up, he certainly rocked them a little.

In fact *American Notes* was in many ways a serious discourse on the nature of American society and American institutions in particular, and by far the most controversial and topical aspects of the book concerned the regime of prisons in America. The country was considered by many to be a leader in penal reform, and in particular English penal experts were interested in the "Separate System" which Dickens had seen in Philadelphia and which was about to be introduced at the new "model prison" of Pentonville. The alternative penal method was known as the "Silent System" which was more purely punitive in character; prisoners worked on the treadmill, or picked oakum, while rigid silence was maintained. Dickens infinitely preferred the latter system. He believed the "model prisons" to be too lenient to their inmates and extolled instead the virtues of hard and unrewarding labour. Certainly he preferred a regime which relied more upon punishment than upon moral improvement; ". . . it is a satisfaction to me," he wrote some years later, "to see that determined thief, swindler or vagrant, sweating profusely at the treadmill or the crank."

Almost as soon as they had returned to England, he and Catherine were planning to make what had now become an annual visit to Broadstairs, and on the first day of August they set off with the children to that resort which in a fake legal deposition Dickens described now as a "seaside dipping, bathing, or watering-place". They were back in a house on Albion Street, along the front and facing the sea, and it was here that Dickens began the fifth chapter of *American Notes*. Throughout the whole of this summer he kept up a steady pace of a chapter a week, his own antagonism towards America, and to the American press in particular, being refreshed by the publication of a faked letter purporting to come from him and in which he attacked friends and enemies alike. It was a clumsy forgery, but the interest in the scandalous Boz was enough to place it on several American front pages. Dickens sent off a series of angry letters to his American friends denouncing this fake, but there was little action he could take except, perhaps, to direct his anger into his writing. It is notable that in the chapter he began to write after he had been informed of the forged letter he dwells once more with some disgust upon the American habit of spitting in all places and on all occasions. And yet even as he was writing *American Notes* he was turning over in his mind the possibilities for a new novel. According to his contract with Chapman and Hall it was to begin in November, but at this stage he seems to have had no clear idea of the direction in which he wanted to move.

Dickens had almost finished *American Notes* by the time the family returned to London at the beginning of October; he had only two chapters to write and, for the first of them, he simply reprinted a number of newspaper cuttings to give his readers some idea of the horrors of slavery in the Southern states. The last chapter, an odd mixture of exhortation and comic observation, was also written hurriedly, and this principally because Dickens's time was taken up by an unexpected visitor in the shape of Henry Wadsworth Longfellow. There had been other interruptions. William Hone, a radical author and compiler of miscellanies, was dying and asked for him on his death-bed. Dickens knew him as a friend and collaborator of George Cruikshank, but it seems that Hone had recently been reading nothing but Dickens's novels and wanted to shake hands with the author before he died; a touching last request and one which Dickens could hardly refuse. So great was his power that even those leaving the world wanted to see and to thank him. So he visited the dying man in the company of Cruikshank. And then, that same night, Longfellow arrived unexpectedly at Devonshire Terrace. Dickens had met and liked the man in the United States and, in his usual impetuous and convivial manner, had invited him to stay with him on his next journey to London; and now he was here. "I write this from Dickens's study," he told a compatriot. "The raven croaks in the garden; and the ceaseless roar of London fills my ears." Longfellow was just five years older than Dickens and at this time not particularly well known in England as a poet. No doubt that is why Dickens referred to him as "the American Professor" – he had been Professor of Modern Languages and Belles Lettres at Harvard since 1836 – but he also called him "the best of the American Poets" and admired the three volumes of poetry which Longfellow had published. So for the next two weeks he became his guide, host and social secretary; there were trips to the theatre, breakfasts and dinners with a variety of friends, visits to the available literary grandees, excursions to the country (Rochester, of course, and Bath, to visit Landor). He also took Longfellow on a tour of the "rookeries" or slums of London, to see how the vagrant and indigent population of the city managed to survive in the narrow alleys, courts and passages of the poorer quarters. There are times, in fact, when Dickens's nocturnal expeditions seem indistinguishable from his trips to the London Zoological Gardens or to Astley's, where other forms of entertainment were also guaranteed. Forster and Maclise went with them on this particular expedition to a lodging house in an area of the Borough known as The Mint: the usual stench emanated from the place and Maclise "was struck with such a sickness on entering" that he had to remain outside with the policemen who were guarding them in this area of theft and vice.

Of course Dickens was more accustomed to the odours of the poor, since part of his knowledge of London came from his journeys into its interior where thousands of people lived in close-packed rookeries or jerry-built tenements without ventilation or sanitation. But familiarity did not breed neglect. He was never anything other than appalled by what he saw, as all were who ventured into what for most respectable nineteenth-century citizens was unknown and forbidden territory. And he knew, too, how dangerous in every sense such places were. Westminster, Southwark, Bermondsey, Whitechapel, Rotherhithe, St Giles, a world within a world. Dickens had been reading Edwin Chadwick's *Report on the Sanitary Condition of the Labouring Population*; not a document for the squeamish, Chadwick himself being a social reformer of the direct, Benthamite breed who never allowed propriety to interfere with his good intentions. Indeed it was after reading Chadwick's report that he emphasised the importance of sanitary reform in the last and hurriedly written chapter of *American Notes*. We shall see at a later date how a number of important themes rise up from this sanitary activity and find their place in Dickens's novels but it is important to note here that, from the beginning, he was deeply concerned with the most important reform activity of the day – the reform of public health.

For London was growing too fast. The "Great Oven", as Dickens sometimes called it, was spreading through Bloomsbury, Islington, and St John's Wood in the North and, in the West and South, through Paddington, Bayswater, South Kensington, Lambeth, Clerkenwell and Peckham. The population of London at the beginning of the nineteenth century was something like one million but, by the end, it had reached four and a half million; in the 1840s alone it has been estimated that there was a net migration into the city of some quarter of a million people. One survey of the Forties found that, in the area of St Giles, the rookery close to the Seven Dials and immortalised by Hogarth in 'Gin Lane', 2,850 people were crowded into just 95 small and decrepit houses. It was not unusual for

217

families of seven or eight people to inhabit one room. And we must not see London as the city so familiar today; much of *that* was a later development of the Victorians themselves who, by the closing years of the century, had transformed whole areas of the metropolis.

Disease spread like a stain. There were four epidemics of cholera within Dickens's own lifetime and, beside these mortal visitations, there were periodic and regular outbreaks of typhus, typhoid fever, epidemic diarrhoea, dysentery, smallpox and a variety of ailments which were classified only as "fevers". Between November and December of 1847 500,000 people were infected with typhus fever out of a total population of 2,100,100, and it seemed to many that London was indeed becoming what *The Lancet* described as a "doomed city". The average age of mortality in the capital was 27, while that for the working classes was 22, and in 1839 almost half the funerals in London were of children under the age of ten. Dickens is often criticised for the number of child-deaths which occur in his fiction but, again, he was reflecting no more than the simplest truth. Dead, and dying around him every day. That is the forgotten aspect of Victorian London. No Londoner was ever completely well, and when in nineteenth-century fiction urban life is described as "feverish" it was a statement of medical fact and not a metaphor. In the opening pages of *The Old Curiosity Shop* Dickens describes the capital as "the stream of life that will not stop, pouring on, on, on . . .", and here we see the image of feverish sweating superimposed upon a city that was filled with the dank cold perspiration of its inhabitants.

On 21 October Dickens and Forster travelled from London to Bristol in order to "see off" Longfellow on his voyage back to the United States and on the following day, now that all his duties in London had been dispatched, he began to make plans for another journey – this time to Cornwall with Forster, Maclise and Stanfield. He was sup-

218

posed to deliver the first instalment of his new novel within a month to Chapman and Hall, but it was already clear that publication would have to be deferred, at least for a short while. Of course the new book was very much on his mind, and in fact his decision to go to Cornwall seems to have been determined by it; he wanted to visit the "very dreariest and most desolate portion of the sea-coast" and, in addition, he wanted to go down one of the tin mines there. Only a few weeks before he had written in support of Lord Ashley's Mines and Collieries Bill and clearly he was aiming to strike at the mines and mine-owners as once he had struck at Yorkshire schools in *Nicholas Nickleby* and the New Poor Law in *Oliver Twist*. After the historical fiction of *Barnaby Rudge*, and no doubt fired imaginatively by his recent experiences in America, he wanted to write another fiction of the present day. So he set off in search of material. However, what gained Dickens's attention did not necessarily engage his imagination, and nothing of that trip finds any place in the novel he was just about to begin; unless it be the fact that *Martin Chuzzlewit* has initially a rural rather than an urban setting. The tin mines were to appear elsewhere, however, when Dickens came to write *A Christmas Carol* in the following year: nothing he saw was ever really lost, but the right conditions were necessary for it to emerge transformed.

Dickens was back in London by 4 November and almost at once began to plot his new work. He needed a name to begin. On a sheet of paper he transcribed all the titles of his previous novels, and then wrote Martin chuzzlewig, then Martin chubblewig, then chuzzletoe and chuzzlebog. Then on another sheet he wrote down a whole range of surnames; Martin was clearly right, but now he put after it chuzzlewig, Sweezleden, chuzzletoe, Sweezlebach, Sweezlewag. Then he decides on Chuzzlewig, writes out a longer title, only to change his mind and on another sheet put Martin Chuzzlewit. He had found it. For names were very important to Dickens. When he started a new periodical he told Forster that "I shall never be able to do anything for the work until it has a fixed name", and it is the same with his characters also. They did not exist for him until he had given them a name and it is that which, like a spell, brings forth their appearance and behaviour in the world. Whenever he saw or heard an odd name he would remember it and then later note it down. He kept lists of them – one such was in fact compiled from a Privy Council Education List – and he had a copy of *Bowditch's Surnames*. Perhaps that is why there are such odd and perhaps not coincidental clusters of names in areas which he knew; Fanny Dorritt is on a gravestone beside Rochester Cathedral, and at the small church at Chalk are Guppy, Twist, and Flight on three adjacent tombstones. In the church register at Chatham are Jasper, Sowerby and Weller while in the register of St Andrew's, Holborn, are to be found Chadband, Twist, Krook, Boffin, Guppy, Dorrit, Marley and Varden. He devoted so much care and attention to the name because within it, when eventually it emerged, he saw the lineaments of the character who possessed it; when he brooded over his lists he was selecting and defining all the qualities he needed. The name, then, works as an almost objective pressure on the novelist's imagination. The fact that he gave his friends and his own family various nicknames – the Ocean Spectre, the Lincolnian Mammoth, the Prince – suggests also how readily he converted the people of the real world into characters of his own devising, all of them inhabiting that private imaginative world which he had constructed for them. And can we not also trace at least part of his constant preoccupation with names to the fact that his own name, Dickens, now so hallowed because of its association with the great novelist, was at the time considered funny and even vulgar? In *The Merry Wives of Windsor* he would have read, "I cannot tell what the Dickens his name is"; he would also have known the phrases of the time, "how the Dickens" and "I'll play the Dickings with you", where variants of his name were used as a euphemism for the devil. He even plays with his own name in all the Dicks of his fiction, as well as in such surnames as Pickwick and Wickfield.

And even Chuzzlewit. Now that he had the name he could set to work upon the complete title and he eventually emerged in the fifth draft with: "The Life and Adventures of Martin Chuzzlewit, His relatives, friends, and enemies. Comprising all His Wills and his Ways, With an Historical Record of what he did, And what he didn't. Shewing Moreover who Inherited the Family Plate; who came in for the Silver Spoons, And who for the wooden ladles. The whole forming a complete Key To The House of Chuzzlewit. Edited by 'Boz'. With illustrations by 'Phiz'." So this is to be the story of a family or a dynasty, its concerns money and inheritance. He began with a parody of genealogical research, then went on to chronicle the progress of an autumn wind in evening as it blows its way towards Mr Pecksniff and his two lovely daughters, Charity and Mercy ("Not unholy names, I hope?" as he is later to ask). The youngest Miss Pecksniff is all simplicity and innocence, all girlishness and playfulness, a tender gushing thing. The elder Miss Pecksniff, in lovely contrast, is all gravity and demureness. Mr Pecksniff himself is a very pattern of the moral man, an architect, a pillar of the little community, who warms his hands before the fire "as benevolently as if they were somebody else's, not his . . ." These opening chapters were written quickly – he had finished them by the middle of December, only six weeks after his return from Cornwall – but they are composed with extreme carefulness, almost self-consciousness, on Dickens's part. Two number plans of the novel survive in which he plots the course of particular chapters, sometimes foreshadowing events which will transpire much later in foreshadowing events which will transpire much later in the narrative, and from this evidence alone it is clear that he was now beginning to take care over the construction and elaboration of his fictions where before he had been happy to proceed on an almost spontaneous or improvisatory basis, most of his plots having been of a picaresque nature which allowed him to introduce characters and arrange incidents as he went along with his characters in the discovery of their world.

In fact Dickens was so pleased with the opening chapters – so pleased, in other words, that his grand conception was coming to life in front of him – that he rushed around to Forster's rooms and, as his friend lay ill, read to him the descriptions of Pecksniff and Tom Pinch. As soon as he had finished it seemed to him, as always, the best thing he had done. The manuscript was delivered to the printers by 18 December and, on the last day of that month, the first number of *Martin Chuzzlewit* was published. From now on he set himself a routine of writing the next episode in the first half of the month, and correcting proofs in the second half. He was on his way again.

But soon there came alarming news; the monthly sale of *Martin Chuzzlewit* was of only twenty thousand copies, far fewer than that of his other serials, and within a relatively short time advertising revenue from the inserts in each monthly number also declined. Dickens was in fact extremely pleased with what he had achieved in the new novel, and believed himself to be in some ways at the height of his powers, and so he was not ready to blame himself for this decline in his popularity. In fact posterity may largely support his own judgment: *Martin Chuzzlewit* is among his greatest novels, primarily because of its rich comic mood, and there was a general book trade depression in the period which was making it difficult for writers and booksellers of every kind. But Dickens was severely disappointed, not to say alarmed, about the course of his finances, now that he was earning much less than he had anticipated. As soon as he had seen the Chapman and Hall accounts in March, he gave up the idea he had envisaged of buying a house or cottage out of town.

Instead he took rooms at Cobley's Farm in the rural retreat of Finchley, and here he contemplated the relative failure of *Martin Chuzzlewit*. The eventual shape of the novel was still at this stage fluid enough for him, if he wished, to change its course and catch more public attention. One possibility was to align the novel even more closely with the most important issues of the period; after all, he had originally considered including the abuses of the Cornish mine-owners. It might have been fortuitous, then, that Dr Southwood Smith, one of the members of the Children's Employment Commission, should now have sent him a copy of its second report. Southwood Smith is one of those social reformers who in large part illuminate the active forces of the era; once a Unitarian minister, he had been private secretary to Bentham and all his life had interested himself both in the problems of sanitation and in the working conditions of the poor. The report exposed the harsh and sometimes unbearable conditions in which children, some as young as five or six, were forced to work. Suddenly all the Dickens's instinctive sympathies came into play and, even as he was writing *Martin Chuzzlewit*, he dashed off a letter to Southwood Smith in which he declared that he would write a pamphlet on the question. A few weeks later he had changed his mind, however, and decided to forget about any pamphlet in order to exert a "Sledge hammer" blow at a later date. It is indeed possible that Dickens had decided to include in *Martin Chuzzlewit* an exposure of child employment. In theory it might have been a good idea and a welcome addition to the range of the novel; in practice it was to emerge in quite a different form.

But there still remained the problem of the novel itself,

223

a novel which Dickens knew to be good but which had failed to capture or to hold the public imagination. And it seems likely that it was at this time, while he was trying to get ahead with the narrative in his retreat at Finchley, that he conceived the idea of sending his "hero", Martin Chuzzlewit, to the United States – a decision which, if it did owe something to his desire to provoke public attention, was also in large part determined by the venomous and abusive tirades which had been reaching him from across the Atlantic. He always said that he made a point of never reading such material in the American newspapers but this sounds like the defence of tremulous and wounded pride; it seems probable that he had learnt the gist of their attacks and, after the relative restraint of *American Notes*, decided to unleash all the fury of his comedy upon them.

This was a period in which Dickens seems to be uneasy and unsettled at every point. Catherine was expecting another child and, although this condition can scarcely be blamed solely upon her, his references to her during this period are notably bad-tempered; he had already called her "a Donkey" at one point. He was also more than angry with his father, seeming positively to disown him and refusing to have any communications with him. "He, and all of them, look upon me as a something to be plucked and torn to pieces for their advantage," he said later in the year. ". . . My soul sickens at the thought of them . . . Nothing makes me so wretched, or so unfit for what I have to do, as these things . . ."

And yet this was also the period when Dickens was writing some of the funniest passages in *Martin Chuzzlewit* – not only the American episodes but also the events at Todgers's, the boarding house in darkest London where Pecksniff and his lovely daughters temporarily reside. As so often in the past, Dickens's private unhappiness, restlessness and anxiety seem only to fuel still further the extravagances of his comedy. It was now, for instance, that he creates the character of Mrs Gamp. The midwife and night nurse, the decrepit party who announces herself, mysteriously but unforgettably, "Gamp is my name, and Gamp my nater," the female whose rallying cry in company is, "Drink fair, wotever you do!", is perhaps the most famous and certainly the funniest of all Dickens's creations. There was a real Mrs Gamp, or, rather, there was an original upon whom the monster was established. A certain Miss Meredith, known to Dickens, had recently been taken ill but not so ill as to be unaware of her nurse's strange habits; one of which was "to rub her nose along the top of the tall fender", and another to sup vinegar with the flat of her knife while eating cucumbers.

By the end of June Dickens was "quite weary and worn out" with *Martin Chuzzlewit* and at the beginning of July he travelled with Catherine and Georgina to stay in Yorkshire with the Smithsons at Easthorpe Park, a late eighteenth-century house which Dickens called ". . . the most remarkable place of its size in England and immeasurably the most beautiful . . ." Here he rested, organised picnics and games, embarked on nocturnal expeditions to the local ruins, and took long rides into the surrounding countryside. While here he read the newspapers, too, and in *The Times* he saw reports of American support for Daniel O'Connell and his campaign for Home Rule in Ireland, support which was hastily withdrawn in some quarters when O'Connell attacked slavery in one of his more fiery speeches. Dickens kept the material, and on his return to London from Yorkshire included it in one of the novel's American chapters which he was now writing. He was starting work at about eight in the morning, in order to make up for the time spent idling in Yorkshire, and once again his humour was in full flood; that "distilled essence of comicality" which he had noted at the time of his American travels was now suffusing his own pages. It would be

225

a weary task to compare, page for page, *American Notes* with *Martin Chuzzlewit*; it need only be said that the random experiences portrayed in the book of travels are here thoroughly condensed and lent what might be described as a thematic purpose. The river journeys into the interior had in *American Notes* contained some "pure delights", for example, whereas in *Martin Chuzzlewit* the journey is one which offers only "the weary day and melancholy night", a journey that reminds Dickens of the progress of time and a passage to the "grim domains of Giant Despair". There had been an incident which Dickens retold in *American Notes* — how a young woman had taken the riverboat to St Louis in order to be reunited with her husband and how she found him waiting eagerly for her, "a fine, good-looking, sturdy young fellow!" The incident is recast in *Martin Chuzzlewit* as concerning a young woman who crosses the Atlantic in order to be reunited with her husband; in the novel she finds him, too, but he is now only a "feeble old shadow". The difference is one of symbolic intent, Dickens's imagination recasting the duller shades of reality to suit his native chiaroscuro.

He had started the September number of the novel after his return to London from Easthorpe Park in July but now, restless as ever, he and the family decamped to Broadstairs for their annual visit. Here Dickens set to work on *Martin Chuzzlewit*, continuing with the American chapters even as they seemed increasingly to create problems for him. In a sense, the form of the novel was becoming irksome to him; it was proceeding along the lines of its internal development which accounts for its organic firmness and consistency, but clearly there were now many things that he wanted to say, and could not say, in such a book. It was only when Dickens travelled up from Broadstairs to London, in order to visit a ragged school, that a new imaginative approach came to him.

He was visiting the Field Lane ragged school in Saffron

Hill. An advertisement had appeared in *The Times*, seeking charity for this particular establishment, and it seems to have been this which originally attracted his attention. Saffron Hill was of course not unknown to him. He had lived very close to it for some years, and had set parts of *Oliver Twist* in its vicinity. When he visited the school, in fact, he described it as being on exactly the same spot where Fagin had once worked, that coincidence emphasising how certain parts of the old city were haunted, haunting, filled with the blackened relics of the real and the imagined past. The establishment itself was sufficiently real and has some claim to being the first of the self-styled ragged schools, although charitable schools were not in themselves a new thing. There had always been a concern in England for the general reclamation of the very poor (education or training of any specific kind was really out of the question) and the Ragged School Movement, under the guidance of a certain Mr Starey, was established to make use of that tradition and properly to direct it.

The Field Lane school which Dickens visited was wretched enough, three rooms on the first floor of a dilapidated house among the swarming courts and alleys of Saffron Hill and its environs. The area itself was considered by many to be the worst in London, a place of filth and disease and every kind of vice, the inhabitants of which were separated from their fellow-citizens by a gulf wider than any city thoroughfare, a separate race who found the shortest route to prison or the gallows, and who were in a very real sense steeped in what Dickens called "profound ignorance and perfect barbarism". It was their children who were enticed to come to the ragged school, set up by Evangelicals primarily to reclaim the souls of the errant young but at the same time trying to inculcate in them the rudiments of learning. Many of these young boys and girls already earned their miserable "living" by thievery or prostitution, and all of them were filthy, reckless and of course illiterate; when Dickens visited them, he found ". . . a sickening atmosphere, in the midst of taint and dirt and pestilence: with all the deadly sins let loose, howling and shrieking at the doors". He was wearing a pair of white trousers and bright boots and, as soon as he entered the room, they began to laugh at him; his companion, Clarkson Stanfield, found the smell too much and quickly left. But Dickens stayed, and by dint of perseverance got them to answer some of his questions. But he was appalled by the ragged figures he had observed here. It was out of this vision of the world that Dickens now found his new subject; his imagination was seized by the conditions of the school and within a few weeks he had created *A Christmas Carol*, the wonderful story of redemption in which appear the two children, Ignorance and Want, infants who are "wretched, abject, frightful, hideous, miserable". This was the book he had been wanting to write all along; and so this powerful Christmas tale, which has achieved a kind of immortality, was born out of the very conditions of the time.

He worked on it quickly, the plot itself deriving from a memory, conscious or unconscious, of the story of Gabriel Grub in *The Pickwick Papers* – an interpolated tale in which a surly old man is visited by various goblins who show him past and future. He had a bad cold, tried not to attend too many social engagements, but as he worked the story grew under his hand. Clearly the narrative of Scrooge and his conversion had been simmering within him for some time, emerging now and again in the history of Martin Chuzzlewit, but it took all the accidental circumstances here related to release it. That is why it emerges almost ready-made. Forster recounts with what "a strange mastery it seized him", how he wept over it, laughed, and then wept again; in the course of its composition he took long night walks through London, sometimes covering ten or fifteen miles, and during these lonely nocturnal excursions he no doubt recalled that sense of life – and that vision of the world — which he had experienced in these same streets as a child. For in *A Christmas Carol* he returns to his childhood and relives it. Not just in the sense that this Christmas story itself is strangely reminiscent of the tales and chapbooks which he had read as a child ("No one was more intensely fond than Dickens of old nursery tales," Forster wrote, "and he had a secret delight in feeling that he was here only giving them a higher form") but also in the more important sense that, for the first time in his published writings, the whole nature of Dickens's childhood informs the little narrative.

In Scrooge's infancy, after all, the familiar elements of Dickens's own past are dispersed. The blacking factory and Gad's Hill Place are wonderfully knit together in an image of a decaying building which is made of red brick and has a weathercock on the top of it: it is here that Scrooge sees, literally *sees*, the heroes of his boyhood reading just as Dickens had once done; and it is from this place, where the plaster falls and the windows are cracked, that his sister, "little Fan", rescues him. How much a reworking of Dickens's own fantasies is this, as the young sister, whom he had thought had abandoned him, returns and leads him "Home, for good and all . . ." But the resemblances to Dickens's own childhood do not end here. The Cratchit family live in a small terraced house which is clearly an evocation of that house in Bayham Street where the Dickens family had moved after their arrival in London, and their crippled infant had first been christened not Tiny Tim but "Tiny Fred" — the name of his own brother who was two years old at the time of their journey to the capital. Some of his earliest memories are here fused together, creating such an entirely new shape that it is perhaps pointless to look for the various scattered "sources" of which *A Christmas Carol* is made up. It is enough to say that much of its power derives from the buried recollections which animate it.

He finished *A Christmas Carol* at the beginning of December so that, in total, it had taken him a little over six weeks to compose. He had already come to an agreement with Chapman and Hall that they would publish the book solely on the basis of a commission and, since it was to be very much *his* Christmas book, he went to great pains to procure for it the best possible appearance. It was bound in red cloth, with a gilt design on the cover and the edges of the pages themselves were gilt; John Leech provided four full-colour etchings, and there were also four black-and-white woodcuts within the text of the book. Altogether a handsome volume and, at the relatively low price of five shillings, it became the most successful Christmas book of the season; some six thousand copies were purchased by Christmas Eve, and it kept on selling well into the new year and beyond. Indeed the response of the public was so enthusiastic that it seems quite to have blotted out both the relative failure of *Martin Chuzzlewit* and any fears Dickens might have had about his waning popularity as a writer.

He knew instinctively what he had done, namely, created a modern fairy story, and in subsequent years his Christmas Books and Christmas Stories make up as important a part of his writing as they constitute a significant extension of his relation to his audience. He did not invent Christmas, however, as the more sentimental of his chroniclers have suggested. Robert Seymour, the suicidal first illustrator of *The Pickwick Papers*, had in 1835 been responsible for *The Book of Christmas* which has many of the genial ingredients of Dickens's own commemorations of the period. But Dickens could be said to have emphasised its cosy conviviality at a time when both Georgian licence and Evangelical dourness were being questioned. It was not yet the "festive season" which Dickens desired to make of it; it did not possess what he described as the "Christmas spirit, which is the spirit of active usefulness, perseverance,

cheerful discharge of duty, kindness and forebearance!"
Christmas cards were not introduced until 1846, and
Christmas crackers until the 1850s. Typically it was still a
one-day holiday when presents were given to children,
but there was no general orgy of benevolence and generos-
ity. It was a time of quiet rest. Acting. Reading aloud.
Music. Games. What Dickens did was to transform the
holiday by suffusing it with his own particular mixture of
aspirations, memories and fears. He invested it with fantasy
and with a curious blend of religious mysticism and popular superstition so that, in certain respects, the Christmas
of Dickens resembles the more ancient festival which had
been celebrated in rural areas and in the north of England.
In addition he made it cosy, he made it comfortable, and
he achieved this by exaggerating the darkness beyond the
small circle of light. The central idea of the book is one of
ferocious privacy, of shelter and segregation, and it was in
*A Christmas Carol* that Dickens divined it and brought it
forth to the surface. Once again his own obsessions take
on the very shape and pressure of the age.

That is why the effect of *A Christmas Carol* on Dickens
himself should not be underestimated. Most importantly,
he had for the first time been able to complete an entire
fiction without being compelled to write in serial portions.
He had had the opportunity to design the book in every
sense, and carefully to calculate the plot in advance. He
had done it all in one bound, as it were, and as soon
as he had written "The End" he added three double
underlinings. Then, he said, he ". . . broke out like a Madman". On 26 December he attended a party given by Mrs
Macready (her husband being away in America). Jane
Welsh Carlyle was also there and told a friend, "Only think
of that excellent Dickens playing the *conjuror* for one
whole hour – the *best* conjuror I ever saw . . ." And then
came the dancing: "Dickens did all but go down on his
knees to make *me* – waltz with him!" as the party grew

madder and madder still. Madder and madder as Charles Dickens whirled through the last days of 1843.

Yet all the pressures of his life were still there, and the only alternative still seemed to him to be escape. Even as he was writing *Martin Chuzzlewit* and *A Christmas Carol*, he was planning to get away. He wanted to make a clean break. To travel in Switzerland, France and Italy. He wanted a rest after his labours on the novel and, always now aware of the perils of over-production, to disappear from public view for at least a year. He had made the decision as *Martin Chuzzlewit* continued with its relatively small sales, but he was defiant about that. "You know, as well as I," he told Forster, "that I think *Chuzzlewit* in a hundred points immeasurably the best of my stories." But the low sale of the novel made it also a matter of pressing economy that the Dickens family should decamp, let their house in Devonshire Terrace, and live more cheaply on the Continent. So everything propelled him in this direction, and not even the fact that Catherine was still expecting the baby could deter him – "We have spoken of the baby, and of leaving it here with Catherine's mother. Moving the children into France could not, in any ordinary course of things, do them anything but good." Clearly no one except himself wished to travel abroad; certainly not Catherine, now in the last stages of her pregnancy. But Dickens's will was not something to be questioned in such matters. If it was good for him, it must be good for them; "And the question is, what it would do to that by which they live: not what it would do to them." In fact as soon as Catherine had given birth to their new son, Francis, Dickens began to write about her with more than a trace of irritation and annoyance. Once more she was suffering from post-natal depression, of which Dickens reports ". . . her health is perfectly good, and I am sure she might rally, if she would". Later he was complaining about how slow she was, and seems to have had no very strong affection for the new baby who would place a further drain upon his dwindling resources. "I decline (on principle) to look at the latter object," he wrote in what may or may not be a mock facetious tone. And this the man who had only a short time before been extolling the familial virtues of Christmas with his final words, "God Bless Us, Every One!" In fact neither the sentiments nor the success of *A Christmas Carol* materially affected his resolve to leave England, and his decision to do so was if anything now being strengthened by the behaviour of his always importunate father; although Dickens's finances were far from healthy, John Dickens seems to have made further and further demands upon him. Dickens wrote to Thomas Mitton, from whom he had already borrowed money, and who acted as his agent in all transactions with his father, "I really think I shall begin to give in, one of these days. For anything like the damnable Shadow which this father of mine casts upon my face, there never was – except in a nightmare." God Bless Us, Every One!

Other problems beset him. Within two weeks of the publication of *A Christmas Carol*, Parley's Illuminated Library brought out a "condensed" but essentially pirated edition of that work. Two days later Dickens had filed an injunction to stop publication; his wrath against American "pirates" might do him no good, but he could at least win some kind of victory in the English courts. And indeed he did: he hired Talfourd to represent him, and the injunction was granted while Dickens sued the printers and publishers for breach of copyright. "The pirates are beaten flat," he said in his triumph but, unfortunately, his was something of a Pyrrhic victory. The defendants declared themselves bankrupt and as a result Dickens had to pay his own costs, which amounted to the not inconsiderable sum of seven hundred pounds. Nothing seemed right in England any more and then, when no worse could be expected, the accounts of *A Christmas Carol* arrived. He

233

had expected to earn something like one thousand pounds from the sale of the book, but the costs of producing it had cut heavily into the profits. He wrote to Forster, "The first six thousand copies show a profit of £230!" – in fact the profit was closer to £130, and Forster seems to have misread Dickens's hand when he transcribed the letter into his biography. In any case the sum was very small, far smaller than anything Dickens had anticipated, and he fell at once into an anxiety which came close to hysteria. "Such a night as I have passed! I really believed that I should never get up again, until I had passed through all the horrors of a fever . . . I shall be ruined past all mortal hope of redemption." And indeed this was his panic fear: the fear of ruin, of being thrust down again into poverty, to go the way of his father into a debtors' prison, all the success and fame he has achieved to be stripped from him as he is cast back into the state of childhood. There must have been times when it seemed to him that all his achievement was a dream, and that he would wake up once again in Bayham Street or the little attic room of Lant Street. There was still so much fear behind the bright appearance of the eminent novelist.

Yet his financial panic seems to have been connected with anxieties about the future as well as those induced by the past, since it is linked to what was becoming a general uncertainty about the course his life was about to take. From this time, for example, one can trace a certain loss of affection for, or connection with, Catherine; as if in some way she was hemming him in, narrowing his possibilities, consigning him to a domestic fate. In fact his disaffection with his wife was signalled in a very curious manner. It happened in Liverpool. He had agreed to travel there once more in the cause of adult educational reform – to speak at a *soirée* of the Mechanics Institution in Liverpool. During the proceedings, a native of Liverpool, Miss Christiana Weller, then eighteen years of age, was called upon to give a piano recital. Her name, with its echo of a more famous Weller in *The Pickwick Papers*, seemed to amuse Dickens and a local newspaper said that as she played the famous novelist "kept his eyes firmly fixed on her every movement". Then he was introduced to her and also to her father, "at the same time making some observation which created much laughter among those immediately around". Then, in his concluding remarks, Dickens went on to say that "the last remnant of my heart went into that piano". (He actually finished by quoting Tiny Tim, "God Bless Us, Every One!", a sure sign that he knew on what basis his current and immediate popularity rested.) Clearly he was in some way attracted to Christiana Weller since he invited himself to lunch with her, at her brother-in-law's house, the very next afternoon, and on that occasion inscribed some verse in her album, part of which read:

> "I love her dear name which has won me some fame
> But Great Heaven how gladly I'd change it!"

In other words, how glad he would be to marry her. If he could. If he were free of Catherine.

In fact this first attraction came somewhere close to infatuation, an infatuation all the more significant in light of the fact that Miss Weller was thought to resemble Mary Hogarth – at least this is what other members of the Hogarth family came to notice about her. On his eventual return to London Dickens told T. J. Thompson, the friend with whom he had stayed in Liverpool, that "I cannot joke about Miss Weller; for she is too good; and interest in her (spiritual young creature that she is, and destined to an early death, I fear) has become a sentiment with me. Good God what a madman I should seem, if the incredible feeling I have conceived for the girl could be made plain to anyone!" Clearly all the thwarted yearning of Dickens's nature became attached to this young woman, that endless appetite for love and affection once more aroused by the sight of a girl who looked so much like Mary Hogarth; and yet how odd, too, that his feelings for her should also be associated with the idea that she would die young.

It is interesting to note, however, that she was not the only young woman to resemble Mary Hogarth. Certainly Georgina Hogarth recalled Mary to his mind, and she was now living with the rest of the Dickens family in Devonshire Terrace. And, if he had to control or to deny certain feelings which he had for his young sister-in-law, is that yet another reason why they broke out again so ferociously in the company of Miss Weller? And is it not also possible that the lament of Tom Pinch, cruelly deprived of the love of Mary Graham in the chapters of *Martin Chuzzlewit* which Dickens was just about to write, is in part established upon his own yearning and his own sense of loss? But the overriding impression of this incident must surely be the extent to which he was dissatisfied with his wife at a time when she was continually bearing his children. How else can one explain almost the hysteria or at least the desperation of Dickens's attachment to a young girl of eighteen, if it did not spring from real emotional unhappiness which his wife had been able neither to divert nor to assuage?

From Liverpool and Miss Weller he went on to Birmingham to give a speech at the Polytechnic Institution. It was in this city, in the town hall crowded with people, that he declared, "As long as I can make you laugh or cry, I will . . ." The next day he returned to London "dead, worn-out, and Spiritless". He knew already that fame and applause could not in themselves assuage that aching, empty yearning, that perpetual "want of something" which the sight of Christiana Weller had provoked once more within him.

The "want of something" which made him restless. Eager to move on. He still wanted to get away, even if, as

Forster maintained, he was being driven away principally by what were "imaginary fears" about his own work. He had also now decided definitely to leave Chapman and Hall and to make new agreements with his printers, Bradbury and Evans, all this merely because of the chance remark by William Hall about the terms of his contract. How much Dickens resented slights, and how impetuously but implacably he reacted to them, is evident from this alone. In the agreement which he eventually signed with Bradbury and Evans, he promised only to provide another little Christmas book on the lines of the albeit very successful *A Christmas Carol* and, in addition, to explore with them the possibility of starting a new periodical. (It was a period when printers often transcended their technical skills, and became publishers as well.) But he had a travel book in mind and was also eager, after he had finished *Martin Chuzzlewit*, to start work on a novel which would have a continental setting; this was another reason why he wanted to move to Europe. But he did not wish to write the projected novel in monthly numbers. His experience with *A Christmas Carol* had led him to believe that it would be better for any new novel to come out in complete and coherent form. The fact was, also, that he was happy to consider these various schemes because he needed money badly. That is perhaps why he approached the publisher, Thomas Longman, in the period after his break with Chapman and Hall; and why he opened negotiations with the *Morning Chronicle* for a series of regular articles. Neither of these two ideas came to anything, but they are indicative of his generally unsettled state of mind just at the point when he was about to leave England.

By spring his plans for his European journey were very well advanced: after much hesitation and consulting of better-travelled contemporaries (like Lady Holland) he had decided upon Genoa as his headquarters, a city which was inexpensive, picturesque and, as he thought, healthy. So he asked Angus Fletcher, the sculptor whose eccentricities had amused him both in Broadstairs and in Scotland but who was now living in that city, to find an appropriate house for the family. Dickens had also been looking for suitable transport. It would have been difficult and no doubt expensive to hire coaches or carriages at every stage of their journey, and he went to the Pantechnicon near Belgrave Square where he found what seems to have been an old stage coach – large enough, in any case, to hold a party of twelve people and equipped, according to Dickens, "with night-lamps and day-lamps and pockets and imperials and leathern cellars, and the most extraordinary contrivances". It was a shabby giant of a coach, priced at sixty pounds, but he bargained it down to forty-five.

They had managed to let Devonshire Terrace and, since the new tenants wished to move in without delay, a detailed inventory was made of the contents of the house, in the course of which it was stated that the library contained more than two thousand volumes. Then the whole family decamped to the house in Osnaburgh Street where the children had stayed during the American tour; the dog, Timber Doodle, was to go with them on their journey but Dickens left with Edwin Landseer a pet raven and pet eagle. Even as the complicated preparations were going ahead, Dickens was still trying to finish *Martin Chuzzlewit*. Never had the composition of any of his books been so beset by the general accidents of life, and yet he still pushed forward; during the last stages of Catherine's difficult pregnancy, during the Chancery suit against the pirates of a *A Christmas Carol*, during his infatuation with Christiana Weller, he had been able to write rapidly, sometimes improvising as he went along, sometimes making minor mistakes as a consequence. It was not in fact until June, and after their removal to Osnaburgh Street, that Dickens finally completed *Martin Chuzzlewit*. Finished at last, perhaps the most comic of his books, the novel in which he immortalised Mr Pecksniff and Mrs Gamp, but written during one of the most difficult periods of his life. There was no time for him to "break out like a Madman" after this novel; he barely had time to make all his farewells before departure, although of course he ensured that his affairs were left in secure hands. Those of Thomas Mitton, for finance; those of John Forster, for publishing. The final number of *Martin Chuzzlewit* was published on the last day of June. Two days later he and his family left for Italy, an event which Forster described as "the turning-point of his career".

# *Fifteen*

THEY left on the Channel boat from Dover on 2 July
– Charles Dickens, Catherine Dickens, Georgina
Hogarth, Charley Dickens, Mamie Dickens, Kate
Dickens, Walter Dickens, Francis Dickens, Louis Roche
(the courier), Anne Brown (Catherine's maid who had
accompanied her mistress on the American tour) and two
domestic servants who will become much less anonymous
in Italy than they ever were in London. A party of twelve
in all, plus dog, travelling together inside the ancient coach
across the countryside of France and Italy. At Boulogne
Dickens entered a French bank to change some money
and made a long request in his inexpert French. "How
would you like to take it, sir?" – the clerk replied to him,
in English. And from Boulogne to Paris. A city he had
never seen, and at once he was enthralled by it. "My eyes
ached and my head grew giddy, as novelty, novelty, novelty; nothing but strange and striking things; came swarming before me." It was all new to him, and he told Forster
that it was as if he had grown another head beside his old
one. On later occasions he would describe Paris as variously light, brilliant, sparkling, glittering; he was affected
by its glare rather than its gloire and, since it is well known
how Dickens always loved to have mirrors around him
in his own homes, it is clear that the French city fulfilled
his own needs for light and brilliancy.

Eventually they reached Italy. Angus Fletcher had hired for them a large house, the Villa Bagnerello, in Albaro, which was then a district just outside the city. It was on the slope of a hill and was reached by a narrow lane which wound its way from the sea-coast to the via Albaro above: a large but not a grand house, surrounded by high walls but overlooking vineyards and the Bay of Genoa; the courtyard opened onto a small front hall, where a marble staircase led upwards to commodious and well proportioned rooms. And yet it did not seem altogether to please Dickens or his family. His name for it was the "pink jail", despite the magnificent views over the Bay, and, in addition, it was swarming with fleas. Genoa itself seems at first to have disappointed Dickens as well. It was a very frowsy and dirty city, not at all that place of Mediterranean brightness which he must at least have half-anticipated. It was crowded. It was noisy. It was slow. And yet he came to love it for, if America had been a journey into an unworkable future, this was a journey into the dismal and ruined past which he had already recreated in his novels. It is not hard to see how he came to appreciate it, even at its worst — with the alleys and high buildings of its ancient town; the palaces and the fine public buildings which crowd against each other on streets no more than twelve feet across; the cavernous dim churches filled with the prayers or sighs of worshippers and fitfully illuminated by the splendour of gilt and marble. But there was another reason why he came to love this place. The frescoes on the walls of the public buildings, the gestures of the people, the very life of the streets, must have given him an unmistakable impression of some theatrical reality, the frescoes themselves looking uncannily like backdrops for the voluble and excited life of the inhabitants. It may well be that the stinking alleys reminded him of London, but this was London seen as a form of theatre. He was at home.

An outline for a new travel book may already have been

241

clear to him but nevertheless, in this ancient place, he had to turn his mind to the Christmas Book which he had promised to Bradbury and Evans and which he wished to finish by mid-October, only three months away. The atmosphere, however, was not yet conducive to work. His daughter, Kate, was very ill for a time but then recovered, and the servants were at first horrified by Italian food and Italian manners; their usual method of communication with the natives was to speak English very loudly and very slowly, as if they were deaf rather than Italian, and Dickens later employed this mannerism in *Little Dorrit* when the inhabitants of Bleeding Heart Yard try to converse with John Baptist Cavalletto: "E pleased," Mrs Plornish interprets for him in what she believes to be very good Italian, "E glad get money." Dickens's cook was the first to master enough of the language to buy whatever food was wanted, and very shortly after the servants began, as it were, to settle in. They remain the permanent but alas unacknowledged backdrop to Dickens's life. We hear little from him about his valet, Topping, for example, no more than that he had violent red hair and a habit of becoming confidential when not entirely sober. In turn Topping, who of all the men of the period was probably the one who knew Dickens best, left no memoir and no reminiscences of his employer. Perhaps he never read his novels. It is not even clear whether he was in Italy with the family — since Louis Roche acted as guide, interpreter and manservant on most occasions, it is likely that he was left behind in some supernumerary capacity in Devonshire Terrace.

Meanwhile, as the family began to start its new European life, Dickens lazed in the Villa Bagnerello. He continued to learn Italian and, although on most occasions he left Catherine to deal with unexpected guests, he attended a few parties and visited the theatres of the town. But most of all he loved to walk, through the city and through the countryside, getting lost in the narrow streets, coming upon "the strangest contrasts; things that are picturesque, ugly, mean, magnificent, delightful, and offensive, break upon the view at every turn." In this period he also managed to complete a task which he did not even think worth mentioning in his correspondence: he completely revised *Oliver Twist* in readiness for its publication by Bradbury and Evans for the first time in a single volume. (Since he was once more suffering from agonising pains in his side, is it possible that the return to Oliver's infancy had reawakened once more something of his own anguished childhood?) This exercise in revision would in itself only be of interest to textual scholars were it not for the fact that, in the process, he imposed a quite new system of punctuation upon his narrative. He seems to have gone through it thoroughly, making many small excisions and changes, but most importantly he gave his words a punctuation which suggests a more rhetorical or declamatory style; it is almost as if he had revised it so that it could be more easily read aloud. It has been suggested that this is an anticipation of his later public readings, but this seems improbable; he had recently been delivering many speeches, in England and just previously in America, and it is more likely that, for the first time, he was now beginning to realise both the power of his voice and the sense of an audience listening to him. It was a new conception of himself, gathered largely in America, his own presence as somehow central to his authorial personality; which is no doubt why he wished to rush back to London later this year precisely in order to read his second Christmas Book out loud to his friends.

With the help of an expatriate Englishman, he managed to rent a palace in Genoa itself; it was a real palace, known as the Palazzo Peschiere, on account of two large and ornamental ponds at the front of the house which were filled with goldfish. It had been built in the late sixteenth century, and was conceived on a very grand scale; the sala on the ground floor was some fifty feet in height, covered with frescoes, and most of the rooms Dickens and his family used led off from this large hall. The walls and ceilings of the rooms were also painted with frescoes, and Dickens later recalled how he wandered from room to room, from bed chamber to bed chamber, as if he were in a vision. The Palazzo Peschiere was also reputed, according to Dickens, to be "very badly haunted indeed" but in the months the Dickens family stayed there they saw nothing.

Dickens himself did in fact experience *something* but he would not have described it as a haunting: he explained it variously as a dream, or a vision within a dream. For, almost as soon as he moved into their new quarters, he saw Mary Hogarth once again. It was the first time she had appeared to him since she had vanished in the wilds of Yorkshire, after he had told his dreams to Catherine, but here in Italy she came again. It happened like this. He had been suffering his old childhood pains, in his back and side, and had found it difficult to sleep. But when eventually he managed to slumber he dreamed of a Spirit wrapped in blue drapery, like a Madonna by Raphael. His memory of Mary Hogarth was now rather generalised – he was not even sure of her voice – but somehow he knew that this was "poor Mary's spirit". He stretched out his arms and called her "Dear". And then, "Forgive me! We poor living creatures are only able to express ourselves by looks and words. I have used the word most natural to *our* affections; and you know my heart." The Spirit said nothing and Dickens began to sob. "Oh! give me some token that you have really visited me!"

*The Spirit*: "Form a wish."
*Dickens*: "Mrs Hogarth is surrounded with great distresses. Will you extricate her?"
*The Spirit*: "Yes."

*Dickens*: "And her extrication is to be a certainty to me, that this has really happened?"

*The Spirit*: "Yes."

*Dickens*: "But answer me one other question! What is the True religion? You think, as I do, that the Form of religion does not so greatly matter, if we try to do good? Or perhaps the Roman Catholic is the best? Perhaps it makes one think of God oftener, and believe in him more steadily?"

*The Spirit*: "For *you*, it is the best."

Then Dickens awoke, roused Catherine from her sleep, and repeated the words of this strange visitation over and over again so that he could the more easily remember them.

By any standards a curious incident, but one not without its echoes and parallels deep within Dickens's own consciousness. His previous Christmas Book, which had at the time so powerfully affected him, did of course introduce Spirits to a sleeping Ebenezer Scrooge in much the same manner. So the imaginative conditions were appropriate, perhaps, for a further nocturnal visitation. The dream was not easily forgotten by Dickens: the hooded figure of a woman reappears in his later fiction and his next Christmas Book, *The Chimes*, was also to deal with ghosts and spirits and visitations.

Of *The Chimes* itself he was soon to say, ". . . it has a grip upon the very throat of the time". This was the Christmas Book he had agreed to write for Bradbury and Evans but, in Genoa, he found it difficult to begin. It was the first time he had attempted to write a book outside England, and "plucked . . . out of my proper soil" he felt ill at ease; a cavernous Italian palace was perhaps not the best place to paint the careful miniatures of benevolence and good will which he needed for the Christmas season. He could not work, and he was vexed by the clangour of Genoa's bells borne upon the wind. These were the noises which eventually saved him, however, and at the beginning of October he sent a one-sentence letter – or, rather, quotation – to Forster: "We have heard THE CHIMES at midnight, Master Shallow!" This short missive has often been quoted as an example of Dickens's boisterous good spirits, but it seems more remarkable for its entire but perfectly unconscious preoccupation with himself and with his own problems.

So he set to work. The bells of Genoa had reminded him of Time, and Time had reminded him of the Sea. Of Motion. Of necessary Progress. Everything came together in a story in which the poor man has a vision of death and sorrow, only alleviated at the end by one of those acts of mercy and charity which Dickens always tried to celebrate in his Christmas fiction. He had started by the second week of October and images of his violence, anger, excitement, are to be found in his description of the writing: "I am in regular, ferocious excitement with the *Chimes*; get up at seven; have a cold bath before breakfast; and blaze away, wrathful and red hot . . ." There could not be a better description of Dickens when "taken by the throat" by a conception. He could not rest until he had got it down on paper. He blazed away through the whole of October, having to take violent exercise to still his beating mind. One day he walked twelve miles in mountain rain; another day he walked six miles under the hottest sun of the day; another day he walked fifteen miles. He sent each section of the tale to Forster, who then took it to Bradbury and Evans; Dickens meanwhile, faithful to his old profession, kept a shorthand copy of each instalment. He worked on, and when he finished at the beginning of November "had what women call a 'real good cry!'"

He had already decided that he wanted to come to London when it was printed; and not just because he wanted to see the volume itself, which he believed would knock *A Christmas Carol* "out of the field". More importantly, he wanted to read the story out loud. He was so pleased by it, so excited by its novelty, that he wanted to see its effect upon a group of chosen friends; particularly those like Carlyle and Jerrold who would understand what a leap Dickens had made from his other fiction. In fact the book did cause something of a sensation and, because of its overtly radical tones, was more vigorously attacked and more stoutly defended than any of Dickens's previous works. Here he brands himself as a true radical, even revolutionary: in this Christmas Book, so hard a present for those who defended the status quo, it is quite clear that Dickens really did despise the political system of his country as much as he loathed its social mores. Of course there were more personal objections to the book too. Sir Peter Laurie, whose campaign against suicides had been satirised here under the name of Alderman Cute, called it "most disgraceful". In fact Laurie had once taken Catherine Dickens to a Lord Mayor's dinner and thought he was on good terms with the famous author. "He is a dangerous man to meet," he said. *The Morning Post* went further and accused Dickens of romanticising "the ruffian and the wanton, the rickburner and the felon". But all this was to come – now that he had finished *The Chimes*, Dickens first had to make his way across the continent to London.

Back in London he took rooms at the Piazza Coffee House in Covent Garden (his house in Devonshire Terrace of course still being let) and then went at once to see Forster in Lincoln's Inn Fields. Forster remembered many years later ". . . the eager face and figure, as they flashed upon me so suddenly this wintry Saturday night that almost before I could be conscious of his presence I felt the grasp of his hand." But of course he had really come back for *The Chimes*, and the next night he read the whole Christmas story to Macready. "If you had seen Macready

247

last night – undisguisedly sobbing, and crying on the sofa, as I read – you would have felt (as I did) what a thing it is to have Power." This was how he described that reading to Catherine. "Power." Power over others. Power to move and to sway. The Power of his writing. The Power of his voice.

And it was that same Power which he demonstrated the following evening when he read his story to a selected group of friends. Forster had called them together in his rooms – Carlyle, Daniel Maclise, Clarkson Stanfield, W. J. Fox, Laman Blanchard, Douglas Jerrold and of course Forster himself, all of them keenly in sympathy with the political and social emphases of *The Chimes*. "It is a tea-party," Forster told one of them in advance, "D. objecting to anything more jovial, and we assemble *punctually at half past six . . .*", that last emphatic command sounding suspiciously like something from Dickens's own lips. Such an early start was necessary because, on an approximate reckoning, *The Chimes* would have taken over three hours to read; which is longer even than Tennyson took to read *Maud* out loud to his friends (although the poet did on occasions read it more than once if he believed that it was not being properly understood). But there was no mistaking Dickens's intention or his effect. He gave a second reading two evenings later, at which the principal guest was Albany Fonblanque, and it might fairly be said that the success of these occasions gave Dickens the first hint, the first intimation, that he might be just as successful with other readings of his works – readings, perhaps, to a larger audience than that comprised of his friends. Certainly it was on one of these evenings, as Forster relates, that Dickens and others conceived the idea of enacting plays in private with a sort of radical amateur theatricals. In fact the stage was never far from Dickens's mind and even now, on this brief and hectic visit to London, he gave permission to Gilbert a'Beckett and Mark

Lemon to dramatise *The Chimes* at the Adelphi. From this time forward, Dickens never wrote a Christmas Book which did not at least have the potential for dramatic adaptation; when this is taken in conjunction with the rhetorical punctuation which he was perfecting (he had been recasting *Oliver Twist* in precisely that style) one can see how Dickens's art was changing even as his own sense of his role was being transformed. He was back in Genoa by 20 December and, pausing only long enough to resolve some difficulty with his passport, he rushed back to the Palazzo Peschiere and to Catherine, whom Forster has described as "disconsolate" at his earlier departure. She was about to be more troubled, however, by her husband's behaviour on his return. For within three days he had started mesmerically to "treat" a certain Augusta de la Rue, the English wife of a Swiss banker residing in Genoa. Thus opens a curious episode in his life, not least because it represents the first notable occasion when his wife opposed his will.

Madame de la Rue suffered from a pronounced and disagreeable nervous "tic" or spasm on her face but this was only the physical symptom of a debilitating anxiety. It is said that she resembled Dickens's sister, Fanny, and this may in part account for his interest in her: in any event, he told her husband that he had particular powers of animal magnetism and that he was "ready and happy" to assist her. So began a course of treatment which was to last some months, Dickens seemingly able effortlessly to induce a trance in Madame de la Rue; in that hypnotised sleep he was able not only to assuage the nervous spasms but also, by the technique of verbal free association, to help to elicit the fears which had induced this nervous disorder. It became for him an intense, consuming, interest. He had no book to write, not yet, and all his energies focused upon the sad state of a helpless woman who was lost in her dreams and who sometimes so recoiled in fright that she became almost unmanageable. At first he tried only to cure her physical disorder but very quickly he became drawn in to the very depths and caverns of her consciousness.

Eventually, Catherine must have complained to Dickens about his close relationship to his "patient". He in turn felt compelled to speak to the de la Rues, transmitting, if nothing else, his wife's concerns. Catherine was already pregnant once more and it may be that her condition renewed that old nervous depression and anxiety from which she always seemed to suffer at these times, but the fact that she found the courage to speak to her husband suggests how upset she was by his intimate association with Augusta de la Rue – the phrase to describe the process, "animal magnetism", perhaps sufficiently suggests the emotional element which must surely have entered into the transaction. Not sexual in overt ways but physical nonetheless. Yet it is also quite clear that Dickens was indignant about any such suggestion; he remembered the whole incident well enough to refer to it some eight years later when he returned to Genoa, and even at such a late date he manages to convey his annoyance at his wife's intervention. There is always a kind of innocence about Dickens on such occasions; his self-righteousness and denial of harm were no doubt quite genuine, but always there is a striking inability to see his conduct on anything other than his own terms. Suspicion normally aroused him into a fury, and there is no doubt that Catherine's doubts (perhaps they went as far as accusations) provoked in him his usual intense response. It may have been one of defiance, however, since he stayed with the de la Rues when the preparations for departure from Italy made life in the Palazzo too chaotic for his tidy temperament. But at least Catherine had spoken out and, perhaps for the first time, had temporarily checked or diverted his wishes.

Dickens was now seeing more of Italy. The Dickens family spent New Year in the Palazzo Peschiere where, with other English residents, they played charades and performed country-dances in the old style. And it was in Genoa, too, that the children were given their first dancing lessons. "Our progress in the graceful art delighted him," Mamie remembered many years later, "and his admiration of our success was evident when we exhibited to him, as we were perfected in them, all the steps, exercises and dances which formed our lessons". They were all still very young. Charles Culliford Boz Dickens was seven, Mary Dickens was six, Kate Macready Dickens was five, Walter Landor Dickens was now three and Francis Jeffrey Dickens was only a few months old. He gave each of them nicknames; Mary or Mamie was known as "Mild Glo'ster", Charles or Charley as "Flaster Floby", Katey as "Lucifer Box", Walter as "Young Skull", and the baby as Chickenstalker – the fact that Francis was named after a character in *The Chimes* suggests how easily Dickens moved from his fictional family to his real family, and how in giving them all nicknames he was in a sense turning them into fiction, too. But with them he was, as one of them put it, ". . . always considerate, always gentle to them about their small troubles and childish terrors". It might even be said that, with his children, Dickens could retrieve his own early and happy childhood. In fact he became increasingly distant with them when they grew older, and more than one of them commented upon the puzzling reserve he displayed as they grew into adolescence. But small children are still quite aware of the atmosphere which attaches itself to either parent – perhaps more aware in infancy than in later life – and there seems no doubt that even at their relatively young ages these children sensed what Henry Dickens was later to call his ". . . heavy moods of deep depression, of intense nervous irritability, when he was silent and oppressed". Touching, too, how the children realised their father hated saying goodbye – ". . . we children, knowing this dislike, used only to wave our hands or give him a silent kiss when parting."

Nevertheless Dickens was constitutionally restless and, in the middle of the first month of 1845, the whole family left Genoa and began their Italian travels. Or perhaps better to say that Dickens began *his* travels, dragging alongside him Catherine, Georgina and all five small children. To Carrara, where the large pieces of earth being thrown over the side of the marble workings reminded him of the scene in the tale of Sinbad the Sailor where merchants "flung down great pieces of meat for the diamonds to stick to". To Pisa where the leaning tower reminded him of all the pictures of it he had seen so many years ago in his schoolbooks. Both Pisa and Carrara, then, seen as images of his childhood reading. On by rail to Leghorn. And then to Rome where he took the opportunity of attending the beheading of a murderer. Dickens's keen observation noticed how the neck of the dead man seemed to have disappeared in the process: "The head was taken off so close, that it seemed as if the knife had narrowly escaped crushing the jaw, or shaving off the ear; and the body looked as if there were nothing left above the ear."

From Rome, the Dickens party travelled via Capua and Naples to Herculaneum and Pompeii where amid the ruins of Time stray objects and moments of the distant past are preserved for ever in the stone. Thus, from the great market-place of Pompeii, Dickens stood and looked at the smoking cone of Mount Vesuvius in the near distance, with "the strange and melancholy sensation of seeing the Destroyed and the Destroyer making this quiet picture in the sun". The destroyer and the destroyed in the same even light – is this an image which Dickens came to remember many years later when, in *Great Expectations*, thirty-two men and women are condemned to death by a judge? "The sun was striking in at the great windows of the court, through the glittering drops of rain upon the

252

glass, and it made a broad shaft of light between the two-and-thirty and the Judge, linking both together . . ." Destroyed and destroyer united in a shaft of light; it is a fine image, and it may well have filtered down from the bright day of Italy to the gloomy interior of London.

The party then travelled on to Florence before returning to the Palazzo Peschiere in Genoa; the whole journey had taken some three months, and it was already spring when they came to spend their last few weeks in Italy. There followed a succession of clear bright days, and the family lived quietly here until the first week of June – quietly, that is, except for the extraordinary news that their cook had decided to stay in Genoa and marry an Italian. By now Dickens was eager to go back to England. He had heard from Bradbury and Evans about the success of *The Chimes*, from which he had already earned some fifteen hundred pounds, and he was arranging for the house in Devonshire Terrace to be repainted and redecorated. His first choice for colour was *bright green*; this was no doubt because the colour of most of the shutters in Genoa was (and still is) just such a green, and Dickens wanted to recreate in part the atmosphere of the city in London. He wanted his house to look *Italian* – "I should wish it to be cheerful and gay . . ." he said, and it seems more than possible that Dickens himself became somewhat Italianate while remaining in the city. When in America, he had discovered some of the virtues and vices of that country within his own nature; now that he was in Italy he recognised some of the great theatrical strengths of the Italians, their vivacity and their humour, also within himself. Catherine objected to the Genoese green, however, and Dickens acquiesced. In any case it was time to go back to his real life in the whirling, active world; time once more, as he used to put it, to "earn my bread". Various projects, which he might undertake on his return to England, were already in his mind. So great had been the success of *The Chimes* that he knew he ought to write another Christmas Book, for example; and he must already have been contemplating the prospect of a new novel opening out in front of him. It was now over a year since he had finished *Martin Chuzzlewit*. Of course he could get to work at once upon the book of his Italian travels, eventually to be called *Pictures from Italy*, but he was a little uncertain how to use the letters he had already written. And there was also the prospect of a new periodical which he had discussed with Bradbury and Evans before his departure for Italy.

They left Genoa in the second week of June, returning to England by way of the St Gothard Pass; yet another wild and treacherous journey of the kind Dickens loved but which the rest of his family must have viewed with less than total enthusiasm, their carriage on this occasion slipping and sliding on the brink of abysses. Charley Dickens, then eight years old, remembered making part of this journey with his father across ". . . an extremely rocky and icy walk, from one part of the steep winding road to another by way of a short cut. Indeed I can see the pair of us now, he stalking away in the distance, I struggling in vain to keep up, very tired but extremely proud of being with him . . . finally very nearly collapsing when the phantom path we had been following was found to disappear over a half-frozen little torrent, which had to be crossed by the insecurest possible arrangement of stepping stones before the road and carriage could be regained." Then on to Zurich, Frankfurt and Brussels, where they were met by Forster and Maclise who accompanied them on the journey home.

# Sixteen

AND what was Dickens's sensation of travel? Nothing changes. The identity remains. All that surrounds it remains. Nothing had changed in his absence; ". . . nothing new in London," he complained four weeks after his return and, in addition, he caught a bad cold almost as soon as he arrived home. The day after that return he visited his parents who were now living in Blackheath, and he of course did the usual round of dinners and meetings with his friends; a dinner with Lady Holland, an outing to Greenwich with Christiana Weller and T. J. Thompson, even a courtesy call upon Maria Beadnell, the young woman who in his youth had captivated him and who had now married. In the carriage back, according to Georgina Hogarth, Dickens laughed at the thought of his previous attachment — Maria Winter, as she now was, being, again according to Georgina, a "good natured woman but *fearfully silly*". Forster has described how it was also in this period that he revisited his childhood home in Bayham Street, Camden Town; a common enough phenomenon, this urge to revisit the haunts of childhood, so shrunken and debilitated in comparison with the memory of those places, but it may well have been connected with his half-formed idea to write his life. (If he was planning anything at all, it would have been along the lines of Thomas Holcroft's *Memoirs*, a book he admired and one which described the poverty and misery, as well as the excitement, of childhood in a graphic if somewhat breathless manner.) Often this return to the haunts of childhood coincides with some change in life, however, some turning point; and so it was to prove with Dickens.

He was "continually weeping" with his cold. After the decaying splendours and theatrical miseries of Genoa, London seemed "as flat as it can be". Camden Town, Greenwich, Devonshire Terrace, everything just as it was and as it would always be. Bayham Street. Maria Beadnell a laughable Maria Winter. Even the old memories of childhood become staler. No one can evoke that mood of sad and embittered weariness better than Dickens – Arthur Clennam's arrival in London on a Sunday morning in *Little Dorrit* is a perfect picture of urban melancholy – and few people can have experienced it so intensely. But if there is one constant and admirable quality in Dickens it is his tendency to fight against such moods with the same unwearying endurance with which he fought against circumstances that hampered him; "Never *say* die" was one of his mottoes. In any case he had work to do; he had another Christmas Book to write and he had agreed with Bradbury and Evans to consider the prospect of a new periodical to be edited by him. Almost as soon as he returned, in fact, he thought of a name for it, *The Cricket*, perhaps inspired by the constant chirruping of the cicadas in his Genoese garden but filled too with folk-tale associations of the hearth. It would be, he told Forster, a journal which would continue the "*Carol* philosophy" and which would allow him to enter people's homes in "a winning and immediate way".

Yet something for the near future engaged his attention much more easily. When he had returned briefly to London the previous winter, in order to read *The Chimes* to his friends, he had discussed, as we have seen, the idea of putting on a play; a private performance, to be paid for

256

by the cast and to which each member of the cast would invite especial friends. In other words, an amateur night. If *Little Dorrit* is in part about the permanence and solidity of human identity, so firmly rooted that no mere change of scene or air can affect it, and if his return to London filled him with weariness and ennui, here was a way of fighting back against those sensations. His eagerness to play a theatrical role was at least in part a way of combating that stale and weary sense of familiarity, of adopting a new identity if only for an hour or so, of exorcising the London gloom by promoting all the colour and brightness of a play. Dickens himself wanted to be dressed in "a very gay, fierce, bright colour" as if in echo of his Italian experience: he was to play Captain Bobadil in a performance of Ben Jonson's *Every Man in His Humour*. Forster was to be in it, too. Clarkson Stanfield, as well. And T. J. Thompson. But it is most important to note that the rest of the cast – Mark Lemon, John Leech, Henry Mayhew, Douglas Jerrold, Gilbert a'Becket – came from a specific group, a little band of journalists who were known as the *"Punch* brotherhood" to themselves and as "those *Punch* people" to outsiders, *Punch* being the name of a magazine founded only four years before and now under the editorship of Lemon himself. Dickens's connections with the new magazine were already evident; his new publishers, Bradbury and Evans, printed it and many of its contributors came from that world of radical journalism which Dickens had known in his days as editor of *Bentley's Miscellany*. Some of them of course were already his friends. John Leech had provided the illustrations for both of Dickens's Christmas Books; he was a quiet man, nervous and somewhat melancholy (as many cartoonists of the period seem to have been). He had attended the same school as Thackeray, but he was to a large extent self-taught in his own art; he also had a notoriously penurious and spendthrift father, and this no doubt endeared him to the novelist

257

who always seems to have preferred the company of men who were in some way like himself. Certainly this was true of Mark Lemon, a large and even portly man who had all the geniality and boisterousness conventionally associated with fat men, but whose conviviality concealed an extremely sensitive nature; Dickens, again, always warmed to such people. The shy, the nervous, and the melancholy were to be found among his closest friends. Both Leech and Lemon were also very fond of children, a trait which further endeared them to him; Lemon was known to Dickens's own children as "Uncle Mark" or "Uncle Porpoise" (his wife was "Aunty Nelly").

Dickens was, according to his eldest son, "a born actor" and he is remembered by one friend as "saying he believed he had more talent for the drama than for literature, as he certainly had more delight in acting than in any other work whatever". Macready called him "unskilled" as an actor, which in a technical sense was true; one common remark seems to have been that Dickens was too "hard" in performance, by which was meant too careful, too contrived, too rigid. He was better at the detail than the broad effect, it seems, which sounds like the fault of a man who was thoroughly self-trained in the art, who had, in a sense, studied its effects too carefully and was too assiduous in applying them. Yet he had the genuine instincts of an actor; first and most importantly, as he admitted, he loved ". . . feigning to be somebody else". Those of an analytical turn of mind might suggest at this point that the drama was for him a form of therapy, helping him not only to "blow off my superfluous fierceness", as he put it, but also to discover and recreate himself by adopting a new identity or series of identities. At a time when he was not engaged in writing his fiction, as in this period, it is almost as if all that imaginative appetite for the creation of character was transferred to his own self; so that he became, as it were, a series of characters in search of an author.

Dickens had been going down to Broadstairs to rest during the rehearsals, since the entire family had once again encamped there. Catherine, now heavily pregnant, did not of course accompany him on his forays into London. By now it was mid-autumn and he needed to prepare a Christmas Book for the end of the year; already for him it seems to have become a seasonal custom in which he and his "audience", as he liked to call it, reaffirmed their close and enduring ties. It was less of a story now, more of a communal fairy tale in which all malevolence is lifted and all disputes resolved. Certainly this was the moral of a theme he had in mind which, largely revolving around the plot of a husband's mistaken jealousy, might have been inspired by Catherine Dickens's complaints about his magnetic relationship with Madame de la Rue. But he had no time to begin work on it: almost as soon as he tried to do so, he became involved in a different project altogether.

It had really all begun the year before when Bradbury and Evans had, in the course of their negotiations with Dickens, proposed the idea of establishing some kind of newspaper which Dickens would edit. On his return from Genoa, as we have seen, he contemplated a cheerful weekly periodical chirping away as *The Cricket*, but now a much more important enterprise was suggested to him. Bradbury and Evans, with the financial backing of Joseph Paxton, had decided to set up a radical liberal paper to rival such established prints as *The Times* and the *Morning Herald*. The moment was propitious; Dickens had returned to England at a time when "railroad mania", the issuing of shares in various railway companies amid the rapid extension of that transport, was at its height. The railway itself was to enter Dickens's next novel as both saviour and destroyer – he took the popular image of the moment and in the alembic of his imagination turned it into something both profound and strange – but, more immediately,

259

it was precisely the ready availability of capital that persuaded Bradbury and Evans to launch a paper which would promote and publicise the interests which the railways served. The interests, in particular, of industrialists, of free traders, of manufacturers, all of whose radicalism in this period was directed against the people whom Dickens himself despised.

And who better than Charles Dickens to edit a newspaper which would appeal to such an audience? It was already clear from the effect of *The Chimes* (not to mention *Nicholas Nickleby*) that Dickens could directly intervene in social matters of the day, and he had been a more than capable journalist in his youth. It seemed like a good idea to Dickens, too, and, after being approached by Bradbury and Evans, he went down to Chatsworth to meet the other principal backer, Joseph Paxton. Paxton himself was an unusually gifted man who, in almost quintessential Victorian fashion, had risen in the world by perseverance, ingenuity and energy; he had begun as a gardener's boy and now, in his early forties, he was a railway promoter, architect, and manager of the Duke of Devonshire's estates. Self-help was not in the nineteenth century a mere idle slogan, but a genuine and specific course of action; it has often been said that Victorian society was authoritarian and hierarchical, but there were really no barriers to the advancement of those with ambition and the appetite for power or wealth. So it was that Paxton and Dickens, both self-made men, sat down together in order to discuss the founding of a national radical newspaper. George Hudson, another self-made man and the "railway King", was also backing the project. And Paxton himself, according to an excited letter from Dickens to his friend and financial adviser, Mitton, "has command of every railway and railway influence in England and abroad except the Great Western . . ." Thus, by the curious affiliations of technological development, a mode of transport was the single most important factor in the founding of a newspaper. With a novelist as its editor.

Once more he was in active, whirring life. Catherine was pregnant, he was planning another performance of the Jonson play to raise funds for Southwood Smith's Sanatorium, he was having more difficulties with his father over money, he was arranging for the education of his son Charley, and he still had not written the Christmas Book which was to appear in two months' time. In addition, he had his Italian travels to chronicle. Now he had agreed to take on the editorship of a daily newspaper and, even though his annual salary of two thousand pounds was to be twice that normally offered to editors, it might have seemed rash of Dickens to take on more duties than one man could ever reasonably perform. Yet, although he did not make a formal acceptance for a few days, he seems privately to have accepted the post almost at once. Almost, you might say, without thinking. With the benefit of hindsight it seems odd that a writer of genius should even wish to become the editor of a newspaper, consuming most of his time and his energy as it inevitably must do, but it has to be recalled that *Martin Chuzzlewit* had not been as great a success as the preceding novels, that the Christmas Books were considered by some to be sentimental fancies merely, and that there were critics who were already writing off Dickens as a man who had exhausted his talents before his time.

From this time forward he went down every day to his new offices in Fleet Street, writing letters to the reporters he wished to hire, organising the administration of the business; in fact he was behaving on the *Daily News*, as it was called, with exactly the same firmness and decision he displayed as a stage manager. But the obvious truth that this was not a play, and that he was the editor of a project for which there were already managers in the shape of Mr Bradbury and Mr Evans, was soon to cause

261

difficulties. Some of his friends had reservations, too; when Forster showed Macready the prospectus which Dickens had written, the actor wrote in his diary that Dickens ". . . was rushing headlong into an enterprise that demands the utmost foresight, skilful and secret preparation and qualities of a conductor which Dickens has not. Forster agreed in many if not all of my objections, but he did not seem to entertain much hope of moving Dickens." Macready, in other words, considered Dickens to be the wrong man in the wrong job. There was a celebration dinner for many of those connected with the project, at which Dickens spoke extravagantly of the potential of the *Daily News*; afterwards someone said to Charles Wentworth Dilke, then editor of the *Athenaeum*, "It is your knowledge that will be called upon to remedy the mischief done by Dickens's genius to the new paper." Which, in fact, turned out to be close to the truth.

Very quickly Dickens had his staff in place and readiness, and nothing is more characteristic of Dickens's wish to stamp his own personality upon the paper than the fact that he hired several members of his own family; George Hogarth, his father-in-law, became the music and dramatic critic; John Henry Barrow, his maternal uncle, became its Indian reporter; and, most surprisingly of all, perhaps, Dickens hired his father to be the manager of the parliamentary reporting staff. Bradbury and Evans had taken offices at 90 Fleet Street next to their own printing presses – the buildings had been gutted and then rearranged as the headquarters of the new paper, and consisted essentially of two tumbledown houses with access to one another. To reach them you passed beneath an archway, out of Fleet Street, and down a narrow lane. In one house was Dickens's "sanctum" and an office for the leader-writer; the editor's office, despite absurd rumours at the time of such luxuries as a silver salver for his letters, was in fact very plain with an office table, an armchair, a reading desk, six leather-bottomed chairs, a sofa and a small bookcase in which there were such necessary works as the *Annual Register* and *Hansard*. Above Dickens were two rooms for the sub-editors and for general journalistic use; above them, and up a flight of wooden stairs, were the compositors' rooms. A staircase gave access to the house next door where the printing presses were kept. The whole works were "ill-lighted" and "ill-ventilated", and one of the journalists there recalled ". . . the worn steps, the soiled cocoa-matting, the walls that ever seemed to require painting and polishing, the windows grimed with smoke, the gas, the glare and the smell of oil and paper. The ceaseless noise of presses, moved by hand or by steam, produced a busy hum, whilst in the foggy atmosphere one could see flitting, like ghosts, the forms of men in paper caps and dusty shirt-sleeves . . ." An evocative memory of a printing era before our own, but one that lasted into the eighth decade of the twentieth century.

For Dickens himself, the preparations for the new paper marked a period of intense excitement: apart from anything else, they revived for him those days as a reporter on the *Morning Chronicle*, just as his recent amateur theatricals had brought back memories of the play-acting of his youth. Time was returning. There is nothing more exhilarating, at least for a period, than old time being restored. It is like the restoration of youth itself. Old time revived. "I can't sleep," he said. But this excitement also increased his propensity to manipulate and to dominate people; "Pray order your Carpet Bag, and get into the train INSTANTLY," he ordered Paxton on one more than usually fraught occasion. The fact that he had shares in the new project suggests, also, that he hoped his initial success would allow him to reap benefit in later years.

And what, meanwhile, of his Christmas Book? He called it *The Cricket on the Hearth*, as if he wanted to redeploy the material he had been ready to pour into his once projected periodical, *The Cricket*. He had arranged for the illustrations to be executed by Leech, Doyle and Maclise, but had himself been able to work on the text only sporadically, beginning and continuing it with interruptions over the late months of 1845, at a time when "insuperable obstacles crowded into the way of my pursuits". It is possible that his work upon the *Daily News*, in particular, meant that his social and political passions were deflected into the newspaper rather than into his fiction. Certainly *The Cricket on the Hearth* lacks the social dimension of its predecessors and the *Edinburgh Journal* noted that here Dickens had "turned his attention to a subject of purely moral interest", that subject being the unfounded suspicions of an elderly husband about the fidelity of his much younger wife. It is a pretty enough tale, and perhaps most affecting still for its portrait of a blind girl whose father has over the years created for her a wonderfully bright and luxurious world in which she believes she lives; no one was better at such effects than Dickens. Once again, as in all of the Christmas Books, he employs the tones of his own voice as if he were reading aloud to his audience, as if he wanted to come close to them, to take them by the arm and show them such sights as the spirits had once shown Ebenezer Scrooge. And once again, as in the other Christmas stories, the theme is concerned with a dreadful prospect which is at the last minute snatched away, a ghastly fear which is raised only to be dispelled on the last page. The effect of all of these books, quite unlike the effect of his novels, might be described as one of cheerful catharsis.

But he had been writing *The Cricket on the Hearth* in a much more discontinuous way than he had ever worked on *A Christmas Carol* or *The Chimes*, each of which seemed to have poured from him in a prolonged fit of imaginative reverie. And, to a certain extent, the difference shows. Not necessarily in its construction, which is intricate, or in its prose, which has moments of great beauty and pathos; but rather in the fact that this most recent story seems to contain certain components of Dickens's experience which he has not bothered to sharpen or suppress. It is in some ways a much more personal book than its predecessors, therefore. Is it not his mother, for example, who is satirised in the shape of a somewhat elderly woman with "a waist like a bedpost" and the distinct impression of having once been very genteel indeed? Certainly his wife enters the narrative in a direct way; first as Tilly Slowboy, the maid who is constantly grazing her legs and falling over stray objects. These were the characteristics by which Dickens had once described his wife's own clumsiness. But Catherine appears, too, in the unwarranted suspicions of infidelity which poison relations between husband and wife. And is Dickens describing his own wife, when he has the elderly and suspicious husband declare: "Did I consider how little suited I was to her sprightly humour, and how wearisome a plodding man like me must be, to one of her quick spirit; did I consider it was no merit in me, or claim in me, that I loved her, when everybody must, who knew her?" The quick spirit belonged to Dickens, and the plodding nature to Catherine; and, by the same act of fictional transference, must everybody have loved Dickens when they knew him? Was this his way of reworking the de la Rue episode in his own mind so that no blame could possibly be attached to him? For if there is one constant and pervasive presence in this book it is really that of Dickens himself; he is like the father of the blind daughter, the loving father who spreads fancies around us to beguile us and to keep us from pain. The loving friend, the loving father, the loving narrator – Dickens places himself on every level of the narrative, as if when he is working quickly and almost unconsciously his own preoccupation with himself comes most clearly forward. Even at the end we return to the narrator himself. ". . . I am left alone. A Cricket sings upon the Hearth; a broken child's-toy lies upon the ground; and nothing else remains."

It was a popular but not a critical success; it sold something like twice as many copies as *The Chimes* but those who were seeking to find evidence for Dickens's fading powers pounced upon it as an example of what one critic called "sentimental twaddle". *The Times* called it "the babblings of genius in its premature dotage", although its reviewer's critical asperity might in part have been connected with the fact that Dickens was just about to set up a rival newspaper. But he, too, seems to have been more concerned with public success than critical approval; his own popular social role was becoming of much more importance to him, and one of the reasons he accepted the editorship of the *Daily News* was to confirm his position as an arbiter of public affairs and to establish an intimate relationship with a large audience who had not necessarily read his fiction. It was in this spirit that Dickens made sure that *The Cricket on the Hearth* would be effectively dramatised as soon as it was published; he allowed Albert Smith to produce a theatrical version, to be performed by the Keeleys at the Lyceum (the Keeleys being a well respected husband-and-wife team who specialised in domestic melodramas of this kind), and he went so far as to send proofs of the story before publication so that the play could be ready at the same time. He even assisted at some of the rehearsals.

While, all the time, the excitement over the *Daily News* grew. Among the staff were now Forster and Albany Fonblanque, Douglas Jerrold and Mark Lemon. It had been agreed some time in advance that the first edition should actually be published on the day that Parliament began its crucial next session, a session which would be dominated by the battle over the Corn Laws. An advertisement had appeared in the *Morning Chronicle* and the *Morning Herald* (*The Times* refused to take it) in which a "NEW MORNING

PAPER" was announced, one of "Liberal Politics and thorough Independence". And, once more testifying to the importance of railway development at this precise period in English history, "in Scientific and Business Information on every topic connected with Railways, whether in actual operation, in progress, or projected, will be found to be complete". Forster still had misgivings about his friend's hectic involvement and told Macready that Dickens was "intensely fixed on his own opinions and in his admiration of his works"; but in part this may have been because his own advice was being ignored. The chief leader writer of the paper, W. J. Fox (himself an important member of the Free Trade movement), told a friend that "Dickens and I are regularly against him [Forster] in almost everything, involving difference of opinion".

By the middle of January everything was ready, and a "dummy" edition was prepared on 17 January, 1846, the real first issue of the new paper being finally produced four days later. It was not a complete success, however; it had been printed on poor-quality paper, and had in places been very badly "made up". In other words, the design and lay-out of the pages, perhaps superintended by Dickens himself, were ungainly. And there were also some misprints, the most egregious being in the account of stock prices, an area where accuracy above all else is necessary. One colleague at this time remembered how on the first day ". . . there was a wild rush for the first number. At the sight of the outer sheet, hope at once lighted up the gloom of Printing House Square, the Strand and Shoe Lane [the offices of rival newspapers] . . . I am not sure there were not social rejoicings that night in the editorial chambers, which had been so long beset by dread."

Dickens was, as ever, an energetic and hard-working editor and, as in all the affairs of his life, he paid a great deal of attention to those details of the project which ensured its efficient operation but which are sometimes scorned by greater minds as trivial or merely technical. He knew well enough that in attention to detail, efficiency, and sheer technical competence the secret of success is to be found. In fact there are occasions when he seems more concerned with the speed with which news is transmitted than the content of the news itself, an interest which might profitably be linked to his own fiction where images of free flow as opposed to barriers and hindrances, of unimpeded circulation compared to stagnation and blockage, occur. Perhaps it is not surprising that certain metaphors in his next novel should arise from the theme of movement and release, just after the time when his major aim was to ensure the rapid and successful circulation of the *Daily News*. In fact the paper itself did improve after the near-fiasco of the first number, and that improvement was at least partly the result of the editor's own contributions; in the next few weeks he was to concentrate upon the discussion of the social questions which had always beset him, and in quick succession produced articles or "letters" on capital punishment and on ragged schools.

All of this is perfectly laudable; there is some evidence to suggest, however, that Dickens may have been a very energetic editor without necessarily being a very good one. In later years, when he was managing and editing his own periodicals, his authoritarian self-sufficiency would be a great advantage; but he was too much a man of his own opinions and prejudices, too dominant a figure, too self-assertive and in some ways too *peculiar*, to be a good editor of such a large and complex undertaking. What is needed in such a post is a man of flexible and catholic temper, who at least professes to believe (as Mark Lemon certainly did on *Punch*) that his contributors are likely to be more intelligent, and better writers, than himself. This of course was quite beyond Dickens's power to manage. One contemporary put it simply: ". . . Dickens was not a good editor. He was the best reporter in London and as a journalist, he was nothing more."

Indeed, soon Dickens became restless and dissatisfied with his role. There seems little doubt that he had by now realised that he had made a mistake, that he was essentially a novelist and that any long disruption of his real work would be injurious to him. In fact he already had vague schemes of a new novel and it seems highly likely that, as soon as he had been granted shares in the company (on the first day of publication, he formally signed an agreement in which he was given shares without any need to bring in capital), he started planning to leave. On 9 February he formally resigned and at once he became much more cheerful. His must have been one of the shortest editorships of a national daily, just eighteen days, and the manner of his departure does suggest a degree of wilfulness or even ruthlessness in any matters pertaining to himself and to his own concerns. He often dropped such causes as copyright legislation very soon after he had taken them up with enthusiasm, and there seems little doubt that he "dropped" the newspaper as soon as he felt it to be interfering with his own real pursuits. Now that he had a book in mind, all the high hopes and high declarations about the *Daily News* weighed less than nothing against his own resolve. But his was not, as it turned out, a calamitous decision. Forster took over as editor and Dilke was appointed as manager; between them the *Daily News* stayed in business and eventually began to flourish as a truly radical newspaper.

Dickens was not wholly free of his connection with the paper, despite the fact that he liked to pretend that his decision was swift and final. Of course he retained his shares in it, and it seems that he continued drawing a salary from Bradbury and Evans until the end of April. But at least he was free of editorial responsibilities, and in these months he went back to his writing while planning another long sojourn on the continent; he wanted to live with his family in a country where expenses were less heavy than in England, and the writing of *The Chimes* in Genoa seems to have persuaded him that he could compose as easily abroad as at home. Nevertheless he did not want wholly to lose that position as public reformer which the editorship had provided for him, and over these next few months he contributed a series of articles on social matters which were published in the *Daily News*.

At the same time as he was composing these short social essays he was busily preparing for the volume edition of *Pictures from Italy*; he was asking friends for his letters to them during that period and he was consulting his own diary, primarily to introduce new sections and not to rely totally on the "Travelling Notes" currently appearing in the *Daily News* (in fact that newspaper carried only about half of the subsequent travel book). There was one problem. Clarkson Stanfield had agreed to illustrate the text for Dickens but, when he read those passages of the narrative in which Dickens satirises the excesses of Catholic devotion, he resigned from the project. Stanfield was himself a prominent English Catholic, after all, as Dickens knew, and he could scarcely be connected with a publication which treats his Church's ritual as little more than a parade of mummers; it is difficult, too, to see how Dickens could have been so cavalier or thoughtless in choosing Stanfield for such a project. Until we remember one important fact already illustrated in his departure from the newspaper. Nothing he ever did was wrong. Nothing he ever wrote was wrong. If other people saw things differently, well, that was entirely their problem; and a problem with which he had little sympathy. In his letter to Stanfield, for example, he offers no apology. "You are the best judge whether your Creed recognises and includes, with men of sense, such things as I have shocked you by my mention of. I am sorry to learn that it does — and think far worse of it than I did." It was the Church's fault, in other words, and not Dickens's. As usual, he went at once into action in order to find a substitute; fortunately and curiously, he chose a young artist who then had no real reputation, Samuel Palmer, whose wonderful illustrations are not the least of the merits of *Pictures from Italy* in its final state.

But, perhaps most importantly in the months after his resignation, he was considering once more the possibility of a new novel. He knew that his public expected and wanted another, despite the sneers of the more intellectual of the critics, and it was in his usual uneasy, vexing, open state of mind that he began his search for a theme and a story. Certain minor incidents seem to have entered his consciousness even as he was making his preparations. He managed somehow to run over and kill a dog in Regents Park "and gave his little mistress – a girl of thirteen or fourteen – such exquisite distress as I never saw the like of". Clearly the incident shook Dickens, for he restores the little dog to life in the novel he was contemplating, *Dombey and Son*, where Diogenes is given by Mr Toots to its own "little mistress", Florence Dombey, of much the same age as the distressed girl in Regents Park. That is one of the secrets of Dickens's art in miniature: to compensate for life, to restore the dead, to revive the past, to make amends in fantasy and like the fairy to grant his own wishes. Other aspects of Dickens's life in this period enter *Dombey and Son* as well. He had met, through Joseph Paxton, the "railway King" George Hudson, and in this next novel the theme of business or at least the men of business takes a central place. A famous broker had failed just before the publication of the newspaper; in *Dombey and Son* there is a similar business failure. The "railway mania" had suffused the entire period, and in this novel the railways of course play a central part; in the narrative he names one area of Camden Town soon to be engulfed by the railways as Staggs's Gardens, and a "stag" was the

271

slang of this period for a speculator in railway stocks. In *Dombey and Son*, too, there are echoes and reflections of Dickens's Italian trip, particularly in his meditations on the need for progress amid the decaying stillness of those who try to forestall or ignore such advance. It would not necessarily be true to say that all of these themes and meanings were consciously deployed by Dickens, only that they are the circumambient life in which he moved and in which he planned his novel. All the while restoring lost time and reviving lost contours; connecting the world and making it lucid; brightening the colours and bringing forth the meaning.

Yet still he could not start the novel, and, it is at this time that he embarked upon yet another philanthropic venture. His Idea was to set up a "Home" or "Asylum" for "fallen women". Almost as soon as the plan for it was broached he outlined the nature and the regimen of the Home to be founded. The system of discipline. The practical training. The daily routine. The very lay-out of the building itself. It is curious how the plans are so detailed that they appear to be ready made; as if Dickens had in his imagination been constructing such a place for some time.

Before his second departure for Europe, now imminent, there were also the usual excursions and celebrations. He went to Richmond with Forster, Macready, Maclise and Stanfield; "we had," Macready noted in his diary in his usual rather lugubrious way, "a very merry — I suppose I must say *jolly* day — rather more tumultuous than I quite like . . ." The fact that Clarkson Stanfield joined the party, despite his refusal to illustrate *Pictures from Italy*, suggests that his anger at Dickens's attitude to his faith had already subsided. It was difficult to stay angry for long with Dickens, when he himself was so mercurial. There was also some kind of celebration when the latest member of his family was christened — by the name of Alfred D'Orsay Tennyson Dickens, in honour both of the poet and of the

272

French count whose wit and judgment Dickens readily admired. But the name was enough to delight those who secretly, or not so secretly, considered Dickens to be rather vulgar.

And he was still waiting for some decision about the *Daily News*. Waiting to find out what might happen to his shares. Waiting to see if his resignation had inflicted a fatal blow on its prospects. Waiting until he could wait no longer, and finally, in April, he decided to leave for Switzerland at the end of the following month. His preferred choice had been Genoa but Catherine, still no doubt concerned about his magnetic relationship with Madame de la Rue, seems to have vetoed that idea; so it was Switzerland, and Lausanne. Two weeks before his departure *Pictures from Italy* was published, in the preface to which Dickens confessed to "a brief mistake I made, not long ago, in disturbing the old relations between myself and my readers . . ." He meant his editorship of the *Daily News*, of course, although the proprietors of that paper might have been excused for believing that the mistake was theirs in hiring him in the first place. *The Times* commented tartly on Dickens's statement about his old "relations" with his public: "Let him not, we entreat him, be too eager to resume them. He has not only to sustain his past reputation, but to repair the mischief which we assure him has been done by his latest publications . . ." Dickens may not have seen this complaint, since it was published the day after he had left for the continent, but no doubt its reproaches and its sentiments were very well known to him by now. He had invited Tennyson to join him in Switzerland but the poet had said to a friend, ". . . if I went, I should be entreating him to dismiss his sentimentality, and so we should quarrel and part, and never see one another any more . . ." So even among his admirers there were some who had disliked the tone of the Christmas Books. It was indeed time to resume his old pursuits.

It was time to embark upon his novel. There was another reason for his departure; he wanted to put as much distance as he could between himself and the *Daily News*. It is quite likely that, despite his best efforts, he still felt some residual guilt about his role in its affairs; more than any single person he had come close to ruining it. But he never could have admitted such guilt. And what did he wish to do instead? To leave the scene of the crime. To take flight. To Switzerland.

# Seventeen

H E planned to be away for a year, enough time to complete a great deal of the novel he now had in mind. So once more the whole large family set forth on its travels, accompanied again by their courier in Italy, Louis Roche. Set forth for Lausanne. Many years later, Dickens remembered the mountains. The wooden cottages. The little wooden bridges. The streams. The hillside pastures. Of course Switzerland was not at all like Italy, and Lausanne was not at all like Genoa – except for the fact that they were both built beside water which was such a potent imaginative force for Dickens (in his next novel the doomed little Dombey gazes out at the waves), and that both were surrounded by mountains. Mountains which haunted certain aspects of Dickens's fiction, too, with a vision of cold and brightness which D. H. Lawrence was to explore in another century in *Women in Love*.

They arrived in Lausanne eleven days after their departure from England, in three separate coaches, and took rooms at once in the Hotel Gibbon. For the next two days Dickens roamed around the town, looking for a suitable house for what was now a family of nine, with servants. It was not a large town but, unlike Genoa, it was neat and clean and orderly – all the things which appealed to Dickens, and it was quite in character that just after writing a Christmas story about a maker of dolls he should

275

now find something which he described as a "doll's house" for his family. It was a villa called Rosemont, lying upon a hill which overlooked the lake and the mountains beyond; only a few minutes' walk to the water's edge among green fields and vineyards. Altogether a different atmosphere from Genoa, then; quiet, industrious, and almost studious in its retirement; Dickens noticed the number of book-shops he passed on the daily walks which soon became his speciality here.

It took only a little while for Dickens to settle in this new environment, and almost at once his attention turned to the two projects which were absolutely necessary for him to complete: the new novel, which he had now already promised to Bradbury and Evans, and the Christ-mas Book which had become almost a seasonal necessity both for him and for his readers. His study was on the first floor of the villa, with a long balcony and a window which looked out upon the lake and mountains: beside him was the town of Lausanne, its steep streets seeming to him like the streets in a dream, and the green hills beyond. It was his custom to walk nine or ten miles every evening, all the time thinking of the books he was about to write; he already had a notion for the Christmas Book, one which concerned the peace that suffuses an ancient battlefield. And in this vision of calm succeeding battle, was he per-haps trying to create a mood in which his own recent struggles on the *Daily News* could be co-opted into a saner and more comprehensive vision of the world? Certainly there is something of this eventually to be discovered in the novel he was also contemplating, *Dealings with the Firm of Dombey and Son. Wholesale, Retail, and for Exportation.* A novel which ends, too, on a note of peace and hope after the struggles of the day. And as he walked through Lausanne, planning *Dombey and Son*, he was looking towards just such an ending, constructing much of the plot in advance so that, by the time he began, he had a clear view of the narrative he wished to complete. This is the first novel for which Dickens's number plans survive and, although it cannot be assumed that there were not similar number plans for his previous fiction, it can at least be tentatively suggested that this was the first novel in which Dickens paid as much attention to construction as he did to composition. The number plans themselves are simply sheets of blue paper, one for each instalment of the novel, folded in half; on the left side he would write down general themes or topics which he wished to introduce, and on the right side the contents of each chapter were summarised. The plans acted, then, both as a structural key and as an aide-mémoire, a way of organising his material in easily accessible form and of maintaining a close scrutiny upon the dynamics of each number. There are often occasions in the novels of Dickens where he introduces a chapter or scene simply to alter the mood or tempo of the narrative, and there is no doubt that it was only by constant reference to his abbreviated notes that he was able to achieve what might be called the symphonic effects in his writing.

So it is that, in the first of the number plans for *Dombey and Son*, on the left hand side of the sheet, Dickens jots down among other references "Wet nurse – Polly Toodlie" and "Wooden Midshipman"; the name is eventually changed to Toodle but the contrast here, implicit and not necessarily conscious, "Wet" and "Wooden", is one that recurs throughout a novel in which various types of solidity and hardness (male) are placed against free movement and liquidity (female). His central female character, Florence Dombey, breaks down in tears some eighty-eight times and this sub-text of tears, of flowing water, of the sea at which Paul Dombey gazes, lends the novel much of its power. Many of the events of this year take their place somewhere within Dickens's wonderfully capacious consciousness, to be transformed into fiction, and it can also

277

be said that the world of commerce and offices which Dickens describes in *Dombey and Son* bears at least oblique relationship to the world of newspapers and railways which he had just quitted. There is a sense in which Dickens seems to wish to separate himself from the world of men, the solid world, and in *Dombey and Son* to reach out to the water and the sea, to describe and to celebrate those specifically female virtues which he longed for – the absence of which had so disheartened him in his own struggles with the commercial men who owned the *Daily News*.

At this time, Dickens walked among the hills behind Lausanne; he walked beside the lake; he looked across at the mountains; all the time thinking of the work in hand. But he could not begin, not yet, not until the "big box" which contained all the appurtenances of his desk arrived at Rosemont; these were not just his writing materials, his goose-quill pens and his blue ink, but also the bronze images of two toads duelling, of a dog-fancier with the puppies and dogs swarming all over him, a paper-knife, a gilt leaf with a rabbit upon it. He grouped all these images around him on his desk; as his son-in-law explained after Dickens's death, these were the images "for his eye to rest on in the intervals of actual writing", and so great was his love of habit and order that he could not write without their silent presence in front of him. As soon as they were placed in his study at Rosemont, he began.

He also began work on what he called *The Life Of Our Lord*, a handwritten manuscript which was not completed for three years, in which he recounts the story of the New Testament (largely drawing upon the gospel according to Luke) in the simple language of a children's tale or fairy story, the latter influence perhaps suggesting the extent to which Dickens turned all of the most significant aspects of his life into just such a story. A story to be read aloud since, in a later letter, Dickens recounts how his children "have had a little version of the New Testament that I wrote for them, read to them long before they could read, and no young people can have had an earlier knowledge of, or interest in, that book". It can fairly be said that the New Testament was at the core of Dickens's own religion. "I hold our Saviour," he once wrote, "to be the model of all goodness, and I assume that, in a Christian country where the New Testament is accessible to all men, all goodness must be referred back to its influence." He told his youngest son, on the eve of the latter's departure for Australia, that the New Testament was ". . . the best book that ever was or will be known in the world . . . I now most solemnly impress upon you the truth and beauty of the Christian religion, as it came from Christ Himself . . ."

Of course his life and opinions are one thing, his art quite another. It is interesting to note that in his actual novels no character seems ever to be primarily impelled by Christian motives, and churches themselves tend to be portrayed as dusty places of empty forms and rituals. He usually mentions ministers only to parody or to attack them. And in fact this disparity, between his vigorous public expression of Christian sentiment and his almost total lack of interest in Christian institutions or Christian representatives, is close to the essence of the matter: he was a man of religious sensibility, but his beliefs were determined by his own vision of the world rather than by any inherited or specific creed. That is why the Christian faith becomes, for him, a larger and brighter version of the sentiments he promulgated in his Christmas Books; at no point does it seem that Dickens relied upon any religious "authority" other than his own will or temperament. In the last resort, he believed no one other than himself. His religion was in that sense part of his extraordinarily self-willed and self-created personality, and cannot be separated from it.

If this is the religious spirit which permeates *Dombey*

*and Son*, as has often been suggested, it is not something deliberately introduced by Dickens but is rather part of the very act of creation. So much part of the writer that he did not choose to reveal it. It is simply revealed. That he was contriving the plot of the novel well in advance is not of course in doubt: he was at work upon his number plans, as we have seen, and the cover design which Hablot Browne completed on his instructions shows the main design of the novel. So, on the long evening walks at Lausanne, Dickens meditated on what he called the "general idea" or the "leading idea"; he was planning so far ahead that he already knew that his proposed removal to Paris in November would, with its "life and crowd", materially help him with a much later number. From his own notes it becomes clear, however, that he is looking forward in terms of story and character rather than of theme; despite the extraordinary amount of attention which has in the past been lavished upon Dickens's symbolic intent, from his own correspondence and working plans it is clear that he did not pay attention – at least any conscious attention – to matters which are conveniently paraphrased as "symbols" or "images" or "emblems". He was concerned with the story and with his characters, and with the complicated relationships which can spring up as both move forward. As he moved forward with them. Seeing nothing but them all around him in the evening air of Lausanne.

It was time to begin. Being a superstitious man he used his own variant of the *sortes Vergilianae*, and took a copy of Laurence Sterne's *Tristram Shandy* from his shelf, opened it at random and, with his eyes closed, placed his finger somewhere upon the printed page; then he read, "What a work it is likely to turn out! Let us begin it!" And so he began, looking out over the lake, with a birth and death; the birth of Paul Dombey and the death of his mother, both caught up in the stern presence of Dombey Senior and the timorous gestures of little Florence Dombey. Here in miniature is the whole family saga in which lineage and commerce go together, a fatal union expressed in the title, *Dealings with the Firm of Dombey and Son. Wholesale, Retail, and for Exportation*. He was proud of the title, and wanted it to remain a secret until the last possible moment; he was nervous about the illustrations, too, and kept sending Browne a variety of often imperious instructions. But this was really only part of his general nervousness at the prospect of once more resuming his old relations with the public. The first number seems to have come relatively easily to him. He had planned well ahead, he knew where he was going, and his prose has a new measure of deliberation and restraint; despite the relatively clean state of his manuscript, with far fewer emendations than usual, it is almost as if he were actively working against his fluency, working to create more prolonged effects and to unite the narrative from its very opening. The novel is in part about the loss of natural affections within one family, and how without them nothing else can grow, and Dickens builds upon the achievement of his previous novel, *Martin Chuzzlewit*, by attempting something close to moral analysis. In these opening pages Dickens sets himself the task of creating a more elaborate interior life for his protagonists; a life which of course will be revealed in speech and in action but which is less theatrical, more measured and more powerful than anything in his previous fiction.

But he had not proceeded far with *Dombey and Son* before he was forced to break off; he had rashly agreed to join an expedition to the Great St Bernard with his "ladies" and with a small group of expatriate English friends. It was a cold journey, and a rough one, but they climbed the mountain and made their way to the famous convent where travellers are welcomed. "Nothing of life or living interest in the picture, but the grey dull walls of the convent," Dickens wrote. "No vegetation of any sort or kind. Nothing growing, nothing stirring." The scene was later to be transposed by Dickens to *Little Dorrit*, where it is viewed as yet another kind of prison, but the ice, the absence of life, the deadness, also find their way into the portrait of Mr Dombey. The English party stayed one night in the place and then made their cold and cumbersome journey back to Lausanne. Where once again Dickens took up his novel, and where once again he worried about the Christmas Book which he had to start almost at once in order to meet the deadline for publication by the end of the year. Within a few days he had in fact been able to finish the second number of *Dombey and Son*, and, two days later, he began on the Christmas tale which he had already entitled *The Battle of Life*. He had hoped to finish it by the end of September; but he could not manage any such rapid composition. He found it extremely difficult to work on two books at once; any creative effort expended on *The Battle of Life* should have been reserved for *Dombey and Son*, or so he thought, and in any case *The Battle of Life* now seemed to him to contain too good a story to be thrown away as a seasonal offering. In his earlier years he had been quite confident of his powers to work on two novels at once — *The Pickwick Papers* and *Oliver Twist* were of course written contemporaneously — but now that particular elasticity of imagination appears to have deserted Dickens. In addition he had never *begun* two books at the same time, and the difficulty of keeping both in his head (as it were) seemed to disconcert and even to paralyse him. Towards the end of September he told Forster that "I fear there may be NO CHRISTMAS BOOK!" Never before had he abandoned a project already begun and he felt "sick, giddy, and capriciously despondent. I have bad nights; am full of disquietude and anxiety; and am constantly haunted by the idea that I am wasting the marrow of the larger book, and ought to be at rest." So he was worried about *Dombey and Son*, an anxiety redoubled in view of the fact that it was his first full-length novel for so long; he was worried about *The Battle of Life*, and the fact that he might have to sever the relationship he had established with his Christmas audience; he was worried about worrying; he needed rest and ease, but he could not get it. He had neuralgic pains across his brow, and thought that he might have to be "cupped" – that is, to have blood drawn from him. He was to say later that at this point he felt himself to be "in serious danger", by which he must have meant some kind of nervous collapse, but he rallied. He found streets, after all, streets in which he could grow more self-forgetful, for in pursuit of that urban "magic lantern" he had made the short journey to Geneva and restlessly walked the narrow and winding thoroughfares of that city.

Within three days he felt well enough to begin the second part of *The Battle of Life*. "If I don't do it," he had told Forster, "it will be the first time I ever abandoned anything I had once taken in hand; and I shall not have abandoned it until after a most desperate fight." So he carried on, working against the grain, using all his massive powers of will to urge himself forward, until by the time he left Geneva for Lausanne, two days later, he knew that he would be able to complete it after all. Six days on, and he had finished the second part; his eye, he said, was now "pretty bright!" Then, as a relaxation from his labours, he used that bright eye to transfix a small audience when he read to them the second number of *Dombey and Son* and provoked "the most prodigious and uproarious delight", the success of which venture led him to think aloud to Forster about the possibility of undertaking public readings in England. Dickens was heartened, too, by the initial success of *Dombey and Son*; the first number had sold approximately 25,000 copies and he wanted to complete *The Battle of Life* as soon as possible in order to return to a novel for which he had great plans – plans enough to retain the interest and excitement of his readers. So he worked at the Christmas Book in a fury, finishing its third and final part within five days; as he did so, he dreamed that the book was "a series of chambers impossible to be got to rights or got out of . . ." Even the short (and remarkably well conducted) radical revolution in Geneva seemed to be aligned to it in his dreams, as if the battle of his title was being mocked or copied by the sparse and scattered battles near Lausanne.

On 17 September *The Battle of Life* was completed. And what of it now? Written with difficulty and in despondency, almost abandoned and then completed in a rush, it is not the most successful of Dickens's stories. And, with its theme of two sisters loving the same man, it has been considered too close to Dickens's own domestic situation to have that objectivity which his best work commands. Of course the theme of two loving sisters, their love devoted to the same male, is one that seems always to have attracted Dickens; but the real importance of the story is to be found in its title. *The Battle of Life* was a phrase which meant a great deal to mid-Victorian Englishmen: it was even something of a truism in a world for which struggle and domination were the twin commandments, where the worship of energy and the pursuit of power were the two single most significant activities, where there was a constant belief in will, in collision, in progress. Darwin and Malthus both described "the great battle of life" and "the great battle for life", the important confusion between the two phrases materially assisting the evolutionist's case; Gladstone was to talk of life as one "perpetual conflict"; Browning wrote, "I was ever a fighter, so – one fight more . . ."; and Samuel Smiles, that wonderful exponent of what we have now come to call Victorian values, noted that "all life is a struggle".

Two days after he had completed the Christmas story Dickens went back once again to Geneva; he had to start work on *Dombey and Son*, simply in order to maintain the monthly publication which had already begun, but he needed to rest first and for a week he managed to subdue his nature to a regimen of complete idleness. Nevertheless he knew where he wanted to go, and what he wanted to do, with the novel; immediately on his return to Lausanne, he began the third number and wrote of Paul Dombey, of Mrs Pipchin, of Captain Cuttle and of Major Bagstock who, when he meets the proud and cold Mr Dombey, begins his course of rubicund flattery: "'By G—, Sir,' said the Major, 'it's a great name. It's a name, Sir,' said the Major firmly, as if he defied Mr Dombey to contradict him, and would feel it his painful duty to bully him if he did, 'that is known and honoured in the British possessions abroad. It is a name, Sir, that a man is proud to recognise. There is nothing adulatory in Joseph Bagstock, Sir. His Royal Highness the Duke of York observed on more than one occasion, "there is no adulation in Joey. He is a plain old soldier is Joe. He is tough to a fault is Joseph:" but it's a great name, Sir. By the Lord, it's a great name!' said the Major, solemnly." One of the marvels of Dickens is the way that he can create a kind of speech which effortlessly evokes a character, a speech both unique and identifiable, a speech which he hears among all the others lodged in his imagination and which he can draw out at will. He had begun the number at the very end of October and completed it on 9 November; a rapid movement forward, but the manuscript contains so many heavy corrections that he was clearly telling the truth when he described himself in "agonies" over the last chapter. Then almost as soon as he had finished, according to prearranged plans, the Dickens family left for Paris. "I have no doubt," he wrote to Forster, "that constant change, too, is indispensable to me when I am at work . . ." This had not always been the case but, from this time, Dickens's general restlessness becomes a marked feature of his life. He had to move on. To take flight. To match his external surroundings against the great restlessness that he harboured within his own self.

# *Eighteen*

I T took three carriages to get the whole family to Paris, on a journey which took them five days. It was impractical as well as expensive for them all to stay in an hotel so, on the first day of their arrival, Dickens looked for a suitable residence. And he quickly found one; a small house in the Rue de Courcelles, an extravagantly shaped and oddly furnished place which appealed to the more whimsical aspects of his imagination. On the night of his arrival he also took a long walk through the city "of which the brilliancy and brightness almost frightened him", according to Forster; and yet he was really quite used to brilliancy and brightness. They were in fact the two qualities most often associated with his own presence in the world, and there is no doubt that he took amazingly to the city on this second visit; he was soon to think more highly of the French than of the English as ". . . the first people in the universe", and in later years Paris became for him a place of refuge, a bolt-hole, when he grew tired of England and of that less bright or brilliant London life. On this second visit it was very cold. It snowed. And yet Dickens did not seem to mind. According to his son Charley, he and his father visited a "good many theatres to 'consolidate my French' as my grandfather once expressed it", and in Paris Dickens by his own account went ". . . wandering into Hospitals, Prisons, Dead-houses, Operas, Theatres, Concert Rooms, Burial-grounds, Palaces, and Wine shops." This was a whole "Panorama" of "gaudy and ghastly" sights, the metaphor itself suggesting just how theatrical Dickens's vision of the world could sometimes become, the painted or scenic representations of the Panorama being one of the chief entertainments of the day.

In particular he enjoyed going alone to the Morgue, a typically French institution where the unidentified bodies of those recently found dead were put on display for the Parisian public at certain times of the day. In later years Dickens was to describe this spectacle in horrified terms – ". . . the ghastly beds, and the swollen saturated clothes hanging up, and the water dripping, dripping all day long, upon that other swollen saturated something in the corner, like a heap of crushed over-ripe figs . . ." Yet he kept on visiting it. He came back all the time, since the Morgue had infected him with a state which he liked to call "the attraction of repulsion". On later visits to Paris he confessed that "I am dragged by invisible force into the Morgue", and he recounted how on one occasion he became obsessed for some days with the image of a man found drowned (a man who was to resurface in *Our Mutual Friend*), an obsession which he himself connected with the fears of childhood.

There were other intimations of death, too, in this period. He had an imaginary death to arrange with all due ceremony: "Paul, I shall slaughter at the end of number five," he wrote to Forster. And he had just heard that his sister, Fanny, "was in a consumption", then a generally fatal illness and one which showed all of its distressing symptoms in advance. There was even a connection between the imagined death and the real disease; Fanny's son, Henry Burnett, was a weak crippled child upon whom Dickens had actually based the character of the ailing Paul Dombey. At least this was how Fanny's pastor, a Reverend

James Griffin of Manchester, told the story: "Harry was a singular child – meditative and quaint in a remarkable degree. He was the original, as Mr Dickens told his sister, of little 'Paul Dombey'. Harry had been taken to Brighton, as 'little Paul' is represented to have been and had there, for hours lying on the beach with his books, given utterance to thoughts quite as remarkable for a child . . ." Perhaps Harry, who had been born in 1839, had also suggested to his famous uncle the character of Tiny Tim in *A Christmas Carol*; Tiny Tim did *not* die while Paul Dombey did, of course, and it seems surprising that Dickens should decide to "slaughter" a child based upon his own ailing nephew. Yet it was fiction. Only fiction. And in the coldest days of the year Dickens was planning the death of little Paul.

There was one interruption when, in the middle of December, he went back to London for a few days. As effective if not titular head of the Dickens family, he came over to discover more about Fanny's mortal illness. And then swiftly back to Paris where he began once more to contemplate the coming death of Paul Dombey. *Presently he told her that the motion of the boat upon the stream was lulling him to rest. How green the banks were now, how bright the flowers growing on them, and how tall the rushes!* New Year's Day was bitterly cold, and in a later description of this occasion Dickens emphasises only his own visit to the Théâtre des Gaîtés that cold evening; but really his mind is elsewhere. Paul Dombey must die. *Now the boat was out at sea, but gliding smoothly on. And now there was a shore before him. Who stood on the bank?* "Everything that is capable of being frozen," he writes of his house in the Rue de Courcelles, "freezes". He is working very slowly upon the novel. "I am slaughtering a young and innocent victim," he says with barely suppressed satisfaction. *He put his hands together, as he had been used to do at his prayers. He did not remove his arms to do it; but they saw him fold them so, behind*

289

*her neck.* The story now had such a hold upon him that he was working upon it both night and day. *"Mamma is like you, Floy. I know her by the face! But tell them that the print upon the stairs at school is not divine enough. The light about the head is shining on me as I go!"* He killed Paul Dombey on Friday night. *The golden ripple on the wall came back again, and nothing else stirred in the room. The old, old fashion! The fashion that came in with our first garments, and will last unchanged until our race has run its course, and the wide firmament is rolled up like a scroll. The old, old fashion – Death!* Then he walked through the streets of Paris until dawn.

With the death of Paul Dombey Dickens created the same sensation as he had with the death of Little Nell in *The Old Curiosity Shop*. He was to do it again, with the death of Dora in *David Copperfield* and with the death of the crossing sweeper, Jo, in *Bleak House*. There were some critics who felt that Dickens had, once again, gone too far in pathos. Others who believed that he killed off any interesting child within reach simply in order to maintain the allure of his narrative. There is some truth in this. Truth enough to provoke a parody of Paul Dombey's death in a satirical magazine, *The Man in the Moon*, where, during a fake inquest into the death of the Late Master Paul Dombey, Dickens himself is called as a witness – "Had once thought of making 'Son' the agent of retribution on 'Dombey'. Abandoned the notion. Did not see his way in working it out. Considered that he had a right to do what he liked with his own. Took things as they came. Did not know what a chapter or a page might bring forth. When he had no more use for a personage, or did not know what to do with it, killed him off at once. It was very pathetic and very convenient . . . If he was asked to name the disease of which Paul had expired, thought it was an attack of acute 'don't-know-what-to-do-with-him-phobia'. Had it not supervened, he would have suffered under, and probably succumbed, at last to a chronic affection, technically called 'being-in-the-way-ism'. These complaints were very prevalent in the literary world, and very fatal . . ." And yet the public loved it, loved the pathos, loved the deaths, and some years later there was still a popular song based upon Paul's demise and entitled "What are the Wild Waves Saying?"

By now, Dickens's purpose in *Dombey and Son* was to throw all the interest after the death of Paul onto his sister, Florence. The story needed this shift of emphasis, for the death of the boy was only a prelude to a story in which the intrigue must grow and in which the collapse of Dombey has to be all the more powerfully conveyed. But again, after all the excitement of little Dombey's death, he was working slowly; he was feeling ill, it was snowing, and he could not seem to find his way forward. He turned down social invitations in order to remain at his desk – no book had caused him so much endless concentration and trouble – and at a late stage reversed the order of two chapters so that the pain of Paul's death in the previous number might be more pleasantly dissipated. But to his horror he found that this new first chapter was two pages too short, so on the following day he travelled to London in order to work near the printer. His son was already back at King's School in Wimbledon, and on this visit he remembers his father taking him for "a long tramp" around Hampstead Heath before they dined with Lady Blessington at Gore House; a dinner, incidentally, at which Charley sat next to Louis Napoleon. Dickens spent only three or four days in London and, on the day he left for Paris, Charley contracted scarlet fever. His father learnt of this the day after he had returned to the French capital and so, with that energy and address so customary to him, he returned at once to London with Catherine. They could not stay at Devonshire Terrace, which was still let to tenants, and instead they moved to Chester Place. This was just a street away from the Hogarths, where Charley was now lying during the worst stages of his illness; Catherine, being pregnant once more, was not allowed to go near her son and Dickens was also forced to remain at a distance until the contagious period had passed.

His concern over his son's scarlet fever made it imperative to stay in London with Catherine, and so he rented the temporary accommodation in Chester Place until the end of June. It was here, in the small street off Regent's Park and only a short distance from the Polygon as well as other haunts of Dickens's childhood, that Sydney Smith Haldimand Dickens was born. The seventh child. But, if even by nineteenth-century standards this was now a large household, there are clear signs that Dickens's financial anxieties, at least, were coming to an end. *Dombey and Son* itself was selling very well, and from the first four numbers alone he received something like fifteen hundred pounds from Bradbury and Evans; in fact, from the sales of all his books during the last six months of the previous year, he earned altogether more than three thousand pounds. He was also banking on (almost literally) the imminent publication of a new and inexpensive edition of his novels; this was known as "working the copyrights", and the plan was to issue all of Dickens's previous novels in cheap weekly and monthly formats. In order to emphasise the novelty of the venture new illustrations were to be used, and Dickens himself decided to write original prefaces for each of his works. He dedicated this new series somewhat grandiosely to "the English people", and in a preliminary advertisement he touched upon all those issues which remained most important to him; he wished his work to become "easily accessible as a possession by all classes of society . . .", and in addition he was happy to become "a permanent inmate of many English homes where, in his old shape, he was only known as a guest . . ." Of course there was also his belief that ". . . the living Author may enjoy the pride and honour of their widest diffusion, and may couple it with increased personal emolument . . ." This last phrase, so redolent of his father in more loquacious moments, represented something of great importance to Dickens; he expected to make a great deal of money out of this venture and, although the receipts for the first year were not altogether satisfactory, within a short time he was earning a relatively large income from what was known as the Cheap Edition. In a sense he was merely keeping up with his time, since the ever-cheaper methods of printing and the ever-widening audience of literate readers meant that novels of his kind could be diffused far more widely than had been the case even ten years before. Certainly he was now one of the highest-paid authors of his day, and it was in these summer months of 1847 that he bought six hundred pounds worth of Consols, the first of many investments he made from this time forward.

And then he was attacked by a horse. A silly accident, perhaps, but one that seemed severely to shake Dickens. He had been working very hard on the eighth instalment of *Dombey and Son* and, in pursuit of physical activity at a time of mental exhaustion, he had gone down to Chertsey for some riding. It was here that a horse in the stable attacked Dickens's arm and shoulder; his coat sleeve and shirt sleeve were torn off and the horse had come close to actually ripping the great muscle of his arm; luckily, as it turned out, it was merely heavily bruised. But something about this incident unnerved Dickens, for he became very ill; not only with the bad bruising upon his arm but also with something which he described as "a nervous seizure in the throat". He felt much more unwell than he told anyone at the time – the remedy seems to have been the sniffing of pungent salts and the taking of wormwood – and admitted only to "a low dull nervousness of a most distressing kind". It is impossible to know precisely what he meant. The nervous prostration may have had entirely

293

physical origins but it is also possible that he had an underlying fear of being attacked, and that even the sudden violence of an animal provoked those fears. In addition he told his sister, dying of consumption, that at times of great anxiety or exhaustion he was sometimes gripped by "dreadful" ideas and oppressive mental "sufferings". The "nervous seizure in the throat" may be another clue to his suffering; a few years later, when he was again affected by nervous exhaustion, he would sometimes wake up in the night with the sensation of choking. A man of immense nervous and imaginative susceptibility could become just such a prey to various horrors. Hence the distress which he experienced now; and, when Landor saw him in the month of the accident, he wrote that he seemed "thin and poorly". Certainly he felt "poorly" enough to travel down to Brighton for peace and sea air; he found lodgings there and worked on the next number of *Dombey and Son*, the novel in which he made imaginative use of his accident some time later when Mr Dombey himself is thrown from his horse and is kicked insensible.

For nothing in his life was so strong as his desire to keep on working, to keep on with business and busy-ness. Even while in Lausanne and Paris he had been contemplating the scheme for the building of a "Home" for "fallen women", and within a month of his return to England he was consulting with prison governors about possible candidates for benevolence while looking in the suburbs of London for a suitable house. By May he had found one, in Shepherds Bush, and at once made an offer for the lease. All of this activity meant that Dickens was leaving his novel to the last minute, not beginning work until the middle of the month and finishing some ten days later, thus leaving just a few days for the setting and correcting of type. Clearly he felt confident enough of the narrative to work on it in this fashion; he was quite sure both of what he wanted to do and the speed with which he could

294

do it. Nevertheless there are signs in these sections of undue haste: in point of invention, and even seriousness, the chapters are some of the weakest in the novel.

The Dickens family now moved down to Broadstairs, as had become the custom when they were in England. Dickens came up to London during this period, and stayed at the Victoria Hotel. Now that he had found the right property to establish his Home, he visited the prisons in order to find likely candidates for its shelter; he was on terms of close friendship with the governors of Cold Bath Fields prison and the Westminster House of Correction and it was primarily to these institutions that Dickens went in search of what might be called the right material. As soon as the Home, Urania Cottage, was formally opened (in the November of this year) he began to attend meetings there regularly and to oversee the major part of its routine. Even here he was in a sense still the novelist, still keeping in touch with the poor, still attending to their habits and their ways of speech, still keen to penetrate their mystery. "My anxiety to know that secret reason of Sarah's," he wrote about one of the girls, "is so intense that I will call on Monday between one and two . . ." When he was not able to discover all that he wanted, he readily used his powers as a novelist imaginatively to reconstruct events and details. Perhaps his own sense of "power" here is the most appropriate. It is in fact also the word that Dickens used when, in the course of an argument that the girls should always emigrate together, he added that "it would be a beautiful thing, and would give us a wonderful power over them, if they would form strong attachments among themselves . . ." This sounds very much like one of the situations he idealised in his fiction; the idea of young women forming strong attachments with each other was at the centre of his last Christmas Book and plays some role in the development of *Dombey and Son*. In this context it might be noted how Dickens believed that these girls with

295

"wretched histories" might be improved by a course of "education and example" and thus be led to a happier fate; there should be "variety in their daily lives" but "rigid order" introduced into their habits so that they might all become an "innocently cheerful Family". They were, also, to be implicitly guided by rules but would never be informed of them. But is this not precisely what happens to the characters in his fiction, characters who are guided by forces which they do not understand and who proceed through tribulation to a generally happier fate, and does it not give extra point to his suggestion that each inmate should have a "book" of her life at Urania Cottage with a final page entitled "Subsequent History"?

After the exertions of Urania Cottage, Dickens went back to Broadstairs and to his family. Hans Christian Andersen, so recently met, came to visit him here and described the ". . . narrow little house, but pretty and neat . . . The windows facing the Channel, the open sea rolling in almost underneath them; while we were eating the tide went down, the water ebbed at amazing speed, the great sandbanks . . . rose mightily up, the lighthouse was illuminated." And so the little town of Broadstairs was in turn illuminated by the imagination of the world's greatest writer of fairy-stories. Unfortunately his English was not as good as his imagination, and during this and subsequent meetings there seems to have been a large degree of misunderstanding and general social difficulty. But there were differences of other kinds, too; as so often with authors, their conversation turned to the question of payment and Dickens seemed quite unable to believe the low royalties which Andersen received. "Oh," he said, in that echo of his speech which so vividly brings him to life, "oh, but we must be misunderstanding one another." The morning after Andersen's arrival Dickens walked with him the two and a half miles to Ramsgate in order that his guest might catch the steam-boat to Copenhagen; Andersen's last sight of England was of Dickens, "in a green Scotch dress and gaily coloured shirt", standing on the quay as the boat slipped over the water.

Two and a half miles was of course no distance at all to Dickens (the "Scotch dress", by the way, is less likely to be a kilt than a pair of fashionable plaid trousers) for, in this first full year he was spending in England for some time, he was filled with restlessness and energy; what he described as his "superfluous steam". And there were many ways of distributing it. He had a sudden idea of editing a standard series of great British novelists, but dropped the plan almost as quickly as he had picked it up. Then, while he was writing *Dombey and Son*, he began to make preparations for the next Christmas Book, even though his experience in the previous year had shown him how difficult it now was for him to work on two fictions concurrently. But again he changed his mind and postponed his next Christmas Book for a year, despite the fact that he was "loath to lose the money" and more importantly to leave "any gap at Christmas firesides". So there was "superfluous steam" left, and he promptly expelled it in a new scheme he had conceived; a scheme for a mutual insurance fund for writers and artists. It was to be called The Provident Union of Literature, Science and Art, and the funds for it were to be raised by a series of amateur theatricals every year. Thus did Dickens hope to combine business with pleasure, and to turn his always much-anticipated and much-longed for theatricals into a *system*; just as he turned the routine of Urania Cottage into a *system*; just as he organised his responses to begging-letter writers into a *system*.

Even as he planned the Provident Union, he was coming to the climax of *Dombey and Son*. Edith Dombey flies from the Dombey household and elopes with Carker. (At the urging of Forster and ever mindful of public taste, he decided that she would not commit adultery; but, in any

297

case, sex rarely enters his novels except in the shape of grotesque lust. For the simple reason that sex renders people all alike, while the whole momentum of Dickens's fiction is towards uniqueness and peculiarity.) Dombey in his furious anger strikes his daughter, Florence, who runs from the house. Dombey pursues his wife and Carker. The chapter concerned with Edith Dombey's elopement was written by Dickens in a furious passion, but even as he wrote so rapidly he included passages which touched upon his other concerns of the moment. For here also was a plea for the outcast – ". . . some ghastly child, with stunted form and wicked face . . ." – in the very week when Urania Cottage was opened. And he was writing here too about "the polluted air, foul with every impurity that is poisonous to health and life" just a few days after he had read a report in *The Times* about the possibility of yet another cholera epidemic in the poorer parts of London.

Dickens went with Catherine to Scotland, the scene of his first public triumph, in order to attend a soirée for the Glasgow Athenaeum. They travelled to Edinburgh, and then from Edinburgh to Glasgow; but on this later ride Catherine was suddenly taken ill and suffered a miscarriage on the train. She was put to bed and was compelled to remain there as her husband experienced "unbounded hospitality and enthoozymoozy". He goes on, ". . . I have never been more heartily received anywhere, or enjoyed myself more completely." Even though his wife was forced to remain in bed after her miscarriage. Is there not in the contrast between these two scenes of domestic life some warning for the future? They returned to London on the third day of the new year, 1848, a date which began the succession of what in his biography Forster called Dickens's "happiest years". And why should he not be happy? He was now wealthy enough no longer to need to worry about money, he was very famous and very well loved. The enthusiasm at Glasgow had been enormous and, just a month before, when he had walked onto the platform of a meeting for the Leeds Mechanics' Institute, "the whole audience rose, and the applause became almost deafening . . ."; it was several minutes before silence could be restored.

But if this year marked a certain happiness and excitement in Dickens's life, now more than ever firmly planted in public affection and respect, it also inaugurated a period during which his actual pre-eminence as a novelist was first seriously called into question. It has to be remembered that in 1847 had appeared *Jane Eyre*, *Wuthering Heights* and of course *Vanity Fair*, all of which novels were recognised as great or at least as significant works. It had been in this year, too, that Dickens entered a more private relationship with William Makepeace Thackeray. His position among his friends of *primus inter pares* meant that he was sometimes called upon to resolve disputes or give assistance in various domestic or financial crises, so it is not surprising that he should have been asked to intervene in a quarrel between Thackeray and John Forster. The details are no longer particularly interesting. Forster told a mutual acquaintance that Thackeray was as "false as hell", the remark was repeated to Thackeray who then "cut" Forster in public. In fact through the agency of Dickens the dispute was quickly resolved, and it is significant now only for the ambiguous position of Thackeray with regard to Dickens and Dickens's intimate friends.

And so by 1848, in his thirty-sixth year, Dickens entered a new age in which writers of more recent celebrity than himself entered the field. The éclat of his sudden rise to eminence had faded, and he was no longer the unique and almost inexplicable phenomenon which in his youth he had been. He was now one novelist among others. There were those who applauded the new "naturalism". There were those who admired the classical or at least neo-classical serenity of Thackeray's writing. There were those who praised the moral passion of *Jane Eyre*. It was natural that all these changes in the literary world around him provoked changes in Dickens's sense of his own art. In his sense of his own self. He always rose to any challenge and, if Thackeray or Charlotte Brontë had achieved effects outside his own range – well, then, he would extend that range. He would go further. There was much still to be done.

And what is the nature of this change? It has often been suggested that, from this time forward, Charles Dickens's imagination became imbued with subtler colours. That the transition from *Martin Chuzzlewit* to *Bleak House*, for example, represents a significant strengthening of his social vision. That he no longer attacks merely rich or proud individuals in the old theatrical fashion but rather explores a whole society in order to discover the forces latent within it. There is no more than a certain truth to this since, from the time of *The Chimes* four years earlier, Dickens had a pretty shrewd idea of the nature of the society in which he lived. There is an unmistakable change in his art during this period, of course, but it would have been astonishing if it had *not* changed in so rich and self-conscious an artist. Something else was happening, something connected with his own sense of literary challenge but also working under the surface of Dickens's own life and opinions, a change which is best exemplified by the extraordinary amount of conscious and unconscious self-revelation that was about to issue from him. All the evidence suggests, as we shall see, that he was turning back to face his own past and to understand the forces that had shaped him; he was begin- ning to observe himself in the context of time and history, in other words, and this new sense of himself spread out- ward, changing everything that it touched, creating new perspectives, encouraging Charles Dickens to recognise the broader and less easily identifiable aspects of the world around him.

Certainly he had every opportunity to do so, for this new year also marked a transition of another kind. John Forster had just taken over from Albany Fonblanque the editorship of the *Examiner* and, no doubt in deference to his close friend's new role, Dickens agreed to write occasional articles and reviews for the newspaper. He had once been a successful reporter, he had once been an unsuccessful editor, but now he took on a task which seemed to combine the best of these roles; he could be both observer and pundit, combining his interest in the local and specific detail with the broadest of moral brush strokes. That is why these occasional pieces, no longer read except as extensions of his fiction, are still entertaining. They are lively, opinionated, ironic, animated by sarcasm or by pity and adopting an expressive style which uses italics, dashes, brackets, short sentences, pithy phrases to encapsulate a point or to offer an opinion. His first article was an unsigned review of a book about ghosts, but over the next twenty-three months he wrote essays upon crime, urban sanitation, poverty, capital punishment – in fact upon all the issues that touched him most deeply.

Thus the public affairs of the year progress with Dickens as observer, all the time in his own journalism providing further evidence for his confession that ". . . the ideal world in which my lot is cast, has an odd effect on the real one . . ." Thus everything became an echo chamber for Dickens's secret voice, the voice of his imagination. This was the voice he must at all costs listen to; and, at the end of February 1848, he went down to Brighton in order to finish *Dombey and Son* in the relative tranquillity of that resort. Yet, restless once more, he came back again to London a fortnight later in order to be "near the printer" as the final pages of his novel emerged. He actually completed it in the last week of March, bringing this extraordinary study of one man's broken pride to an end with his usual feeling of desolation at being parted from the characters of his imagination. Finished. Finished at last. Until he suddenly remembered that he had left out Florence's little dog from the happy tableau at the end of the novel. So he instructed Forster to add a sentence on that theme and, four days later, tried to work up his spirits once more in an expedition to Salisbury and Stonehenge. Forster, Lemon and Leech went with him and all these men formed part of a *Dombey* celebration dinner which took place two weeks later, a dinner at which Henry Burnett sang. Dickens was still describing his "forlorn" condition some days after this event, so bereft did he feel after despatching his novel into the world, but at the dinner itself he was, according to Macready, "happy". He had every reason to be; the sales of *Dombey and Son* had risen to something like thirty-five thousand, at least ten thousand more than those for *Martin Chuzzlewit*, and Dickens declared that ". . . I have great faith in Dombey, and a strong belief that it will be remembered and read years hence". So he had recovered all of his old hearty self-confidence; the fact that he did not feel it necessary to begin another novel *at once* suggests also that his new financial security removed that anxiety about the future which had dogged him through all the years before.

But Dickens's sister's health was failing now and indeed she was dying. Dickens had visited her in Manchester and had frequently written to her with his characteristic messages of hope and encouragement, but it was clear by the end of June that she had little time left; with her husband she came down from Manchester to Hornsey, both to be near her family and close to the doctors who might best be able to treat her. But there was no hope; she was thin to the point of emaciation and worn down by the constant cough of the consumptive. Dickens visited her often, almost daily. "She shed tears very often as she talked to her brother," Mamie Dickens recalled many years later. ". . . He was deeply moved, and greatly impressed by her calmness and courage." Dickens has left his own account of one such painful interview. "I asked her whether she had any care or anxiety in the world. She said No, none. It was hard to die at such a time of life —" for she was only thirty-seven years old — "but she had no alarm whatever in the prospect of the change; felt sure we should meet again in a better world . . ." This was the sister with whom he had grown up and first gone to school, the sister who seemed to have deserted him when he was consigned to the blacking factory, the sister who sang and acted with him in their early years. She had seen him grow into a famous man, and now she was dying. "She showed me how thin and worn she was; spoke about an invention she had heard of that she would like to have tried, for the deformed child's back; called to my remembrance all our sister Letitia's patience and steadiness; and, though she shed tears sometimes, clearly impressed upon me that her mind was made up, and at rest." He came back from this meeting and, before going to bed, wrote out a detailed account and sent it to Forster; in moments of great emotion he could only understand his feelings when he wrote them down. That is the time when they became real for him, and when he could begin to understand himself. And it was at this time, too, that he began to contemplate the next Christmas Book, a book concerned with "the revolving years", with "the memory of sorrow"and the significance of time past.

So it was in no very sanguine frame of mind that he went down to Broadstairs for the annual summer holiday. Georgina and the children were already there; and so was Catherine, who was once again pregnant and once again in poor health as a result. Dickens now cancelled most of his own social engagements; he needed time to rest. And to think. The next Christmas Book was very much on his mind, and the shadow of a coming novel, itself concerned with time past, might also have brushed across him. He went up to London on at least one occasion, mainly on business concerning the Home for Fallen Women, and it was on his return from this visit that he was greeted by the sight of Catherine ensconced in a carriage-and-pair and surrounded by a large crowd. It seemed that the pony which drew her phaeton had panicked for some reason and started bolting down a steep hill; Dickens's servant, John Thompson, had thrown himself out of the phaeton while Catherine, screaming in fright, was borne down the hill. The pony plunged down a bank, the shafts of the phaeton broke, the carriage came to rest, and Catherine emerged shaken but unhurt. In the past he had always been annoyed by her propensity for accidents, and had often directed against her that momentary irritation and annoyance which were very much part of his attitude towards her. But not now. Not when she was pregnant again. Not when his sister was dying.

They left Broadstairs at the end of August, and returned to Devonshire Terrace. Fanny was sinking, and she knew now that she had only a little time. As soon as he had returned, Dickens went once more to see her and she told him that "in the night, the smell of the fallen leaves in the woods where we had habitually walked as very young children, had come upon her with such strength of reality that she had moved her weak head to look for strewn leaves on the floor at her bedside". It was a remark which Dickens did not forget and he revives it in his next novel, *David Copperfield*, ". . . I remember how the leaves smelt like our garden at Blunderstone as we trod them underfoot, and how the old, unhappy feeling, seemed to go by, on the sighing wind." The death of his sister is associated here with the death of David Copperfield's young mother, and in that strange concatenation we see the presence of time past. Time returning. On the second of September, Fanny died, in the presence of her father. The funeral was conducted at Highgate cemetery where her Dissenting pastor noted that "Mr Dickens appeared to feel it very deeply . . ."

The next day he went back to Broadstairs where he stayed for three weeks before returning to London via Rochester, making his way back through the town where he and Fanny had once walked. He had not written his next Christmas Book, but was still considering it even as he was being visited by "dim visions of divers things"; this might be the first mention of the semi-autobiographical novel he was about to write, *David Copperfield*, but it is also possible that he had something else in mind. Had he decided, while consumed with remembrance of things past, to write down his own life story? Certainly the past was much with him now. Only a few months before, he had attended the funeral of William Hall, the publisher who had printed his first story, and now with the death of Fanny it was as if the whole period of his childhood had re-emerged within him – all the sensations and emotions of which could only be understood by him when he wrote them down. And so he began. It is not clear precisely when he composed the autobiographical fragment which he sent to Forster, and which Forster was later to publish; Dickens himself was to say that he had written it "just before Copperfield" which strongly suggests this period just after Fanny's death. But he had been considering the possibility of writing his life for some time. "Shall I leave you my life in MS when I die?" he had written two years before to Forster, although this sounds very much as if he were simply leaving material for a putative biographer: "Remember that for my Biography!" he once counselled Forster after he had told him how he had got out of bed one winter's night to practise the polka for his son's birthday party the next day. But events of this period hastened his approach to the more private aspects of his past and of his character. The hero of *Great Expectations* was to say of a passage in his own life that ". . . the secret was such an old one now, had so grown into me and become a part of myself, that I could not tear it away". But Dickens did now tear it away. He had reached a point where the episode of his childhood humiliation could remain his own "secret" no longer. For it was now that Forster told Dickens a story. He told him that Charles Dilke, a friend and colleague of John Dickens, had once seen Dickens working in a warehouse near the Strand, "at which place Mr Dilke, being with the elder Dickens one day, had noticed him, and received, in return for the gift of a half-crown, a very low bow". When Forster told his anecdote, Dickens was silent for a few minutes. Clearly he had touched upon a theme too close to Dickens for comfort. The secret of his past, which had played so large a part in his later self-development, was one that he had been able to keep to himself. No longer.

He eventually sent what he had finished of his autobiography to Forster who was no doubt pledged to secrecy as to its contents; which may be why in *Bleak House* Tulkinghorn, the lawyer who knows the secrets of the great, is placed by Dickens in Forster's own chambers in Lincoln's Inn Fields. It has been stated by one of Dickens's sons that his father also showed what he had written to Catherine, who persuaded him not to publish his childhood memories on the grounds that they defamed his own mother and father. This may or may not be true. It seems more likely that he had already decided not to publish anything in this form.

Yet the urge to write about his past was still very great and, as soon as he returned from Broadstairs to London, he started work on the Christmas Book he had for so long been contemplating, a book about lost time. *The Haunted Man and the Ghost's Bargain* is concerned with the power of memory, with family life which is destroyed and replaced only by the wretched anxieties of a distinguished but solitary man; it is a story in which the central character's mournfulness is linked closely with the death of a beloved sister. It is a strange and powerful book in which memories "come back to me in music, in the wind, in the dead stillness of the night, in the revolving years". The theme itself revolves around Dickens's belief that memory is a softening and chastening power, that the recollection of old sufferings and old wrongs can be used to touch the heart and elicit sympathy with the sufferings of others. In his autobiographical fragment he had written of his parents' apparent neglect only to add that "I do not write resentfully or angrily: for I know how all these things have worked together to make me what I am . . ." Now, in the last words of this Christmas Book he was writing, he put it another way; "Lord, keep my memory green . . ." For it was his suffering and the memory of his sufferings which had given him the powerful sympathy of the great writer, just as his recollection of those harder days inspired him with that pity for the poor and the dispossessed which was a mark of his social writings. It has been said that in this autobiographical fragment Dickens is only suppressing his feelings of hurt and jealous rage, but it seems more likely that he was actively involved, after Fanny's death, in the process of transcending them.

*The Haunted Man and the Ghost's Bargain*, the first Christmas Book for two years, was carefully planned; the manuscript shows evidence of forethought and afterthought, as Dickens crosses out, amends, and adds to such an extent that in its original form it is actually very hard to read. He was working on it slowly through November, while Mark Lemon was preparing a dramatic version of the same story, and by the third week of that month he had finished the first two chapters. Then he went to Brighton, to finish the third and last chapter in the winter's quiet of that seaside town which always seemed to him to be a place of "gay little toys", a small and bright resort where somehow he could master his material with more ease. By the end of the month he had completed it. On the first day of December he told his publisher, William Bradbury (no doubt eager for "copy"), that "I finished last night, having been crying my eyes out over it"; and indeed the manuscript does look in part as if the ink has been blotted by tears. He read it to Mark Lemon, so that Lemon could finish the dramatic version, and then he sent it off to Bradbury and Evans. Twelve days later he was reading it "with his usual energy and spirit" to a group of friends which included Forster and Clarkson Stanfield. In the larger world it was received with rather more enthusiasm than the less approachable *Battle of Life* but it was not a particular commercial success, not at least when compared to the sales of *A Christmas Carol* and *The Chimes*. Indeed this was to be Dickens's last Christmas Book, as if in this tale of memory restored he had come to the end of that series which had combined private memory, religious feeling and social satire in equal measure. In *The Haunted Man and the Ghost's Bargain* particularly, intense personal feeling had been closely allied with a religious message of hope and redemption; thus it was that the death of Fanny and the abandoned autobiographical fragment worked together to form a purer and larger statement. This was indeed Dickens's genius: to remove his private concerns into a larger symbolic world so that they became the very image of his own time.

But, even as he infused the power of grace through these pages, his forgiveness of his own real family was only partial. In the last month of the year he attended the marriage of his younger brother, Augustus, but firmly refused to have anything to do with that of Frederick to Anna Weller. For a while he set his face against a brother who, he believed, had all the worst attributes of their father. And once more he was restless. There were vague plans of Italy, which came to nothing. For he had something else to do, something for which travelling would have been a poor
308

substitute; he was restless because another novel, closely related to everything he had just written, was stirring within him. He had been contemplating a new book in the last months of 1848, and at some point in this period Forster suggested to him that he use a first-person narrative – a suggestion which Dickens took very seriously. It has often been said that Dickens was thinking of *Jane Eyre*, and the success of that novel in creating a narrator who tells her own story, but it is also likely that he was aware of his own success in dealing with Paul Dombey's illness from the child's point of view and wished to achieve such an effect on a much larger scale. He always possessed the ability to build upon his achievements. He had written in *Dombey and Son* about the loss of natural affection, he had written in *The Haunted Man and the Ghost's Bargain* about the importance of memory, and from both of these there now emerged another story.

In this period Dickens was also writing a series of articles for the *Examiner* on the plight of mistreated and wretched children. They were the victims of what was known as "baby-farming", by which the parish and local authorities gave the orphaned or the abandoned into the care of minders who were paid a certain amount each week per head of child; "a trade," as Dickens wrote, "which derived its profits from the deliberate torture and neglect of a class the most innocent on earth, as well as the most wretched and defenceless . . ." He was writing about the deaths of no less than one hundred and eighty children at the Juvenile Pauper Asylum in Tooting run by a certain Benjamin Drouet, deaths which had mostly occurred during the cholera epidemic of that winter but which were materially assisted by under-nourishment as well as lack of basic care and hygiene. The Board of Health had recommended that the uninfected children should be moved to some other place, but the Poor Law Commissioners rejected the suggestion; so more children died. Drouet was indicted for manslaughter; but then he was acquitted on the grounds that the children, even when they first entered Drouet's "care", would probably have been too weak to resist the disease. This incident called forth from Dickens four separate articles, an apt measure of his disgust at the systematic starvation and mistreatment of children who were emaciated, covered in boils, unable to eat, and who ran the risk of being horse-whipped if they complained of their treatment. The episode helped to focus and to systematise Dickens's feelings about the need for proper urban sanitation and rigorous administrative control of institutions such as the pauper asylum, but it is significant, too, that he was writing about child neglect at precisely the time he was fashioning *David Copperfield* in his mind. Everything was coming together.

In February he went down to Brighton once again, with his own family and with the Leeches; he wanted to be near what he called now the "great hoarse ocean" which seemed in its roar to be asking, "won't anybody listen?" But Dickens did. He listened to everything. He saw everything. And was sometimes granted the strangest recompense: he believed that extraordinary things were always likely to happen to him and, true to form, the landlord of his lodgings as well as the landlord's daughter went "mad" before being taken away in strait-waistcoats, raving, to the local asylum; ". . . quite worthy of me," Dickens said with less than charitable concern for the poor couple, "and quite in keeping with my usual proceedings." And as he looked out at the hoarse ocean his own mind was "running, like a high sea" on the possible names for his new novel. He knew by now that it was going to be a narrative couched in the first person, and he knew that it was to become the saga of a young man's life; that is no doubt why he was thinking of Henry Fielding's *Tom Jones* and why Hablot Browne in his cover drawing gave only the most general incidents of a life from cradle to grave.

But the names were now the important things. Without the names, he had no characters and no real story. Without the names, he could not begin. His working notes provide evidence of the care with which he was proceeding. *Mag's Diversions and experiences, observation Being the personal history, of Mr Thomas Mag the Younger of Copperfield Blunderstone House* went through a variety of changes, some seventeen in all, until Dickens emerged at the end triumphant with *The Copperfield Survey of the World as it rolled. Being the personal history, adventures, experience, and observation, of Mr David Copperfield the Younger of Blunderstone Rookery.* All this in a firm hand, with his characteristic two underlinings of each word; and then, in a fainter and slightly narrower hand, he added: "which he never meant to be published, On any account." The name Copperfield had itself emerged through a rehearsal of such names as Wellbury, Magbury, Topflower, Copperboy and Copperstone. Just as Murdstone was to emerge through Harden, Murdle (later revived as Merdle in *Little Dorrit*) and Murden. Announcements of a new novel were made at the end of February; at which time, too, Charles Dickens began.

# Nineteen

A ND how did he begin? He began by considering what
he called the "central idea" or the "leading idea"
which he then, according to his publisher, "revolved in
his mind until he had thought the matter thoroughly
through". Finally, again according to his publisher, he
"made what I might call a programme of his story with
the characters" and on that rough base he would begin
his work. Dickens himself said that at this early stage he
also needed to be sure of the "purport of each character"
as well as the "plain idea" each might come to embody.
Of course he might still be struck by, or imagine, scenes
and characters (even incidents) which had an independent
existence of their own; there were occasions when he
chose a particular London street or district, for example,
before detailing the plot which would eventually lead into
it. But all the time he was looking for that one chain of
being, that one clear line to which everything else could
be attached – the important point being that he invariably
saw this in the form of a *story*. The story which would bring
ideas or characters to light and life.

It was not an instant or an easy process, and throughout
Dickens's writing life the symptoms at the beginning of a
new novel are the same. "Violent restlessness, and vague
ideas of going I don't know where . . ." And then again,
". . . it is like being *driven away*." Here is the idea of a new

312

story actively repelling him, thrusting him outside its own field of force. Dickens became irritable, solitary, preoccupied, ". . . going round and round the idea . . .", not being able to settle on any one thing and therefore not able to rest; ". . . walking about the country by day – prowling about into the strangest places in London by night – sitting down to do an immensity – getting up after doing nothing . . ." This was for him the agony of birth, ". . . wandering about at night into the strangest places . . . seeking rest, and finding none". That last phrase is strikingly reminiscent of the fate of the unclean spirit in the Bible, as Dickens stalks the streets of London, both by day and by night, the amorphous shape of the narrative within him like some burden from which he needs to be relieved. Then, as the time came close for the strange story to be born, he would shut himself away in his study, contemplating, looking out of the window, not writing a word.

Thus did he "lay the ground". And it is not surprising that a man who went to so much trouble to arrange and to learn his speeches in an orderly fashion should wish to take infinitely more trouble over his novels; never was a writer so exact, so thorough, so careful in his plans. He told one contemporary that ". . . the plot, the motive of the book, is always perfected in my brain for a long time before I take up my pen". And he told another that ". . . he never began to write before having settled the work in its minutest detail, in his head". But this is not to say that he knew every aspect of his novel in advance; far from it. He had the architectural plans drawn up, as it were, but he needed to build freely and instinctively. He began with the story and with the ideas which that story suggested; but then, as he writes, he lets that story take on its own most appropriate shape. Then the characters come and settle within the narrative, bringing with them their own lines of force which complicate the essential plot. And so a double focus is at work; the characters seem for a while

313

to career off at a tangent, but then the "leading idea" draws them back again and reasserts itself until the characters once again break free and roam before being once again retrieved.

And what of *David Copperfield*, now that Dickens had walked and contemplated, had found a title and a theme? Now that he was ready to begin? Since he had decided to set part of the narrative in Yarmouth, he purchased a copy of *Suffolk Words and Phrases* in order to find expressions he might use to lend authenticity to his local characters' speech. In fact the intensity of his care over, and work upon, the new novel is a mark of its importance to him; there were no theatricals and no foreign excursions in this first year of its writing, nothing but hard and constant effort upon a novel which he was always to consider his best. It was in this early stage of preparation that he concocted the name of Murdstone and the first entry on the right-hand side of his working plan says simply, "Father dead – Gravestone outside the house". Murdstone. Gravestone. So did name and theme intertwine in an immediate and almost instinctive pattern of association. He began the actual novel slowly and with some difficulty in the last week of February and worked on it steadily for much of the next month; the first page is filled with emendations as Dickens made his way through the thicket of memories and inventions in a chapter simply entitled "I Am Born". Dickens wrote, "Here is our pew in the church" in the second chapter, entitled "I Observe", and in his own copy of the novel Forster has written "actual" in the margin beside it – no doubt Dickens told him of the truth of this. And in the same chapter, beside the account of David reading to Peggotty from a book about crocodiles and alligators, Forster has written "true". He makes no such mark a little earlier, where the young David is terrified by the story of Lazarus rising from the dead, and associates it with his own dead father; but that was for Dickens "true" and
314

"actual" in quite another sense. He was making slow progress — so slow, in fact, that in the end he was forced to write quickly in order to finish the number in time for publication. But still he had written too little, and at a late stage added passages on the characters both of Mrs Gummidge and of Little Em'ly, whose fate is for an instant unveiled. So the scene was gradually being established: in these first three chapters Dickens had introduced David, Mr Murdstone, Little Em'ly, Peggotty and Betsy Trotwood. Their story is set in the 1820s and 1830s, and Dickens makes sure that David Copperfield is of an appropriate age so that, when he is eventually sent to work in a factory, he is the same age as Dickens was at the time of his arrival in London. Thus did autobiography merge wonderfully with fiction. Each chapter was sent to the printer as soon as it was completed, and then at least two sets of proofs were despatched back to Dickens who, in turn, sent one set to Hablot Browne for the purposes of illustration. This was a much more sensible arrangement than the conveyance of messages from Lausanne and Paris while Dickens was deep in *Dombey and Son*, and in fact the relationship between author and illustrator now returned to its previous cordial and professional shape. So the first number was completed and ready at last, everything prepared for Dickens's long sojourn in the Shadowy World.

And yet which for him was the world of shadows and which the world of reality? There are occasions when he does not seem to know and, even as he wrote the first number, Dickens was also completing his articles on the deaths of the children at the Tooting juvenile pauper asylum. He was dealing with two kinds of child abuse one after another; the private abuse of David Copperfield at the hands of the Murdstones, and the public abuse of the abandoned children in the baby farm, the emotion induced by both spilling over into each other. And it was at this time, too, that the real world assumed the shape of

315

Dickens's own fiction. Just at the end of his labours on the first number of *David Copperfield*, he was walking along the Edgware Road with Mark Lemon when a young man picked Lemon's pocket. In Dickens's own words as recorded in the police court, "I was with Mr Lemon, and saw him turn suddenly round upon the prisoner, who speedily ran away: we pursued him, and when he was taken he was most violent; he is a very desperate fellow, and he kicked about in all directions. There was a mob of low fellows close by when he tried Mr Lemon's pocket, and we were determined that he should not effect his escape, if we could prevent it." "A mob of low fellows" – here is the authentic voice of Dickens.

After this episode, he went down to the Isle of Wight with John Leech, his purpose being to find a suitable spot for the summer months. They stayed at a lodging house in Shanklin while they reconnoitred the area, and within a couple of days Dickens had found "Winterbourne" in Bonchurch, a converted barn some hundred and fifty feet above sea-level with an estate which extended down to the seashore and included a stream as well as a waterfall. It was owned by the Reverend James White, an aspiring playwright whom Dickens had met through Macready some time before (he described White as "comically vari- ous in his moods", which suggests that he was not entirely in sympathy with him – in fact, as so often with Dickens, he preferred the company of White's wife, Rosa), and it was here that he decided to retreat while he carried on with his writing through the summer months. He returned to Devonshire Terrace in order to pick up family and servants, and a week later came back to Bonchurch with all of them in tow; Thackeray by chance encountered them on the pier at Ryde and, as he put it, saw them "all looking abominably coarse vulgar and happy".

By the end of August he had finished the fifth number and almost at once set to work on the next. It was at this time too that, in proof, he hit upon the idea of Mr Dick being haunted by King Charles the First's head; just as, now, his own head was filled with ague and fever. His symptoms were alarming; ". . . an almost continual feeling of sickness, accompanied with great prostration of strength, so that his legs tremble under him, and his arms quiver when he wants to take hold of any object." He was writing this account to Forster in the impersonal third-person, as if he wanted to distance himself from his own sickness, and it is typical of him that despite his loss of strength and concentration "I make no sign, and pretend not to know what is going on". He blamed the climate of Bonchurch for his condition, but the symptoms he describes sound like some sort of generalised nervous debility: "Extreme depression of mind, and a disposition to shed tears from morning to night . . ." it was now also that he began to make plans to leave the island and consequently finished the number of *David Copperfield* later than usual.

Dickens abandoned the Isle of Wight at the very end of September and travelled down with the family to Broadstairs. It was here, ensconced once more in the house next to Ballard's Hotel by the sea-front, that he set to work on *David Copperfield*. By the time he left, almost three weeks later, he had in fact completed an entire number. But he was also the recipient of bad news: the sales of the novel were markedly down on those of its predecessor, and were to average something like twenty thousand copies a month as contrasted with approximately thirty-five thousand for *Dombey and Son*. Dickens did not yet have the exact figures but their drift was clear enough; he was not going to earn as much on this novel as he had anticipated. But he was not wholly cast down. Not now. He had other plans. After the relative failure of *Martin Chuzzlewit* he had turned eagerly to the *Daily News* as a form of recompense, of release, of refuge. Now once again he was maturing the

317

idea for another periodical, albeit of a more personal kind. He had in fact been considering it throughout the summer, even while at Bonchurch, but the bad news about *Copperfield* made it of more pressing and even paramount concern. He was already discussing specific details with Forster: a weekly periodical at a price of three-halfpence or twopence, and featuring a character to be called "THE SHADOW" who would be a kind of correspondent at large and who might be assumed to have some secret intelligence on the latest subjects of the day. This journalistic spectre would also provide the kind of framing device for various pieces which Dickens always seemed to prefer; it is yet another example of that unity in diversity which is the mark of his fiction as well as of his journalism, and might without portentousness be described as an aspect of his aesthetic sense. As soon as he returned to London he informed Bradbury and Evans of his plans, in which they broadly concurred. Dickens was, you might say, back in business.

But it was a difficult period for him. In December, particularly, he was being harassed on two sides. The first instance was certainly the most disagreeable, and the most invidious. One Thomas Powell, an employee of Thomas Chapman and colleague of Dickens's younger brother, Augustus, had three years before been detected embezzling money from the firm; he tried to commit suicide by taking laudanum and, out of pity for his situation, Chapman never pressed charges. On a later occasion he was detected in forgery but feigned madness and was for a while detained at a lunatic asylum in Hoxton. Then he had decamped for America where he earned his living as journalist and writer of cheap books. Powell had known Dickens reasonably well and, through the agency of Augustus, had even dined with him; it was not a connection he was likely to forget and, in this year, he had written a distinctly unflattering life of Dickens which was even

318

now appearing in the American newspapers. In this account Dickens is branded as a snob and parvenu; perhaps more importantly, he is also accused of having based the character of Mr Dombey upon Thomas Chapman himself. Dickens had already learnt of all this in October, and immediately took steps to denounce Powell as a liar and forger (which undoubtedly he was). Now, in December, he had dispatched to America a series of documents convicting Powell of the offences charged, plus a pamphlet of his own in which he went through the same charges. It was at this point that Powell threatened to sue him for libel, to the amount of ten thousand dollars.

Of course he had no real chance of launching let alone winning any such case, and Dickens was more angry than anxious about the matter. But unfortunately it coincided with another threatened action, and this time from a more unlikely source. A certain Mrs Hill, a chiropodist and manicurist, a neighbour of Dickens, and a dwarf, felt that she was being portrayed as the untrustworthy and tiny Miss Mowcher in *David Copperfield*. She was right; Dickens had obviously seen her on many occasions, and had caricatured at least her appearance in the novel without any thought of the consequences to Mrs Hill herself. So she sent a pained letter about his use of her "personal deformities"; "Should your book be dramatised and I not protected madness will be the result." Dickens sent her a conciliatory reply, in which he admitted the justice of her rebuke in part but went on to say (quite untruthfully) that the main element of the characterisation was based upon someone else. But immediately he wrote a more honest letter to Forster in which he concluded, ". . . there is no doubt one is wrong in being tempted to such a use of power." Again that word with which he characterises his fiction. Power. A few days later he received a letter from Mrs Hill's solicitor, in which an action for libel was vaguely threatened. Dickens tried to mollify the man, and promised to repair the damage by changing the character of Miss Mowcher in order to throw a creditable light upon Mrs Hill herself. He was as good as his word, eventually, but there can be little doubt that he was perturbed by all that had taken place. Perturbed in other ways, too. A few days later he resigned from the Garrick, for reasons which remain unknown, and in the same period he was offended by Daniel Maclise apparently because he had been unable to attend the usual Christmas celebrations at Devonshire Terrace. In other words, there was anger and resentment in Dickens during this period, particularly against Thomas Powell. Certainly it is possible that the memory of the experience of these feelings was one he used to direct David Copperfield's hatred against Uriah Heep in the chapter he was then writing. And so it goes on, this shuttling between literature and life, this cross-fertilisation; no doubt the closest examination of each day in Dickens's life, if such a process were at all possible, would reveal other associations and resemblances. But they are not to be unearthed now, not at this late date, and in any case *David Copperfield* must temporarily give way to what had become for him more pressing matters. For, at the end of December 1849, Dickens announced in handbills that he was about to begin editing a "WEEKLY MISCELLANY OF General Literature". It was a role he would maintain until the end of his life.

# Twenty

THE old year ended and the new decade began with his work on the new periodical, and he was attending quickly to the next instalment of *David Copperfield* in order to give himself more time to concentrate on its preparation. He was receiving manuscripts from friends, and even soliciting useful material, as early as January 1850; he was preparing "dummy numbers" (he had learnt something from his brief editorship of the *Daily News*) and even before he had thought of an appropriate name for the journal he was already announcing its aim as the ". . . raising up of those that are down, and the general improvement of our social condition". He had in mind some clear aspects of that social condition; in particular sanitation, education and housing. These were the three issues that lay beneath the "condition of England question", as it was still being called, and it was genuinely part of Dickens's determination to fight for those causes even as he tried to beguile and to entertain. But after his experience on the *Daily News*, as well as on *Bentley's Miscellany*, he was determined that this time he should be in sole charge of the editorial content of the periodical; he knew himself well enough to realise that he could brook no interference in the pursuit of his own designs. But he needed assistance; he could not edit a weekly periodical on his own and, on Forster's advice, Dickens decided to employ W. H. Wills, once his secretary on the *Daily News*, as sub-editor of the magazine. He could not have made a better choice. Wills was already experienced in what might be described as the administrative side of publishing, having been assistant editor of *Chambers's Journal* as well as Dickens's quondam secretary.

So the ground was being laid for the new periodical and, on the second day of February, Dickens, after several attempts at finding a title (among those considered were *Charles Dickens* and *Everything*), hit upon *Household Words*. It was taken from one of the many Shakespearian tags he seemed to carry in his head. "Familiar in their mouths as Household Words" was placed upon the masthead of the periodical, although the actual line from *Henry V* is slightly different and reads "Familiar in his mouth as household words". Now that he had found a name he also needed a local habitation, and a few days later he took a lease upon 16 Wellington Street North, a small and narrow thoroughfare just off the Strand, the headquarters of the new periodical itself being "exceedingly pretty with the bowed front, the bow reaching up for two stories, each giving a flood of light". Like much of London it stood upon a haunted spot, the site of an old tenement where, according to legend, Hogarth had seen the final tableau of "The Harlot's Progress". In the first-floor front of the older house the artist had seen the woman in her coffin, the ancient drunken crones in various postures around her, and it was this scene which Dickens often "conjured up", he said, as he sat beside the bow window on the first floor. He soon became as familiar in this area as in many other parts of London, and local tradesmen told one of his earlier chroniclers that "they noted regularly his lithe figure briskly flitting past as the clock struck, his little bag in hand".

Dickens also began writing a small book which he was eventually to finish some three years later. In his spare time, while resting from his labours on his fiction or on

322

the new periodical, he was in the habit of dictating to Georgina Hogarth a narrative which he entitled *A Child's History of England*. It was meant primarily for his own children, but it was also in part serialised in *Household Words* so that it can fairly be said to have some general or public import. The actual contents are not in themselves particularly original; Dickens seems to have derived most of his information from Keightley's *History of England* and from Charles Knight's *Pictorial History of England*. Certainly the latter book was in his library, and was heavily annotated by him.

All of this activity meant that in London Dickens was too pressed and too bothered to work properly on *David Copperfield*, for which project he needed at least two weeks in every month. So at the beginning of March he took lodgings in King Street, Brighton, in order to work in peace. Here he began those chapters which deal with Copperfield's burgeoning romance with Dora Spenlow, a romance in which there are shades of Dickens's love for his mother and his sister, as if the novelist himself were looking helplessly back at the time of his own infancy. Back towards his dream of a girl or young woman; young, beautiful and good. A dream which descended on him again as he travelled on the railroad, which he described as ". . . a wonderfully suggestive place to me when I am alone . . ." He was coming from London back to Brighton, and was concerned with the want of "something tender" in the second issue of *Household Words* which he was even then preparing. As the train made its way towards the coast Dickens looked up at the stars through the window of his carriage, and something in that sight of immensity reminded him of the night-sky of his own childhood – of the time when he and his now dead sister had looked out the window of their little room in Chatham, had seen the adjacent graveyard, and had looked up at the heavens together. Even as he is writing about Dora Spenlow, therefore, his mind is roving back towards his young sister; out of his nocturnal meditation came "A Child's Dream of a Star", a short but in many ways attractive piece which certainly contributed to the tenderness of *Household Words*. "'My age is falling from me like a garment, and I move towards the star as a child.'" It was not the only time in this year when he went back to his infancy; in the seasonal story he eventually wrote, "A Christmas Tree", he returned to the scenes of his childhood and described them in vivid and exact detail. In both of these shorter pieces there is both nostalgia and true memory; it is almost as if his work on *David Copperfield* had unlocked the mysteries of his own childhood, so that at last he is able to go much further back than the period he described in his explicitly autobiographical fragment; to go back to the beginnings of his life, to the Eden time.

The first issue of *Household Words* bears the date 30 March, 1850; this was a Saturday, and the periodical actually appeared on the Wednesday before. Underneath this title, on the front page, were the words "Conducted by Charles Dickens", which also appeared as a running head throughout its twenty-four pages of double-columned and unillustrated type. Contributions were anonymous but, when Douglas Jerrold saw this constantly reiterated phrase, he said that it was really "*mono*nymous throughout". It was published weekly and priced at twopence – although it was also released in monthly form and, eventually, as a bound volume. This first number contained an "Address" to its readers written by Dickens, in which he once more staked his place beside the hearths of English families and pledged that nothing in his journal would render his readers "less ardently persevering in ourselves, less tolerant of one another, less faithful in the progress of mankind, less thankful for the privilege of living in the summer-dawn of time".

Dickens was pleased with this first issue, and sanguine

about the prospects of the periodical in general: "The Household Words I hope (and have every reason to hope) will become a *good property* . . . The labor, in conjunction with Copperfield, is something rather ponderous; but to establish it firmly would be to gain such an immense point for the future (I mean *my* future) that I think nothing of that." Some of his contemporaries were not as impressed, and Mrs Browning said that it "won't succeed, I predict, especially as they have adopted the fashion of not printing the names of contributors". She was wrong: the circulation settled down to approximately thirty-nine thousand and, although this figure is not nearly as high as for other periodicals of the period, it was enough to generate a reasonable profit.

Dickens's writing within the pages of *Household Words* took many different forms. He closely and carefully revised articles for the periodical which, as it were, diffused his spirit through the nation. But there were also many occasions when with Wills or others he would collaborate in "composite" articles, Dickens characteristically providing the opening and ending to set the tone of the piece, while his collaborator filled in the rest. Sometimes these articles were the result of a joint expedition by Dickens and his companion to a post office, or to a factory, or to a market, or to a school, or to a race-meeting; they would visit the site of their investigation together, and then write separately the portions of the article to which each had been assigned. Dickens would then knit the pieces together.

Some of his articles were also written in collaboration with their subjects, and in these first months of the new journal Dickens was arranging to meet various members of the Detective Department at Scotland Yard in order to obtain material or anecdotes for *Household Words*; one of these men, Inspector Field, was later assumed to be the original of Inspector Bucket in *Bleak House*, and there is no doubt that Dickens was sufficiently impressed by him to turn him into yet another token of his always-admiring interest in the efficiency and doggedness of the London police. Inspector Fields's recollections of his cases were not always reliable, however, and there is some evidence that Dickens's own tendency to exaggerate the facts was amply assisted by the officer himself; the famous detective had once been an amateur actor at the Catherine Street Theatre, and once more in that typically nineteenth-century association with the theatre there is a clue not only to the somewhat melodramatic nature of the New Police but also to the Victorian temperament. Even its representatives of authority and of the law had theatrical as well as investigative instincts. Is that not what Dickens was trying to reveal in his accounts of Parliament or of Chancery? Society as theatre?

And all the time Dickens continued his work on *David Copperfield*. By the beginning of May he had come to a crucial point in the narrative. "Still undecided about Dora," he wrote to Forster, "but MUST decide to-day." The decision was whether Dora, David Copperfield's child-wife, was to live or to die. As was his custom on such mortal occasions he took long walks to contemplate the matter and spent some of his evening simply thinking; keeping his mind steadily on the object of his thought and trying to trace its path forward. Tracing its path through the avenues of his own life also. He was reading Carlyle's *Latter-day Pamphlets*, even then being issued, and he was about to read Tennyson's newly published *In Memoriam*; both of these books would have an influence upon *David Copperfield* itself.

Eventually he was able to plan the novel to its end. The last four numbers were sketched out in his working notes, and the main stages of the narrative signalled well in advance. He set to work upon the number in which Little Em'ly is finally discovered (a chapter over the melodrama of which he expended great pains), but clearly he was finding it very difficult to write during the London summer, quite apart from the fact that he was constantly being waylaid by office business and by reportorial excursions. So he negotiated the summer lease of Fort House in Broadstairs; this relatively large house, a little away from the main town and sea-front, had always attracted his attention, and for him and his family it must have seemed the perfect seaside retreat – the house itself separated from the harbour by a cornfield, overlooking the sea and the lighthouse.

On the fifteenth of August, before he left London, he made up another issue of *Household Words* with the assistance of Wills; on the next day Catherine was confined and gave birth to a daughter, Dora Annie Dickens; that same afternoon Dickens and the rest of the family travelled down to Broadstairs as had been originally planned to take up their newly rented summer quarters. Georgina went with him in order to look after the children, while Catherine remained in London with the new baby; not necessarily an unusual or unsympathetic arrangement. What *is* odd, however, is that, just five days after Dora was born, he wrote to his wife – ". . . I have still Dora to kill – I mean the Copperfield Dora . . ." As if he could mean anything else. But how strange it is for him to call his infant child after a character whom he intended to "kill".

Dickens and family were to stay at Broadstairs from the middle of August until the end of October; by now a town, according to George Eliot, "which David Copperfield has made classic". She is talking here of the location of "Betsey Trotwood's cottage" in the vicinity; thus did Dickens's work descend like a tongue of fire upon a locality, its scorch marks lasting for ever. Fort House was the ideal location for Dickens himself and his study, reached by a small staircase, had large windows letting in the brightness of the day, as well as affording a fine view of the open sea.

327

But in some respects Broadstairs was becoming less attractive than before. In particular Dickens was bothered by the sounds of street-sellers and street musicians as well as by noise in the vicinity of Fort House itself. There was a coastguard station not far from the house, and the wife of the coastguard gave her recollections of the famous novelist to one of his first biographers. "Mr Dickens," she said, "was a very nice sort of gentleman, but he didn't like a noise." Whenever the children were too raucous, Dickens would gently ask the coastguard "to take the children away" or "to keep the people quiet". There were other kinds of disturbance, too. When Forster came to stay he snored so loudly at night that Dickens could not sleep; he wandered around the house and even woke up Georgina to keep him company. The scene was suitably transformed by Dickens in the chapter of *David Copperfield* he was just about to write, the chapter in which the fatal storm at sea keeps David up. "For hours I lay there, listening to the wind and water . . ." Is it too fanciful to imagine Dickens lying in his own room, listening to the wind and water of Broadstairs and revolving so many matters in his head?

In his study, looking out to sea, Dickens completed the next number of *David Copperfield* by the middle of September; this instalment is perhaps the most notable of all, since it contains the chapters which describe the emigration of Little Em'ly and the Micawbers as well as the death of Steerforth in the terrible storm. Images of the sea here as he gazed out of his window – the sea which propels new life or the sea which destroys; and, in his notes about the storm, Dickens wrote in his memoranda, "at Broadstairs here, last night" although in fact no storm has been recorded during this period. These are some of the most memorable passages in the novel and, although the storm scene has been justifiably described as a fine piece of marine description, the departure of Little Em'ly with Mr Peggotty has a tone and resonance that bring it close to the poetry of Dickens's being, the slow, sad music which is often to be heard within his fiction and indeed which may be its most enduring presence. "Surrounded by the rosy light, and standing high upon the deck, apart together, she clinging to him, and he holding her, they solemnly passed away. The night had fallen on the Kentish hills when we were rowed ashore – and fallen darkly upon me." As he wrote he had "been believing such things with all my heart and soul . . .", and, afterwards, he was so disturbed by his own powerful narrative that ". . . I can't write plainly to the eye . . . I can't write sensibly to the mind". Yet almost as soon as he had finished this number he began the next and last, the double number in which David Copperfield travels abroad, as Dickens had done, and in which all his travails are finally resolved with his marriage to Agnes Wickfield. He was still in Broadstairs on the twenty-third of October when, finally, he completed the novel.

Immediately after David Copperfield was published, the general critical reaction was favourable and, it soon became clear that this was his "masterpiece" although, even so, Dickens himself retained a peculiarly private relationship with the novel. ". . . I never can approach the book with perfect composure," he once wrote, "( it had such perfect possession of me when I wrote it) . . ." And in his preface to the novel he declared that ". . . no one can ever believe this Narrative in the reading more than I have believed it in the writing". For, yes, he was sending part of himself into a shadowy world where the novel becomes a narrative among other narratives, part of a larger history than that of his own self, revolving slowly with the borrowed motion of its creator and of its time until it takes its place in the permanent literature of its country. Compared with Dickens's previous novels *David Copperfield* has much less movement, much less speed and glitter; it is stiller, retrospective, the sentiment chastened, the comedy deepened. This tone had been implicit in *The Battle of Life*, apparent even in the miniature, "A Child's Dream of a Star", but this is the first occasion when it can be detected on a sufficiently large scale to represent a change of direction. It is a change towards a certain kind of plangent lyricism, and it is not unrelated to the fact that this is the first novel in which Dickens consistently uses the first-person singular, the first novel in which he *sees* himself as he breathes and moves.

Of course we might say in the modern idiom that this is a fiction which is really "about" itself. It is both a novel of memories and a novel about memory. Memory brightens: ". . . I have never seen such sunlight as on those bright April afternoons . . ."; memory creates in the mind fresh associations: ". . . the Martyrs and Peggotty's house have been inseparable in my mind ever since, and are now;" memory revives the clearest and most detailed impressions: "the scent of a geranium leaf, at this day, strikes me with a half comical, half serious wonder as to what change has come over me in a moment . . . ;" memory retains the sharpest of all impressions: "the face he turned up to the troubled sky, the quivering of his clasped hands, the agony of his figure, remain associated with that lonely waste, in my remembrance, to this hour. It is always night there, and he is the only object in the scene." And memory brings back the earliest and most permanent impressions of childhood, like the occasion when David sees his mother for the last time: "I was in the carrier's cart when I heard her calling to me. I looked out, and she stood at the garden-gate alone, holding her baby up in her arms for me to see. It was cold still weather; and not a hair of her head, or a fold of her dress, was stirred, as she looked intently at me, holding up her child. So I lost her. So I saw her afterwards, in my sleep at school – a silent presence near my bed – looking at me with the same intent face – holding up her baby in her arms." But there is also the mystery of other memories, preconscious memories: ". . . a feeling, that comes over us occasionally, of what we are saying and doing having been said and done before, in a remote time . . ." Memory, then, as a form of resurrection and thus of human triumph; as David Copperfield looks out of the window he had known so many years before and sees the old sorrowful image of himself as a child. "Long miles of road then opened out before my mind; and, toiling on, I saw a ragged wayworn boy forsaken and neglected, who should come to call even the heart now beating against mine, his own." Thus does memory recreate the self out of adversity, linking past and present, bringing continuity and coherence, engendering peace and stillness in the very centre of the active world. It is the purest and best part of Dickens's self, the source of his being, the fountain of his tears. All of his writing and experience over the last two years had brought him to this point, this resurrection.

Dickens soon returned to London where he had other enterprises to superintend. In particular he had to write a seasonal piece for the first Christmas number of *Household Words*. No longer would he have the time or the inclination to write a Christmas Book; the last of them, *The Haunted Man and the Ghost's Bargain*, had appeared two years before. So now he wrote a short essay, "A Christmas Tree", in which he evokes in extraordinary and wonderful detail the toys of his childhood; it is perhaps not a coincidence that, only a few weeks later, he was explaining to a correspondent how he dreamed characteristically of his youth and early manhood. Of those enchanted days before his marriage, before his success, before his fame. When he turned his attention away from those lost years and looked at the present life surrounding him, he was nothing if not gloomy. He wrote two other pieces for *Household Words* in the same period; one entitled "A December Vision" and the other "The Last Words of the Old Year". In the first he depicts England as a place of ruin and disease, a place where children are neglected or whipped for small crimes, ". . . hunted, flogged, imprisoned but not taught . . .", where illiteracy and brutishness and death triumph, where "not one miserable wretch breathed out his poisoned life in the deepest cellar of the most neglected town, but, from the surrounding atmosphere, some particles of his infection were borne away, charged with heavy retribution on the general guilt". In the second essay he portrays a country in which degradation and neglect are rampant, and where the Court of Chancery shockingly mismanages justice. Both essays are powerfully written, and it is of some interest to note that they foreshadow the themes which he was to explore only a few months later in *Bleak House*. He was slowly approaching a deeper understanding of the world, but it would take some private miseries of the next year to act as the lightning rod of the vision even now taking shape.

He had been sitting to the portrait-painter, William Boxall, but he broke off the sessions when he found that on the canvas he first resembled a famous boxer, Ben Caunt, and then a murderer, Greenacre. He was inordinately restless and he was also feeling extremely unwell; what he called a "bilious attack", but one which has all the marks of nervous prostration. Then, on the last night of the old year, he held a country dance at Devonshire Terrace. A party that heralded a year in which Dickens would be forced to endure much distress and many changes, the year in which all the bleakness of *Bleak House* seems to descend upon him.

# Twenty-One

CHARLES DICKENS was now approaching middle-age. His "bilious attack" was succeeded by a very bad cold. His tenancy of Devonshire Terrace was coming to an end, and so he was planning to move house. A restless and disagreeable start to the new year in every way, and one which was compounded by the behaviour of his brother, Frederick, who was using his name to obtain credit from various sources; ". . . rasping my very heart," Dickens said. But, more importantly, his father's health was failing. Both his parents had moved to Keppel Street, near Russell Square, in order to live with a certain Mr and Mrs Davey; Davey was a surgeon acting as a medical attendant to John Dickens, who was now severely afflicted by the urological complaint (probably bladder stones) which had beset him for the last thirty years. Mrs Davey recalled later that Dickens would often visit his parents here. "He was not a very talkative man," she said, "but he could be extremely pleasant when he chose." An implication here, perhaps, that with his parents Dickens relapsed into silence or monosyllables.

At this time too Catherine had become "exceedingly unwell", as Dickens put it, although her illness was really only the culmination of a prolonged period of anxiety and distress. Not that this was always visible to Dickens's acquaintances; it was in this year that Henry Morley, one of the contributors to *Household Words*, declared that "Dickens has evidently made a comfortable choice. Mrs Dickens is stout, with a round, very round, rather pretty, very pleasant face, and ringlets on each side of it. One sees in five minutes that she loves her husband and her children, and has a warm heart for anybody who won't be satirical, but meet her on her own good natured footing. We were capital friends at once, and had abundant talk together. She meant to know me, and once, after a little talk when she went to receive a new guest, she came back to find me when I had moved off . . ."

But Catherine's condition was now serious enough to persuade Dickens that she ought to travel at once to the more bracing air and water of Malvern; together they went down and took Knutsworth Lodge, where Dickens stayed with her for two or three days before returning to London. Over the next few weeks he was to commute between Malvern and London, spending two or three days each time with Catherine at the health resort; in other words, at a time of great personal business and vexation, he was behaving as a considerate and careful husband. Even at Malvern in these conditions, however, his sense of humour did not desert him and his descriptions in a comic account of the "Cold Waterers" to Forster might be applied to "fitness fanatics" of any period; especially an old man who was engaged in the Victorian equivalent of "jogging" and "who ran over a milk-child, rather than stop! — with no neckcloth, on principle; and with his mouth wide open, to catch the morning air".

From the scene of these monstrosities he came up to London to continue with his always-pressing business and, in addition, he was still actively looking for a family dwelling to succeed Devonshire Terrace. His offer for a certain Balmoral House in North London was rejected but this was fortunate since a few years later a barge filled with gunpowder, travelling along the Regent's Park Canal, exploded opposite the house and all but destroyed it.

But then the world rushed in upon him, too. He was told that his father was seriously ill and about to undergo an operation from which it was doubtful he would recover. The bladder stones had now grown so large that John Dickens could no longer urinate and the operation, "the most terrible . . . known in surgery" according to Dickens, would entail an incision being made between the anus and the scrotum so that the stones could be physically removed. And this John Dickens would be forced to endure without anaesthetic. His son arrived soon afterwards and found his father's room awash with the consequences of what must have been a terrifying and almost unbearable surgical procedure; "a slaughter house of blood," as Dickens described it to his wife. And yet the native optimism of the father, which may have played some part in his son's description of Mr Micawber, helped him to rally; he was according to Dickens "wonderfully cheerful and strong-hearted". But Dickens felt the blow himself almost as if he were a part of his father. "All this goes to my side directly," he said, experiencing once more the terrible agonies of his childhood (when, it has been said, his own kidneys became inflamed in response to his father's urinary troubles of that period), "and I feel as if I had been struck there by a leaden bludgeon." He returned to Devonshire Terrace, and, while his father slept, awaited more news. The next morning he went to the *Household Words* office. It was a miserably wet day in late March, and he looked down from his first-floor study onto the scene in Wellington Street North. "It is raining here incessantly . . . A van containing the goods of some unfortunate family, moving, has broken down outside – and the whole scene is a picture of dreariness." A family moving, just as his family had moved when he was a child, just as he was attempting to move now. Dreariness. The past and present coming together through a prospect of rain as he waited

335

for news of his father. He attempted to carry on with his normal work, and on 28 March he went down to Malvern once again to see Catherine. But by now it was clear that his father was dying; Dickens was sent for and returned to London. He arrived at Keppel Street at a quarter past eleven on the night of 29 March, and with his mother stayed at the bedside of the dying man. ". . . he did not know me, nor any one. He began to sink at about noon . . . and never rallied afterwards. I remained there until he died − O so quietly . . ."

John Dickens was buried at Highgate Cemetery on 5 April, and upon his gravestone Dickens had composed a tribute to his "zealous, useful, cheerful spirit". After the funeral Elizabeth Dickens stayed for a while at the home of her daughter, Laetitia, in Notting Hill and planned later to travel up to Yorkshire in order to stay with Alfred. And what of Dickens, after the first shock of the death had passed? From now on, when he referred to John Dickens, characteristically he used the phrase "my poor father"; all his resentment and anger seemed to have been dissipated, leaving only the pity of circumstances behind. Circumstances to which John Dickens had been as much a victim as his son. (It is not inapposite to note that it is precisely the power of circumstance which envelops his next novel.) Dickens still could not sleep and, from one letter, it is clear that he began once more to worry about his finances, as if the death of John Dickens had revived in him all the old fears of debt and imprisonment. For three nights he walked the streets of London until dawn − just such a night as he recreated in *Bleak House*, his next novel, when ". . . every noise is merged, this moonlight night, into a distant ringing hum, as if the city were a vast glass, vibrating".

After the funeral of his father, Dickens again took up his routine of going between London and Malvern; and, as he did so, he was making his plans for the year ahead.

He had already decided to spend the summer once more at Fort House in Broadstairs, and was hoping to begin a new novel during the late autumn or winter in London; at least as soon as he had found a suitable new house, and had settled there. On 14 April he came up to London in order to take the chair at a meeting of the General Theatrical Fund, one of those theatrical charities which appealed both to his sense of justice and to his delight at the professional actor's skills. Of course, with Catherine recuperating in the country, Dickens was also trying to spend as much time as possible in the company of his children; so on this day he went straight from the station to Devonshire Terrace and, according to one of his daughters, spent much of his time "playing with the children and carrying little Dora about the house and garden". Little Dora, named after the heroine of *David Copperfield* who dies. The "ill-omened" name. Then the time came for him to change and to go on to the London Tavern for the annual dinner. The affair was conducted as usual but, half an hour before Dickens was to speak, Forster was called out of the room. When Dickens rose he was greeted with "prolonged cheering", and after a few words on the general subject of the Fund he went on to express his gratitude to the theatrical profession: "Not because the actor sometimes comes from scenes of affliction and misfortune – even from death itself – to play his part before us; all men must do that violence to their feelings, in passing on to the fulfilment of their duties in the great strife and fight of life."

Forster himself was soon to speak but he knew now that he had a much harder task to face; he had left the room at the urgent bidding of one of Dickens's servants, who came with the news that the infant Dora had died quite suddenly. Forster decided to keep the news from Dickens until all his part in the proceedings had been completed, and in his biography Forster recalls how with anguish he listened to Dickens's remarks about the need to leave even the scene of death in order to carry on with the battle of life. No doubt Dickens had been thinking of his father's death then, steeling himself to go forward into the world once more, but how apposite his words were in another sense. Forster rose to speak; when, in the course of his speech, he referred to Dickens's "practical philanthropy" someone at the back of the hall called out, "Humbug!". But Forster carried on unperturbed. It was only at the end of the proceedings, and with the help of Mark Lemon whom he had called to assist him, that he told Dickens about the sudden death of his infant daughter. She had been seized with "convulsions" and expired within a few minutes. Dickens did not then break down but came back home. "I remember what a change seemed to have come over my dear father's face when we saw him again," Mamie recalled, ". . . how pale and sad it looked." All that night he sat beside the death-bed, keeping watch over the little girl's corpse with Mark Lemon. The next morning he wrote a tender and careful note to Catherine, clearly anxious that this latest news might augment her own suffering and even lead to some kind of breakdown. "I think her *very* ill," he told her, although he knew his daughter to be dead. Forster went down to Malvern with the letter and, when the news was eventually broken to her, Catherine fell into a state of "morbid" grief and suffering. Then, after some twelve hours or so, she seemed to recover something of her self-control. Dickens himself remained "in control" for a while, but his daughter remembered the time when he could no longer restrain his grief: "He did not break down until, an evening or two after her death, some beautiful flowers were sent." He "was about to take them upstairs and place them on the little dead baby, when he suddenly gave way completely". There are only one or two other recorded occasions when Dickens "gave way", but those who saw it never easily forgot.

So the shocks of this year had been great indeed: the sickness of Catherine, the death of his father and the death of his child. Yet pre-eminent in Dickens's mind was the need for self-sacrifice and for continuing ardent labour; in this he was so much like his contemporaries that we might even on this occasion describe him as "Victorian". But he laboured on, and eventually began his arrangements for the summer. He managed, as planned, to rent Fort House once more; Catherine, Georgina and the children went on ahead of him while he completed his business in London. But he did not stay in Devonshire Terrace; he was so dismayed at the prospect of so many people arriving for the Great Exhibition, some of them no doubt bearing with them letters of introduction to the famous novelist, that he rented out his house and himself took refuge in the office of *Household Words*. He also went down to Epsom for two days, in order to work up some material for the periodical, but he did not linger over the Great Exhibition itself. It had formally been opened at the beginning of May and Dickens's reaction was notably reserved about an event which, for most of his countrymen, marked the plain supremacy of England in the world of commerce and invention.

And it was now, with the family ensconced in Broadstairs, that Dickens at last managed to buy a house: Tavistock House, a plain brick building just off Tavistock Square and screened from the public thoroughfare by iron railings, a garden and trees. It was of some eighteen rooms, larger than Devonshire Terrace and in a grander district; it had been owned by a friend of Dickens, Frank Stone, but the Stones were to move to the next house but one. And so Tavistock House was prepared for its new family. In fact it was to have something of a chequered history; a later owner, Georgina Weldon, suffered a nervous collapse within its walls and subsequently issued a pamphlet entitled "The Ghastly Consequences of Living in Charles

Dickens's House", in which, among other things, she claims that her fate was "that of a sane person shut up in a lunatic asylum, put there for the purpose of being slowly or 'accidentally' murdered". She might be said intuitively to have picked up something of the atmosphere which was to be engendered here. Dickens himself always believed in the personality of houses, too, in that constant slow life which accrues to them, but at this early stage there seemed no reason to believe that Tavistock House would not be for him and his family a perfectly happy place.

It was now also that the shades of a new book were beginning to thicken around him, and as usual he became affected by that "violent restlessness . . ." which presaged a new novel. But he could start nothing until Tavistock House, described by Frank Stone's son as a "dirty, dismal, dilapidated mansion", had been redecorated and thoroughly repaired. For throughout the summer Dickens had also been directing busy letters to his brother-in-law, Henry Austin, asking for advice and assistance on various domestic and sanitary arrangements. Turning painting rooms into drawing rooms; preparing curtains and carpets; lengthening the entrance passage; attending to the drains; turning a recess into a cupboard or perhaps, on second thoughts, a bookcase; arranging a shower bath, ". . . *a Cold Shower of the best quality, always charged to an unlimited extent* . . ."; shielding the water closet from that shower, since "I have not sufficient confidence in my strength of mind, to think that I could begin the business of every day, with the enforced contemplation of the outside of that box. I believe it would affect my bowels." And, as usual, he wanted everything done *at once*. "I have to request that no time may be lost in executing this work"; "VITALITY OF EXPEDITION"; "*punctuality and dispatch*"; speed, always. What Henry Austin thought of his brother-in-law's state of permanent hyper-activity is not recorded. Nor are the impressions of the workmen who were constantly being stared at, questioned, and generally chivvied by Mr Dickens.

In the middle of November, the family were at last able to take possession of Tavistock House. It had been transformed; now it was indeed a grand house, fully refurbished and redecorated, and one of Dickens's first concerns was to keep the iron gates in front of the driveway locked. In this way he hoped to avoid the depredations of the street traders and the street musicians, whose noise was one of the principal discomforts of his London life. He had already promised his daughters that their old attic room in Devonshire Terrace would be replaced by what he called a "gorgeous" room in Tavistock House; but "they were not allowed to see the room at all until it was quite finished, and then he took them up to it himself. Everything that was pretty, dainty and comfortable was in that room . . ." Hans Christian Andersen was later to visit the house and recalled how "in the passage from street to garden hung pictures and engravings. Here stood a marble bust of Dickens . . . over a bedroom door and a dining room door were inserted the bas-reliefs of Night and Day after Thorwaldsen. On the first floor was a rich library with a fireplace and a writing-table, looking out on the garden . . . The kitchen was underground, and at the top of the house were the bedrooms." Andersen's room itself looked out over the towers and spires of London which "appear and disappear as the weather cleared or thickened". But no weather, no fog or rain, could affect the neatness and orderliness inside the house. Marcus Stone, his neighbour's son, recalled that in the newly refurbished house Dickens's influence was everywhere visible, with ". . . his love of order and fitness, his aversion to any neglect of attention, even in details which are frequently not considered at all. There was the place for everything and everything in its place, deterioration was not permitted

. . . There was no litter or accumulation of rubbish, no lumber room or glory hole."

His study at Tavistock House was a large room with sliding doors which led into the drawing room; Dickens liked to open these doors and thus, during the mornings given over to composition, walk up and down the whole length of the house. Pacing around as he contemplated the next sentence, the next word. And it was here, in his new study, that he began work on *Bleak House*. This title was only given to the novel after much experimentation, perhaps while at Fort House in Broadstairs; the first title was almost as simple as the last, and on off-white paper he had written in black ink "Tom-All-Alone's" and, beneath it, "The Ruined House". There had been a place known as Tom-All-Alone's near Chatham, a patch of ruined houses cleared to make way for a new prison, and it seems likely that at this point Dickens was imagining the setting of his story in some similar ruined house in the country. His second attempt at a title included: "That got into chancery/And never got out." So already he saw this ruin as part of the interminable processes of the law, the Court of Chancery being notorious for its inefficiency and dilatoriness. There is a pun here too, the phrase "in chancery" being used for a hold in boxing. Then he added "Building/Factory/Mill", as if he wished to incorporate the state of industrialised Britain. After a few more attempts he tried out "Bleak House Academy", as if some part of the national education were to be included in his plan. Then "The East Wind" was introduced as a title, a wind which to Londoners was often a harbinger of disease, spreading as it did from the East End of London to the more salubrious areas of the West. Until eventually the title emerged plainly as *Bleak House*. But how important the process had been to him, how many half-formed ideas and images had attached themselves to Dickens's search for a name.

And so he begins. In his new study in Tavistock House

he takes out his blue paper, dips his quill pen in black ink, and begins. "London. Michaelmas Term lately over, and the Lord Chancellor sitting in Lincoln's Inn Hall. Implacable November weather. As much mud in the streets, as if the waters had but newly retired from the face of the earth, and it would not be wonderful to meet a Megalosaurus, forty feet long or so, waddling like an elephantine lizard up Holborn Hill." A Megalosaurus in Holborn Hill – he had invented a similar image just a few months before when in *Household Words* he had imagined a "scaly monster of the Saurian period" in a creek of the Thames. The image had appealed to him, and so he had retained it; it is precisely what he was to call, in the preface to this novel, ". . . the romantic side of familiar things". A fact balanced against an unfamiliar impression, reality suffused with wild fancy so that it both is and is not the same – the kind of magic Dickens had imbibed from his childhood reading and now somehow recreated in this present world of mud and November weather. The balance between fact and marvel, reality and grotesquerie, sense and romance – a balance which for some reason seems quintessentially of the mid-nineteenth century when all forms of scientific and historical enquiry were discovering the marvellous within the domain of the familiar. It had been precisely this sense which Dickens wished to capture in the early stages of preparing *Bleak House*. He had a notion of setting his ruined country house in a valley in Gloucestershire because it reminded him of a valley in Switzerland; thus, in conflating them, he would be able to introduce the foreign into the familiar.

But it was of London which he now wrote. The city where the Megalosaurus might stalk and which on this November day is suffused with fog. "Fog everywhere . . . Chance people on the bridges peeping over the parapets into a nether sky of fog, with fog all round them, as if they were up in a balloon, and hanging in the misty clouds."

So the fog brings mystery, too, diffusing "the romantic side of familiar things" as the people hurry through the pearly darkness. And yet such a fog was real enough. It was no wraith of Dickens's invention. One contemporary wrote about "the vast city wrapt in a kind of darkness which seems neither to belong to the day nor the night . . ." The fogs of London were famous then. White, green, yellow fogs, the exhalation of coal fires and steamboats, factories and breweries; one afternoon, only a few years before, ". . . the mingled vapour and smoke grew thicker and thicker until it was literally pitch-dark. Torches appeared on all the streets . . ." The city as the mystery. That is at the heart of *Bleak House*. The city where the familiar becomes foreign, just as the words of the law are "foreign" to those who cannot read.

There was a sense in which Dickens loved this alien city; he loved that unearthly darkness which made it a place of fantasy and a harbinger of night. This was the city that harboured all the grotesques and the monsters which he created in *Bleak House*, fashioning them out of the mud and dirt which fill its pages. Dickens loved the city of mist, the city of night, the city lit by scattered lights – perhaps it might be described as a form of urban Gothic, like the architecture which was even then appearing in the grander thoroughfares of London. "There is nothing in London that is *not* curious," Dickens once wrote. But that which was the most curious was also "the most sad and the most shocking". This was "the great wilderness of London" in which we are able even at this late date to fix the precise places which Dickens chose to depict. The graveyard outside which Lady Dedlock dies was located at the corner of Drury Lane and Russell Street, with its entrance through Crown Court. It is now a playground for children. Krook's Rag and Bottle Warehouse was to be found in Star Yard, near Chichester Rents; at the time of writing, this whole area has been demolished to make way for new building.

But, even if by a feat of the historical imagination we stand upon the same pavements and see the old buildings and gates rising up once more, they would still not be the same places which Dickens saw. For him they were emblems of a new order and thus charged with unfamiliar mystery, the whole great city becoming as extraordinary as the Thames of his vision, the Thames which in *Bleak House* "had a fearful look, so overcast and secret, creeping away so fast between the low flat lines of shore: so heavy with indistinct and awful shapes, both of substances and shadow: so deathlike and mysterious". One other thing ought to be remembered, too: London was as interesting to its own inhabitants as it was to Dickens himself, and there is no doubt that they were eager to see, to read, and to learn all they could about their novel circumstances in a city which was growing and changing at an unparalleled speed. It was their sensibility, for example, that encouraged the growth of a more strident melodrama in the "low" theatres, in its dramatic contrasts mimicking the change and uncertainty of metropolitan life; there were new forms of comedy, too, particularly the comedy of shiftless street life; and a harsher kind of romanticism emerges, the romanticism which springs from the urban dark. The urban dark which Dickens was even now creating as he worked upon *Bleak House*.

By the first week of December he had finished all but the second chapter of its opening instalment, but then he had to break off in order to start work on his Christmas essay for *Household Words*. Never was he able to free himself from the trammels of his weekly periodical and in this short piece, "What Christmas Is, As We Grow Older", he establishes a melancholy note in his memories of the dead, and in his memories of past Christmases. "Lost friend, lost child, lost parent, sister, brother, husband, wife, we will not so discard you!" But in this little seasonal vignette there is also a plea for forbearance, for acceptance and understanding of the past; this Christmas, the Christmas after the death of his father and the death of his daughter, this Christmas becomes for Dickens a time of reconciliation. A time to sit and pause. A time to cease to complain and to strive. A time to incorporate the past. This, at the end of 1851, when he was beginning *Bleak House*.

# Twenty-Two

A TIME, too, for festivity. *Laus Deo!* was his general response to the birth of a new year and, for the first party in Tavistock House, Dickens organised a New Year's Eve celebration. He had also built a stage in the back room of the first floor of Tavistock House for the usual Twelfth Night entertainments, which rivalled those of Christmas and the New Year, and he called it "The Smallest Theatre In The World". This year he and the children put on a burlesque by Alfred Smith, *Guy Fawkes*, but such festival productions became an annual event in the Dickens household. Charley has described his father's omnipotent role in these proceedings: "He revised and adapted the plays, selected and arranged the music, chose and altered the costumes, wrote the new incidental songs, invented all the stage business, taught everybody his or her part . . ." No wonder the male children of Dickens were in later life to feel inadequate (the daughters had more of Dickens's own spirit) – how could it be otherwise with such a father?

Nothing now was so important to him as the writing of *Bleak House*. By the end of January he had come close to completing the first two numbers; he had interpolated a new chapter, "In Fashion", which he paginated from A to E and then inserted between the original first two chapters. Now "In Fashion" could be seen as a parallel to the first chapter, "In Chancery", and the structural principle on which Dickens was working becomes quite evident. His notes on this new second chapter — "*Lady Dedlock. Law Writer.* work up from this moment" — make it clear also that the elaborate parallels he was setting up in the narrative were accompanied by a very clear sense of the direction of the plot. As he writes he sees the comprehensiveness of what he is about to achieve like a half-glimpsed vision in front of him. It is this vision towards which he proceeds. And now he wanted to move ahead as quickly as possible.

His early routine for *Bleak House* was now settled. He generally worked on the novel from ten until two and, under normal circumstances, he hoped to finish his work by the twentieth of each month. At the end of this period he generally found himself in a state of what he once called "blackguard restless idleness", and would be constantly asking friends to join him on nocturnal tours, walking expeditions and various country jaunts. The paucity of references to *Bleak House* in his correspondence during the time of composition strongly suggests that he was quite in command of his material and felt no need privately to agonise over its composition; in a way it could be said that he had been preparing for this novel all his life and, despite the calamities and general weariness which had helped to provoke it in the first place, there can be little doubt that while he was actually working he remained relatively content. Despite the generally oppressed and oppressive tone of the book, in fact, there is ample evidence to suggest that Dickens was even happy while he was writing it — certainly happier than he had been in the previous year, when no proper creative work had been accomplished. Any amount of misery can afflict a writer, but in the actual process of writing that misery is dissolved. It might even be said that *Bleak House* cured the very malaise which was responsible for its composition.

348

By 7 February Dickens had finished the second number of *Bleak House*, and only now did he discover that he had overwritten and had to delete some seventy-six lines. At least it looks as if they were excised for reasons of space, although it is interesting to note that the majority of these cancelled lines concern the manner and conversation of Leonard, later hurriedly changed to Harold, Skimpole. The point was that, for the "model" of this irresponsible and fickle creature, Charles Dickens had taken Leigh Hunt, a friend of long standing. That it was meant to be a close study of the original is evident in Dickens's admission later that "I suppose that he is the most exact portrait that ever was painted in words! I have very seldom, if ever, done such a thing. But the likeness is astonishing ... It is an absolute reproduction of a real man." He had even lifted some of the material of Skimpole's conversation from a book which Leigh Hunt had written eight years before, *A Jar of Honey from Mount Hybla*. So astonishing a likeness, in fact, that he asked Forster and another friend to look over these passages in early proof stage; both men told him that the resemblance was too close, and that changes or excisions ought to be made. So Dickens altered the name from Leonard to Harold, cut out some of the more egregious parallels, and hoped for the best. But in truth nothing could alter the obvious identification with Hunt, and it soon became common knowledge that Dickens had pilloried his friend in the latest number of *Bleak House*. It was soon well known in London, at least, and, according to one contemporary, ". . . the general opinion was strongly in favour of Hunt". Another contemporary recalled that when the portrait of Skimpole was published the reaction among friends of Leigh Hunt was "intensely painful" and had "the effect of estranging one from the friends of Dickens who were most like flatterers and partisans".

But the origins of characters are deeper and more

disturbing. Of course there are the easy identifications to be made in the pages of *Bleak House*, from the grand (Lawrence Boythorn was meant to be a sketch of Walter Savage Landor) to the trivial (Inspector Bucket bears some idealised resemblance to Inspector Field and Mooney the beadle is apparently taken from a real beadle, Looney, who superintended Salisbury Square). But the point is that all of these characters, in the very act and art of composition, become, as we have had occasion to note elsewhere, part of the author himself.

Dickens worked on through February, and at the end of that month the first number of *Bleak House* appeared – on this occasion in bluish-green wrappers (Dickens did not return to the bright green wrappers of his earlier novels until the commencement of *Our Mutual Friend*, his last completed work). Such was the pressure of time that some of the narrative was set very hurriedly, and in fact over forty different compositors worked upon it over the months that followed, but the advertising space included in each number was at a higher premium than ever. On the inside cover of the first number there was an advertisement for Edmiston's Pocket Siphonia, or waterproof overcoat, which was followed by a section called "Bleak House Advertiser"; advertisements here included one for Rowland's Macassar Oil, for Life Pills, for Chrystal Spectacles, for Cough Lozenges, Pulmonic Wafers, Hair Lubricant, Shawls, Self-Acting Pipe Tubes, and Parasols. Some twenty-four pages of advertising in all, and on the inside back-cover an "Anti-Bleak House" advertisement for overcoats and trousers. The back cover itself was devoted to Heal and Son's Bedsteads. So did the life of nineteenth-century England surround, and even compete for attention with, Dickens's own evocation of it.

As Dickens finished each chapter or each number of *Bleak House*, proofs would be sent on to Hablot Browne with Dickens's specific recommendations for subjects to be illustrated. Then, customarily, Dickens would see a proof of Browne's plate for final approval. He was writing quickly now, in any case; he wanted to get ahead on the novel so that he could find time for journeys of the Amateur Players – an amateur theatrical group established by him – to Manchester and Liverpool which he had arranged on the Guild's behalf for February. In Manchester they played at the Free Trade Hall, and then went on for two performances at the Philharmonic Hall in Liverpool. And, as far as Dickens was concerned, there was always the same "triumph", the same "rapturous auditors", the same prodigious scenes in which he and the cast were ". . . blinded by excitement, gas, and waving hats and handkerchiefs". There never can have been a man whose enthusiasm expressed itself in such hyperbole, and throughout his life everything is either the *best* or the *worst*; there was no middle way. When he returned from this short tour he suffered the usual symptoms of withdrawal from the gas and the excitement; he was, as always, exhausted, stiff, and with weakened voice. As he used to tell his correspondents, he made fourteen costume changes each night. Nevertheless the festivities could not be allowed to end so abruptly, and a few days later he gave a dinner for the whole cast at Tavistock House.

It was at Tavistock House, too, that in the middle of March Catherine Dickens gave birth to her tenth child – named, in honour of the baronet, Edward Bulwer Lytton Dickens (Bulwer-Lytton himself was godfather). It was to be her last child, the conclusion of her long and unhappy history of pregnancy. The tour or perhaps the birth seemed to have unsettled Dickens; although he had to finish as much of *Bleak House* as possible in order to make room for yet more provincial theatricals in May, he was working on the novel only fitfully, felt "anxious", and was taking eighteen to twenty-mile walks in order to quieten or exhaust his restless spirit. He remained relatively content

351

as long as he could work systematically and consistently on the novel; but to work on it discontinuously, abruptly, quickly — this he disliked. He was also concerned about Leigh Hunt's reaction to the portrayal of Harold Skimpole (he still found himself automatically writing Leonard, and then crossing it out). Once more he was thinking of going abroad; to Paris, to Geneva, anywhere. In fact, in the end, he only went as far as Dover; but he did visit Rockingham Castle for one night, no doubt in part to refresh his memory concerning the model for his own Chesney Wold in the novel. But this was his normal reaction at times of self-imposed or external stress; to escape, to get away, to flee. And this despite the fact that all the news concerning *Bleak House* ought to have cheered him. Bradbury and Evans reported that sales were very high, and indeed they remained at over thirty thousand for the whole run of the novel.

It is not hard to see why, despite his mood, he needed to work quickly on *Bleak House*; not only was he in charge of all the administrative arrangements concerning a second provincial tour but a glance at his engagements for the first week of May, even before he departed with the Amateurs, reveals just how occupied he was. On the first day of May, a Saturday, he was trying to finish the next number of the novel (chapters eleven to thirteen), before attending a dinner for the Royal Academy that evening. On Sunday he had to prepare another large section of his *A Child's History of England*, ready to dictate it to an amanuensis at Wellington Street North. On the mornings of Monday, Tuesday and Wednesday he had to be present at the office, in order to "make up" the next two numbers of *Household Words*. On Wednesday he took the chair at a meeting for the removal of trade restrictions on literature; George Eliot was also present on that occasion and remarked how Dickens was ". . . preserving a courteous neutrality of eyebrows, and speaking with clearness and decision", but she did add that he was "not distinguished-looking". Two days later there was a dinner at Tavistock House to celebrate his son's christening, and on the following afternoon his time was taken up by a number of welcome and unwelcome callers. Then, two days later, he was off with his Guild players for performances in Shrewsbury and Birmingham.

There were only a certain number of days, therefore, when he was able to concentrate upon *Bleak House* and, almost as soon as he returned from the short provincial tour, he was once more "hard at work" on the fourteenth chapter, trying to keep free of interruptions and making sure that all his attention was concentrated on the working out of the story. Presumably that is why he went down to St Albans as soon as he had corrected the proofs of that number; he was thinking ahead, thinking of poor Jo's vagrant route, Jo, who, in his mortal illness, talks of travelling along "the Stolbuns Road". Certainly he was in his mind now, since the number he had just finished had concentrated upon the sufferings of the poor street-crossing sweeper; to such an extent, in fact, that the narrator *becomes* Jo as he shuffles through the streets of London. "To be hustled, and jostled, and moved on; and really to feel that it would appear to be perfectly true that I have no business, here, or there, or anywhere . . ." And it is in this spirit, and with this access to Jo's consciousness, that Dickens reflects upon a world controlled by what Jarndyce calls "this monstrous system". As the poor Chancery litigant, Gridley, puts it, "The system! I am told, on all hands, it's the system. I mustn't look to individuals. It's the system."

At the beginning of October the children were left in London (Mamie and Katie being superintended by a French governess) while Dickens, Catherine and Georgina travelled across to Boulogne. He wanted to finish the next number of *Bleak House* in France and, as soon as he had done so, to return to London and his ordinary professional life. It is remarkable, incidentally, for a man of such fixed habits, how easily he could accommodate his writing to any surroundings; London, Folkestone, Dover and now Boulogne seemed to provide no distraction or difficulty in the constant daily process of writing. Only a man who was so fully in his imagined world that the real one no longer obtruded could manage such changes of scenery with Dickens's equanimity. They stayed in Boulogne for two weeks, at the Hotel des Bains, and clearly appreciated the area; it was in fact to take the place of Broadstairs as their summer retreat, although on this first visit Dickens brought back with him only one souvenir – a little figure of a Turk seated, smoking, as the sign for a tobacconist's shop, which he considered to be unmatched for its "grotesque absurdity". As soon as he had returned to London, he went straight to the office in order to discuss with Wills the shape of the coming Christmas issue. He also brought back the next two chapters for *Bleak House* and, since he did not in fact return until 18 October, less than two weeks before publication, he was cutting his "deadline" rather fine.

And then straight on to the next number, leading up to what he called "the great turning idea", by which he clearly meant the revelation to Esther Summerson that her mother is indeed Lady Dedlock. Gustave Flaubert used to say that he suffered with his characters even as he created them, that he became invaded by nervous anxiety at the same time as his characters, and even shared in the agony induced by the arsenic poisoning of Emma Bovary. Dickens's symptoms were not so severe but he did manage to contract a very bad cold at the time he was consigning Esther Summerson to a bout of smallpox; although, curiously enough, W. H. Wills became, like Esther, temporarily blind at the time that particular episode was published. And then there was rain. Rain in London for three months;

heavy rain through which Dickens insisted on walking; hallucinatory rain, since with his bad cold "my whole room looks swollen and giddy, and it seems to be incessantly *raining* between me and the books"; fictional rain in *Bleak House*, the rain which further weakens Jo in his short passage to death.

By the middle of December Dickens had at last come close to "the great turning idea" and at the last minute he added, on a separate piece of paper, the passage in which he used various authorities to confirm his use of spontaneous combustion when Krook dies. Already he could see to the end of the story. He was planning to complete it by the following August, and then to travel once more to Switzerland. In the interim, between numbers in this bleak December, he rushed out once more into the world in order to refresh himself. With Wilkie Collins he went on a prowl around Whitechapel, and with Frank Stone he went back to Chatham, revisiting this site of childhood memories just after completing a short essay, "Where We Stopped Growing", in which he evokes some of the sharpest memories of his own childhood. He was also dictating sections of *A Child's History of England* concerned with the reign of Henry VIII, and in the number of *Bleak House* he had just finished he had written of ". . . the lamplighter going his rounds, like an executioner to a despotic king, strikes off the little heads of fire that have aspired to lessen the darkness. Thus, the day cometh, whether or no."

Dickens was now working hard on *Bleak House*, but his time was also being taken up by *Household Words*: Wills was ill, and for the last few weeks Dickens had to conduct all the usual business of the journal. He went down to Brighton for a fortnight specifically in order to work in peace, Catherine and Georgina having gone ahead of him in order to make sure that their lodgings in Junction Parade were in perfect order for him. Then, as soon as he was back in London, he was rising at five o'clock even on a Sunday morning in order to carry on with the novel. He was writing, and then reading episodes to family and friends; constant toil over the book which had taken so strong a hold upon him, constant toil leading up to the climax of the story. It seems likely, also, that he rented rooms in this period where he might work undisturbed. Certainly at a later time he took an apartment for just such a purpose at the corner of Hatcham Park Road and New Cross Road, and there is some evidence to suggest that he had taken up the accommodation while he was composing *Bleak House*. The other location mentioned as Dickens's temporary habitation is (or was) Cobley's Farm in North Finchley; the site of the rented rooms is less significant, however, than the fact that Dickens was beginning what would become a lifelong habit of providing himself with a "bolt-hole" for the purposes of work and anonymity. New Cross, or Finchley, was a long way from his normal centre of operations; and a long way, too, from Tavistock House. For there had been interruptions even there. He had wanted to hire a gun, with small shot, in order to get rid of some dogs which barked in Tavistock Square and then, a little later, he had been horrified to see the local baker's man relieving himself outside the gates of Tavistock House itself. Dickens, who was always aware of his personal dignity on such occasions, remonstrated with him; the man was *"very impertinent"* in return, and Dickens threatened to have him taken into custody under the Police Act. This was not the only occasion when Dickens threatened less distinguished members of the community with the law — another thing he detested was swearing in public places — but nevertheless he saw the humorous side even of his own actions. The baker's man, he said, ". . . was rather urgent to know what I should do 'if I was him' — which involved a flight of imagination into which I didn't follow him".

The dominant note of his life at this time is still one of overwork: ". . . the journey is ever onward and we must pursue it or we are worthy of no place here." His appearance, too, began to show signs of his stress and exhaustion. There were people who now commented that they "would not recognise him" as the young man they had once known, and Mrs Yates, a quondam actress who had not seen him for fifteen years, told her son that ". . . save his eyes, there was no trace of the original Dickens about him". The young man with the flowing locks had gone; only the bright eyes remained the same. He had said the whisperings of sickness were "hypochondriacal" but he became truly sick; once more it was the inflamed kidney of his childhood, now causing him such discomfort that he took to his bed for six days; his pain rendered his face gaunt, his eyes wide, and, as he told Wilkie Collins a few years later, "I was stricken ill when I was doing Bleak House, and I shall not easily forget what I suffered under the fear of not being able to come up to time". On doctor's advice, from this time forward, he always wore a broad flannel belt around his waist to protect his weak kidney. And he had to get away. He went down to Folkestone, and then to Boulogne, where arrangements for a summer residence had been made.

Immediately after his arrival there he rested for a week, and began to recover his strength. As soon as he had done so he set to work once more upon *Bleak House*, even now reaching its climax as Lady Dedlock is tracked down by Inspector Bucket and Esther Summerson. By the end of the third week of June – less than two weeks after his arrival – he had managed to complete the number; and, by the end of the month, he had fully sketched out all the steps which would lead him to the end of the book. As soon as he had done so he was once more asking friends to join him in the château; clearly his intention to finish the novel in the course of August meant that he could have companions with him by the time he was ready to celebrate its completion. He even planned a banquet at the château formally to signal that event. Before he began this final entry into *Bleak House* he rested again for a few days, if rest it can be called, with his daily and energetic expeditions to fêtes and fairs, theatres and markets. He even took a two-day trip to Amiens. Then on the first day of August he began the final double-number, his aim being to finish it by the eighteenth or nineteenth and then to take the final chapters personally to London. Dickens set timetables for himself with an iron determination, as if he could work best within punishing and self-imposed constraints, and on this as on many other occasions he fulfilled his own demands to the letter. So it was that in the first seventeen days of August he completed *Bleak House*.

He had finished on time too, and at once set off on the short trip to London in order to complete all necessary preparations in person. In the preface which he now wrote, he declared that, "In 'Bleak House' I have purposely dwelt upon the romantic side of familiar things. I believe I have never had so many readers as in this book. May we meet again!" He stayed in the capital only for two or three days, and then returned to Boulogne where in the Château des Moulineaux, he read the final number to his family. "May we meet again!" This was how he now saw his intimate relationship with his readers, as if he were about to shake hands with them, fix them with his bright eyes, and hold them in leisurely converse. The interest was to a certain extent reciprocated; as the *Illustrated London News* now said, ". . . 'What do you think of *Bleak House*?' is a question which everybody had heard propounded within the last few weeks." Clearly there was something different in it, something odd, something unexpected to prompt the question. In later years it was seen by nineteenth-century commentators as the beginning of Dickens's unfunny and ponderous "decline", and even the criticism at the time was not as laudatory as the actual sales of the novel might suggest; once more the power of his characterisation was acknowledged, and the word favoured to describe it was "daguerreotype" with all its contemporaneous associations of sharpness and clearness of focus. But the *Spectator* was not alone in ". . . having found it dull and wearisome". Even Forster believed that it lacked the "freedom" and "freshness" of Dickens's previous novels, and thus inaugurated works of quite a different and more cumbersome kind. Apparently there were few readers able to detect the pattern which Dickens had laid down within his story. Chancery? The ruined slums? The churchyard? These were not seen as emblems of some larger design, but rather Dickens's specific response to specific abuses.

But what of it now, this narrative which now stands in a sense outside of time? It has often been suggested that *Bleak House* does indeed mark a change in Dickens's style but one that is to be welcomed; the novel, according to many recent critics, inaugurated the novelist's "dark period". It is agreeable thus to mark off the stages of Dickens's progress, but it is hard to find any real evidence with which to do so. The development of a novelist can really best be understood, not in terms of his "moods" or even of his "themes", but rather in that slow process of experimentation and self-education which changes the techniques of his prose. In that sense, the "darker" aspects of Dickens's novels are merely an aspect of their more assiduously unified structure. There are scenes in *The Pickwick Papers* and in *Oliver Twist* as dark as anything in *Bleak House*; what has changed is the way in which he closely packs together all the aspects of his vision, thus excluding that free play and improvisation which we consider to be the "light" pitted against the "darkness" of his structural control. There is another change as well; as Dickens wrote each novel he came to a much more intimate understanding of his own vision of the world, and this closer acquaintance with his own genius inevitably precluded a certain kind of improvisation or elaboration which in a lesser novelist can be seen as "charming" or "ingenious". Forster had noticed it, too, this loss of "freedom"; but it was a necessary part of the restraining and refining force of Dickens's imagination. He was seeing things more clearly, he was seeing them as a whole.

A general feeling of restlessness after the completion of *Bleak House* seems to have affected Dickens and it was now that he set off upon a long excursion to Switzerland and Italy in the company of Wilkie Collins and Augustus Egg. They were a well-matched trio, and, although there were times when their misadventures seem to come very close to those of Jerome K. Jerome's later trinity of imagined travellers, they got on well enough. Dickens was back in London, though, by the second week of December and, although he was once more deep in *Household Words* business as well as the management of Tavistock House theatricals for Twelfth Night, his main concern was with some readings he had promised to give in Birmingham for the Industrial and Literary Institute. There were to be three of them — *A Christmas Carol* on 27 December, *The Cricket on the Hearth* on the following day and then, on the thirtieth, *A Christmas Carol* once more. This last performance was the one in which he was most interested, since the audience would be comprised entirely of the "working people" who would be sold tickets at the low price of sixpence. Catherine, Georgina and the older children accompanied him to Birmingham, while Wills seemed to be acting in the capacity of manager for the occasion.

For the first Reading, in the Town Hall, he rose a little nervously before the seventeen hundred people who had endured a snowstorm in order to hear him. But he soon got into his stride and, as he told a friend a few days later, ". . . we were all going on together, in the first page, as easily, to all appearance, as if we had been sitting round the fire". This was the first large public reading he had ever given, and all his skills as an actor could not have prepared him for such an occasion; yet he took to it very easily, he took to it *naturally* simply because it was natural for him to become intimate – as if "round the fire" – with seventeen hundred people. One of the secrets of his genius was his ability to project himself in just such a fashion so that, although his own domestic life might not always have been a model of sympathetic union, he could represent and instil the idea of domesticity and comfort in those who watched and listened to him. A reporter from the *Birmingham Journal* noted "how Mr Dickens twirled his moustache, or played with his paper knife, or laid down his book, and leant forward confidentially . . ." He misjudged only one particular; it took him three hours to read *A Christmas Carol*, where he had predicted two, but judicious cutting in later years substantially shortened this tale of comfort and joy. It always remained his favourite among his readings, at least until his last years, since of its very essence it conveyed precisely the mood of familial and national harmony which he was even then attempting to instil with his presence in Birmingham. Although the second night's reading of *The Cricket on the Hearth* seemed to have been equally successful, Dickens never enjoyed it so much.

So the great triumph of his Birmingham visit was his reading of *A Christmas Carol* on the third night to the "working people". Two thousand of them packed the Town Hall – it had been at Dickens's own instigation that the tickets were priced so cheaply – and as soon as he appeared on the platform the *Birmingham Journal* recorded how they all "rose up and cheered most enthusiastically, and then became quiet again, and then went at it afresh". Before he began to read, he stepped forward to address them. "My Good Friends . . ." he started to say, and at once there was "a perfect hurricane of applause". They

were his good friends indeed, and as he made his preliminary speech he was interrupted by cheers and laughter
and applause, as if he were the very first man who had
understood them and who represented them. For had he
not in his Christmas Books stood up for the rights of the
poor? And here he was, telling them that he had always
wished "to have the great pleasure of meeting you face to
face at this Christmas time" – more applause and cheering
– and going on to instil the central lesson of his own political philosophy. "If there ever was a time when any one
class could of itself do much for its own good, and for the
welfare of society – which I greatly doubt – that time is
unquestionably past. It is in the fusion of different classes,
without confusion; in the bringing together of employers
and employed; in the creating of a better common understanding among those whose interests are identical, who
depend upon each other, and who can never be in unnatural antagonism without deplorable results, that one of the
chief principles of a Mechanics' Institution should consist."
He went on in this vein, again with much cheering and
applause, until he ended with "I now proceed to the
pleasant task to which I assure you I have looked forward
for a long time".

He began, "Marley was dead . . .", and carried on
through that great lament for the poor and that insistent
wish for pity and for sympathy. "They lost nothing,"
Dickens reported afterwards, "misinterpreted nothing,
followed everything closely, laughed and cried with the
most delightful earnestness." Here he had full proof of
what he called his "Power", evidence of his ability to sway
large masses of men and women, and to "imbue" them,
too, with something of his own beliefs. And at the end, to
renewed cheers and applause, he came forward to say
". . . I am as truly and sincerely interested in you . . . any
little service to you I have freely rendered from my
heart . . ." It had been a triumph, and there is no doubt
362

that the reception he received from this working-class audience materially affected his description of the same men and women in the novel he was just about to begin, *Hard Times*. But now he also knew more about his own gifts and capacities, and Wills wrote to his wife, "If Dickens does turn Reader he will make another fortune. He will never offer to do so, of course. But if they *will* have him he will do it, he told me today." He was ready to enter one of the most extraordinary periods of his own life.

# Twenty-Three

*C*HARLES DICKENS: "Mrs Morson, this is the girl who wants to go, I believe."

*Mrs Morson*: "Yes."

*Charles Dickens*: "Take her at her word. It is getting dark now, but, immediately after breakfast tomorrow morning, shut the gate upon her for ever."

Thus Dickens with some of his first words of the New Year, at Urania Cottage. And, as always, he listened eagerly to the words of these young women in reply, noting them down as precisely as if they had stepped out of one of his own novels: ". . . she didn't suppose, Mr Dickerson, as she were a goin to set with her ands erfore her . . ." And then again: ". . . which blessed will be the day when justice is a-done in this ouse." The banished girl was left in a state of miserable consternation for the night but then, as Dickens had planned all along, the order was revoked for the sake of "the great forgiving Christmas time". Thus authoritarianism is mixed with pity, and may be seen as a picture in miniature of Dickens's attitude towards the poor and the dispossessed.

Similarly it was in the spirit of the great Christmas time that once more he organised the Twelfth Night theatricals; in fact the children had already settled upon some form of play but Dickens saw them rehearse it, decided that it was not good enough, at once began to marshal them in *Tom*

*Thumb*, and observed that "they have derived considerable notions of punctuality and attention from the parental drilling". No doubt they did. Dickens himself played the ghost of Gaffer Thumb (under the stage name of "The Modern Garrick"), and in fact was dressed for the part in so "hideous and frightening" a manner that his young son remembered being taken up to the dressing room to see his father in advance, so that he might not break down in terror on the stage of the "Theatre Royal, Tavistock House".

It was also the birthday of Dickens's eldest son, Charley, but for him it was not a particularly happy time. He was a disappointment to his father, who perhaps saw in his eldest son a distinct and unflattering contrast to those like himself – those who had been compelled to force their way through an uncongenial world. Yet what he did so quickly and peremptorily in his life, what he felt and believed, soon sent down echoes into the darker and stranger regions of his imagination. What kind of education should a parent give a son? How much was the ambition of the self-made man really worth? These were the questions which he began to explore in his next novel.

He set to work in the third week of January 1854. He took out a sheet of his characteristic light blue writing paper, and calculated the amount he would need to fill five pages of *Household Words* each week. He was no longer used to writing in the weekly format and so, to expedite matters, he actually decided to arrange the new novel in monthly parts which he would then subdivide into the necessary weekly portions. On the same day he took out another sheet of paper and began to consider titles. On the left hand side he wrote simply, "Mr Gradgrind/Mrs Gradgrind". Then on the other side he began with his title, "Stubborn Things". Then he wrote "Fact". Which was followed by "Thomas Gradgrind's Facts". It is clear in which direction his imagination is running. Only a few months before he had written in Boulogne an article entitled "Frauds on the Fairies" in which he took exception to his old friend, George Cruikshank, and his attempts to introduce temperance propaganda into the fairy-stories of childhood. As a child he had detested books which had discounted the wonderful and the bizarre in favour of precept or homily, and now his old faith in the stories of his youth was crystallised in this little essay with his declaration that "In an utilitarian age, of all other times, it is a matter of grave importance that Fairy tales should be respected". This of course had wider ramifications. Mr Gradgrind, whose name he had found at once, was a teacher, and clearly was always meant to be; thus we have such alternative titles as "Two and Two are Four" and "Prove it!". A theme continued in the first words of the novel, echoing around a schoolroom, "Now, what I want is, Facts."

The opening of the novel was proving difficult, however. In the manuscript of *Hard Times*, the first page is covered with deletions and emendations; and two days later Dickens was asking W. H. Wills to obtain for him ". . . the Educational Board's series of questions for the examination of *teachers* in schools". He needed material evidence, in other words, on which to base his attack upon false education. But at some point over these first few days Dickens, in one of those acts of imaginative combination which set him apart from his contemporaries, saw through the matter of the schools to the larger question. "Facts" in an utilitarian age also meant the vogue for statistics and figures which was even then being used to abstract and anatomise the suffering of the urban poor. So everything once more was coming together; the horrors of a childhood unalleviated by Fancy could be aligned to the horrors experienced by the urban poor and by the working people of the great industrial cities. Now the real subject was in place. *Hard Times*. He had actually written it out three times in his list of possible titles, and its recurrence suggests the direction in which his imagination had been moving all along. This was the theme that had been waiting for him, and it took the question of education to act as a catalyst for it.

Hard times. He had been in Birmingham, after all, where, among the workers of that great industrial city (that "machine" as Dickens once described it), his support for the new Educational Institute had been cheered and applauded. In an essay he wrote for *Household Words* directly inspired by travelling on the Birmingham railway he created a landscape which was to reappear in *Hard Times* itself; with the "glare in the sky, flickering now and then over the greater furnaces ... Tongues of flame shoot up from them, and pillars of fire turn and twist upon them." And of course his reception had encouraged him in his belief that the labouring classes needed the sustenance of Fancy as embodied in *A Christmas Carol*; the connection between childhood, fairy-tales and the labouring poor was made again. Just as importantly, his enthusiastic welcome confirmed him in his belief that they were on the whole generous and true people.

But why sometimes did they behave in a manner quite inconsistent with Dickens's belief in them? He had been reading about a strike of weavers in Preston, which quickly became a crucial test of the relative powers of Capital and Labour; the mill-owners closed their factories in order to prevent the workers from picking them off one by one, and the dispute over whether it was a straightforward strike or a management "lock out" was only one issue during a protracted struggle in which each side waited for the other to surrender. The strike was in its fourth month when Dickens visited Preston and attended one of the workers' meetings. As he explained in an article which he wrote for *Household Words* two weeks later, he was impressed by the workers themselves and their "astonishing fortitude and perseverance; their high sense of honour among themselves . . ." but, if blame were to be found, it should be directed against "some designing and turbulent spirits". This was precisely the line he had taken before, and ". . . I left the place with a profound conviction that their mistake is an honest one . . ." The strike was an honest mistake – rather cool comfort for those engaged upon it but his sentiment emphasises the central message which he had been repeating in articles and speeches and correspondence; there must be some mutual trust and regard between employers and employees because they needed each other, and in harmony between them lay all the hopes for the prosperity of the country. In the same article he also declared that ". . . into the relations between employers and employed, as into all the relations of this life, there must enter something of feeling and sentiment; something of mutual explanation, forbearance, and consideration . . ." Now these are precisely the virtues encouraged by Fancy, as Dickens had also often repeated, so in condemning the aggression between workers and masters at Preston he was also implicitly condemning the loss of Fancy in their lives. That is why he was so concerned to support educational institutes in the large industrial cities; the delight in Fancy, the delight in literature, would encourage just those virtues of harmony and sympathy which were necessary in the maintenance of good industrial relations.

And so he set to work on *Hard Times* after his return from Preston. The narrative had been conceived for *Household Words* and everything about it reflected that condition, even to its appearance on the front page of the periodical as if it were a cross between a journalistic report and an editorial. He began writing it in a deliberately sparse style and the fact that he still had "motes of new stories" floating in front of him as he did so suggests what is evident enough from a reading of this small book: Dickens did not in any sense think of it as a novel in his usual vein. In fact it reads like a fable, in a style which is very close to Victorian translations of fairy-stories in the same period. Its intentional simplicity also brings it much closer to the tone of his Christmas stories and it is possible that, in the absence of his old Christmas Books, Dickens was trying to write something on a similar scale and with a similar purpose – to bring his listeners together around the fireside of his imagination, just as he had managed to do at the Birmingham meeting, and to impress upon them the virtues of comradeship and sympathy. Of course it is "topical", too, in the same way that *The Chimes* had been topical. It was even associated with a series of articles which Dickens was about to publish in *Household Words* on industrial accidents: in fact he added a passage about such accidents, and a footnote drawing attention to the series in the periodical, but both references were excised at proof stage. His satire on the facts of Mr Gradgrind's classroom was aimed at a number of specific targets as well; primarily the Department of Practical Art, as we have seen, but it was also directed against the contents of Charles Knight's *Store of Knowledge* (which in fact introduced the ludicrously literal definition of a horse); against the "tabular reports" of library reading compiled by the Manchester Free Library and discussed in *Household Words* one month before; against the new regimen of pupil-teachers who were even now issuing from the training colleges only recently established; and of course against those people in general "who see figures and averages" only. In a later letter he attacked what was generally known as the "Manchester School" of political economics for what he called ". . . its reduction to the grossest absurdity of the supply-and-demand dogmatism" and its belief that self-interest was the major factor in human decisions. "As if the vices and passions of men had not been running counter to their interests since the Creation of the World!" The vices and passions of men;

369

these are what Dickens wanted to chasten and reveal as he moved steadily forward upon his story.

Through the early months of 1854 Dickens worked on. He said later of *Hard Times* that ". . . the idea laid hold of me by the throat in a very violent manner", but at the time all he could see was the labour and difficulty of a narrative which was being serialised in weekly parts almost as he wrote it. The requirements of "compression and close condensation" gave him "perpetual trouble", and in a letter to Forster he complained that ". . . the difficulty of the space is CRUSHING. Nobody can have an idea of it who has not had an experience of patient fiction-writing with some elbow-room always, and open places in perspective. In this form, with any kind of regard to the current number, there is absolutely no such thing . . ." In fact the form he had chosen was less strict than that of the familiar monthly numbers, at least in the sense that he was writing for his own periodical and could increase at will the space given to the story in each issue; which he did, for example, in the last instalment. But his constant meticulous effort, week after week, was in itself exhausting; his doctor ordered him to have a "regimen of fresh air" for a week, and it is likely that his need for a respite became obvious just after he had finished, at the beginning of March, an instalment of some eleven thousand words.

At the beginning of April the first number was published; it was displayed on the front page as "HARD TIMES by Charles Dickens", the only time that a signed article had appeared in its pages. No illustrations. Just two columns of print going from page to page, and presented in such a way that it might just as well be a leading article as a story – a confusion which undoubtedly proved fruitful to a novelist who was as keen to catch the atmosphere of the time as to create a fable of the machine age. It was, in a sense, an inauspicious time, for this was the month that Britain declared war against Russia, ostensibly over the defence of Turkey but in reality as a check against the growing power of that nation under Czar Nicholas. This war, described by one historian as initiated by a potent combination of British liberalism and jingoism, was not one which would necessarily be criticised by Dickens; but his early comments on the issue are concerned only with its effect upon the sale of books. (There would come a time when the conduct of that war, however, provoked some of Dickens's most bitter condemnations of the "system" by which Britain was governed.) But the publication of *Hard Times* was inauspicious in a much smaller way as well: Mrs Gaskell had already started writing a novel, eventually entitled *North and South*, which anticipated Dickens's location and broad theme. In January Forster had written to tell her to ". . . go on with the story whether it be for Dickens or not". In fact it was for Dickens, and appeared in *Household Words* almost immediately after the conclusion of *Hard Times*. By April, however, it was clear that there was more than a passing resemblance between the two tales, but Forster wrote to encourage her. "As to the current which Dickens's story is likely to take I have regretted to see that the manufacturing discontents are likely to clash with part of your plan but . . . I *know* with what a different purpose and subsidiary to what quite opposite manifestations of character and passion *your* strike will be introduced, and I am your witness, if necessary, that your notion in this matter existed before and quite independently of his." It has been suggested that Dickens was guilty of plagiarising Mrs Gaskell's novel but there is no evidence or justification for this. Dickens really did not begin editorial work upon her manuscript until he was well into his own and, if anything, he went to some pains not to clash with *North and South*. That is why, in *Hard Times*, the theme of union and management is quickly raised and just as quickly forgotten. In any case the two novels are barely alike in any respect, Dickens's mythical

371

and fabulist imagination working on quite different principles from Mrs Gaskell's more naturalistic and domestic preoccupations.

But Dickens was finding it hard to get on with the novel. It was not until the end of June that he began in earnest, and he worked steadily through into July; his aim now was to finish by the nineteenth of that month. He was what he called "... stunned with work ..." He was coming close to the discovery of Stephen Blackpool in the deserted mine-shaft, leading ineluctably to the millhand's death. Dickens's head was feeling "hot"; he was for some reason nervous; and it was at this moment that he has Rachael, the hapless friend of Stephen, declare, "... I fall into such a wild, hot hurry, that, however tired I am, I want to walk fast, miles and miles." A wild, hot hurry: that was Dickens's state now as he came to the concluding chapters. Stephen dead. Gradgrind's son fleeing from the scene of his crime. And in Dickens's notes: "Wind up – The ashes of our fires grown grey and cold." He had, in the interim, sent a letter to Carlyle asking if he might dedicate the book to him; which was duly done, although Carlyle's reply was not as enthusiastic as perhaps it might have been. To lend his name to a *fiction*?

Dickens finished two days sooner than he had anticipated, in his own wild, hot hurry. But by now he was feeling very tired and "used up". In fact he was more exhausted than he realised and he claimed to be suffering from the "... very hot, close, suffocating, and oppressive" weather. The climate, as always, seemed to reflect his moods. He was now preparing an edition in volume form, and he gave titles to all of the chapters and divided the novel into three "Books". This may or may not have been partly in imitation of Thackeray who had divided *The History of Henry Esmond* in such a manner; whatever the cause, Dickens liked the arrangement, and he was to employ it for all subsequent completed books. He commuted in the hot weather between Tavistock House and the office of *Household Words*. He was sitting for yet another portrait. He was annoyed by Catherine's mother, who for some unaccountable reason wished to take out life insurance at her advanced age. And then something strange occurred, something which might be put down to Dickens's own state of nervous exhaustion. He was walking along the street one morning when "I suddenly (the temperature being then most violent) found an icy coolness come upon me, accompanied with a general stagnation of the blood, a numbness of the extremities, great bewilderment of mind, and a vague sensation of wonder. I was walking at the time, and, on looking about me, found that I was in the frigid shadow of the Burlington Hotel. Then I recollected to have experienced the same sensations once before precisely in that spot. A curious case this, don't you think?" The hotel itself was at 19 Cork Street (the building now contains an art gallery), on the corner of Burlington Gardens, and assiduous research has yielded no earthly clue to the source of his sensation. Yet it is a case "curious" enough, especially for a man who had only recently been condemning the contemporary craze for "spirit rapping" and who was in the habit of poking mild fun at people interested in the occult. But he did attend seances, with whatever misgivings, and he did have a real sense of the numinous. What could be more natural, then, that his own nervous debility should render him susceptible to all those influences which linger in the avenues and alleys of the great, wild city? Of course he could feel his tiredness; but it was not his way to yield to such things and in his own hot way he tried to conquer that feeling of being exhausted, frayed, empty, "used up". He met a friend at the theatre, the playwright Buckstone, and proceeded to drink gin-slings with him until dawn. Not a usual practice of Dickens's, but he was on his own and, most importantly, he was intent upon ". . . knocking the remembrance of my work out".

Dickens now travelled to Boulogne, and at last began the "country holiday" of which he was so sorely in need. He lay on the grass and read, he lay against the haystacks and slept; ". . . reading books and going to sleep" was his phrase, the luxury of retreating to his childhood experience of reading and resting. But with it too there was now the intimation of adult exhaustion – the dropping of the book, the page unturned. He visited the fêtes and fairs, as he had last year, and went for his usual fifteen or sixteen-mile walks; since he was walking in the rain for some of the time, however, he suffered an inflamed ear for several days and placed compresses of poppies against his head to relieve the swelling and the pain. Thackeray was in Boulogne, too; his daughters were now on very friendly terms with Dickens's daughters, and it seems likely that it was the children who brought the two novelists together here. They dined on at least one occasion, and then played "forfeits" with the boys. There were also house-guests of course and Wilkie Collins, suffering agonies of rheumatic gout, stayed for some weeks.

Boulogne itself was untypically animated. The outbreak of the Crimean War explained the presence of a large army camp which had been established in the vicinity, and what with Napoleon III, and what with the Prince Consort, the whole place came alive (in Dickens's descriptions at least) with flags and bugles and guns. And fires. If there was one thing that Dickens enjoyed, both in art and in life, it was a good fire; so he was positively enthusiastic when a theatre in Boulogne was burnt to the ground. He went to the scene of the accident as quickly as he could, and found that ". . . the spectacle of the whole interior, burning like a red-hot cavern, was really very fine, even in the day-light".

By now Dickens had reached middle-age, and he had attained unprecedented success, and yet he was still not

374

content. Not happy. This must have seemed the strangest thing of all to him, to have achieved so much and still to be looking for contentment. And what could he see ahead of him except further disquiet? If he had not found that one thing he was always looking for by middle-age, how could he be expected to find it later? That need for love and admiration, born in childhood, was still not satisfied; that wound which had opened in his earliest years was still not healed. And perhaps this is the most terrible thing of all, so disconcerting as to provoke all his intense restlessness and his desire for escape – it had been the dislocation and privation of his childhood in the blacking warehouse which had helped propel him towards success. But, now that he had achieved that success, and its novelty had waned, all the miseries of his childhood were returning with redoubled strength. The fame and fortune of his years as a novelist had effectively repressed all the symptoms of his old panic and disorder but now, as he entered middle-age, they were reasserting themselves once more. He had never escaped his past – he knew that as well as anyone – he had merely prevented it from swallowing him up. There is a curious passage in Forster's biography, when discussing the problems of this time, which takes us to the heart of one of Dickens's fears; ". . . there were moments (really and truly only moments) . . ." but a moment can last a lifetime! – ". . . when the fancy would arise that if the conditions of his life had been reversed, something of a vagabond existence (using the word in Goldsmith's meaning) might have supervened. It would have been an unspeakable misery to him, but it might have come nevertheless." If the conditions of his life had been reversed . . . and he had returned to the precarious existence of his childhood. This is what Dickens feared; he had feared it as a child, when he saw how easily he might have taken up the street-life of the other children around him; and now, even at the pinnacle of his success, that childhood

375

terror of vagabondage had revived. He could not escape his past, or the anxieties of his past which sometimes had more reality than the real world all around him. There is that image at the end of *Hard Times* – Gradgrind sitting in the Clown's chair in the middle of the circus-ring, his son capering around him with blackened face and hands. The scene has the quality of a vision or what Dickens would have called a "picture"; and could not the son, covered in blacking, be a "picture" of the young Dickens? A young Dickens, in a nightmare of degradation, capering before his father? Or is it the young Dickens capering and gibbering before the older version of himself? Swallowed up, at last, by his past.

# Twenty-Four

W HEN he returned to England, he had grown very brown in the sun (an indication of the fact that Dickens had a slightly dark or what was once termed a "muddy" complexion). But he said that he was feeling "too old"; clearly the recuperation in France had not materially affected his anxious state. He plunged himself into work as if it were some shower bath of the spirit and at once began composing the Christmas issue of *Household Words*, using the idea of the Watts's charitable hostel in Rochester as a venue for certain moving or entertaining stories written by several hands. Of course some of these stories were Dickens's own, and in his account of Watts's Charity itself he managed to arouse the anger of the Rochester worthies; the *Maidstone and Kentish Journal* berated him for inaccuracy and bad taste, since ". . . the matron of the Charity has been vulgarised and the provisions of the founder's will misunderstood". A reminder that Dickens was not often concerned with the reaction of those real people about whom he chose to write; in a sense, he did not see them when he was writing, he saw only his *idea* of them. In addition he was preparing another round of public readings; this was only the second year in which he had agreed to give them, but already he had come to think of them as a settled and satisfactory activity into which he could pour all his ferocious energy. So satisfactory in fact that, despite Forster's protestations and his own occasional misgivings, he was happy to increase their number when the opportunity arose.

Dickens arranged to read for various charitable or civic institutions. In fact his success at Birmingham the year before had been so "prodigious", to employ one of his own favourite words, that he had been obliged to refuse most of the many requests which were now made to him. It was this enthusiasm for his new role as reader that persuaded him to make more commercial arrangements in future years, but, for the moment, he was the charitable speaker; on 19 December he went to the Literary, Scientific and Mechanics' Institution in Reading, and then two days later read at Sherborne for the Literary Institution; immediately after Christmas he went to Bradford and read on behalf of the Temperance Educational Institution. On all three occasions Dickens had decided to read *A Christmas Carol*, so obviously appropriate for the season, but now a new element was introduced into its delivery. Before he began to read, he announced that he would be treating his audience as if it were grouped around a Christmas fire; then he went on to say, ". . . if you feel disposed as we go along to give expression to any emotion, whether grave or gay, you will do so with perfect freedom from restraint, and without the apprehension of disturbing me."

His largest audience was at Bradford, where some 3,700 people were packed into St George's Hall; as was now becoming his habit, he and Wills went up the night before in order to inspect the reading arrangements, and on this occasion Dickens found to his consternation that two rows of seats had been set up behind his lectern. "These (on which the committee immensely prided themselves) I instantly over-threw: to the great terror and amazement of the bystanders . . ." Dickens *never* allowed anyone to sit behind him; partly no doubt from some half-superstitious, half-obsessive, fear that he might be attacked, and partly because much of the power of his reading lay in his eyes and in his gestures. He was asked where the Mayor was supposed to sit and, characteristically, he replied that ". . . the Mayor might go – anywhere – but must not come near me". The reading was another success, with all the laughter and the tears and the cheering he hoped for, expected, demanded. And there was a little private drama as well; he seems to have been greatly taken by the landlady of the hotel in which he was staying. Restlessness again. The restlessness of the heart revealed in half-joking asides, as if the subject were never very far from his thoughts.

Two days after the Bradford reading he gave an address for the Commercial Travellers' Schools at the London Tavern. The fact that Dickens was to speak meant that ". . . as dinner hour approached the ticket bureau of the tavern was literally besieged by applicants . . .", an anticipation here of the extraordinary scenes which were to accompany Dickens on his later reading tours. When he spoke he was greeted with "loud and protracted cheering"; whatever the critics might say, it was Dickens the popular author who was still triumphant.

In this same spirit of communal entertainment Dickens was also rigorously marshalling his own children for the next Twelfth Night play at Tavistock House – on this occasion, *Fortunio and His Seven Gifted Servants* – in which Dickens played the part of the angry "Baron Dunover (A Nobleman in Difficulties)". Georgina Hogarth presided at the pianoforte, and Mr "Wilkini Collini" played Gormand. A comic song against the Czar was performed, and there was dancing afterwards. Another year had gone by, a year for Charles Dickens of arduous labour followed by low spirits, exhaustion swiftly succeeded by intolerable restlessness.

And how did his public reputation stand now? There is Nathaniel Hawthorne's comment, confided to his notebook after a visit to England in this new year, 1855: "Dickens is evidently not liked nor thought well of by his literary brethren – at least, the most eminent of them, whose reputation might interfere with his. Thackeray is much more to their tastes." A true enough assessment, for there is no doubt that the intellectual and literary leaders of opinion were considerably less impressed by Dickens than the middle-class or working-class audiences whom he addressed. Of course he had his loyal allies – Forster, Collins and the regular contributors to *Household Words*; but even they were somewhat suspect and Ruskin wrote in this same year that "he is in a bad set . . . Yet he is I believe a good man (in the common parlance) and means well – ". In the same month that Ruskin made this comment, *Blackwood's Magazine* observed that Dickens was "a *class* writer, the historian and representative of one circle in the many ranks of our social scale . . . it is the air and breath of middle-class respectability which fills the books of Mr Dickens". There is a certain truth here, too, and it is that particular kind of middle-class appeal which was responsible for some of the more highbrow disdain of the man Trollope was to dub "Mr Popular Sentiment". But there was more to it than that. *Hard Times*, and his subsequent address to working men in the pages of his periodical, had also laid him open to the charge of what Macaulay termed "sullen socialism". This was what Marx had in mind when he told Engels that Dickens had "issued to the world more political and social truths than have been uttered by all the professional politicians, publicists and moralists put together".

Dickens's resentlessness was, if anything, aggravated still further now, and, within a week or two of the New Year, he was planning a few days in Paris with Wilkie Collins, Dickens turning more and more often to Collins for relief from all his familiar responsibilities. Certainly these responsibilities were getting no lighter, and from this time forward there emerges in Dickens's correspondence a line of pained and anxious rumination over the fate of his children; none of whom, daughters excepted, were "turning out" as he had once hoped and expected. Charley was trying to find work with a London firm; Walter was about to enter a school in Wimbledon where he would be specifically trained for his duties in India. And their father, meanwhile, was taking long daily walks through the snow. Thinking of their future. Thinking of his future. Thinking of the further series of readings he had planned; already he was moving on from the success of *A Christmas Carol* and wanted to take extracts from one of his novels. Thinking of a new novel, the "motes" of which had been hovering around for some months. In fact certain elements of it had entered his consciousness, and, in an essay entitled "Gaslight Fairies" which he wrote for *Household Words* in February, many of the characteristics of the Dorrit family – as yet unborn – are to be found. Thinking of these things as he trudged through the snow, walking from Tavistock Square to Highgate and beyond during one of the coldest of winters.

It was now that Dickens learned that Gad's Hill Place, the house just outside Rochester, hallowed by its association with Falstaff, and hallowed, too, because of its association with his father, was for sale. This was the house which John Dickens had shown his small son, and which he had held out to him as the possible reward for a successful man. At once he made enquiries about purchasing it; "The spot and the very house are literally 'a dream of my childhood'," he told Wills. And how strange, that this dream should have persisted through all the years of his fame. Particularly since Gad's Hill Place is not in itself an altogether prepossessing house – certainly not as grand as Tavistock House itself – and yet so strong was the hold of Dickens's infancy upon him that it remained an enchanted spot. Perhaps he also wanted to placate his father's shade by purchasing it, just as his father had once wished. He had decided to visit it again three days later, but then suddenly he changed his mind. Something more significant had just occurred. Quite by chance, another aspect of his past had returned. The night before he was to leave for Rochester, he received a letter.

He had been reading by the fire, when some letters were given to him; he looked at them in a desultory fashion (he received and sent so many that he used to refer to himself as a sort of Home Office), and then found his mind to be "curiously disturbed" and "wandering away through so many years to such early times of my life"; he could find no reason for the change of mood, but he picked up the pile of letters once again and looked through them. It was then he saw certain handwriting, for the first time in over twenty years, and he recognised it at once: it was that of Maria Beadnell, the girl for whom he had conceived such a strident passion in the days when he was working as a shorthand reporter in the House of Commons. The days before any of his novels had been conceived. The days before his fame. So it was exactly to that time of his life that her letter sent him spinning. At least this was how Dickens described his reaction to Maria Beadnell herself, since he needed something of a theatrical overture for the recommencement of a friendship which had once been so important to him.

He wrote to her the next day, and it was no doubt in order to do so that he cancelled his arrangement with Wills to visit Gad's Hill Place; he explained to Wills that it was because of the heavy snow, but in fact only a few days before he had walked from Gravesend to Rochester through banks several feet high. He really needed time and quietness to reply to this letter from an emblem of his past. What Maria Beadnell (now in fact Mrs Maria Winter) wrote is not recorded, although to judge from Dickens's reply it was simply a letter to a famous friend in which
382

she recounted news of her marriage, of her daughters, and of her family. It was later reported that she was fond of a little drink in the afternoon, and she may have decided to write to Dickens at a time of more than usual sentimentality or nostalgia. Dickens himself replied in a full flood of the same commodity. "I forget nothing of those times," he told her. This was almost the literal truth; he could still recall the details of conversations and clothes as if the events of his youth had happened just the day before. When we talk of Dickens's "nostalgia", then, it is wise to remember that it was of a special kind; he still *saw* and *heard* everything very clearly. "They are just as still and plain and clear as if I had never been in a crowd since, and had never seen or heard my own name out of my own house. What should I be worth, or what would labour and success be worth, if it were otherwise!" He ended with something of a peroration, indicating not for the first time that he was stylistically most conscious when his deepest emotions came into play. "In the strife and struggle of this great world where most of us lose each other so strangely, it is impossible to be spoken to out of the old times without a softened emotion."

Dickens received another letter from Maria Beadnell, and at once he sent another long reply addressed now to "My Dear Maria". Clearly it was sent to a secret address, or sent privately to her by some other means, because only two days later he was addressing a perfectly discreet letter to "My dear Mrs Winter"; in other words, he was writing her a letter which could be shown to her husband without embarrassment. It all sounds very much like a reprise of the subterfuges of youthful lovers. The first and more private letter was in response to an obviously impassioned communication from Maria, in which she tried to explain her coquettish behaviour so many years before. The game of "might have been" was one that Dickens on occasions liked to play, and in his response he dealt in tremulous tones with his own thwarted passion; ". . . nobody can ever know with what a sad heart I resigned you . . . My entire devotion to you, and the wasted tenderness of those hard years . . . whether any reputation the world can bestow is repayment to a man for the loss of such a vision of his youth as mine . . ." That was what he lamented, the vision of his youth. In these letters to Maria there is revealed an almost hysterical willingness to love or to be loved, an eagerness to return to his youthful state matched only by the sorrow which he experiences when he realises that such a retreat is not possible. Yet none of these letters would have been written, none of this terrible thwarted feeling could have existed, if it were not for the deep unhappiness of Dickens's present life. He now found London dreary; a thaw had followed the snow. "Everything is weeping," he said. The city was damp and dirty and wet, and the jangling of church bells disturbed him.

They decided to meet, but as soon as he saw her, all his longing and his passion fled. Georgina described her later; she "had become *very* fat! and quite commonplace . . ." The youthful Maria, conjured up so delicately and tenderly by Dickens, turned out no longer to exist. As he put it only a few months later in *Little Dorrit*, and in a passage which Maria herself was sure to read, "Clennam's eyes no sooner fell upon the subject of his old passion, than it shivered and broke to pieces". It is difficult to envisage Maria's feelings when Dickens goes on to write, ". . . Flora, who had seemed enchanting in all she said and thought, was diffuse and silly . . . Flora, who had been spoiled and artless long ago, was determined to be spoiled and artless now." But there was something crueller still. In one of her letters to Dickens Maria had pointed out that she was now "toothless, fat, old and ugly" but Dickens had brushed aside this as the merest playful nonsense. But now he remembered it, all too well: " 'I am sure,' giggled Flora, tossing her head with a caricature
384

of her girlish manner, such as a mummer might have presented at her own funeral, if she had lived and died in classical antiquity, 'I am ashamed to see Mr Clennam, I am a mere fright, I know he'll find me fearfully changed, I am actually an old woman, it's shocking to be so found out, it's really shocking!' "

The brief episode with Maria Beadnell only emphasises the miseries with which he felt himself to be surrounded. In "Gone to the Dogs", an ironic essay on private and public misfortune, which he now wrote for *Household Words*, he once more laments the loss of his first innocent love and chronicles the growth of seedy worldliness in men and women; themes which he has deployed before but here they are explicitly linked first to financial chicanery and disgrace, then to national ruin itself. The last two subjects were also to be explored in *Little Dorrit*, the novel which he was now contemplating. So, in his short essay, the loss of innocent love, the prevalence of financial malpractice and the conduct of the Crimean War are linked together as expressions in miniature of the same anger and bitterness which were soon to break out elsewhere. That there was anger in him now is not in doubt. He let slip in one letter that he was ". . . dead sick of the Scottish tongue in all its moods and tenses", which can only be a reference to his wife and to her family.

It was now though that he turned in earnest to the new novel. Never since *Barnaby Rudge* had any novel so long a period of gestation, for though he had finished half of the first number by the middle of May, he had broken off to perform with his amateur players. (The first number would not in fact be published until December.) But this interval was only the symptom of a larger confusion and difficulty. His son, Charley, was to say of *Little Dorrit* that ". . . my father started [it] in a panic lest his powers of imagination should fail him", a domestic comment which lends weight to Forster's description of his friend's "sluggish fancy" in the preliminary stages of composition and Forster's belief that ". . . the old, unstinted, irrepressible flow of fancy had received temporary check". All these factors are meant to explain what Forster called ". . . a droop in his invention". Posterity has not shared that judgment, however, and the signs of delay and confusion in the early stages of writing have less to do with any diminution of inventive skill than with what was for Dickens almost a unique problem; he had no "guiding idea", or leading theme, which would propel him through the narrative, and all the preliminary memoranda suggest that he was casting around for some time in an effort to make all of his "pictures" and preoccupations cohere.

He worked straight on from the first to the second number, taking up the threads he had so lately introduced. He was still more tentative than usual, casting about in his notes to himself for the proper continuation, until it was clear that a girl named "Dorrit" was to be given a larger context and a home; the home being the Marshalsea Prison where Dickens's own father had once been imprisoned and where now "Little Dorrit", as he had decided to call her, returns to her father and her ungrateful siblings. The novel was growing, and changing, all the time. Wilkie Collins came down to spend some time with the Dickens family in Folkestone, and some relatives also arrived, but he was now confident enough of the drift of his story to inform his German publisher, Tauchnitz, about the publishing arrangements for the new novel. And, as he moved on to its third instalment, all those elements which had been lying quietly unworked beneath the surface of his imagination could now be used. He wrote a satirical chapter on the Circumlocution Office, that epitome of "tuft-hunting" amateur bureaucracy; ". . . I have been blowing off a little of indignant steam," he told Macready, "which would otherwise blow me up . . ." But this was no longer just to be the satirical novel which Dickens had at first intended; he was now extending his theme, so that Circumlocution becomes the whole vast babble of the world, the world of travellers, the world of hypocrisy, the world of imprisonment. He now decided, too, that he would raise up the Dorrit family from poverty and make them rich, and in that transition show the emptiness of wealth. Now the story was "everywhere – heaving in the sea, flying with the clouds, blowing in the wind . . ."

In early October, just after he had finished the third number, he recited *A Christmas Carol* in aid of the Mechanics' Institution of Folkestone; he read in a carpenter's shop and was, according to Mark Lemon's daughter, "very nervous". At any event, the next day he reported himself to be climbing, swimming and generally leading the life of a "fighting-man" in training. Five days later he went up to London in order to preside at a dinner for Thackeray, who was about to cross the Atlantic in search of American gold, and then returned to Folkestone. But he was still travelling. Travelling now back to France, where he was spending more and more of his time – partly, at least, in order to keep away from London while he was writing. With Georgina he went across to Paris and, after some difficulty in finding the right apartment, rented strange lodgings in the Avenue des Champs-Elysées for the next few weeks.

It is clear that he liked Paris because he was now very famous there; in shops any presentation of his card was met with, "Ah! C'est l'écrivain célèbre!" He was invited to grand dinners, some of which he described in tones worthy of the *Arabian Nights*, and he knew or was introduced to most of the literary "lions", among them George Sand, Lamartine and Scribe. He struck up a particular friendship with the actor, Régnier, and the demands of amity were such that he congratulated Régnier on a drama, *La Joconde*, which in a private letter to Forster he condemned. He was sitting to the painter, Ary Scheffer; the

*Moniteur* was serialising *Martin Chuzzlewit*; the eminent French critic, Hippolyte Taine, was about to write at length about him in *La Revue des Deux Mondes*; the French publishing firm of Hachette were negotiating with him on the terms for a complete edition of his novels. In other words, Paris had taken to him as once London had done, and part of his pleasure in living in the capital has to do with the fact that the early stages of his English fame were here being revived. Yet it would be wrong to consider Dickens in Paris as some wholly new or different creature; his restlessness and frustration were apparent even here and, if he criticised England for its narrowness and its mercenary values, he was in turn criticising the French drama for its absurd and frozen classicality at the same time as he was noting that the Parisians in particular seemed mesmerised by the Bourse. False-seeming; the worship of money; stale theatricality; narrowness. These were conditions which he seemed to confront wherever he turned.

In the beginning of November he returned to London for a week; he had at last decided to buy Gad's Hill Place. At this stage he thought of it only as an investment, and had no definite plans of inhabiting it, but he had come back to the city to supervise negotiations for its purchase. So he returned to the capital which was as unwelcoming as if it had taken on the murky colours of his description in the opening chapters of *Little Dorrit*. "Perpetual rain," Dickens wrote to his wife from the office of *Household Words*. "Storms of wind." There were charity children in the street outside, braving the gusty showers in order to attend a morning performance by Anderson the Wizard in the Gaiety Theatre just opposite in the Strand. He had a bad cold, and his eye was infected. London. A few nights after his arrival he went wandering with Albert Smith through the streets of the East End, and quite by chance came upon a forlorn group who had been refused entry to the Whitechapel Workhouse on a "very dark, very
388

muddy" night; ". . . five bundles of rags," he called them. Dickens at once rang for the Master of the Workhouse in order to speak to him, but the man was not at fault; the casual ward of his institution was already full, and nothing could be done for these five souls. Dickens then went up to question them; they were all women, and when one of them told him that she had not eaten for a day and a night he seemed not to believe her. "*Why, look at me!*" she said. Then: "She bared her neck, and I covered it up again." He gave her a shilling for supper and a lodging (in that part of London, such a lodging would have been of the meanest sort). "She never thanked me, never looked at me – melted away into the miserable night, in the strangest manner I ever saw." In this silent flight she resembles a young man who had, chattering at Dickens, twisted himself out of his rags on an earlier London night; and it is as if in these worn and silent creatures he was beginning to see the soul of London itself.

At the beginning of December the first number of *Little Dorrit* was published. Bradbury and Evans had in advance conducted a large publicity campaign, with some four thousand posters and no fewer than three hundred thousand handbills. The first instalment was itself, in Dickens's phrase, a ". . . brilliant triumph" and the printing order for the second number was increased to thirty-five thousand. In the middle of that month he returned to London to savour his triumph, and then went on to Peterborough to give a reading of *A Christmas Carol* at the Mechanics' Institute there; a member of the audience on that occasion remembered how ". . . a broad high forehead and a perfectly Micawber-like expanse of shirt collar and front appeared above the red baize box . . ." Then back to London where ". . . the people I met, on their way to offices, were actually sobbing and crying with cold". Then off to Sheffield where once more he read *A Christmas Carol*; when he came to the line, ". . . and to Tiny Tim, who did

NOT die", there was a tremendous shout from the audience who in that act of revival perhaps saw something of themselves. One contemporary report explains how ". . . a universal feeling of joy seemed to pervade the whole assembly who, rising spontaneously, greeted the renowned and popular author with a tremendous burst of cheering". And what of the author himself who had managed to create that universal joy, who seemed somehow to have the force of the world flowing through him? He could not sleep that night. He felt like "an enormous top in full spin". He purchased his usual almanac from a shop in Oxford Street, and then returned to Paris.

Now at last he could work on *Little Dorrit*, and in these final days of the old year Dickens depicted the passage of his heroine through the waste of London. The narrative seemed to enlarge and expand as he wrote it; originally it was to be only part of a chapter, but now he renumbered the chapters so that the whole instalment ended with that sad nocturnal expedition. The footsteps and the street-lamps. The rushing tide and the shadows. The sounding of the clocks. The homeless. The drunken. The vision of Whitechapel Workhouse is here enlarged and deepened, bringing with it all of the weariness and sadness which Dickens now associated with the city: ". . . the flaring lights . . . the ghastly dying of the night". The strange scene of the woman bending over Little Dorrit: "I never should have touched you, but I thought that you were a child". And her "strange, wild cry" as she turns away. And Dickens himself at the closing of the year? He said that he was overworked. That he was depressed. Here we may see in part the origins of that image of imprisonment which critics have detected running through the novel. For even in Paris Dickens was weary, and there was nowhere else to turn.

# Twenty-Five

1856. A year before his life was irrevocably to change. Fourteen years before his death. A year of restlessness. A year of continual movement from place to place. Dickens's plan was to stay in Paris until May, and then move on for the summer to Boulogne. Not that the routine of his life had changed; it had just found another, and perhaps more garish, setting. He liked to walk still. Walk endlessly. He walked the old walls of Paris, and at night he used to wander into "strange places". He invited friends as old as Beard and as new as Sala (a young man who had impressed him so much with his articles on London for *Household Words*) to stay in Paris with him and his family. But there was something wrong, something troubling him ... in one letter in this first month of the new year, he addresses himself in the character of Boots, the servant with whom he had just attained a signal success in his Christmas story. Dickens was always good at imitating servants, and perhaps it has something to do with the fact that his paternal grandparents themselves were both "in service" that in such a voice he comes close to revealing his true feelings. "When you come to think what a game you've been up to ever since you was in your own cradle, and what a poor sort of chap you are, and how it's always yesterday with you, or else to-morrow, and never today, that's where it is." Three months later he was expanding upon the same mood in a more intimate and less facetious letter to Forster: "However strange it is to be never at rest, and never satisfied, and ever trying after something that is never reached, and to be always laden with plot and plan and care and worry, how clear it is that it must be, and that one is driven by an irresistible might until the journey is worked out! It is much better to go on and fret, than to stop and fret. As to repose – for some men there's no such thing in this life."

He went back to England at the beginning of February, specifically in order to bring with him the number of *Little Dorrit* he had just completed but also to continue the protracted negotiations over his purchase of Gad's Hill Place. London was no longer his chosen city, however, and he told Catherine that "the streets are hideous to behold, and the ugliness of London is quite astonishing". He had a tooth extracted almost as soon as he arrived, and of course plunged into his usual maelstrom of self-imposed activity. "I began the morning in the City, for the Theatrical Fund; went on to Shepherd's Bush; came back to leave cards for Mr Baring and Mr Bates; ran across Piccadilly to Stratton Street, stayed there an hour, and shot off here. I have been in four cabs today at a cost of thirteen shillings. Am going to dine with Mark and Webster at half-past four, and finish the evening at the Adelphi." He ran across streets; he "shot off"; he took cabs in his haste.

While he remained in London there was a spectacular bankruptcy, and only a few days after his return Sadleir, a prominent financier, took poison and killed himself on Hampstead Heath; this was another aspect of England which he detested, its burgeoning and often corrupt financial empire, and he was to introduce it at once into *Little Dorrit* in the character of Merdle, the financier whose power is proportionate to his chicanery. Of course commercial speculation was not confined to England alone; at the same time there was a fever of speculation in Paris, and the strong smell of what Dickens called a "pecuniary crisis", but it was of England which he wrote. So it is that within a week of his return to the French capital he started work on a new instalment of the novel, and began his portraits of Merdle and of that fashionable "Society" which is no less a prison or forcing-house than the Marshalsea gaol itself.

He worked on through the next instalment, correcting the proofs in Paris as soon as they were returned to him by the London printers. Then once more back to London with the final sections of the number, arriving at eight o'clock in the morning on 10 March and returning to Tavistock House only briefly before going to his office in Wellington Street. Then straight on to inspect the ruins of Covent Garden Theatre, which had burnt down only four days before; he loved fires, as we have seen, and, next to fires, the blackened relics of the conflagration. ". . . the theatre," he said, "still looked so wonderfully like its old self grown gigantic that I never saw so strange a sight." And he noticed everything; the iron pass-doors, the chandeliers, and even pieces of material from the men's wardrobe from which ". . . I could make out the clothes in the Trovatore".

There had been one especial reason for his return to London; he had finally, after delays and negotiations that seemed to him to be stretching on as long as an amateur Chancery suit, purchased Gad's Hill Place. The house he had seen with his father, so many years before, was at last his own. There are certain people who seem doomed to buy certain houses. The house expects them. It waits for them. Gad's Hill Place and Dickens had just such a fatal affinity. It was the house which had once been pointed out to him as the very summit of achievement, and it was the house in which he was to die. He paid £1,790 pounds for it. "After drawing the cheque I turned round to give it to Wills . . . and said: 'Now isn't it an extraordinary thing

— look at the day — Friday! I have been nearly drawing it half-a-dozen times, when the lawyers have not been ready, and here it comes round upon a Friday, as a matter of course.'" The point was that Friday had become a sort of superstition with him, being the day on which he considered that the most important things in his life always happened to him. It was his "lucky" day. Unfortunately he could not move into the house he had purchased in so timely a fashion; it still had its tenants, a rector with his daughter, and Dickens's plan was eventually to refurbish it before letting it out by the month. If there were no tenants, it could then become a retreat for himself and for his family. A few days after he had signed the agreement he travelled down with his son, Charley, together with Mark Lemon and Wilkie Collins. "We inspected the premises as well as we could from the outside — " his son later recalled, "my father, full of pride at his new position as a Kentish freeholder, and making all manner of jokes at his own expense, would not take us into the house for fear of disturbing the rector and his daughter who were then inhabiting it — and we lunched at the Falstaff Inn opposite, and walked to Gravesend to dinner, full of delightful anticipation of the country life to come."

Now that matters were settled, Dickens felt able to return to Paris. Wilkie Collins joined him there and, although on a previous visit he had stayed in bachelor apartments a few doors away from their own lodgings, now he stayed with the Dickens family and dined with them every day. The fact that Collins himself was often ill from gout or rheumatic fever did not in any sense strain their relationship, as illness was wont to do in other cases with Dickens, ". . . my old Patient" he called him once, as if his position were that of doctor as well as friend. In fact he also had another role to play, perhaps the most important of all, since it is clear that in this period Dickens was in a sense training Collins to be a writer. Of course there were their usual walks, nocturnal or otherwise, on one of which, incidentally, Collins found some of the material for his finest fiction. "I was in Paris wandering about the streets with Charles Dickens," he said, "amusing ourselves by looking into the shops. We came to an old book-stall – half shop and half store – and I found some dilapidated volumes and records of French crime – a sort of French Newgate Calendar. I said to Dickens, 'Here's a prize!' So it turned out to be. In them I found some of my best plots." But Dickens played much more than this passive role in Collins's development as a novelist; he counselled him on publication arrangements, he discussed "Fiction" on many occasions (one of the few recorded examples of Dickens taking anyone into his confidence on that subject so close to him, so close to his most secret impulses), he listened to Collins's stories and then endeavoured to correct or advise the younger man. "Keep all this a secret," Collins wrote to his mother in this year, ". . . for if my good-natured friends knew that I had been reading my idea to Dickens – they would be sure to say when the book was published, that I got all the good things in it from him . . . He found out, as I had hoped, all the weak points in the story, and gave me the most inestimable hints for strengthening them . . ." In other words Collins became something of an apprentice and those critics who have suggested that it was Dickens who learnt from Collins (*The Mystery of Edwin Drood* is always cited for an example, as a work to a certain extent modelled upon *The Moonstone*) should look again at the available evidence. Dickens may have learnt some things from Collins, but they were not of a literary nature.

By the first week of April he had written the first two chapters of the next instalment of *Little Dorrit*; then Macready came to Paris for a short visit, and after he had gone Dickens fell to work and finished the number at once. He took a long walk through Paris in preparation for the next, but in fact did not begin. Not yet. There were dinners. There were other visitors. And his internal restlessness always came back to the surface, leading him into those "strange places". One night, in a cheap venue where there was wrestling as well as other more familiar nocturnal pursuits, he was attracted by the face of a young woman, "handsome, regardless, brooding . . ." He did not speak to her, but the next night he returned to the same place in order to look for her — ". . . I have a fancy," he told Wilkie Collins, his old companion on such pilgrimages who had now returned to London, "that I should like to know more about her. Never shall, I suppose." Here is the yearning of the famous man, ready to return to a tatty Parisian "night-spot" in order to seek out an anonymous woman.

He went back once more to England at the beginning of May; he was supposed to be staying in London at Tavistock House but his wife's family, the Hogarths, were there and his dislike for them was now so intense that he preferred to stay at the Ship Inn, Dover, for four days until they had left the premises. He had told Wills from Paris that "the Hogarth family don't leave Tavistock House till next Saturday, and I cannot in the meantime bear the contemplation of their imbecility any more. (I think my constitution is already undermined by the sight of Hogarth at breakfast.)" On the same day he wrote to Mark Lemon that ". . . I cannot bear the contemplation of that family at breakfast any more . . ." And this about a family he had once admired and about a man, George Hogarth, of whom he had been especially fond. What had gone wrong? It was in part the result of the sometimes extraordinary behaviour of Mrs Hogarth, a woman of apparently volatile temperament, but his rage against "that family" had much more to do with his growing estrangement from Catherine herself. It is not easy to chart the course of this. In the letter to Forster already quoted, in which Dickens had discussed his restlessness in vivid terms, he had gone on to say, as if in extenuation, "I find that the skeleton in my domestic closet is becoming a pretty big one . . ." So here was the root of his dislike of the Hogarths, his growing dislike of a wife who seemed to him to have inherited, in what might be described as a typically Dickensian manner, all of the less amiable characteristics of her parents.

Over the years he had complained about her clumsiness, her slowness and her occasional absent-mindedness; characteristics especially irritating to a man as quick, neat and decisive as Dickens. There were times, as we have observed, when he had also been rather callous about her child-bearing propensities, especially since she suffered from post-natal depression amounting almost to mental disorder; it was as if Dickens had no responsibility at all for the emergence of his children into the world. Reports about his actual behaviour to his wife differ and, as is usual in such cases, rely more upon rumour and conjecture than evidence. One young contributor to *Household Word* noted that "it had been obvious to those visiting at Tavistock House that, for some time, the relations between host and hostess had been somewhat strained; but this state of affairs was generally ascribed to the irritability of the literary temperament on Dickens's part, and on Mrs Dickens's side to a little love of indolence and ease, such as, however provoking to their husbands, is not uncommon among middle-aged matrons with large families."

So Dickens stayed at the Ship Hotel, Dover. He had hoped to work upon *Little Dorrit*, but he could do nothing. Instead he went for what were now becoming his customary twenty-mile walks; the more restless he was, the more imprisoned he felt himself to be, the longer his walks became. Dover itself was "out of season" and in an essay he wrote for *Household Words*, on the very subject of not being able to write, he described the closed shops, the empty theatres and the deserted bathing-machines. He looked in at a window of a shop selling literature, and saw *Dr Faustus*, *The Golden Dreamer* and *The Norwood Fortune Teller* at sixpence each. He walked on the Downs and there encountered a "tramping family in black" to whom he gave ". . . eighteen-pence which produced a great effect, with moral admonitions which produced none at all". And there again is the essential Dickens, an unhappy man standing on the Downs and giving "moral admonitions" to a family of vagrants. As soon as the Hogarths had left Tavistock House he moved back to London; one of the things that irritated him most about his wife's family was their general untidiness, and on his return to the house he swept the floors, washed the study and drawing room, ". . . opened the windows, aired the carpets, and purified every room from the roof to the hall". The carpet was in the corner "like an immense roly-poly pudding, and all the chairs upside down as if they had turned over like birds and died with their legs in the air . . .", this last image one which can truly be given the much-abused term "Dickensian". And then he returned to his London life – a party at the *Household Words* office, a visit to Drury Lane Theatre, an evening with Macready, a visit to the Egyptian Hall in Piccadilly. He was given permission to mount the dome of St Paul's in order to see the fireworks and illuminations in celebration of the end of the Crimean War, and there had a vision of "blazing London" so much like his own description of it in *Barnaby Rudge*.

He continued all through May with his work on *Little Dorrit*, now so much in command of his narrative that he made for himself only the briefest of notes and memoranda. Even as he was hastening around the city this spring at his usual feverish pace, therefore, he was at the same time writing about a melancholy, deserted London of summer, on ". . . a grey, hot, dusty evening". A city that contained "Wildernesses . . ." In these chapters of the novel he infuses the narrative once more with images of travellers, of the strange roads down which they all drive, of uncertain futures. There is also a wonderful image here of the Thames as a symbol of change, of forgetfulness, of destiny; ". . . and thus do greater things that once were in our breasts, and near our hearts, flow from us to the eternal seas." And is he here also mourning the loss of his love for Catherine?

He stayed in London for the whole month, and then in the second week of June he travelled to Boulogne where the rest of his family had already established themselves for the summer in the Château des Moulineaux. Dickens grew a beard, to complement his moustache, and dressed in what John Forster called a "French farmer garb" of blue blouse, leather belt and military cap.

And he had his work still to do. ". . . Now to work again – to work! The story lies before me, I hope, strong and clear. Not to be easily told; but nothing of that sort IS to be easily done that *I* know of . . ." He was writing the final chapter of the instalment he had started in London, and the whole of the next number; difficulties did exist even so, as he confessed, but these were primarily the result of the fact that he had now to prepare for the ending of Book One, for that moment when the Dorrit family walk free from the Marshalsea and Little Dorrit herself collapses at the prospect of liberty.

Dickens was inviting guests to stay with the family at Boulogne even as he resolved his difficulties with *Little Dorrit* – Mary Boyle, Mark Lemon, Thomas Beard and Clarkson Stanfield among them – but he realised that these were people who knew him too well to dream of interrupting him at his work. Most other social invitations he declined, even one from Lord John Russell for dinner, since he knew that such excursions unsettled and delayed him. He entertained "at home", as it were, and the only variation from this self-imposed quietness lay in his frequent trips across the Channel to London, bearing with him some more pages of manuscript or proofs. Gradually he was reaching the end of the first "Book", only to discover from the proofs that he had underwritten the last chapter of all. So at this point he added a scene in which the other debtors in the Marshalsea watch the Dorrits depart: "It was rather to be remarked of the caged birds, that they were a little shy of the bird about to be so grandly free, and that they had a tendency to withdraw themselves towards the bars, and seem a little fluttered as he passed." How apposite, perhaps, that while staying in Boulogne Dickens had his own caged bird, a canary which he called *Dick*. And that when finally he left Boulogne he described the grounds as resembling a ". . . dreary bird-cage with all manner of grasses and chickweeds sticking through the bars". Images of cages emerged everywhere around him as he wrote the novel and, in this same period, he wrote a brief résumé of his biography to Wilkie Collins only to add that ". . . I feel like a wild beast in a caravan describing himself in the keeper's absence". He felt himself to be imprisoned, perhaps, but was there not a part of him that believed that he *deserved* to be imprisoned?

He took the remaining pages of the last chapter to London with him and then, three days later, travelled back to Boulogne on the Folkestone boat; on which he discovered his old friend, Chauncy Hare Townshend. There may have been no car ferries in 1856 but the mid-nineteenth-century version certainly existed, and Townshend was sitting in his private carriage which had been hauled onto the deck. "I could not but mount the Royal Car," Dickens wrote, "and I found it to be perforated in every direction with cupboards, containing every description of physic, old brandy, East India sherry, sandwiches, oranges, cordial waters, newspapers, pocket handkerchiefs, shawls, flannels, telescopes, compasses, repeaters (for ascertaining the hour in the dark), and finger-rings of great value." And here is an example of

Dickens's instinctive irony: "He was on his way to Lausanne, and he asked me the extraordinary question 'how Mrs Williams, the American actress, kept her wig on?' I then perceived that mankind was to be in a conspiracy to believe that he wears his own hair."

Dickens had been expecting to spend at least another two months at the Château des Moulineaux, but a sudden outbreak of cholera in Boulogne meant that the entire household had to return hurriedly at the end of August. The children returned first with their mother, then Dickens, and then finally Georgina; the staggered departure necessary because of all the truncated arrangements involved with the disconsolate M. Beaucourt. The Channel crossing was not a success, for Dickens at least, and a fellow-traveller observed that he carried with him "a box of homeopathic globules"; in fact it was Dickens's habit to take a dose of laudanum on such occasions, to steady his stomach and no doubt his nerves, and it seems in later years that laudanum (or tincture of opium) became for him something of a necessary palliative.

As soon as he had returned to Tavistock House he threw himself once more upon *Little Dorrit* and, although he had begun the second "Book" and was "hard at it", he was now in arrears and beginning to lose his reserve of two months' work before publication. He even added one chapter at a late stage, which suggests that, even though he could now see clearly to the end of the whole novel, he was experiencing certain local difficulties. At the same time he was sending out instructions for the next round of stories in the Christmas issue of *Household Words*. One such story, contributed by Dickens himself, was "The Wreck", in which the theme of a beleaguered explorer was taken up in an account of the horrors inflicted upon shipwrecked travellers. Once again he was delineating the extremities of suffering and he told Wills that "I never wrote anything more easily, or I think with greater interest and stronger belief ". Images of ships appear in the chapters of *Little Dorrit* he was also writing in November, but the concept of "The Wreck" goes beyond his customary interest in the sea and the things of the sea; in this story the death of a little golden-haired child, Lucy, becomes the central theme; both in spirit and in content it is closely related to the death of the boy taken across the Cape by shipwrecked travellers, about which Dickens had read many years before and which he had recently commemorated in verse. It has also been surmised that the "Golden Lucy" of the Christmas story is related to Lucy Stroughill, a small girl who was one of his neighbours during his childhood days at Ordnance Terrace. So the memories of childhood return in a story of suffering and desperation. Then in the last month of the year he included this passage about marriage in *Little Dorrit*: ". . . and after rolling for a few minutes smoothly over a fair pavement, had begun to jolt through a Slough of Despond, and through a long, long avenue of wrack and ruin. Other nuptial carriages are said to have gone the same road, before and since . . ." "The Wreck of The Golden Mary". *Little Dorrit*. Travellers both. The journey suddenly stopped. Wreckage. A broken marriage. Lost love. Dead children. The struggle to endure. The quietus found only in death. Dickens was feeling strangely unwell; ". . . a digestion, or a head, or nerves, or some odd encumbrance of that kind . . ." He was living amid the "usual uproar", which are the last two words of his novel, and yet, as he put it in a letter before he reached that ending. "Calm amidst the wreck, your aged friends glides away on the Dorrit stream, forgetting the uproar for a stretch of hours . . ." One more the image of shipwreck. Yet he worked on amidst "the wreck", into the year that was to signal the end of his marriage and the start of a very different life.

# Twenty-Six

I N January 1857 Dickens went down to Brighton for a few days with Collins, and while he was there Benjamin Webster, the theatrical manager and actor, read to him a play, *The Dead Heart*, a tale of self-sacrifice at the time of the French Revolution which leads to a substitution at the foot of the guillotine. The story made such an impression upon Dickens that it emerged two years later in *A Tale of Two Cities*. All his life Dickens used such external influences or coincidences to reinforce his imaginative impulses. Just before going down to Brighton he had visited the Zoological Gardens, for example, and seen the snakes there being fed with live guinea pigs and rabbits — ". . . I have ever since been turning the legs of all the tables and chairs into serpents and seeing them feed upon all possible and impossible small creatures . . ." And that is why, while working on *Little Dorrit* in Brighton, he described the hands of Rigaud ". . . with the fingers lithely twisting about and twining one over another like serpents. Clennam could not prevent himself from shuddering inwardly, as if he had been looking on at a nest of those creatures." Exactly as Dickens had done in the Zoological Gardens.

He was embarked upon the twenty-eighth chapter of the second Book, and now he had to prepare for the final double number and the conclusion of his story. He organised his notes carefully and, in order to remind himself of precisely what he had already done, he summed up the action for himself in a series of memoranda. He came back to London after a few days but then went down to Gravesend, partly to work on the conclusion of the book in peace, but also partly to superintend the repairs which were being made to Gad's Hill Place. But he was back in London at the beginning of May, and it was in his study at Tavistock House that he finished *Little Dorrit*. He had at this time been writing to a novelist, Emily Jolly, and in his letters he had besought her to "strive for what is noblest and true" in her work; it was in this spirit that he approached the closing pages of *Little Dorrit* itself. Certainly there is a religious sense at work in the book. "Set the darkness and vengeance against the New Testament," he wrote in his working notes, and in his description of a sunset over London he introduced this new sense of life. "From a radiant centre, over the whole length and breadth of the tranquil firmament, great shoots of light streamed among the early stars, like signs of the blessed later covenant of peace and hope that changed the crown of thorns into a glory."

Sales of *Little Dorrit* were good; they held up until the end, and the final double number, when finished, had a circulation of approximately twenty-nine thousand copies. Dickens, in his preface, remarked upon the number of his readers and repeated the phrase he had used at the end of *Bleak House* — ". . . May we meet again!" The critical reaction, if he had cared to read it, was less encouraging. In fact it was largely treated as a failure, a bad novel, a sign of Dickens's sad decline; this reaction was partly political, partly the "intellectual" response to a popular author, partly the need to pull down an idol. *Blackwood's Magazine* called it simply "Twaddle" (a reference which Dickens saw by accident and which upset him for at least a moment). And one of his first biographers, writing a sixpenny pamphlet which was published in the following year, said of *Little Dorrit* and of *Bleak House* that they "have not been greatly relished by the public any more than they have been praised by the critics". It was in this period that a handsome Library Edition of Dickens's novels first started to be published (it was yet another way for him to "work" his copyrights), and one of the reviewers of that edition suggested that "it does not appear certain to us that his books will live . . ." But what did Dickens make of such criticism? A few weeks later he was walking with Hans Christian Andersen, who had been hurt by the reviews of his latest book (in fact he had been found lying face down, in tears, on the lawn of Gad's Hill Place). "Never allow yourself to be upset by the papers," he told Andersen, "they are forgotten in a week, and your book stands and lives." They were walking in the road, and Dickens wrote with his foot in the dirt. "That is criticism," he said. Then he wiped out his marks with his foot. "Thus it is gone."

The completion of *Little Dorrit* meant that he could turn his attention properly to Gad's Hill Place. He had frequently made trips into Kent in order to superintend the repairs he had ordered, but it was only now that he began seriously to move into his new house; as usual, he was hurrying along the various workmen still on the premises, who were only to "be squeezed out by bodily pressure". He was demanding speed because he wanted Catherine to come down on 19 May, which was her birthday, and on this occasion the family party was joined by his extended family of Wills, Collins and Beard. But this was only a preparatory "house-warming", and on the first day of June the family travelled down for the entire summer; Tavistock House meanwhile was left in the charge of Anne Brown, Catherine's old maid, so that it was ready for Dickens to use on his frequent business trips to London.

At this time Dickens was also arranging for some

readings of *A Christmas Carol*, and at the end of June he read his story at St Martin's Hall, near Leicester Square. The hall itself was crowded hours before he walked on stage and, as *The Times* reported, "so large was the number sent away from the doors through want of room that long before the assembly had dispersed placards were affixed in various parts of the building . . . announcing a repetition of the 'reading' at the same place on Friday, the 24th instant". *Town Talk* suggested that many had come simply "for the purpose of looking at the man who has, for so many years, been an unknown though most familiar friend . . ." – a salutary reminder that, in these early days of photography (M. Daguerre's new process had not been perfected until 1839), Dickens's face was not necessarily familiar to those who knew his works (although in February of this same year, 1857, he had declared himself in danger of being "mobbed" if he went to India House). For those who had not seen him, *Town Talk* provided a brief portrait; of a man now in his forty-sixth year, slight, with long brown hair, moustache and pointed beard. The journalist also noted, as had others, that he had a slight lisp or hiss when he tried to pronounce 's'. As soon as Dickens appeared there was such prolonged applause that "it threatened to postpone the reading indefinitely". The occasion was a success; particularly noted were Dickens's expressive eyes, his hand movements, his well-controlled voice and his ability dramatically to render the speech of his characters. At the end there was ". . . a long outburst of cheers, mingled with the waving of hats and handkerchiefs".

In the period he was preparing for these readings Dickens was also rehearsing his amateurs in *The Frozen Deep*, a drama set in the Arctic regions, ostensibly written by Collins, but heavily revised by Dickens. He had to attend to all the details of lighting and setting (the fact that he seems to have been a master at lighting *The Frozen Deep* may itself provide an interesting light upon similar effects in his novels). One participant in these proceedings remembered how he was to be found in the Gallery, ". . . resting one arm in the hand of the other, looking at the drops and cogitating upon their effect for the coming night, or working like any scene-shifter at the properties". His participation did not end there, however, and on at least one occasion he acted as ticket-seller. A certain Mr Hipkins recalled how Dickens ". . . related to me how a Yorkshireman had applied for a ticket and told him (of course not knowing him) that the purpose of his long journey was to see him". Dickens did not reveal himself to this admirer, and Hipkins suggests that the Yorkshireman might in fact have been disappointed since Dickens had lost his "jauntiness of appearance" and ". . . looked furrowed and careworn".

The cycle of his readings and performances was only momentarily interrupted when he travelled down to Southampton in order to witness the departure of his son, Walter, for India. He had joined the East India Company as a cadet and, after suitable training in England, was now at the age of sixteen about to set sail. He was in fact sailing to the place of his death. He died six years later, and Dickens was never to see him again, one of the many tragedies and disappointments that were to mark Dickens's children; as if his own great success had left some kind of stain upon his offspring. As if, in some form of natural compensation, they *had* to fail. Dickens had always found Walter "a little slow", with a good sense of "duty" and "responsibility" but with no "uncommon abilities"; no doubt he saw in him something of his wife, and there is in the extant photographs of the boy a hint of Catherine's "sleepy" expression. But now, at this time of separation, Dickens wrote that ". . . I don't at all know this day how he comes to be mine, or I his . . ." And yet, watching Charley and Walter mount ahead of him onto the gangplank which led to the ship, Dickens saw himself as a young man in their shapes. He had always found partings difficult but now he had come to believe, in his own uneasy and restless state, that ". . . the best definition of man may not be, after all, that he is (for his sins) a parting and farewell-taking animal . . ." There is no evidence to suggest, however, that Dickens was particularly upset about Walter's departure for Walter's own sake; his lament is generalised, and his own response to seeing his son leave was to think of himself at a similar age. With him, the pity here seems to be a form of self-pity, as if in parting with his son he was parting with some aspect of his own self.

Two further performances of *The Frozen Deep* followed at the Gallery of Illustration and, at the end of one of them, John Deane, the manager of the Great Manchester Art Exhibition, suggested to Dickens that he might like to perform in that city's New Free Trade Hall. Dickens went up to Manchester in order to read *A Christmas Carol* there, and took the opportunity of inspecting the Hall itself. It was certainly adequate for the play itself, but clearly it was too big for Georgina or for his daughters to act in; they were not trained in the arts of the stage, and would be neither seen nor heard to best effect in a building which could hold upwards of two thousand people. They had managed extraordinarily well during other public performances, but the time had come to find professional actresses and, the day after his return from Manchester, he began to search for them.

He was assisted in this by Alfred Wigan, the manager of the Olympic; he had already engaged two young actresses, Fanny and Maria Ternan, at his theatre and now at Dickens's suggestion he approached them to see if they would take part in *The Frozen Deep*. Wigan in turn recommended to Dickens their younger sister, Ellen Lawless Ternan, and their mother, Frances Eleanor Ternan. And so the Ternans enter this history. A family which would otherwise have remained unknown to posterity, a family of struggling actresses who have been caught in the brilliant light which has fallen around Charles Dickens. When at least one member of that family would have preferred to remain in subdued shadow.

There exists a certain amount of information about the Ternan girls in the year of *The Frozen Deep*. The eldest, Fanny, said of her family that "we are a nervous crew, but we have our compensations . . ." Fanny herself was always considered to be the cleverest of the three and, in fact, she was to have some sort of career as a novelist and general writer in her later life; Maria was the liveliest and the most entertaining; Ellen, the youngest, was described by an intimate of the family as "outwardly placid but firm underneath". She was also the least gifted actress in the family and, despite her early experience of the theatre, she never seems to have created much of an impression in her theatrical roles. She was an actress by inheritance, in other words, and not by vocation. Yet since there was something about her which powerfully affected Charles Dickens, perhaps in the exploration of her personality we may learn something of the novelist himself. She was just eighteen when she played in *The Frozen Deep*; the same age as Dickens's daughter, Kate. She had in fact been born in Rochester, and her uncle, a barge-owner, still lived there. One might call this a coincidence, to have been born in the very place which was at the centre of Dickens's imagination, if it were not for the fact that, as the novelist himself knew, there is really no such thing as coincidence. "And thus ever, by day and night . . . coming and going so strangely, to meet and to act and react on one another, move all we restless travellers through the pilgrimage of life." It is clear enough that Dickens knew of the Ternan family before he met them in the course of the Manchester production; the father had appeared at the Theatre Royal, Rochester, when Dickens was a boy in that place, and he might have seen Mrs Ternan on the stage at Covent Garden in the late Twenties. He would no doubt have heard of the Ternans in any case through Macready who knew them well and had acted with both parents. So when Dickens encountered them he was in effect encountering a known quantity, a branch of that theatrical life which he understood so well and which he never ceased to appreciate. He might even have already seen Ellen Ternan upon the stage since, four months before, she had appeared at the Haymarket as Hippomenes in Frank Talfourd's *Atalanta*. There is a story that he comforted her "behind the scenes" when she feared that, in her male part, she was too scantily clad; but this is undoubtedly one of those apocryphal stories which spring up unaided about the lives of great authors. Certainly he comforted Maria Ternan during *The Frozen Deep* but that is, as they say, quite another story.

And what of Ellen herself at this time? Dickens's daughter, Kate, described her as ". . . small, fair-haired, rather pretty . . ." She went on to say that she was not a particularly good actress but that "she had brains". The *Era* described her in *Atalanta* as ". . . a debutante with a pretty face and well-developed figure . . ." but noticed her apparent lack of confidence on the stage. Ellen emphasised that lack of confidence when she described herself as having ". . . a figure like an oak tree and a complexion like a copper saucepan". But the fact that she did not consider herself to be pretty, despite the opinions of others, may have something to do with her growing up in the company of two older and more vivacious sisters. It seems that she also suffered from occasional migraines and from "nettlerash", a skin condition now more commonly linked with psychosomatic tension; so we are entitled to think of her as a somewhat nervous young woman. In later life she showed herself to be practical and clever; the daughter of her closest friend, a certain Helen Wickham, has remarked that, in later life, she was witty, warm, sympathetic,
410

charming, cultured and charitable. If this litany of praise sounds perhaps too fulsome, the same observer adds that she also occasionally "victimised" her household, that she let her husband "make a perfect doormat of himself for her", that she read all of her daughter's letters until she was twenty-five and that sometimes "when she didn't get her own way" she made extraordinary scenes. She could also be "rather a cruel tease" and "quite a little spitfire".

This, then, was the young woman who brought to the surface Dickens's most dangerous and powerful emotions. He first encountered her at rehearsals of *The Frozen Deep* with her mother and sister, rehearsals which took place intensively for three days just before they all travelled up to Manchester on the railroad. At first, from Dickens's own descriptions, it would seem that he was most struck by Ellen's slightly older sister, Maria — struck, at least, by the ready emotionalism of her response to his performance. She had already seen one of the performances of the play and, when she arrived for the rehearsals, she said, according to Dickens himself, "I am afraid, Mr Dickens, I shall never be able to bear it; it affected me so much when I saw it, that I hope you will excuse my trembling this morning, for I am afraid of myself." She might have said something like this, but the actual speech bears all the marks of having been half-invented by Dickens himself; "I am afraid of myself" being, as we have seen, one of his own favourite expressions. In another account of the same conversation Dickens has her saying, "I cried so much when I saw it, that I have a dread of it, and I don't know what to do." Which sounds more likely to be correct.

The play opened at the New Free Trade Hall on 21 August, and the night belonged to Dickens. Wilkie Collins recalled that "he literally electrified the audience". As Dickens put it himself, "It was a good thing to have a couple of thousand people all rigid and frozen together, in the palm of one's hand . . . and to see the hardened

411

Carpenters at the sides crying and trembling at it night after night." The carpenters were not the only ones to cry. At the end of the play Maria Ternan had to cradle the dying Dickens in her lap, and "when we came to that point at night, her tears fell down my face, down my beard . . . down my ragged dress – poured all over me like Rain, so that it was as much as I could do to speak for them".

There was of course a party after the last night, but Dickens retired to bed early. And the cause was Ellen Ternan. "I have never known," he wrote to Wilkie Collins some while later, "a moment's peace or content, since the last night of *The Frozen Deep*. I do suppose that there never was a man so seized and rended by one spirit." He had returned to London but was embroiled in a state of intense restlessness, dreariness, misery. It had broken out at last, that feeling which he had kept under control with hard work and long walks and vivid theatricals and constant activity. There was no escape from this feeling which had always been latent within him – this weariness, misery and blankness so much like the sensations of his childhood. The feeling of being "neglected and hopeless"; the "miserable blank" of his life; the time when "I felt as if my heart were rent". All these are words from his own memories of his childhood, but they could equally well be applied to this period of his life also, all the old feelings triggered off by the sight of a young, attractive and unattainable girl. And compounded now by the sense of his own ageing, of life closing down. Forster was to say of this period in his friend's life that "there was for him no 'city of the mind' against outward ills, for inner consolation and shelter". But this is to do Dickens less than justice; he had a "city of the mind" in his fiction itself. But he had to suffer the disadvantages of his gifts; his quick imaginative excitement and his loss of self-possession in the characters of his imagination were now the very qualities which unnerved him, saddened him, rendered him desperate. He saw too

412

much; he *experienced* too much; he conjured up too readily images of decay and suffering. Perhaps, at such moments, he turned too easily to tragedy or melodrama. All the characteristics that made him a great novelist were now directed against his own self. Yet, in Dickens's life, there was always somebody else to blame and even as his own misery increased so did his disaffection from his wife; ". . . the years have not made it easier to bear for either of us," he told Forster, "and, for her sake as well as mine, the wish will force itself upon me that something might be done. I know too well it is impossible. There is the fact, and that is all one can say." Some months before he had written in *Household Words* that "the Law of Divorce is in such condition that from the tie of marriage there is no escape to be had, no absolution to be got . . ."

But his was not a character to succumb to mere resignation. He followed Ellen Ternan, and some words in *Our Mutual Friend*, a novel in part concerned with helpless passion, may be significant here. "You draw me to you. If I were shut up in a strong prison, you would draw me out. I should break through the wall to come to you. If I were lying on a sick bed, you would draw me up — to stagger to your feet and fall there." These are sufficiently alarming sentiments and Dickens immediately observes, "The wild energy of the man, now quite let loose, was absolutely terrible."

By the beginning of October Ellen Ternan was engaged at the Theatre Royal, Haymarket, where she remained for much of the next two years; this seems like a natural move, but in fact Dickens had more than a small role in negotiating it. For in the middle of the month, after Ellen had joined the company, he was thanking the manager, Buckstone, for his help in arranging matters so well; "I need hardly tell you that my interest in the young lady does not cease with the effecting of this arrangement . . ." And, in the meantime, something had happened further to

413

estrange Dickens from his wife. It is not clear what it might have been; there were any number of misunderstandings between them and, according to Dickens's own report to Emile de la Rue, Catherine was often jealous of his relations with other women and was inclined to suspect the worst. Finally, irrevocably, Dickens turned away from Catherine. On 11 October he asked her maid, Anne Brown, radically to alter the sleeping quarters for his wife and himself; what had been a shared room was to be cut in two and henceforth Dickens would sleep alone, a partition between his wife and himself. He was withdrawing from her, literally sealing himself off from her. Three or four days later he left Tavistock House after a quarrel with Catherine; he left his bed at two o'clock in the morning, unable to sleep, and walked all the way to Gad's Hill Place. A distance of some thirty miles. "The road was so lonely in the night," he wrote later, "that I fell asleep to the monotonous sound of my own feet, doing their regular four miles an hour. Mile after mile I walked, without the slightest sense of exertion, dozing heavily and dreaming constantly." More than seven hours' walking. In his broken pedestrian sleep he made up verses, spoke in a foreign language, believed that he was about to breakfast in an "Alpine Convent". Seven hours, never once stopping. And of what else did he dream in this extraordinary nocturnal expedition? Only a few weeks later he was telling Mrs Watson about the Princess of the fairy-stories, ". . . you have no idea how intensely I love her!" In fact on more than one occasion he obliquely describes Ellen as a "princess" out of the story-books. Yet how strange it is that she seems already to have become less a living human being than a creature from his imaginary world and a figment of his heart's desires. Even in the heat of Dickens's passion we may look for explanations to Dickens the fabulist.

But there was also and always Dickens the public man,

who even in these days must work on; work on with *Household Words*, work on with his speeches and engagements, work on with the next Christmas issue of the periodical. For the latter, at least, he found his theme readily enough; the Indian Mutiny had erupted earlier in the year, and the carnage inflicted upon the British community in India by the native inhabitants seems to have provoked in Dickens a rage which blended easily with his private discontents. He gave two readings of *A Christmas Carol*, one for the Mechanics' Institute at Coventry and one for a similar organisation in Rochester. He also issued invitations to dine "with us" at the end of November, so there was at least some pretence of, or approximation to, ordinary domestic life in the Dickens household. But there was no Christmas party this year at Tavistock House.

Uncertainties pursued him into the following year. He was not sure whether or not to begin a new novel; he had written down notes which had occurred to him during *The Frozen Deep*, but he could not yet settle to such a long task. He wanted something to divert and preoccupy his "worried mind" but he found that, for the first time in his life, he could not properly discipline himself. He still planned to work on the novel through the summer in order that he might begin publishing in the late autumn; he even had a title in mind, of a sufficiently foreboding kind, *One Of These Days*; and yet, and yet . . .

Instead in March he began seriously to plan an extended season of readings, beginning in London and then extending to the provinces, although even still he was keenly aware of the possible dangers involved in turning himself into what was essentially a public entertainer. Ever since the early Forties he had emphasised the dignity and the value of the novelist's calling, of course, and now he began a series of conversations with his friends and his publishers to test whether that calling would be in any way diminished by his new role. He asked Bradbury and

Evans about the possible effect upon his next book; and of course he talked to Forster, who seems to have been alone among his friends in objecting to the idea as an abrogation of his powers and his responsibilities. Since Dickens's mind seems to have been firmly made up even before he began to take advice from his friends, he quickly dismissed Forster's objections as "irrational". By the end of the month, in fact, his plans were set; he would read *A Christmas Carol* both in London and in the provinces, by the end of which tour he hoped to have netted ". . . *a very large sum of money*".

A large audience assembled for the first reading at St Martin's Hall in London. Dickens stepped onto the platform, flower in his buttonhole and gloves in hand. He showed no outward signs of nervousness but, according to Edmund Yates, he was "walking rather stiffly, right shoulder well forward"; but at once he was greeted by a "roar of cheering which might have been heard at Charing Cross". Dickens remained composed. Before he began, he made an announcement. He had decided, he said, to take up "reading on my own account, as one of my recognised occupations" and he went on to say that "firstly, I have satisfied myself that it can involve no possible compromise of the credit and independence of literature. Secondly I have long held the opinion, and have long acted on the opinion, that in these times whatever brings a public man and his public face to face, on terms of mutual confidence and respect, is a good thing". Then he went on to speak of the ties almost "of personal friendship" between himself and his readers. "Thus it is that I come, quite naturally, to be here among you at this time; and thus it is that I proceed to read this little book, quite as composedly as I might proceed to write it, or to publish it in any other way." One of the audience remembers Dickens's "clearness of articulation, as though he were particularly desirous that every word should be thoroughly weighed by his

416

Dickens reading to his daughters
Mamey and Katey on the lawn of Gad's Hill

John Forster

Wilkie Collins

Caricature of Dickens and Dolby,
*c.* 1868

Dickens, 1867

Ellan Ternan

Gad's Hill Place

The Swiss Chalet

'The Empty Chair', Gad's Hill, June 7, 1870.
Painting by Luke Fildes
on the day of Dicken's death

Dickens after death, by J.E. Millais

Dickens dreaming
about his characters,
*c.* 1870.
From a painting,
*Dicken's Dream* by
Robert William Buss

hearers . . ." Dickens was in fact trying to suggest that it was a natural and even almost inevitable development of his art, that there was nothing unusual about reading in public, and that it could only confirm the relationship he had already established with his audience. That he believed this there is no doubt; but of course he had left out of account the two most pressing reasons for his decision to read. He did not mention the feverish restlessness which had destroyed his domestic happiness and which had almost driven him to this fresh activity, and he did not mention (as he had done to his friends) his hopes of earning a great deal of money in a relatively short space of time.

He still recognised problems, of course, and was particularly nervous about reading *The Chimes*. "To tell you the truth," he told Thomas Beard, ". . . I *can not* yet (and I have been at it all the morning) command sufficient composure at some of the more affecting parts, to project them with the necessary force, the requisite distance. I must harden my heart, like Lady Macbeth." He had struck upon the real secret of any such undertaking: in order to move his auditors he must not himself be moved. He was determined to acquire whatever skills he needed for such work; all his life, he had taken on challenges only to wrest victory from them. And this was now something that he knew he had to do. "I must do *something*," he told Forster, "or I shall wear my heart away." Here the single most important reason for the readings emerges once more in his own words; his misery at home, his unsatisfied longings for Ellen Ternan, were pushing him forward and ". . . the mere physical effort and change of the Readings would be good, as another means of bearing it". It is even possible that he rehearsed his readings in front of Mrs Ternan (and perhaps Ellen, too), since she knew a great deal about the art of elocution. And so he had begun, his unsatisfied love for a young woman turning his life around.

417

# Twenty-Seven

DICKENS had once told an actress, "in his rapid, earnest way, and with the slight lisp which he had, 'Ah! When you're young you want to be old; when you're getting old you want to be young . . .'". It was in this spirit that Dickens was about to set in train a series of events which would forever change his life. "Who then could have conceived or prophesied," Percy Fitzgerald wrote later, "that in the year of grace 1858, the whole fabric should have begun to totter, and that a strange, sudden change should have come about. This literally – I remember it well – took away all our breaths . . .". And if Dickens could have foreseen precisely what would happen, would he have changed his course? No. No will could ever be set up against his own and, at a time when he seems to re-experience something of his old childhood misery and sense of abandonment, he exhibits once more that firmness of purpose, that ardour against the barriers of the world, that belief in self-transformation, which had animated his earliest years. This was his second battle, even if it were essentially a battle against himself, and he was not about to shirk it. So much of his life and struggle seemed to him at such times to be a dream, and yet what of his own dreams now? "Only last night," he told Macready in the middle of March, "in my sleep, I was bent upon getting over a perspective of barriers, with my hands and feet bound. Pretty much what we are all about, waking, I think?"

In the early months of 1858 he was just as disaffected from Catherine, but the tone of his remarks is one of solemn weariness and endurance. "A dismal failure has to be borne," he said to Forster, "and there an end." At the beginning of May, though, something happened that was to provoke from him rather more than weariness at the unhappy state of his marriage. There were one or two specific episodes which affected the events of the next few months, even though the incidents themselves have since been obscured in a cloud of gossip and speculation. One had to do with a small piece of jewellery. It was not unusual for Dickens to reward members of his amateur cast with "keepsakes" at the end of a season; Francisco Berger, who organised the musical aspects of Dickens's theatre, was for example given a pair of cuff-links. So it was that he had given a piece of jewellery to Ellen Ternan. In some accounts Dickens presented her with a brooch which contained his portrait or his initials; in other accounts he gave her a bracelet. Whatever the item, such a gift would have been given to the young actress in the autumn of 1857. Reports differ again about the revelation to Catherine of this gift; in one, the brooch needed to be mended and the jeweller to whom it was sent, seeing the initial or the portrait of Charles Dickens, had returned it to Tavistock House. Georgina told Catherine, who then "mounted her husband with comb and brush". But in another account the jeweller informed Mrs Dickens that "her" bracelet was ready for collection and it was at this point that she discovered her husband's gift to the young actress. Both reports are further muddled by the fact that, in the story of the brooch, Georgina Hogarth is said to have told Catherine because she was jealous of *Mrs* Ternan. Ellen Ternan is also described as Dickens's "god-daughter". In other words all the confusions which can be expected from hearsay and rumour abound in these accounts. But whatever the true facts, it was at this point that Dickens decided he must separate from his wife.

He wanted the actual process of separation to be handled as informally and as discreetly as possible; a man in his prominent public position could hardly act otherwise, and he proposed to his wife that they should lead separate lives while remaining to all outward appearances the same married couple as before. At first he suggested that she should have her own apartment in Tavistock House, and should appear at parties in her old role; a neat and agreeable solution for him, but not one that was likely to recommend itself to Catherine who would be forced to live a kind of charade. Then Dickens suggested that they should take it in turns to occupy the town house and the country house – she remaining at Tavistock House while he lived at Gad's Hill Place, and vice versa. There even seems to have been an idea that Catherine should live abroad, without her children, while Dickens remained in England. Of course Catherine rejected all such suggestions; or, rather, she and her family rejected them. Faced with her husband's sudden and no doubt bewildering desire to break all marital and domestic ties, she went for advice and for comfort to her parents. Her sister, Georgina, it seems, tacitly supported Dickens in his desire for new arrangements in which she inevitably would play a much larger role although her own somewhat anomalous position in any new household would have been (and was) a distinctly uncomfortable one.

Within days of his proposals for an informal separation being rejected, Dickens suggested that Catherine should set up house elsewhere and that he would then give her four hundred pounds a year, plus brougham – the latter article, the carriage, suggesting just how precisely Dickens thought he could "tie up" matters in this way. Certainly he seemed intent upon something as carefully arranged as one of his own fictions. Later he would declare that Catherine had first broached the idea of leaving home, but that is clearly not the case: whatever shortcomings she possessed as a mother (and these were only suggested by Georgina and Dickens) she had no desire whatever to abandon her children. It was he who wanted her to leave but, as soon as the Hogarths themselves began to take an active part in the negotiations, his hope for a quick, clean resolution evaporated. He was slowly but inevitably drawn into a protracted dispute, and part of the reason for his subsequent extraordinary, in some ways inexplicable, behaviour can be laid to the fact that he had lost control of events – a situation almost unique in his life, and one with which he really did not know how to deal. Mrs Hogarth came to stay with Catherine at Tavistock House, and on the following day Dickens left the house and moved into his offices at Wellington Street North. Forster was deputed to act for Dickens (he was to negotiate directly with Mrs Hogarth, whom Dickens detested), while it was agreed that Mark Lemon, a friend of both parties, should act as Catherine's representative.

And so, through the first two and half weeks of May, Forster and Lemon, with Catherine and Mrs Hogarth, tried to draw up a suitable deed of separation which would satisfy all parties without the need to enter a court of law. But Dickens's hopes of keeping the business secret were necessarily misplaced; rumours about the impending separation began to spread and, as is usually the case, rumour begat rumour. That he was having an affair with an actress. An actress at the Haymarket. Ellen Ternan. Maria Ternan. Mrs Ternan. No one seems to have been sure about the exact identity. That Mrs Dickens had written to the Haymarket, exonerating the said actress. That he had eloped with the very same actress to Boulogne. And then there were rumours, infinitely more damaging, that he was having an affair with his own sister-in-law. With Georgina

421

Hogarth. That she had given birth to his children. More astonishing still, it seems likely that these rumours about Georgina were in fact started or at least not repudiated by the Hogarths themselves. The point was that Georgina had elected to stay with Dickens and his children even as Catherine was being forced to leave them and, in addition, it seems likely that she knew in advance of Dickens's plans to separate from his wife; his letters to her in the months before these events suggest that she was altogether in his confidence. As a result her mother and her younger sister, Helen, turned upon her; *she* was still in the confidence of the great novelist, while *they* were repudiated and despised. Could it be from these feelings of jealousy that so much malice spread? It can happen even in the best of families. "The question was not myself; but others," Dickens later wrote to Macready. "Foremost among them – of all people in the world – Georgina! Mrs Dickens's weakness, and her mother's and her younger sister's wickedness drifted to that, without seeing what they would strike against – though I had warned them in the strongest manner."

Events were now slipping even further out of Dickens's control, and it was at some point in these crucial days that Mrs Hogarth seems to have threatened Dickens with action in the Divorce Court – a very serious step indeed since the Divorce Act of the previous year had decreed that wives could divorce their husbands only on the grounds of incest, bigamy or cruelty. The clear implication here was that Dickens had committed "incest" with Georgina, which was the legal term for sexual relations with a sister-in-law. At Dickens's instigation Forster wrote an urgent letter to Dickens's solicitor, asking for clarification of the new Act; and at the same time, too, Georgina was examined by a doctor and found to be *virgo intacta*. At this point, it seems, the Hogarths implicitly dropped the threat of court action. Yet the bare facts of the matter can hardly suggest the maelstrom of fury and bitterness into which the family, now divided against itself, had descended. And what of Dickens himself? From the beginning he had tried to keep everything as neat and as ordered as everything else in his life, but it had spiralled out of control. The case for an informal separation had degenerated into a series of formal negotiations which in turn threatened to lead to public exposure of his domestic life; he, the apostle of family harmony, had even been accused of incest with his own wife's sister. He reacted badly to stress and now, during the most anxious days of his life, he ceased to behave in a wholly rational manner.

Shortly after this, however, Catherine sent a letter to Mark Lemon, which she asked him to pass on to her husband; the contents are not known but Lemon now made it clear that he wanted to extricate himself from what was becoming a more and more unpleasant and difficult business. And then, the day after, perhaps in defiance of her mother's wishes, Catherine agreed to accept the deed of settlement; to accept, in other words, her husband's terms. Trustees were now appointed to look after her interests – Lemon, despite his reservations, being one and Frederick Evans, Dickens's publisher, being the other. In fact Catherine also employed Evans's solicitor, and eventually set up house only half a mile from Evans himself; he clearly felt the need to protect her, even at the cost of incurring the enmity of his most profitable author. But, at this stage, Dickens was eager only that the whole affair should be settled. On the Saturday, the day after Catherine had accepted the terms, her solicitors conferred with her father and then, three days later, they met Dickens's solicitor, Ouvry, and began the formal preparation of the deed of settlement. As far as Dickens was concerned the matter was over now, and he asked Wilkie Collins to visit him so that he might tell him the whole long story.

Dickens was now hearing the abuse on all sides and, in a number of letters, he refers to the "lies" which were being spread about him everywhere. He heard that Mrs Hogarth and Helen Hogarth were, even as the negotiations about the settlement were being concluded, still spreading rumours about Georgina. If Catherine had agreed to the settlement against the advice of her mother, as seems likely, then Mrs Hogarth's own bitterness was leading her into a fresh assault upon the integrity of the daughter who had taken Dickens's side against her own sister; it ought to be noted, however, that Catherine herself seems to have borne no grudge against her younger sister, and in fact seems to have been relieved that the children remained under her care. But as soon as Dickens heard of this fresh outbreak of rumour he wrote to his solicitors and demanded that they obtain an undertaking from the Hogarths that all such gossip would stop; otherwise, he would proceed no further with the negotiations. Catherine's solicitors then wrote back and declared their ". . . conviction that the Hogarth family could not have originated them". But this was not enough for Dickens; he was still hearing a variety of lies and slanders directed against him and Georgina, and he wanted Ouvry to be "relentless" with Mrs Hogarth. In the event, on the same evening, George Hogarth, the mild-mannered, gentle man who must have been immensely distressed by all this familial rivalry and hatred, wrote a letter to his solicitor in which he assured him ". . . that the report that I or my wife or Daughter have at any time stated or insinuated that any impropriety of conduct had taken place between my daughter Georgiana [sic] and her Brother in Law Mr Charles Dickens is totally and entirely unfounded". Of course Hogarth himself was not being accused of anything and, in any case, the slanders against Dickens went wider than the charge of incest with Georgina. So Dickens's solicitor wrote back to say that ". . . Mr Dickens will not sign any deed with these charges hanging over him, and supposed to be sanctioned by some members of his wife's family". He enclosed a statement which he wished only Mrs Hogarth and Helen Hogarth to sign. In the meantime, Dickens was reading *A Christmas Carol* at St Martin's Hall, followed on the next evening by *The Chimes*. Stories of familial harmony after discord. Peace. Good will upon earth. No record remains of his appearance or demeanour on these occasions.

The choice for Mrs Hogarth was obvious; either she signed the statement prepared for her by Dickens's solicitor, or Dickens would refuse to proceed with the deed of settlement, a settlement which now raised Catherine's annual income to six hundred, rather than the first proposed four hundred, pounds. Catherine's misery would only be lengthened by any delay, and Mrs Hogarth must have known well enough by now that her son-in-law was not the man to yield to any entreaty. But still she held out against signing the piece of paper which would be tantamount to confessing she had spread rumours about her own daughter, Georgina – until, that is, Mark Lemon and Dickens's eldest son pleaded with her to do so and thus to end the uncertainty under which they were all now living. Clearly, for Catherine's sake as much as for anyone else, the matter should finally be resolved. So, on 29 May, Mrs Hogarth and Helen Hogarth reluctantly put their names to a document which said in part, ". . . certain statements have been circulated that such differences are occasioned by circumstances deeply affecting the moral character of Mr Dickens and compromising the reputation and good name of others, we solemnly declare that we now disbelieve such statements. We know that they are not believed by Mrs Dickens, and we pledge ourselves on all occasions to contradict them, as entirely destitute of foundation." Catherine's solicitor then proposed to present this document in return for the deed of settlement itself, but Dickens believed that such a transaction would be an outrageous attempt at something close to a "bargain"

425

where only simple justice was involved. Catherine's solicitor immediately gave way, and the statement was handed to Dickens. On the same day Catherine left Tavistock House for the last time, and travelled to Brighton with her mother.

Two days later Dickens was back at the house. Georgina and the children were with him, and in a letter to a friend Dickens spelled out the nature of the separation; Charley was to live with his mother while his eldest daughter, Mary, was to be "mistress of the house". She was, in other words, to be in titular command of the servants and household management while in fact Georgina herself was really in charge of such matters. It was Georgina who now wrote to Maria Beadnell about the whole affair, although the tenor and vocabulary of the letter strongly suggest that Dickens simply dictated it to her. Once again it was written ostensibly "more in sorrow than in anger" and, once again, the real responsibility for what had happened was heaped upon Catherine; a strange letter for her sister to write, even at Dickens's dictation, but an indication of how far the ordinary loyalties of family life had broken down under the pressure of Dickens's anxiety and uncertainty. But such private letters were not enough for him, and on the following day he consulted his solicitor about the possibility of issuing some kind of public statement exonerating himself from all the false charges that had been levelled against him. Ouvry's private advice is not recorded, but it is doubtful in any case if anything would have stopped Dickens from taking the extraordinary step of issuing to the newspapers a personal statement on his "domestic trouble". Yet, even as he began to draft it, he was clearly ill at ease and, when he took a walk that day to prepare for a speech he was about to give for The Playground and General Recreation Society (how strangely his private and public lives conflicted now), "the first thing I saw, when I went out of my own door, was a policeman hiding among the lilac trees apparently lying in wait for some burglar or murderer. After observing him with great dread and anxiety for a minute or two . . .'' he realised that the policeman was on a harmless errand. But why had he been filled with such "great dread and anxiety" at the mere sight of a policeman? Was it already some guilt which was haunting him, not letting him rest? Some irrational fear of imprisonment?

By the beginning of June the two sets of solicitors had agreed upon a draft of the terms of the separation. Catherine was to be given an income of six hundred pounds; at Dickens's instigation, she was granted unlimited access to the children; and both parties agreed not to "disturb" each other or take legal action against each other. In other words Dickens was to give his wife exactly what she would have been granted if there had been an act of judicial separation, while in turn Catherine (and of course by implication her mother) would no longer hint or threaten any proceedings under the new Divorce Act. Catherine's solicitor sent a copy of the document to her in Brighton. At the same time Wills travelled down to see her, with a copy of Dickens's personal statement; he found her on the pier, reading a novel (the title of which remains unknown). Dickens intended to issue his statement to the newspapers and also to publish it in *Household Words*; he had already shown it to several friends, such as John Forster and Edmund Yates, who advised him not to issue such a private account of domestic conflicts. But Dickens also consulted the editor of *The Times*, John Delane, who believed that it should so be published. It was his advice Dickens decided to take, although it is of course unlikely that he ever had any other plan in mind. With a copy of this statement he sent to Catherine a letter, asking her to read the "article" since it contained a reference to herself (although at no point requesting her permission to divulge the details of their married life), and adding, "Whoever

427

there may be among the living, whom I will never forgive alive or dead, I earnestly hope that all unkindness is over between you and me." Catherine (perhaps somewhat weakly) said that she did not object to the allusion to her, but then sent a copy of it to her solicitors. They promptly asked Dickens to postpone its publication, but events were already in motion. On the following day it appeared in *The Times* and then in the succeeding issue of *Household Words*. In part it read as follows: "By some means arising out of wickedness, or out of folly, or out of inconceivable wild chance, this trouble has been made the occasion of misrepresentations, most grossly false, most monstrous, and most cruel – involving, not only me, but innocent persons dear to my heart . . . and so widely spread, that I doubt if one reader in a thousand will peruse these lines, by whom some touch of the breath of these slanders will not have passed, like an unwholesome air."

But in this respect, if in no other, he misjudged the extent of his fame. A pamphlet about Dickens's life, printed later in this year, suggests that very few people outside the London literary "world" knew anything about the matter. Nevertheless, "called upon by the first novelist of the day thus to ventilate a vague denial of nothing that anybody seemed to know about, the press generally printed the manifesto". One of his first biographers was a boy at the time this statement was issued, and he said that ". . . I well remember the feeling of surprise and regret which that article created among us of the general public . . . So far as one could learn at the time, no great dissimilarity existed between the author and the man . . ." But the statement, simply entitled "Personal", altered that equilibrium; a gap opened between Dickens the novelist and Dickens the husband and father. Percy Fitzgerald recalled that "people were all but bewildered and almost stunned . . . Everyone was for the most part in supreme ignorance of what the document could possibly refer to

428

. . . the delusion that all of his readers had heard of some particular slander that had grown out of the domestic trouble, the fact being that nearly everyone who had read the dark allusion was in the completest ignorance".

Of course Dickens genuinely thought that everyone was talking about him. There is what might be considered an anticipatory passage in *Dombey and Son*, anatomising Dombey's feelings after the flight of his wife from the Dombey home. "The world. What the world thinks of him, how it looks at him, what it sees in him, and what it says – this is the haunting demon of his mind. It is everywhere where he is; and, worse than that, it is everywhere where he is not." Dickens literally could not bear it; he, the celebrant of the domestic hearth, was even now being whispered against, accused of hypocrisy, condemned for putting away his wife, disparaged even for "preferring" his wife's sister. His anger and bitterness could simply not be held in check; he believed himself to be a good man who had been wronged, and this was the truth which he had to convey to his public.

And what were the reactions of those closer to him than the public itself? It has to be remembered that a separation of this kind, on the grounds of incompatibility, was a relatively rare occurrence. And that adultery itself (which comprised part of the rumours about him) was considered a very serious offence; in the staple fiction of the period, for example, marriage is a sacred institution, the destruction of which leaves the man a wretch or miscreant for the rest of his life. Of course there were those who took his part – Wills, Forster and Mrs Macready among them – but it is hard not to suspect that there was a general uneasiness about his behaviour even amongst his closest friends. Forster admitted to Landseer that "both are in the wrong . . . But yet I wish you could know *everything* – because, upon the whole, Dickens bears this test better than you would be prepared to think . . ." But others were not so charitable or, perhaps, so partisan. Harriet Martineau, who knew Catherine's trustee, Evans, declared that Dickens was really "wild" with "conflict of passion". Mrs Gaskell thought that it had made him "extremely unpopular" and James Payn described it as "a public outrage, a blazoned defiance of all ordinary rules of conduct". Elizabeth Barrett Browning said of Catherine, "Poor woman! She must suffer bitterly – that is sure."

And what of the other principal players in this drama? Of the reactions of Ellen Ternan or Mrs Ternan nothing is known; their silence at the time can be taken for granted. Catherine herself removed to 70 Gloucester Crescent; she made little outward comment upon her misfortune, although in a letter to her aunt she declared that ". . . you will understand and feel for me when I tell you that I still love and think of their father too much for my peace of mind . . . I trust by God's assistance to be able to resign myself to His will, and to lead a contented if not a happy life, but my position is a sad one, and time only may blunt the keen pain that will throb at my heart, but I will indeed try to struggle hard against it." About two months after the separation her eldest son came to live with her, as she had wanted, and there were occasions when she was visited by her other children. But her position was indeed a "sad" one, a wife only in name, publicly alienated from her famous husband's affections, and a woman who became increasingly lonely through the passage of years. Her husband's remaining letters to her are short and infrequent, beginning formally with "Dear Catherine" and ending with his usual signature and flourish; the letters are addressed to "Mrs Charles Dickens". But not the least touching aspect of her long privation is to be found in the efforts which she made to keep up with her husband's career; she avidly read the novels that were to follow, and often went to the theatre to see dramatic adaptations of his fictions. And, in a sense, he and his work were so close to her that he could never really be separated from her. "She was always kind," it was reported later. "She delighted to give children's parties at her house, although on these occasions her own loved children were never among her little guests."

And what of the children? Walter was in India; Francis was in Germany; Alfred, Harry and Sydney were at Mr Gibson's boarding school in Boulogne; and Charley was at Baring's Bank (he left for Hong Kong a year later). Edward, still only six years old, remained at home under Georgina's care. Dickens said of his eldest children that, "between them and myself, there is a confidence as absolute and perfect as if we were of one age". A curious remark, echoed in a 'letter' where he said of his children that "all is open and plain among us, as though we were brothers and sisters"; interesting, perhaps, as much for his own implicit reduction of his age as for the manner in which he instinctively idealises the relationship between brother and sister. It is not at all clear, however, that his children would have agreed with him about the amicable relationship he had formed with them; most of them were in any case out of England, and played no part in the separation proceedings. And Edward (or Plorn) was too young to understand what was taking place.

But Dickens now began to suffer from the consequences of his behaviour. And, when a letter he had written attacking Catherine appeared in the English press (as he must have known it would, sooner or later), he became even more fiercely and justifiably criticised. There were times when his depression became so great that he was utterly cast down. "Sometimes I *cannot* bear it," he told Mary Boyle. Desolation. A feeling of loss. Bewilderment. Rage. Misery. Is this also the feeling he pours into Rogue Riderhood of *Our Mutual Friend* – ". . . like us all, every day of our lives when we wake – he is instinctively unwilling to be restored to the consciousness of this existence, and

431

would be left dormant, if he could". Years of overwork and of pressing anxiety had finally taken their hold upon him; there was no doubt that he was suffering from nervous exhaustion, and his sometimes extraordinary behaviour, seeing plots against himself in every quarter, suggests strongly that he was now experiencing something very close to a nervous breakdown. There had been reports in earlier days of Dickens's "madness" – that is often how people respond to such extraordinary energy and productivity – and even after his death there were critics who described his "monomania" or his "hallucinations". But there was nothing "mad" about Dickens at all. In this period of nervous exhaustion it would seem that all of his usual characteristics simply became exaggerated to the point of unreality. Of course it is easy to wield such terms as madness, and there are times when such a description becomes simply a way of avoiding any real understanding of the subject. But one thing is certain: it is hard not to see in Dickens's behaviour during the separation all the fears and anxieties of his childhood revived, all the latent and necessary confusions of his own personality brought to the surface.

# *Twenty-Eight*

IT was a hot summer, the summer of 1858. The Thames stank, and the sewage of three million people boiled under the sun in what was now no more than an open sewer. In the public buildings along the banks of the river, blinds were soaked with chloride and tons of lime were shovelled into the water itself. Boiled bones. Horse meat. Cat gut. Burial grounds. All of them putrefying and fermenting in the heat. This was the climate in which Charles Dickens began his London readings in the second week of June, to be succeeded in August by a provincial tour. He had changed his programme from the original series of Christmas Books, and began the London season in St Martin's Hall with the story of *Paul Dombey*. A week later he added two of his Christmas stories, the *Poor Traveller* and *Boots at the Holly Tree Inn*, as well as including a monologue entitled *Mrs Gamp*. *Paul Dombey* itself was "a prodigious success", Dickens reported, and the audience wept so much that his manager, Arthur Smith, was not sure about using it again. But Dickens knew better; he repeated the reading twice in the next month.

Dickens also knew that he now needed his audience more than ever. Ellen Ternan was about to go up to Manchester for two months, since the whole company at the Haymarket was due to open in the Theatre Royal there. It has sometimes been suggested that by now Dickens was having some kind of "affair" with her, but all the evidence suggests otherwise. He seems still to have been in that dazed and infatuated state with which he had first seen her; certainly all the protestations of innocence which mark his public statements in this period have the ring of genuine and literal truth. It was almost a childish innocence, in fact. As he said to Mary Boyle in an affectionate letter, one of the many he wrote to her, his heart itself was "like a child," in the sense that it was both tremulous and uncertain even in the company of those he knew well. But his relationship with the whole Ternan family was clearly growing stronger. In the summer, even as he was continuing with his reading tour, he was trying to find a proper singing master for Ellen's sister, Fanny; she wanted to study in Italy, and he went to some trouble to assist her. In fact he was even forced to defend Fanny Ternan's innocence against rumours which connected her name with his own, and on one occasion he was obliged to thank her cousin, Richard Spofford, for believing in his honesty and in her blameless integrity. He even compares her to his own daughters, which suggests that Dickens found in the Ternans something of an extended family without the discord which had overpowered his own household.

No doubt there was gossip about all of the Ternans, and perhaps about Ellen in particular. It should be remembered that, in this period, a woman who was thought to have sexual relations with a man outside marriage was considered to be little more than a prostitute and that, in addition, the term "actress" still carried a certain amount of moral opprobrium. Ellen could have been, and no doubt was, as virginal as Dickens always insisted; but this would not have stopped the malice and the rumour. It is for this reason, no doubt, that Dickens became incensed about what has become known as the Berners Street affair. Dickens's efforts to find a singing master for Fanny Ternan in Italy had been successful, and it seems likely that he helped to pay for her trip to that country together with her mother who was to act as chaperone; the two other daughters, Maria and Ellen, were still working in London but they had moved on Dickens's advice from Canonbury to rooms at 31 Berners Street (just off Oxford Street and closer to the theatres). It was during their residence here that the policeman on that particular "beat" questioned the two women. Ellen told Dickens what had happened, and at once he flew into one of those indignant passions during the course of which he lost all sense of reality; if the incident was reported in *The Times*, he told Wills, there would be "public uproar". In his vociferous letter he went on to tell Wills to see the two women, and then to make a complaint at Scotland Yard against the officer. Dickens seemed to think that the policeman had been bribed to find out more about the Ternan girls from some "Swell"; this seems likely, but his reaction to the incident suggests the extent to which he felt himself threatened from all sides. And, to complicate matters still further, his own family were behaving in a less than "respectable" manner. His brother, Frederick, had left his wife, and Anna Weller had now applied to the recently-established Divorce Court for a legal separation on the grounds of adultery. Yet another brother, Augustus, had deserted his wife, too, and gone to America with another woman. Who in the period, knowing of these matrimonial entanglements as well as that of Charles Dickens himself, would have failed to consider the whole family to have, in one of the phrases of the time, "bad blood"? And who even now can doubt that the legacy of John Dickens's fecklessness had not in some sense imprinted itself upon his children – even if, in Dickens's case, it was to be all the more sternly repudiated?

Yet there is a sense in which Dickens, despite all of these familial and amatory anxieties, seems to have confronted the worst and to have overcome it. He had of course removed one source of discomfort. He had separated from Catherine and, in so doing, he had sloughed off the life he once thought that he wanted. Instead he had now got the life he *really* wanted all along; all the available evidence suggests (though of course it does not prove) that he had entered a strange mythical relationship with the idealised virgin of his fiction, and that his affection for Ellen Ternan was quite outside the familiar Victorian pattern of clandestine mistresses. He was happy to have faced down the world, too, and the idea for a Christmas story which occurred to him suggests precisely his attitude at this time; it was to be a story that ". . . shows beyond mistake that you can't shut out the world; that you are in it, to be of it; that you get into a false position the moment you try to sever yourself from it; and that you must mingle with it, and make the best of it, and make the best of yourself into the bargain." It was the same force of life which made him always watch the world; while on a railway trip, he told Georgina, "it was a most lovely morning, and, tired as I was, I couldn't sleep for looking out of window".

In fact the actual Christmas story he wrote was of a quite different complexion and, furthermore, it was the last to be published in *Household Words*. The grievance which Dickens had held against Frederick Evans since the time of the separation had not perceptibly abated and he set to work now to sever all connection with the publishing firm which had served him so well and for so many years. In particular he wanted to take *Household Words* away from them; so in November he appointed Forster as his representative and, through him, asked his publishers to agree to the dissolution of the periodical. In the meantime Dickens went down to Gad's Hill Place and prepared to start work upon the next, and last, Christmas issue of *Household Words* with Wilkie Collins. For a while he had thought of using his Christmas contribution as the opening of a new novel – he had been jotting down notes for one at the beginning of the year – but in fact it was eventually combined with some stories of Collins and others to produce *A House To Let*. Dickens's own piece, "Going Into Society", was a moral fable on the dangers of "Society"; a subject, you might say, which he now knew by heart. So perhaps something of Dickens is to be found in the "Showman" who tells this story, a man who ". . . had led a wandering life, and settled people had lost sight of him, and people who plumed themselves on being respectable were shy of admitting that they had ever known anything of him".

Negotiations with Bradbury and Evans were proceeding even as he wrote and published this cautionary tale. The publishers refused to discontinue *Household Words* and in fact they denied the legality of Dickens's proceedings; he then asked them, instead, to sell their interest in the periodical to him. They replied that they might be interested in selling their share, but only as part of an arrangement in which he would purchase their interest in all of his works. Dickens then offered one thousand pounds for *Household Words* alone. Again, they refused. It was a complex and acrimonious dispute as Wills and Forster, directed by Dickens, refused to do anything other than purchase the periodical or dissolve it. (It is not recorded how difficult it was for Wills to take a stand against men whom he had previously liked and admired, yet another instance of the havoc which Dickens could wreak in private relationships when he was set upon some end of his own.) Matters were further complicated by the fact that Dickens was already thinking ahead to a new periodical, to be conducted wholly by himself. He had also decided to return to Chapman and Hall for the publication of his novels, despite the fact that this was the firm which he had left in a similar outburst of anger and indignation so many years before. But that was now long in the past; Hall was dead and Chapman was about to retire, leaving the running of the company in the hands of his cousin, Frederick. Once more Dickens was fighting against his "enemies" real or imagined, changing his old allegiances, abandoning those who stood opposed to his will, forcing his way through the world.

It was with something like fellow-feeling, therefore, that towards the end of the year he delivered a speech at a prize-giving of the Institutional Association of Lancashire and Cheshire; it was an occasion when he gave prizes to working men who had completed courses of study under difficulties, men who represented the individual triumph of skill and assiduity over poverty and disadvantage, men whose will to succeed had overcome all obstacles. And how close such men were to Dickens at this time of his life! Two poor brothers who worked in coalmines during the day and then, three nights a week, walked eight miles to a college. A moulder in an iron foundry who got up at four o'clock in the morning to learn industrial drawing. A piecer who at the age of eighteen had been illiterate, but who then taught himself how to read and write, how to work in algebra, and who wrote of himself ". . . that he made the resolution never to take up a subject without keeping to it . . ."

On the day after the prize-giving he left Manchester for Coventry, where he was to be presented with a seventy-five guinea watch (purchased by subscription after Dickens had read for the Coventry Institute in the previous year). He made an agreeable speech, as everyone expected, and then at the end he made an impromptu toast to the women. "We know that the Graces were all women (*renewed laughter*); we know that the Muses were women, and we know every day of our lives that the Fates are women (*Roars of laughter*). I think that as we receive so much from them, both in happiness and pain, we ought at least to drink their healths. (*Cheers.*)". No one who knew anything of Dickens's domestic trials could doubt the significance of what were, for him, remarkably frank words;

". . . both in happiness and pain . . ." The last days of the year, at Gad's Hill Place, were wet and dreary. Dickens, the painter W.P. Frith and Collins played bagatelle and talked.

He had no desire to celebrate his forty-seventh birthday two months later. "I have not had the heart to make any preparation for it," he wrote to Wilkie Collins, "— you know why." But he did not want his gloom to infect his children, and he planned to take them down to Brighton for a few days. He also had a bad cold, always a sure sign with Dickens that he was either depressed or overworked. "— you know why . . .", he had said, and it is likely that the reason was that "little reason", that "riddle", Ellen Ternan. Fanny Ternan and her mother were about to return from Italy, and Dickens seriously thought of letting Tavistock House to the entire family; until, that is, Forster argued him out of the idea. It would no doubt have been a provocation to those who already suspected "the worst". Even so, when the Ternan family were reunited, they took steps to move from the unfurnished lodgings in Berners Street; somehow the two older sisters were able to afford to take a lease on 2 Houghton Place, Ampthill Square, in Camden Town. It has been suggested that Dickens himself provided the money with which they purchased the lease, but the evidence for this remains circumstantial — consisting mainly of the fact that, a month before, Dickens sold at least fifteen hundred pounds' worth of government stock and, a few weeks later, agreed to write a short story for the *New York Ledger* at the then astonishing price of one thousand pounds. Clearly he needed money for something, but it may just have been for "improvements" at Gad's Hill Place. Whatever the truth of the matter, the Ternans (without Fanny, who had decided to remain at her studies in Italy) moved into the new house in March. Five months later Ellen appeared for the last time on the stage and, from that time forward, seems to have earned her living in Houghton Place as a teacher of elocution. The house itself was a four-storied, terraced affair in a suitably residential and middle-class area of London. Francisco Berger, who had met the Ternans when he was arranging the music for *The Frozen Deep*, often visited the new family residence; he remembered the occasions when he met Dickens there, too, playing cards and singing duets with Ellen at the piano. Perhaps they sang together two popular songs of that time, Mendelssohn's "Fast, ah, too fast fade the Roses of Pleasure" and John Barnett's "I will gather the Rose".

In the first months of this new year, 1859, Dickens was sitting to Frith; Forster had commissioned a painting of his friend, and Frith had willingly accepted it. Dickens was, he said later, "a delightful sitter, always punctual to the moment, and always remaining the full two hours . . ." He even went to the trouble of having himself photographed by a celebrated exponent of the new art, Watkins, and to the photographer's studio were brought Dickens's table, chair and velvet jacket — the point being that Frith could work from the artificial image when the great original was absent. The photograph itself shows a grave, rather tired man, his hair pushed back from his forehead, sitting back in his chair in an indefinably wary or uneasy posture. He seems to be holding a paper knife, or quill pen, in his right hand. Frith thought nothing of the photograph itself, although he used the basic position. In his portrait the tiredness has been replaced by something very much like exaltation, and the gravity has been combined with intense watchfulness. When Dickens was not talking during each of the two-hour sessions, he had time to think.

Thinking of more readings. Thinking of a reading tour of America, although there was what he called a "private reason" for his regretting a long absence from England. Thinking of the successor to *Household Words*, which he was still determined to dissolve. Thinking of titles for a new periodical. Astonishingly enough, considering his present
440

position, he first came up with *Household Harmony*, and became rather annoyed when Forster gently hinted at the incongruity. "I am afraid we must not be too particular about the possibility of personal references and applications: otherwise it is manifest that I never can write another book." But he assented, and considered *Charles Dickens's Own* and *Time and Tide* among other titles. Until triumphantly he arrived at,

" 'The story of our lives, from year to year.' — *Shakespeare*.

ALL THE YEAR ROUND.

A weekly journal conducted by Charles Dickens."

He had even found an office for the new periodical, only a few doors down Wellington Street North from his old headquarters; but a much plainer set of rooms than those for *Household Words*, described by Percy Fitzgerald as ". . . a shop rather than an office". One visitor noticed the plainness of the new offices, too, and remarked that there was not ". . . a square yard of carpet of any kind, but daily scrubbings had made the floors and stairs scrupulously clean. Nowhere in the building did I see a single article of furniture excepting an oblong table and a pair of large rush bottomed armchairs in the editorial room". Nevertheless Dickens did fit up for himself an apartment on the top storey of the house; he was planning to let Tavistock House and needed somewhere to stay in London on his frequent trips from Gad's Hill Place.

There was of course still the pressing necessity to wind up *Household Words*, before his attention could be fully engaged upon the new journal, and he went about that business with his usual speed and steely determination. He had three hundred thousand handbills and posters printed, in order to advertise the new journal, at which point

Bradbury and Evans issued an injunction to stop the distribution of leaflets announcing his departure from *Household Words* and the imminent publication of *All The Year Round*. For once Chancery acted speedily; the case came up the next day, and judgment was largely given in Dickens's favour. The Master of the Rolls also ordered that *Household Words* be put up for auction, and the proceeds distributed fairly between all the parties concerned. Dickens's determination to buy the periodical, now that the opportunity presented itself, could only have been strengthened by a rumour that Bradbury and Evans wished themselves to purchase *Household Words* and make Thackeray its new editor. So at the auction Dickens, represented through the bidding of Arthur Smith and the diversionary tactics of Frederick Chapman, bought out his old journal for £3,550, a sum which he later recouped by selling the stock of stereotype plates to Chapman and Hall. He had won, as he had always insisted he would, and in the last number of *Household Words* he could not resist proclaiming the fact of his own rightness. "He knew perfectly well, knowing his own rights, and his means of attaining them, that it *could not be* but this Work must stop, if he chose to stop it. He therefore announced many weeks ago, that it would be discontinued on the day on which this final Number bears date. The Public have read a great deal to the contrary, and will observe that it has not in the least affected the result." In a private letter Dickens said of his old publishers, "What fools they are!"

*Household Words* and *All The Year Round* finally merged in the issue of Saturday, 4 June, 1859, after *All The Year Round* had been issued by itself for the previous five weeks. In some respects the two periodicals were identical – the same size, the same sober appearance, the same double-columned page, approximately the same mixture of articles, and the same price of twopence. The first issue of the new journal began, on the front page, with the opening

442

episode of a new novel he had been working on, *A Tale of Two Cities*. It was a beginning, too, in another sense. He had been thinking about the nature of the new periodical, and the defects of its predecessor, and had come to the conclusion that *All The Year Round* would always carry the serialisation of a novel (sometimes, in fact, two novels were published concurrently); he remembered how *The Old Curiosity Shop* had once saved *Master Humphrey's Clock*, and *Hard Times* had materially assisted *Household Words*. In fact novels were now to be the main feature of the new periodical, among them *The Moonstone* and *The Woman In White*, as if in obeisance to a culture which demanded more comfortable and leisurely reading.

By the time the first issue of *All The Year Round* appeared, Dickens had already written at least the first three weekly episodes of *A Tale of Two Cities*; he had in fact been working quickly upon it, after so long a period of gestation, and would continue to do so. But it did not spring fully-armed, as it were, from his imagination. He had always admired Carlyle's *History of the French Revolution*, and asked him to recommend stuitable books from which he could research the period; in reply Carlyle sent him a "cartload" of volumes from the London Library. Apparently Dickens read, or at least looked through, them all; it was his aim during the period of composition only to read books of the period itself, and so great was his enthusiasm for the story that it had indeed "taken possession" of him. He was a "slave" to it by the middle of May and managed to complete it by the beginning of October. Dickens's knowledge of the French Revolution was strengthened by Carlyle's wonderful history, which had appeared twenty-two years before, but it was a subject which seems always to have fascinated him. In truth his opinion on the matter never really changed, since it was his primary belief that the French *ancien régime* had itself created the conditions which provoked the revolution. ". . . It was a struggle on the part of

443

the people for social recognition and existence," Dickens had written in the *Examiner*, in the heady period of the Forties when Chartism itself seemed to bear witness to the threat of an English revolution of a similar kind. ". . . It was a struggle for the overthrow of a system of oppression, which in its contempt of all humanity, decency, and natural rights, and in the systematic degradation of the people, had trained them to be the demons that they showed themselves when they rose up and cast it down for ever." It was a social philosophy, or, rather, a social obsession, which he had emphasised in all his writings.

*A Tale of Two Cities* was unusual for Dickens, however, in the sense that he explicitly conceived it as a novel of story and incident rather than of character or dialogue. He was reading the first four of Tennyson's *Idylls of the King* through the summer months while he was working on the book, and that is perhaps why he also described it as ". . . a *picturesque* story". He was often susceptible to stray influences of this kind, although this in turn raises the troubled question of the sources which affected his composition of the novel. Troubled in the sense that he was now being directly charged with plagiarism – not plagiarism of Carlyle but of *The Dead Heart*, a play by Watts Phillips which opened three weeks before the conclusion of *A Tale of Two Cities* in *All The Year Round* and which had the same historical setting, much the same story and approximately the same climax. Nevertheless many other sources have also been suggested for it; among them Bulwer-Lytton's *Zanoni*, Matthew Lewis's *The Castle Spectre*, Arthur Young's *Travels in France*, Louis-Sébastien Mercier's *Tableau de Paris* and Beaumarchais's account of his imprisonment during the Terror (the last three were no doubt recommended by Carlyle, who also employed them). It was perhaps Carlyle who was the biggest influence at this time. There are linguistic echoes of Carlyle in the novel itself – "Indeed they were at sea, and the ship and crew were in peril of

444

tempest" is a notably Carlylean image of the state of France – but they would have been purely instinctive on Dickens's part. Just as his most powerful feelings were comprehended by him in terms of *words*, so the words of others most powerfully affected him. According to Carlyle's biographer, Froude, Dickens carried with him everywere a copy of *A History of the French Revolution* at the time of its publication in 1837; that he referred to it often is exemplified by a photograph of him later in life, reading upon the lawn of Gad's Hill Place, with an edition of that same volume in his hands. Dickens, in his preface to this novel, called it a "wonderful book". Certainly some episodes from *A Tale of Two Cities* are established upon Carlyle's own narrative, particularly the accounts of the revolutionary crowds and the events of the September massacres. Carlyle's history may also have prompted Dickens's use of hidden documents which play so large a part in the working out of his plot. But it would be hard to establish, from these borrowings, that Dickens derived anything like a "philosophy of history" from Carlyle; he took from him what he needed for his immediate purposes, that is all, and it seems likely that whatever general inspiration Dickens received from him in earlier days was now largely dissipated.

There is an interesting anecdote from this period, which perhaps expresses the nature of their relationship better than any disquisition. Carlyle went to hear Dickens read the trial scene from *The Pickwick Papers* and, when Dickens arrived on the platform, the two men nodded at each other. They were on the best of terms and, in fact, shared a similar sense of humour; one contemporary observed of this occasion that "I thought Carlyle would split, and Dickens was not much better. Carlyle sat on the front bench, and he haw-hawed right out, over and over again till he fairly exhausted himself. Dickens would read and then he would stop in order to give Carlyle a chance to stop . . ." During the interval Carlyle went backstage, and had a brandy-and-water. "Carlyle took his glass and nodding to Dickens said, 'Charley, you carry a whole company of actors under your hat.'" A compliment, of course, but there is little doubt that, even at this relatively late stage in Dickens's career, Carlyle could really only think of him as an entertainer, his constant bias against fiction leading him to disregard the more serious aspects of that pursuit. Dickens was too keen an observer not to realise this and, in turn, he treated Carlyle with an admiration and friendliness not unmixed with reserve. It would in any case have been quite alien to his own self-sufficiency and self-regard ever to take wholesale from Carlyle any of Carlyle's broader themes; in particular Dickens distrusted his love of the past and his worship of power, and it is noteworthy that both these aspects of Carlyle's history are missing from the novel.

But what of Dickens's general borrowings? Goldsmith, Smollett, Sterne, Marryat, Addison, Scott, Fielding, and Hogarth are only a few of the artists from whom Dickens is supposed to have taken effects, characters or scenes. Of course it is true that Hogarth, for example, provides Dickens with something very much like a mythology upon which he could draw when necessary; but, in general terms, the materials which Dickens stole or borrowed are never as important as the principles upon which they are transformed by him into the constituents of his own especial art. There are in fact two types of borrowing in his work. One is purely instinctive and unconscious, and it is fair to say that he would have been astonished by the number and variety of passages or characters he is alleged to have taken from previous novelists. The work of Smollett or Sterne, of Defoe or Addison, was simply part of the world in which he moved; one might as well say that he stole the image of Newgate from the actual Newgate Prison as to suggest that somehow he consciously plagiarised material from the favourite authors of his early years. The second type of borrowing is more deliberate. As in the case of Carlyle's *History of The French Revolution*, he took certain passages or incidents which struck him as being significant and then redeployed them. These passages were for him a source of inspiration; he abbreviated them, elaborated upon them, adapted them, but in all cases the original material is only of significance by reason of its place in the fresh combinations of Dickens's fiction. To suggest that they are "stolen" or "borrowed" or "plagiarised" is little different from stating that the words Dickens used are "stolen" or "borrowed" from the English language itself. So it is that in *A Tale of Two Cities* Dickens took from Carlyle what he needed and then refashioned it in the light of his own highly idiosyncratic or immediate preoccupations with imprisonment, with rebirth – and, more particularly, with self-sacrifice and the renunciation of love.

# Twenty-Nine

H E was planning to stay at Gad's Hill Place for the whole of this summer of 1859, while he carried on with the weekly instalments of *A Tale of Two Cities*. And how different his life was now. This was the first full year in which he was separated from his wife and, perhaps just as importantly, the first full year in which he maintained his isolation from such old companions as Mark Lemon. Friends saw and heard much less of him now, as if he had decided to deliver some kind of reproof to all those who had even a partial sympathy for Catherine. He had also contracted a heavy and prolonged cold, complete with sore throat and congested chest, which left him tired and enervated for weeks at a time.

These spring and summer months of 1859 marked the period after the first series of public readings, too, and as always the applause and brightness of his travelling life were succeeded by a period of increased gloom and disappointment. Somehow he needed to find a fresh source of excitement, some new stimulus – all the more reason, then, for his being taken into "complete possession" by the novel he had now started to write. For him it was the next best thing to *acting*, the excitement which he poured into his presentation of Sydney Carton and of this world of terror. He planned to stay in the country until October, time enough to complete *A Tale of Two Cities*, at which point he would be ready to set off on a second provincial reading tour. As always the most orderly and methodical of men, he quickly developed a routine; going to London on Monday afternoon and spending Tuesday at the office in Wellington Street, returning to Gad's Hill Place on Wednesday and working there on the novel until the next Monday. For a short time he was diverted from his main work by the story he had agreed to write for the *New York Ledger* for a thousand pounds – "Hunted Down" it was called, and it is not in itself a particularly memorable piece of fiction, except perhaps for its demonstration of Dickens's general fascination with the idea of the murderer and his particular interest in the case of Thomas Wainewright, the poisoner whom Oscar Wilde was later to immortalise in his much more interesting composition, "Pen, Pencil and Poison". There will soon be occasion to describe daily life at Gad's Hill Place, but it is enough at this point to suggest that, for Dickens, it was a sufficiently quiet and retired place to allow him to work undisturbed upon his novel. Of course there were visitors – Thomas Beard, W. H. Wills and Edmund Yates among them – but Georgina now organised the household very competently. The only incidents seem to have been those of ordinary rural life at this period in the nineteenth century; the celebration of various rustic occasions at the Falstaff Inn just across the road; the long country walks accompanied by Turk, a bloodhound, and Linda, a St Bernard. It was a very hot summer, and the nights were for Dickens particularly disagreeable; but he worked on, buoyed up by the success both of his serial and of *All The Year Round* itself.

In a letter in this period he asked Wills to send proofs of the current number of *A Tale of Two Cities* to Ellen Ternan (it is conceivable that he wanted her to see how he had portrayed Lucie Manette) but he was not inseparable from his new companion. There was, after all, his notion of travelling to America. A country which promised him *money*. It had been a New York journal which had paid him a thousand pounds for one short story, but there was the prospect of yet larger sums if he would agree to an extended reading tour of the major cities. His interest in what was already a much-discussed project had been revived by the arrival in England of James Fields, a young publisher and partner in the Boston firm of Ticknor, Reed and Fields; he was very enthusiastic about Dickens's work in any case, and came down to Gad's Hill Place specifically to persuade him that the time had come for him once more to take the United States by storm. It was something of a personal misfortune, then, that the Civil War should break out not long after. Dickens was not to visit the United States for another five years, at a time when his own health was much less able to withstand the rigours of the journey.

Even now he could not shake off the persistent low illness which so enervated him, and he decided to travel down to Broadstairs to see if the sea air and sea-water might help him to recover. He was with Wilkie Collins's brother, Charles, and seems to have diverted himself as much as he could under the circumstances; spending one evening, for example, enjoying the performance of a particularly bad mesmerist in the Assembly Rooms. But he was too ill to bathe in the sea, and his head felt "addled". Throughout these months, in fact, there is a general feeling of dilapidation and weariness about him; just before he left for Broadstairs he wrote a letter to Forster which ended with a prospect of death. "I am a wretched sort of creature in my way, but it is a way that gets on somehow. And all ways have the same finger-post at the head of them, and at every turning in them." This is very much the mood that suffuses the passages of *A Tale of Two Cities* which he was now writing, the mood emerging, too, in one of his characters who reveals that, ". . . as I draw closer and closer to the end, I travel in the circle, nearer and nearer

450

to the beginning". And how close this is to his own life, reading now in public as he had once performed in public as a child, once more haunted by the theme of imprisonment as he had been when his father was incarcerated in the Marshalsea. Could it be that Dickens himself felt that he was also close to the end of his own full circle, returning to the anxieties and loss of childhood?

Soon after Broadstairs he went to London for a few days, and then returned to Gad's Hill Place where, at the very beginning of October – just in time to prepare for the public readings a week later – he finished the novel. It was published in volume form by Chapman and Hall in the following month, although it seems less to require a book than a theatre. For in some sense it is the most dramatic of his novels; almost literally so, since its theatricality and rhetoric spring from his stated wish to act out the life and death of Sydney Carton. Clearly Dickens has learnt something from his public readings as well as from his amateur theatricals; the style is insistent, repetitive, and almost gestural. It is significant, too, that almost as soon as he had completed it he was making plans to have the story dramatised both in Paris and in London. The French scheme was abandoned because of the possibility of government censorship, but Tom Taylor adapted the novel for the Lyceum under the management of Madame Celeste. Dickens was in fact so eager to provide a proper dramatic version that he played a large role in the rehearsals – there is evidence that he practically directed the play – and even changed the famous ending specifically for theatrical purposes. The last lines of the novel, " 'It is a far, far better thing that I do, than I have ever done; it is a far, far better rest that I go to than I have ever known", were now supplemented in the stage version with a final "Farewell Lucie, Farewell Life!". *Curtain*. The fact that the Lyceum was only a hundred yards away from his office made his participation in the play all the easier; we must imagine him walking briskly down Wellington Street, recognised by those he passed, and crossing to the other side of the street just before he reached the Strand. The theatre is still there, a dark, grimy adjunct to a now undistinguished thoroughfare.

And of the story itself? In some ways a dark one, filled with images of horror and of destruction, of dirt and disease, of imprisonment and violent death. The central image is one of resurrection, but this encompasses the stealing of dead bodies from their graves as well as the more spiritual resuscitation which Sydney Carton so much longs for. This is a world of enormous shadows, of the setting sun, of night; the only illumination occurs in the glare of the French Revolution itself, as if the only alternative to the darkness of despair lies in the rage and destructiveness of that event. And yet in his fiction (as opposed to his journalism) Dickens never really adopts an attitude without at the same time embracing its reverse and it cannot be expected, particularly at this time of his life, that he would be able to resolve all of those contradictory impulses and ambiguous attitudes that comprise so large a part of his genius. The force of the novel springs from its exploration of darkness and death but its beauty derives from Dickens's real sense of transcendence, from his ability to see the sweep of destiny. "Eye to eye, voice to voice, hand to hand, heart to heart, these two children of the Universal Mother, else so wide apart and differing, have come together on the dark highway, to repair home together, and to rest in her bosom." Forster was wrong to say that Dickens had no "city of the mind", no inner resource to combat the changes of the world; he had a sense of the numinous, and he had a sense, too, of that common fate which transcends all social divisions and diurnal battles. This, in the year after the start of his new life, is what emerges most clearly from one of his shortest and most powerful novels.

The brief provincial tour began on 10 October with a reading in Ipswich and ended on the 27th with one at Cheltenham; fourteen performances in all, punctuated by visits to Gad's Hill Place or Tavistock House, and of which nothing need be reported except the usual prodigious enthusiasm and Dickens's own restless energy. He went back to Gad's Hill Place at the conclusion of the readings in order to celebrate Katie's twentieth birthday (Forster and Wilkie Collins joined him there) and then at the beginning of November he returned to London and to Tavistock House; he had decided to remain here at least until Easter, and to lease Gad's Hill Place in the interim. Now that he had returned for the duration, he at once set to work; not only to clear up the vast arrears of correspondence but also to settle down to his regular periodical business. In particular he wanted to decide well in advance the length and nature of the serial stories which would follow *A Tale of Two Cities*, to be completed at the end of the month; he had already arranged for Wilkie Collins's *The Woman In White* to begin in *All The Year Round* immediately after the conclusion of his own story.

He was busy in another sense, too, since, between reading tours and between novels, he went back to a largely public role. He visited a commercial travellers' school in Pinner the day before making a speech to the Commercial Travellers' Association, for example, but even on this occasion he made a reference to the dominant note in his life at this time. "Gentlemen, we should remember tonight that we are all Travellers, and that every round we take converges nearer and nearer to our home; that all our little journeyings bring us together to one certain end . . ." Death. After his speech the orphan children of dead commercial travellers were paraded around the dining hall and "excited the deepest interest"; they sang several songs and then a toast was given to Dickens himself ". . . who appeared overcome by the manner in which his health was received". Now it was time for his annual series of Christmas readings in St Martin's Hall (his last performances here, since the hall burned down eight months later), and then four days after Christmas he travelled to Wales to see, and to report on, a terrible shipwreck of the *Royal Charter* off the coast near Llanallgo. The local clergyman had played the major part in retrieving the bodies of the dead and in a little Welsh church Dickens ". . . remarked again and again . . . on the awful nature of the scene of death he had been required so closely to familiarise himself with . . ." Death. He stayed in Wales for four days.

When he returned to London, the long illness from the earlier part of that year manifested itself once more and, on doctor's orders, he was forced to remain in the city. So it was in this first month of the New Year, closeted in London, that he took advantage of an idea which seems to have occurred to him when he addressed the Commercial Travellers three weeks before – for it was now that he took on the persona of an "Uncommercial Traveller" in order to write a series of essays for *All The Year Round*. Over the next few months he wrote essays in which he raised once more the spectre of a lost past. The spectre of lost childhood. In a letter from this period he said that ". . . the old time never grows older or younger with me". It remains as it was, always present and always being invoked. As it is in these essays themselves, sixteen of them written between January and October of 1860 – essays concerning the Paris Morgue and the bodies of the dead; concerning broken sleep; concerning his lonely walks through the streets of London at night; concerning sad and dismal metropolitan neighbourhoods; concerning suicides and paupers in Wapping; concerning the figure of "the very queer small boy" who is the spirit of his own infancy; concerning the lonely chambers in the Inns of Court; concerning the deserted churches in the City of London,

St James Garlickhithe, St Michael Paternoster Row, St Martin Vintry, St Michael Queenhithe; concerning his visit to his childhood haunts from which he returns with his early imaginations ". . . so worn and torn, so much the wiser and so much the worse!"; concerning the grim and frightening stories of his childhood nurse. These are chronicles of sometimes desolate and unhappy wandering, filled with nostalgia, solitude, weariness and melancholia (even his letters in this period are much quieter and much plainer, less buoyant with the vivacity of Dickens's inventiveness). The wanderings of a man haunted by his past and by images of death – and we recall once more the words in *A Tale of Two Cities*, "For, as I draw closer and closer to the end, I travel in the circle, nearer and nearer to the beginning." And yet how much Dickens still sees and notices of the world around him, how much he is still part of his world even if the London which he resurrects in his "Uncommercial" essays is a faded or faint city with nothing of that crowded and almost "modern" life which burgeoned during the Sixties. These are the essays of a man who remembers an earlier time with infinite longing and infinite regret, a writer who could not help but pour out these thoughts between the writing of *A Tale of Two Cities* and the writing of *Great Expectations*.

He went down to Gad's Hill Place in April but then was back at Tavistock House where he wanted to remain until June. But he no longer liked this house, this harbour of so many memories. He wanted to get rid of it. He wanted to sell it. A few weeks later he began to suffer from rheumatism which attacked his left side, yet another involuntary memory of childhood, and so he decided to leave London a little earlier than he had planned in order to recuperate in the country air. The month before he had also been attacked by neuralgia of the face; all these were in fact harbingers of serious ill-health, but they were signs which he chose to disparage or to ignore. And now another part of his past was about to leave him. His daughter, Kate, was going away from home – and this the daughter who in manner and in temperament was most like her father, who had the same slow pulse and the same occasionally fiery temper, the same nervous habits and the same ready wit. She had always been her father's favourite, the one who was pushed forward by the others to ask for special dispensations, but now she was leaving him. She had decided to marry Charles Collins, the younger brother of Wilkie; not because she was in love with him, she explained later, but simply because she wanted to get away from "an unhappy home". Dickens was very much opposed to the match, not least because he was unsure of Collins himself; he had already employed him to write for *Household Words* and *All The Year Round*, and thought enough of him to take him to Broadstairs with him ten months before, but for one reason or another he objected to Kate's marriage to him. It has been suggested that he was homosexual. Kate herself seems to have told her father that her husband was impotent. Certainly they had no children, and in addition he suffered from a mysterious, wasting illness throughout most of their married life. He was also a timid and rather melancholy man, who in later years seems to have wilted under Dickens's fierce glare.

There were to be family problems of other kinds, too, and only a few days after Kate's marriage Dickens's brother, Alfred, died of pleurisy. He had been an engineer working in Manchester, and the only one of Dickens's brothers to have made anything of his life – Dickens had already given up on Frederick and totally rejected Augustus, both of whom had been almost criminally careless with money and both of whose lives seemed like some broken reflection of their father's. Now Alfred was dead, leaving behind a widow, Helen, and five children. Dickens went up to Manchester at once, and brought his brother's family back with him to London. The funeral was held at Highgate, where John Dickens was buried, and then Dickens returned to Gad's Hill Place with the bereaved family. He found a farmhouse nearby where Helen and the children could stay while he looked around for a London house, all of which activity meant that he was preoccupied with their affairs for some weeks. It is even possible that the five children reappeared in *Great Expectations*, the novel he was soon to begin, as the five lozenge-shaped tombs in Cooling Churchyard (there is in fact a row of six stone lozenges there). Not an indication that he wished them dead, not that, but rather a sign of how powerfully the events of his life intruded into his fiction, even the most stern and obvious realities being transformed into the shape of his own fears and preoccupations. Another part of his past was about to be abandoned, too; after having lived there for some nine years, he was now in the process of selling Tavistock House. He was planning to spend the summer and autumn months in Gad's Hill Place and then renting a furnished house in London from February to March.

So this is what it had come to by the late summer of 1860. His favourite daughter married and living away from home, his brother dead, his old house sold. In addition, his mother was now dying. All these were marks of loss or separation, and, suffering from low spirits, he now found that he could not sleep; and it was at this low point, at the beginning of August, that he began "meditating a new book", as if the only cure for this depression of spirits was a return to his imaginary world. "But we must not think of old times as sad times," he explained to Mrs Watson in September, "or regard them as anything but the fathers and mothers of the present. We must all climb steadily up the mountain after the talking bird, the singing tree, and the yellow water, and must all bear in mind that the previous climbers who were scared into looking back got turned into black stone." DON'T LOOK BACK. That is the sentiment here, and it can be seen to act as some kind of anticipation of the novel he was to begin three weeks later, *Great Expectations*; a novel in which he is engaged in exorcising the influence of his past by rewriting it. The talking bird and the singing tree sound like the very emblems of his fiction, but he can only reach them by climbing steadily forward and ignoring the path which has brought him to this point. DON'T LOOK BACK.

And, in the month when he handed out this injunction, he burnt all of his past correspondence. It was part of the general "clear up" necessitated by the selling of Tavistock House, but it has wider ramifications as yet another example of his desire to resist his past, to efface it, to rewrite it, to turn his separation from his wife and the start of his new life into something much more real, more tangible. He burnt the letters in the field behind Gad's Hill Place; Mamie and two of her brothers brought out basketful after basketful of them, from Carlyle, Thackeray, Tennyson, Collins, George Eliot . . . the letters of twenty years. Mamie asked him to keep some of them, but he refused. No. They all had to be burnt. And as he completed this sacrificial pyre it began to rain very heavily; ". . . I suspect my correspondence of having overcast the face of the Heavens." In his new life there is almost some kind of hatred of the past.

At the end of September he began work on *Great Expectations*; or, rather, he began writing another essay in the guise of the "Uncommercial Traveller". Forster had suggested to him that he might try his hand once more at the humour which had been so much a part of the sketches of his early years (it was Forster, too, who had deplored the relative absence of humour in *A Tale of Two Cities*), but as he started writing in the old manner there occurred to him what he called "a very fine, new, and grotesque idea". ". . . I begin to doubt," he went on, "whether I had not better cancel the little paper, and reserve the notion for a new book . . . I can see the whole of a serial revolving on it, in a most singular and comic manner . . ." Forster states that this "grotesque" idea contained the germ of the relationship between Pip and Magwitch which was to be at the centre of *Great Expectations*. This is certainly possible, but it is also true that the actual form of *Great Expectations* had much more to do with the troubled state of *All The Year Round* than with Dickens's own creative imperatives. He had begun the story almost as soon as the "idea" occurred to him, apparently believing that he was starting work on the basis of the usual twenty numbers, but then certain commercial considerations altered his plans. The problem lay with Charles Lever's novel, *A Day's Ride: A Life's Romance*, which was then being serialised in the periodical but was proving to be a heavy liability in terms of falling sales. Something had to be done quickly before *All The Year Round* suffered what might have been irretrievable damage to its circulation. So, on 2 October, only a few days after he had begun the new novel, Dickens decided that it would have to be written as a weekly serial for the periodical and that it should be of approximately the same length as *A Tale of Two Cities* – this despite his previous complaints about the shortness and difficulty of weekly instalments. So was *Great Expectations* born. By 4 October he had determined upon a name and started work upon it in its new format – the first episode was to be published at the beginning of December, and he wanted to have at least two months of the book in hand before that date. At least he had his broad theme already prepared; it was to concern the adventures of a "boy-child, like David" but, in order to avoid any kind of unconscious repetition, ". . . I read *David Copperfield* again the other day, and was affected by it to a degree you would hardly believe . . ." So did his past, inserted within the narrative of the earlier novel, still haunt him; even now as he was beginning the life of Pip,

459

an anxious and guilt-ridden child, sensitive to the point of hysteria and altogether a very queer, small boy.

By the middle of the month he had completed the first four chapters, so spontaneously and so instinctively that he dispensed with working notes and barely used anything from the notebook which he still kept (all he took from his memoranda are a few names). Then he went down to Gad's Hill Place in order to work undisturbed, and by the end of October he had completed seven chapters; he was back in his old routine, of fierce work followed by equally fierce exercise, and at least for a while he seemed more cheerful. Yet he was no longer so resilient, no longer able to maintain the same rate of composition. He felt himself to be overworking; he was suffering once more from pains in his left side, which seem to have been an extension of his summer rheumatism; and he could not sleep. The longevity of these pains in his left side suggests that even now he was suffering the preliminary symptoms of the stroke which would finally kill him. And yet, he said at the beginning of December, ". . . I MUST write". He was now in his fiftieth year, growing a little bald, unwell, driven by no stern economic necessity but nevertheless driven by something. ". . . I MUST write." He was feeling so ill that he went back to Gad's Hill Place, and here he continued with his self-imposed routine of work. ". . . I MUST write" were words he had used in a letter from his country "retreat", and the chapters he wrote during this period of ill-health, effort and exhaustion are invested with a strange, hallucinatory, murderous tone. Orlick's irrational attack upon Mrs Joe Gargery, as if he were a surrogate for Pip's own suppressed feelings of rage and hurt; allusions to George Barnwell, the murdering apprentice made famous in song and story; Pip's confession to Biddy of "the madness of my heart"; the appearance of the strange Mr Jaggers; Pip's last visit to Miss Havisham before his departure and his entering into his great expectations. The humour is here as much as in any of Dickens's earlier books, but it is darker now and somehow more vicious. It was bitterly cold at Gad's Hill Place, and he was still feeling very unwell; the thermometer was well below freezing, the pipes stopped, the water in the bedroom jugs froze and broke the crockery.

He spent Christmas Day with the household (because of the low temperature they could barely sit at the dinner table), and then on the following day he went back to London; primarily this was in order to be close to his doctor, Frank Beard (who was Thomas Beard's brother). It was warmer in London and, in addition, Beard advised him not to continue his "commuting" between Gad's Hill Place and Wellington Street, the new bachelor quarters he had taken up. So he stayed in his quarters at the office, writing on, pleased by the early success of his serial which was hailed at once as a return to his old "humorous" manner. In fact he stayed in London until the middle of January, while the rest of the household were still ensconced at Gad's Hill Place – doing nothing but work, swallow his medicine, and take a stall at the theatre every night. No doubt he was seeing Ellen Ternan (although no word of her escapes into his correspondence) but his principal male companion in these wintry London days was Wilkie Collins, whose irregular love life Dickens now viewed with equanimity. In fact he often visited Collins's lodgings in Harley Street where the young writer lived with Caroline Graves and her daughter, Harriet; Dickens even invented affectionate nicknames for them.

While he stayed in London Dickens's progress on *Great Expectations* was rapid. "As to the planning out from week to week," he told Forster later, "nobody can imagine what the difficulty is, without trying. But, as in all such cases, when it is overcome the pleasure is proportionate." He had decided to divide the novel, like its predecessor, *A Tale of Two Cities*, into three books; he had issued the previous

461

novel in monthly numbers as well as in the weekly instalments of the periodical, but the experiment had not been a success and Dickens did not repeat it; *Great Expectations* accordingly appeared only in thirty-six consecutive numbers of *All The Year Round*. His innate and instinctive orderliness was such, however, that the three books (or "Stages", as he called them) were almost exactly the same length even though the weekly portions sometimes varied in quantity. And he had not entirely forgotten his original plan to write his usual twenty monthly numbers; he still calculated the series on a monthly basis, and paginated afresh at the beginning of each month's manuscript.

By the middle of January his health had improved sufficiently for him to return to Gad's Hill Place, and for the next few weeks he travelled back and forth in his usual manner; although at first much of his time in London was taken up with house-hunting rather than with writing. It was his plan to spend the next five months in rented accommodation in the capital – primarily for Mamie's benefit, since she enjoyed the delights of the "season" – and it did not take him long to find a "really delightful house" at 3 Hanover Terrace, facing Regent's Park. Here he wrote, went to the office, gave dinners, met his friends; and from here too he emerged to take his long walks through London, that ambulatory routine he had begun in his childhood and of which he had never grown tired. Four days before he moved into Hanover Terrace, in fact, he took just such a walk from his offices in Wellington Street – along the Strand which passed Wellington Street, then down Whitehall to Westminster, then through Westminster along the Thames to Millbank; ". . . the day was so beautifully bright and warm," he told de Cerjat in a letter the following day, "that I thought I would walk on by Millbank, to see the river. I walked straight on *for three miles* on a splendid broad esplanade overhanging the Thames, with immense factories, railway works, and whatnot erected on it, and with the strangest beginnings and ends of wealthy streets pushing themselves into the very Thames. When I was a rower on that river, it was all broken ground and ditch, with here and there a public-house or two, an old mill, and a tall chimney. I had never seen it in any state of transition, though I suppose myself to know this rather large city as well as anyone in it . . ." This was the very area where, in *David Copperfield*, the prostitute Martha is tracked – Dickens now, on the last day of January 1861, following her route in a neighbourhood which he had then described as ". . . oppressive, sad, and solitary by night, as any about London. There were neither wharves nor houses on the melancholy waste of road near the great blank prison. A sluggish ditch deposited its mud at the prison walls. Coarse grass and rank weeds straggled over all the marshy land in the vicinity. In one part, carcases of houses, inauspiciously begun and never finished, rotted away. In another, the ground was cumbered with rusty iron monsters of steam-boilers, wheels, cranks, pipes, furnaces, paddles, anchors, diving-bells, windmill-sails and I know not what strange objects . . ." But now this area of wooden piles, and rotten buildings, and discarded machinery, had been transformed into the broad esplanade along which Dickens walked.

How much London had changed in just ten years of his life. Where once this place had been no more than the outer reaches of a tumbledown eighteenth-century city, it was now the harbinger of the modern capital of the late nineteenth century – cleaner, more stately, more organised. The great arterial sewers north and south of the river were now in place, and the Thames itself was no longer the open cesspool which it had been in the earlier decades of the century. Seventeenth and eighteenth-century London was now being altered beyond recognition by street improvements; cut up and excavated by the encroachment of the railways; razed in the commercial redevelopment of the City. Even the early nineteenth-century London of Nash was itself being destroyed in the course of the enormous transition through which the capital now was passing. Queen Victoria Street cut through from Blackfriars to the Bank of England. Cannon Street extended. Farringdon Street. Garrick Street. New Oxford Street. Clerkenwell Road. Southwark Street. All now being built on the "open cut" or "cut and cover" methods, which turned parts of London into vast building sites of dust and wooden scaffolding. Westminster Bridge and Blackfriars Bridge rebuilt. The Hungerford Suspension Bridge torn down. Hungerford Market torn up. Cannon Street terminus. Victoria Station. St Pancras. Broad Street. The line from Shoreditch to Liverpool Street. And, most spectacular of all, the underground railway from Paddington to Farringdon Street was opened in 1863 – the vast building programme which this particular development entailed meant that much of the old Clerkenwell, described in *Oliver Twist*, was gone for ever. For inhabitants like Dickens, who had known London since the Thirties or Forties, it might well have seemed as if the old city were being extirpated and a new one erected in its place. It is only in the earliest photographs of London, those taken in the Thirties and Forties, that it is still possible to see the lineaments of the city in which Smollett lived and Defoe worked; the stillness and quiet of these first photographs truly give the impression of a place rescued from the oblivion of lost time. But later photographs, of the Sixties and Seventies, show a different capital; the advertising hoardings, the omnibuses carrying men in stove-pipe hats, the cabs, all the rush and blur of the traffic, evoke a city much closer to modern times. Much closer to ourselves. The old and the new lived precariously together just for a moment – this moment, with Dickens striding between the two.

And so, even as Charles Dickens strolled along the new esplanade of the embankment, London was being transformed. It was no longer the city which he had known as a child and young man. This was now becoming the London of wide streets and underground railways, the orderliness and symmetry of the old Georgian capital quite displaced by the imperialist neo-Gothic of mid-Victorian public buildings. Something of the old compactness had gone for ever and with it, too, the particular gracefulness and colour of the previous century. In its place rose a city which was more massive, more closely controlled, more organised. The metropolis was much larger but it was becoming emptier, as the suburbs around London took up some of the displaced population, and it was also much more anonymous; it was a more public city, the seat of empire and of commerce, but it was also a less human one. It is not possible to see Ebenezer Scrooge or Miss Havisham, Fagin or the Artful Dodger, in the new thoroughfares and squares of the 1860s; this was no longer the wild and barren place of Dickens's imagination, nor was it the extravagant and eccentric locale where all his characters had met and moved together. And yet Dickens never ceased to live in that old city. Even as he walked along the Thames Embankment, he was still walking with Pip through the city of forty years before. Dickens was observing the new city at a time when his own imagination was dwelling in the older London of *Great Expectations*, when his own vision was of a lost past. For the old city was the one in which he always lived. It was the city that had made him. It was the city which had almost destroyed him but which had then raised him up. It was the city of his dreams and the city of his imagination. In his work it is the city that will live for ever. But, with all the change around him, did he think now that he, too, was part of a vanished dispensation — that he, in this new city, was himself growing old?

# *Thirty*

O N his next birthday, perhaps as a present to himself,
Dickens bought Mary Green's *Lives of the Princesses
of England* and Agnes Strickland's *Lives of the Queens of
England*. On the same day he held a dinner for himself at
3 Hanover Terrace; his old friend, Beard, was among the
guests and most of his family were also present. His son,
Charley, had now returned from China and was working
in the City — he had in fact already had an effect upon
his father's *Great Expectations*, in which the young Herbert
Pocket was originally a "merchant" who was to trade
". . . to China for teas". But Dickens struck out these references at proof stage. He did not strike out a description of
Herbert, however, which might almost be that of Dickens
about his son, "There was something wonderfully hopeful
about his general air, and something that at the same time
whispered to me that he would never be very successful
or rich". It is worth noting in this place that Dickens was
angered and distressed by the fact that his son was still
intent upon marrying Bessie Evans, the daughter of the
publisher whom Dickens had utterly rejected and abjured
ever since the time of the separation. Was fiction one way
for Dickens, then, to express all those aggressive impulses
which could not emerge in ordinary waking life? Frank
was at home, too; Dickens, despairing of his competence
in business matters, had taken him on as a general fac-

totum in the *All The Year Round* offices. Mamie of course was present, as was Georgina who, in the 1861 Census, was described somewhat unflatteringly as "servant-housekeeper". Kate and Charles Collins were living in the apartment of Kate's mother-in-law at Clarence Terrace. Dickens still did not think much of that marriage, either, and at the same time he was being compelled to subsidise his other children from a distance; Walter had already been accruing large debts in India, and in the previous months Dickens had sent him £115. 14s. Then there was his brother Alfred's widow, Helen, and her five children; and then there was his mother in her senility. It is no wonder that in a letter the following month he was describing how ". . . I am quite weighed down and loaded and chained in life" – and this just after he had written in *Great Expectations* of the convicts who were ". . . handcuffed together, and had irons on their legs . . ." In the narrative at this point Pip tries imaginatively to understand the plight of these chained criminals, but surely we can see behind the text itself the shadow of Dickens identifying himself with the prisoner if not with the outcast.

He was being pressed in by his own engagements also. He wanted to complete *Great Expectations* as quickly as possible – he had a date early in June in mind – but his work upon it was disrupted by a series of six readings which he had undertaken to give in St James's Hall in March and April. When the time came to give them, some people in the front row ". . . plainly saw the tears provoked by the wonderful reception given to Dickens directly he stepped upon the platform". One member of the audience at St James's Hall was Thomas Beard himself, but he always sat at the end of the row and was too shy to go "backstage" in order to drink brandy and water with Dickens. He did not wish to impose upon his old friend. He was both too stalwart and too bashful to do so, and perhaps a better companion for Dickens than some of his more effusive

467

contemporaries. As Thackeray said at this time, "There is nobody to tell him when anything goes wrong. Dickens is the Sultan, and Wills is his Grand Vizier". At the end of the readings Dickens was delighted to have made five hundred pounds, after all expenses had been paid, but nevertheless he was relieved to be able to concentrate on the continuing story of Pip and Magwitch. At some point it seems that, for quietness, he took rooms near the Five Bells public house in New Cross (he had stayed in lodgings here once before), and by the end of April he was well into the third "stage" of Pip's expectations and his knowledge that all of his wealth and his status as a "gentleman" had come from the pocket of the convict Magwitch.

He continued to write and yet he was almost constantly in pain. He was suffering from what he called "facial neuralgia", and was too ill on 20 May to take the chair at the annual dinner of the Newsvendors' Benevolent Association (Wilkie Collins, rather reluctantly, took his place). But he was able, two days later, to hire a Thames steamer so that he might more accurately convey the chase and recapture of Magwitch on the river. Forster and other friends joined him on this excursion and Forster noticed that ". . . he seemed to have no care . . . except to enjoy their enjoyment and entertain them with his own in shape of a thousand whims and fancies; but his sleepless observation was at work all the time, and nothing had escaped his keen vision on either side of the river." When he returned, Dickens made out a list of the tides and their times. On the following day he went down to Dover for a week, principally so that he could work undisturbed on the last chapters of the novel but also because he hoped the sea air might cure his neuralgia. He went for his customary walks (on one day he actually walked from Dover to Folkestone and then back again, a distance of some fourteen miles) but he was concentrating upon the book so that he might finish it by the middle of the following month. "I work here, like a Steam Engine, and walk like Captain Barclay", the "Captain" being a famous pedestrian who once walked one thousand miles in one thousand hours. And, by the time he returned to London, he was indeed coming to the end of his story; in order to help himself with the construction of its last scenes, he drew up memoranda on dates and characters which had already occurred. He had been expecting to finish the book on 12 June and so orderly were his calculations that he in fact completed his narrative just the day before. More remarkable still is the fact that his neuralgic pains vanished as soon as he had finished his work.

Dickens now returned to spend the summer at Gad's Hill Place; it was his custom to come up to London on Wednesday, in order to arrange the "make-up" of the next issue of *All The Year Round*, but most of the week was spent in Kent. The younger boys were also back from school for the summer, and now there were opportunities for cricket, for country expeditions, for walks, for hours on the lawn. But of course for Dickens there also had to be time for work; there never was a period in which he could be truly said to relax, and even during these quiet summer months he began assiduously and earnestly to prepare for the series of readings which were to begin in the autumn. For a long time he had been wanting to devise a reading out of *David Copperfield* and, now, with almost four months before the start of his tour, he had found the perfect opportunity to do so. In the same period he prepared reading scripts which were provisionally entitled "Nicholas Nickleby at the Yorkshire Schools", "Mr Chops, the Dwarf", "Mr Bob Sawyer's Party", "The Bastille Prisoner" and "Great Expectations". The last two were never performed but all of the others were, the reading version of *David Copperfield* being some two hours in length while the extract from *Nicholas Nickleby* ran for one and a quarter hours.

Yet even as he planned for the reading tour he was

disturbed by news that threatened to ruin it before it had begun: Arthur Smith, his manager, had grown dangerously ill; Dickens was greatly worried and did not know what to do. He could make no definite plans while Smith lay sick but, on the other hand, he did not want to employ anyone in his place; it was only when Dickens perceived that Smith would not recover that he decided to employ a certain Arthur Headland. And then Smith died — the friend who Dickens said was his "right arm". The day after Dickens returned from the funeral, his brother-in-law, Henry Austin, the man to whom he had often turned for support and advice, died also. More deaths crowding in. And yet he declared that the coming readings ". . . must be fought out, like all the rest of life". This was always Dickens's reaction in the face of death — to fight. The world was one in which we are ". . . all to suffer, and strive, and die"; but for Dickens the emphasis is upon the *striving*. In fact he felt the death of Arthur Smith much more keenly than that of Henry Austin. Nothing now could be the same, and, without him, he felt quite lost and helpless. Smith had arranged everything, had dealt with tickets and audiences, with transport and with hotels. What he also missed, in his absence, was the sense "of compactness and comfort about me" which was so important to him in the long and arduous travels around the United Kingdom.

So it was that in the autumn of the year he set out upon the second series of readings which, he feared, would be dull and wearisome without the presence of Arthur Smith. The tour was to last until the end of January and was to encompass places as far apart as Brighton and Edinburgh, Hastings and Preston. But it did not begin well. The audience at Norwich, the first stop, "were not magnetic", he reported, by which he meant that there was no current of energy between himself and his listeners; sometimes he described this in moral terms as a "common bond", but as often as not it seems to have been almost a more tangible link. It is significant, too, how on this second major tour he was able subtly to discriminate between the responses of the various audiences whom he addressed, which suggests in turn how much his own performance depended upon his "peculiar personal relation" with each audience. It was for him almost a physical charge, a surge of energy that lent him the power to impersonate the scores of characters whom he "read" each night. Even now it was beginning to take its physical toll, however; one child was allowed into his dressing room after a reading in Colchester at the beginning of November, and even many years later remembered the way Dickens ". . . in his shirt-sleeves, was walking rapidly up and down, as a means of getting through with the cooling and calming process . . ." Later he ate a large supper but ". . . was absolutely never still, mentally or physically . . ."

In the middle of November he returned to Kent; he had arranged for a break of ten days in the intense schedule of readings in order that he might work on that year's Christmas issue of *All The Year Round*, but then once more he was back on his travels. It was from this time forward, however, that all the problems he foresaw in the absence of Arthur Smith began to plague him. It was in the third week of November that the readings started to go wrong, with an accident at Newcastle-upon-Tyne. The audience "were all very still over Smike" when the gas apparatus which illuminated Dickens fell over; one woman screamed and ran towards him, and there was "a terrible wave" in the crowd. But these were times when Dickens was effortlessly able to keep his composure. He spoke out loudly to the woman, "There's nothing the matter, I assure you; don't be alarmed; pray sit down." The panic subsided, the equipment was reassembled, and the reading continued. But it had been a difficult moment; the packed halls, the excitement of the crowd (often seeming to

471

amount to hysteria), the difficulties of exit, the fragility of the gas equipment, meant that such occasions carried a constant risk of fire or fatal crushing. And it was at this time, of all times, that Dickens had cause to regret Arthur Smith's absence even more. Handbills advertising the readings went astray; the wrong readings were advertised; printed cards contained the wrong details. Dickens, who of all people demanded the utmost precision and rigour in business arrangements, was as concerned as he was enraged.

By the end of the reading tour, in January 1862, he could not sleep and was ". . . dazed and worn by gas and heat . . ." He came back again for rest to Gad's Hill Place, but in February he decamped with his family to another London residence which he had taken for the season (not rented on this occasion, but exchanged for Gad's Hill Place), 16 Hyde Park Gate South, just a few yards from Kensington Gardens. But he did not like it all all – ". . . this odious little house," he called it, this "London box". And his work was not over yet. He had agreed to give further readings in London in the Hanover Square Rooms, and these were to continue until the end of June; in other words, he had characteristically determined to keep himself occupied the whole time he remained in the capital. Clearly he had no thought of rest or recreation – perhaps for the sake of the money, perhaps for the sake of the applause and glare to which he had now become accustomed, more likely for the potent combination of all of these. He also had plans to begin work on a new novel, for which characters and subjects had already occurred to him – a strange father and son he had seen in Chatham, "Found Drowned" posters by the London wharves – but it proved impossible to work in the little house in Kensington. So after breakfast he left each morning for the office, no doubt making a habit of walking the four miles to Wellington Street, and spent many evenings in the company of friends like Yates, and Wills, and Collins. He was now also well acquainted with two other men who were to become almost "fixtures" in his life from this time forward, men for whom he had the strangest affection, and whose friendship casts another light upon Dickens's own character.

The most interesting of these two companions was Charles Fechter, an actor of French parentage whose strong accent had not inhibited his success upon the London stage. He had first achieved that success with his portrayal of Hamlet at the Princess's Theatre in 1861, and the remark of a theatre employee on that occasion is still worth recording today – "Sir, it's wonderful. We all know Mr Kean. Mr Kean was great. But with 'im '*Amlet* was a tragedy, with Mr Fechter it's quite another thing. He has raised it to a mellerdrama." In fact melodrama was not quite Fechter's forte; he was a remarkable actor on the stage of the period precisely because of his ability to subdue the rant and gestural theatrics which were so common amongst his contemporaries and to replace them with something which seemed at the time much more "natural-istic", more "romantic", more "picturesque". These were precisely the qualities to which Dickens aspired in his own amateur dramatics, and it is perhaps not surprising – given Dickens's own sensitive condition during this period – that he first recognised Fechter's genius when he saw him playing a lover. He had seen him in Paris. "He was making love to a woman," Dickens told a friend, "and he so ele-vated her as well as himself by the sentiment in which he enveloped her, that they trod in a purer ether, and in another sphere, quite lifted out of the present. 'By heavens!' I said to myself, 'a man who can do this can do anything.' I never saw two people more purely and instantly elevated by the power of love." It is hard not to think of Dickens's own situation at this time in his extraordinary attachment to a man who could play the elevated and romantic lover, the man who took love into a purer sphere than that of earthly pleasure.

Another constant visitor to Gad's Hill Place was Henry Chorley, a music critic and occasional novelist; he was on such good terms with Dickens, in fact, that he was one of the few men who was able to invite himself down to Kent for weekends. Yet he was a stranger partner for Dickens than Fechter – Chorley was a mild, broken-down, sad bachelor in late middle-age (he was five years older than Dickens). He had a thin voice, a shuffling gait, and a depressive temperament which he never could quite quench with drink. Yet Dickens understood him, liked him and tried on all occasions to cheer him. By all accounts Chorley was a disappointed man who thought he had failed in life, and no aspect of a man's character was more likely to win Dickens's instinctive care and sympathy; we need go no further than his fiction to recognise to what extent Dickens could "identify" with those who had been vanquished in the "battle of life". Of course he himself had never failed, but the fact that he had spent half a lifetime terrified of any such eventuality meant that he could be wonderfully generous with those who had not been able to avert it. But there was another tie between men otherwise so dissimilar in their destinies. Chorley, too, was almost entirely self-educated, thwarted from his early vocation by a mother who put him to work in a mercantile office when he was still a boy. Here, in this congruence of early life, we see also one of the roots of Dickens's sympathy – no story could stir him as much as that of maternal mistreatment, and there were times indeed when he seemed to treat Chorley almost as some sad alter ego, some version of Charles Dickens if Charles Dickens had failed. So it was that, during these spring months in London, he and Chorley would make long expeditions together – on one occasion, for example, after listening to Arthur

Sullivan's music for *The Tempest*, walking from Crystal Palace back to Chorley's house in Knightsbridge.

Yet as soon as the period of house exchange was over, and he could remove himself from the disagreeable "box" in Kensington, he returned to Gad's Hill Place for the summer; another summer of sports in the afternoon (cricket in the field behind the house or croquet on the front lawn), and evening games of whist, of riddles, or of conundrums. But these idle pleasures were not to be enjoyed for long since, in June, Georgina Hogarth became ill. Dickens described her condition as "degeneration of the heart", or "aneurism of the aorta", and in fact she grew so seriously ill that he began to doubt whether she would be able to recover. She was low-spirited, confused, and suffered great pain in her chest. Dickens himself, seeing the rapid decline of the woman who had stood by him during the time of the separation, went around in an "altogether dazed" condition. She had recovered a little by the end of June, but was still very ill indeed and suffered something of a relapse towards the end of July. But was his own anxiety at Georgina's condition in part amplified by guilt? Why was it that Georgina's "heart" had been so suddenly afflicted? It has been suggested that she had heard, or knew, of something about her brother-in-law's life which deeply disturbed her. This would be merely fanciful speculation, were it not for the fact that in this very period of Georgina's illness Dickens's own movements become strangely and even mysteriously uncertain.

In the third week of June, even while Georgina remained very ill, he went to France for a week, returned for his last London reading on 27 June, and then almost at once set off for France again – these two journeys being only the beginning of a number of short but regular visits to France he made over the next three months. Certainly his wandering back and forth between the two countries, combined with his anxiety about Georgina's illness, meant

475

that he could settle down to nothing in any continuous way; it is clear that he wanted to begin the novel which he had already been contemplating for some months, but he did not find sufficient time or peace of mind to do so for another two and a half years. His correspondence during the period is remarkably uninformative, however, compared at least with the wealth of detail which he usually lavished on his travels. "I have been in France . . . I am away to France forthwith . . . going back there immediately . . . a visit at a distance . . . My absence is entre nous . . . On the Sunday I vanish into space for a day or two . . ."

Significant, and probably unintentional, is his employment of the word "visit" – whom was he visiting? And where, at a "distance", did he go? The second question can, at least, be answered with some certainty; Dickens was crossing the Channel to Boulogne, and then travelling a few miles south to the village of Condette. The Mayor of the Commune of Condette at that time has recorded how "Charles Dickens, le célèbre écrivain, a habité la maison de M. Beaucourt-Mutuel – il y faisait en 1864 son séjour favori et y restait, de temps en temps, une période de 8 jours; il a laissé quelques souvenirs parmi quelques habitants . . ." The house which M. Beaucourt-Mutuel owned in Condette was a modest chalet, certainly modest by the standards of the previous dwellings he had owned in Boulogne and in which Dickens had stayed. But there lies the story itself: M. Beaucourt-Mutuel's expenditure on the "Property" of Boulogne was so large that he went bankrupt, and in 1860 he was forced to sell up and to purchase instead the modest bungalow some ten miles outside Boulogne. This is the "chalet" where Dickens stayed. The plaque affixed to its wall states that he resided here from 1860 to 1864, while the Mayor of Condette gives 1864 as the time of the first visit; in fact all the evidence from the hints and indirections in Dickens's correspondence suggests that he visited Condette regularly from this time, 1862, until the summer of 1865. So what was the attraction of such a place for Dickens? It was a quiet, even secluded, village; and the chalet itself, with its courtyard and gardens, had nothing close to it except for the scattered dwellings of the small farmers of the locality. It can be inferred, in other words, that Dickens liked the privacy of this area and of this particular house.

And so to whom did he pay these "visits"? It is unlikely, to say the least, that he would be constantly crossing the Channel in order to pay his respects to the Beaucourt-Mutuels. The answer lies closer to home, but it would probably never have been revealed had it not been for a railway crash which occurred in June 1865 – at the time of the terrible accident at Staplehurst, as we shall see, Charles Dickens was travelling in a first-class carriage with Ellen Ternan and Mrs Ternan. They had all come over from Boulogne. There can be no certainty in this matter but the balance of probabilities tilts one way: that, from 1862 onward, Ellen Ternan and Mrs Ternan were paying guests at the chalet of the Beaucourt-Mutuels (who now needed any additional income rather badly) and that Dickens's frequent and continuous journeys to France were for the sole purpose of visiting them in their seclusion. Perhaps just as significantly, the constant travelling of 1862 (one might almost say that Dickens was "commuting" between France and England) coincided with a period in which, as he told his closest friends, he was consumed by "misery". In September he told Wilkie Collins that "I have some rather miserable anxieties which I must impart one of these days . . ." Three months earlier he had written to Forster about ". . . the never to be forgotten misery of this later time . . ." which he compared to the miseries of his child-hood (the miseries of the time when he felt himself to be abandoned). In December he also told Laetitia that he had ". . . quite enough of my own cares".

And what provoked this anxiety and pain? It is hard to avoid the conclusion that it had something to do with his continual visits to Ellen Ternan and her mother in Condette. There have as a result been many speculations about the exact nature of the relationship between Dickens and Ellen in this period – that they were unhappy lovers, that Ellen had had a child and was bringing it up secretly in Condette, that she had had a miscarriage or abortion, that the child had died. It has to be said at once that no evidence has been found for any of these more dramatic possibilities, and we may perhaps approach a little closer to the truth of Dickens's unhappiness in a letter which he wrote in October to his sister, Laetitia, who was still in deep distress after the death of her husband. "But in this world," he said to her, "there is no stay but the hope of a better, and no reliance but on the mercy and goodness of God. Through these two harbours of a ship-wrecked heart . . ." A shipwrecked heart – a strange although not entirely inapposite phrase to use to a widow, but how easily it springs from Dickens's pen. How much it seems to reflect his own concerns, too, is evident when he adds that "the disturbed mind and affections, like the tossed sea, seldom calm without an intervening time of confusion and trouble". Again Dickens seems in part to be addressing himself here; it has already been conveyed how often he employed the imagery of storm and sea to describe this period in his own life. Just as instinctive as his reference to the "shipwrecked heart", and to that underlying faith in God which bolsters it.

But these do not sound like the remarks of an adulterer, or of a man who has fathered a child upon a young woman living in banishment in France. It is unlikely, too, that Madame Beaucourt-Mutuel or Mrs Ternan would have permitted anything other than the greatest respectability of manner and conduct under what might be considered to be their joint roof. But we are left, then, with the enduring and perhaps unanswerable question: what precisely was the nature of the relationship between Ellen Ternan and Charles Dickens? That he was obsessed with her, there can be little doubt. That he maintained his relationship with her until the end of his life, there can be no doubt. That he maintained his affection for her, also, is undeniable. Perhaps an "ordinary" man might in such circumstances have become her sexual partner, but one needs only to look back over these pages to realise at once that Dickens was not "ordinary" in any sense. In many ways he was decidedly odd. His hysterical reaction to the death of Mary Hogarth – his keeping her clothes so that he might on occasions take them out and look at them, his longing to be buried with her – indicates as much. And since his behaviour was always quite exceptional, we should not fall into the trap of expecting him to behave in a conventional way with Ellen Ternan.

It has generally been assumed, however, that their relationship was indeed consummated, and that Ellen Ternan became his mistress. The rumours were only given wide currency in the 1930s when a certain Thomas Wright passed on the remarks of a Canon Benham – to whom, it seems, Ellen "disburdened her mind" in later life in an apparently very generalised way. Where there is a mistress, however, there may be also a child; and in recent years there has as a result been a constant game of "hunt the baby", complete with its panoply of scholarly misunderstandings, family secrets, biographical gossip, asides in letters marked "confidential", elaborate investigations into rate books and parish registers and railway timetables – all of it, in the end, amounting to nothing. This pursuit is only to be expected, however; legitimate children are rarely a subject of any great interest since their relationship to their famous parent tends to be quite transparent. But the idea of Dickens siring an illegitimate child who grew up in the late nineteenth century, and even survived into the

479

twentieth, has more resonance; an illegitimate offspring seems somehow to acquire more power, as if its status as an outcast brings it closer to the genius who was its father. At least two people have been nominated for this role but, again, the suggestions have proved to be quite without foundation. It is true that a servant who had worked for Ellen Ternan claimed that "there were children", but for every statement suggesting a sexual liaison there is an equally authoritative one asserting quite the opposite. Ellen Ternan's maid, Jane Wheeler, who was in her employment from 1866, left a message for Ellen's daughter – ". . . if you had asked she would have told you the truth, your dear mother never was the mistress of Charles Dickens".

There can be no certainties here. But it is appropriate, at least, to recall the words of Ellen Ternan's daughter: "My mother very often talked about Dickens. She always spoke of him with affection and said what a good man he was. Never was there a suggestion of sadness or sorrow or trouble in her references to him. She just spoke of him as a great man, and a great and well-liked friend . . ." Perhaps this is too anodyne a description, but it seems likely that there is a truth somewhere within it. Nevertheless we are not talking of any ordinary friendship between a "great man" and a young woman; it was something very extraordinary indeed, more extraordinary than an adulterous liaison and almost bewilderingly odd. We must imagine Dickens, in middle-age, haunted by a young woman who became for him a surrogate sister, daughter, virgin mother, child; a man obsessed, and unhappy with that obsession to the end of his life; a writer who had formed in life precisely the kind of relationship he had so helplessly created again and again in his fiction; a genius who held on to his ideal against all the odds and who, it might be said, was eventually destroyed by it. His was the "ship-wrecked heart" after all, and could it not have been Ellen's reluctance to take on so strange a role that accounted for all the misery piling up against him in this year? The year when he first started travelling to Condette?

By now Georgina had slowly begun to recover her health and in early October Dickens took her down to Dover to try his favourite remedy of sea-air and sea-water. Then he was mysteriously absent again for a few days but, on his return, decided to remain with her at Gad's Hill Place because, since his departure, she had stayed there alone; Kate and Charles Collins had been in Scotland, while Mamie had been with friends. In the middle of October he travelled back to France, on the understanding that Georgina and Mamie were to follow him four days later. It was probable that he spent those four days at Condette, since he planned to meet his two relatives at Boulogne; but the sea was too high, the wind too strong, and eventually the channel boat found its harbour in Calais. Dickens went to meet them there and they travelled on by train to Paris – to an apartment at 27 rue du Faubourg Saint-Honoré which was very expensive but ". . . pretty, airy, and light". Of course he now knew Paris very well, and his general sense of being "at home" in France (indeed it had become almost literally his second home) was increased by the fact that "I see my books in French at every railway station great and small". Wills came over for a few days to decide the contents of the next Christmas issue, his journey indicating that this was no longer a mere routine part of the periodical – each Christmas number sold in the region of two hundred thousand copies, and represented an important part of Dickens's income. Wills reported back to his wife that "Dick" was "very cheery".

He went from Paris to Condette, "touching the sea at Boulogne" as he put it rather vaguely to his daughter, Mamie, in a letter which makes it quite clear that she, at least, did not know about Ellen Ternan or about the chalet. He was away for ten days, on a kind of "tour" which took him to Amiens and Arras, and then just after the middle of February he returned to London. To work. To activity. He proceeded with some London readings which he had already planned, beginning with two a week but eventually cutting them down to a reading each Friday. Then once more he travelled back to France on "anxious business" and he remained as a result "in dull spirits". Back to London where in a speech at the beginning of April he declared, "Depend upon it, the very best among us are often bad company for ourselves (I know I am very often) . . ." Then he was again summoned back to France by "a sick friend". Those biographers who have suggested that the sickness in question was either Ellen Ternan's miscarriage or her pregnancy must explain why it had been continuing now for almost a year. And there is something more to be said on this matter. We have seen how the young women whom he idealised in the past seemed always to be destined, in his eyes, for an early death – as if the image of Mary Hogarth imprinted itself upon their outlines. Ellen's protracted sickness, if such it was (and it should be remembered that in later life she did suffer from prolonged ill-health) would only have had the effect of endearing her more to him, of persuading him to idealise her all the more hopelessly. Then, after this visit to a sick friend, he returned to hear news of Augustus Egg's death. "We must close up the ranks and march on . . ." he told Wilkie Collins, and two weeks later repeated the phrase during a speech on behalf of the Royal Free Hospital. Death and mortality all around him. The first four months of 1863 have in this bare biographical account comprised nothing more than work and sickness, constant travelling and constant anxiety. But anxiety can twist time out of shape. A moment may last a lifetime. Four months in this account, therefore, but of how long a duration to Dickens?

There are happier things to record, however, since it was while he remained in London now that he finally healed
482

his breach with Thackeray. Dickens claimed that it was he who made the first move, while he was hanging up his hat in the Athenaeum. He looked up and saw Thackeray's haggard face. "Thackeray," he said, "have you been ill?" And thus, according to Dickens, were they reconciled. A rather more convincing account is given by Sir Theodore Martin who was speaking to Thackeray at the time when Dickens came into the club. He passed close to Thackeray "without making any sign of recognition". Suddenly Thackeray broke away from his conversation, and reached Dickens just as the latter had his foot on the staircase. "Dickens turned to him, and I saw Thackeray speak and presently hold out his hand to Dickens. They shook hands, a few words were exchanged, and immediately Thackeray returned to me saying 'I'm glad I have done this.'" This sounds much more likely to be true than Dickens's self-serving version, particularly in light of the fact that he was notoriously bad at being the first to "make up" in such circumstances. He said once that ". . . quarrelling is very well, but the making up is dreadful", and this was largely the result of his own shrinking sensitivity in emotional matters of this kind. He could not bear even the prospect of being rebuffed, and so he held his peace.

He divided his time between Kent and his London office (since he had been forced to spend so much time in France, he had not rented a London house) but even here, in the midst of his familiar life, he was dreaming of Ellen Ternan; dreaming of her in a red shawl with her back turned towards him. And again he was unwell. For a man who had always prided himself upon the vigour and elasticity of his physical spirit, he had become surprisingly susceptible to all the ills of the flesh. He was also growing tired of London; it was in this period, as the "Uncommercial Traveller", that he was describing the hopeless shabbiness of the city, and he now spent as much time as possible at Gad's Hill Place. There had been occasions in the past when he had discussed with Forster the possibility of renting or even selling that house, but now it had truly become his domain.

# *Thirty-One*

T HE summer of 1863 was as unsettled as the spring.
He went back once more to France in August, but
had returned to Gad's Hill Place by the end of the month,
with two projects now firmly on his mind; one was the
Christmas issue of *All The Year Round*, the writing of which
had become part of his settled routine, and the other was
the novel which he had been contemplating for at least
the previous two years. Now, at last, he thought he was
ready to begin; he wrote to Chapman and Hall in order to
fix the appropriate terms for what would be his first long
novel for seven years; he wanted six thousand pounds for
half the copyright, and he got it. He was so eager to begin
now that nothing really could stop him, not even the
deaths of those around him. He had once said that to live
through middle-age was to walk through a kind of cemetery, and so it was to prove in this last half of the year.
His hated mother-in-law, Mrs Hogarth, died in August but
this was of no real interest to Dickens; he sent a very curt
note to Catherine about her rights to the grave where Mary
Hogarth was buried. And then in September his own
mother died — not a moment too soon, Dickens seems to
have felt, since for some time she had been in a state of
bodily and mental decay. She had been living with her
daughter-in-law, Helen, in a house at Grafton Terrace (for
which Dickens paid), and it was here that he had occasion-

ally visited her, in her "fearful state". But there are no real signs of loss or grief in Dickens's response to her death; certainly nothing remotely comparable to the bleakness which had descended upon him after the death of his father. But, if there was no explicit or even conscious grief on Dickens's part, something close to sorrow emerges in the work upon which he was now engaged. Mrs Dickens was buried on a Thursday at Highgate Cemetery, next to her husband, and only three days before Dickens had begun that year's Christmas story with the portrait of a garrulous female, Mrs Lirriper, who seems not unlike the mother whom he was about to bury. But there is a difference now; Mrs Lirriper, far from being one of the silly women so characteristic in his fiction, is, despite her tendency to talk, a kindly and sensible old party. Surely it is possible to see in this contemporaneous portrait some kind of oblique, posthumous tribute to Mrs Dickens which her son could not give her in her lifetime? He had been too close to her, and she had wounded him too much, for any such emotional openness in his life; but, in his art, and after her death, she lives again as a good and decent woman. In the story, too, she has a male lodger, Major Jemmy Jackman, who is not unlike John Dickens in speech: "I esteem it a proud privilege to go down to posterity through the instrumentality of the most remarkable boy that ever lived . . ." This might have been John Dickens talking about his son, Charles, but this "remarkable boy" is a young orphan whom Mrs Lirriper and Major Jackman bring up. Just the three of them – a mother not a mother and a father not a father, with one male orphan; almost a holy family, one might say, but a holy family of Dickens's imagination.

On the last night of what had been for him an anguished year Dickens played charades at Gad's Hill Place with his guests; they had to guess, among others, his rendition of The Pathetic History of the Poor Little Sweep, Mussulman

Barbarity to Christians, and Merry England. One of his props for this game was placed against the wall of his bedroom and, when he noticed that it looked like one of "the dismal things that are carried at Funerals", he quickly cut off the black calico draped around it. On retiring to bed that night he saw that the prop was still in his room, and that its shadow still kept its resemblance to a funereal pike. That same evening, at a quarter past five, his son Walter fell dead in Calcutta with a gush of blood from his mouth. More death. Walter left nothing behind, only a little trunk which contained some changes of linen, some prayer books, and the photograph of "a woman believed to be a member of the family". Could that have been a photograph of his mother, Catherine, living alone in Gloucester Crescent? A friend later recalled that she was "in great grief" at the death of her son. Her estranged husband sent out to India an inscription for the boy's tomb, but he sent not one word of condolence to Catherine herself. Death and gloom and estrangement everywhere around him.

And what of the novel being written all through this time? He had decided to call it *Our Mutual Friend*. He had begun it in November, and he already had the "main line" of the story in front of him; now, after more than two years of attempting to write, he was desperately eager to carry on with it in case he lost the impetus or became in any other way unsettled and distracted. Certain characters and themes had stayed with him for a long time; he had jotted down notes for the character known as Podsnap as early as 1855, and the title itself was one of those stray phrases which seemed to lodge in his memory like a talisman. It occurs in truncated form on at least three occasions in *Little Dorrit* — ". . . very proper expression mutual friend", as Flora Finching says. But, more importantly, the themes and emblems of the book can be traced much further back; for, in *Our Mutual Friend*, the songs of his childhood re-occur in almost hallucinatory state as the wooden-legged Silas Wegg recites the words of a sentimental ballad, "The Light Guitar", which Dickens learned as a child and which he had quoted almost thirty years before in his first published volume.

> "And if my tale (which I hope Mr Boffin might excuse)
> should make you sigh.
> I'll strike the light guitar."

Now that he had the "main line" of the story he worked upon it closely and continuously. He knew from the beginning how the story was slowly to be divulged, his suggestions for each instalment in his working notes closely following the writing of the one before, his memoranda emphasising how sustained and unified a design he had in mind – "lay the ground carefully . . . *This to go through the book* . . . clear the ground, behind and before . . . Lead on carefully . . ." Sometimes his notes to himself in the course of the composition mention just a name, or a place, as if the whole vast panorama were ready to unfurl in his mind at the smallest hint. Yet he was writing much more slowly than before, the style of the narrative so much more elaborate, the conversations reading in part like ritualised drama; his handwriting is small now, sloping downwards to the right, with many additions and emendations. He even told Wilkie Collins that the effort of going back to the large scale of twenty monthly numbers, after the serials in *All The Year Round*, left him "quite dazed".

It is almost as if he were starting again, starting something in quite a new vein, and this sensation of novelty was emphasised by the fact that he was now working with Marcus Stone rather than Hablot Browne as illustrator. He had dropped Browne abruptly and the illustrator, an innocent, shy and unworldly man, never really understood the reasons for Dickens's decision: ". . . lately (Authors and Artists will sometimes squabble) I have not been on very good terms with him . . ." he had said before their separation and, after the event, he told his partner, "I don't know what's up any more than you do . . . Dickens probably thinks a new hand would give his old puppets a fresh look . . . Confound all authors and publishers, say I; there is no pleasing or satisfying one or t'other. I wish I had never had anything to do with the lot."

Marcus Stone designed the cover of the monthly parts after seeing only the first two numbers and, although Dickens had specific corrections to make to it, he seemed altogether pleased by the result. "Give a vague idea, the more vague the better," he told the young man, and Dickens was for once himself quite vague. When Stone asked him which of Silas Wegg's legs was wooden, for example, he did not know, "I do not think I had identified the leg." Stone also quotes him as saying, on the subject, "It's all right – please yourself." This in turn suggests that Dickens himself was less interested in the illustrations to his work, perhaps because he realised that they were no longer as necessary to his design as once they had been. In fact the story of his collaboration with Stone over these months indicates a certain decline of enthusiasm and concern. At first he gave him specific instructions, but soon he permitted him his own choice of good "moments". Then, towards the end of the serialisation, Dickens allowed Stone to choose and illustrate whatever subjects he liked best, scarcely bothering to raise any objection. But this is to anticipate the entire composition of *Our Mutual Friend*. By the third week of January 1864, he had just written the first two instalments, and at once he started work upon the third, his assiduity largely a result of the fact that he wanted to have five numbers in hand before he began publication. A large amount, perhaps, but he realised that he was now working much more slowly than before, and that he could not automatically rely upon that old exuberant inventiveness which had always brought him up to the deadline with enough material. In addition he was about to rent another London house for the "season", which in its turn would cause further interruptions.

It was while he was looking for a house, at the beginning of February, that the news arrived of Walter's death in India; he did not tell Georgina of the proximate cause of his son's sudden collapse, because it turned out that he had been suffering from precisely the same "aneurism of the aorta" which afflicted Georgina herself. He was distressed, but not exactly prostrated with grief, and in any event went ahead with the renting of 57 Gloucester Place just north of Hyde Park. It was here that he was to settle until June, and it was here in February that he worked on the third number of *Our Mutual Friend*. The last chapter of the previous instalment had turned out to be too long to be used, and it was while Dickens was contemplating a fresh subject to fill the gap that Marcus Stone arrived with news which was to change the entire narrative. Stone had been looking for a stuffed dog to act as a model and had in the course of his enquiries come across a certain Willis, a taxidermist whose shop was in St Andrew's Street near Seven Dials. Stone had already heard Dickens say that he needed to find a peculiar avocation for *Our Mutual Friend* – "it must be something very striking and unusual," he said to him one night in a theatre they were visiting – and, as soon as he had found the taxidermist, Stone went around to Gloucester Place in order to tell him that he had come across something very striking indeed. At once Dickens accompanied him back to the shop and, although Willis himself was not there, he took note of everything; in a novel which came to anatomise society and the confusion of human identity, this articulator of skeletons and stuffer of dead animals proved to be precisely the man he needed for the purposes of his design. And so Mr Venus was born.

By June of 1864 Dickens was writing the seventh number of *Our Mutual Friend* and at last managed to get away from London; he went down to Gad's Hill Place and there continued work on the novel. Since he was planning another journey across the Channel he was working very hard and very steadily. He was about to reach the moment when Jenny Wren, from the roof of the counting house in St Mary Axe, calls down, "Come up and be dead! Come up and be dead!"; he knew the strength of his story now and, perhaps for the first time in his life, was not unduly concerned by falling sales. (There had been a drop of something like five thousand between the first and second numbers, and by the final double number sales were down to nineteen thousand after beginning at thirty-five thousand.) Of course he no longer needed to be concerned with any disastrous financial loss; for one thing, he could rely for his livelihood upon his readings and his ownership of *All The Year Round* as well as the steady "working" of his copyrights in the various editions of his previous novels. Indeed his annual income climbed steadily year by year in this period, and it seems likely that increased financial security materially assisted his artistic self-confidence; or, rather, he was no longer so troubled by extraneous factors. He just kept on with his steady hard work, and managed to complete the seventh number on time, just before leaving the country in the last week of June. He might have been going to France, as he told one acquaintance, or he might have been travelling to Belgium, as he informed a second correspondent; he was either unclear himself, and planned to take a touring holiday with Ellen Ternan and her mother, or he was deliberately if vaguely trying to cover his tracks. Certainly, in a letter to Wills, he joked about another "Mysterious Disappearance". He was back at Gad's Hill Place in the first week of July, however, and immediately started work on correcting proofs: his brief holiday meant that he had already almost "lost" one number of the five he wished to hold in advance. Matters were not helped, either, by a sudden illness of Wills which meant that Dickens had to take on more editorial work than was customary.

But his main complaint seems to have been quite a new one with him; he told Forster that he was now "wanting in invention, and have fallen back with the book". This had always been one of his greatest fears, to lose his creativity, to break down, so it is no wonder that he was also feeling "very unwell". He had been suffering from a sore throat, and now he was visited by some more serious but non-specific physical affliction which left him weak and depressed. It was very hot at the beginning of August, too, and as a result he still could not work properly. But by the middle of the month his health and spirits had sufficiently improved; he was "working hard" again, and was turning down invitations so that he might write undisturbed and catch up on the amount by which he had fallen behind. By the beginning of October he had in fact managed to finish the ninth instalment, and was thus, at last, almost half-way through the novel. But he still had to write his Christmas story for the year. It had now become of serious financial moment to him, and time was pressing. So he stayed at the office in Wellington Street and there worked steadily upon "Mrs Lirriper's Legacy", the successor to "Mrs Lirriper's Lodgings" with which he hoped to achieve a similar success. He went to see *The Streets of London* at the Princess's Theatre one evening in order to "cool" his "boiling head" after his work, and then a few days later he finished the seasonal story. He was so concerned about its success, in fact, and so worried about the possibility of piracy or imitation, that he told his printer to lock up the type once it had been set and to pull no proofs without Dickens's written instructions. It is a pleasant enough tale, with its kindly and garrulous heroine at the centre, and even in this comic format Dickens was able once more to

492

spread a moral for his audience – in this case not his old Christmas message of comradeship and conviviality but rather the more sombre theme which was also at the heart of the novel upon which he was now engaged, that "Unchanging Love and Truth will carry us through all!".

In November he travelled again to France – no doubt once more to see Ellen Ternan, whose presence (it can be surmised) was also casting a shadow over his writings. The danger is of seeing her everywhere, in fact. Can it be Ellen Ternan who stands behind Lizzie Hexam, for example, the "low born" but gentle heroine of *Our Mutual Friend*? Is it she who informs Dickens's description of Bradley Headstone's passionate and violent attachment to Lizzie: " 'Yes! you are the ruin – the ruin – the ruin – of me. I have no resources in myself, I have no confidence in myself, I have no government of myself when you are near me or in my thoughts. And you are always in my thoughts now. I have never been quit of you since I first saw you. Oh, that was a wretched day for me! That was a wretched, miserable day!' " Then, again, there is Charley Hexam's rejection of her: " 'But you shall not disgrace me . . . I am determined that after I have climbed up out of the mire, you shall not pull me down'." Can we sense in this ambivalence, projected into the contrasting responses of two characters, something of the complexity of Dickens's own feelings? Or perhaps we may see the shadow of Ellen Ternan behind the portrait of Bella Wilfer in the same novel, the girl who says that " '. . . I am convinced I have no heart as people call it; and that I think that sort of thing is nonsense'". Which is uncannily reminiscent of Estella's declaration in *Great Expectations*: " 'You must know,' said Estella, condescending to me as a brilliant and beautiful woman might, 'that I have no heart . . . I have no softness there, no – sympathy – sentiment – nonsense.' " Are these, too, echoes of a real woman?

Perhaps. Perhaps not. A writer whose life had been

marked by astonishing and abundant invention cannot be presumed to rely upon Ellen Ternan for his portraits of young women. What is certainly true is that in these last two novels, *Great Expectations* and *Our Mutual Friend*, Dickens has for the first time given serious consideration to the theme of unrequited love. In earlier books it may have been secret or ill-timed, but there was always an equilibrium in which both parties seem to accept that they loved or can be loved; and that, when eventually they declare their love, it is not rejected. But in these last two novels – and in his uncompleted final fiction also – there is torture in love, and despair, and madness. There is some necessary connection between courtship and death in them, too, so that in these last works it is possible to trace the strange curve of Dickens's temperament exploring extremity in art if not necessarily in his life.

The Christmas gathering that year comprised Charles and Kate Collins, the Fechters, Marcus Stone and Henry Chorley; as the *Gad's Hill Gazette* stated, "The guests remained on and off from Dec. 24th 1864 until Jany 5th 1865." It was not necessarily a very merry gathering. In particular Dickens seems to have been uneasy about the protracted ill-health of his son-in-law, Charles Collins, which in fact proved in the end to be cancer of the stomach. "I have strong apprehensions," he said, "that he will never recover, and that she will be left a young widow." The complexity of his feelings towards his favourite daughter suggests that the wish here was very much the parent of the thought itself. As for the others at this happy time? "All the rest are as they were. Mary neither married nor going to be; Georgina holding them all together . . ." But there was some relief. Some excitement. As his Christmas present Fechter had brought to Dickens a Swiss chalet – a real one, disassembled into pieces. It was too cold to participate in any outdoor games, and so Dickens suggested that the "bachelor guests" (by which
494

he presumably meant the strong Stone rather than the weak Collins) should unpack the pieces – ninety-four altogether, in fifty-eight boxes – and help to put them together. But it was too complex and difficult an undertaking for the men to manage and Fechter's French carpenter at the Lyceum, M. Godin, was summoned from London to help. It was in fact larger than anyone (except, perhaps, Fechter) had anticipated – a real chalet on two floors, with a ground floor room and a first floor room, the latter having six windows. So Dickens arranged for it to be erected on that piece of ground belonging to him on the opposite side of the Rochester High Road; there the chalet was shaded by the cedars and stood in a place from which Dickens could see the fields of corn beneath him and, in the distance, the Thames with its yachts and steamboats. Eventually he also had a tunnel excavated beneath the road itself, so that he might pass from his house to his chalet undisturbed; the building of this, like the building and furnishing of the chalet itself, filled him almost with boyish delight. One of his children remembered how expectantly he watched as the workmen approached each other from the opposite ends of the tunnel, and how he ordered an impromptu celebration when they broke through and completed the work. And the chalet itself was like a fantasy of boyhood, this secret place among the trees. It became his place of work in the spring and summer, an alternative to his study in the house, one which was even brighter and lighter. He had a telescope placed there so that he might observe the world around and above him but, more importantly, he had mirrors fastened along the walls so that the whole interior sparkled and shone with the sunlight even as he wrote at his desk.

His routine in the early months of 1865, as he continued his work on the last half of *Our Mutual Friend*, was one in which he "commuted" between Gad's Hill Place and the office of *All The Year Round*. In January he was asking for

495

a copy of *Merryweather's Lives of Misers* in order that he might detail the reading matter of the Golden Dustman, Mr Boffin: " 'Now, look well all round, my dear, for a Life of a Miser, or any book of that sort . . .' " Working on Mr Boffin's decline and fall; watching from his office window at the crowds streaming over Waterloo Bridge; Silas Wegg singing "auld lang syne"; a fire at the Surrey Theatre. So did his life, interior and exterior, continue. At the beginning of February he was again in France "for a week's run"; apart from anything else he seems to have been crossing the Channel "perpetually" because his visits to Condette helped to soothe the neuralgia from which he was now constantly suffering. But it was never entirely alleviated, and in the third week of February he became troubled by a swollen left foot. Yet it was only the harbinger of greater pain and distress; as Forster justifiably said, it represented "a broad mark between his past life and what remained to him of the future". So did the signs multiply, the bars of the prison house closing round. Dickens, who believed always in triumphing over illness by determination and hardihood, declared that he had simply contracted frost-bite from too much walking in the snow around Gad's Hill Place. This was where the first fierce attack came upon him, after all – he was walking with his two dogs, Linda and Turk, when he suddenly fell lamed to the ground. He managed to rise only with much difficulty and then had to limp home for three miles, the dogs creeping beside him and never turning from him as he slowly made his way. He was greatly moved by his pets' reaction, in fact, which provided him with further proof that they had distinctive intelligence and temperament (a belief that was not necessarily widely shared at the time). "Turk's look upward to his face was one of sympathy as well as fear", according to Forster, "but Linda was wholly struck down".

He remained in pain and ill-health until the spring, only

finally recovering in the last week of April. He went out to dinner for the first time on the twenty-seventh of that month and then, almost immediately, took himself off to France where he spent the first week of May. But his general nervous exhaustion, of which the swollen foot may have been one manifestation and of which his previous "want of invention" was certainly another, was not to be so easily cured. He gave a speech for the Newsvendors' Benevolent Association, on which occasion he "covered" for Edmund Yates who lost the thread of his own speech ("I saved you that time, I think, sir!" he told him. "Serves you well right for being over-confident"). He was away again for some three days, and then on the twentieth of the month delivered an address to the Newspaper Press Fund in which he recounted his memories of his own days as a newspaper reporter. So many years ago now. A time when he could stand for hours in pelting rain in order to transcribe political speeches, could gallop through the dead of night in post-chaises, could sit huddled in the House of Commons; the audience, according to one reporter present, were ". . . carried away by the extraordinary charm of that speech". But, for Dickens, what were the feelings as he recounted those bright and dashing days? So long ago. Clearly there was something wrong with him even as he made the speech. For some reason he wrote two identical letters to Austen Layard on succeeding days, having forgotten that he had written the first. And he needed to get away. ". . . Work and worry," he told Forster before he left once more for France, ". . . would soon make an end of me. If I were not going away now, I should break down. No one knows as I know to-day how near to it I have been . . ." He told Mamie that ". . . I had certainly worked myself into a damaged state". He left for France at the end of May, therefore, and at once began to feel better; perhaps the company of Ellen Ternan itself was enough to assuage much of the nervous tension under

497

which he seems to have laboured. But then something happened, something which was to affect the rest of his life.

While in France he had managed to work on the second chapter of the sixteenth number – he was drawing towards the close of *Our Mutual Friend* – and he brought the manuscript back with him in the pocket of his overcoat (he had a Gladstone bag, which he took everywhere with him on his travels, but for some reason he never trusted his own work to it). With Mrs Ternan and Ellen Ternan he boarded the ferry which took them from Boulogne to Folkestone, and it may well have been on this occasion that a fellow-passenger noticed him: "Travelling with him was a lady not his wife, nor his sister-in-law, yet he strutted about the deck with the air of a man bristling with self-importance, every line of his face and every gesture of his limbs seemed haughtily to say – 'Look at me; make the most of your chance. I am the great, the *only* Charles Dickens; whatever I may choose to do is justified by that fact.'" The three of them were booked into a first-class carriage and they took the 2.38 tidal train from Folkestone to London. They passed the town of Headcorn thirty-three minutes later and were approaching the viaduct over the river Beult just before Staplehurst at a speed of fifty miles an hour on a downward gradient. At that moment repair work was being conducted on the viaduct itself (in fact it was little more than a bridge) and two of the rails had been lifted off and placed at the side of the track. Even as the train was speeding down towards them. The foreman in charge of these works had consulted the wrong time-table; he did not expect the tidal train for another two hours and, against regulations, the flagman who was supposed to give warning to oncoming trains of any obstruction was only 550 yards from the site of the work. So everything happened too late. The driver of the train saw the red flag and applied his brakes, but he had no time.

He whistled for the guards to apply their brakes (there was no consistent braking system then) but it was not enough. The train approached the broken line at a speed of between twenty and thirty miles per hour, jumped the gap of forty-two feet, and swerved off the track as the central and rear carriages fell down from the bridge onto the bed of the river below. All of the seven first-class carriages plummeted downwards – except one and that one, held by its couplings onto the second-class carriage in front, was occupied by Charles Dickens and the Ternans. It had come off the rail and was now hanging over the bridge at an angle, so that all three of them were tilted down into a corner.

With a makeshift arrangement of planks he managed to extricate the Ternans from the upturned carriage, and it was at this point that he saw the other first-class carriages lying at the bottom of the river bed. With his familiar cool self-possession he went back into the carriage, and took out a travelling flask of brandy as well as his top hat. He filled the hat with water, clambered down the bank, and then started his work among the dying and the dead. He found a man with his skull cut open; he gave him a little brandy, poured some water on his face, and laid him on the grass beside the stream. He said only "I am gone", and then died. A woman was propped against a tree, her face covered in blood; he gave her a little brandy from his flask, but the next time he passed her she was dead. The dead and dying lay everywhere. "No imagination can conceive the ruin . . ." he said in a letter, and this was one of his constant remarks – unimaginable, I could not have imagined it – the reality of the scene too great even for him. One young passenger, Mr Dickenson, recalled later how it was the urging and assistance of Dickens which ensured that he was rescued from beneath a pile of twisted wreckage. Another passenger recalled how Dickens, with his hat full of water, was "running about with it and doing

499

his best to revive and comfort every poor creature he met who had sustained serious injury". One other instance will suffice. A man was looking for the woman he had just married, so "Dickens led him to another carriage and gradually prepared him for the sight. No sooner did he see her corpse than he rushed round a field at the top of his speed, his hands above his head, and then dropped fainting." And then, as he prepared to quit the scene of death, Dickens did a remarkable thing. He remembered that his manuscript was still in the pocket of his overcoat and, ". . . not in the least flustered at the time", he clambered back into the swaying carriage and retrieved it. He said that it was soiled only, although any such marks of the accident have now faded from the pages themselves. Then he travelled back to London with the other survivors on an emergency train, and was met by Wills at Charing Cross station. It was only now that his self-possession and calmness vanished; now that he was safe in London once more, he felt "quite shattered and broken up". He spent the night at his quarters in his office, with Wills sleeping next door in case Dickens should need him.

Some days later Dickens was still overwhelmed by the experience. He felt weak, but he experienced a "faint and sick" sensation in his head rather than in his body; his pulse was low, he felt generally nervous and when travelling by train he suffered from the illusion that the carriage was "down" on the left side. In fact this was not the side which went down in the actual crash, but we may recall that it was his left foot which had been attacked earlier in the year and that he suffered from renal colic on the left side of his body — in other words it is possible that the accident had materially affected Dickens's weak side, and that the vascular damage already recorded had been increased by his general nervous strain after the Staplehurst disaster. In fact travelling became for him the single most distressing activity, although he tried to get over his fear of trains by going back in them almost at once. He returned to London in one, for example, in order to see his doctor and no doubt to call upon Ellen Ternan. But it was not easy for him; he had to travel on a slow train rather than the express, and even the noise of his London hansom distressed him. He withdrew from all public engagements, and "the shake" certainly affected his writing in more than a physical sense; the rest of that number of *Our Mutual Friend*, snatched from the crash, is curiously dull. In addition it was far too short – ". . . a thing I have not done since Pickwick! . . ." – and he had to lengthen it at proof stage.

But the permanent results were equally serious. The effect of the Staplehurst accident "tells more and more", he noted in 1867, and then a year later he confessed that ". . . I have sudden vague rushes of terror, even when riding in a hansom cab, which are perfectly unreasonable but quite insurmountable". This sudden sensation of horror remained the most obvious consequence. How could it not be so in a man with a visual memory as powerful as his imaginative capacity, forever reliving the old crash and forever *seeing* the crash into which he might again be plunged? His son, Henry, recalled that "I have seen him sometimes in a railway carriage when there was a slight jolt. When this happened he was almost in a state of panic and gripped the seat with both hands." And Mamie remembered that ". . . my father's nerves never really were the same again . . . we have often seen him, when travelling home from London, suddenly fall into a paroxysm of fear, tremble all over, clutch the arms of the railway carriage, large beads of perspiration standing on his face, and suffer agonies of terror. We never spoke to him, but would touch his hand gently now and then. He had, however, apparently no idea of our presence; he saw nothing for a time but that most awful scene." The great conceiving power of Charles Dickens was thus turned into a medium for recurrent and conscious nightmare; once he had seen the characters of Smollett and Fielding around him, now he saw only the dead and the dying. There were even times when he had to leave the train at the next station, and walk the rest of the way home. But surely there must have been some further reason for this scene to be etched upon his consciousness in characters of fire? In much of his fiction the railway is seen as a terrifying and destructive force, no more so than when it tears up the landscape of London and runs down the guilt-ridden Carker in *Dombey and Son*. Was it as if some terror from his own imagination had now come alive, just as the dead had surrounded him at Staplehurst even as he was writing a book about death itself? Not only had he been involved in a crash but that accident may have injured Ellen Ternan and certainly threatened to expose his "other life" with her. His own worst fears must then have loomed in front of him, and was there not also some sense of guilt and punishment following him as relentlessly as the train once pursued Carker? We know only that, as his son said, Dickens "may be said never to have altogether recovered" and that he actually died on the fifth anniversary of the Staplehurst disaster.

He was back in the office by early July, but he now had no intention of being away from Gad's Hill Place for more than a day or two at a time. It was the usual summer, with his children back from school and his friends visiting for long weekends. The *Gad's Hill Gazette* has news of a cricket match, too, but one son was noticeable for his absence; at the end of May, Alfred had finally departed for Australia. He wanted to become a sheep farmer and there is no doubt that Dickens, always feeling himself beset by the number and demands of his dependants, was pleased to see him start out in life on his own account. And Dickens himself still had much to do. He had by now the whole plan of *Our Mutual Friend* sketched out, and was hoping to finish the novel by the end of August. To that end he was working very hard, and his notes demonstrate the care with which he was now completing the pattern of his narrative: "*Back to the opening chapter of the story* ... Back to the opening chapter of the book, *strongly.*" On the reverse side of his notes for the last double number, he explains the intricacies of the plot to himself in preparation for the denouement of the story. And in fact the relative dullness of the instalment written after the Staplehurst accident seems to have lifted; by the time he begins the next his customary inventiveness and humour have returned with his cutting portrayal of the stately but gloomy Mrs Wilfer who could assume, ". . . with a shiver of resignation, a deadly cheerfulness".

He continued working at Gad's Hill Place and was, by August, working on the final double number. He had finished it by the very beginning of September and then, for the first time in his life, wrote a "Postscript" (rather than his usual preface) in which he justified his method of narration and described briefly his experience in the Staplehurst crash. "I remember with devout thankfulness that I can never be much nearer parting company with my readers for ever, than I was then, until there shall be written against my life, the two words with which I have this day closed this book: – THE END." It would be the last time he would be able to use those words. In this postscript he was also concerned to explain the difficulties of monthly serialisation in the exposition of his "pattern", which indicates that he was to a certain extent concerned about the critical reception of the book. It was, to use the common term, "mixed", and perhaps the most severe commentary came from the young Henry James – ". . . the poorest of Mr Dickens's works. And it is poor with the poverty not of momentary embarrassment, but of permanent exhaustion . . ." E. S. Dallas in *The Times*, however, claimed that *Our Mutual Friend* was ". . . infinitely better than *Pickwick* in all the higher qualities of a novel . . ." It is not known whether Dickens read James's review in *The Nation* but certainly he read the notice in *The Times*. And it says something about his need for praise, especially the kind of praise that preferred his later novels to his early ones, that he in fact presented Dallas with the manuscript of *Our Mutual Friend* itself. Of all things this was what he most wanted to hear: that he had never deteriorated, that he was still at the height of his powers, that his early popularity had not been succeeded by what Henry James had called "permanent exhaustion". That he did not feel himself to be exhausted, despite the effects of the Staplehurst crash, is clear enough from the fact that even as he was completing *Our Mutual Friend* he was thinking ahead to his next novel, at least to the extent of soliciting an offer from an American publisher.

As soon as he had finished he wanted again to get away, this in part to cure the neuralgia which had been so badly affecting him. He met Wills at the office in London to expedite urgent business, and then made the journey to France. It can be assumed that he was returning over the same route as the train in the Staplehurst disaster, so this desire to leave as soon as the novel was finished must in part have been related to his need to fight out, and triumph over, his fears of travelling after the crash. He was in Boulogne for a few days; since it is clear that from this time Ellen Ternan and her mother resided in England, he may have been involved in winding up their affairs in Condette. Nevertheless he reported to Forster that ". . . I am burnt brown and have walked by the sea perpetually". He also reported that his foot was swelling again but it appears not to have prevented this perpetual walking – another example of Dickens's refusal to "surrender", as he might have put it, to physical debilities. From the Boulogne area he went on to Paris, where he stayed a few days, before crossing the Channel once more. On his return he shuttled back and forth between Gad's Hill Place and the offices in Wellington Street, and it may well have been about this time – certainly it was in this year – that the young Thomas Hardy encountered the great English novelist. It ought to rank as one of the most significant meetings in nineteenth-century literary history but, as on most such occasions, it was nothing of the sort. Hardy was then studying architecture in London and on this auspicious day he entered a coffee-shop near Charing Cross when he saw Dickens. "I went up and stood at the vacant place beside the stool on which Dickens was sitting. I had eaten my lunch, but I was quite prepared to eat another if the occasion would make Dickens speak to me. I hoped he would look up, glance at this strange young man beside him and make a remark – if it was only about the weather. But he did nothing of the kind. He was fussing about his bill. So I never spoke to him."

It was while he was in London now that the idea for the next Christmas story occurred to him – a sentimental piece, as it turned out, but remarkable for its depiction of the central character. Dickens described how it occurred to him. ". . . I sat down to cast about for an idea, with a depressing notion that I was, for the moment, overworked. Suddenly, the little character that you will see, and all belonging to it, came flashing up in the most cheerful manner and I had only to look on and leisurely describe it . . ." The character was that of a "Cheap Jack", a travelling salesman who moved around in his wagon from village to village, and precisely the sort of person whom Dickens would have seen in the lanes of Kent. The curious thing is that into the character of this itinerant salesman Dickens should pour so much of his own feeling – as if such a traveller were, at this point in his life, closer to him than anyone else. The Cheap Jack's wife has gone, his child is dead, and he takes a strictly paternal interest in a young girl with "a pretty face" and "bright dark hair" who also happens (no doubt for the purposes of Christmas sentiment) to be both deaf and dumb; together they travel around the country. He is "King of the Cheap Jacks" whose own sense of professional responsibility means that he has to hide his true feelings from the public. "Being naturally of a tender turn, I had dreadfully lonely feelings on me after this. I conquered 'em at selling times, having a reputation to keep (not to mention keeping myself), but they got me down in private, and rolled upon me. See us on the footboard, and you'd give pretty well anything you possess to be us. See us off the footboard, and you'd add a trifle to be off your bargain." This is so close to Dickens's own private lamentations in the same period, and so close to his own role as a public performer during his readings, that it is hard to resist the belief that he was in a sense writing out his own misery; or, rather, *seeing* his misery in this guise. It is perhaps only to be expected, then, that when he came to adapt this story for his real public readings, it was an enormous success, and *The Times* reported that ". . . perhaps there is no character in which the great novelist appears to greater advantage".

He had finished the story by the third week of September, just days after returning from France, but it cannot be said that he had in any sense recovered his health. The journey may have done something to restore his confidence in train travel, but there is evidence that it was precisely in this period that he suffered a mild or transient stroke. He himself told a friend only that he had suffered from "sunstroke" and had been ordered to bed for a day. In fact one of his earliest biographers, writing in 1871, has indicated that Dickens suffered a stroke in the previous summer — ". . . whilst on a trip to Paris," he wrote, "Mr Dickens met with a sunstroke which greatly alarmed his friends. For many hours he was in a state of complete insensibility, but at length recovered and in due course returned home." This sounds very much like the same event, which the biographer has misdated by a year, and the evidence itself is clear; he was receiving advance warning of what might one day be a massive stroke or haemorrhage. Nevertheless he preferred to pass off the symptoms as local and specific, and continued with his usual heavy round of activity: in the latter half of September he was once more embroiled in Guild business and *All The Year Round* affairs, for example, as well as assisting Fechter at the Lyceum with an adaptation of *The Master of Ravenswood*. Mrs Ternan herself had been recruited into the cast (one more indication that she and her daughter had left Condette), so Dickens's efforts as an unofficial and unannounced "play doctor" were no doubt redoubled.

Then, at the beginning of a new year, 1866, he decided, against the advice of friends, to embark upon another reading tour of England and Scotland. He had learned from his mistakes with Arthur Headland four years before, however, and had decided that he would leave all the administrative and managerial business to a firm of professionals; in the middle of January he went up to London in order to negotiate with Chappell and Company of New Bond Street, using Wills as his principal agent in the transactions (Forster, quite opposed to Dickens's readings in any case, would not have been suitable for the role), and eventually a satisfactory agreement was reached. But the point was that Dickens should not really have been working hard at all, let alone contemplating a long and arduous tour of the whole country. It was, Forster said in his biography, a "startling circumstance". In fact Dickens himself was feeling unwell through much of January and February, and there is no doubt that the effects of the train crash, as well as more general arteriosclerotic weakness, were operating within him. His doctor, Frank Beard, diagnosed "want of muscular power in the heart" and Dickens himself recognised some diminution in his usual "buoyancy" and "tone". His pulse was abnormal, too, and he was advised

507

to rest. But of course he could not rest: he had reasoned himself into believing that the readings might actually be of some benefit to him, and he said that the doctors themselves (he sought a second opinion, which was very much the same as Beard's) encouraged him to read occasionally. Which sounds very much like an anxious patient putting words in the mouths of others. Forster explained Dickens's eagerness to tour at this time as part of his self-imposed task ". . . to make the most money in the shortest time without any regard to the physical labour to be undergone". This is true, but there is another truth. He could no more stop himself than he could stop breathing. He had to go on. He had to face his audience in the brilliance of the gaslight. He had to confirm his own sense of being loved. He had to recreate a family around him. He had, even, to confirm to himself the efficacy and strength of his own fictions.

By March he had reached agreement with Chappell and Company on the nature and extent of the proposed tour. He would give thirty readings for which they would pay him fifteen hundred pounds. Originally he had been thinking of something in the region of two thousand guineas, but he accepted the lower offer with no misgivings. Indeed he seems to have been making some sort of point; he said later that he had informed the firm that "I offer these thirty readings to you at fifty pounds a night, because I know perfectly well beforehand that no one in your business has the least idea of their real worth, and I wish to prove it". And as always (as he might have said) he was right. Chappell themselves agreed to take care of all business and administrative arrangements, as well as paying for his personal and travelling expenses. They also appointed, with his agreement, a certain George Dolby to take care of all the business management; Dickens had met him on occasions before, but it was only now that they really came to know each other. Dolby was a tall, bald, thick-set man with a loud laugh, and a supply of humorous stories matched only by theatrical gossip. Precisely the kind of man, in other words, that Dickens liked. He was to "manage" Mark Twain at a later date, and Twain described him as ". . . large and ruddy, full of life and strength and spirits, a tireless and energetic talker, and always overflowing with good nature and bursting with jollity". He could be a little noisy and was "not over-refined" as one acquaintance put it; but there was also a quieter and sadder side to him, an aspect manifested in his stammer which, as Dickens noticed, always disappeared when he was imitating other people. The forced proximity of Dolby and Dickens, over a number of years, did nothing to destroy the true friendship which grew up between them – both of them "professional" men, both of them funny and observant. In addition, and most important of all to Dickens, Dolby remained punctilious and trustworthy. He has left his own account of his relationship with the novelist, which reveals a more humorous and light-hearted man than most biographers of his later years have cared to suggest. There is no doubt, however, that Dolby brought out the best in him; he used to make him laugh, for one thing, and was always prepared with new anecdotes and stories for "the Chief", as he came to call him. Dolby also had a fund of animal spirits – he had a trick of standing on his head upon a chair, which Dickens made a point of attempting – and a wide vocabulary.

So it was in his company that Dickens began his new series of readings. It was his first extended tour for four years, and of course he prepared himself with his usual thoroughness. He also took pains to adapt a reading from the Christmas success of the previous year, the story of the Cheap Jack, and rehearsed it to himself some two hundred times. But still he was not altogether sure of it, and so he arranged for a private reading in front of friends at Southwick Place – a reading which Dickens, true to his methodical disposition, timed to the second. Among the audience were Forster, Browning, Collins, Fechter and, according to Dolby, ". . . the verdict was unanimously favourable". Even his closest friends were now surprised by Dickens's skills as a reader; again according to Dolby, they (as well as the general public) ". . . were convinced that up to that time they had had but a very faint conception of Mr Dickens's powers either as an adapter or an elocutionist . . ." So, with Dickens thus heartened, the readings began. With Dolby as business manager and Wills as travelling companion, he opened his tour on 23 March, 1866, at the Assembly Rooms in Cheltenham. He saw Macready here after his performance and noted to a mutual friend later that he seemed "on the whole much older", a condition which he ascribed to the fact that Macready had retired from the theatre. It is as if Dickens were in a sense cheering up himself – proving to himself that he should go on with his remorseless activity, the decay of a retired Macready reinforcing his determination to do so. From Cheltenham the Dickens party travelled back to London (Dickens had to give a speech at the Royal General Theatrical Fund) but then on again to Liverpool, to Manchester, to Glasgow, to Edinburgh, to Bristol, to Birmingham, to Aberdeen, to Portsmouth . . . until coming to the end of the tour in London in June. The great novelist was now the great entertainer.

# Thirty-Two

P UBLIC readings had once more taken their place at the centre of his life, and perhaps through them we may see something of the true nature of his genius. He had acquired his skills only with great effort and determination, precisely as he had once mastered shorthand when he was a young man. The most important first step was preparation – not just the idle rehearsal of an hour or so but a consistent, methodical and laborious process of dramatisation and memorisation. He rehearsed the story of the Cheap Jack more than two hundred times before he felt able to put it on stage, and in fact most of his readings were the product of at least two months' work; on expressions, gestures, intonations, everything. In the margins of the "reading books" which he created out of his stories and novels he would add small notes as keys to his own delivery; "cheerful", "stern pathos", "mystery" and "quick on" appear in *A Christmas Carol* while in *The Cricket on the Hearth* are to be found instructions such as "very strong to the end". It is not at all clear whether he worked entirely on his own; many observers noticed how his delivery improved as he went on, and in his own advice to other speakers there is a clear professional understanding of matters to do with elocution. All of which suggests – or at least raises the possibility – that he was coached by Ellen Ternan or by Mrs Ternan. Certainly it has been suggested as a reason for his close friendship with the family, and it is not one that can entirely be discounted. And as he rehearsed his words, shouting out loud in the lanes around Gad's Hill Place, declaiming in his study, cutting and altering his stories as he went along, it was his own fiction that was being revivified. With it, too, his own identity. In a speech he gave in 1869, he refers to the fact that "it was suggested by Mr Babbage, in his *Ninth Bridgewater Treatise*, that a mere spoken word – a mere syllable thrown into the air – may go on reverberating through illimitable space for ever and for ever, seeing that there is no rim against which it can strike: no boundary at which it can possibly arrive". Perhaps Dickens had this imaginative sense of his own voice, as the words of Sam Weller or Mrs Gamp ascend into the air and travel through the infinite universe.

In the process, too, these had become new creations. It was often remarked that Dickens did not like members of the audience to consult copies of his books as he was reading from them, and this was for a very good and very specific reason; they were rarely the same narratives, and certain people even complained about the fact that he departed from the text. In preparation for the readings he had already condensed and changed various passages, removed references to gesture and appearance, altered the jokes, and so forth. He also revised passages in the light of the audience reaction itself, and on more than one occasion was known to "gag" or improvise on the spot. He felt able to do so because he had his stories by heart after hundreds of previous rehearsals. Sometimes he would announce the title of his reading and then ostentatiously close his prompt book and recite from memory, but there were also occasions when he would hold the book only for effect or turn the pages mechanically without ever seeing them.

The tour continued through the spring of 1866. Dolby was taking care of all business matters and spent very little time with Dickens. Wills was the reader's principal companion and, much to Dickens's discomfort, he cross-examined Dolby on the preliminary journey to Liverpool in order to decide upon his suitability. In fact Dickens, too, had worried that Dolby might not be "a man of resources". But he passed all the tests and soon he was not only sharing the first-class carriage with Dickens but also using the sitting room which he invariably booked at each hotel. It was Dolby, too, who, on this first trip together, has left a record of Dickens's own excitement and enthusiasm. How he visited the circus whenever he could; how he danced a hornpipe in the train carriage as Wills and Dolby whistled an accompaniment; how he always provided the sandwiches of egg and anchovy, and made the iced gin punch; how he was once told off by the manageress of a station refreshment room for helping himself to milk and sugar; how he lay down like a pantomime clown along the steps of the houses in his home town. It is a striking portrait of Dickens with, as Dolby said, "the iron will of a demon and the tender pity of an angel"; with his pea-jacket, his d'Orsay cloak and soft felt hat "broad in the brim" and "worn jauntily on one side"; with his "wiry moustache", "grizzled beard", and deeply lined, bronzed face like the face of "a Viking". In Liverpool three thousand people were turned away from his reading; in Glasgow two files of policemen kept the crowds from the doors of the City Hall; in Manchester there was so wild a demonstration of cheering and applause that Dickens, for once, was overcome. But there was no doubt that the whole tour, in the long intervals between those demonstrations of joy and gratitude which revived him so easily, was wearying in the extreme. Railway travelling now disturbed and exhausted him; Dolby has recorded how he used to nerve himself with a pull of brandy from his travelling flask. (On one occasion, compounding his terror of travelling by express, a fire broke out in one of the carriages.) It was a hard life: getting up at six-thirty, travelling on to the next place, lying in a hotel bed unable to sleep, eating very little, the whole process repeated day after day. Forster said that "it was labour that must in time have broken down the strongest man . . ." but Dickens, now in his fifty-fifth year, was not so strong as that. Even during the tour he was still suffering from what he called "irritability of the heart", and his general restlessness and insomnia made the condition worse. Only the performances themselves seemed to help him and, during the short interval, he always took a dozen oysters with a little champagne in order to refresh himself. He ate but little apart from this. He was hoarse with cold at Manchester, and was compelled to read with a husky voice; and one observer at a Birmingham reading noticed "how fatigued" he seemed in comparison with his visit in 1859. In May Wills informed his wife that Dickens was suffering from headache and what he called "brow neuralgia"; Dickens himself said that he was feeling very gloomy and "dull" but, as was his habit, he tried never to show this to his travelling companions. To them he remained cheerful – what Wills called "plucky" – and it would be hard from Dolby's own account of Dickens's animated behaviour to realise that he was a man who had just suffered from a terrible nervous shock and the effects of a transient stroke. But the effects were nevertheless there; towards the end of the reading tour he began to suffer severe pain in his left eye, and his left hand, too, was in the grip of "neuralgic" spasms. He went on, in low spirits each day, only to spring up again at the expected time. He went on but, by the time he had finished the tour in June, he said that he felt "very tired and depressed". But there is the extraordinary thing – even before this tour was over he had already opened negotiations with Chappell and Company to undertake another in the following winter. Nothing could stop him now.

He had been away for some three months; when he

went down to Gad's Hill Place in order ". . . to rest and hear the birds sing", it was his first visit since March. No doubt he was comforted, too, by the fact that the gross receipts of the tour amounted to some five thousand pounds; he had kept his bargain with Chappell, and they had been rewarded. Then he went back to London, partly in order to be "disposed of" at various dinners and social engagements (although he seems to have been able to limit himself now to three or four days each week) and partly to catch up with all the arrears of office business and correspondence. He also had to set to work upon a projected new edition of his works, the "Charles Dickens Edition", each of his novels appearing once a month in a single volume for 3/6, freshly set, with new prefaces by Dickens himself and, as the prospectus explained, "a descriptive headline will be attached by the author to every right-hand page". In fact this became the most popular of all Dickens's editions in his lifetime; with the gilt lettering on the back, and a facsimile signature on the red cover, it might be seen as encompassing and defining a lifetime's work. It was truly his memorial. His last edition.

In July he was spending much of his time at Gad's Hill Place, and this because he had a great deal of entertaining to arrange there, what with guests he and his family had invited, or guests who had invited themselves. He travelled up to the office for at least two days a week, however, and future work was very much on his mind. It was not long before he had come to an arrangement with Chappell for the next series of readings, although the success of the first tour was such that Dickens could now more or less dictate his own terms; he was to receive sixty pounds a night (an increase of twenty per cent on the last series) and would perform for forty-two nights, with Chappell as usual paying all of his travelling and business expenses. He would begin in the new year and he calculated that, in the six months remaining of the old, he could write the next

Christmas story for *All The Year Round* and make some progress upon a novel which he wished to serialise in that periodical during the following spring. Again he had ideas and conceptions floating somewhere within the recesses of his consciousness, but as yet no firm thread upon which to bind them.

Throughout the summer Dickens was never completely well. He was bothered by flatulence and stomach pains and was on two occasions seized "apparently in the heart". More warning signs, but again Dickens chose to ignore their seriousness by suggesting that they had to do with something "in the atmosphere". And of course he carried on with his duties regardless, including time-consuming but not necessarily unwelcome work with Fechter at the Lyceum; the actor-manager was about to put on Dion Boucicault's sensation drama, *A Long Strike*, and Dickens was a constant and regular adviser in all the theatrical preparations. But he was also getting on with his own necessary business. He had begun the Christmas story for that year, and used as his starting point his embarrassment at being reprimanded during his last reading tour by the manageress of the station refreshment room; he took his belated literary revenge by parodying and mimicking the harridans behind the counter in "The Boy at Mugby". But this was only one of his contributions to that Christmas issue of *All The Year Round*; he also appended a number of other stories, among them the famous ghost tale, "The Signal-Man", which serves as an apt reminder of Forster's remark that Dickens liked nothing so much as to tell or to be told ghost stories. In fact he wrote almost half of that year's Christmas issue, and was at work on it throughout September and the first half of October. Certainly there was no diminution of inventiveness in this last period of his life; the comic impersonation of the boy in the refreshment room was followed by the ghost story, both of them preceded by the sentimental narrative of a disappointed

516

man. The last is perhaps the most interesting for in two stories, "Barbox Brothers" and "Barbox Brothers and Co", Dickens reverts to what had become his most enduring fantasies and images. Here once more is a weary and anguished man – disappointed in love, disappointed in life, disappointed in the absence of any real childhood and youth. And here again, as in two of his previous Christmas stories, a melancholy middle-aged man takes up with a small girl and protects her; there is no suggestion of a sexual tie here, of course, but rather the kind of plaintive infantilism (Dickens was adept at creating "baby talk") which seems now to spread over any story of his which is at all concerned with human love.

It sounds like a quiet summer and autumn, then, after the excitement of the readings, but it was not without its moments of local drama; he was forced to shoot the dog which Percy Fitzgerald had given him, Sultan, because of its propensity to lunge at any human shape apart from that of Dickens himself (he was led ceremoniously out to the field, and there shot through the heart); he was in the process of suing a Mr Cave, the proprietor of the Marylebone Theatre, who had accused Dickens of turning up drunk at a production of *The Black Doctor* (untrue); his renegade brother, Augustus, died in Chicago. And then his daughter, Kate, became seriously ill with something known then as "nervous fever", which sounds as though it might have been related to Lehmann's observation earlier in the year that she was ". . . burning away both character and I fear health . . ." And so the year came to an end: a houseful of guests at Christmas and Dickens reading his adaptation of "The Boy At Mugby" to the assembled company, a sports competition on Boxing Day with Dickens as judge and referee ("The All Comers' Race. Distance – Once round the field. First Prize, 10s . . ."), and Ellen Ternan close by in Rochester where she was staying with her uncle.

In the new year, 1867, Dickens was to embark upon the second reading tour. There were on occasions incidents which broke the monotony; like the time Dickens was improvising a song-and-dance routine in a railway carriage when his sealskin cap was blown out of the window, or the excitement of the journey to Ireland during a period when the Fenian crisis was at one of its intermittent heights. As always, of course, he was at least momentarily cheered and revived by the reactions of the audiences who came to see him; his letters speak continually once more of huge crowds, incredible applause, tears, laughter. But by the time it had come to an end he was sick to death of it all – of the hot rooms, and the glare, and the exhaustion. In his diary entry for 13 May, 1867, beside his brief notation that he read "Dombey & Bob" at St James's Hall, he underlined the word *Last*. It was all over. Yet even before reaching this happy quietus he was contemplating yet another tour; and, this time, the most arduous and exacting yet. He had for a long time been receiving letters and invitations to read in the United States and these offers of engagement had now become "the chief topic" of his discussions with Dolby. Should he travel to America, to the "Loadstone Rock", as he called it? He believed that he could make a "fortune" there, but he could not bring himself to contemplate the absence from Ellen Ternan. He wanted to triumph in the United States as he had already triumphed in England, to stamp his image upon the moving spirit of the age, but he could only do so at the risk of his mental and physical health. But Dickens was now preoccupied with America. It had become for him ". . . this spectre of doubt and indecision that sits at the board with me and stands at the bedside". And yet, and yet ". . . the prize looks so large! . . ."

He decided that he could come to no real conclusion without the benefit of a first-hand report about his prospects and so, one July morning as he and Dolby walked
518

across Hyde Park to the office from Paddington Station, it was agreed between them that Dolby should travel to the United States at the beginning of August in order both to judge the financial prospects of an extended reading tour and to inspect halls for likely venues (he would in addition take with him the manuscript of "George Silverman's Explanation", and another story, which Dickens had written for the American journals). At the same time Dickens was intent upon changing his life in a more immediate way. Since the end of March he had been sporadically searching for a house in the London suburb of Peckham, which he might lease for Ellen Ternan and her mother. Peckham was anonymous and still preserved an air of remoteness from metropolitan concerns; more importantly still, it was only about twenty minutes' walk from the apartment which Dickens seems intermittently to have kept near the Five Bells Inn in New Cross. It took some time, however, to find an appropriate house. On the sixth of that month he had sent a letter to Wills on stationery embossed with the legend "ET", in which he admitted that the "Patient" (Ellen) was the "gigantic difficulty" in the way of his travelling to America. And, later in the month of June, Ellen's sister, Fanny, certainly stayed there during a visit from Italy (where she now lived with her husband, T. A. Trollope). The evidence of Dickens's diary strongly suggests, however, that he or Ellen had found a suitable house by the twenty-first of the month, and that on the following day he waited there some time for her in order to examine the property. It was at 16 Linden Grove, a comfortable two-storeyed house surrounded by a large garden and settled among fields. A more prosperous house than the previous one; a more *genteel* house. But first it had to be redecorated and the Ternans remained in temporary accommodation until it was ready for occupancy. They moved in on 18 July, at which point it seems that Dickens returned to Gad's Hill Place. It has generally been assumed

519

that he shared both the temporary and permanent houses with the Ternans, although there is no direct evidence to that effect; the notations in his diary are too elliptical to afford any real clues. In fact it seems just as likely that Dickens maintained his lodgings near the Five Bells during this whole period – what better reason could there have been for choosing a house in this vicinity in the first place? He paid the rates for Linden Grove (under the assumed name of Charles Tringham), but it is at least possible that he simply visited the Ternans regularly rather than lived there. The fact that he sometimes travelled back to Gad's Hill Place from New Cross Station (which is just a short stroll from the Five Bells) certainly suggests that he still maintained his old quarters even at the time when the Ternans were close by.

On the second day of August he accompanied Dolby to Liverpool in order to "see him off" on his Atlantic crossing. He made the journey even though he was once again suffering from a swollen and painful left foot which made it necessary for him to walk everywhere with a stick – when the two men boarded the ship he was recognised everywhere, and both men and women offered him their seats. Nothing seemed to minimise his own curiosity, however, and Dolby records how "he examined everything, even to the little bunk in the state-room, as if it had been a bed at Gad's Hill, to see that it was comfortable". Dickens returned to London the next day, dined that evening at the Athenaeum and, because he was too lame to go the railway station, took a hansom cab out to Peckham. The following day was a Sunday, but he came to London expressly in order to receive the advice of an eminent surgeon, Sir Henry Thompson. Thompson diagnosed "erysipelas" – a fevered inflammation of the skin – consequent upon walking, which might be classed as yet another example of a doctor telling the patient precisely what the patient most wants to hear. Erysipelas itself was a serious
520

disorder, however, and was sometimes known as "St Anthony's Fire" because of its connection with severe nervous affliction. Dickens returned to Peckham at once, but on the following day came back again to London in order to consult the doctor once more; the condition of his foot was now so bad that he was "laid up" at the Wellington Street offices for the next four days.

By the end of this week of being "laid up", Dickens felt strong enough to undertake a ride in the open air and a visit to the Olympic Theatre; and, from that time forward, he commuted between Wellington Street and Peckham while also of course making sure that he made regular visits to Gad's Hill Place. All the time he was waiting anxiously for Dolby to telegraph his news from America but, in this interval, he could not of course be expected to *stop working*. So he began that year's story for the Christmas issue – so much a matter of routine now, but Dickens was too great an artist not to distil something of himself in even the most minor or improvised piece. The new story, or rather serial, was entitled "No Thoroughfare" and it was once again a collaborative effort by Dickens and Wilkie Collins. It is, in general terms, a mystery story in which murder and flight and embezzlement are played out against that setting of the Alps which so haunted Dickens's imagination. It was characteristic, too, that Dickens should once more direct his imagination into the mind and consciousness of a murderer, the same smooth, hypocritical murderer who had appeared in "Hunted Down" and would reappear in *The Mystery of Edwin Drood*. He was working on the story at Peckham and, at the end of August, he read the first portion of it to Wilkie Collins at the office. He wanted to finish it as quickly as he could, and this primarily because America was so much on his mind that nothing else seemed to be of much consequence.

Dolby returned to England in late September, having fulfilled the commands of his "Chief" to the letter. He

521

had inspected various halls in Washington, New York and Boston; he had carefully calculated the likely profits of the enterprise, down to the most recent rate of dollar conversion; he had spoken to the most eminent and influential men of the country, including the famous P. T. Barnum. Dolby immediately travelled down from London to Gad's Hill Place – he was greeted on his arrival at the house by the sound of a dinner gong which Dickens described as "real show business" – and it was here that he announced to "the Chief" his overwhelming conclusion. Dickens should go to the United States. It was then agreed that Dolby should make out an official written report on the subject, which Dickens could show to his advisers (foremost among them Wills, Forster and his solicitor, Ouvry). But these three gentlemen were scattered all over the country and could not conveniently be brought together so, instead, Dickens wrote out his own account which he entitled "The case in a nutshell". Dolby's advice is tendered, but the main thrust of this "nutshell" report is directed towards the probable financial gains from the American tour.

There were a great many arrangements to be made, but none more sensitive and more important than the question of Ellen. She had been "the gigantic difficulty" of his going at all, principally because he could not bear the contemplation of such a long absence from her. And so, throughout these months of planning and negotiation, he had been scheming to bring her with him to the United States. Of course she could not travel with such a public man in any compromising capacity, and it seems that at first he thought of taking her with him ostensibly as a companion to his daughter, Mamie. Mamie herself has said that her father had asked her to accompany him to America, and only reluctantly abandoned the idea when it was clear that his would be only a "business trip". Certainly there is a note in his pocket diary about a ladies' state room for the

Atlantic crossing, "2 berths for'ard in front of machinery". The importance here lies in the note about *two* berths; Ellen, if she should come, was not to come alone. Mamie did not go, however, although the excuse of a "business trip" does not sound entirely plausible. It seems that she had in any case a fear of travelling by sea, and it is possible that she rebelled at the prospect of travelling simply in order to legitimise Ellen's position. Whatever the reason, that particular plan had to be dropped. But Dickens had not given up. Not yet. Dolby was to travel to the United States ahead of his employer, in order to make sure that preparations for the readings were well advanced, and three days before his departure he dined with Dickens and Ellen Ternan. Some new plan had already been concocted, and it is clear from the extant correspondence that Dolby was to consult with James Fields, Dickens's publisher in Boston, and his wife whom the novelist had already met and liked — to see if it was at all possible for Ellen to come over without causing undue scandal or offence. Since Ellen had a cousin, Richard Smith Spofford, who lived just north of Boston it was at least possible that Ellen might travel separately to the United States on the excuse that she was visiting her relative. In any case, Dolby was to send back a transatlantic cable with the message either "Yes" or "No"; but Dickens was not so sanguine about the prospects that he did not readily envisage a negative response to Dolby's discreet enquiries.

Meanwhile, in the first days of October, he prepared himself for his journey, which could now be undertaken without Ellen since Dolby had cabled "No". Amidst the press of business one occasion stood out, however, and this was the farewell banquet given to him by his friends and contemporaries at the Freemasons' Hall seven days before his departure. It was a lavish affair, even by mid-Victorian standards; there were some four hundred and fifty guests at the banquet itself while, according to custom, some one hundred women were sitting in the gallery above. The lobbies and the corridors had already been decorated with statuary and exotic plants, there were English and American flags entwined together, and the walls of the hall itself had been decorated with twenty panels, representing the works of the novelist, each one announced in gold lettering. It seemed to one observer that "the noble room had all the semblance of a temple especially erected to the honour and for the glorification of England's favourite author". The doors were thrown open and, when Dickens appeared "a cry rang through the room, handkerchiefs were waved on the floor and in the galleries . . . and the band struck up a full march". During the dinner the band of the Grenadier Guards played music by Mozart, Meyerbeer, Verdi, Strauss and Offenbach. Grace was sung, various speeches were made (by, among others, Landseer, Trollope and Bulwer-Lytton) until eventually Charles Dickens himself rose from his seat. But he could not make himself heard, since the assembled company rose and cheered continually; some people crowded the aisles around him while others leaped upon chairs. Dickens now almost lost control of himself. He tried to speak but could not do so and, according to one observer present, "the tears streamed down his face". Eventually, he went on to talk of America, and he took this occasion to make peace with the men and women among whom he was soon to move by repeating some words from one of his Christmas essays. "I know full well, whatever little motes my beamy eyes may have descried in theirs, that they are a kind, large-hearted, generous and great people. [*Cheers*]." And this was how he ended a speech which had been interrupted so many times by cheering and applause: " 'And so,' as Tiny Tim observed. 'God bless us every one!' " He sat down to the sound of continual cheering.

At the beginning of the following week, just four days

before his departure, he was back in the office, making his final preparations for departure. Percy Fitzgerald came to see him there and observed ". . . the worn, well frayed man, now looking at a letter brought in hastily, now engaged with some businessman". It was from there, also, that he wrote a short and somewhat curt note to Catherine, who had clearly written to him with her own message of *bon voyage*. It read only, "I am glad to receive your letter, and to accept and reciprocate your good wishes. Severely hard work lies before me; but that is not a new thing in my life, and I am content to go my way and do it." On 8 November he travelled in a special railway carriage – a "royal saloon carriage", someone called it – from London to Liverpool. Wills travelled up with him and noticed curiously how, after lunch, Dickens "actually took out a clothes brush and flicked away all the crumbs from seats and floor". Then, on the ninth of the month, Dickens sailed on the *Cuba* for the United States.

# Thirty-Three

H E had been given the second officer's cabin — on deck, which meant that with his window and door open he received all the fresh air he needed. But he was still not entirely sanguine about the pitching and rolling of these cross-Atlantic ships, and so he carried with him a medicine chest filled with laudanum, ether, and sal volatile. In the event, however, he found that baked apples were the best precaution against sea-sickness. With him, but in less commodious quarters, were Scott, his new valet; Lowndes, the new gas-man; and a general factotum called Kelly whose ill-health seems to have infuriated his employer. He also took a large number of books with him, among them the proof sheets of a new life of Garrick; he was, as he said to his daughter, a "great reader" on board ship. From his own account it was a voyage punctuated by the intense merriment which Dickens's joviality produced and interrupted by gales of the most frightful nature; par for the course, one might say, on any journey involving the author. He took particular pleasure in describing the Sunday service during a heavy sea, when clergyman and congregation rolled around together and provided what Dickens called an "exceedingly funny" spectacle. As usual in these circumstances, he could not restrain his laughter: ". . . I was obliged to leave before the service began." But no doubt he had time amidst all this comicality to reflect once more upon the country he was about to visit again after an absence of some twenty-five years, years in which, it must be said, Dickens had not materially changed his opinion about it at all. Despite his friendship with various Americans, it is clear that he still distrusted the country as a place where "smartness" vied with financial malpractice as the chief household god.

Dolby's advance arrival in Boston had alerted that city to Dickens's coming and just before he docked, according to a report in one newspaper, ". . . everything was immediately put into apple-pie order. The streets were all swept from one end of the city to the other for the second time in twenty-four hours. The State House and the Old South Church were painted, offhand, a delicate rose pink." The booksellers' windows were filled with his novels, and once more there appeared the "Little Nell Cigar" and the "Pickwick Snuff" and the "Mantalini Plug". It had already been arranged that Dickens, true to his custom on his reading tours, would stay in an hotel for the duration of his stay; and, for this "first stop" in Boston, rooms had been prepared for him at the Parker House. Dolby had already decided that Dickens should not be exhibited free of charge, as it were, and had demanded strict privacy for his employer; so the manager of the hotel assigned a private waiter to serve Dickens's meals in Dickens's own sitting room, and placed a servant outside the door at all times to prevent access to the apartment. And already, days before his arrival, the queues for tickets for his "readings" were enormous; the attraction consisted not only in his own fame and genius but also in the novelty of the enterprise, since no one in America had ever seen public readings of the kind which he proposed. On the first morning the tickets were on sale the queue was over half a mile long, and many people had arrived the night before with straw mattresses, food and tobacco.

Two days after his arrival Dickens had dinner with his

publisher, James Fields, and his wife Annie Adams Fields; the two became his closest friends during this visit, Annie herself being then thirty-three while her husband was fifty, and from Annie's diaries it is possible to elicit a sympathetic if occasionally too romantic portrait of Dickens himself. The first dinner went well enough – "he bubbled over with fun," Mrs Fields wrote. But his real thoughts were elsewhere and on the same day he wrote to Wills, explaining that he would send letters to Ellen Ternan ("my Dear Girl . . .") through him. On the following day he had breakfast in his sitting room, before commencing what would become a daily rehearsal of the readings; in this room there was a large mirror surrounded by decorated black walnut, and it is likely that he paraded his facial impersonations in front of it. Then, after a light lunch, he took the first of his long walks which varied somewhere between seven and ten miles. A reporter noticed what he was wearing for this first excursion: "Light trousers with a broad stripe down the side, a brown coat bound with wide braid of a darker shade and faced with velvet, a flowered fancy vest . . . necktie secured with a jewelled ring and a loose kimono-like topcoat with wide sleeves and the lapels heavily embroidered, a silk hat, and very light yellow gloves . . ." A gorgeous specimen among the conventionally dark-suited and dark-coated inhabitants of Boston and one small boy, a certain John Morse junior, "remembers distinctly that Dickens was the most magnificently attired pedestrian that he had ever seen". Whenever he stopped a crowd gathered but, on the whole, the Bostonians left him to himself. He was compelled go to the local theatre incognito, however, to avoid any inconvenient demonstrations.

His first reading was held on 2 December at the Tremont Temple. There had been a snow-storm that morning, but the evening was bright and clear; according to the *New York Tribune*, "The line of carriages ran down all manner of streets and lost itself in the suburbs . . . the gay, struggling, swarming multitude that was trying to get inside the doors, watched by the long-faced silent multitude that crowded round the doorways without tickets . . .'' Among the audience were Longfellow, James Russell Lowell, Oliver Wendell Holmes, R. H. Dana and Charles Eliot Norton. It took time for the audience to settle but then Dickens, to an accompaniment of loud cheers and applause and waving of handkerchiefs, walked briskly onto the platform in his evening tail-coat with its lapels faced in satin, and with two small red and white flowers in his buttonhole. The ''set'' was unchanged – the same maroon back-cloth, the same maroon carpet, the desk and the array of gas pipes. Without acknowledging the applause in any way, he began to read from *A Christmas Carol*. The reception was by all accounts (and not only that of Dickens) remarkable for its length and vociferousness.

He read three more times in Boston and then travelled down to New York, where he stayed at the Westminster Hotel in Irving Place. The hotel manager had thoughtfully arranged for his sole use of a private staircase which led to his door and, as in Boston, a servant was posted outside Dickens's apartment to prevent any unwanted intruders. The next morning he and Dolby visited the Steinway Hall, where the readings were to be given, and then spent the rest of the day walking about the city. He read six times in the Steinway Hall and, once again, he received tremendous ovations. As the janitor of the hotel said to him, in words beautifully transcribed by Dickens, ''Mr Digguns, you are gread, mein-herr. Ther is no ent to you! Bedder and bedder. Wot negst!'' One senses, in his evident delight in reproducing the sound of these words, his old sharpness and observation. It could not be said, however, that he was seeing much of the country on this visit – in these first weeks, he was travelling only between Boston and New York – but, then, he had no interest in seeing it. He was no longer the young man of 1842, wide awake and desperate to know everything. Now he was interested only in his performances, and in the amount of money which he was able to earn from them; he sent his "takings" back to England almost as soon as Dolby had collected them, and his correspondence in this period is rendered almost wearisome by his constant emphasis on the sums acquired and the sums expected.

In the first month of 1868 he read in New York, Boston, Philadelphia, Baltimore and Brooklyn; hard work for him, but hard work also for his staff which had to be augmented with some American recruits. Numbering and stamping six thousand tickets for Philadelphia, eight thousand tickets for Brooklyn; answering business correspondence; arranging advertising; preparing accounts; organising all travel arrangements. And, in response, the excitement of the American public. "People will turn back, turn again and face me, and have a look at me . . . or will say to one another, 'Look here! Dickens coming!' " When he sat in his carriage people would gather around it and "in the railway cars, if I see anybody who clearly wants to speak to me, I usually anticipate the wish by speaking myself". But he was in poor health still and would remain so for the rest of his visit, the "influenza" having settled down into a cold and catarrh which stayed with Dickens while he remained on American soil. This often made him very depressed; he was sleeping only for about three or four hours each night, and he told Georgina that he was losing his hair "with great rapidity". He was indeed almost visibly growing older, day by day and week by week. But the most extraordinary aspect of this extraordinary tour was the extent to which he was able to recover when he stood on the public platform for his readings; he had a strange power of "coming up to time", no matter how drained and debilitated he seemed beforehand, and indeed it was often the case that the more prostrated he was in advance
530

the more powerful his performance. All his nervous energy seemed at once to expel the signs of ill-health, like an organism through which an electric current is passed. Then afterwards the faintness, the sickness and the depression: they had not been expelled but simply suppressed, and Dickens himself fully realised that ". . . one's being able to do the two hours with spirit when the time comes round, may be co-existent with the consciousness of great depression and fatigue".

On the first day of February, he travelled down to Washington for his readings there; he visited President Johnson ("Each of us looked at the other very hard . . ."), and attended one dinner at which a guest noticed how he was ". . . extremely nervous, quick in his motions and changing his expression like a flash". On this occasion he heard many stories about the last days of Abraham Lincoln, and in particular his strange dream before his assassination. And then, after Washington, off to Baltimore, Philadelphia, Hartford, and Providence where, when he marched up the steps of his hotel accompanied by two policemen and surrounded by a crowd, he remarked to Dolby, "This is very like going into the police van in Bow Street, isn't it?" But everywhere the cold, the snow-storms, the gales. He was now so exhausted that he had decided to cancel some of the readings already planned; he cut out Chicago, the West and Canada, so that he might be able to return home a month earlier than he had originally envisaged. And all the time he was writing letters to Ellen Ternan – four in February alone. For a few days at the beginning of March he was able to rest, since his projected readings had to be cancelled in the week of the President's impeachment. But then he was off again. Syracuse ("We . . . supped on a tough old nightmare called buffalo . . ."), Rochester, Buffalo, Albany, New Haven, Hartford, even though the brief respite had done nothing to ease his depression or fatigue. His only relief seemed to lie either in the constant calculation of the profit he was making — he estimated, rightly to within a thousand, that he would make for himself some twenty thousand pounds — or in his excitement at witnessing the enthusiasm of his audiences. "They have taken to applauding too whenever they laugh or cry," he said of the Bostonians, "and the result is very inspiriting." Particularly he noticed, one night, that "one poor young girl in mourning burst into a passion of grief about Tiny Tim, and was taken out". He was dosing himself with laudanum by now simply in order to sleep (although the soporific had an enervating effect upon him the next day) and his foot had once more broken out in all the agonies of swelling. He was so badly lamed, in truth, that he hobbled everywhere, through the snow and the slush of the American streets, on a stick. Dolby now never left him and, even during the readings, sat by the side of the platform and carefully watched his progress.

But soon only the last readings in New York were left. He was clearly exhilarated by the prospect of his imminent departure, and after the first reading there his spirits once more rose in an improvised routine of comic songs and "patter" in the company of his friends. He read again the next night and Mrs Fields noticed that one of the signs of his fatigue was ". . . the rush of blood into his face and hands". Four days later, on 18 April, a farewell banquet was held for him in New York; so serious was his lameness, however, that he arrived very late. He had been in such pain all day that he could not fit a boot on his foot, and in the end Dolby had to drive all over the city looking for such a thing as a gout-stocking. But eventually he arrived, an hour after the appointed time, hobbling in on the arm of Horace Greeley, the editor of the *New York Tribune*, with his foot swathed in something resembling a carpet-bag. Dinner was conducted to the sound of national airs being played by a band and, at the end, he rose to speak. "When the storm of enthusiasm had quieted," one guest remembered, "Dickens tried to speak but could not; the tears streamed down his face. As he stood there looking on us in silence, colour and pallor alternating on his face, sympathetic emotion passed through the hall. When he presently began to say something, though still faltering, we gave our cheers . . ."

A few days later he was unable to rise from his bed, so tired he had become. That night Fields told him that a statue ought to be raised in honour of him and of his heroism. "No, don't," he replied characteristically, "take down one of the old ones instead!" Then, on the following day, he sailed for England. He was surrounded by a large crowd as he left his hotel for the last time, and bouquets were thrown to him from the windows nearby. It was a fine day as he went down to the harbour by Spring Street, to step onto the private tug which would take him to the *Russia* which was lying off Staten Island. As soon as Dickens saw the water, he said, "That's *home*!" Fields and other friends had accompanied him to this final point of departure. "As the tugboat hooted, all left save Fields . . . The lame foot came down from the rail, and the friends were locked in each other's arms. Fields then hastened down the side, and the lines were cast off. A cheer was given for Dolby, when Dickens patted him approvingly upon the shoulder, saying 'Good boy'. Another cheer for Dickens, then the tug steamed away." The group left on the shore shouted, "Goodbye!" Dickens ". . . put his hat upon his cane, and waved it, and the answer came 'Goodbye' and 'God bless you every one'". Anthony Trollope, who had arrived in New York that same day, visited Dickens in his cabin just before the *Russia* sailed; he found him with his foot bound up, but remarkably cheerful.

And what of Dickens himself now? What had been the effect of his American tour? Both his sons believed that it injured him. Henry said that it actually shortened his life, and Charley has written that ". . . the American work had told him upon him severely. The trouble in the foot was greatly intensified, and he was gravely out of health." But there is something more to be discovered in the record of these five months, something which Carlyle discerned when he read Forster's account of them in his biography: "Those two American Journies especially transcend in tragic interest to a thinking reader most things one has seen in writing." It is reasonable to assume, for example, that Dickens almost killed himself in order to make more money; he risked everything in order to become more "secure". And yet this had always been the case. Certainly it had been true at the time of his earliest childhood, when the search for security was the one constant aspect of a life so bedevilled by pain and anxiety. And it may be precisely here that the proper significance of his American journey can be understood – that, somehow, in the vision of the mature Dickens making his way through an alien country, we catch sight, from time to time, of the young Dickens making his way through the streets of London.

There was that same desperate need for security, and that same sense of the "dreariness" of life which he had experienced as a child; his Christmas journey on the train from Boston to New York, when he sat in silence and looked out of the window, evokes the journey he made in the coach which brought him from Rochester to London as a child. A journey in which ". . . I thought life sloppier than I expected to find it". In adult life as in childhood, also, he was racked by pains of a predominantly nervous origin; what he called his "ailing little life" as a child, when as Forster said, he was "subject to continual attacks of illness", had surely now returned. But now, as then, he preferred to keep his agony to himself and once more "suffered in secret". There was a similar attempt to conceal his life in other ways, too. Where once he had hidden from Bob Fagin and his warehouse companions the fact that his father was in the Marshalsea, so now he hid from most people his liaison with Ellen Ternan. There was the same need to perform as well; in the blacking warehouse he had entertained his little companions "with the results of some of the old readings" just as now, in America and England, he entertained audiences with readings from his own books. As a child he had been considered a "prodigy" by the adults, and he was considered a prodigy still. As a child he had also felt the need to work skilfully and hard, saving as much money as he could in the process; and nothing of that had changed. The continual fevered sicknesses, the sense of dreariness and desolation, the secret life, the need to entertain, the urgent desire to work, the interest in money – all these echoes of his childhood resound through these last years. Of course many things had changed. He no longer took his breakfast in prison, he no longer hated his mother and his older sister, he no longer felt himself to be "beyond the reach of all such honourable emulation and success", he no longer felt himself to be neglected and humiliated, and the crowd no longer watched him tying up the labels of blacking pots in the window of Chandos Street. But do we not feel the pressure of these things still propelling him forward through all the days of his life? It is not so tragic as Carlyle would have it, but, rather, part of the ineluctable process of life – Charles Dickens returning, despite his genius and all his fame, to the state of his childhood. As if nothing that had ever happened to him could exorcise the presence of that child. As if nothing, in the end, were of any account beside that sense of the world which first visited him as a child.

# Thirty-Four

THE *Russia* arrived at Queenstown Harbour on the last day of April, 1868, but Dolby and Dickens did not hurry home. They dined in Liverpool on the following day and then took the morning train the day after that, arriving back in London in the middle of the afternoon. But Dickens did not go down to Gad's Hill Place. He went instead to Peckham in order to be with the Ternans, Ellen and her mother having returned from Italy only two days before. He stayed here for a week, making occasional visits to London.

He was still preoccupied with business at *All The Year Round*, and managed to organise for himself a summer routine from which he rarely, if ever, departed; from Monday to Thursday he worked and lived in London, while at the weekends he returned to Gad's Hill Place where he entertained the various guests who arrived throughout the summer months (among them Longfellow and Frith). In fact his work on the periodical was at last providentially lightened, although for a reason with which Dickens could possibly have dispensed. His son, Charley, was involved in bankruptcy proceedings, having lost all of his money in his paper-mill business and owing something like one thousand pounds. This was for him a very serious matter, since he had a wife and five children — Dickens was at a loss to know what to do for him, but eventually arrived at the conclusion that he was best placed to work with him at Wellington Street. So Charley reported on the daily "mailbag" and answered most correspondence. There were family problems of another kind also; his daughter's husband, Charles Collins, was now in very bad health and, Dickens reported, "*I* say emphatically — dying". In fact Collins had stomach cancer and would die in 1873 but, as far as Dickens was concerned, his demise could not come a moment too soon. This was partly because of his resentment at Collins marrying his daughter in the first place (after Dickens's death Georgina told Annie Fields that he had for a long time been exercised by the "dreary unfortunate fate" of Kate), but partly because of his deep dislike of constitutional weakness of any kind.

But it was also in this period that Dickens's problems wore a more private aspect. It seems that the Ternans left Linden Grove in Peckham — by October Mrs Ternan was staying at 32 Harrington Square, and from December to June she and, most likely, Ellen were staying at 10 Bath Place in Worthing. After that they moved into an apartment house at 305 Vauxhall Bridge Road. The evidence is circumstantial and incomplete but it does suggest that, from this time forward, Charles Dickens and Ellen Ternan no longer lived with or near each other; Dickens himself seems to have kept on the Peckham house for a while, and perhaps paid someone to maintain it for him. Nevertheless there is no evidence of any estrangement between them — it seems clear, as we shall see, that Ellen accompanied him on all or part of his next reading tour — and it is even possible that she sometimes remained *sub rosa* at Peckham after her mother had moved away. In what capacity, if such is the case, is of course not known. But perhaps one might pick out some stray sentences from the novel which Dickens soon began to write, and repeat the words of Rosa Bud to her "lover", Edwin Drood. " 'That's a dear good boy! Eddy, let us be courageous. Let us change to brother and sister from this day forth.'

'Never be husband and wife?'

'Never!' "

And, when Longfellow came to visit Dickens at Gad's Hill Place, he noticed his "terrible sadness".

What else was there for Dickens to do, now, except to work on and to work hard? By the end of July he was trying to begin that year's story for the Christmas issue of *All The Year Round*, but he was starting drafts only to abandon them; he could see nothing beyond what had now become for him a dreary routine of stories around a theme. One such draft, written partly in Peckham, may be what has since become known as the "Sapsea Fragment"; it is a short episode narrated by a pompous auctioneer which bears the seeds for some parts of *The Mystery of Edwin Drood*. It may actually be this piece of narration which Dickens described to Wills as tending towards a new book rather than a Christmas tale but, even so, it remained only a fragment. Eventually he abandoned altogether the idea of writing a Christmas number for that year, despite the evident financial advantages of the old scheme. He simply seemed unable to work at his old pace or with his old instinctive energy, and it is significant that Forster should notice this summer ". . . manifest abatement of his natural force, the elasticity of bearing was impaired, and the wonderful brightness of eye was dimmed at times". He added, more ominously, that on one occasion ". . . he could read only the halves of the letters over the shop doors that were on his right as he looked". Dickens ascribed this to the effects of the medicine he was taking for his injured foot and, according to Forster, no one really understood ". . . the fact that absolute and pressing danger did positively exist".

Perhaps it says something about his frayed state in this period that, when his son Edward ("Plorn") emigrated to Australia, he was plunged into a quite uncharacteristic paroxysm of grief; and this despite the fact that Dickens himself had been largely instrumental in sending Plorn, not yet seventeen, to seek his fortune in the outback. He had seen in him what he had observed in other of his children, a lack of determination and application which he blamed upon their mother but which might equally have been ascribed to his own family. In preparation for Plorn's emigration he had sent him to Cirencester Agricultural College for eight months – he considered this quite long enough under the circumstances – and then dispatched him to join his brother, Alfred, in New South Wales. But he had always been an impressionable and rather vulnerable boy, and it seems somewhat rash of Dickens to send him to a life in the outback which he himself knew only from "books and verbal description". (How typical of him, though, to trust in "books" for a true depiction of the reality.) But, when the time came to take his leave of Plorn on the platform of Paddington station, "the scene that followed was tragic in its emotional intensity". These are the words of Dickens's son, Henry, who went on to describe how "my father openly gave way to his intense grief quite regardless of his surroundings". On another occasion he added that "I never saw a man so completely overcome", which suggests that Dickens's passionate outpouring of sorrow must have been of an extraordinary kind. Certainly Plorn himself was not accustomed to seeing his father so moved, except perhaps when he gave public readings, and he looked the other way until the train was ready to depart. He took with him, however, a complete set of his father's books; how touching that this young man should be seeing his father for the last time, while carrying with him the novels by which Charles Dickens would be remembered for ever.

Henry Dickens was now spending a great deal of time with his mother. While he remained at home he was a burden about which Dickens still often complained; he had expressed a wish to go to Cambridge rather than immediately to embark upon a professional career, but it was only with misgivings that Dickens allowed him to attend university. In fact Henry had gone up to Trinity Hall just a week before Plorn sailed, and Dickens was very careful about ensuring that his son received just enough money *and no more*. His refrain is always the need to keep out of debt, and to depend upon his own resources; his injunctions are always the same, too. Do not waste your father's hard-earned money. Remember what your father's life was like at the same age. Nevertheless he was genuinely proud of his son, and was delighted when in the following year Henry won a scholarship at Trinity Hall which promised him an annual stipend of fifty pounds. Henry told him the news when he arrived from Cambridge at Higham station and was met by his father in the pony carriage. At first Dickens only murmured "Capital! Capital!" but, half way home, he ". . . broke down completely. Turning towards me with tears in his eyes and giving me a warm grip of the hand, he said, 'God bless you, my boy; God bless you!'" Henry was the only one of his children to have achieved any success in life, and it must have sometimes seemed to Dickens that he had attained his great distinction at the price of everybody else's happiness. But now, in Henry, he had some proof that at least a particle of his extraordinary talents might survive his passing.

In other respects the world was, as he had said, very much a cemetery. Just a few weeks after Plorn had left him for ever, his younger brother, Frederick, died of asphyxia induced by the bursting of an abscess on his lung — Frederick, the boy whom Dickens had taken into chambers with him when he was a young reporter, whose education and prospects had always been a source of concern to him, the brother to whom he always felt closest. He had

540

become something of a lounger, something of a wastrel (although he had always retained that sharp humour and sense of the comic which his older brother also possessed) and, in recent years, his improvidence and irresponsibility had been yet another burden on Dickens. But the news of his death erased all traces of their previous arguments and Dickens remembered only the bright, active boy for whom he had taken all the "parental" responsibility. He had been, as it happened, his last surviving brother. "It was a wasted life," Dickens wrote to Forster, "but God forbid that one should be hard upon it, or upon anything in this world that is not deliberately and coldly wrong . . ." There is a tone of resignation and forgiveness in this that consorts easily with Dickens's more fragile state, a new tone that also found relief in a friendly letter which he now wrote to Mark Lemon after twelve years of cold hostility and suspicion. Towards the end of his life he was beginning to see matters in a longer perspective, even those affairs which had once so closely moved him and enraged him.

It was Dolby who told him about his brother. He had received the news of Frederick's death from a friend who lived in the same town and, when he broke it to Dickens, it had a "serious effect" upon him – to such an extent that his "distress of mind" seemed to make it impossible for him to read that same night in London. And yet the sight of the hall and the little reading desk acted as a kind of drug; they "banished all this depression, and he forgot himself and his own sufferings in the excitement of his duty". This of course was, for him, one of the inestimable benefits of his public readings; even now, ill, prematurely old, depressed (as he so often announced himself to be), he was revived by the momentum of his reading scripts and literally forgot himself in the excitement of taking on the very characters he himself had created. He could forget his own mortality. That is why, even at the very height of

541

his exhaustion and overwork, he knew that he would greatly miss these public performances once the "farewell" season was over.

Yet those closest to Dickens were still unhappy about the effects of the readings. They watched Dickens in agonies upon the stage in front of them, and knew how it was affecting him. There may even have been something too dangerous, too alarming, almost *too* odd, in the sight of this man tearing himself to pieces in front of an audience. But nothing could stop Dickens now. At least two of those present at one reading from *Oliver Twist*, Charles Kent and Wilkie Collins, had more technical objections. They were unhappy at the sudden termination of the reading at that point where Sikes drags the dog from the room of the murder and locks the door. Perhaps the flight of Sikes should be shown, and then his death as he falls from the rooftop on Jacob's Island? At first Dickens was much opposed to this – ". . . no audience on earth could be held for ten minutes after the girl's death," he told Kent. ". . . Trust me to be right. I stand there, and I know." But this was just his usual tone of certainty, and in fact he did append a short narrative to the murder itself. In three pages of manuscript he condensed all that part of *Oliver Twist* which deals with the flight and death of Sikes, and the whole reading was as we have it now. Dickens also arranged an addition to his familiar set in order to take account of the unusual nature of this particular reading. Two large maroon screens were placed on either side of the regular back screen, like wings, and curtains of the same colour were placed to enclose any other opening upon the stage. Dickens, in other words, was creating a confined space in which the figure of the actor and reader was entirely isolated – each gesture distinct, each movement lit by gas against the dark cloth. It had become a Theatre of Terror.

He gave his first public performance of "Sikes and

Nancy" on 5 January, 1869, in St James's Hall. He had been rehearsing it for some days and, when it was completed, according to Dolby, he was "utterly prostrate"; it was only after he had quickly left the platform that the audience was able to recover its composure, too, and realise what had taken place upon the stage – ". . . that all the horrors to which they had been listening were but a story and not a reality". The accounts in the press were generally very favourable and nothing further was needed to steel Dickens's determination to make it an essential, and indeed the central, part of his repertoire. He read it approximately four times a week and nothing on earth seemed able to prevent him from doing so, even at the cost of life and health. It took on, for him, an hallucinatory reality. It became almost a monomania. It was, Dolby said, ". . . one of the greatest dangers we had to contend against", and still Dickens went on.

On the night after the first London reading he went on to Ireland. Percy Fitzgerald saw him when he was about to catch the train and noticed how his face was "worn and drawn, and delved with wrinkles, and scored with anxiety, bronzed and burnished, and also wearing a very sad expression . . ." Had Ellen Ternan come to see him depart, too? Or even to travel with him? There is an oblique aside in Percy Fitzgerald's account which suggests as much for, when he took this opportunity of telling Dickens that he was to be married, "I recall his saying that I must let him tell it to one who was with him." One who was with him . . . Fitzgerald does not amplify upon the unnamed companion, but it is hardly likely to have been Dolby, Georgina or any of the other frequently mentioned members of Dickens's staff or family. It is clear, too, from Dickens's own unusual confession later, that Ellen Ternan had been with him for at least one of the later readings in the North of England; so she was his companion still and, again according to his own unexpected reference, was the only person who could tell him those "home truths" about his health which others like Dolby tended to avoid.

But there were times when the symptoms of his ill-health were impossible to ignore. By the middle of February his foot was so bad that his doctors insisted the next London reading be cancelled, and that a forthcoming tour of Scotland be postponed. For a few days Dickens remained in London – to judge by his correspondence, clearly impatient and fretful but determined to rise triumphant from his pain. Eventually the swelling abated, and Frank Beard allowed Dickens to travel only five days after the original diagnosis, despite the fact that this was against what Forster called the "urgent entreaties" of his family and close friends. Dolby noticed, when his "Chief" did arrive in Scotland, that he was "very lame" but that he tried to "disguise the fact" of his ill-health with his usual "vivacity of manner". On that visit he read "Sikes and Nancy" in Edinburgh, and afterwards he was again so "prostrate" that he had to lie on the sofa in order to regain something of his strength and composure. After a glass of champagne he returned to the stage for the second reading "as blithe and gay as if he were just commencing his evening's work". Nevertheless Dolby noticed with some alarm that "these shocks to the nerves were not as easily repelled as for the moment they appeared to be, but invariably recurred later on in the evening, either in the form of great hilarity or a desire to be once more on the platform, or in a craving to do the work over again". That is the strangest aspect of all, this craving to go on and do it all again.

His foot had recovered but the constant slow wearing down of his health and vitality proceeded apace; the sudden death of his old friend, Emerson Tennent, and the necessity of attending his funeral, for example, meant that one reading at York had to be almost desperately quickened. In order to reach the train to London on time that night, he went through his readings without a normal interval, stepping behind the screen only to moisten his lips with champagne before continuing from "Boots" to "Sikes and Nancy" to "Mrs Gamp". On the train back to London Forster found his friend looking " 'dazed' and worn". There is something almost maniacal about this constant effort, this constant travel and this no less constant fatigue – and how like him, at this juncture, to spend a whole morning in clearing up Wills's office, throwing away everything, straightening out shelves and corners, getting himself covered in dust, relentlessly determined to reduce everything to "good order".

Dickens returned to Gad's Hill Place, feeling now "greatly shaken". In a joint communiqué by his doctor Beard and a specialist Watson, part of his illness was ascribed to his "long and frequent railway journeys", and this was a diagnosis with which Dickens agreed; he said that his ailment was in large part due to railway "shaking" and he found suddenly that he could not bear to travel on express trains. The Staplehurst disaster, in other words, continued to haunt him. He was sleeping and eating normally, but he admitted that he felt dazed and very tired. He was avoiding stimulants of any kind and, instead of his usual tea or coffee, was now drinking homoeopathic cocoa. He had to stay very quiet for at least a month, and was of course severely disappointed by the necessary cancelling of the readings and by the subsequent loss of revenue. Yet it says something about his remarkable will, as well as his powers of apparent recovery, that a few days later he announced himself to be in a "brilliant condition" and was even ready to resume his London life. But did he also now have some sense that his death was coming; or had he, even, in that incipient paralysis, had some intimation of what death was *like*? Two days after his return to London he wrote to his solicitor, Ouvry, asking him to draw up his will. Which was speedily done – it was made out by

12 May and then executed at the office of *All The Year Round*. He had rented no house in London this season but instead, when he did not wish to be confined to the office, he took rooms at the St James's Hotel in Piccadilly. While "in town" he would go to the theatre, dine at Verey's or at the Blue Posts tavern in Cork Street; other favourite inns, where dinners were served, were the Cock and the Cheshire Cheese in Fleet Street as well as the Albion opposite Drury Lane Theatre. One of his most constant companions now was Dolby and, during this period in London just after the enforced retreat from Preston, he noticed ". . . the change that was coming over him. I missed the old vivacity and elasticity of spirit . . ."

But he put a brave face upon his condition, not least because his American friends, the Fields, had come to England and Dickens had decided that they were to be entertained and diverted on a very large scale. One of the reasons he took rooms at the St James's Hotel was to be close to their own hotel in Hanover Square. Certainly he was concerned to put them at their ease about the condition of his general health and, in a letter before he saw them, he explained that he had been disturbed by railway travel but was now "myself again". On the first day he met them, almost as if to prove his fitness, he took James Fields on a long walk beside the Thames. Both Fields and his wife have left records of their time with Dickens. How he took them to the rooms in Furnival's Inn where he had begun *The Pickwick Papers*. How he guided them through the Temple, and showed them the room where Pip had lived in *Great Expectations*, the dark staircase on which Magwitch had stumbled and the narrow street where Pip had found lodgings for his unwanted benefactor; yet how strange a picture this is, Dickens pointing out these dwellings as if his characters had been real. As if his novels were now part of the bricks and stone of London. As if he had filled the city with his own creations. Dickens walking through the streets of London on a spring evening, evoking the very contours of his fiction, as ". . . a belated figure would hurry past us and disappear, or perhaps in turning the corner would linger to 'take a good look' at Charles Dickens".

In the following month, James and Annie Fields went down to stay with Dickens at Gad's Hill Place; again there were more expeditions, more long walks, more parties, more dinners. They all went to Canterbury in large four-horse carriages, complete with postillions in red coats and top-boots, and it was here that Dickens found another clue to the novel he was about to write. In the cathedral there, he was depressed by a service which seemed no more than a token of worship and which would find its place in the pages of *The Mystery of Edwin Drood*. It was in Canterbury that Dickens also gave one intimation of his fictional method when, asked which house was the original for Dr Strong's school in *David Copperfield*, Dickens laughed and replied that several "would do". It was here, too, that he was happy to lose his identity. A crowd collected around the carriages and one man, pointing to James Fields, shouted out, "That's Dickens!" Dickens then handed Fields a small parcel and said, in tones loud enough to be heard by the crowd of onlookers, "Here you are, Dickens, take charge of this for me."

It was the last full summer of Dickens's life – "a very happy summer", too, according to both Kate Collins and Georgina Hogarth. He spent the weekends, as usual, in Gad's Hill Place but made a point of being in London on Thursday for "make-up" day at the office. Wills was now almost retired from the business and Dickens's son, Charley, rescued from the disgrace of bankruptcy, now seems to have taken on many of his old duties. Dickens himself wrote only a few short articles for the periodical during the period of recuperation. But he did also manage to write an essay on Fechter, destined for the *Atlantic*

*Monthly* and designed to bolster the actor's reputation just before he began a tour of the United States, an essay which has an interest beyond that of the mere "puff" since within it Dickens reverts to his one apparently inescapable subject. For he talks about Fechter as a romantic actor and mentions in particular how the loved object is redeemed, rendered brighter and worthier, by the very interest and passion of the lover himself. "I said to myself, as a child might have said, 'A bad woman could not have been the object of that wonderful tenderness, could not have so subdued that worshipping heart, could not have drawn such tears from such a lover.'" And once again in this account of love it is remarkable how Dickens puts himself in the place of a child and, with a child-like vision, describes an earnest and almost spiritual passion.

It was now, too, in the summer of 1869, only a little while after the physical suffering induced by his readings, that Dickens became once more eager to begin the composition of a new novel. He had considered the possibility the summer before, and had managed to produce at least one fragment, but it was only now he felt that he could begin seriously to write. This probably had less to do with the "free time" available to him (he had had just as much to spare in the previous year) than with the fact of his illness; the shock of his debility and the first intimations of death seem to have propelled him once more towards expression, towards the writing of a novel which would be dominated by images of death and by the presence of unacknowledged passions running beneath the observable surface of life.

As so often, other ideas swiftly followed his initial determination to write, and in August he told Forster that he had "a very curious and new idea for my new story". By 20 August he was already considering titles for the new novel; he set down a list of seventeen of them on a sheet of paper, beginning with "The loss of James Wakefield" and ending with "Dead? Or alive?". On the same day he wrote to Frederick Chapman, projecting the idea of a new story in twelve shilling numbers, thus suggesting that Dickens, aware for the first time that his powers could be exhausted as rapidly as his readings had been terminated, was not eager to trust himself to a twenty-month series on the old pattern. Market conditions had also changed, and what had been acceptable in the Forties and Fifties was not, in the days of Mudie's Lending Library and the railway bookstalls, necessarily the right formula for the late Sixties and Seventies. Dickens himself was never afraid, in the cant phrase, to move with his times. It was one of the secrets of his permanent and growing success. Contracts were soon drawn up, but it is another indication of his anxieties that, at his insistence, a clause was inserted which stipulated that, in the event of the author's death or incapacity, arbitrators would estimate the amount to be repaid to Chapman and Hall. He did not want to sign any contract under false pretences, and his worries about the financial loss to Chappell and Company after the abandonment of the readings suggest how careful he now wanted to be with his publishers. Contracts were not finally completed and accepted until the winter of this year but, in the event, Dickens was paid £7,500 and a half share of the profits for the copyright in this last book.

By the middle of September Dickens began his real planning for the novel. At some point in this month, or the one before, he explained to Forster the "very curious and new" idea that had occurred to him. It was one that concerned the murder of a young man by his uncle, and how the truth of this familial slaying would not be revealed until the murderer himself reflects upon the stages of his fatal career in a condemned cell. This is an intriguing plot and, with its use of opium as an agent of revelation, bears a passing resemblance to Wilkie Collins's *The Moonstone*. But it does not consort very well with the list of titles and themes which Dickens had propounded to himself on 20 August, the drift of which indicates that the main character was to vanish only to re-emerge at the end of the book. It seems likely that the idea of murder, and thus the permanent disappearance of Edwin Drood, only occurred to Dickens once he had begun to draw up the main lines of the plot in his number plans. This in itself would explain his strange treatment of a story by Robert Lytton, "The Disappearance of John Acland", for which he had already arranged publication in *All The Year Round* – this is a short narrative in which the disappearance of a young man is only later discovered to have been, after all, murder. Dickens accepted this story when he was not sure about the main lines of his own novel but, as soon as he had decided that *his* disappearing character should also be murdered, he abruptly terminated Robert Lytton's story with only the briefest of excuses. He did not want his new thunder to be stolen, in other words, and "The Disappearance of John Acland" was sacrificed to *The Mystery of Edwin Drood*.

But Dickens was not interested simply in the machinations of crime and detection; his was to be a crime based upon the experience of violent and thwarted love, and it was to be explored through the consciousness of the murderer himself, John Jasper. This was not a new development – he had been working towards a similar effect with Bradley Headstone in *Our Mutual Friend* and with Obenreizer in "No Thoroughfare". But although there are hints of both these characters in Jasper, in the portrayal of this divided, driven man there is a greater intensity of focus on the nature of aggression and sexual obsession. Even as Dickens was able in conversation to outline the plot and the theme of his novel to Forster, his real and incommunicable interests were working their own way towards resolution. So it is that *The Mystery of Edwin Drood* becomes essentially the mystery of his murderous uncle, Jasper, and the real theme of the novel lies not in its complicated plot but rather, as Dickens's daughter, Kate, has expressed it, in Dickens's ". . . wonderful observation of character, and his strange insight into the tragic secrets of the human heart . . ." And how could it not be so, at a time when his public life was dominated by his reading of "Sikes and Nancy" and his private existence conditioned by what seems to be an increasingly sorrowful love for Ellen Ternan?

Certain key themes were evident, however, from the beginning. The first number plan opens with the line "Opium-Smoking", and at once we are in the world of Limehouse and Bluegate Fields: an area which in the months before Dickens had visited as guide to his American publisher. But then, in that same first number plan, another locale emerges – "*Cathedral town running throughout*". In the novel it is called Cloisterham but every available detail suggests how strongly it is related to the city of Dickens's childhood, to Rochester and its environs. London, then, conjoined with Rochester. At the end of his life he is returning to the twin sources of his creativity. Not only returning to them, but actually seeing them as one. For, in a novel which is concerned with the nature of the divided life and the dual personality, it is not so strange that Limehouse and Rochester should meet, should in a sense be superimposed upon one another to create a composite landscape of the imagination; even down to the very details of topography when St George's-in-the-East, the wonderful and barbaric church which looms over the opium dens of Bluegate Fields, comes to resemble Rochester Cathedral itself. The visions of his childhood and his experience as a man, mingled together.

Certainly these were the elements which were in his mind when, at the end of September, he began seriously to work upon the new story; the extant number plans suggest that he could see his way through the first stages of the novel without undue difficulty. He had already

551

agreed that Charles Collins should undertake the illustrations to the new monthly series. Whether this was at Collins's suggestion, or at Dickens's actual request, is not certain; but it seems likely that he was happy to grant a commission which would not only occupy his son-in-law's time but also afford him at least the basis of an income. In any case Collins himself, as Dickens knew very well, had a higher reputation than Marcus Stone who had illustrated Dickens's previous novel. In order to prepare Collins for the work ahead, Dickens asked Frederick Chapman to send down to Gad's Hill Place copies of the old green covers which Hablot Browne had designed in the past. He wanted Collins, in other words, to work on the basis of approved models. Now he, too, was ready to begin. During the autumn and winter he often went to the office in Wellington Street but he did not set up living quarters there, as he had in the past; he went there only to work. The rest of his time was spent either at Gad's Hill Place or at Peckham, in which retreat some of the planning and composition of this final work were undertaken.

By the third week of October he had finished the first instalment of the novel, and promptly read it out at Forster's house "with great spirit". Stone. Dust. Old churches. The presence of the past. These are some of the aspects of the vision which Dickens was now imparting to his listeners. It is the smallest and most intense world that he had ever created, beginning with the strange opium dreams of Bluegate Fields and then moving on the "old Cathedral town" of Cloisterham. Or shall we say Rochester? Transformed now, in any event, to an oppressive and echoic place; it is as if Dickens were finding within himself, and within the landscape of his childhood, a stranger aspect of human passion and a permanent reminder of human mortality. Stories of antiquity. Stories of the English past. It was not for Dickens a new theme — in an essay for *Household Words* nineteen years before he
552

had spoken of "an old Cathedral town" characterised "by the universal gravity, mystery, decay, and silence", but one so badly embodied in "the drawling voice, without a heart, that drearily pursues the dull routine . . ." How odd and how significant, then, that he had been dismayed by just such "drawling" voices when he had visited the cathedral at Canterbury a few months before. There are times in Dickens's life when a perception suddenly returns with undiminished vigour.

In *The Mystery of Edwin Drood*, however, all the old perceptions are shadowed and deepened with Dickens's own painful reflections on the nature of time and of mortality, reflections which elicit in turn some of his finest writing. "Old Time heaved a mouldy sigh from tomb and arch and vault; and gloomy shadows began to deepen in corners; and damps began to rise from green patches of stone; and jewels, cast upon the pavement of the nave from stained glass by the declining sun, began to perish . . . In the Cathedral, all became grey, murky, and sepulchral, and the cracked monotonous mutter went on like a dying voice, until the organ and the choir burst forth, and drowned it in a sea of music. Then, the sea fell, and the dying voice made another feeble effort, and then the sea rose high, and beat its life out, and lashed the roof, and surged among the arches, and pierced the heights of the great tower; and then the sea was dry, and all was still." It is the nearest Dickens came to a Gothic novel, a novel springing out of his own childhood memories, compounded by hard experience, and mixed with the strange promptings of his own heart – " 'If the dead do, under any circumstances, become visible to the living . . .' " The mingling of the living and the dead is at the centre of nineteenth-century Gothic but of course it had also been at the centre of Dickens's own imagination; the opening of *David Copperfield*, with the infant fear of the father rising from his grave, is only one indication of the extent to which it affected him. But now, at the end of his life, with how much troubled ambiguity does he approach the dead and address the question of death itself.

Dolby has said that the writing of the novel came with more difficulty to Dickens; it gave him "trouble and anxiety", and Dickens told him that he "missed the pressure" of former days. But in fact the manuscript suggests that the writing of it came to him with relative ease, since there are fewer emendations than in some of his previous novels. His major alterations, indeed, are in the sphere of addition and augmentation; which in turn emphasises how in this novel Dicken's prose seems instinctively more economical and more restrained. *Our Mutual Friend* had been established in part upon periphrasis and comic grandiloquence but *The Mystery of Edwin Drood* is much more austere, all the corrections and additions adding only to the specificity and detail of the narrative. This may partly spring from Dickens's desire to harbour his powers at a time when he was not sure how long they would last or how far they could be extended; but, more importantly, it may be that the power and significance of his final vision did not encourage any of the free-wheeling exercises of the past. Of course he had in his most recent novels explored the theme of the "secret" life, of dual identity and self-division, just as he had also analysed the necessity of masks and camouflage in a world which depends upon appearances. And of course all these matters must have seemed germane to the life which, even as he was writing the novel, he felt compelled to lead. But in *The Mystery of Edwin Drood* they are enlarged and strengthened in the pursuit of a larger vision, a vision which depicts the "lanes of light" between the dark pillars of a crypt and which reflects upon ". . . that mysterious fire which lurks in everything . . .", even in the cold stone walls of an ancient church.

He had been writing the second instalment during November, despite being affected by a heavy cold, and he managed to finish it by the end of the month. He was trying to move on quickly, not least because he knew that he now had to prepare for that short season of "farewell" readings which his doctors had permitted. But he completed these first two numbers only to discover, to his horror, that he had underwritten both of them; each one was something like six pages too short, and he had at once to set to work to make up the deficiency. He added an entirely new scene, transposed a chapter from the second instalment to the first, and then added another chapter to the second – all of which meant that he was using up his material too fast. He was also vexed by his illustrator. Charles Collins, having sketched out a cover, found that he could no longer draw without weakening his health. Some other artist had to be found at once and Dickens went up to London in order to consult with Frederick Chapman. In the event he discovered a young artist, Luke Fildes. Or, rather, it was John Everett Millais who found him for Dickens – the painter, who was staying at Gad's Hill Place, went into Dickens's study one morning and showed him the first issue of *The Graphic*. "I've got him!" he shouted and then pointed out to his host an illustration, "Houseless and Hungry", which Fildes had executed. It was exactly the kind of realistic and detailed examination of social misery which would have appealed to Dickens, and he wrote to the young artist asking to see other specimens of his work. These, too, proved satisfactory and so he gave him the commission, an extraordinary honour and indeed opportunity for so young an artist. Thus, it was settled. Three days before Christmas, too, Dickens had managed to finish all the necessary rewriting.

But once more, only a week or so away from his last season of readings, he was suffering great pain. Dolby noticed "... a slow but steady change working in him ...", and on Christmas Day his foot was so swollen that he had to remain in his room. He could not walk because of the pain and discomfort but, in the evening, he managed to hobble down to the drawing room in order to join his family in the usual festivities after dinner. It was his last Christmas on earth; he, who had in his own work so often celebrated the blessings of that season, could now experience it only as an invalid. He lay on the sofa and watched the others at their games. And of what was he thinking now? There is one clue, at least, to his state of mind. His family had been playing "The Memory Game"; it was one which Dickens could hardly ever resist and, after observing the others for a while, he decided to join in. Henry recalled one of his contributions. "My father, after many turns, had successfully gone through the long string of words and finished up with his own contribution, 'Warren's Blacking, 30 Strand'. He gave this with an odd twinkle in his eye and a strange inflection in his voice which at once forcibly arrested my attention and left a vivid impression on my mind for some time afterwards." Warren's Blacking, 30 Strand. The blacking warehouse. The site of his childhood labour and humiliation. The source of all his agony. And yet the name meant nothing to his family; none of them knew of his past. Just another phrase in the course of a Christmas game; but, to Dickens, how pregnant with the whole mystery of his life. Yet it remained a mystery, even to those who knew and loved him best. Although he was here for the first time openly alluding to that terrible period, his family would not know the truth about his early life until they read of it in Forster's biography.

The following afternoon, after the usual Boxing Day sports, Dickens made a little speech to the assembled guests and contestants, at the end of which he said that ". . . please God we will do it again next year". But they did not. On New Year's Eve he attended a party at Forster's house, where he read out the second instalment of his new novel. At the stroke of midnight the company stood with their glasses in their hands to mark the turn of the time. Later one guest said that "I never saw him again".

# Thirty-Five

I N the New Year, the last year of his life, Dickens broke
the rule he had always maintained – he was both writing a novel and doing a series of public readings at the
same time. He was trying not to allow the readings to
interfere with his composition but, nevertheless, he was
now appearing at St James's Hall approximately twice a
week and, in addition, he felt it necessary to spend some
time in "getting up" his subjects once more. There is no
evidence, however, that he would willingly have forgone
the opportunity of this "farewell" series of twelve performances; he needed the money (or thought that he did, which
is much the same thing) but he also felt a sense of responsibility to others beside himself. He had been much
impressed by the considerate behaviour of Chappell and
Company towards him at the time of his infirmity the year
before, and according to Forster this sense of duty alone
". . . supplied him with an overpowering motive for being
determinedly set on going through with them".

In fact Dickens had actively looked forward to his next
engagements with his public. Dolby reveals that, when Sir
Thomas Watson gave him permission to undertake these
last readings, it "inspired him with new hope, and did
much to promote what we all hoped would be his perfect
recovery". So he began in good heart on 11 January, and
Forster noticed that, after the slight roughness of delivery

noticeable on his return from the United States, he now spoke with "the old delicacy" and with "a subdued tone" which had all the "quiet sadness of farewell". He also gave readings on three separate mornings, and this for the benefit of "the theatrical profession" whose other engagements meant that they could never attend his evening performances. This of course also materially affected his stamina and now, no doubt at his family's urgent request, Frank Beard stayed with him and monitored his pulse both before and after each reading. His records survive, showing clearly how Dickens's pulse leaped up as he came to the conclusion of each narrative. His ordinary pulse on the first night was 72 but soon it was never lower than 82 and, on the last nights, rose to over one hundred; during the readings themselves it rose rapidly higher and, at the close of his last reading from *David Copperfield*, it had risen to 124, which was in fact the mark it reached after all the "Sikes and Nancy" performances. So did his body respond to its work, manifesting evidence of slow but steady deterioration. Indeed his son, Charley, believed these final readings to have actually killed him and he remembered Frank Beard addressing him in words that were hardly reassuring. "I have had some steps put up against the side of the platform, Charley. You must be there every night, and if you see your father falter in the least, you must run up and catch him and bring him off with me, or, by Heaven, he'll die before them all."

Dickens had rented a house at 5 Hyde Park Place for the duration, principally because he wanted to remain in the capital during the readings, and thus avoid any of the railway "shaking" involved in commuting between Gad's Hill Place and London. He was once more back in "Tyburnia", and this last of his London houses directly overlooked Hyde Park, with what is now Bayswater Road beneath its windows. His bedroom and study were on the first floor, directly above the road, but Dickens seemed in no way to be affected by the constant roar and hurry of the traffic; he told Dolby that even at dawn he liked to hear the noise of the waggons bringing produce from Paddington station to the markets of the city, because it reminded him of that active and busy world which revolved even as he slept. And why should he care about London noise now? He had known it all his life. Of course he still had his "secret" retreat in Peckham, and his charwoman there remembered that at the time "Mr Tringham" was writing "a mystery story"; so it may be assumed that parts of *The Mystery of Edwin Drood* were composed in Linden Grove.

There were occasions now when he talked of death, particularly of his desire for a sudden death. "A death by lightning most resembles the translation of Enoch," he is supposed to have said, although the words do not sound like those of Dickens. But the sentiment is clear enough. Nevertheless he still made a determined effort to remain cheerful, at least when he was in the company of others. His left hand was swollen, and he had to support it in a sling; as a result he cancelled dinner with Gladstone at the end of January, but of course carried on with the third instalment of his novel in the dull and gloomy weather of the later winter. He respected Gladstone to a certain extent, but it cannot be said that at this stage he had any more real faith in him than in any other legislator or parliamentarian. Indeed his very last words on the subject of political life are as plain as they could possibly be; he told Bulwer-Lytton in February, four months before his death, that ". . . our system fails". He had been moving towards this conclusion all of his life and now, in a sense, he was returning to all his old allegiances in his hatred and contempt for Parliament; he was as proud now of what he called his "radicalism" as he had been when he was a young man.

The days passed by. The last days. He gave his final reading from *David Copperfield* on the first evening of March. Two days later he attended, with Wills, a birthday party for Ellen Ternan at Blanchard's in Regent Street. On the eighth of the month he gave his last performance of "Sikes and Nancy", the reading which more than all others had weakened him. It was while he was on his way to the platform in order to play murderer and victim for the last time that he whispered to Charles Kent, "I shall tear myself to pieces." A few weeks before he had confessed to Dolby that ". . . it was madness ever to have given the 'Murder' reading, under the conditions of a travelling life, and worse than madness to have given it with such frequency". Yet even though he saw his madness he could not stop it. He went on.

The day after this reading he had an interview with the Queen in Buckingham Palace, at the sovereign's own request. Despite his lame foot he had to stand throughout the audience, according to protocol, while Victoria leaned against the arm of a sofa. He thought her "strangely shy", he told Georgina, "and like a girl in manner". In her journal the Queen described him as ". . . very agreeable, with a pleasant voice and manner". And of what did they talk? The servant problem. Lincoln's dream before his assassination (a topic of which Dickens never grew tired). Dickens's own public readings. The time when, thirteen years before, she had attended a performance of *The Frozen Deep*. The American attitude towards the Fenians. National education. The price of butcher's meat. Thus did the two greatest representatives of the Victorian era address one another, just as if they were unaware of their place in the history of their time. There were rumours afterwards that Dickens had been offered a knighthood or even a peerage, but there was nothing to them; he had in any case decided that he would remain what he had always been. Charles Dickens.

The time had now come for him to prepare himself for his final reading, his last appearance before the public. Two days before, he gave a dinner for all those connected with

561

the business side of the reading tours and then, on 15 March, he prepared for his final reading that night. He was suffering from a bad throat, and had to have a poultice placed on it. He saw Luke Fildes about the illustrations for the fourth number of *The Mystery of Edwin Drood*. And then in the evening he went from Hyde Park Place to St James's Hall in order to read "A Christmas Carol" and "The Trial from Pickwick"; for the last time his audience would hear the voices of Ebenezer Scrooge, Bob Cratchit and Sam Weller. A huge audience had assembled, and many hours before the time of the reading crowds had gathered outside the two entrances in Regent Street and in Piccadilly. But punctually, at eight o'clock, Dickens walked onto the platform with his book in hand, "evidently much agitated", Dolby said, by the emotion of this final performance. The audience then rose to its feet, cheering and applauding, and he could not proceed for several minutes. Everyone watched him as he stood smiling behind his desk, that "spare figure . . . faultlessly attired in evening dress, the gas-light streaming down upon him, illuminating every feature of his familiar flushed face . . ." And then eventually he began. "I thought I had never heard him read . . . so well and with so little effort," Charley said. Charles Kent believed that ". . . he was keyed to a crowning effort". After he had finished the second of his readings, the trial scene from *The Pickwick Papers*, once more the audience burst into applause and cheering which lasted for several minutes. He had left the platform but had been recalled by the enthusiasm – almost the hysteria – of the audience several times. Until finally the noise and sensation abated. Dickens stood in front of them for the last time, and delivered a short speech that he had prepared for this occasion. "Ladies and Gentlemen, it would be worse than idle – for it would be hypocritical and unfeeling – if I were to disguise that I close this episode in my life with feelings of very considerable pain." Then he spoke briefly of the fifteen years in which he had been engaged in his readings, of his duty to the public and of their ready sympathy in return. He mentioned the imminent appearance of *The Mystery of Edwin Drood*, and then his voice faltered as he came to the end – ". . . but from these garish lights I vanish now for ever more, with a heartfelt, grateful, respectful, and affectionate farewell." There was a brief hush in the audience followed by something very like a common sigh and then, as his son recalled, "a storm of cheering as I have never seen equalled in my life". His head was bowed and the tears were streaming down his face as he left the platform. But the cheering and applause would not stop; after several minutes he returned, faced his audience once again, raised his hands to his lips in a kiss, and then left the platform for the last time. "He was deeply touched that night," his son said, "but infinitely sad and broken . . ." So much had come to an end now. So little left ahead of him. For a man who could never bear to say farewell, and for whom that direct relation to his public had been at the centre of his life, it was a moment of terrible sorrow.

In the third week of March, just a week after his final public reading, Dickens read the fourth number of *The Mystery of Edwin Drood* to Forster; the fact that Forster had once again become his confidant, and that he was still to a certain extent estranged from Wilkie Collins, suggests that Dickens at the end of his life was now returning to some of his oldest allegiances. He also told Forster on this occasion about the problems he was once again having with his sight. He could not read the right-hand half of the names above shop-doors. Then, a few days later, he experienced a massive haemorrhage of blood from his piles. All the signs were now pointing in the same direction. But there were also things to cheer him. At the beginning of April the first number of *The Mystery of Edwin Drood* was published in the familiar green cover, and it was an immediate success. Something like fifty thousand copies

563

were sold, and the critical reaction was largely concerned to celebrate the fact that the novelist had reacquired his "old" manner. The actual peculiarities of the novel were not generally noticed, and instead the reviewers praised the humour present in characters like the stonemason, Durdles, and the Tory "jackass", Mr Sapsea. That is why the *Spectator* believed Dickens to have returned "to the standard of his first few works", and yet of what a different world those first works had been a part. In the "Advertiser" purchased with *Nicholas Nickleby* there had been advertisements for such things as the Poor Man's Pill and Hussar suits for boys. Now, in *The Mystery of Edwin Drood*, the advertisements were for washing machines and self-raising flour.

His deteriorating sight and the disorder of his piles meant that he was seeing Frank Beard at least once a week, generally on the day before "make up" day at the office of *All The Year Round*. Nevertheless, when he gave a speech to the Newsvendors' Benevolent Association on 5 April, one spectator observed that ". . . he was full of merriment and overflowing with humour". The next day he attended a Levee at Buckingham Palace, for which notable occasion he was forced to wear court dress, including a cocked hat which, unsure of the proper direction it was meant to point, he tucked under his arm. Then on the following evening he gave a grand reception at Hyde Park Place, complete with Joachim playing Schumann and Tartini as well as the sound of the massed ranks of the London Glee and Madrigal Union. "Everyone" was there – it was, you might say, his final tryst with "Society" – but Dolby noticed that Dickens himself, although as bright and as animated as ever, was "suffering very much" and looked "jaded and worn".

It was a busy month. He went to the circus on one evening and saw an elephant standing on its head, which feat led him to wonder out loud why "they've never taught the rhinoceros to do anything . . ." He visited the theatre. He attended private dinners with friends. And, of all marks of respect and homage, he seemed most pleased by the gift from a successful Liverpool timber merchant, George Holme, of a silver table ornament. Georgina, in a letter to Annie Fields, said that Dickens could not remember anything more "gratifying" and "pleasant" during the whole of his career. One part of the gift was a silver centre-piece for the table, on the sides of which had been etched designs to represent the seasons – spring, summer and autumn only, however, so that Dickens might be reminded simply of the more agreeable and hopeful months. But he told Forster, in words that disclose his state of mind during this last period, "I never look at it, that I don't think most of the Winter." Even if the real winter was never to surround him again.

Mamie said that in this period of busy activity he "grew quickly and easily tired", and in truth he just as rapidly became bored with dining out and general socialising. He was growing restless and even by the middle of April had made up his mind not to accept any public engagements for the rest of the year. He was also tired of London and longed for the country, a mood which he expressed in the instalment of the novel he was writing at this time – ". . . deserts of gritty streets, where many people crowded at the corners of courts and bye-ways, to get some air, and where many other people walked with a miserably monotonous noise of shuffling feet on hot paving-stones, and where all the people and all their surroundings were so gritty and so shabby." He was working slowly on the story now, transposing chapters in order to create the pre-cise dramatic effect he desired, moving on carefully but anxious in case he was using up his material too quickly.

But his concentration upon the narrative was then pro-foundly disturbed by the death of Daniel Maclise, one of his oldest companions, the young man who with Forster and Ainsworth had comprised the first real circle of friends to which Dickens ever belonged, the oddity and solitude of whose final years only served to remind Dickens of how much they had all gone through, how much they had all changed. He could not really "get over" the artist's death – in a letter to Forster he said that he was "at once thinking of it and avoiding it in a strange way" – and it is almost as if in the shock of that fatality he had some intimation of his own end. He had already agreed to deliver a speech at the annual dinner of the Royal Academy three days later, and he took the occasion – he had, at least, that much command of himself – both to mourn the passing of his old friend and to lament the loss to his chosen profession. Towards the close he added this: ". . . I already begin to feel like that Spanish monk of whom Wilkie tells, who had grown to believe that the only realities around him were the pictures which he loved [*cheers*], and that all the moving life he saw, or ever had seen, was a shadow and a dream. [*Cheers*]." One of the guests said of Dickens that night, ". . . he then looked like a man who would live and work until he was four score. I was especially struck by the brilliance and vivacity of his eyes." But in fact it was the last public speech that Dickens ever made.

On an evening that month he had been visited at Hyde Park Place by a young author, Constance Cross, who had been recommended to him by Bulwer-Lytton. They spoke together for about an hour and in the course of their conversation he told her that he was considering a stay of two years in Germany, and that he was hoping to travel there "accompanied by his daughter". He told her also about Gad's Hill Place – ". . . I love the dear old place; and I hope – when I come to die – it may be there." Then he described his evenings "generally in the society of a much-loved daughter, to whom he often affectionately referred". Or perhaps this was his way of talking of Ellen Ternan, these references to his "daughter"? Constance Cross eventually asked him what might happen if he died before one of his books was completed. "That has occurred to me – at times." But then he added, more cheerfully, "One can only work on, you know – work while it is day."

Dickens was now on the last chapter he would ever write, concerned that he had already used up too much of the material he had prepared and anxious lest he had inadvertently disclosed too much of his complete design. But he wrote on now, as Rosa Bud arrives in London and glides in a boat along the Thames, ". . . and, all too soon, the great black city cast its shadows on the waters, and its dark bridges spanned them as death spans life, and the everlastingly green garden seemed to be left for everlasting, unregainable and far away." He wrote only a few thousand words after this, and the fact that he left the novel unfinished has in turn led to what has generally been called "the Drood controversy". Was Drood really dead? Was Jasper really the murderer? How was Drood murdered? Who is the strange figure of Datchery? Woman, or man? But in a sense all these enquiries miss the central point; that Dickens was not really concerned with plot at all, at least not in the mechanical sense which such speculations imply. Of course it has afforded a great deal of harmless amusement to those who enjoy games and puzzles but it has left out of consideration the true nature of Dickens's art which, in this final novel, was so deeply implicated in the extraordinary and haunting portrayal of John Jasper – a murderer perhaps, an opium addict certainly, an artist, a frustrated lover. Jasper who, even when he plays his music, is "'. . . troubled with some stray sort of ambition, aspiration, restlessness, dissatisfaction, what shall we call it?'" We may call it the very conditions on which Charles Dickens himself held his life, a life of struggle and work and anxiety lit by the intense glare of fame. Again, of Jasper, Dickens writes that, although "constantly exercising an Art which brought him into mechanical harmony with others . . .", he possessed a spirit which was ". . . in moral accordance or interchange with nothing around him". It may well have been on the afternoon of this day, after writing his novel all the morning, that Dickens was seen near the Athenaeum ". . . grey-haired, careworn, and so absent and absorbed in his thoughts . . ."

Dickens returned to Gad's Hill Place that night, and was never to leave it again alive. He spent the weekend walking and writing letters. On the Sunday afternoon he became very tired after a relatively short walk and his daughter, Kate, was shocked to see him "a good deal changed". But he seemed to improve during dinner and then, afterwards, he smoked his usual cigar and took a stroll in the garden with both his daughters, the air filled with the sweet scent of syringa shrubs. Afterwards he sat in the dining room and contemplated his new conservatory, which had just been completed as an extension to that room. Mamie had gone into the drawing room to play the piano, and Dickens listened to her solitary music as he sat looking at the flowers. Kate had mentioned to her father that she wanted to talk to him about a decision she was about to make – she wanted to go on the stage, in order to earn some money for herself and her ailing husband – and at eleven o'clock, when Georgina and Mamie had retired to bed, and the lights in the conservatory had been turned down, father and daughter talked together. They discussed her plans, of which Dickens disapproved since there were people in the theatrical profession "who would make your hair stand on end". They considered the matter for a while but then, when Kate rose to leave, Dickens asked her to stay because he had more to say to her. He talked of his hopes for *The Mystery of Edwin Drood*, "if, please God, I live to finish it". Then, he added, "I say *if*, because you know, my dear child, I have not been strong lately." He went on to talk of the past but not of the future, and it seemed to his daughter that "he spoke as though his life were over and there was nothing left". Then he went on to regret that he had not been "a better father — a better man". Kate said, in a later unpublished account, that he also mentioned Ellen Ternan. Father and daughter did not leave each other until three in the morning.

But Dickens was up the next day, Monday, at 7.30 — "Sharp, mind," he had said to his parlour-maid, since he had a great deal of work to manage that week. He went over to the chalet early in order to continue with his writing of the novel, and it was here that Kate came to see him before she left for London with Mamie. She knew how much he hated partings, so she had merely left her love to be given to him by Georgina; but, as she waited on the porch for the carriage to take her to the station, she had "an uncontrollable desire to see him once again". So she hurried to the chalet on the other side of the road, and mounted the wooden staircase to the upper room where he always worked. "His head was bent low down over his work, and he turned an eager and rather flushed face towards me as I entered. On ordinary occasions he would just have raised his cheek for my kiss, saying a few words, perhaps, in 'the little language' that he had been accustomed to use when we were children; but on this morning, when he saw me, he pushed his chair from the writing-table, opened his arms, and took me into them . . ." It was the last time they would speak to one another. That afternoon he walked to Rochester with the dogs and, in town, he bought a copy of the *Daily Mail*. He was seen by several people leaning against the wooden railing across the street from Restoration House, and "it was remarked at the time that there would be some notice of this building in the tale then current . . ."

On the next day he wrote, as usual, and then drove to Cobham Wood with Georgina, dismissing the carriage once they had arrived there and walking round the park back to Gad's Hill Place. It is impossible not to quote an account of precisely the same walk from his first novel. "A delightful walk it was: for it was a pleasant afternoon in June, and their way lay through a deep and shady wood, cooled by the light wind which gently rustled the thick foliage, and enlivened by the songs of the birds that perched upon the boughs. The ivy and the moss crept in thick clusters over the old trees, and the soft green turf overspread the ground like a silken mat." A June day. So it was then, and so it was now. In the beginning we see his end. It was his last walk, but it had been beautifully anticipated thirty-four years before. That evening he fixed some Chinese lanterns in the conservatory, and sat in the dining room to consider their effect in the twilight.

He awoke early on the following day, Wednesday, 8 June, in excellent spirits. He talked a little with Georgina about his book and then after breakfast went straight over to the chalet in order to continue work on it. He came back to the house at one o'clock for lunch, smoked a cigar in the conservatory and then, unusually for him, returned to the chalet where he remained occupied on the novel which had taken such a hold upon him. These last pages were written with relative ease, marked by fewer emendations than usual, and Dickens's final passage of narrative opens with an encomium to light – "A brilliant morning shines on the old city" – which echoes the very first sentence of his first novel, *The Pickwick Papers*. "The first ray of light which illumines the gloom . . ." Light calling to light, the figure of Dickens bent between them. That light even penetrates into the cold stone of the cathedral and manages to "subdue its earthy odour", again in echo of his first novel where Jingle had spoken of the same place, "Old cathedral too – earthy smell . . ." The circle was almost complete. His first novel and his last novel. One opening with the light and with Rochester, the other closing on the same two notes. The circle of life.
570

"For, as I draw closer and closer to the end," it had been said in *A Tale of Two Cities*, "I travel in the circle, nearer and nearer to the beginning." Charles Dickens coming to his end now, in the house he had seen as a child and which he had never forgotten. He wrote the last words of *The Mystery of Edwin Drood*, "and then falls to with an appetite"; after which he formed the short spiral which generally marked the end of a chapter. The end. He came back to the house an hour before dinner and seemed "tired, silent and abstracted". While waiting for his meal he went into the library and wrote two letters. One to Charles Kent, in which he arranged to see him in London at three o'clock on the following day: "If I can't be — why, then I shan't be." The other to a clergyman to whom, in response to some criticism, he declared that "I have always striven in my writings to express veneration for the life and lessons of Our Saviour . . ."

Georgina was the only member of the family with him and, just as they sat down together for dinner, she noticed a change both in his colour and his expression. She asked him if he were ill, and he replied, "Yes, very ill; I have been very ill for the last hour." She wanted to send immediately for a doctor but he forbade her to do so, saying that he wanted to go to London that evening after dinner. But then something happened. He experienced some kind of fit against which he tried to struggle — he paused for a moment and then began to talk very quickly and indistinctly, at some point mentioning Forster. She rose from her chair, alarmed, and told him to "come and lie down".

"Yes," he said. "On the ground."

But as she helped him he slid from her arms and fell heavily to the floor. He was now unconscious. A young servant went at once on the pony, Newman Noggs, into Rochester in order to summon the local doctor, Mr Steele, who arrived at 6.30. "I found Dickens lying on the floor of the dining-room in a fit. He was unconscious, and never

571

moved. The servants brought a couch down, on which he was placed. I applied clysters and other remedies to the patient without effect." Rugs were wrapped around him and pillows were put beneath his head.

Telegrams had already been sent to Frank Beard, and to Dickens's daughters. When they arrived at Gad's Hill Place, Kate could hear her father's deep breathing, "We found him lying unconscious on a couch in the dining room where he and I had talked together; a sudden gloom had fallen upon the place, and everything was changed; only the still, warm weather continued the same, and the sweet scent of the flowers he had so much admired floated in through the open doors of the new conservatory." They watched him through the night, taking it in turns to place hot bricks against his feet which were now so cold. He did not move at all, and yet they could not help but still believe that, suddenly, he would revive and be himself again. They could not believe that this unconscious form was Charles Dickens. But he never stirred.

"On the ground." His last words. And is it possible that he had in some bewildered way echoed the words of Louisa Gradgrind to her errant father in *Hard Times*, " 'I shall die if you hold me! Let me fall upon the ground!' "? And were his other characters around him as he lay unconscious through his last night? He had often recalled the image of Sir Walter Scott dying ". . . faint, wan, crushed both in mind and body by his honourable struggle, and hovering round him the ghosts of his own imagination . . . innumerable overflowing the chamber, and fading away in the dim distance beyond". He had spoken these words, as a young man, in America, at the height of his fame. And can we see them now, the ghosts of Dickens's imagination, hovering around him as he approaches his own death? Oliver Twist, Ebenezer Scrooge, Paul Dombey, Little Nell, Little Dorrit, the Artful Dodger, Bob Sawyer, Sam Weller, Mr Pickwick, Barkis, David Copperfield, Pip, Quilp, Fagin, Stephen

Blackpool, Nicholas Nickleby, Mrs Nickleby, Bumble, Jo, Martin Chuzzlewit, Bob Cratchit, Fagin, the Crummles family, Edwin Drood, Peggotty, Mr Dick, Mr F's Aunt, Mrs Gamp, Uriah Heep, Pecksniff, Micawber, the Infant Phenomenon, the Jellybys, the Smallweeds, the Mantalinis, the Father of the Marshalsea, Barnaby Rudge, Rogue Riderhood, Miss Havisham, Bill Sikes, Nancy, Smike, all of them now hovering around their creator as his life on earth came to an end.

But there were other shadows hovering about him which he could not have seen. Shadows of the future. Shadows of the real people he was now leaving behind him. Of John Forster kissing his friend's face as he lay in his coffin and writing, "The duties of life remain while life remains, but for me the joy of it is gone for ever more." Of Ellen Ternan visiting Mamie and Georgina in the years ahead, marrying a schoolmaster, teaching French and elocution to schoolchildren. Of Mamie and Georgina sharing a house with Henry. Of his children fighting bitterly amongst themselves. Of Kate painting and looking after her invalid husband, until he died and she married again. Of Georgina and Catherine Dickens reconciled at last. Of Catherine herself, living out a true widowhood after the enforced separation of twelve years. Of Sydney buried at sea two years later. Of Plorn bankrupt. Of Alfred lecturing on his father. Of Charley giving readings from his father's books. Of a Christmas fund raised for the benefit "of the descendants of Charles Dickens". Of the sale of his effects two months later, when the stuffed body of Grip, his favourite raven, was sold for one hundred and twenty pounds. All this came to pass.

They watched him through the night – Frank Beard, Georgina, his daughters – but he never stirred from his unconsciousness. Doctor Steele returned in the morning and observed that "there was unhappily no change in the symptoms, and stertorous breathing, which had commenced before, now continued". He and Frank Beard advised that another doctor should be summoned and Charley, who himself had now arrived, sent a telegram to London: "Mr Dickens very ill. Most urgent." But there was nothing now to be done. When Russell Reynolds arrived in answer to the urgent entreaty he said at once, on seeing him, "He cannot live." Ellen Ternan, summoned by Georgina, came that afternoon to be present at the side of the dying man. He lingered all that day, his breathing becoming louder. And then at five minutes before six o'clock in the evening his breathing suddenly diminished and he began to sob. Fifteen minutes later he heaved a deep sigh, a tear rose to his right eye and trickled down his cheek. He was dead. Charles Dickens had left the world.

# Postscript

NONE among those who stood around him that day really wished him back. He had suffered too much. He had become too sad. It was Kate who remarked that "if my father had lived, he would have gone out of his mind".

Lived through what? There were thirty more years of the century. Charles Dickens died at the very height of the "Victorian" age, and yet in his death one of its moving spirits had crept away. Part of its soul had gone. So, looking back at the record of this one life, can we see the traces of the larger world in which he moved? He was born at the beginning of the century and never quite reconciled himself to the developments which took place in his maturity. He was already the most famous novelist in England when Victoria ascended the throne, and throughout his life Dickens was unmistakably an early Victorian; anyone who knew him in the Fifties and Sixties would instinctively have known that his temperament and vision came from an epoch that had already disappeared, just as even in our period it is possible to recognise the salient characteristics of men and women who came to maturity in the Thirties or Forties. He was an early Victorian, or perhaps more accurately a pre-Victorian; in his capacity for excitement and exhilaration, in his radicalism, and in his earnest desire for social reform, he was one of those who came to prominence in the first three decades of the century. The joy in discovery, the belief in progress, the largeness of spirit – all these were characteristics of the men who grew old with Dickens. In his ardour, in his theatricality, even in his vulgarity, he is a man from the beginning of the century. By the time of his death most of these characteristics had left the English; or, rather, they had become less prominent and had been supplanted by a certain practicality and a certain steadiness. Just as the larger movement of the age was towards centralisation and uniformity, so the single-mindedness and indeed eccentricity of the early Victorians were in turn replaced.

There is no doubt that such changes occur, but perhaps it is only in the processes of an individual human life like that of Dickens that they can be mostly clearly discerned. Yet they can be recognised, too, in Dickens's own fiction, no less in its comedy and sentiment than in its brooding poetry and in its capacity to transform the world into myth. In Dickens's work – in Dickens's life itself – there is the same unmistakable urge to encompass everything, to comprehend everything, to control everything. In this he is a part of his period, the man exemplifying the spirit of his time in his energetic pursuit of some complete vision of the world. The intricacy, the complexity, the momentum, the evolution, the very length of his narratives indicate as much – narratives which contain so much humour (and there never was a period so capable of laughing at itself), so great a concern for the central human progress of the world, and yet such a longing for transcendence also. Charles Dickens was the last of the great eighteenth-century novelists and the first of the great symbolic novelists, and in the crushing equilibrium between these two forces dwells the real strength of his art. The newspaper editorials after his death noted how fully he had chronicled his period but he had done more than that; he had made it larger, brighter, more capacious than anything they could

576

possibly have imagined for themselves. It may be true that he created or recreated his age in his own image but, as we have seen in this history, in his own person he experienced powerfully the most genuine forces of his time. The plunge from relative gentility, the manual labour in the blacking warehouse, the ambition, the endless hard work, the energy, the battle against circumstance, and then the triumph of the will. To be followed in turn by exhaustion and illness. And by the ultimate triumph of sorrow and fatality. So do all ages, and all men, go into the dark.

In some ways it can be said, therefore, that he represented the Victorian character, both in his earnestness and in his sentimentality, in his enthusiasm and in his sense of duty, in his optimism and in his doubt, in his belief in work and in his instinct for theatricality, in his violence and in his energy. For him life was conflict, it was "battle" always, but one which contained vivid colours and grandiose visions. The nature of that "battle" is clear enough. It was not just his own private battle against the world and against the demands of his own divided nature; it was also a struggle in which all the forces of his time were ranged beside him, for it was a struggle to maintain a vision of the coherence of the world, a vision of some central human continuity. In this sense it was also a battle against all the self-doubt, anxiety and division which lay beneath the surface of his own nature, just as they dwelt beneath the progressive formulations of nineteenth-century power.

But these are generalities, no longer close to the life as it was conducted or to the century as it moved forward. ". . . trifles make the sum of life": David Copperfield's words have a place in this history, for surely it is in the "trifles" of Dickens's life that we have found the source and measure of the works which comprise his greatness. Not trifles, then, but origins. For what do Dickens's own novels tell us, but that a passing gesture, an image, or mood, can form a whole network of meaning. That the coincidence, the chance remark, the unexpected meeting, can change a human being. That the significance of a whole lifetime of endeavour can be altered by the sudden confusion of events. But this is not simply a novelistic device. It is a perception into the very nature of the world, and it is one which biography itself must strive to exemplify. To see Dickens day by day, making his way, the incidents of his existence shaping his fiction just as his fiction alters his life, the same pattern of emotion and imagery rising up from letters and novels and conversations, the same momentum and the same desire for control – to see Dickens thus is to turn biography into an agent of true knowledge, even as we remember that the greatness of his fiction may lie in its absolute *difference* from anything which the life may show us. But once we have made that leap, from the man to his works, then we can also begin to carve out that unimaginable passage from the single human being to the age in which he lived. Seeing in his gestures, his conversations, his narratives, his dress, his moods, even in his moments of blindness and self-deception, the lineaments of the age itself – an age which existed in him and through him, but which also existed beyond him. An age which may also be seen as an exhalation of human lives. The spirit of the time. The breath of the time. People, known and unknown. And among them Dickens, whom we have come to understand.

A few weeks after his death, just as everything had been prepared for the auction of his effects, Georgina, Mamie and Kate walked through Gad's Hill Place, "going into every room, and saying goodbye to every dear corner". Mamie wrote that ". . . We three, who have been best friends and companions all our lives, went out of the dear old Home, together". Three years later Catherine Dickens attended the first performance of *Dombey and Son* at the Globe Theatre in London. But she could not watch it. She broke down and wept.

# Index

animal magnetism, 249–50
*Arabian Nights*, 34, 168
Arras, 482
*Athenaeum* (journal), 262
Athenaeum (London club), 483, 520
*Atlantic Monthly*, 547–8
Austin, Henry (CD's brother-in-law), 133, 340; death, 470, 478
Austin, Laetitia Mary (*née* Dickens; CD's sister), 13, 133, 303, 336, 477–8
Australia, 502, 539

Babbage, Charles: *Ninth Bridgewater Treatise*, 512
Ballantyne, James, 91
Balmoral House (North London), 334
Baltimore, Maryland, 205, 530–1
'Barbox Brothers' (CD; story), 517
'Barbox Brothers and Company' (CD; story), 517
Barclay, 'Captain', 469
Baring Brothers, 392
*Barnaby Rudge* (CD): writing and serialisation, 105, 134, 138, 166–7, 181, 184–8, 192–3, 385; publication, 154–5; Bentley advertises, 166; CD ends Bentley's contract for, 167; father–son relations in, 187; historical themes, 187–8, 219; mobs and riots in, 187, 191; pain in, 195; on London, 398
Barnum, Phineas P., 522
Barrow family (CD's maternal grandparents), 4, 36
Barrow, John Henry (CD's uncle), 73, 80, 86, 262
Barrow, Thomas (CD's uncle), 7, 24, 36
Bartley, George, 76–8
'Bastille Prison, The' (monologue), 469
Bates, 392
Bath (city), 216
*Battle of Life, The* (CD), 282–4, 308, 330

Bayham Street *see* Camden Town
Beadnell, Maria (*later* Winter): CD in love with, 71–3, 80; rejects CD, 78–9, 83; appearance, 92; CD calls on, 255–6; resumes contact with CD, 382–5; portrayed in *Little Dorrit*, 384–5; letter from Georgina on CD's separation, 426
Beard, Dr Francis: treats CD, 94, 461; and CD's health decline, 507–8, 545; and CD's swollen foot, 544; attends CD in final year, 559, 564; and CD's death, 572–4
Beard, Thomas: friendship with CD, 86, 116; and John Dickens's debts, 89; character, 105; invited to Broadstairs, 136; visits CD in Paris, 391; visits CD in Boulogne, 399; at Gad's Hill Place, 405, 449; and CD's reading of *The Chimes*, 417; dines with CD, 466; attends CD's London reading, 467
Beaucourt-Mutuel, Ferdinand, 401, 476–8
Beaumarchais, Pierre Augustin Caron de, 444
*Bee* (journal), 168
Belgium, 134
*Bell's Life in London* (magazine), 94
Benham, William, 479
Benning, Dr, 142
Bentham, Jeremy, 223
Benthamites, 86
Bentley, Richard: publishes CD, 106, 111–12; relations with CD, 112, 151; CD borrows from, 124; and CD's editing of Grimaldi *Memoirs*, 135; publishes *Barnaby Rudge*, 135, 138; CD believes himself exploited by, 155; advertises *Barnaby Rudge*, 166–7; CD buys release from contract with, 167, 184, 192

Bridgman, Laura, 200
Brighton: CD in, 185, 294, 301, 307, 310, 323, 355, 403; Catherine moves to after separation, 426–7; CD's public readings in, 470
Bristol, 218, 510
*Britannia*, S. S., 196, 197, 209
British Museum, 80
*British Press, The* (journal), 61–2
Broadstairs, Kent: CD visits, 134, 192; CD rents houses in, 162, 178, 189, 195; CD stays in, 176–7, 180, 214, 226, 259, 295–6, 303, 317, 327–9, 450; H. C. Andersen in, 296; CD leases Fort House, 327–8, 337, 339, 342
Brodie, Sir Benjamin, 110
Brontë, Charlotte: *Jane Eyre*, 299–300, 309
Brontë, Emily: *Wuthering Heights*, 299
Brooklyn, New York, 530
Brown, Anne, 206–7, 240, 405, 414
Browne, Hablot Knight ('Phiz'): CD chooses to illustrate *Pickwick Papers*, 104–5, 158; character, 105; visits France and Belgium with CD, 134; accompanies CD on Yorkshire trip, 136, 140; travels to Midlands and North Wales with CD, 152; illustrates *Nicholas Nickleby*, 158; illustrates *Martin Chuzzlewit*, 221; illustrations for *Dombey and Son*, 281; illustrates *David Copperfield*, 310, 315; illustrations for *Bleak House*, 350–1; CD ends partnership with, 488–9; cover designs sent to Charles Collins, 552
Browning, Elizabeth Barrett, 325, 430
Browning, Robert, 284, 510
Buckingham Palace, 561, 564
Buckstone, John Baldwin, 373, 413
Buffalo, New York, 531

Bulwer-Lytton *see* Lytton
Bunyan, John: *The Pilgrim's Progress*, 179, 184
Burdett-Coutts, Angela Georgina, Baroness, 368
Burnett, Frances Elizabeth (*née* Dickens: CD's sister; 'Fanny'): birth, 3, 8; on CD's recollection of early childhood, 10; boating expeditions, 19; schooling, 21–2; CD's relations with, 22; character, 22; accompanies CD at audition, 77; and CD's trip to America, 196; ill with consumption, 288–9, 302–4; in *David Copperfield*, 304; death, 304–5, 308, 323–4
Burnett, Henry (CD's brother-in-law), 302
Burnett, Henry (son of Fanny and Henry), 288–9

Camden Town, London, 38–41, 43, 49, 53, 229, 255–6, 271
Campbell, Thomas: 'Ye Mariners of England', 20
Canada, 531
Canterbury, 547, 553
*Carlton Chronicle, The* (newspaper), 106
Carlyle, Jane Welsh, 231
Carlyle, Thomas: influence on and relations with CD, 170–2; political views, 172–3; and CD's *The Chimes*, 247–8; *Hard Times* dedicated to, 372; sends books on French Revolution to CD, 443; influence on *Tale of Two Cities*, 445–6; on novelists as showmen, 446; CD burns letters, 458; on effect of US tour on CD, 534–5; *Heroes and Hero-Worship*, 170–1; *History of the French Revolution*, 170, 443, 445, 447; *Latterday Pamphlets*, 326; *Past and Present*, 171–2

583

Carrara (Italy), 252

Caunt, Ben, 332

Cave (proprietor of Marylebone Theatre), 517

Celeste, Madame (Celeste Elliott), 451

Cerjat, William de, 462

Chadwick, Edwin: *Report on the Sanitary Condition of the Labouring Population*, 217

Chalk, Kent, 103, 119, 124

Chancery, Court of, 65, 342, 348, 353

Chapman and Hall (publishers): publish *Pickwick Papers*, 99–102, 107–8; John Dickens requests loan from, 119, 156; publish *Nicholas Nickleby*, 135; publish *Sketches by Boz*, 135; agreements with CD, 161; and *Master Humphrey's Clock*, 161; payments for *Nicholas Nickleby*, 161; discuss new novel with CD, 191–2, 215, 219; finance CD for year off, 192; CD borrows from, 213; and *Martin Chuzzlewit* sales, 223; agreement over *A Christmas Carol*, 230; CD breaks with, 237; CD returns to, 437; buy plates of *Household Words*, 442; publish *A Tale of Two Cities*, 451; terms for *Our Mutual Friend*, 485; agreement for *Edwin Drood*, 549

Chapman, Frederick, 438, 442, 549, 552, 555

Chapman, Jonathan, 203

Chapman, Thomas, 99, 104, 318, 437

Chappell and Company: organise CD's reading tours, 507–8, 514–15, 549, 558

Charlton, Elizabeth Culliford (CD's great aunt), 63

Chartism, 187

Chatham, Kent: CD's childhood in, 14, 15–19, 245; CD at school in, 31–2; CD portrays

in *Oliver Twist*, 120; CD revisits, 177, 355, 472; remembered by CD, 323, 342

Chatsworth, Derbyshire, 270

Cheap Jack (character), 505–6, 509, 511

Cheltenham, 453, 510

Chertsey, Surrey, 293

Chester Place, London, 291–2

Chesterton, G. K., 98, 170

Chicago, Illinois, 531

Children's Employment Commission, 223

'Child's Dream of a Star, A' (CD; story), 33, 324, 330

*Child's History of England, A* (CD), 323, 352, 355

*Chimes, The* (CD): spirits in, 245, 256; writing of, 245–6, 264, 270; CD reads aloud, 247–8; radicalism in, 247, 369; success and sales, 247, 253, 266, 308; dramatised, 249; CD's public readings from, 417, 425

choledra epidemics, 216, 298, 309, 401

Chorley, Henry, 474–5, 494

Christian, Eleanor, 178–9

Christianity, 279

Christmas, 230–1, 233, 345–6

*Christmas Carol, A* (CD): public readings by CD, 30, 360–2, 381, 406, 408, 415–16, 425, 511, 529, 562; religion in, 33; boyhood reading in, 34; portrays Bayham Street house, 41; and Cornish tin mines, 219; origins and writing of, 228–32, 264; qualities, 231; pirated, 233, 238; success of, 233, 237, 308; profits from, 234; spirits in, 245; character of Tiny Tim in, 289

'Christmas Tree, A; (CD; essay), 331

Cincinnati, 206

Cirencester Agricultural College, 539

Cobham Wood, Kent, 569

**Dickens, Charles – *cont.***

BIOGRAPHY – *cont.*

leaves Chatham for London, 36–41; education neglected, 40; work at Warren's blacking factory, 44–6, 50, 535; lodges with Mrs Russell, 49; leaves blacking factory, 54–8; attends Wellington House Academy, 58–61; attempts violin, 59; leaves Wellington House, 63; works as lawyer's clerk, 63–7; theatrical ambitions, 66, 75–8; learns and uses shorthand, 67–8, 74; as parliamentary reporter, 67, 73–4, 93, 95, 497; as reporter at Doctors' Commons, 68–9; 73, 103; romance with Maria Beadnell, 71–3, 78–9; works on *Morning Chronicle*, 81–2, 86–8, 95, 106, 263; considers bar career, 85–8; helps father with debt repayment, 88; leaves home, 88–90; contributes to *Evening Chronicle*, 90–3; engagement and marriage, 91–2, 94–5, 103; early success, 108–9; social circle and friends, 115–17; marriage relations and domestic life, 117–19, 125–6, 164, 232, 234–6, 259, 385; moves to Doughty Street, 124–6, 151; and servants, 124, 155–6, 162, 242, 253, 391; clubs, 126, 185, 320; grief at death of Mary Hogarth, 128–30, 207, 479; visits Yorkshire school, 136–9; riding, 140, 150, 293; sends parents to country, 156–7; moves to Devonshire Terrace, 165–6; earnings and finances, 174, 222–3,

233–4, 292–3, 298, 491, 530, 532, 545, 549; pet raven, 180, 185–6, 573; describes self as Gentleman, 185; asked to stand as parliamentary candidate, 188; and Sanatorium project, 188–9; borrows from Chapman and Hall, 192; dogs, 209, 238, 449, 496, 517; gives nicknames to family, 220, 251; and Ragged School movement, 227–8; and Christmas, 230–1, 233, 345–6; conjuring, 231; infatuation with Christiana Weller, 234–6; buys coach, 238; library and books, 238, 323; walking and exercise, 246, 297, 336, 348, 351, 374, 381, 388, 391, 395, 397–8, 414, 462–3, 468, 504; practises mesmerism, 249; treats Augusta de la Rue mesmerically, 249–50, 265; relations with children, 251–2, 337, 380–1, 407, 431, 467, 537–40; attends beheading, 252; holds shares in *Daily News*, 263, 269, 273; accidentally kills dog, 271; plans and sets up home for fallen women, 272, 294–7, 364; attacked by horse, 293; investments, 293; Powell's life of, 318–19; and father's operation and death, 335–6, 339, 486; and death of daughter Dora, 337–9; buys and refurbishes house, 339–42; London retreat, 356; threatends baker's man, 356; revives interest in Maria Beadnell, 382–5; purchases Gad's Hill Place, 392–3; dislikes wife's

**Dickens, Charles – *cont.***

CHARACTERISTICS – *cont.*
beard and moustache, 339;
love of fires
(conflagrations), 374, 393;
discontent, 375;
complexion, 377;
nostalgia, 383; sense of
numinous, 452; romantic
passion, 479–80; hair-loss
and ageing, 530

HEALTH: spasms and
seizures, 50; facial pains,
108, 181, 468; headaches,
108; unexplained illnesses,
151; fistula operation,
194–5; seasickness, 197;
nervous exhaustion, 283,
294, 431–2; illness after
attack by horse, 293–4;
bilious attack, 332; kidney
trouble, 357; inflamed ear,
374; eye infection, 388;
tooth extracted, 392; takes
laudanum, 401, 532;
depression and
near-breakdown, 431–2;
recurrent illness, 450, 454,
461; neuralgia, 496, 504;
swollen foot and lameness
(vascular disorder), 496–7,
500, 504, 520, 532–4, 538,
544, 555–6; reaction to
railway accident, 500–2,
513; stroke, 506–7, 514;
general health decline and
debility, 507–8, 516,
530–3, 538, 544–5; effect
of readings on, 514,
543–5, 559, 561;
erysipelas, 520–1; pulse
rate, 559; swollen hand,
560; piles, 563–4; sight
limitations, 563; collapse
and death, 571–4

IDEAS, BELIEFS AND
OPINIONS: theatre, 26–9,
40, 42, 60, 65; religion,
33–4, 129–30, 230–1,
279; child neglect, 57,
309–10; political
radicalism, 87, 170, 172–3,
187–8, 247, 321, 371, 560,
576; money, 106;
education and schooling,
137–8, 141, 227, 366–7;
child labour, 153, 223;
penal system, 214;
Christmas, 230–1, 233,
345–6; Church, 270–1;
superstition, 280; fancy
and entertainment, 367;
working classes and strikes,
367; Crimean War, 371,
385; supernatural, 373;
financial speculation, 392;
marriage, 402, 413;
coincidence, 409; French
Revolution, 443–4; death,
454, 554

LITERARY LIFE AND
ENDEAVOURS: creation of
characters, 1–2; and
childhood recollections,
10–11, 20–1, 23–5;
spelling, 60; depiction of
law, 65; and shorthand
transcription, 67–8; early
journalism, 74–5, 91; first
published writings, 83–6,
90; 'Boz' pseudonym, 85;
comic power, 85, 145–7,
225–6; pirated, 86;
journalistic influence,
92–3; Chapman and Hall
publish, 99–101; fluency
in writing, 107, 124; early
success, 108–10; edits
*Bentley's Miscellany*, 111,
151; autobiographical
elements, 121–2, 265, 300,
305–6, 308, 314–15; and
innocent girlhood, 129;
poetic style, 132–3; lack of
ralism, 142–3; social
effects and consequences,
143–8; identification with
characters, 144–5, 353–4;
garrulous women, 146;
working routine, 150, 152;
theatrical effect, 158–9;
inventiveness, 159, 162,

183, 386, 516; and
contracts, 161, 168, 184,
192, 230, 237, 485, 549;
plans *Master Humphrey's
Clock*, 161–3, 168;
narrative stance, 169;
sentimentality, 183–4; and
international copyright,
199, 212; and US speech
style, 201; and names,
219–21, 311; and home
copyright breaches, 233;
punctuation, 243;
editorship of *Cricket*, 256,
259; edits *Daily News*,
259–68; resigns from *Daily
News*, 269–70; and
Christianity, 279; religious
content, 279–80;
simultaneous writing, 282,
297; speech in, 285; cheap
editions, 292–3; restraint,
298; rivalries, 299–300,
379–80; development of
social vision, 300, 360;
writings for *Examiner*, 301,
309; planning of novels,
312–14; editorship of
*Household Words*, 320–5,
352, 355; 'dark period',
359, 492; reputation, 380,
404; Tauchnitz editions,
386; discussion with
Collins, 395; block
(inability to write), 397;
Library Edition of works,
405; and dissolution of
*Household Words*, 436–7,
441; return to Chapman
and Hall, 437; starts up
and controls *All the Year
Round*, 441–2; influences
and sources, 446–7; writes
as 'Uncommercial
Traveller', 454, 458, 483;
and illustrators, 488–9;
'Cheap Jack' stories,
505–6; 'Charles Dickens
Edition' of works, 515
PORTRAITS: by Maclise,
163–4; by Boxall, 332; by
Scheffer, 387; by Frith,
440; photographs, 440
PUBLIC READINGS: of *A
Christmas Carol*, 30, 360–2,
378, 381, 387, 389–90,
406, 408, 415–16, 425,
511, 529, 562; CD's gift
for, 243, 248, 283, 361–2,
416–17, 510, 541;
Birmingham beginnings,
360–2; planning of,
377–8, 381, 415–16,
448–9, 469–70; early
tours, 378–9, 387,
389–90; first paid
performances, 416–17,
433, 468; Carlyle hears,
445–6; effect on CD, 448,
513–14, 541–4; planned
tour of America, 449–50;
1859 tour, 453–4; conduct
and presentation of,
467–8, 470–2, 511–12,
542; and Smith's death,
470; 1866 tour, 507–9,
512–13; 'Cheap Jack'
readings, 509, 511;
importance to CD, 511,
541; 1867 tour, 514, 518;
financial success of, 515;
American tour, 518,
522–5, 526–34; 'Sikes and
Nancy' monologue, 542–5,
551, 559, 561; farewell
series, 555, 558, 561; final
appearance, 561–3; *see*
individual readings and
towns
SPEECHES AND
ADDRESSES: Royal
Literary Fund, 126;
Liverpool Mechanics
Institution, 234;
Birmingham Polytechnic
Institute, 236; Commercial
Travellers' Schools, 379;
Playground and General
Recreation Society, 426;
Institutional Association of
Lancashire and Cheshire,
438; Commercial

Dolby, George: and CD's shorthand, 68; manages CD's reading tours, 508–9, 546, 560; friendship with CD, 509–10, 512, 514; advance trip to USA, 518–23, 527; with CD in USA, 527, 529–33; returns from USA, 536; and death of CD's brother Frederick, 541; on CD's farewell readings, 543, 558, 561; and CD's health decline, 544, 546, 564; and CD's reading of 'Sikes and Nancy', 544; on writing of *Edwin Drood*, 554; attends CD's final reading appearance, 562

*Dombey and Son* (CD): portrait of Portsmouth landlady in, 10; marine store in, 43; weeping in, 183, 277; business failure in, 271; dog episode, 271; railways in, 271; Italy in, 272; water in, 275; planning and writing, 276–83, 285, 291, 294, 297, 301, 315; title, 276, 281; themes, 278, 281, 291, 295, 297–8; religion in, 279–80; CD reads from, 283; sales, 283, 292, 302, 317; child's death in, 288–91, 309; celebration dinner for, 302; ending, 302; and loss of natural affection, 309; and marriage separation, 429; public readings from, 433, 518; railway accident in, 502; dramatised, 579

Doughty Street, London, 124–6, 134, 151, 162, 165

Dover, 352, 354, 396–7, 468, 481

Dowling, Vincent, 94

Doyle, Richard, 264

Drouet, Benjamin, 309–10

Easthope, Sir John, 86–7

Easthorpe Park, Yorkshire, 225–6

Edinburgh: CD visits, 189–91, 198; CD given Freedom of, 190; CD's public readings in, 470, 510, 544

*Edinburgh Journal*, 264

Egg, Augustus, 360, 482

Egyptian Hall, Piccadilly, London, 398

Eliot, George (Mary Ann Evans), 327, 352–3, 458

Elliotson, John, 211

Ellis and Blackmore (law chambers, London), 63–7

Engels, Friedrich, 380

Epsom, Surrey, 339

Evans, Bessie *see* Dickens, Elizabeth

Evans, Frederick, 423, 430, 436, 466

*Evening Chronicle*, 90–3

*Examiner, The*: Fonblanque edits, 116; CD contributes to, 151, 212, 301, 309; Forster succeeds Fonblanque as editor, 301; prints CD's views on French Revolution, 444

Fagin, Bob, 45

Fechter, Charles: actinvb, 473; friendship with CD, 473; at Christmas gathering, 494; gives chalet to CD, 494–5; CD works with, 507, 516; CD reads Cheap Jack story to, 518; CD writes essay on, 547–8; US tour, 548

Felton, Cornelius, 203–4

Fenians, 518

Field, Police Inspector Charles Frederick, 325–6, 350

Field Lane Ragged School *see* Saffron Hill

Fielding, Henry, 88, 446; *Tom Jones*, 310

Fields, Annie Adam: and CD in USA, 523, 528, 532; and CD's concern for daughter Kate, 537; with CD in England, 546–7; letter from Georgina Hogarth, 565

Lemon, Mark – *cont.*
nature, 258; works at *Daily News*, 266; at *Dombey and Son* celebration dinner, 302; dramatises *The Haunted Man*, 307–8; pocket picked, 316; CD meets in London, 392; visits Gad's Hill Place, 394; and CD's dislike of Hogarths, 396; visits CD in Boulogne, 399; and CD's separation from Catherine, 421, 423, 425; CD's isolation from, 448
Lever, Charles, 459
Lewis, Matthew: *The Castle Spectre*, 444
*Library of Fiction* (Chapman and Hall), 100, 102
*Life of Our Lord, The* (CD), 278
Limehouse, London, 551
Lincoln, Abraham, 531, 561
Literary Fund *see* Royal Literary Fund
*Literary Gazette*, 109
Little College Street, London, 48–9, 53
*Little Dorrit* (CD): speaking to foreigners in, 242; urban melancholy in, 256; Great St Bernard Pass in, 282; names in, 311; Maria Beadnell portrayed in, 384–5; attacks English society and values, 385–7, 390; CD plans, 385; financial speculation in, 385, 392; Marshalsea in, 386, 393; writing of, 386–7, 390, 393, 395, 397, 399–401; depicts London, 388; sales, 389, 404; serial publication, 389, 392, 403–4; marriage and travel in, 402; ships in, 402; critical reception, 404–5; religious sense, 404; and 'mutual friend', 487
Liverpool, 234, 351, 510, 513, 520
Lloyds (insurance office), 62
London: CD's early life in, 12–13, 36–8, 42; as subject of CD's writing, 133, 218,
224, 343–5, 398, 454–5, 463, 465, 483, 546–7, 551; CD's vision of, 169–70; conditions in, 172, 216–18, 227; CD's knowledge of, 216–17, 462–3, 560; Longfellow in, 216; population and growth, 217; sanitary reform in, 217; epidemics, 218; fog in, 343–4; CD's unhappiness with, 392; alterations and rebuilding, 463–5; CD shows Fields around, 546–7
London Library, The, 443
London Tavern, 337, 379
Londonderry, Charles William Stewart, 3rd Marquis of, 213
Longfellow, Henry Wadsworth, 215–16, 218, 529, 538
Longman, Thomas, 237
Looney (beadle), 350
Louis Napoleon *see* Napoleon III, Emperor
Louisville, Kentucky, 206
Lowell, James Russell, 529
Lowndes (gas man), 526
Lyceum Theatre, London, 266, 451, 507, 516
Lytton, Edward George Earle Lytton Bulwer-, 1st Baron: friendship with CD, 117; on poetry, 133; as godfather to CD's son, 351; at CD's farewell banquet, 524; CD complains of political system to, 560; recommends Constance Cross to CD, 566; *Zanoni*, 444
Lytton, Robert: 'The Disappearance of John Acland', 550

Macaulay, Thomas Babington, Baron, 380
Maclise, Daniel: character, 115–16; friendship with CD, 115–16, 164, 566; portrait of CD, 163; invited to Broadstairs, 176; visits

143; comic qualities, 145; sales, 150; dramatised, 154; dedicated to Macready, 158; theatricality, 158–60; neglected, 160, 162; payment for, 161; celebratory dinner for, 163; completion, 163; and CD's childhood, 164; stories within, 168; public readings from, 469; and advertising matter, 564

'Nicholas Nickleby at the Yorkshire Schools' (monologue), 469

'No Thoroughfare' (CD; story, with Wilkie Collins), 520, 550

Norfolk Street, Fitzroy Square, London, 69

'North, Christopher' *see* Wilson, John, 529

Norton, Charles Eliot, 529

Norwich, 470

O'Connell, Daniel, 95, 182, 225

*Old Curiosity Shop, The* (CD): gambling in, 44; Russells portrayed in, 49; schoolchildren in, 57; characters, 174–6; origins, 174–6; serial publication, 175–6, 191; writing of, 175–7, 180; mixed character of, 179–81; and death of Little Nell, 181–3, 290; dramatisation, 181; sorrow in, 183; completion, 184–5; volume edition revisions, 184; on London, 218

*Oliver Twist* (CD): child labour in, 45; CD plans, 85; writing and serialisation, 120–3, 130, 133–4, 138, 140, 150–2, 175, 177, 282, 443; child hero, 121–2; Cruikshank illustrates, 121, 153; and death of Mary Hogarth, 130–2; polemical nature, 131; shaped as novel, 131; themes, 131–2, 139, 219; poetic style, 132; read by young thieves, 144;

completion, 151–2; dramatised, 153–4, 249; revisions, 153, 243, 249; three-volume edition, 153; romantic vocabulary, 158; and CD's childhood, 164; setting in, 227; one-volume edition, 243; dark scenes, 359; London in, 464; CD's readings from, 542–3

Olympic Theatre, London, 521

Ordnance Terrace, London, 402

Orsay, Count Alfred d', 272–3

Osnaburgh Street, London, 211, 238

*Our Mutual Friend* (CD): wooden leg in, 26; drowned man in, 288; wrappers, 350; helpless passion in, 413; misery in, 431; origins and sources, 487; title, 487; writing of, 487–91, 495–6, 498, 502–3; Marcus Stone illustrates, 488–90; taxidermist (Venus) in, 490; sales, 491; Ellen Ternan portrayed in, 493; unrequited love in, 494; manuscript rescued from railway accident, 500; Postscript, 503; reception, 503; murderer's conscience, 550; style, 554

'Our Parish' (CD; series), 93

Ouvry, Frederic, 423–4, 426, 545

Palmer, Samuel, 271

Paris: CD visits, 240, 280, 380, 387–8, 390–1, 393–6, 481, 504; Dickens family stay in, 285, 287–9; Morgue, 288, 454; CD's reputation in, 387–8; finance in, 392

'Parish, The' (CD' series), 85

Parley's Illuminated Library, 233

Parliament, British, 67, 73, 93, 95, 497

Parthenon Club, London, 185

603

604